Books by James D. Horan
FICTION

King's Rebel
Seek Out and Destroy
The Shadow Catcher
The Seat of Power
The Right Image
The Blue Messiah
The New Vigilantes
Ginerva

NONFICTION

Action Tonight
Desperate Men
The Pinkerton Story (with Howard Swiggett)
Desperate Women
Confederate Agent
Pictorial History of the Wild West (with Paul Sann)
Mathew Brady: Historian with a Camera
Across the Cimarron
The Wild Bunch
The D.A.'s Man
The Great American West
C. S. S. Shenandoah: The Memoirs of Lieutenant-Commanding James L. Waddell
Timothy O'Sullivan: America's Forgotten Photographer
The Desperate Years: From the Stock Market Crash to World War II
The Pinkertons: The Detective Dynasty That Made History
The Life and Art of Charles Schreyvogel: Painter-Historian of the Indian-Fighting Army of the American West
The McKenney-Hall Portrait Gallery of American Indians
North American Indian Portraits
The Authentic Wild West: The Gunfighters
The Authentic Wild West: The Outlaws
The Great American West (Revised Edition)

THE JINGLE BOB PRESS SERIES

The Trial of Frank James for Murder
The Life of Tom Horn
The Daltons

GINERVA

GINERVA

A NOVEL
by James D. Horan

CROWN PUBLISHERS, INC.   NEW YORK

Designed by Ruth Kolbert Smerechniak

Printed in the United States of America
Published simultaneously in Canada by
General Publishing Company Limited

Library of Congress Cataloging in Publication Data

Horan, James David, 1914–
    Ginerva.

    I. Title.
PZ3.H78383Gi [PS3558.065]   813'.5'4   79–12733
ISBN 0–517–53392–8

For Gertrude,
who stayed with Ginerva to the very end

CONTENTS

Author's Note

It is important to state emphatically that Ginerva and her Society of the Chosen are completely imaginary, that none of the Society's officers, staff, or members represents a living person.

I also wish to point out the manuscript of this novel was delivered to my editor months before the grisly happenings of Jonestown revealed the inside story of the People's Temple. The workings of my Society of the Chosen and the events surrounding it had their origins in the author's imagination. The actual writing of this book took place in the winter and summer of 1977–78.

What is not imaginary is the disturbing question which faces many of the characters of this novel: what can law enforcement and Congress do about the nation's sects and cults tinged with fascism and criminality while continuing to protect the constitutional rights of their members to worship as they please?

It is a question which will face us all in the 1980s.

For my thoughts are not your thoughts
Nor are your ways my ways . . .

ISAIAH 55:8

I do not know why this confronts me,
       This sadness, this echo of pain;
A curious legend still haunts me,
       Still haunts and obsesses my brain.

HEINRICH HEINE
The Lorelei

GINERVA

GINERVA

The Limping Survivor

When that young lieutenant died he took a lot of me with him. I heard him when he began calling out orders. First to his sergeant, next his corporal, but the VC's mortars had left them torsos and disjointed dummies clad in rags.

Then he began calling to me. "Mr. Hillers, are you all right? Mr. Hillers, can you hear me? Keep your head down, Mr. Hillers, we're clearing 'em out. . . ."

It seemed hours but in reality it had to be only a few minutes; how long can a man last with both legs blown off? Finally he moaned softly and died.

I could see him out of the corner of my eye as I pressed my face into the jungle muck. He was only twenty-two, a brown-haired Boston boy who had won a battlefield promotion in the Highlands. He had seemed delighted and slightly awed that a war correspondent would be tagging along with his platoon on this routine patrol. I had to keep reminding him it was only because he and three of his kids were from the circulation area covered by the Ranks newspaper chain in New England. This patrol was to prove how the magnificent heroes of New England, descendants of the Minute Men, were outthinking and outfighting the cowardly guerrillas of North Vietnam. All this would appear in a column I wrote with the hideous title of "Dear Buddy." I didn't tell the lieutenant I came to Nam only because Mr. Ranks, the publisher, had been my father's roommate in college and it was either this or Canada for me.

As I pushed my nose, mouth, and teeth into the mud I prayed that none of Charley's mortars, now blowing to bits the skin, bone, and rags left of the platoon, would find me. I had witnessed combat many times but this time I was inside its violent heart. The air seemed composed of millions of pieces of metal screeching overhead, shredding trees, leaves, and grass. For the first time since I was a little boy I cried; cried for myself, the lieutenant, for the kids who had piled out of that copter, brave but scared, a few minutes before we hit this miserable spot.

We had walked into a typical VC ambush. They set off a Claymore-type mine, sprayed the patrol with automatic weapons fire, then started in with mortars. Finally it ended and they faded into the jungle, leaving behind sixteen dead young Americans and a weeping war correspondent. I was the sole survivor of Company H's platoon. The entire action lasted about five minutes; to me it was longer than my lifetime.

I forced myself to crawl to where the lieutenant was propped against a tree. I thought at first he had been only wounded, then I saw his legs were gone. I don't remember anything after that. When a Dustoff with medics appeared they found me sitting alongside the dead lieutenant. They later told me I had torn my shirt into strips and was trying to stop the boy's massive bleeding.

I didn't come out of it until I woke up in a bed in Saigon. The nurse told me they had taken quite a bit of iron out of the back of one leg but there wasn't anything serious. She made me a present of one of the pieces; it was an ordinary chunk of metal about as big as the top of my thumb and shaped like a triangle. One of the orderlies had drilled a hole in it. I later put it on a chain and wear it to this day.

A week later a general pinned the Purple Heart on me. I had been walking around but the wire service guys I knew insisted I get back into bed for the ceremony. Mr. Ranks put the AP wirephoto he had ordered on page one of his ten dailies and four weeklies along with the pictures of the four dead kids from Boston and various parts of New England. The head said, DEAR BUDDY COLUMNIST DECORATED FOR BRAVERY IN RAID.

I almost threw up.

Mr. Ranks kept cabling me to write the story of the patrol. Instead I sent him a note thanking him for all he had done for me and resigning as "Chief Correspondent of the Ranks Newspapers Covering New England Men and Women in the Vietnam War." The truth is, I was the only chief, there were no braves, not even a Minute Man.

I had been in Nam for almost five years, through Nixon's White House ringed with protesters, until the patrol was ambushed. Since those minutes of terror in the mud, an icy hand seemed to hold my guts in its grip. To stay any longer would have frozen me forever.

In the beginning it had been a dream assignment; all I had to do was fill that ridiculous "Dear Buddy" column with names. A thousand years ago Mr. Ranks had given me my marching orders during lunch at the Princeton Club:

"Names, names, names. Names of mothers, fathers, sisters, brothers, uncles, aunts, nephews and nieces, neighbors—even their dogs. Any name as long as it is in our circulation area."

The plan as he outlined it was to get the grunt's name and address and let him add a sentence:

"Hi Mom and Dad. This is Rudy. Everything is great. I love you. Don't forget to give Dusty a good run every day."

Or:

"Hi, Honey. I'm fine. I love you. Send me Kevin's last picture."

Looking back, it was no more bizarre than anything else connected with that absurd war. I came to Saigon, found an apartment, collected my boots and fatigues, got my little plastic-covered MAVC (Military Assistance Command, Vietnam) accreditation card, met the eager information officers, and began collecting names, names, names, and more names.

It went on and on and on until I discovered the real war, the one covered by the free-lancers, the drifters, the loners who appeared to write for papers or magazines I had never heard of. But they were covering the war as it should have been covered and I joined them, perhaps as a protest to the obscenity of my column.

Mr. Ranks sent irritating cables ordering me to stop playing Richard Harding Davis and go back to collecting names. The information officers were only too happy to have someone on their staff do just that, so Mr. Ranks got his names, along with stories of a war most of his readers never wanted.

In Saigon I met Ben Rice in the Crystal Bar, one of the many on notorious Tudo Street. The bar had a Vietnamese name but the free-lancers who made it their headquarters called it that after the huge imitation crystal chandelier in the dining room. Ben and I hit it off immediately. He was a fellow New Yorker slightly more than five eight—I'm six two—but what he lacked in height and heft he made up by brains and shrewdness. He was a lawyer, working in a theatrical firm when he was drafted; his fantastic repertoire of erotic stories about Broadway and Hollywood could hold the Crystal's packed bar so still you couldn't hear ice tinkle in a glass. He liked long thin cigars, they were always tilted upward like FDR's cigarette holder in the newsreel shots I recalled seeing when I was a kid. He had thick black curly hair, dark eyes that didn't miss a thing, loved to keep a secret and then surprise you. He was the sloppiest officer on the Judge Advocate's staff but from what I heard he was a brilliant lawyer who loved to defend the hard rocks and make fools of the trial officers.

It had taken him only a few weeks to know where to find good-looking—and agreeable—girls, motorcycles, petrol—just about everything a good clean American boy would want in that pathetic city.

When I showed Ben my note of resignation to Mr. Ranks, he shook his head.

"You're foolish, Hilly," he told me. "You gained a reputation out here. Stay on and wait for the end. We both know it can't last much longer. Then go back, say good-bye to Mr. Ranks, and latch on to a big city newspaper."

I couldn't. The newspaper business no longer interested me. After five years I cringed inwardly when a kid would say very shyly he was from New England and could he get his name and message to his parents in the "Dear Buddy" column.

In a way I was glad I had been hit because it brought me back to my senses. What the hell was I doing in this nightmare? For me there was no myth of wartime heroics, no gallant moments spent under fire with soldiers who were teenagers. I had found war exactly as Sherman had described it. Now all I wanted for the rest of my life was the peace and quiet I knew I would find at St. Timothy's, a private school I had attended in New Jersey. I had written to Johnny Masters, head of St. Timothy's history department, asking for a job. Johnny had been my roommate at St. Timothy's and at Princeton, where we had majored in history. Johnny European, I American. Pilgrims to the Civil War was my field, I love history but I have no desire to make it. Johnny cabled the job was mine.

The day I was to leave for stateside, Ben came to say good-bye.

"You look great, Hilly," he said as he hugged me. "How are you feeling?"

I tapped my leg. "Fine except for this. They told me I'll have a slight limp for the rest of my life."

He looked thoughtful. "You know the shrink with the white beard who thinks he looks like Hemingway?" When I nodded he went on. "Well, we're both from Brooklyn and I decided to look him up. The other night I cleaned him in a poker game. By the way, doctors are the worst cardplayers in the world. After, we went over to the Crystal and had a few. Naturally I pumped him about you. He insisted that limp is definitely psychosomatic, Hilly."

"Come off it, Ben," I told him. "I know what hit me." I pulled up my pants leg to reveal the healing scars with the stitch marks like neat embroidery up and down the outside of my leg. Then I bounced the flattened triangle of iron in the palm of my hand. "Believe me, this is not imaginary. When I walk on that leg for a while it hurts like hell."

"That could be true, Hilly," he said doggedly, "but the mind can be very tricky. That shrink took me back to his office and showed me a number of books with all kinds of case histories. He convinced me that you can *feel* pain when actually you are *not* in pain. It's all in the mind." He paused, then added gently, "He said you have a guilt complex, Hilly, and you are only punishing yourself. That limp is your personal whip. The shrink said it's not unusual. You were the only survivor of that platoon and no matter how you explain it to yourself, you feel guilty. You keep telling yourself it was only because of you that they died. . . ."

I guess he could see in my face he was touching a nerve end, and he quickly changed the subject.

"What the hell, the shrink said it will disappear after you get back," he said cheerfully.

I yawned involuntarily, and he said quickly, "Are you getting any sleep? Are the pills they gave you doing any good?"

Sleep? When every night was filled with exploding mortars and flying arms and legs and that dying lieutenant's clear voice asking if I was all right. Was *I* all right?

"It's getting better," I said, but it wasn't. I wondered if the nightmares would ever go away.

"My tour is up in six months," Ben said after a moment. "Then there's another month or so in Washington, and I'll be out. I sent in my resignation to the firm. By this time next year I'll have my own office."

"That will be great, Ben."

"I want to see a lot of you, kid." He used this expression even though we were the same age.

"We'll have a great time together." He added with a grin, "Maybe I'll even get you a couple of freebies to a show."

"Sure. You have the phone number of St. Timothy's. Call me when you get back to the city, Ben."

We stood there in a tight embarrassed silence, then he reached over and gripped my hand.

"Hilly, it was great knowing you," he said. "Believe me, it won't be the same when you're gone. . . ."

An orderly came in and picked up my gear.

When I limped to the doorway, he called out, "Remember what that shrink said, Hilly—it's all in your head."

"That shrink reminds me of the guy who wrote that manual on

jungle fighting," I told him. "How about the line I read to you? 'The jungle can be your friend. . . .'"

He stood at the doorway, and when the elevator door opened, I turned and he waved.

An information officer drove me to the field, and after we had said good-bye I waited at the end of the runway for the transport. It came in and discharged a load of marine replacements, bewildered, awkward, and, God, how young! They looked like high school freshmen. When I thought of what awaited them I wanted to shout, "Go home! Get out of here! There's nothing for you here but death and corruption!"

But I didn't. I silently watched them march off in columns to the waiting convoy. Then I climbed the ramp into the near-empty transport. As the plane climbed into the cloudless sky I looked down for the last time at the dwindling rice paddies, endless green valleys, and hills where I had buried my dreams and my youth.

As the transport moved across the sparkling China Sea, I considered the changes in my life that had taken place during the last few years.

I was a New Yorker, born Richard Preston Hillers, III, Hilly to my friends, at the end of World War II, after my father returned from France where he had been wounded in Patton's drive. I grew up in one of those spacious old apartments in the east Seventies, the kind with enormously high ceilings and a crotchety Irish doorman who smiled only during Christmas week. I knew the Strawberry Festival at the New-York Historical Society and their Sunday afternoon programs before I saw my first Flash Gordon serial on TV. My mother, an artist, hated the tube; only after she had become seriously ill did she allow one in the house. Ironically, she got to love those silly soap operas and the outrageous commercials in which early television sold everything from dog leashes to onion choppers. She died when I was in the fourth grade at P.S. 7. I can vividly recall her waxen face and the overpowering smell of flowers.

A series of housekeepers followed, none very satisfactory. This along with the growing problem of drugs in New York City's schools helped to make up my father's mind to send me to St. Timothy's, a preparatory school he had attended.

St. Timothy's was in New Jersey, two hours from Times Square, but as far as I was concerned it was this side of the Great Wall of China. However, by the time I entered high school there I loved its rigid discipline, English public school air, and basketball team. In senior year I was captain and recipient of three athletic scholarship offers. But my father would have none of it. I went off to Princeton, his alma mater, where Johnny Masters and I were high scorers. I was a stringer for the *New York Times* sports page and owner of an MG that would be a collector's item today.

Like all Americans who grew up in the 1960s—the draft era—I faced the dilemma of either serving in the armed forces or finding some way to get out of it. I can still feel the shock and dismay I experienced the morning I heard my number called in the draft lottery—eight!

That same afternoon a bored clerk estimated I had the summer but suggested that I not make any plans after Labor Day. She didn't even look up when she pronounced sentence. I was dismissed when her phone rang and she began a detailed description of what she intended to wear at her sister's wedding.

I didn't go to Canada, not that I lacked the guts but simply because of a ravishing blonde, Bobby, who should have written the *Kama Sutra*.

One night my father came home with great news; he had eaten lunch with his college roommate, Charlie Ranks, publisher of a New England newspaper chain. Mr. Ranks had offered me the job of "Chief War Correspondent." I instantly saw myself in a trench coat, looking handsome and daring as Errol Flynn as I covered our troops in Vietnam. Those dreams still held after I had lunch with Mr. Ranks at the Princeton Club, where he described his plan of introducing the "Dear Buddy" column.

I smiled to myself as I recalled that naive kid of almost five years ago who had so conscientiously sought out soldiers, sailors, marines, and airmen who came from New England. Curiously, the column caught on. It did have its value; some of the one-line messages were the last families heard until the military escort rang their bell. I was mentioned in *Time* and had my picture in a *Life* layout on Nam. Then I became one of the Crystal Bar's zealots, going along on missions whose memory today makes me break into a sweat, willing to witness how grim-faced grunts played Cowboys and Indians in the jungle with heavy automatic rifles, mortars, rockets, and gunships.

One day an information officer told me about this kid from Boston who had been given a field commission for performing an extraordinary bit of heroism. The information officer had discovered there were three other kids in the same company who came from New England, and he suggested they put together a routine sweep.

"Strictly a noncontact operation," he said. "Great hometown stuff for that column of yours. Interested?"

I was. I became the seventeenth member of Company H's Second Platoon.

On a "strictly noncontact operation" set up just for me.

Sixteen died—only Dear Buddy survived.

As I stepped off the plane in San Francisco, I recalled what happened to my father during World War II when he was granted his first pass from Halloran Hospital in Staten Island to visit his mother in Manhattan. While he waited for the St. George Ferry, strangers invited him to have a drink. On the boat a woman kept calling him "one of our nation's heroes," and when he stepped off the ferry at the Battery a man volunteered to drive him home. Later that evening a friend took him to the Stork Club, a famous watering place of its time. He was given the best table in the Cub Room and Sherman Billingsley, the owner, presented him with a pair of bright red suspenders, which my father sheepishly revealed to me was quite a status symbol of his day.

But I soon discovered it was a hell of a lot different in this war. There were no kindly strangers or gracious old ladies at the airport, no one offered to buy me a drink, give me a pair of suspenders or a ride—there were only a surly cabdriver, a bored room clerk, and a greedy bellman.

But my father made up for all of that when I got him on the phone. He gave me a rousing welcome, and to my surprise revealed he had a scrapbook of all my articles. Only recently, he said, he and Mr. Ranks had had dinner at the Princeton Club, at which time Mr. Ranks called me one of the best reporters he had ever hired and said anytime I wanted a job his door was open. I told my father how I felt, what I wanted to do at St. Timothy's; all he said in his quiet way was that he understood and when I got home we would have the finest meal the city could offer and we could talk all night if I wanted.

The next call I made was to Johnny Masters. A member of the faculty informed me he was out of town attending the funeral and to the affairs of an aunt who had died. I remembered the aunt, she had raised Johnny. However, he did read a message Johnny had left for me: relax for a few days and he would get in touch with me about staff schedules and when I should report.

At first I thought of returning home immediately, but San Francisco looked so attractive, so full of life after what I had seen in the last five years, I decided to stay out the week and do the tourist bit. I called my father and he agreed it would be a good city to unwind in, then I sent a note off to Johnny letting him know where I was staying.

In the morning I set out to do everything expected of a tourist, from riding a cable car to visiting the wineries.

The tourist role lasted three days before I found myself getting bored. One night, after a lonely dinner, I decided to walk about the city. During the last few days my leg had ached; now as I walked it began to pain. I gave up after a mile, hailed a cab, and to stretch out the evening, I told the driver to take a roundabout route to the hotel.

I don't know what section of the city it was when we turned into a side street filled with a slow-moving, singing crowd gathered in front of what appeared to be an old movie theatre. The driver told me they were Disciples of Ginerva, who claimed God had given her a warning to the world that Armageddon was at hand. Her Society of the Chosen, he added, was now the biggest cult on the West Coast.

His hands fashioned her figure in the air. "She's built like that," he said. "Man, would I like to save her!"

Watching a beautiful evengelist do her act sounded better than riding around in a cab and sitting alone in a hotel room, so I paid him and joined the chanting crowd. A smiling couple in their early twenties took my hands.

"Welcome, brother," the boy said. "Welcome to God's circle."

"I'm a stranger in town, just stopping by," I said.

"There are no strangers in the Society of the Chosen," the girl said solemnly.

"Who is Ginerva?" I asked.

"God's courier to the world," the boy explained.

Several young people nearby swung up their clasped hands and cried: "Glory to Ginerva! She will save us all!"

"God came to Ginerva and warned her he will destroy the world by a Sea of Flame unless we abandon our evil ways," the boy said. "But he showed her his mercy and how we can be saved by becoming a Chosen One. Would you like to be a Chosen One, brother?"

I quickly assured him, "I'll think about it."

Whistles shrilled behind us. The street was now jammed from curb to curb.

When we reached the lobby, I found it covered with posters of a beautiful woman gazing heavenward under block letters which read FOLLOW GINERVA AND BE SAVED AS A CHOSEN ONE!

Several young men firmly but courteously kept the lines moving into the theatre. Their cold stares were intimidating.

At first something about them was puzzling, then I realized what it was: they all looked alike, crew cut, clean shaven, blue suit, white shirt, dark tie, white carnation. They could have been flash frozen.

"The Avenging Angels," the boy whispered. "Ginerva's bodyguards."

I wondered why God's courier needed bodyguards. . . .

Ushers escorted us to aisle seats midway in the orchestra and gave us hymn sheets.

"Would you like to hear the story of Ginerva?" the boy asked when we sat down.

Without waiting for a reply he went on: "Oh, it's a glorious story, brother, full of God's love and mercy for us. Several years ago when Her Holiness was working in the mountains with poor people—her whole life has been dedicated to doing God's work—she went for a walk in the woods to pray. Suddenly there was a great white light and God spoke, giving her his message to the people of the world, warning them to put aside their evil ways and follow the Way of the Cross or he will destroy the world by a Sea of Flame. . . ."

"Only Disciples in the Society will be saved," his solemn girl friend interjected.

"The Society of the Chosen!" the boy continued. "You must join it, brother, so you can be with us on God's great white cloud!"

A fat woman in front of us turned and cried: "Praise to Her Holiness, Ginerva!"

"A great white cloud?" I asked.

"The largest cloud ever to appear in the heavens," he replied. "It will come down with angels and we all go aboard to be taken into Paradise. Oh, brother, please join us. . . ."

"And is this what God promised Ginerva?"

"That and many other things." He leaned toward me, his eyes glowing. "Do you know that he gave Her Holiness control of his lightning? Oh, yes, brother, one day to prove to the unbelievers that she is truly God's courier, the Almighty will send down his lightning and she will play with it like a child with a toy."

"God also gave her power to heal the sick and give peace to the troubled," the girl added.

The boy pointed across the orchestra. The far aisle was filled with crippled men, women, and children, sitting on chairs, holding their crutches; others were in wheelchairs, and some on stretchers.

"Wait until you see how the power of her healing lets them throw away their crutches and jump out of their wheelchairs," he said. He turned to his girl friend. "We saw it happen many times, didn't we, honey?"

She nodded and reported in a monotone, "Oh yes, many times. God has given Her Holiness great powers."

The boy glanced down at my foot and said softly, "Let her bless you, brother, and the pain will be gone."

You poor dumb misguided kid, I told him silently, it would take more than your lovely phony to repair the damage done by VC's mortars that afternoon.

To pass the time and avoid any more of his babbling, I looked about the theatre, estimating it held about four thousand seats. Everyone was taken, with crowds standing in the rear. The stage was large and bare except for a lectern; the backdrop was a screen reaching to the ceiling. A carpeted ramp, entwined with flowers, led from the stage to the orchestra. Although there was an ancient cooling system, the place was stifling. Faces glistened in the dull yellow light; all around makeshift fans of folded newspapers and cardboard were in action.

Softly, very softly, came the first organ notes. The boy nudged me. "It's beginning," he whispered excitedly.

There was a warning chord, followed by the swelling noise of *"Bringing in the Sheaves."* One hymn followed another, each increasing in tempo until the booming notes seemed to shake the walls. When the last one finally died away, a big chunky blond man with a rough-cut ravaged face, a crew cut, and dressed like the Angels in the lobby, walked out of the wings.

"Brother Russell," the boy said. "He's in charge of the Angels. He does the readings."

"Welcome, Brothers and Sisters," Russell announced in an incongruously high stilted voice, "Tonight Her Holiness will speak on the Last Hours of Christ and after will give her Blessing. Now if you will turn to your white sheets. . . ."

He appeared self-conscious, uncertain, as he nervously led us through a reading of the Acts of the Apostles. He finally ended and the audience sent him off with a relieved *"Amen."* Now the air was filled with tension; it was clear everyone was waiting for Ginerva.

Suddenly the theatre was plunged into darkness; red exit lights glowed like fierce one-eyed cats. Then a golden shaft speared across our heads to encircle a woman on the stage. She was the most beautiful I had ever seen. Young, surely not thirty, stately, tall, slender. Her hair, like burnished copper glinting in the soft light, fell to her shoulders. She was dressed in a long white gown with a blue velvet sash encrusted with tiny stones that glittered as she walked.

That night she talked about the passion and death of Christ. She had a wonderful gift of imagery and made that great drama come to life. She pictured the weary heartsick Jesus, the days of his miracles finished, returning to Jerusalem for what he knew was his confrontation with death. Then, as Luke wrote, the frightened, puzzled disciples at the Last Supper breaking into song, their voices flat in that room so filled with fear; the agony in the garden with his drops of blood staining the earth; then Judas leading the soldiers, their mail clinking in the silence as they surrounded Jesus to take him prisoner. At this point she paused and walked very slowly to the edge of the stage.

There wasn't a sound, a cough, an impatient shuffling of feet. A hush lay over the theatre. I found myself impatiently waiting for that magnetic voice to continue. She had bowed her head, and when she looked out at us I could see her eyes were glistening with tears.

Suddenly she pointed, and like the rest of the audience I was startled.

Behind her on the screen, in shocking vivid color, was the head of the crucified Christ, blood trickling down his forehead from under the crown of thorns, the deeply lined stricken face, the curve of the cheek, the pleading dying eyes. It was a slide, but a powerful one.

"Do you see his torn flesh?" she cried. "*Flagra* is the Greek word in the Bible, iron chains with iron balls at the end to rip a man's skin from his bones. That was the Roman punishment for criminals, but for Jesus they refined it. The guards relished their task. They whirled the chains about their heads and laid on with a will. Jesus suffered as a mortal. There was no divine assistance. All he could do was try to pull aside his battered body as the chains fell, to wrench his head about in agony. Then at last, when the scourging was finished, they crossed his hands on his breast, gave him a ragged red cloak and a circle of thorns as the guards jeered and laughed, not realizing what they were destroying was themselves."

I could see the tears on her cheeks, there were sounds of sobbing, and someone cried out.

"He was unable to carry the cross, so Luke tells us, 'They seized one Simon of Cyrene, who was coming from the country, and laid on him the Cross to carry it behind Jesus. . . .'

"Now on the peak of that bleak hill they gave him the punishment fit only for slaves, but again they went further. Instead of tying his hands and feet, they nailed him to the wood."

Everyone around me leaned forward in their seats to catch every word.

"The women below huddled together in grief and horror as the hours passed. The soldiers gave him gall and pierced his side with a lance. What little life was left was going fast. The clouds thickened, a great silence fell over the earth, the birds were still. He cried out one more time and died."

As the spot became brighter, she pointed to herself and then to the audience.

"That man was condemned by me, by you! And you! And you! We placed him on that cross, day after day. Each one of us stabs his side with a spear and gambles for his garments." She held out her hands, pleading. "This is what God told me that night on the lonely mountain trail! 'Your world is evil and full of sin,' he said, 'Full of wars and hate and even the corruption of my children! If the world does not follow the way of my Son I will destroy it with a Sea of Flame, and when it is done there will not be left standing a blade of grass, a bird in the sky, or a leaf on a tree. There will be nothing but ash, and the only sounds will be the wailing and gnashing of the teeth of those who have been condemned to the deepest pits of Hell.'"

The color of the spot had subtly changed. Now it was the blue of twilight. She stood there, arms held out, a stunning alabaster statue. Slowly she knelt down, her voice quivering.

"God gave me this warning, but he also showed me his mercy. He asked only that we obey his commandments, love one another as brothers and sisters. He also wants us to know that the terrifying Cross of Calvary was good news! Good news, my dear Disciples, because by that Cross came eternal life! The mighty heart broken that day let flow a glorious healing power to cure all of us of evil and of sin. Listen to John as he tells us how from that Cross came not only eternal life in the sense of resurrection to life after death, but in the sense of life so precious even this side of death, that to love it is to stand with one foot in all eternity!"

She got up and ran to the ramp.

"Who will follow me to Calvary and promise the man on that Cross he will obey his Father's plea to me to help straighten out this world? To help cast out its evil ways and bring our nation—and the world—to the ways of the Lord!"

Rather than be conspicuous, I rose with the rest of the audience who were chanting: "We will, Ginerva! We will, Ginerva!"

"Let is sing out the praises of the Lord!" she cried. "Sing out! Sing out, my dear Chosen Ones—sing out!"

As the organ notes boomed, the boy and girl gripped my hands and shouted out the chords of an old tent-meeting hymn. I stood there feeling like a fool.

"Come join me," she ordered when it ended. "Come join me and find peace in the blood of the Lamb of the Cross."

A row of Angels almost magically appeared, moving swiftly to form a ring about her as the crowds surged down the aisle. Towering above them was Brother Russell, who kept shouting:

"Kneel down and be blessed by Her Holiness, Ginerva!"

I was far from being lost in a mystical ecstasy, and when the kids tried to pull me with them, I held back.

"Let her bless you, brother," the boy whispered. "Let her bless away the pain in your leg."

When I shook my head, they pushed past me and knelt in the aisle. The Angles forced the crowds to make a passage for her, and she passed along the kneeling men and women, smiling, touching. She was more beautiful up close. I could see her eyes were large and green, the color of the China Sea. Her lips were perfectly formed, her skin unblemished. Occasionally she tossed back her long copper-colored hair, like a filly bursting with life.

The two kids returned to their seats, and we watched Ginerva bless her kneeling followers. When someone tried to hold her hand, kiss her fingers or the hem of her robe, there was always an Angel to intercept the move. When she returned to the stage the organ began again. After the last note died away, she walked down the ramp and stood at its bottom, waiting, Angels at either side. Her face was set and I thought somewhat troubled.

"Now comes the Blessing of the Sick," the boy whispered.

There was a stirring in the far aisle where the crippled and ill were waiting. When Brother Russell raised his hand, a grotesque march began. Men and women on crutches lurched from side to side, wobbled with canes, eagerly guided their wheelchairs, while nurses and aides pushed stretchers to where Ginerva was waiting.

It was an eerie and I thought sickening sight, as the Angels brought them up one by one. After being blessed by Ginerva, a man flung aside his crutches and cried: "God Almighty! I can walk again! Ginerva cured me!"

"What horrible nonsense," I muttered.

"Do you see, brother?" the boy said. "Her Holiness has the power of the Lord in her!"

"Hallelujah!" his girl friend called out between sobs.

A woman flung her cane into the air and did a mad dance before falling on her knees and reaching out to clutch Ginerva's robe, but an Angel grabbed her hand, gently lifted her and led her away.

I felt instinctively that this was distasteful to Ginerva. Her smile seemed forced, and once when a child on a stretcher was wheeled before her, she stepped back and vigorously shook her head, but Russell leaned over, whispered something to her, and she reluctantly touched the child's forehead.

Finally the last wheelchair and stretcher had been taken away; Ginerva returned to the stage and again took the microphone.

"And now, my dear Disciples, the time to end our rally is near at hand. We have been to the Last Supper, journeyed to the foot of the Cross; we have promised the Almighty Father we will do his bidding —rid the world of evil! But as I have told you, he also promised me that if the world turns its back and continues to listen to the Devil, he will send down a great white cloud to lift us into Paradise before his mighty Sea of Flame consumes the earth. That is his promise, the promise he gave me that night on the lonely trail! So now let us sing out in gratitude for his mercy! Sing out, my dear Disciples! Sing out in joy!"

The organ boomed, "It's That Old Time Religion" as Angels went up and down the aisles, waving their hands like orchestra conductors, urging all to sing at the top of their voices, while Ginerva, smiling, looked down on us.

As the tempo of the hymns increased, the image of Christ on the

Cross grew larger and larger until it filled the entire rear of the stage. When she turned and pointed to it, the lights dimmed and the organ notes died away. Lightning flashed and peals of thunder shook the theatre. The manufactured storm was incredibly real, and I expected at any moment to hear the agonized voice of that man on the cross cry out:

"Father, Thy will be done. . . ."

Flashes of lightning now enveloped Ginerva, bathing her in a weird luminous light as she raised her hands to heaven. Winds howled and her exquisite body was outlined against the taut silken gown.

This violent scene touched hidden hungers within some of her Disciples and brought them flaring to the surface. The fat woman in front of me leaped out into the aisle and began a wild jerking dance, waving her hands and babbling incoherently as the sweat flew off her red, round face. The boy and girl next to me tried to pull me with them, but when I held back they joined the woman, their heads rolling about, eyes blank, lips wide with ecstasy.

The aisles were soon filled with men and women, dancing and shouting, some writhing on the floor and barking like animals. All this against the background of the make-believe crashing thunder and lightning which seemed to bounce harmlessly off the rigid statuelike figure of Ginerva. It was both a fascinating and a frightening mixture of fanaticism and spectacle.

Suddenly, as if a switch had been pulled, the thunder and lightning broke off. The wild dancers wound down, their frantic movements slowly diminishing until they stopped, eyes glazed, lungs pumping like bellows. The boy and girl returned to their seats, slumping down, staring straight ahead as though they were in a hypnotic trance.

Once again the bluish spot found Ginerva looking to heaven like a bad painting of Mary listening to the voice in her heart. It slowly faded, winked out, and she was gone.

The boy abruptly came out of his trance. "She's leaving," he cried. "Her Holiness is leaving!"

Crowds surged toward the stage. Again the line of Angels, linked arm to arm, held back the chanting crowd.

"Ginerva! Ginerva! Courier of God! Bless us!"

"O Blessed Holiness, remain with us always!"

"Help us drive the evil from the world, Ginerva!"

The fat woman was kneeling, tears streaming down her cheeks, while the woman who had tossed aside her cane was dancing about and singing, "I can walk again! The power of God is in Ginerva!"

The boy vigorously shook my shoulder. "Wasn't that a glorious rally, brother?"

I mumbled something and joined the slow-moving crowd headed

for the front door. The organ was now pounding out, "Onward, Christian Soldiers," and some Disciples who appeared to be reluctant to leave were shouting the words.

The boy and girl remained at my elbow. "You must join the Society, brother, and be saved from God's wrath," the boy bellowed in my ear. I smiled and waved good-bye as we entered the lobby. A number of smiling, eager young men and women, whom I assumed were Disciples, held out wicker baskets and containers. When one was rapidly filled with bills, another took its place. I reluctantly put in a dollar; after all, this nonsense had helped me to pass the evening.

Some were holding up stunning wallet-size color photographs of Ginerva looking as if she was about to ascend into heaven.

When I held out a dollar, one said gently, "That will be *five* dollars, sir."

I was about to refuse but decided the photograph would be my souvenir of San Francisco. Other Disciples in the lobby displayed trays of plastic statues, all sizes, of Ginerva in her robe, arms beseeching heaven. Still others sold a shabby-looking tabloid called *The Call*. I bought a copy; another dollar.

Whoever was running this show was certainly pulling in the coin, I told myself.

Near the door an Angel inside a booth was handing out leaflets. He thrust one into my hand.

"Join the Society of the Chosen and be saved from God's wrath," he intoned.

"How do I join?" I asked.

He looked me quickly up and down. "All the instructions are there, sir," he said politely. "We have several Houses of Preparation in the city. . . ."

I pressed him, "What is a House of Preparation?"

A group was now gathering about the booth holding out their hands for leaflets.

"A place to prepare you for God's work," he said calmly, "and to learn how to help Her Holiness drive the evil from this world."

"But there will always be evil as long as there is man," I said.

"Not so!" he suddenly thundered. "Those are the devil's words! Join the Society, brother, and be cleansed of those thoughts."

They were all looking at me as though I had suddenly sprouted a tail and horns, so I quickly melted away into the crowd.

Outside, a chanting mob jammed the entrance of the alley next to the theatre.

"What's going on?" I asked a cop.

"Aw, that's where she comes out," he said wearily. "Okay, folks, now let's move on and let those people behind you in the lobby get out. . . . Please move on. . . ."

As I tried to make my way clear of the crowd, the chanting stopped and someone cried out, "Here is Her Holiness!" A flying wedge of Angels swept out of the alley. In the center was Ginerva, wearing a dark blue velvet cloak covered with tiny pearls. She looked drawn and weary. When a glittering black Cadillac pulled up to the curb, the crowd surged forward.

I was almost swept off my feet and slammed against the car door as the Angels pushed back the crying, chanting, shouting mass of people. One Angel reached out and yanked me violently to one side. Outraged and sick of the whole evening, I pushed him as hard as I could.

I'm over six feet, but he towered over me and was built like a professional linebacker. Nimble as a cat, he whirled around, his fist drawing back.

A hand in the blue robe reached up and stopped him.

"No," Ginerva said, looking at me. She was about to move on when she paused. Then a curious thing happened; it was no sudden glow or burst of light, nothing really that could be measured. I was probably the only one who noticed a slight change in her manner, but it was enough of a signal to let me know she had made up her mind not to pass me.

"Do you remember what Mark wrote, brother?" she said, in a voice so soft I could barely hear it above the shouting and the chanting. "When it was evening there came a rich man from Aramathea named Joseph, who was also a disciple of Jesus. He went to Pilate and asked for the body of Jesus. Then Pilate ordered the body given to him, and Joseph took the body and wrapped it in a clean linen shroud and laid it in his own tomb which he had hewn in rock; he rolled a great stone to the door of the tomb and departed. . . ."

While the crowd pushed and swirled about the barricade of Angels, I looked deep into those green eyes.

"Will you watch with me outside the tomb, brother, for the glorious day when Christ returns?"

I found myself saying, "I will, Ginerva. . . ."

She slowly reached out and touched my cheek. I was transfixed. For the first time since I left Nam, I felt a deep sense of peace.

It happened in a flash, then I was back in the noisy crowd looking at her. The Angel reached past me, opened the car door, and Ginerva got inside, to stare straight ahead. Cops appeared, shoving us back along the curb, and the car pulled away to disappear around the corner, past the hooting, jeering pickets.

I started to walk down the block, hoping to hail a cab, when I stopped, stunned.

I was no longer limping.

2

The Quest

The whole night had made no sense. In the half-lit fuzzy world of waking, sleeping, and waking again, I kept seeing her face, hearing her voice, feeling the touch of her hand on my cheek. I told myself it had been simply stage business, emotionalism, even fanaticism, but the hard fact kept echoing back: the limp was gone. Twice, three times I got up and walked across the room. I was walking normally. I could hear Ben's jeering voice: *What did I tell you, kid? Didn't the shrink say is was psychosomatic?*

Then I fell asleep, the first deep, peaceful sleep I had in months. I woke up feeling refreshed but still confused. I placed Ginerva's color portrait on the bureau and studied it. The face was delicate, almost fragile, the eyes filled with secrets. I saw her again on the stage, heard her clear, almost hypnotic voice as she talked about the man dying on the cross.

I got up and walked across the floor to the window. The limp was gone, I knew, never to return.

I sat on the edge of the bed, only to get up and restlessly pace the room. I finally decided that if I wanted peace of mind there was only one thing to do: find out all I could about this woman who claimed to be God's courier to the world but who could be the best scam artist to appear in a long time. I took out the jagged triangle of metal and studied it. But what scam artist could cure a man's limp and drive the Furies from his mind?

The *San Francisco Chronicle* was a logical starting point. My war correspondent's ID card got me past the guard in the lobby to the newspaper's reference room, where a friendly young woman listened to my fiction of how I planned to write an article on female evangelists and could I see any clippings and photographs they had on a woman called *Ginerva*?

She looked dubious for a moment, glanced at my ID, then winked.

"We don't usually do this for strangers," she said. "Our legal department raises the devil. But seeing as you are a colleague . . ."

She led me to a small table in the far corner, and within minutes I was opening a folder: GINERVA—EVANGELIST. The meager collection of clippings disappointed me, the only two worthwhile were an early interview with Roger Talbot, the *Chronicle's* religious editor, and a brief review in the *Los Angeles Herald-Examiner's* television column of a news segment on evangelists, featuring Ginerva. There was a one-column photo of David Harper, the producer of the news feature, and a superb photograph taken by a *Chronicle* photographer that showed Ginerva sitting alone in a small church.

It could have been late afternoon, a bar of sunshine bathed her in light as she sat alone among rows of empty folding chairs. Her head was slightly tilted, and she almost seemed to be listening to something only she could hear. The eerie quality of the photograph undoubtedly had attracted the night editor, who had spread it across the top of the religion page.

After I had copied the address of her storefront church, the girl told me I could find Talbot, the religion editor, at a nearby motel.

A bellboy pointed him out to me in the lobby. He was frail and white-haired, but he carefully looked me up and down after I had introduced myself and showed him my ID.

"A war correspondent interested in female evangelists?" he asked. "That's a new one." He picked up some magazines from a chair and motioned for me to sit down.

Talbot turned out to be a delightful old gentleman who had been in the newspaper business from the post–World War I years to the *Chronicle's* religious beat.

"This is my last assignment," he said with a grin. "It isn't much, but it's a hell of a lot better than sitting around the lobby with these other old toads waiting for the medical examiner's wagon to cart me away."

Talbot told me the first he knew of Ginerva was someone in the *Chronicle's* advertising department describing to him how crowds were flocking to her storefront church.

"The idea of a woman evangelist sounded interesting," Talbot said, "so I went over to see what it was all about."

Talbot said he found the store jammed with a large crowd overflowing into the street. An usher brought him inside, and he heard Ginerva for the first time.

"She was so good I went back," he went on. "It was then I saw her give what they called 'The Blessing of the Sick.' It was simply a laying on of hands. Two men in wheelchairs jumped up and shouted they were cured, and a woman with a hearing aid kept screaming she could hear."

I asked, "Did it look real?"

He laughed. "You can see the same thing all over San Francisco. Gurus. Faith healers. Self-proclaimed mystics. It's usually some poor hysterical woman or an exhibitionist throwing away their crutches or jumping out of a wheelchair, and you have what they call a miracle." He looked thoughtful for a moment. "However, I can't call Ginerva a *complete* fraud."

"Why not, sir?"

"I've been in this business too long to be taken in," he said. "The Bible-thumpers around here know that and don't try to pull anything on me. When I went to that storefront church the second time, her major domo kept trying to sell me a story of what he called 'Ginerva's miracle cures,' but I decided to look into them myself."

He paused, took out a small tin box of snuff, carefully inserted a pinch into each nostril, sneezed, wiped his nose, and continued.

"I selected three cases and talked to the people themselves, members of their families and their physicians.

"Two were cures but with natural explanations. The tumor on one man's neck had certainly disappeared under the extensive cobalt treatments he had been taking. In the second case, a former marine gunnery sergeant came back from Vietnam with a blood infection. He was a big man who had shrunk to about one hundred and forty pounds. Three weeks after he was blessed by Ginerva, he began to recover. But the doctor at Walter Reed Hospital in Washington who treated him said he had told the sergeant he would begin to recover after several months in the States and with their medicine. That's what happened." He looked out the window. "But then there was the third case . . ."

As Talbot described it, a young leukemia victim had been wheeled into the storefront church. She showed improvement a few weeks after she had been blessed by Ginerva.

"The last time I saw her, she was playing tennis with her brother," Talbot said. "She's in Paris now as an exchange student. I spoke to her doctor, and he agreed there was no medical explanation, but he also said it's not the first case of arrested leukemia he has seen nor will it be the last."

"That fellow you called her major domo, Mr. Talbot," I asked, "what was his name?"

"Names have a way of slipping from your memory when you're my age," he said. "But I remember telling myself he looked like someone milking the main chance."

"A promoter?"

"I would say so. And a good one. You should talk to the *Chronicle*'s photographer who took that picture and have him tell you how that fellow set it up, skylight and all."

After I had identified myself as a correspondent for the Ranks newspapers in the East, doing a series on West Coast television, the television station told me where I could find Harper, the producer. He was filming an interview with two young Mexican-American gang leaders, and after he finished I asked him about Ginerva. He frowned for a moment, then recognition filled his face.

"Oh yeah, I remember her now. That terrific-looking chick in a storefront church on Halsey Street." He shook his head. "But a phony. A real phony."

"Why do you say that?"

"She got five minutes of a twelve-minute segment on gurus, faith healers, and cults, right? Well, after I did a fast exterior and a pan shot of the inside of that crummy church, I also did some close-ups of her when our reporter was interviewing her, because she is a real beauty. But she couldn't talk without this guy at her side. He practically put the words in her mouth."

"Do you remember his name?"

"No, but he was a real pro. You could tell by the way he was operating. He had another guy with him and a good-looking blonde. . . ."

Halsey Street was in a rundown part of the city among tenements and warehouses. The windows of the store were whitewashed, and on a nearby wall were remnants of a poster:——ED AS A CHOSEN ONE. A card on the door referred all inquiries to the superintendent.

The super was suspicious and surly, but as I learned in Saigon, money produces smiles. The five dollars I gave him made him find the key to the store and instantly become a fountain of information.

"Sure I remember Ginerva. I put her down as a goodlooking nut, but my wife thought she was great and wanted me to go with her to that church. But that stuff's not for me. I'd rather look at basketball on TV."

He swung open the store's door, switched on the light, and pointed to a rear partition. "She lived in the back."

The place was long and narrow and very dusty. At one end there was a raised wooden platform with a broken chair. "They put in that platform after she got started," he said.

"Who are 'they'?"

He shrugged. "I dunno. There were two guys and a zoftig blonde. They were runnin' things. But they came after she started to get crowds. One night she had so many they put up a loudspeaker outside so everybody could hear her."

"Did any sick or crippled people come here?"

"Jeez, it was like a hospital corridor sometimes!" he said. "Crazy people in wheelchairs, on crutches—even in ambulances! They all wanted to get blessed by her."

"Did you ever see anyone cured?"

He said, "One night my wife finally dragged me over here. It was a big night. The street was packed. They even had cops directing the traffic. After the usual prayers and singin' there was this Blessin' of the Sick, as they called it. Now I'm really tellin' you what I saw—I can swear a guy threw away his crutch, a woman kept screamin' she could hear again, and a guy jumped out of his wheelchair and began walkin' around. I kept tellin' my wife it's a crock, but she kept pointin' to the guy who had thrown away his crutch and the woman who kept wavin' her hearin' aid. After that the place was always crowded."

We walked to the edge of the platform, and I asked him, "When you first met her, did she ever tell you where she came from or what her name was?"

"No. But I sort of think she was an actress."

"What made you think that?"

"Well, after I got out of the navy, my uncle got me into the stage electricians' union as an apprentice. Me and my uncle were workin' in Pasadena at the Little Strand Theatre when this stock company came in. It was a pissant outfit, mostly kids who wanted experience. But the lead was this knockout. And man, she was good! I remember she was playin' the woman who was a saint. You know, the woman who wore armor and they burned her."

"Joan of Arc?"

His face lighted up. "Right. That's it. Well, when I seen her, somethin' clicked in my head and I said, 'Hey, lady, didn't I see you in Pasadena playin' that saint in armor?' She just shook her head and walked away, but I swear she was the same one. I didn't ask her any more questions; I figgered if she didn't want to talk about it, who am I to care? Then again, maybe I was wrong. I told my wife, and she says, 'Mind your own business,' and that's what I did."

"Wasn't there anyone around here who *didn't* like her?"

He thought for a moment. "I guess you can say the Underwoods hated her guts."

"For what reason?"

"Their daughter, Elly. She was over there every night. Then she joined the Society of the Chosen. I thought the old man was gonna tear Ginerva's place apart. They went down to the cops but the cops said they couldn't do anythin' because Elly was twenty-three. She gave up a good job as a secretary and even dumped the guy who she was goin' with. The kid was so upset he joined the Marines. I told my wife it would have to be three Marilyn Monroes to make me do that." He added casually. "Maybe I could fix it so they will talk to ya. . . ."

I gave his another five and he was off like a shot, disappearing into one of the tenements. He returned in about twenty minutes.

"You won't have any trouble, they're dyin' to talk."

The Underwood apartment on the third floor of the tenement was scrupulously clean. Mrs. Underwood was a petite, nervous, gray-haired woman; her husband, who towered over her, had a belly that bulged over his belt, and arms like tree trunks. They insisted I have a cup of coffee and a piece of cake; before I had taken a bite, Underwood went into a rambling tirade.

"I'll tell you about that gang—thieves and whoremasters, that's what they are! That dame talkin' about how she met God and all that crap while the others keep connin' those kids to join that goddamn Society. I told the wife, 'Don't let Elly go over there—I don't like those people, I think they're phonies.'" He turned to his wife. "Didn't I keep tellin' ya that, Rose? But no, no one listened to me. I saw what was happenin'. First Elly kept tellin' us about this wonderful woman of God who was gonna help everyone be saved from Judgment Day. She had some kind of a story about a cloud comin' down from heaven. And this kid of mine believes it!"

"My daughter was a wonderful girl until she went over there," Rose said. "She graduated from secretarial school and had a fine job. In another year she was going to be made an executive secretary. She worked for a firm that made little wire wheels for some kind of motors."

Tears ran down Underwood's weatherbeaten cheeks and his voice held a note of bewilderment.

"She has everything here. There wasn't anythin' she asked for that she didn't get. . . ."

I nodded to the superintendent. "This gentleman said you went to the police, Mr. Underwood. What did they say?"

"Aw, the cops were all right. They talked to us but that was all. They said the DA had some cases but dropped 'em because these people's rights are protected by our Constitution!" His powerful fist dented the table. "What about my rights! Ain't I got any? These bums come in tellin' a lot of lies and hypnotize my daughter, take her away, and I can't do a thing about it?"

"Do you have any idea why your daughter joined the Society, Mr. Underwood?"

He slowly shook his head and sighed. "Not a one, buddy, not a one. . . ."

When we were going downstairs, the super whispered: "The kid had a reason. Underwood would come home Friday night with a load on and beat up the old lady. I musta called the cops ten times. He's such a big bastard they had to play a tattoo on his head with their clubs before they could get the cuffs on. My wife would go up and help Rose; the kid was always cryin', she said."

Perhaps for Elly Underwood there was a reason to follow Ginerva, but what about the others—the sons and daughters from affluent, educated, happy homes—why did they abandon everything to follow Ginerva?

Outside, the super was silent for a moment. "There's one more thing," he said abruptly. When he hesitated, I gave him a few more dollars, and he told me a strange story of the young woman who had inherited the row of tenements from her uncle. With her husband, a CPA, they maintained the place for a year. When they first came to collect the rents, they brought with them their four-year-old son, a victim of a rare muscle disease. The boy could manage only a few steps with heavy braces. The CPA laughed at the suggestion of the super's wife that they bring the child to be blessed by Ginerva, but one night, unknown to her husband, the mother attended a storefront church meeting and the boy was blessed.

"About three weeks later the guy called me up," the super said. "He was cryin' and babblin' like a baby. At first I couldn't understand what he was sayin'. Then I got it. They had just come from the doctor and were told the kid was improvin'."

"Are you telling me that this child, a helpless cripple, was cured after being blessed by Ginerva?"

"Buddy, I'm only tellin' you what *I* know," he said. "Right after that the kid kept improvin'. Last year they sold the houses and went south, where he got a pretty big job. They came around the day before they left to say good-bye." He shook his head unbelievingly at the memory. "The kid was with them. He wasn't wearin' any braces." His hand traced the journey in the air. "He got up, and so help me, mister, he walked from the curb to the stoop where I was standin'. The kid kept yellin', 'I did it, Mommy! I did it, Mommy! I walked!' I felt like cryin'." He shrugged. "That's *really* all I know, buddy. . . ."

(2 6)

When he turned to leave, I asked about the skylight.

"Oh sure," he said, and we returned to the store. Inside he pointed to the ceiling. "There is a big skylight up there." He walked across the room and unraveled a chain wrapped around a hook. "You pull this chain and the cover comes back—"

As he pulled, a steel cover slid back in the ceiling and a solid bar of sunshine, glittering with dust, lit up the dim room. It was as if a spotlight had been turned on.

"Someone told me this place had been a photographic studio when the navy took it over in World War II," the superintendent said. "Maybe that's why they had this skylight."

He locked the door of the store, waved good-bye, and entered the tenement.

I stood there alone, my mind in a whirl. I had no doubt that the super's story was true. Why would he have made it up? To please a curious generous stranger? That didn't ring right. After all, he had given me details which confirmed what Talbot had told me about the skylight.

The possibility that Ginerva could be a divine courier sent by God in one last effort to conquer the human heart with love and understanding before it vanished in His all-consuming fire crossed my mind, but it was so alien to my private convictions I dismissed it with a smile.

The truth is, I never possessed any deep religious faith; theological arguments always bored me. Even when the VC's mortars were threatening to blow me apart with the rest of the platoon, I couldn't force myself to start praying frantically to an unseen hidden power I had never thought twice about. I simply found it difficult to believe that a good and powerful God would allow men to wage a war like Nam, be indifferent to the needs of the poor, and let helpless children starve and be brutalized in a world that never once in its whole existence had offered peace and understanding. If there was a God, why didn't he make things right in the first place or at least intervene when the creatures he had made to his own likeness became embroiled in murder and genocide on a scale so vast as to numb the mind? Simplistic? Perhaps, but that had always been my private philosophy. So it was against this background that I dismissed the possibility, remote that it was, of Ginerva being God's courier and having divine powers to heal.

Yet as I walked down that dirty deserted street, the question once again rose to nag at me: why had my physical pain, my limp, and the nightmares vanished when she had touched me? And why did the small boy begin to walk after she had blessed him? And the cure of the young artist, investigated by Talbot, an experienced newspaperman who certainly was not naive and impressionable . . .

There was a bench at the bus stop, and I sat there a long time wondering, questioning, trying to sort out the natural explanations. But in the end, like Talbot, I could not find a satisfactory answer.

Not yet. . . .

The last call I made was to the *Chronicle*'s photographer who had taken the stunning picture of Ginerva. He said that when he arrived at the store, a man who appeared to be in charge told him to return precisely at four that afternoon.

"I didn't get it," he said, "but I returned. Before the store was dim; now it was bright—they had pulled back the cover of the skylight. Ginerva was sitting all by herself, looking beautiful, with the sunlight streaming down on her. The guy didn't have to hit me over the head. I just kept shooting. You saw the picture. It won the paper's monthly prize, the best picture of the year, and I sold copies to two photographic magazines. Like I said, they're all phonies. But the guy who was directing things that day certainly knew what he wanted."

Back at the hotel, I discovered I didn't have much of an appetite and left nearly all of my dinner on the plate. A brisk walk failed to clear my head; Ginerva's face was continually before me. When I returned to my room, I placed her color portrait on the bureau and studied it for a long time. I had never met anyone like her in my lifetime; scam artist or mystic, she had completely captivated me.

Sleep was impossible, so I decided to go over my notes, which I spread out on the bed, to plan just how my amateurish investigation should continue. I weighed one statement against another, one claim against another. Starting at the very beginning was Ginerva herself. I could see her on the stage, how she looked, how her splendid sense of imagery and stage presence had moved me. Unquestionably she was beautiful, the most beautiful woman I had ever seen, a self-proclaimed divine courier with a message to the world that God was ready to destroy it unless the world abandoned its evil ways. It sounded like an incredible fantasy, but obviously there were thousands who not only believed her but had joined her Society of the Chosen.

There were two things left to do; find that Pasadena playhouse and talk to her.

I found myself eager to begin. I felt a strange excitement, as if I was preparing for a rendezvous with a beautiful and mysterious woman. In the morning, the last thing I did before I left the room was carefully place her portrait in my wallet.

I discovered the Little Strand Theatre in Pasadena was now a parking lot; the building had been torn down after its owner had died two years before.

"It was an eyesore and I'm glad it's gone," a nearby real estate man told me. "The old guy who owned it loved to play the role of a theatrical producer, but all he could get were the worst of the amateur companies."

The local undertaker who had buried the old man gave me his nephew's name in San Diego. On the phone the nephew was courteous but emphatic; when the building was sold all books and records had been destroyed.

"It wasn't as though some famous actors or actresses had played here in their early days," he explained. "My uncle loved the theatre and year after year hung on to that old place. Nearly all the companies were non-Equity, only losers or kids wanting experience."

The leaflet I had been given at the rally had the address of the Society of the Chosen in San Francisco. It was a beautiful brownstone building with a gold-embossed cross on the door. One of the Angels answered my ring. He was soft-spoken but had eyes as hard as granite. He said simply that Her Holiness was appearing in other cities to give them God's message, then he closed the door on my request to take a message for her.

The following morning I returned to my room after breakfast and was wondering what next to do when the phone rang; it was Johnny Masters, telling me he had returned to St. Timothy's earlier than he had expected and wondering if I could meet him at the school as soon as possible and make a choice of my quarters because an extensive renovating program was to begin.

I hated to leave but there was nothing else I could do, so I ended my search at least in San Francisco. I told Johnny I would meet him at St. Timothy's within a few days. Then I called my father and made reservations for an afternoon flight to New York.

On the way to the airport, I asked the cabbie to pass the St. James Theatre. In the daylight it was shabby, desolate-looking. On either side of the entrance were huge posters:
LISTEN TO GINERVA—COURIER OF GOD, AND BE SAVED!
WILL YOU PERISH IN GOD'S SEA OF FLAME? FOLLOW GINERVA AND BE SAVED!

Almost unconsciously I moved my foot about; there was no pain. Before I left the hotel I had flushed the pills the doctors had given me in Saigon down the toilet; there had been no nightmares since I had attended that rally.

There were still many unexplained gaps in her story and questions that needed to be answered. What had started as a hunt for informa-

She studied there, spent some time with Old Vic, then enrolled in the American Academy of Arts here in the city."

"Is she here now?"

"I'm coming to that. About four months ago, Butler decided to set up his own company. He wanted to do a play a year, open in London, then bring it to New York. The company would be used in his movie making. It was along the idea of Orson Welles's old Mercury Theatre. He asked me to set up the legal structure, and that's what I've been doing in London."

I toasted him with my cup of coffee. "To the greatest solicitor of them all."

"My cup runneth over," he said. He took a sip of coffee and continued.

"About three weeks ago I began to notice a change in Butler. He seemed vague, jumpy, apprehensive. Then one night, very late, he called me over to his apartment and told me the reason: Leah, his daughter, had left the New York drama school and joined the Society of the Chosen."

"Ginerva's group?"

"Your old girl friend. You would be surprised how that phony organization has grown."

"She's not on the Coast any more—they bought that seminary near Purchase."

"I know, you showed me the clipping. For your information, they offer what they call a 'weekend retreat' up there, and it's packed with kids every week. That's what Leah took, and she never came out. That goddam woman is a menace."

"Why is she a menace, Ben? At least the kids aren't hustling, or mainlining, or robbing old women."

"No, but her goons are brainwashing them. You told me you saw kids collecting in San Francisco. The're all over the country, in the waiting rooms of airports. On the streets outside Grand Central. Penn Station. I made a stopover in Chicago and they were at the airport, shaking their containers, selling their wilted flowers or some newspaper they print. I spoke to them, Hilly, they sound like wind-up dolls! And where is all that dough going?"

"You got me. But how do I fit in with all this?"

"Let me go on with Butler. When he found out his daughter had joined the Society of the Chosen, he was furious. Like all rich men, he can't understand why money will not solve his problems. He tried to reach Leah to offer her anything, but she refused to talk to him. Then he called me. I advised him there was little he could do legally. She is twenty-two, on private property, and protected by the First Amendment."

"Even though you claim this whole thing is a fraud?"

"Freedom of religion. You have to prove that something is illegal before the law can act. That's why at Butler's order I hired the best private investigators in the business. But they just can't seem to dig up any evidence that someone is breaking the law." He paused. "I thought it was helpless until I saw this kid, Turner—" He added swiftly, when he saw my look of impatience, "I have to go back, Hilly, to fill you in. Do you remember the law firm I worked for before I was drafted?"

"Sure. The one you said represented everything in the entertainment business from jugglers to movie stars."

"That's correct. They have a fantastic variety of clients in show business. One whom I handled owned what was then the largest gay nightclub in the city. It was a classy place on the East Side. No SM guys, leather, or keys. Good food, entertainment, and more gays in one place than anywhere else in the city. The cops were dragging in the owner and I was in court once or twice a month. Finally I got a Supreme Court injunction and made the cops stop their harassment. The place finally burned down. I always thought someone needed a fire. The owner opened a health club on the West Side which he wanted me to handle, but I declined. However, he was always grateful for the fight I put up for him in Supreme Court and has sent me a few good clients. One day he called and asked as a personal favor if I would talk to the nephew of a friend, who had a legal problem. I agreed and the kid came in. His name is Norman Turner." He leaned back. "And he wanted to talk about Ginerva. . . ."

"Was this *before* you knew Butler?"

"Long before. I had just opened my office after coming back from Nam."

"What did the kid want, Ben?"

"It seemed his mother had been killed in an air crash, and in a time of great emotional stress he joined the Society, gave them his inheritance, which included a $24,000 insurance policy on his mother which they had collected, and a brownstone worth $90,000."

"And now he wants out and his money back?"

"Exactly. He wanted me to start a legal action against the major domo of the entire entourage. He's the absolute boss and the one closest to Ginerva."

"Do you know his name?"

"Foreman—David L. Foreman. He appears to have covered his tracks very well. We can't find anything about him."

"That could be the guy who started out with her when she had that storefront church in San Francisco. Remember how the old religion editor described him to me? 'A promotor who was milking the main chance.'"

"That sounds like Foreman. There is also a woman and two other guys connected with him. We don't know too much about them at this point, but we will. You know, of course, the crap Ginerva's handing out?"

"You mean her meetings with God?"

"The Doomsday bit. How the Almighty gave her control of the lightning—the worst nonsense I have ever heard."

"What about this kid?"

"Turner? Well, the day he came in to the office was slow, so I let him talk. He's a nice kid but mixed up, sad, in a way. He's editor of *The Call*, their excuse for a newspaper."

"Does the kid have newspaper background?"

"From what he told me, he did some sports writing for his college newspaper and was a stringer for a New York City newspaper. I guess he was better than nothing. The kid told me some of the things going on—they run that motherhouse like an army camp, and the only way you can get out of there is to go over the fence and that takes a lot of doing. When someone wants out they are taken to what they call "counseling" and after a few days the rebellious kids come back as good little boys and girls. Obviously they have people skilled in psychological brainwashing techniques and the kids don't have a chance. Now let me get back to Butler. After he told me his daughter had joined the Society of the Chosen, I told him about Turner and at his request got in touch with the kid."

From inside his jacket he took out an envelope that contained several sheets of letterheads, and gave one to me. On the top was "Hillside Press, 309 Wallace Avenue, Jersey City."

"That's the printer who does *The Call*. Turner gave me these letterheads and told me that whenever I wanted to get in touch with him to write a few lines saying he was needed for a consultation on editorial changes and to telephone at once. That's what I did. When he called, I told him about Leah Butler, and he promised to get back to me. A week later, I met him in a small restaurant in the Village. The kid's really scared, Hilly, the way he keeps turning around you would think his head is on a swivel."

"Does he know anything about Leah?"

"He did. Leah, he said, is assigned to the motherhouse. She'd already had one bad experience; soon after she arrived Foreman ordered her to abandon all thoughts of acting. He told her the stage was the 'devil's playground.' Turner found her weeping on a back stairwell. He suggested to Foreman that Leah teach dramatics to the

Disciples who are training as salesmen to sell *The Call* and their phony jewelry. Foreman liked the idea and told Leah she could use her talents for 'God's work.' Leah and Turner became good friends. As I told Butler, Leah isn't all that lost; Turner said she has resisted all attempts by Foreman to exploit her for the publicity value."

"Ben, you still haven't told me how *I* come into this!"

"Just be patient, Hilly. Butler, as you would imagine, has a lot of contacts. Through them we got a private interview with the attorney general in Washington. The AG is a nice guy whose wife happens to love Butler, so he gave us a lot of time. He had an IRS file on his desk when we came in—a file on the Society of the Chosen. But as I told you, the feds couldn't find anything illegal. The AG pointed out that religion, no matter if it's devil worship, is a most delicate matter in this country. What is sacrilege to one man is religion to another—and all protected under the First Amendment."

"What about bank accounts and stuff like that?"

"All legal. The IRS can't find a thing."

"So the Attorney General of the United States couldn't help you or Butler?"

"Don't be sarcastic. As I said, he was very sympathetic. In addition to having been dean of Yale's law school, he has one of the best legal minds in the country. He told us about a former pupil who was elected prosecutor of a midwestern city. He also had trouble with a prophet and a cult that was using young people in his community, but after failing to find any evidence of illegality, he turned to a friend who owned the state's largest newspaper and suggested he start looking into the group. The publisher assigned a reporter, and the hard white glare of publicity did what the law couldn't do; exposed the leader as the charlatan he really was. The group was laughed out of existence."

I said, "And now we come to my part?"

"Right. You may or may not know that Sir Edward's father-in-law, Lord Cavendish, grandfather of Leah, is the media king of England. He not only owns the big newspapers over there but has papers in Canada and across the United States, along with television stations and a syndicate that distributes most of the comics and columns. Notch Hall Publishers, one of the biggest, is a subsidiary of the syndicate."

"I'm beginning to smell something, Ben."

"Hear me out, Hilly," he said quickly. "Let me finish. After we left the AG's office in Washington, Butler and I returned to New York and sat around his apartment exchanging ideas. Closely examined, most of them fell apart. Then it came to me. I gave the idea to Sir Edward and he went for it—"

"And that is?"

"Why shouldn't we take advantage of Sir Edward's father-in-law's newspaper, publishing, and television empire? Do as that guy did in the Midwest—use the media to expose this phony bitch and her Society?"

"But how will that get Butler's daughter back?"

"Leah told Turner that while she still believes in Ginerva, some things about the Society now disturb her. Her father insists she is a levelheaded, intelligent kid who would leave that setup once it's exposed."

He studied me. "So far what do you think of the idea?"

"How would you go about exposing these people? What format would you use?"

"I suggest that a writer—someone who knows the newspaper business—do a devastating series on the Society. The series would be expanded into a book, with both the series and the book given a tremendous push by Cavendish's chain—advertising, promotion."

"But, Ben, where would the material come from? You can't write a series out of thin air from a bundle of clippings."

"Private investigators," he said promptly. "Butler is willing to hire a small army. Everything they dig up will be turned over to the writer."

"Have you worked out an agreement? What will the writer be paid?"

He said quickly, "Cavendish will pay you an advance of $50,000 for a ten-part series and an additional $50,000 for a book-length manuscript of not less than 60,000 words. There will be no trouble on royalties—we can name our terms. You could get a hell of a foreign sale, Hilly, and I bet I can massage those guys in Hollywood so they'll come running with fistfuls of money. . . ."

I groaned. "I thought you would get around to me."

He ground out his cigar. "When I proposed you, Sir Edward was very enthusiastic. He got Lord Cavendish on the phone and talked to him. They're both very high on you, Hilly." He leaned back. "Well, what do you say?"

I protested, "Ben, there are scores of writers you could get—some have excellent backgrounds in investigative reporting. They could do a superb job for Butler."

"Hilly, Sir Edward is no fool. Neither is Lord Cavendish. I talked to Butler for hours—until four this morning, in fact—and many times with his father-in-law. His phone bill will be enough to bail out New York. We are convinced you would do a dramatic, conscientious—and, I might add—truthful job." He hunched forward. "Nobody wants this to be a five-star final tabloid exposé, Hilly. This is important! The more I read the reports of our investigators, the more I am convinced that there is something behind this group. It's more than just a bunch of smart con men with a good-looking dame up front, exploiting thousands of gullible young kids, it's—" He paused, then added fiercely, "It's goddam sinister! I don't know what they're up to, Hilly, but my gut reaction tells me it's bad. Very bad."

"I still can't believe the attorney general, with all his resources, can't do something, Ben!"

"There are laws in this country, Hilly," he said with elaborate patience. "The government just can't start investigating the Society of the Chosen because the daughter of a world-famous actor decided to join a religious cult!" He slammed his palm down on the table. "We must have facts to give the law! A publicity campaign against these people is bound to attract dissident members, people like Turner with an ax to grind! All we need is one tiny opening to get our foot in the door."

"Didn't Turner supply that opening?"

"Of course the kid will be of enormous help." He impatiently pushed aside his cup. "But we need more, much more. Well, what do you say, Hilly?"

"Frankly I don't know. . . ."

"What do you mean, you don't know? All I've been hearing from you for the past few years is how you find this woman so interesting, so mysterious. In San Francisco you spent a couple of days looking into her and not finding a hell of a lot. Here I give you an opportunity to do all the investigating you want and get paid more than $50,000 to do it, and you hesitate! 'I don't know' is all I can get out of you! Hilly, I don't understand."

"There's nothing to understand, Ben. I'm simply not an investigative reporter. I got to Nam as a war correspondent only because of a fluke. My father had lunch with his college roommate who happened to own a string of newspapers and had a crazy idea I could write a column called 'Dear Buddy.' Just how the hell does that qualify me for the job?"

"Very simple," he said calmly. "From what I gather, Foreman is a smart guy. If you go up there and sell yourself as a sympathetic newspaperman who will give him a fair shake, I bet you a bottle of the best scotch he'll go for it." He leaned forward, "After all, Hilly, didn't she work a miracle on you? Suppose you tell him the whole story of the action in Vietnam and what happened to you that night outside the theatre? Isn't it logical to assume he'll welcome you with open arms? You will be a friend in a world of a hostile press. I went over the scrapbook Mrs. Caxton has been keeping for you, and the tone of the articles is getting nasty. That one in the Detroit paper—didn't it charge the Society of the Chosen with brainwashing kids and tell how parents are beginning to organize protests?"

"Not only in Detroit, but the L.A. and San Francisco papers have had series on the Society," I pointed out, "and not complimentary."

"So there you are," he said, throwing up his hands. "What more do you want? Your girl friend is vulnerable, now is the time to move in. You can ride up on a big white horse like Lancelot."

"I don't want to do a hatchet job on anyone, Ben."

He clasped his hands to his forehead in mock horror. "A hatchet job! Who's asking you to do a hatchet job?"

"You are, pal, and you know it."

"Let me ask you this," he said. "Will you promise to write everything as you see it, along with everything either I or my investigators dig up?"

"If you mean gossip, innuendos and half-truths, the answer is no."

He slammed his hand down on the table. "I mean the *facts* you claim to love. Documentary evidence. No gossip. No half-truths. No innuendos—only hard cold facts that could be used in a court or a legal action. Now what do you say about that?"

"Do you have such material?"

He hesitated. "Well, let's say I'm on to something. . . ."

"Well, what is it?"

"I've only started. At this point the information is so tenuous it may peter out. I would rather not discuss it now, Hilly, and get you off on the wrong track."

"But is the information *on* Ginerva?"

Again he hesitated, then slowly nodded. "Yes, I can tell you that much, but don't press me. Let's leave it this way. If it dies out or really builds into something, you will know all about it." He added pleadingly, "Hilly, all I'm asking you is to go up there as a writer who is deeply interested in finding out all he can about this woman who claims to be the courier of God. Let me do the lawyer's job. As I told you, we're hiring a small army of private investigators." He paused. "Who knows what will happen while you're up there? Maybe you can do something to help this guy Foreman, maybe in the way of publicity or promotion, so he could come to depend on you. When we're both finished, we'll sit down and compare notes. I give you my word, and that's from a guy who loves you like a brother, that anything you write, the syndicate and the newspaper chain will print without touching your copy. Now what do you say?"

"How long do I have?"

"Take as long as you want. You don't go back to St. Timothy's until—what, the first week in September? Spend all summer."

"Suppose Foreman says no?"

"Then he's a fool, and I don't size him up as a fool." He said sharply, "But if he does, you can write the series based only on the factual material our investigators come up with. Again, no gossip, no innuendos, no hatchet job. Only facts. We'll also get interviews with parents of kids in the Society, kids who have dropped out, documents of public record—that sort of material."

I could feel a kernel of excitement starting to grow. It would be an absurd thing to attempt, of course. If I did as Ben suggested, I would have to spend weeks *inside* the motherhouse, talking to Ginerva, viewing her up close, trying to answer all the questions which had plagued me about her for years and probing the psyches of her weird followers. I would have to take my chances with Foreman, her slick promoter, Russell, their muscleman, and that group of humorless Avenging Angels. And too, I would be paid more than $50,000! Ben's proposition was completely ridiculous, of course, but I knew it would be impossible for me to refuse. . . . Ginerva at last!

"Okay, I'll do it," I said. "What's the first step? See Sir Edward with you?"

"Not right now," he said. "First you're going with me to see the DA. His son was with me on the Columbia Law Review. I called him and he made a date for me to see his old man."

"Won't you have to call him again to tell him I'll be along?"

He carefully snipped off the end of a cigar with a pair of tiny gold scissors, lit it, and eyed me with amusement through the smoke of the cigar he held clenched in his teeth like FDR's cigarette holder. Then he removed it with a flourish.

"When I made that date I told him you would be with me."

I had heard that the reason for Ben's success in a courtroom was his careful preparation and his particular talent for sizing up his clients and his opponents.

How true.

3

Sir Edward Butler

Sir Edward Butler had one of the largest apartments in the Dakota; it seemed like an estate with elevators. Ceilings soared, the windows were wide, with a fabulous view of Central Park. I hadn't seen parquet floors since our old apartment. Books, magazines, manuscripts, newspapers were everywhere. Ben nudged me and I looked across the room. A portrait of Ellen Terry hung over the fireplace, but she was older, her eyes weary and cynical.

He whispered, "He went wild when he saw my Terry. He wanted me to name a price."

"What did you tell him?"

"I said I would rather give him my right arm. He offered me his tickets to his play if I would tell him how that secret slot in the molding worked."

"You said no, of course."

"You guessed right, my friend. Who needs Butler to get me tickets? Here he is."

First you noticed how handsome he was; chiseled face, deep blue eyes with incredibly long lashes, and thick gray hair in a fashionable cut that fit his head like a warrior's helmet. Then you spotted the obvious signs of dissipation, the slight trembling of his hands and the tiny network of veins beginning to appear along the sides of his nose.

He was tall, and although he was in his late fifties, he was trim and deeply tanned. He had a mechanical trained actor's smile that could be turned on and off like a neon sign, a mouthful of expensively capped teeth.

"Ben, how are you?" He turned to me. "And this is Hilly?"

"Richard Preston Hillers, famous war correspondent and hero, now St. Timothy's celebrated professor of history—Colonial to Appomattox."

Butler held up a glass of Perrier water. "I'm on the wagon for this new play. What will you gentlemen have?"

He quickly and expertly mixed our drinks, and then we sat down after he casually brushed piles of manuscripts to the floor.

"Any news about Leah, Ben?" he asked, the smile gone, his voice anxious.

"Nothing really, Sir Edward, but Hilly has agreed to write that series."

"Wonderful!" he said. "I can't thank you enough, Hilly. I feel so damn frustrated. First your attorney general tells me there's nothing he can do. Then your IRS claims this damn organization is clean. And you don't hold out much hope for the DA, Ben—"

"It's an old story, Sir Edward," Ben said. "The District Attorney would demand evidence of a crime. The organization is completely protected by the First Amendment."

"But we know they're a band of charlatans, Ben!" Butler protested. "They couldn't care less about God! They're only using those poor kids."

"Just so everything is put on the table, Sir Edward, Hilly believes there could be another side," Ben said. "I think you should listen to him."

I briefly told him about Vietnam and what had happened to me in the old movie theatre.

He gave me an incredulous look. "But, Hilly, surely you don't believe in that woman and all she claims?"

"I'm not claiming she is a miracle worker, Sir Edward, but you must consider the facts—beyond my own experiences. I personally looked into three cases of cures—one girl had leukemia—who were cured after Ginerva blessed them."

"I knew an actor in London who had a child with leukemia," he said. "They were ready to bury her when she recovered. I believe she has three children now." He waved his hand. "The girl you looked into probably would have been cured without being touched by that fraud."

I found his arrogance abrasive. "I don't agree, Sir Edward," I told him. "I have no doubt the people who have taken her over can hide in the shadow of a corkscrew but I'm not ready to completely condemn her, not yet, anyway."

He raised his eyebrows. "You seem taken with her."

I replied, "Let's say she interests me."

"I can't understand," he said slowly, "why someone like Leah who could have anything she wanted, chose to leave me and her drama studies to follow this woman! It doesn't make sense."

"Kids today are lost, Sir Edward," I told him. "They don't trust anyone or anything. I will never forget the young Marine who came back on the plane with me. 'I will never trust anyone again,' he told me, 'and that includes my parents and my government.'"

"That's the way it is today, Sir Edward," Ben broke in. "Look at that survey the churches did that appeared on page one of the *Times*. Only older people are going to church, many of the younger ones have dropped out of formal religion. They're looking for something—something with a message of hope—"

"And you believe that is why they follow her?"

"Yes I do. I also know it's a racket, and a big one. Our investigators have been looking into this guru business. One guy who was a former bartender grew a beard, bought a white robe, and founded a temple in Brooklyn. He retired two years ago to an estate in Florida, after an old woman left him over $200,000."

"But what does Ginerva offer?"

I answered, "The way I see it, she offers the kids a challenge to change the world, and it's catching on. In addition, there is also a sense of belonging."

"I don't care what she offers," Butler said fiercely. "That woman is a bloody charlatan."

"We can accuse her twenty-fours a day, Sir Edward," Ben said, "but that won't put her in jail. Only evidence of fraud or better will." He looked over at me. "Maybe Hilly will come up with something."

"I'm not a detective," I warned them.

"No, but you have common sense," Ben said easily. "You may stumble across something."

"Do we know where this woman comes from? Her early background?" Butler asked.

"Our investigators report no more than what Hilly dug up when he was out in San Francisco," Ben said. "Hilly talked to someone who thought she could have been an actress who once played *Joan* in Pasadena but there is nothing in the *Equity* records or in the files of *Variety*." He hesitated. "However, as I told Hilly, Sir Edward, I'm on to something that could really shake them up, perhaps destroy her. . . ."

Butler gave him a startled look. "My God, man, what is it?"

Ben shook his head. "I didn't want to tell you about it because at this stage it is so tenuous the whole lead could go up like a puff of smoke. It's a long way from here, and there is a hell of a lot more work to be done before I can really discuss it. So please, Sir Edward, let's leave it until I have something concrete. If it falls apart I'll tell you both what is was."

"You'll leave me biting my nails," Butler grumbled.

"Better that than be disappointed," Ben said briskly. "But what we do have now is Hilly, and I'm sure he'll give us a first-rate job."

"No doubt about that," Butler added.

"I have made it clear to Ben, and I would like to make it clear to you, Sir Edward," I said, "that I don't intend to do a hatchet job on Ginerva. I will only write the facts as I see them."

"Granted," Butler said coolly. "I don't believe Lord Cavendish would print a mess of lies about anyone, even that fraud. But I do think the simple facts about Ginerva and her horrible Society would be enough. Don't you, Ben?"

"Before Hilly starts writing, I hope to give him facts that will blow her beautiful head right off her shoulders," Ben said, grinning.

"I'll go back to London trying to guess what it is instead of concentrating on my script," Butler complained. He pleaded, "Not even a small hint, Ben?"

But Ben only shook his head at both of us.

4

The Motherhouse

I agreed with Ben that the only way to get a real insight into the Society of the Chosen—and Ginerva—was through Foreman, and we both concluded two preliminary steps had to be taken: Ben would contact Norman Turner, the dissatisfied young Disciple and editor of the cult's newspaper by using one of the printer's letterheads, and I had to make some arrangement with Mr. Ranks.

"Foreman is sure to do some checking on your background. The series you are doing should be for the Ranks chain," Ben pointed out. "It would only take a few phone calls to find out the Notch Hall Syndicate is owned by Lord Cavendish, Butler's father-in-law. Do you think Ranks will go for it?"

"I don't see why not. He praised me to the skies when he last saw my father. What about me? If Foreman does any checking, do you think he could link me with you?"

"I don't see how. I'm Butler's attorney of record, but certainly your name would never appear."

"I'm beginning to feel like a secret agent."

He laughed. "Enjoy it, Hilly! Who can tell? You might wind up hanging a prophetess!"

I saw Mr. Ranks in his Boston office and he was agreeable to any arrangements I wanted to make. When I called Ben from Boston,

Turner had already contacted him and would see us in a midtown hotel room.

He was in his early twenties, slender, with an almost adolescent boniness about him, and worried pale blue eyes.

He sat on the edge of the bed and said, looking at me, "What's up, Mr. Rice?"

"This is my friend, Richard Hillers," Ben said, turning to me. "You can call him Hilly."

"How are you, Norman?" I said, shaking a handful of bones.

"Fine." He looked at Ben. "What's this all about?"

"Hilly is a former war correspondent who will appear very shortly at the motherhouse to sell Foreman the idea of writing a series on Ginerva and the Society for a New England newspaper chain. By the way, Norman, have you had lunch?"

"I had a hamburger on the way over here," Turner said nervously. "I don't see how this concerns me, Mr. Rice."

"I assume you still want to get back your money and the house you gave those phonies," Ben snapped.

"Oh yes, of course."

"When you first came to me, we went over the whole problem of either suing or prosecuting these people. I explained to you how they are fully protected under the First Amendment and have a free tax status as a religious organization. I also told you that to file suit for recovery of your money is one thing, but an investigation to gather evidence to back your claim of duress and conducting a trial is very, very expensive. Do you remember me telling you all this, Norman?"

"Yes, sir."

"Well, you know all about Leah Butler and how furious her father and grandfather are because she joined that nut factory. We've gone to the Attorney General, the IRS, and the New York County District Attorney, but none of them can help us. Now we have decided that only the hard glare of publicity might prod some official agency into doing something about the Society of the Chosen and perhaps attract enough outraged parents to bring a class action or, better still, get on the backs of the politicians representing them in Washington and force a federal agency to go after this group. Do you understand?"

"I'm with you," Turner said.

"That is why Hilly is going up there to try to sell Foreman the idea. I would like you to help him in every way possible." Now he spelled it out very slowly. "In return, Norman, I promise you at the proper time I will start suit on your behalf, use every bit of information dug up by the detectives working for Sir Edward, and bring your case to trial." He paused and smiled. "And it won't cost you a dime. How does that sound?"

Turner intertwined his fingers and looked about the room.

"Foreman is no dope, Mr. Rice," he said slowly, "and Brother Russell—" he swallowed hard, "—is a rough guy."

"Isn't Russell the big blond guy who opened the rally I attended in San Francisco?" I asked Turner.

He nodded. "That's him. He's head of security for the mother-house."

"Why are you afraid of him, Norm?" Ben asked easily.

Turner kept swallowing. "There are a lot of stories about him."

I pressed him. "Like what?"

He studied his clasped hands. "Kids who want to leave are brought to him. Either you don't see them again or they come back walking on their heels. There is a black kid named Thomas. He was making all kinds of threats and Russell called him in. I didn't see him for a few weeks. When I did, he was carrying a Bible, smiling to himself, and telling everyone how he loved the Society."

Ben said, "In other words, they did something to him. Maybe brainwashed him. Is that it, Norm?"

Turner said quickly, "I don't know, Mr. Rice, I really don't know." He swallowed again. "And I don't want to know. All I want is to get out, sue them, and get my money back. . . ."

"And that is exactly what will happen, Norm," Ben said assuringly. "Now, what do you think of Hilly going up there to do a newspaper series on Ginerva and the Society? Do you think they'll go for it?"

"I don't think you'll get very far," Turner said to me, almost apologetically. "Two weeks ago I heard they turned down a New York newspaper and a big TV program that wanted to do an interview with Ginerva."

"Who refused?" Ben asked.

"Foreman. Brother Foreman. Some of the newspapers have been blasting the Society recently, and he really got mad at some guy on the Coast who suggested that the government look into where the money is all going."

"Do you have any idea of where it *is* going, Norm?" I asked.

He shrugged. "Who knows? They say foreign missions. Old age homes. Half-way houses for addicts. Schools. You know, the usual crap." He said bitterly, "What a jerk I was to fall for that line."

"Anything you can do to help us will help yourself in the end, Norm," Ben pointed out.

"Do you see Ginerva often?" I inquired.

He shook his head. "She has an apartment over the Grand Ball-room on the far side of the estate but we don't see her that much. Once or twice when she's coming back from a rally or when she walks about the grounds. Now they have an Angel outside her front door twenty-four hours a day."

"Why? Has there been any trouble?" Ben asked.

"Not that I know of," Turner replied.

"Who is really the boss at the motherhouse?" I asked.

Without hesitation he answered, "Foreman. No one makes a move up there without his okay."

"Does that include Russell?"

"Russell, Andrew—he's sort of assistant to Russell—they all jump when Foreman calls. The national tour is the big thing now."

"Tell us about it, Norm," Ben said.

"I know some of the girls who work for Russell and sometimes for Foreman, and they usually tell me things," he said. "Foreman is making big plans to have Ginerva do a national tour, to appear in almost every city. There are all sorts of plans in the making about using ads on television and in newspapers." He hesitated. "In fact, this might be a good time to hit Foreman. . . ."

"Why is that, Norm?" I asked.

"He's been complaining lately to me about *The Call*—I'm the editor —how it is nothing and he wants to put some money into it and make it look 'classy'—that's the word he used. I'm supposed to give him a report with recommendations sometime this summer. He wants to revamp the whole paper by Labor Day. I know he's looking for publicity for Ginerva and this tour, but as he told me, he can't trust any newspapermen. How did he put it?" He grinned. "Oh, yeah. He called them all 'infidels.'"

"Hilly has something more to offer than the ordinary neswpaper-man who goes up there, Norman," Ben said. "Hilly, why don't you tell Norm what happened between you and Ginerva."

By the time I finished telling Turner the story of the San Francisco incident, his eyes were wide.

"That was a miracle!" he exclaimed.

"Yeah," Ben said dryly. "We'll make it a miracle for Foreman's sake. Do you think that will impress Foreman, Norm?"

"I think that will give you a good edge," he said, shaking his head. "A real good one. Do you have any clippings?"

"My father kept a scrapbook of some of my stories from Vietnam."

"I would bring that along," Turner said. "Foreman is great for visual stuff."

I asked him, "In your opinion, does Ginerva follow Foreman's orders?"

"Definitely," was his answer. "She's no better than anyone else up there. He's the boss and she knows it."

"In San Francisco I was told there was another man and a blonde woman connected with Foreman," I said. "Do you have any idea who they are?"

"The blonde is Sister Sloan, and the other guy is Brother Troy. She works with Foreman in his office as his assistant, and Troy is supposed to be in charge of communications. He told me once that he had been in Vietnam doing a documentary."

Ben looked at me. "Did you ever hear of him, Hilly?"

I shook my head. "No, but that doesn't mean anything. I never met half the print and television reporters in Saigon. There were even war correspondents representing fashion magazines. However, Troy could be a friend in court."

Turner glanced at his wristwatch. "I had better get back up there. When will you see Foreman?"

"In a few days."

He put out his hand. "Good luck. If you convince Foreman to let you do the series, he'll order me to help you."

After Turner left, Ben turned to me with an amused look. "You better make your 'miracle' convincing, Hilly. That's your ace in the hole."

A few days later, carrying the packaged scrapbook, I took the train to White Plains and found a cab at the station. The driver was a huge impassive man with hooded eyes and a stub of a cigarette that hung from the corner of his mouth. When he talked it bobbed up and down, sprinkling his vest with ashes.

"I want to go to the headquarters of the Society of the Chosen in Purchase," I told him.

"Do you have a kid in there?" he asked in a flat emotionless voice.

"No, I'm a newspaperman up here to interview Ginerva."

"You'll never get to see her," he predicted gloomily. "They don't like newspaper people. In fact they asked me not to bring any up but to have them call from here."

I leaned over, the ten dollar bill next to his face. He took it and turned on the ignition.

"I'll take ya to the gatehouse, after that you're on your own. Okay?"

"Fine. Do you get many riders wanting to go there?"

"They come every week," he said in his monotone. "Fathers, mothers, sisters, brothers, girl friends, boy friends—they all want their people out of there. But the kids don't want to leave."

"What makes you say that?"

"I dunno. But it ain't a place I would want my kid to be in. I think I'd break both his arms and legs before I'd let him go."

"Have you seen any of the Disciples?"

"Oh sure, they ride me all the time to the White Plains station. Nice kids but they give me the creeps. They talk like machines and always leave their newspaper." He held up a copy of *The Call*. "I bring it home to the wife for the cat's box."

We rode for a few miles in silence, then he warned, "It's just up the road."

We drove along an endless row of hedges behind a high cyclone fence. Beyond were the peaks and eaves of a beautiful mansion. There was a small wooden house at the open iron gates and a bronze sign which read SOCIETY OF THE CHOSEN.

A guard in a gray uniform standing in the doorway of the gate-house watched me approach. He was young, alert and carefully looked me up and down.

"Can I help you, sir?"

"My name is Richard Preston Hillers and I'm a special writer for the Ranks newspaper chain," I told him. "I would like to see David Foreman in regard to a series of articles we're doing on the Society."

"I'm afraid you're wasting your time," he said. "All press inquiries must be made in writing—"

"I've come here to see Brother Foreman about a particular 'miracle' performed by Her Holiness, which I witnessed," I said. "I don't intend to write for an interview, and I don't think Brother Foreman would like it if he knew you had turned me away without discussing that miracle before I wrote the series."

His eyes wavered, then dropped. "I'll tell the house you're here," he mumbled and went inside. He returned in a few minutes. "Someone is coming down."

The estate looked enormous from where I stood: acres of rolling lawns and shrubbery, a long driveway leading to a stunning Victorian mansion with verandas and dark green awnings. There were graveled paths, other buildings, trees under which groups of young people were studying or talking, and an athletic field where several were playing volleyball. Suddenly a small cart, the type used by golfers, came down the drive.

"This man will take you to Brother Russell in the motherhouse," the guard said, relieved.

A hard-faced Angel was driving. He looked the same as those I had seen in San Francisco: young, crew cut, blue suit, white shirt, dark tie. The only thing missing was the white carnation.

"You have a beautiful place here," I observed as we chugged up the driveway.

"There is only peace and love here," he said in a flat voice as he raised his hand in answer to a group that called out, "Good morning, Brother. Peace be with you."

When he left me at the foot of the steps of the big house, another Angel pressed a hidden buzzer that opened the heavy front door. I found myself in a large foyer facing a magnificent winding staircase. At its foot two Angels sat behind a desk; a third was standing. I recognized him as Brother Russell.

"You told the guard at the gate you are a newspaperman," Russell asked softly. "May I ask what paper?"

"It's a chain," I replied. "The Ranks newspaper chain, the largest in New England, starting with Boston. There are also five newspapers in the South, from North Carolina to Texas. Ten dailies and five weeklies; total circulation according to the last Council audit is in the millions. Here is my identification."

He quickly read my ID card and looked up. "This is a war correspondent's identification card."

"I was in Vietnam five years covering the war for the Ranks papers and writing a column at the request of Mr. Ranks."

Russell handed me back my card. "As I understand, you are interested in doing a series on the Society of the Chosen and Her Holiness, Ginerva."

"That is correct. Mr. Ranks has been impressed by some of the stories about the Society and believes a series of objective articles would interest our readers."

"We have cooperated with the press many times," he said coldly, "and they have been far from objective. You said you wished to see Brother Foreman. Who gave you his name?"

"I heard it at a rally I attended some years ago at the old St. James Theatre in San Francisco. You were also there, Brother Russell."

"You told the guard at the gate you knew of some particular miracle performed by Her Holiness. What about it?"

"It happened to me."

Russell and two Angels stared at me. Then Russell said, "Have a seat. I'll see if Brother Foreman can see you."

He went upstairs and I sat there, trying my best to avoid the cold, hostile stares of the two Angels. After about fifteen minutes, he appeared at the top of the stairs.

"Okay. Send him up," he called out.

On the second floor there were several heavy oak doors bordering a long corridor. Russell opened one, stood aside, and I walked into a small office. Seated at a desk was a blonde I estimated to be about thirty-five. She had cool blue eyes, hair like corn silk stylishly coiffed, a flawless complexion, and pouty pink lips without a trace of lipstick.

Before she identified herself I knew she was Sister Sloan.

"I'm Sister Tura Sloan, Brother Foreman's assistant," she said. "He will be with you in a few minutes. Please be seated."

After a few minutes I said, "I find it's very peaceful here."

She slowly swung around from her typewriter. "That's all there is here—peace and love," she said. I thought I detected just the faintest sign of sarcasm in her voice, and I noticed Russell frown.

A few minutes later a buzzer sounded. "Brother Foreman will see you now," she said, looking me up and down as I followed Russell into the office.

A pretty brown-haired girl with large violet-colored eyes, carrying a batch of letters, passed me on her way out. Sister Sloan stiffened and gave her a scornful look. It was something to remember.

Over Russell's shoulder I could see rows of steel files, a black leather couch, a bank of windows overlooking the spacious grounds, and a large desk.

Darkness. Strange, but that was the very word that leaped into my mind as I studied the man behind the desk. He appeared to be in his early forties, with a thin handsome face, thick coal-black hair, dark eyes, and a smooth, swarthy skin. His conservative suit never came off a pipe rack. In the few minutes it took me to cross the room, I was sure those cold knowing eyes had classified and filed me for future reference. For a moment we studied each other, then he silently pointed to a chair in front of his desk. As I sat down, his fingers started to drum, almost unconsciously, on the onyx desk top, smooth as a slab of polished coal. I could see his fingernails were manicured.

"I haven't too much time, Mr. Hillers," he said in a sure cool voice, "so let's get down to business. Brother Russell has given me the basic information: your name is Richard Preston Hillers, you were a war correspondent for the Ranks newspaper chain, and now you would like to do a series of articles on the Society of the Chosen and Her Holiness, Ginerva." He paused, then asked, "Why should we cooperate with you when we have refused a major New York City newspaper and a national television network?"

My reply was swift and blunt. "Why did you turn them down?"

My aggressiveness seemed to take him by surprise. "Simply because they come up, we cooperate fully, and what finally appears in print is a collection of half-truths, outrageous lies, gossip, and innuendo. Some time ago I decided we can't win, they'll print what they please, so why waste our time cooperating?"

"I don't happen to be the usual reporter, Brother Russell."

"Oh?" he said, "and what makes you different?"

I slowly and very dramatically lifted my pants leg, pointed to the jagged scar on my calf, and rolled down my sock to reveal the pink welt on my shinbone.

"These are shrapnel wounds I received when I accompanied a platoon on patrol action in the Highlands," I said. "We were ambushed by the VC and I was the only survivor. I was forced to watch the young company commander die—both his legs were blown off."

Both were listening intently. I knew I had them.

"God must have had some plan in mind to allow me to survive," I went on. "I came back to the States with what the doctors said was a permanent limp in this leg. One night in San Francisco, just before I returned to New York, my leg was paining so much I took a cab back to the hotel. On the way we were stopped by a large crowd going into a theatre. The cab driver said it was a rally being held by Ginerva, and told me something about her. On a God-inspired impulse, I went into that theatre and listened to her very beautiful sermon on the last hours of Christ. When Brother Russell asked that all those who wished to be blessed by Her Holiness kneel down in the aisle, I joined the others and was blessed by Her Holiness. When I left the theatre, my limp had disappeared."

"And doctors had told you the limp would be permanent?" Foreman asked.

I lied as gracefully as I could. "The bone man at the hospital said the shrapnel had permanently damaged some muscles. . . ."

"We haven't been to the St. James Theatre for years," Russell said. "Why didn't you come to us earlier?"

"I returned from Vietnam feeling disillusioned and depressed," I explained, "and decided to leave the newspaper business to teach at St. Timothy's, a private boys' school in New Jersey. When I read you had moved your motherhouse here, I decided it was time to show in some way my appreciation for what Her Holiness had done for me. I thought of the idea of a series and approached Mister Ranks. He was very enthusiastic and has promised to both promote the articles and give them a great deal of space in his newspapers."

"When you write these articles, do you intend to discuss your own miracle?" Foreman asked.

I hoped I looked surprised. "Of course."

"Then what more can we give you?"

"I think it is time to show the *real* Society and reveal the good it is doing for the young people in our country," I said with a great deal of eagerness. "I was with them in San Francisco, talked to them, listened to what they had to say. I assume the Society is larger now, there must have been many, many cures during the last few years across the country. Now you have this new motherhouse. As I came in, I saw some of the young people on the grounds. They appear very happy to me. I would also like to interview Her Holiness. I would like to tell her my story, get her opinion of today's world, what is happening to all of us, where are we going. . . ."

I didn't want to pile it on too much so I let my words die off. Foreman's dark eyes seemed to bore through me. His face was impassive, but those polished nails had started their drumming.

"May I see the identification card you showed Brother Russell?" he said at last.

He examined it closely and returned it. "By any chance do you have some of your articles?"

I put my wrapped scrapbook on his desk. "My father died last year. I found this among his effects. It's a scrapbook of some of the stories I filed from Vietnam. Immodestly, I might point out I was praised in an article *Time* did on war correspondents stationed in Saigon."

"What would you want to do here?" Russell asked.

"I have no plans for the summer," I replied, "so I would like to spend as much time as possible simply wandering around the grounds, talking to the young people, going over correspondence from those who have been blessed by the powers of Her Holiness as I was, and of course speaking at length to Ginerva."

"Where can I get in touch with you, Mr. Hillers?" Foreman asked suddenly.

"As I said, I have no plans for the summer, so I'm still at St. Timothy's."

"How about Mr. Ranks? I would like to talk to him."

"You'll find him at the Ranks Newspaper Enterprises in Boston. If there are any other references you might want—my father, now deceased, was a Chase vice-president and head of Princeton's alumni for a few years. I believe my dean would—"

He held up his hand with a slight smile. "That won't be necessary, Mr. Hillers. But I would like to talk to Mr. Ranks and read your articles." He paused, then went on. "Frankly, there are some plans for the Society I would like to see receive the proper publicity. Well, we'll see."

He stood up and held out his hand. "We will get back to you in a few days," he said.

"That will be fine, sir."

"Do you have a car, Mr. Hillers?" he asked as I started for the door.

"Why no, but I thought I would call a cab at the White Plains station—"

He said without looking at Russell, "Brother Russell will find someone to drive you to White Plains."

In the outer office, a disgruntled Russell told me to wait, leaving me alone with Sister Sloan.

She smiled for the first time. "Will you be joining us, Mr. Hillers?"

"That will be up to Brother Foreman."

"I understand you are a newspaperman."

"Yes. I hope to write a series on the Society."

She said, still smiling, "Will you promise to give us a fair shake?"

"Definitely, " I hesitated, then decided to take the gamble. "May I interview *you*, Sister Sloan?"

"I'm sure that could be arranged," she said. "After all, I have been with Brother Foreman since the beginning."

"I would love to hear all about it," I said.

The door opened and Russell entered. "I have a car waiting downstairs," he said.

The look she gave Russell told me she didn't like him, but the smile she gave me held a number of promises. . . .

Three days later, Sister Sloan called me at St. Timothy's with the news that Foreman wanted to see me.

Russell didn't meet me, but his Angels passed me along to Sister Sloan, who ushered me into Foreman's office. He was staring into the shiny black top of his desk like a man searching for answers in a pool of ink. When I took the same chair, he nodded and without a word pressed a buzzer. A door opened off to one side of the room and a man stepped in. I was sure he was in his mid-forties, but the flabby figure, moon face, and puffy neck made him look older. I suspected the bluff hard-guy look hid an insecure frightened man eager to please everybody.

He walked over to the desk, gave me a glance, then turned to Foreman.

"That's him, Dave, Richard Preston Hillers, the best newspaperman in Saigon!" He thrust out his hand. "Hello, Hilly, I guess you don't remember me? I'm Steve Troy, who was out there for the Christian Television News Service. We did that tour together of the orphanage with Ky after the Reds blew it up." He said to Foremen, "You wouldn't believe it, parts of kids' bodies all over the place . . ."

Now he was swaggering, just another member of that privileged group of romantic free spirits who recorded so much of history, tumbled with life, and scorned death with a smile.

I was startled. Although I had never seen him before, I had been in a party of correspondents who trooped after Ky, looking like Captain Midnight as he walked through the wreckage of an orphanage shelled by the VC.

He gave me an enthusiastic handshake. "Wasn't that a horrible day, Hilly?"

"Bombs do terrible things," I said vaguely, "and when it's children —"

"You know my documentary won the Church Council award?" he interjected eagerly.

"Congratulations," I replied, hoping it appeared as if I knew what he was talking about.

Foreman looked impatient. "I interrupted Brother Troy at his work to say hello to you." He looked at Troy, who immediately got the message.

"It was great seeing you, Hilly," he said, waving his hand. "I told Dave, anything I can do to help, just shout."

Well, that was an indication I was in. . . .

After Troy left, Foreman said briskly, "Brother Troy is in charge of our communications. He and Brother Turner, the editor of our newspaper, *The Call*, try to take care of publicity. Have you seen our paper?"

"Yes. I have bought a few copies."

"What do you think of it?"

I gave him a cautious answer. "It could be improved."

He grimaced. "It's horrible. I plan to have it revamped." He reached down into a drawer, took out my scrapbook, and pushed it toward me. "Your articles were excellently written and very inspiring. Brother Troy has spoken of his documentary and repeated the story of the orphanage so many times that when I found your article on the incident I brought him in to say hello."

And also have Troy confirm who I was.

"I'm very happy that Brother Troy's documentary won that award."

"Frankly, Mr. Hillers, you didn't appear as if you remembered him," he said with a thin smile, "but that doesn't matter. Brother Troy was born not to be remembered." He leaned back. "Now let's get to you. First of all, your writing impressed me, and so did my brief talk with Mr. Ranks, who, by the way, was very high in his praise of you."

He swiveled around and walked over to the window, where he stood in silence, looking out. The window was open, there was a sound of a lawn mower and a faint smell of freshly cut grass. He looked over at me and said, "Mr. Ranks promised me to promote your series and treat it with dignity. He also guaranteed that your copy will not be touched."

He returned to the desk and leaned on the back of his chair. "I consider that important, because I am sure that because of your experience with Her Holiness you will not only be fair to us but will be—I guess the proper word is—understanding."

He walked around the desk and sat down. Almost instantly, his manicured fingers began their drumming on the desk top.

"I've decided to go along with your proposal, Mr. Hillers, although I should tell you, in all honesty, that some of my colleagues were against it." He studied me in silence. "I hope I won't have any cause to regret this decision."

"I can't guarantee you won't, sir."

"I will arrange an interview with Her Holiness within a few weeks.

Frankly, she doesn't like meeting the press, but she always accepts my recommendations. Now as to the things you will need . . ."

"I was wondering about photographs. Do you work with a free-lance photographer?"

"No. We have one on the grounds, Brother Bruce Stafford, a young Disciple who is very good." He gave me a small card enclosed in plastic. "By the way, this will be your ID card. Sister Sloan will fill it out and Brother Stafford will drop by *The Call*'s office within the hour to take your photograph. Please slip it under the plastic cover. I have informed Brother Russell to advise all our grounds personnel that you are to have access to most areas and will be interviewing Disciples."

"Are there any areas closed to me?"

"Only a few," he said casually. "Our training homes and Brother Russell's headquarters for his security program. I wouldn't want to embarrass any of our young converts during their training, and Brother Russell insists we not publicize our security measures. A few years ago a gang of hoodlums attended one of our rallies on the West Coast and hurled a trash can down into the orchestra from the balcony. Three Disciples were seriously injured. After that, our insurance company insisted we establish our own security force. Thus came the Angels."

"You spoke of plans for the Society, sir."

He studied me for a moment. "You don't forget anything, do you, Mr. Hillers?"

I smiled. "I try not to, sir."

"Perhaps we can talk about it later," he said.

"In my interview with Ginerva—will I be alone with her or will you be there?" I asked.

The steady dark eyes never blinked. "Would you like to be *alone* with her, Mr. Hillers?"

"I would like to."

His reply was a blunt, "Why?"

I started, then faltered. "Well, it would—there are a number of questions I would like to ask her—"

"Personal questions?"

He seemed to be guessing what was on my mind, this scam artist, promoter, and possibly thief. The tone of his voice, his manner, indicated he owned her, controlled her, and this made me furious. To hide my feeling, I bowed my head and said softly, "Well, there are a number of questions I would like to ask her. . . ."

I thought I caught an edge of contempt in his voice. "Like what happened to you that night in San Francisco, Mr. Hillers?"

"Well, yes. . . . There are questions—"

(6 1)

His unwavering eyes were fixed on me. "Very well, you will see her alone, Mr. Hillers," he said with a tightened smile. "Is there anything else?"

I showed him a tiny camera I had brought back from Saigon. "In addition to the photographs I will use, taken by Brother Stafford, I would like to also use this . . . sort of candid camera shots. . . ."

"Perfectly all right," he said briskly. "All I ask is that you avoid the areas which would violate Brother Russell's security measures and our training programs."

A buzzer sounded and he nodded.

"I asked Brother Turner to come over and meet you. He's here now."

The door opened, and Sister Sloan ushered in a very nervous Turner. He gave me a quick glance and, swallowing hard, stood almost at attention before Foreman's desk.

"Brother Turner, this is Mr. Hillers; we spoke about him yesterday. He will be spending some time with us and will stay with you. As I explained, he's doing an objective series about the Society and Her Holiness, and I want you to give him all the help you can. Show him about the grounds. Assist him in interviewing the Disciples—anything he wants. He is to have our complete cooperation. Is that clear?"

"Yes, Brother Foreman," Norman replied. He gave me a quick tentative smile and held out his hand. It was damp with sweat. "Pleased to meet you, Mr. Hillers."

"Perhaps there is one thing you can do for us while you are here, Mr. Hillers," Foreman said as I rose.

"By all means, sir."

"Brother Turner doesn't have your journalistic background. He's making a survey of *The Call* for me. As I told you, I would like to revamp the entire paper, establish it as the *real* voice of the Society. Perhaps before you leave you can give him some suggestions."

"I will be very happy to help," I said.

"Good. Now if there is anything you need, any questions you want answered, please call Sister Sloan. She lives on the grounds and will get to me or Brother Russell immediately. Good luck with the series."

In the outer office, Sister Sloan briskly asked Turner: "Are you parked in the rear?"

"Yes, Sister Sloan."

"Why don't you bring the cart around while I fill in Mr. Hiller's ID card?"

When Turner left, I gave her the card, and she quickly typed in my name and under it VISITING JOURNALIST—APPROVED BY BROTHER FOREMAN.

"The photographer will be over this morning to take your picture," she said, smiling. "You had better wear your ID all the time; Brother Russell makes a big deal about it." She had very blue eyes and this time there was a hint of perfume. "Will you be here all summer?"

"A good part of it." I said. "I hope we can have that interview."

"I'm looking forward to it," she said softly. "Just give me a call—" She broke off when Turner came in.

"Okay, the cart's outside," he said.

"Good-bye, Mr. Hillers," she said. "I'm sure we can make your visit very enjoyable."

"I'm sure you will," I said.

Russell was waiting at the bottom of the stairs. His slate-colored eyes were cold and hostile; it was clear he was one of Foreman's "colleagues" who didn't like the idea of my being here.

"Did Sister Sloan give you an ID card?"

"Yes, Brother Russell," I said very humbly. "Here it is."

He turned to Norman. "I told that kid Stafford to get over to your place right away and take his picture. You make sure that he does." He came back to me. "Wear that ID card every minute you're out on the grounds. Understand?"

"Yes, sir."

He turned to the Angel standing next to him. From what I could see of him in the shadows, he had a battered face, deep-set, smoldering eyes, and lips more like a slash.

"Brother Andrew, this is Mr. Hillers," Russell said. I felt it was more of an identification than an introduction. Andrew gave me a brief nod.

"He's staying with you, right?" Russell asked Turner.

There were beads of sweat on Norman's forehead. "Yes, sir," he said. "Brother Foreman asked me to help Mr. Hillers any way I can."

Russell, Andrew, and the two Angels sitting at the desk stared at me, measuring me. There was such a sense of menace in that dim silent hall, I had to suppress a shiver. Then at last Russell stepped aside, pressed a buzzer, and I followed Turner down the steps to where a cart with a ragged canopy was parked.

"This is Betsy," Turner said with a forced laugh. "She's not much but she'll get you around. I also have a van I use to bring copies of the paper from the printer in Jersey City."

As we chugged down the driveway, I said, "I don't think Russell liked the idea."

"Wait until we get into the office," Turner said quickly. "Sometimes I think they can even read lips. From a mile away."

The Call's office was the former apartment of the mansion's chauffeur. The neat garage had stacks of *The Call* filed in the rear under dates stenciled on the wall. A stairway led upstairs to one large room, two small bedrooms, a kitchen, and a bathroom. The large room had two desks with spindles, paste pots, piles of yellow copy paper, and a telephone. Several clippings were tacked to a corkboard. It looked like the city room of a small newspaper on a Sunday afternoon after the cleaning ladies had finished.

Turner sighed. "I tried to make it look as professional as possible for you," he said. "Welcome to *The Call*, voice of the Society of the Chosen! Now for the grand tour." His wave took in the apartment. "My room, your room, the john, and our city room. They don't allow booze up here or I'd offer you a drink. How about some coffee and a Danish?"

"That will be fine."

After he made two cups of instant coffee and sliced a piece of pastry, he said, "I almost collapsed yesterday when he called me in and told me about you. I was sweating so much I had to change my shirt. What do you want to do first?"

"Let's just talk. What about that guy Andrew?"

"Avoid him and Russell as much as possible. They're mean bastards."

"Foreman gave me this story about some hoodlums who threw a trash can into the audience of a rally and to satisfy their insurance company they had to organize the Avenging Angels. Is that a crock?"

"Sure it is. Foreman made a big deal of that incident on the Coast, but one of the kids who was there told me it was an empty plastic container and no one was hurt. He used that as an excuse to form the Angels."

"Do you know who they are? Where they come from?"

"Some guys were former football players, disco bouncers, even ex-cons, from what I heard," he said. "They all have special training in judo, karate, and street fighting." He lowered his voice. "Now this is only what I heard, but before I came they had classes up here in mind control for a selected few Angels. Two guys gave it, but don't ask me who they were or where they held the classes on the grounds, because I don't know."

"But why do they need the Angels?"

"Any kid who wants out is taken over by Russell and his Angels. I guess they use the Angels as sort of a private police force."

"You told me about that black kid, Tom, and what they did to him," I said. "Will I be able to talk to him?"

He shook his head. "I'll make sure you'll meet him, but it won't do you any good."

"Why not?"

"You might as well talk to the wall. All he does is babble on and on."

"Was anyone ever hurt up here?" I asked him. "Were the police ever summoned?"

He licked his lips and his voice dropped to a whisper. "There were those two girls," he began, but I interjected, "Norman, why the hell are you whispering?"

"I don't even like to talk about it," he said nervously. "After you have been up here for a while, you get the idea they know what you're thinking. . . ."

"Okay. What about those two girls?"

"They were artists working in the midtown office they call The National Tour Headquarters. That's where Foreman is planning the tour for Ginerva I told you about. Any Disciple who has experience or talent for art, works down there on posters and other visuals. Now what I'm telling you is only gossip from some of the kids who work down there. They said Foreman was fooling around with this girl—"

"Wait a minute. You mean he's screwing the young kids who work in his midtown office?"

Turner kept swallowing and licking his lips. "Remember this is only what I *heard*. One day they caught this kid trying to get into the Grand Ballroom to see Ginerva. They took her down to midtown and Foreman talked to her. One of the girls told me she heard Foreman shouting at her and she came out crying. I guess she was one of the kids he was fooling around with downtown. A short time later she jumped from the seventeenth floor of a building on Fifty-seventh Street. Before that, there was a young Chinese girl who took an overdose of pills in a hotel. She also worked in the midtown office, and from what I heard she had been seen leaving with Foreman. . . ."

"How about their parents?"

"No one even claimed the body of the Chinese girl. Foreman had her buried somewhere in Westchester. The girl who jumped only had a grandmother living somewhere in the Northwest. They shipped her body home. Believe it or not, Foreman had a big memorial service held up here for both of them."

"What about the police?"

He shrugged. "They were both open-and-shut cases of suicide, Hilly. One girl jumped, the other took an overdose. That's the way the cops wrote it off."

"Maybe. I'll give that to Ben for his detectives to check out. Now may I ask you something personal, Norm?"

"Shoot. Ask anything."

"What made you join the Society of the Chosen? Ben told me about your mother, but was that the only reason?"

He brooded for a moment in silence. "In the beginning I kept insisting mother's death was the only reason, but now I know I was lying to myself. There's another and more important reason why I came here. The truth is I'm a misfit. I was always one of those kids who could never fit in. I couldn't catch a football. When I tried to dribble I fell over my own feet. In tennis I couldn't get the ball over the net. In high school I tried to be assistant manager of the baseball team, but they fired me because I got some of the away dates mixed up. Not that I didn't have friends, but they always mimicked me in a crowd or made me the butt of their jokes. Instead of laughing back, I went off by myself. My mother was a widow, and I was her baby. She wouldn't let me go away to college so I day hopped. It wasn't bad because the state university was so big; I was just another face in the crowd. But still nothing went right. First I went into physics, but flunked that. Then I transferred to premed, but couldn't make it. And finally I went into communications. That's where I was when mother was killed in the plane crash. Until she was gone, I never really knew how much I would miss her. I was alone, and I panicked. One day I got talking to some kids outside the Library on Forty-second Street. They seemed so warm and understanding that I decided to accept their invitation to come up here for a weekend. By Monday morning I was hooked. It was the world outside that I was scared of—people and failure. I was sure that at last I belonged to something. I was sure I was finally doing something worthwhile with my life, so I joined. And stupid that I was, I gave them most of mother's estate. With the brownstone, it came to more than $100,000."

"Did you ever make it known to Foreman you wanted to leave and get your inheritance back?"

He gave me a frightened look. "Do you think I'm nuts, Hilly? I don't want to go out a window like the kid on Fifty-seventh Street."

"But you did go to Ben."

"That was different. What I plan to do is leave here and let Ben fight it out in court. I have a trust fund which comes due next year. Thank God, I couldn't touch it after mother died—so I can live royally, lying on some California beach and trying to get my head on straight."

I pointed out, "But you would have to testify, Norman."

He smiled. "I'll hire two of the biggest guards I can find before I walk into any courtroom to face them. But they won't let it come to trial. I'm sure they'll settle. The publicity lately hasn't been that good and it's beginning to get under Foreman's skin. That's one of the reasons he agreed to let you come in here."

"What instructions did he actually give you?"

He wiped his face. "Wow! Let me tell you what happened. He just called me in, told me briefly what you were doing, and then turned me over to Russell. That big goon took me into his office, closed the door and sat me down. He didn't raise his voice, but did I sweat! He told me I was going to be responsible for you and to make sure I steered you to those Disciples who were—can you believe it—that bastard used the phrase 'inspired' with the love of Her Holiness?"

"In other words, rig the interviews. Are there kids here who have become disillusioned? Who want out?"

"Leah Butler for one," he replied promptly. "Now that she's been in for a while, she is beginning to ask questions."

"What kind of questions?"

"Where the money is going, for one thing. She's teaching the kids who are street peddlers, and she has an idea of what is coming in. But nothing is going out. No churches. No old age homes. No missionary centers. No halfway houses for junkies. Nothing. Leah now believes what we believe—the Society of the Chosen is one gigantic rip-off."

"Has she tried to leave?"

"No," he said, "and I don't think she intends to."

I was surprised. "But her father told me that once she realizes this is all a fraud she would leave. Or at least try. Why should she want to stay?"

"Ginerva," he said. "Leah is sure Foreman and the others are running a racket, but she still is convinced Ginerva is a holy woman, a courier of God." He shook his head. "Bruce and I have argued with her but she keeps telling us, 'prove Ginerva is a phony.' Only last week I told her she should have studied law instead of dramatics." He added hastily, "But don't get me wrong, Hilly. Leah is a great girl. Really great."

"Will she help us?"

"I don't know. Let me talk to her. She should be back soon."

"Foreman told me I could go anywhere on the grounds, but to stay away from their training programs and Russell's security setup. Why are they so sensitive?"

"The Society has training centers all over the city they call Houses of Preparation," he explained. "The ones Leah and I went to on Long Island and in Brooklyn weren't all that bad but some, we hear, are like concentration camps. The worst one is on Staten Island. They use that to prepare kids as street peddlers. You really have to be out of your skull to sell those wilted flowers and crap jewelry seven days a week, twelve hours a day, in all kinds of weather and living like a pig in some loft or store. Of course Foreman wouldn't want you to see that. Russell has his security headquarters in a small stone house on

(67)

the north end of the grounds, and the Angels also have a gym in an old barn; all are *verboten*." He said wryly, "As I told you, this place is all love and brotherhood."

"By the way, Norm, you said you were going to check when Leah is coming back. Where is she?"

"She is a member of the team sent to Philadelphia to help open a new House of Preparation. Giving out leaflets. That sort of thing."

"What exactly does she do in this dramatics class?"

He grinned. "Teach the street peddlers how to act. Besides the kids selling flowers, jewelry, and other junk, at Christmastime we have Disciples dressed up as Santa Claus. Leah teaches them how to attract little kids and persuade their old ladies to toss a few bucks into our pots. The kids on the street learn how to put on an act. Like this."

He put his hands together, looked sad, and held up an imaginary bouquet.

"Sir," he pleaded, "only a dollar for this beautiful little bouquet for your loved one. God's flowers, sir. Kissed by the sun, blessed by the rain and the wind. They will look beautiful on your table tonight, sir. It's a dollar for our missions. For our old age homes. It's a dollar for God's work, sir." He dropped his pose and looked at me. "Isn't it corny? But believe it or not, it works."

"And Leah does this?"

"In the beginning they told her they planned to form theatrical groups to put on plays in schools, but then Russell decided they wanted more money coming in so they ordered her to teach the peddling teams. She hates every minute but—" he shrugged—"she's staying because she believes in Ginerva. And you just can't change her mind. . . ."

"Maybe we can, Norm. Now how about that blonde in Foreman's office? Sister Sloan. What do you know about her?"

"Not much. Somehow I always figured her to be a round heels."

"Any reason?"

"Who am I that she would make a pass at? I only know what I hear." He gave me a nervous side glance. "If I'm right in what I'm thinking, Hilly, lay off. That's dynamite."

"Is she Foreman's girl friend?"

"I thought so when I first came up here but no more. I think whatever was between them has cooled. Did you see a pretty girl working in Foreman's office? Her name is Margo."

"Long brown hair, violet eyes?" When he nodded, I said, "She was there the first time I went to his office. Wait a minute! Sloan gave her a look that could kill. Is Margo the reason why they cooled it?"

"It's what I *assume*," he warned me, "based only on gossip. Margo

(68)

has been working in the tour office with Foreman. One of the kids who works down there said she saw them leave together."

"Foreman must like young girls."

"From the number he has working for him he certainly doesn't go in for old bags."

"Exactly where is this tour headquarters?"

"In midtown just off Fifth Avenue. I can't tell you too much about it because I have never been there."

"Why does Foreman want this big tour? I've seen Ginerva on television from Chicago, St. Paul, L.A.—"

"But she's still not that *big*, Hilly, not in the class with Billy Graham or Oral Roberts, to name two. Foreman is determined to make Ginerva the biggest evangelist in the United States today. He wants her name on everybody's lips. He wants to be on hand when she's invited to the White House. When they tour Europe. That guy has big plans! He's not planning a simple tour— this is a super-super tour! And from what I understand, he's going to put in a hell of a lot of money." He leaned across the desk and said earnestly, "He also has big plans for the Society of the Chosen."

"What do you mean by 'big plans'?"

"Just that. Combined with the tour will be a recruiting drive for Disciples. I know this from some of the kids who are making posters down there. The tour is another reason why he wants *The Call* to be revamped. It's all part of the big push. As I told you, Hilly, you couldn't have come at a better time."

There were sounds of steps on the stairway. "That's Bruce," he said and opened the door to admit a handsome husky teen-ager carrying a camera case. He could have stepped out of a Norman Rockwell cover.

"I'm Brother Stafford," he said, "Brother Russell—"

Turner pointed to me. "Here's your victim, Bruce. Mr. Hillers. He's here to do a series on the Society and Her Holiness for a chain of New England papers."

"Will you be staying, sir?" Stafford asked as he took out his camera.

"He's bunking in here with me," Norman explained. "Mr. Hillers was a war correspondent in Vietnam."

Stafford looked impressed. "My father, who just came back from Paris, bought me three fantastic books of Vietnam combat pictures," he said. "One was by a French cameraman who was with the VC. Terrific stuff! I would have given anything to have been there with a camera."

I said, "And some of the photographers I knew would have given anything to have been back here."

"That's what I want to do," he said fervently, "photograph what's happening. Work for a wire service or a big city newspaper . . ."

"But Brother Stafford," Norman said mockingly, "I thought you intended to devote your life to Ginerva?"

Stafford flushed a bit. "Well, yes—that too."

"You don't have to worry about Mr. Hillers, Bruce," Turner said assuringly. "He doesn't believe the Society of the Chosen is God's gift to the world." He turned to me. "Bruce, Leah, and I have had a few talks about the Society."

Apparently Bruce was reassured. After he had taken a picture with one camera, he took another with a Polaroid and gave me the print.

"Slip this one under the plastic cover of your ID card," he said, "and wear it all the time."

"What happens to the other print?"

"That goes to Brother Russell for his files."

"You've been in his office, Bruce," Turner said. "What does it look like?"

"Well, he's framed and hung all the pictures I've taken of him and Ginerva. He has them all over the wall. He also has a box on his desk filled with enough keys to open every door to this place along with a picture file of just about everyone who's been here for more than a few hours."

"What is this thing of him and Ginerva?" I asked.

Stafford looked thoughtful. "I've asked myself the same question. Maybe he's in love with her."

Norman said, laughing, "Beauty and the Gorilla."

"That key and picture file indicates he likes security," I pointed out.

Stafford hesitated. "This isn't a fact, but someone told me Russell was once a private detective in California."

I tucked that bit of information in the back of my mind.

"Norman had just finished telling me when you came in why he joined the Society. Would you mind telling me your reason, Bruce?"

Stafford glanced at Turner, then at me. "Well, I had some trouble at home. My father's an importer and does a great deal of traveling, while my mother takes care of the business. I was alone a lot and got into a few jams. One day I took off and wound up here." He looked anxiously at Turner again, who said, "No kidding, Bruce, Hilly is okay."

Stafford said to me, "No names. No quotes."

I promised. "No names. No quotes."

"Well, it's like this with me," he said. "I don't bother anyone and no one bothers me. I've traveled all around the country for the Society and have taken a fantastic number of pictures. Some have appeared in newspapers and magazines. Once AP used a shot of mine as a wire

photo that the *Daily News* ran very big on page three. I now have one
hell of a book of pictures to show when I get out of here." He
shrugged. "To me it's been on-the-job training."

"But what will happen when you want to leave?" I asked him. "I
understand Brother Russell doesn't like Disciples to leave."

"I don't have any problems with Russell," he said easily. "I have
always made sure not to rub him the wrong way." He grimaced. "That
bastard, Andrew, could be difficult but I'll find a way to get around
him.

"Don't be too sure, Bruce," Turner warned.

Stafford smiled. "I have it all figgered out, Norm. I'll be seein' you,
Mr. Hillers. . . ."

So there was Bruce Stafford, handsome high school athlete, son of
well-to-do parents, interested only in photography and using the
Society of the Chosen as "on-the-job training."

"Bruce is only one of his kind up here," Norman pointed out. "It's
true he comes and goes as he pleases, but that's because from the very
beginning he was smart enough to get around Russell. He's taken
excellent pictures of Russell with Ginerva at some of the rallies, and
that goon has them framed and hanging in his office."

"Did Bruce go through the training program?"

"Instead of sending him to a House of Preparation, Russell sent
him around the country taking pictures of every Team Leader and
Angel along with their vital statistics—you know, height, weight, color
of eyes, hometown—that sort of stuff. So now Russell has a complete
file of every one of his musclemen and fanatics. I always wondered
why he wanted that."

"This is only a wild guess, but is it possible he wants a file to keep
track of his people, in case any become dissident? He has both information and photographs to help track them down."

Turner nodded slowly. "That could be it. How do you like that?
Brother Russell, the Heinrich Himmler of the Society of the Chosen!
Hey, all this talking has made me hungry. How about lunch in the
cafeteria?"

The cafeteria in the motherhouse could have been in any one of a
thousand hospitals, schools, or even prisons. The walls were a mus-
tard color, the old-fashioned high ceilings had been lowered with
fluorescent lighting. The steam table extended around the room into
a long L-shape with a stack of battered plastic trays near the door.
The first thing you saw were jellied salads which Norman swore
bounced when dropped, then trays of slabs of meat in congealed
brown gravy, and bowls of weary-looking vegetables. Beyond them

(7 1)

were sandwiches wrapped in clear plastic with identifying tags.

"I always look for a ham and cheese or tuna fish," Norman said, "they can't do much to them."

We both selected ham and cheese sandwiches, got thick white mugs of coffee and tiny packages of cookies. The bread was certainly not fresh—I later discovered the Society bought a nearby bakery's returns—and the ham was fatty. I had tasted better coffee in the jungle.

Disciples kept coming over to our table to talk to Norman, who appeared popular. They were super active, bursting with nervous energy, some unconsciously lifting themselves up and down on the balls of their feet as they talked. They chattered among themselves incessantly until the cafeteria sounded like a bird sanctuary with a cat on the prowl. They were all young, some in their late teens, others in their early twenties. All carried a Bible; some read aloud as they ate, others read in silence.

"Ginerva's Disciples seemed to have been wound up," I observed to Norman.

"This is nothing," he said. "You should see them after a Blessing."

As we were leaving, a young black boy rushed up to Turner. "Hey Norm. How goes it, man?"

"Fine, Tom," Norman said. He looked at me. "This is Mr. Hillers, who is writing a series on the Society. He might like to talk to you. . . ."

"Sure. What can I tell ya?"

His large dark eyes looked almost feverish, and from time to time he snapped his fingers as if keeping in time with a rhythm only he heard.

"Perhaps you can tell me why you joined the Society and—"

The flood of words drowned the rest of my questions. "It's right here, man." He held up his Bible. "It's right here. The word of the Lord. They wrote it, those people who knew the Lord. The truth is here. And God gave Ginerva that truth. She is all his power. All his might. You better believe he whispered in her ear that the black day is comin'! Oh, yes, that big black day when the sky will fall and the fire will come through every crack in the sidewalk. Every tree, every building. You know that World Trade Center Building? Biggest pillar of fire you ever saw! Burnin' bright day and night. No fire department gonna put that one out. No, sir. The whole world gonna be like that. Burnin'. Burnin'. Only us Chosen, we're gonna be saved. We're gonna walk on that great white cloud with Ginerva. She's gonna save us! Lead us to the Lord! And into Paradise."

He closed his eyes and rocked back and forth, hugging the Bible to his chest.

I repeated, "But why did you join the Society of the Chosen, Tom?"

"The Lord directed my feet," he said quickly, popping open his eyes. "The Lord came to me and said, 'Thomas, open your heart and let the Holiness enter.' And that's what I did. Just opened my heart to the Lord!'"

"And Ginerva—what do you think of her?" Norman asked him.

"Ginerva is the courier of God," he repeated, almost mechanically. "Ginerva is come to tell us about the Lord's warning. Ginerva spoke to God and he told her what to do. Hail to Ginerva! She's—"

"Thank you, Tom," I said.

He broke off, blinked, and gave me a vacant smile. "Praise Ginerva," he said and walked away, muttering to himself and hugging the Bible.

"That's Tom," Turner said bitterly. "He didn't even look the same when they got through with him. . . ."

The estate was enormous. Turner said it consisted of more than two hundred acres of lawns, gardens, wooded sections, driveways, beautiful dormitories built more than a half century ago, and smaller buildings used as quarters for staff members and for classes. A cyclone fence topped with strands of barbed wire ran along the highway from the gatehouse, cut through a heavy wooded section, circled around the rear of the larger buildings past a stunning garden, with empty niches which had once held the Stations of the Cross, along the main driveway, to finally end at the gatehouse. As Norman explained, the motherhouse and its surrounding land was completely isolated from the outside world. Visitors were escorted from the gatehouse to wherever they were going, then returned to the gatehouse. Radios were not permitted, and the one color television set had a seven-foot screen in the assembly hall of one of the dorms; its only function was to show Ginerva speaking at out-of-town rallies. Parents were permitted to visit their sons and daughters on the afternoon of every fourth Sunday, when they shared hot dogs and hamburgers. But only those parents, friends, and relatives who were formally "invited" could enter the grounds.

"It's hard to believe, but some of the parents are as nutty as their kids and praise this place to the skies," Norman said in an unbelieving voice. "Those are the only kind invited. The first month I was up here, I gave them the name of one of the few friends I had in college. After all the dough I had given them, I guess they wanted to keep me happy, so they sent him an invitation. My friend was horrified and begged me to leave with him. Angels are always walking around the grove where you eat and one heard this fellow. He was never invited again."

A short time later, as we drove down one of the paths, he pointed to a beautiful blue stone one-story building with barnlike doors. There was no balcony or outside stairway, only the smooth blue wall. The large French windows on the second floor were curtained.

"That's the Grand Ballroom," Turner explained, "where Ginerva blesses special groups of Disciples from out of town. Her apartment is on the second floor. Last year Leah and I were members of a welcoming committee for a visiting group of Disciples from Ohio. After they left, we were taken up to her apartment, where she thanked us. She has a fantastic layout!"

"What does the welcoming committee do?"

"Show the visitors around the grounds and tell them how happy everyone is serving Ginerva while waiting for God's Great White Cloud to come down and lift us all into Paradise. Play a few games of basketball or volleyball with the kids, seat the older ones before the fireplace in the sitting rooms of one of the dorms, serve them tea and cookies, listen to them spout the Bible and tell us how inspired they are after listening to Ginerva. The usual crap."

"Knowing all this is phony, Norm, do you still have doubts about Ginerva?"

He glanced down at my leg. "But *you* are one of her walking miracles, Hilly! And *you* can't make up your mind about her!"

True, very true.

"As I get it," he said pointing to the Ballroom, "the guy who built this estate was a railroad baron who loved the theatre. He built this ballroom not only to hold parties but also to have famous performers come up and put on plays."

He broke off at the chugging sound of a cart approaching from a side driveway. Suddenly it turned around the corner. The Angel was dressed like the others but wore wraparound gold-rimmed shades. It gave him a sinister look. On the seat beside him was a shortwave set with leather straps like a backpack. It suddenly came to life with someone barking: "A2 Block checked." Sitting alongside the set was a huge German shepherd. The instant the dog saw us it bared its teeth. At the driver's command the animal relaxed, savage growls still rumbling in its throat.

"Good morning, Brother Matthew," Norman called out nervously but the driver ignored him as the shades fixed on me as we passed. I could feel them boring into my back.

"Who the hell was that?" I asked.

"Brother Matthew," he replied, staring straight ahead. "He's one of the patrols continually checking the grounds. Did you see that set? They use them to keep in touch with one another and with Russell in his headquarters. Matthew does the night patrol. To him it's all a big game. He likes to scare the hell out of the kids with that mutt, but that animal is dangerous. A couple of months ago he almost took off the arm of the milkman while he was delivering to the cafeteria. I heard the guy threatened to sue, and Foreman had to pay plenty for a settlement. Now do you see how hard it is to get out of here? During the day they have the Angels with their sets patrolling, and at night there's Matthew. If that nut and his mutt catch you on the grounds after dark, you're in for big trouble. Remember that, Hilly—big trouble."

For the next several days I wandered about the estate, visiting classrooms, talking to the staff members, and interviewing Disciples. To make sure Norman didn't get into trouble with Russell, I let him set up some interviews, but I also sought out a number on my own. All bubbled with enthusiasm for the Society of the Chosen and seemed to be intensely devoted to Ginerva. I sat under the trees and listened to them tell me of her confrontations with God on the lonely mountain trail, his threat of Doomsday and his promise to lift all members of the Society of the Chosen into Paradise on his great white cloud if the world ignored her. There was also the story of how God had promised to entrust Ginerva with his lightning to impress the unbelievers.

The commonsense arguments I posed were greeted with vague, polite smiles, glazed eyes, and the usual: "But Brother Hiller—God *spoke* to Her Holiness and told her what was coming! She is only repeating the words of the Almighty! Is it not the same as Paul on his way to Damascus who heard the voice of Jesus?"

The most insistent question they asked was, "Why is it so strange that God should have picked a *woman* as his courier to the world? Didn't God select other women as his instruments? What of Jael? Deborah? Esther? And doesn't the Bible tell us that Judith was marvelously beautiful in the eyes of the troops of Holofernes, whom she beheaded to save Israel?"

After a week, I came to the conclusion that Norman Turner represented in microcosm most of the reasons why they had joined the Society of the Chosen to follow Ginerva; acute feelings of loneliness, a desire to right the ills of the world, and a sense of belonging. The world outside the cyclone fence was full of fears and hidden dangers. Inside was a world where no one was old, everyone was happy, and there was no sickness.

There was an eerie sameness about them, as if their minds had become fossilized by the same anecdotes they told about Ginerva's confrontation with God, the same Biblical quotations they used; there was the same nervous energy, the fixed smiles, the continual flow of words like conversations imprinted on tape pouring out of the mouths of dolls.

There were also the obviously mentally disturbed like Norman's friend, Tom, who followed us about for a whole day, talking incessantly, smiling, singing, shouting, laughing, and always hugging the Bible to his chest.

The Angels were something else; cold-eyed, trim, hard, they moved about the grounds in their carts or on foot, ignoring the Disciples, who quickly made way for them.

Russell was clearly their leader; when he moved or spoke they jumped. I was sure some, like Brother Matthew, were simple package thieves. Once he stopped his cart to stare silently at me for a moment, the big shepherd on the seat beside him snarling and eyeing me as if I were his next meal.

Up close, his young tanned face was bony and pitted. He was smaller than the other Angels, but was the only one I saw who carried a holstered revolver and cartridge belt. As Norman later explained, Matthew was armed because he patrolled the grounds at night.

He passed me several times, slowing down to deliberately look me up and down. I decided to test him. As I had found in Saigon, if you resisted the motorbike thieves they turned and ran.

"Can I help you?" I snapped.

He seemed nonplussed by my aggressiveness. "You're supposed to wear your ID card all the time," he grumbled.

He was right. I had forgotten the damn card. I carefully pinned it to the lapel of my jacket.

"Anything else?"

He shook his head and chugged off. I knew I had made an enemy, but it was time to let Brother Matthew know I wasn't the milkman.

As the days passed, some of the brainwashing techniques used by the Society of the Chosen became evident. On walls, corridors, stairways, in offices, rooms in dorms, study and assembly halls were large striking color photographs of Ginerva looking to heaven, as if she was listening to God's words. At regular intervals throughout the day and evening, a solemn voice narrated over loudspeakers the story of how God confronted Ginerva on a mountain trail in the South where she was a missionary to give her his threat to the world of Armageddon and his promise of deliverance to the chosen who would listen to Ginerva's message.

There were also paintings of Ginerva standing at the side of the Angel Gabriel, welcoming scores of Disciples aboard a white cloud while bars of heavenly light shone about her. During the day, pairs of Disciples would suddenly approach a group sitting on the lawn or under a tree and call out: "Remember, Brothers and Sisters, you are Ginerva's Chosen Ones. . . ."

The day-to-day routine allowed few idle moments; from dawn to evening Disciples attended Bible studies under the trees or in class-rooms, while others crowded the Assembly halls to join a perfectly magnificent choir in shouting out emotional hymns. When I scoffed at Norman's story that Disciples were ordered out of their beds in the middle of the night to kneel in the corridor outside their rooms and pray, he woke me early one morning and led me to a window.

"Look across the lawn at the dorms," he said, glancing at the luminous hands of his wristwatch. "It's just four o'clock." Suddenly rows of lights appeared in the darkness.

"That stuff drives Leah crazy," he said. "When she tried to argue with her dorm leader, she was told it was to give her inner strength to follow Ginerva."

"Suppose you turn over and say the hell with it?"

"They drag you out into the corridor and berate you in front of everyone for listening to Satan. You won't believe half the stuff that goes on here, Hilly!"

I reminded him, "From what I understand, the Jesuit training isn't exactly luxurious, and don't Catholic monks live a spartan life?"

"True," he replied, "but when seminarians and monks want to leave, they walk out. Not here."

From what I could determine, all power at the motherhouse flowed from Foreman, through Russell and his assistant, Andrew, to the Angels and then to a group of slightly older men and women called Team Leaders. Like army noncoms, they made sure the rules were enforced, the orders obeyed. Most of them looked to be in their thirties or early forties; grim, humorless, fanatical. But they were efficient and industrious. All lived by a watch.

One day I was sitting under a tree with a group of Disciples who were singing hymns with a boy who accompanied them with a guitar, when a Team Leader walked up. She was a gimlet-eyed woman who wore her hair in a bun.

"Brothers and Sisters," she called out, "it is now 3:15 P.M. and time for your discussion of the Acts of the Apostles!"

The Disciples jumped up, formed a line, and, still singing, marched behind the Team Leader in the direction of a dormitory. I had the uneasy feeling I was watching an animated cartoon.

Two weeks passed. I had made numerous notes and tape record-ings of interviews with Disciples, most of them monotonous in their similarity. Without appearing to do so, I sought out those Disciples who accompanied street peddling and preaching teams during their training period. I would gradually lead them up to their street expe-riences, then casually ask for an estimate of their daily total.

A puzzling financial pattern slowly began to emerge. The peddling and preaching teams not only covered the city's busy thoroughfares from early morning to late at night in the theatrical district, but also set up what they called "preaching posts," in which a street preacher spoke to noontime and homeward bound crowds, as Disciples with containers passed among the listeners. In the evening they all returned to a central point on the Lower East Side where the leaders of the teams turned in the money. Estimates of totals ran from $150 to $400 a day. Approximately fifty teams worked the city seven days a week from morning until late at night in rain, snow, or freezing cold; there were no holidays. All the veteran street teams were trained on Staten Island. When I asked them about the island training, the Disciples I questioned quickly changed the subject or stared off into space.

Using two hundred dollars a day as the norm figure, I estimated the teams brought in about ten thousand dollars a day, or three million, six hundred fifty thousand dollars a year—tax free!

"And that's only in New York," Norman said with an awed look. "There are street peddling teams doing the same thing in Chicago, L.A., San Francisco, Detroit—nearly every large city in the country! But take only ten cities, Hilly. If they bring in anything like New York, that means a rough estimate of thirty million a year! And that doesn't include mail contributions or money they collect at rallies!"

"How do you know they solicit money by mail, Norm?"

"On one of my first trips to the Jersey City printer to pick up copies of *The Call*, they began loading boxes in the van," he replied. "They looked too small to be newspapers, so I opened one and found the Society's soliciting letters and envelopes. The guy on the loading platform had made a mistake." He whistled softly. "I never realized how big a racket this is."

"And you are sure they are not building any old age homes, missionary centers, halfway houses for addicts, hospitals, or schools?"

"I'm positive," he said firmly. "I have a half-ass string of what are supposed to be my correspondents for *The Call* and I talk to them all the time. When I ask for news of any buildings or centers being built by the Society, they don't know what I'm talking about." He looked at me. "I guess the money is going into their pockets."

"That's what Ben hopes to prove," I said.

He shook his head. "That's impossible, Hilly. Just take a look at this setup. Once you get in, you can't get out. There is Russell and his army of goons. The government won't do anything. The DA says his hands are tied because they are protected by the First Amendment. The cops throw up their hands and say it's up to the DA to move. Just how in the hell can amateurs uncover any proof this is a racket?"

"Maybe someday in some way we will. . . ."

"Forget it," he said. "You're a writer. Concentrate on the mystery of Ginerva. That's enough. Don't go putting your head in a noose. If Russell or any one of them catches you uncovering anything—watch out!"

Of course Turner was right. It was not only dangerous but positively foolish for me to try to play detective to help Sir Edward get his stubbornly foolish daughter out of this place. Let his private investigators do that. I was only interested in what Norman called "the mystery of Ginerva." That was enough for one obsessed history teacher and "Dear Buddy" columnist.

After weeks of listening to and talking to Disciples, I was impatient to get to Ginerva, so one evening I called Sloan and asked her to remind Foreman of his promise to arrange an interview for me. She promised and hung up; I was surprised at the terse conversation. And thinking about it, her voice had sounded slurred. Was Sister Sloan a closet drinker? However, the call worked; two days later an Angel dropped by *The Call*'s office with a summons from Foreman.

He was still cordial but very brisk; the interview with Ginerva would take place at 4:00 P.M. the following day.

"Her Holiness has just returned from a conference with our leaders in the Midwest," he explained, "and I would like her to get some rest before she sees you."

"I would suggest that Brother Stafford come along," I said. "We can have a picture taking session first, and when he leaves I will do the interview."

His fingers started their drumming. "I don't know," he said slowly. "To be frank, Her Holiness was reluctant to do this interview, but as I told you, she accepts my recommendations and she agreed. What about the photographs we have on file?"

"They are fine, Brother Foreman, and I intend to use some but I do think that photographs taken in her apartment or study will give the interview more of a personal touch."

"Very well," he said, "if you think so." He made a note. "I will have Brother Stafford meet you outside the Grand Ballroom at four P.M." He leaned back. "How is the series going?"

There was no doubt in my mind that every interview, every move I made, had been reported back to him, but I nodded brightly and said: "Oh, just fine, Brother Foreman."

"Excellent. Now as I told you, if there are any questions you want answered—"

"In fact, I have one, sir."

He looked surprised. "Oh? And what is that?"

"There is one question most readers will ask, Brother Foreman, and that is how does the Society of the Chosen use the money coming in from the street sales, contributions, and so on?"

He smiled and pressed a buzzer. In a moment Sister Sloan opened the door.

"Do you have that financial breakdown prepared yet for Mr. Hillers, Sister Sloan?"

"I just finished it a few hours ago, Brother Foreman," she said.

"Fine. When Mr. Hillers leaves, be sure and give him a copy. Thank you."

When she had closed the door, Foreman said, "It's a question raised all the time. Some months ago one of the L.A. papers ran a vicious story about the Society, hinting at all sorts of hanky-panky. I called the editor and offered to give him a complete financial report, but did he print it?" He shook his head. "Not a line."

I nodded, sympathetically, I hope.

"Every penny taken in by the Society is carefully recorded," he said now. "We also have an outside firm audit our books. Once a year we give the IRS an accounting. I hope that, in all fairness, Mr. Hillers, you mention the report."

I promised I would, we shook hands, and I left. In her office Sister Sloan seemed a bit tense. She was wearing a blue suit that went with her eyes and blonde hair, but I noticed her hand shook slightly when she gave me the typewritten report.

"I have seen you on the grounds," she said. "How is it going?"

"Fine. Just fine."

Her voice dropped slightly. "Anytime you feel you want to talk to me. . ."

"I'm finishing gathering some of the basic facts," I said. "In a few days I would like to discuss this report."

Her eyes locked with mine. "Anytime, Hilly."

"Perhaps in the evening?"

"That will give us time to talk," she said.

"Hilly, you're making me nervous," Turner protested as we drove back to *The Call*'s office. "That woman could mean trouble."

"You have to touch all bases when you're doing research, Norm," I told him.

"Since when have they called it that?" he said scornfully.

I prepared for the interview as excitedly as if I were going on my first blind date. After all the years of searching, questioning, following her on television and in print, I was to finally meet Ginerva face to face. I studied the portrait in the plastic case in my wallet and vowed that her beauty would not get me off center.

Numerous questions tumbled about in my mind as I walked across the grounds to the Grand Ballroom. Should I start with her background? Question her about those cures—miracles? My limp? If I searched for a mystical enlightenment, what would I find? What answers would I receive? Brief? Tidy? Satisfactory? Or would she answer at all?

I met Stafford promptly at 4:00 P.M. outside the Grand Ballroom. The Angel on guard escorted us into a cavernous darkness and up a stairway that had tiny lights embedded in the wall alongside each step. On the second floor we followed him down a corridor which circled the balcony. At its end he knocked on a door with a gold-embossed cross.

A soft voice told us to enter. I stepped in, and the door closed behind me and Stafford. The room, flooded with late afternoon sunshine, was luxurious; wall to wall carpet was so deep I felt I was walking on marsh grass. A large, almost sensual dark red velvet modular couch dominated the room. There were stunning lamps, original pastoral oils, a smaller couch, and a gleaming marble table with a vase of fresh flowers. Beyond, in another room, I could see part of a Louis XV canopied bed and a mirrored vanity.

Ginerva was standing in front of a desk. She was wearing a black sweater with a single strand of pearls, and a tweed skirt. The sunshine turned her hair into spun copper. I suddenly recalled the skylight in the storefront church and wondered if she had deliberately selected this spot.

"Ah, Brother Stafford," she said, smiling. "Our wonderful cameraman." She looked at me. "And Mr. Hillers."

It was difficult not to let her beauty disturb me; she was stunning.

"Please be seated," she said, motioning to the couch. When we sat down, she went on, "Brother Foreman tells me you have been enjoying your visit with us, Mr. Hillers."

"Very much so . . ."

When I hesitated, she said, smiling, "Call me Ginerva."

"May I ask where the name came from?"

I sensed, rather than saw, a slight stiffening. "From the Almighty," she said. "He told me that was to be my name." She turned to Stafford. "Brother Foreman said you want some new photographs."

"Mr. Hillers requested them, Your Holiness," he said.

So not *everyone* uses Ginerva, I told myself.

She came back to me. "Do you wish anything in particular, Mr. Hillers?"

For about a half hour Stafford took the pictures I suggested; at her desk, on the couch, looking out the window, reading letters, the usual stuff to dress up an interview. Stafford seemed happy with the results as he packed his gear and said good-bye.

(81)

When we were alone, she rejoined me on the couch and leaned back. Her throat was as smooth as porcelain and she had a stirring figure. I quickly got out my notebook and pencil.

"Could you sketch your background, Ginerva? Parents, school, that sort of thing?"

"Well, to begin, my parents were missionaries stationed mostly in Central and South American countries—"

"May I first have your full name, Ginerva? Where you were born? What schools or colleges—"

"I don't consider that important," she said calmly. "Shall I continue?"

"May I ask what order or society your parents were in?"

She frowned. "Is that necessary?"

This time I was determined not to back down. "Well, I do think this interview should be as factual as possible."

"The Society of World Christians," she said reluctantly.

"And their headquarters?"

She looked at me. "Wherever you find misery, poverty, and death." She wasn't smiling any more. "Do you want me to go on?"

"Please do."

"My parents worked for many years among the Indians in the Bolivian jungle northeast of Santa Cruz," she said slowly, as if remembering. "I guess the first thing I can recall is a desk my father made out of a packing case, and how I could look out through the spaces of the wall of our splitlog house, across the plaza to where my father and the natives had built a small wooden church."

Now her eyes were almost closed and she seemed more relaxed. Rather than stop to ask her questions, I decided to let her go on.

"Father would take me out into the jungles in the early morning. I will never forget the sound of the wind through the banana trees. The crowing of the roosters, the thumping sound the women made pounding their mahogany pestles." She paused. "There isn't anything like dawn in the jungle. First there is total blackness, then, as if God had suddenly pulled up a shade in the heavens, the sky is suddenly all pink and yellow with streaks of red. My father had a man named Rogelio who helped him. He came every morning just at dawn." She abruptly got up, walked to the desk, turned and faced me. "I haven't thought of that man in years, Mr. Hillers, but at the moment I mentioned him I could smell the scent of woodsmoke that clung to his jacket. Isn't that strange?"

"Yes, it is," I said.

"I can see Juan, our pastoral leader, and the children of the village hunched over the light of the kerosene lantern in my father's room, studying Scripture with him and my mother. There was a necklace of

(82)

jungle seeds Juan gave me for my birthday . . . the taste of papaya and mango, the great starlit nights and my mother telling me that all things, even the singing frogs, had meaning in God's design of the universe."

That soft musical voice was hypnotizing. "Father tried to teach them English. Every morning they would come over, sometimes with fresh meat, to pay for the lessons. The Indians are very proud and will never take unless they can also give. They would sit on the floor in front of my father's crate desk and slowly pick out the letters of the alphabet. Then they would take their machete and walk to their *chaco* to work. Later I would join mother and the women to get water and Epifanio, who was my age, would help me carry back a bucket. In the heat of midday, the jungle became very quiet, and mother would tell me we would have to take a siesta like the animals and we would both lie down."

She walked to the window and looked out.

"That was my life, Mr. Hillers, until I was sixteen, when both my mother and father were killed by a drunken driver in La Paz.

"How ironic it was," she said, turning around, "that the driver was not a native but an American. A salesman. His car went up on the sidewalk and killed them both instantly."

"May I have the names of your parents? When this tragedy took place?"

"I have always insisted on complete anonymity, Mr. Hillers," she said quietly. "My past means nothing. Where I came from. Who I was. The names of my parents are no longer important. They are with God. What is important is the future. Will the world listen to God's warning?"

The air in the room was suddenly very still. Through the open window I could hear the far-off chugging of a cart. Matthew and Buck on patrol?

"Would you want me to continue, Mr. Hillers?" she asked softly.

"I'm sorry. Please do."

Her tone suddenly shifted and she said, "After I buried my parents, the American consul offered me money for a passage home, but I had wanted to be a missionary since my earliest recollections, so I asked the Society to allow me to remain and continue the work my parents had started. A number of letters and cables convinced them and I was finally approved. I remained in Bolivia for five years, then went on to Peru, Brazil, with a year in Kenya, which I loved." When she turned, the dying sun touched her face with its soft light. "Nakuru is on the shores of Kenya's famous lake of the flamingoes. When they lift in flight, it seems as if a giant pink cloud is rising from the lake. It was a very beautiful place. In Kabujoi I trained native girls in social work.

One of the great thrills of my life was to hear a young girl jump up and shout, 'I can write my name! I can write my name!' "

Her face was glowing, her eyes dancing, and by the movements of her hands I could see the young native girl crying out her great triumph.

"That was my last foreign missionary post. I contracted a fever which held on for some months, then returned to the States to be assigned to do missionary work among the blacks in the South."

I asked, "Is that when you had your confrontation with the Almighty?"

When she had been recalling South America or Kenya she had sounded animated, smiling, gesturing as she remembered, but now the words seemed automatic.

"It was near a small village in the mountains. Please don't ask me the name, the Society of World Christians has asked me not to mention it and I will always respect their wishes. I had been back a year. The fever had taken a great deal out of me, but the mountain air and plenty of good food were helping me to regain my strength. This night I was driving a van back from a Gospel class I had been teaching. Somehow I missed the turnoff and found myself on a mountain road. It was very narrow and there was no place to turn, so I decided to keep on until I found a clearing. Suddenly, there was a great light shining on the road before me. A voice commanded me to get out of the van. It seemed the whole forest was ablaze with light, the brightest I have ever seen. . . ."

She walked to the middle of the room and stood there, her eyes closed, her hands held out, palms up.

"A powerful voice that filled the forest said, 'Ginerva! Ginerva! You have pleased me by what you have done for the lesser of my children. But I am angry at the evil in hearts of all men. I command you to warn the world to follow the way of my Son to the Cross or I will destroy the world with a Sea of Flame. When the last fire dies away, there will be nothing left but ash, the birds of the sky will be no more, nor will there be a flower left or a blade of grass. There will only be the sound of the wailing and gnashing of teeth of those who have been condemned to the deepest pits of Hell.' "

She became rigid and swayed, and for a moment I thought she was about to fall.

"Then God allowed me to see the world in flames. There was fire everywhere, pouring down from the skies, seeping out of the earth. Men, women, and children were screaming torches trying to escape this Sea of Flame that was consuming the universe. . . ."

She buried her face on her hands and began weeping. When I started toward her, she shook her head violently from side to side.

"No, no—you must listen to me! You must! It's important! The whole world must know God's message to me!"

I returned to the couch; the hairs on the back of my neck were beginning to rise.

"I could see mountains crumbling into the burning seas; towns, cities, even villages were vanishing into flames. The whole world was afire—from New York to Moscow, to the tiniest village I knew in Kenya. The cries of the people were so dreadful I covered my ears, but it didn't help. I don't know how long I stood there, watching. Finally and very slowly it faded away, and once again there was only the light in the forest. Then God told me that in his mercy he would give the people of the world one more chance to hold off Doomsday. God said that if mankind turned to the cross of his beloved Son and drove the evil from their hearts, he would bless our lives and give us the strength to want peace and not war; to love each other as brothers and sisters and not as strangers and enemies; to help the less fortunate of the world and not have some wallow in luxury while others hunt scraps from the garbage heaps. . . ."

The last light touched the streak of tears on her cheeks. Suddenly the thought came to me; was this the actress whose performance of *Joan* in that shabby little Pasadena playhouse was so impressive the tenement super never forgot it?

The question was out before I realized it. "Were you ever in the theatre, Ginerva?"

Her face was to the window. The dying sun gave her face a faint gold tinge. Slowly she turned to me. "Why do you ask that?"

I tried to sound casual. "I believe I read it somewhere."

She said with a sad smile, "You mustn't believe everything you read in the newspaper about me, Mr. Hillers."

"And you never played *Joan* in the Little Strand Theatre in Pasadena?"

I thought I caught a flicker of something—could it have been fear?—in her eyes, but then, studying her face, I wasn't sure. It was so impassive. She stood by the window, still as a portrait, serene, beautiful, yet giving off a distinct tension.

"There is more to tell, Mr. Hillers," she said, completely ignoring my last question as if it had been too ridiculous to answer. "God warned me there would be many disbelievers. To prove to them that I was his courier to the world, he promised he would give me control of his lightning during a storm. Bolts from the heavens will dance about me like fountains of fire but I will not be harmed. He also promised that if the world turns its back on me, he would first send down a great white cloud, and all those who had believed in me would be lifted into Paradise. He told me my name would be Ginerva and I was

(85)

to form the Society of the Chosen and welcome those who listened to his warning. . . ."

Silence.

Suddenly the soft challenge came running across the room. "Don't *you* believe in me, Mr. Hillers?"

She caught me off balance. "Is it important that I believe in you?"

She went on as if she had not heard me. "I want you to—so much."

"I have been waiting for this meeting for a long time, Ginerva," I said.

She smiled. "And now you are here."

I said, "One night in San Francisco, you touched my cheek and my limp disappeared."

She stunned me when she said, "I remember. You were standing by the door of my car."

"You remember? It was so long ago."

The quiet voice went on. "I could see the pain in your eyes. You were troubled. Brother Foreman told me you had been a war correspondent and had been wounded in Vietnam."

"I was the only survivor of a patrol," I said.

"And you still think about it. . . ."

"It will never leave me."

She closed the drapes, lit a candle, placed it in a holder on the marble table, and sat on the couch next to me. The soft light gave her deep green eyes a velvety appearance.

"Perhaps it will help to talk about it, Mr. Hillers," she said softly. "Tell me about that patrol. . . . Tell me what happened. . . ."

The nightmare I thought had been buried was actually near the surface of my subconscious, waiting for the proper chemistry to bring it back with a rush. The dimness, the candlelight, those strange eyes, and the soft, sympathetic voice were doing it. I could feel the heat of that far-off afternoon and hear the swish of the elephant grass about my legs, and I ran from the copter to the cover of the brush where the friendly little Polish sergeant was waiting, grinning at me. We argued good-naturedly with the lieutenant about wearing our flak jackets, then moved in single file along the trail through the jungle to the village to be searched for VCs.

There were supposed to be Amtracks but they never came; maybe it was too routine, this "no contact" sweep that had been set up just for me. Once again I heard the sounds of weapons locking, loading, bolts being slammed shut, clicks of safeties going off. The sergeant was kidding me and it all seemed boring; I had done this too many times. I was wondering how I could make this leisurely walk in the sun a heroic action with the descendants of New England's brave Minute Men against the cowardly VC when the Claymore mine went off.

Rounds were cracking around me, mortars were thumping, and the kids in the platoon were like toy soldiers as they ran, crawled, and crouched in terror. The fear in my mouth was like gall. . . .

I found myself saying, "I dove for cover and buried my face in the mud. The earth shook with the mortar blasts. One kid was blown apart and pieces of him were on the back of my shirt. Another nearby didn't have a torso. I heard the lieutenant, and then I saw him. Both his legs were off and he was propped against a tree. He called out to the others and then to me . . . asking me if I was all right. He died slowly. . . . The explosions were all around me. I woke up in the hospital. They told me they had taken pieces of shrapnel out of my leg and I would limp for the rest of my life. . . ."

She reached out and gently touched my cheek. "I will pray to God to let that day fade away and to give you peace."

"It was all my fault," I said. "If it wasn't for me they could be alive today."

The soft soothing voice told me, "Don't blame yourself, Mr. Hillers, what happened was the will of God."

She stared off into space. The room was deadly still and dim beyond the circle of candlelight. I wanted to ask her if there was anything wrong, but something held me back.

Was this some more of that scene-setting, like the skylight that sent down a bar of golden light to make her face glow as if she were listening to God's voice?

Slowly, very slowly, she rose, her eyes dazed and far away. She seemed to have forgotten where she was.

"They are all by the throne of God," she said in a soft monotone. "The lieutenant and the young soldiers who were with you that day. They are in Paradise singing the glory to God. . . ."

What nonsense is this, I wondered? I was about to ask her if we could continue the interview when she continued.

"Yes, they are all in Paradise, including the young Polish sergeant who kept kidding you that day about the correct spelling of his street."

I felt as if an icy hand had touched my back. Suddenly, like a woman in a dream, she turned, walked into her bedroom, and closed the door. For a moment, not knowing what to do, I sat in that weird room, the candlelight casting long shadows on the walls and drapes. There wasn't a sound except for the beating of my heart. Finally I got up and walked out. I found my way along the corridor and down the stairs to the front door. The Angel on guard waved, and a cart chugged up.

"He will take you back to your quarters, sir," he said.

But I wasn't listening. I was still in a state of shock. I was sure I had not identified the sergeant as Polish, and up to this moment I had completely forgotten how he had kidded me about the correct spelling of the name of his street—Kosciusko Street!

After the Angel had dropped me off at the office, I sat on the steps listening to the orchestrations of the night insects and trying desperately to gather my thoughts together. How was it possible Ginerva knew that story? Was she a skilled hypnotist who had used the candlelight and those magnetic green eyes to dredge up minute details of that long-ago afternoon and then present them to me as if by magic or a supernatural gift? Or was she—

"It's all a trick," I said half aloud. "Part of this whole scam operation! She's trying to make me a believer, trying to get me to swallow the nonsense she's handing out to these kids. . . . Nobody has the power to bring back the past. Nobody has the power to predict the future. . . . It's all a con game. . . . I know it is."

The low voice above me sounded frightened. "Hilly? Is that you?"

It was Turner, at the top of the stairs; I had been so lost in my own thoughts I had not heard him open the door.

"Come on down, I have something to tell you," I said.

He was in his pajamas, his face a pale blur in the darkness. "What are you doing out here talking to yourself?" he asked. "You scared the hell out of me."

After I told him the story, he said, "But you said you told her about the sergeant."

"True, but I never said he was Polish, and in fact I had forgotten completely about that spelling of the name of his street."

"Did you intend to use it in your story at the time?"

"It probably would have been only a line or two at the most. Actually, I had been planning to weave the story around the lieutenant and how he had gotten his battlefield promotion in the Highlands, because I was sure the patrol would end up only as a routine sweep."

We sat there in silence for a long moment.

"Sometimes I wonder, Hilly," he said at last. "Could Leah be right? Could Ginerva really be what she claims?"

"I don't know what to believe," I told him. "But I know I've got to find the answers. Some way. Somehow."

"You gave Foreman that scrapbook of clippings," he suggested. "Could he have given it to her? Maybe she read something."

"I never wrote the story of that patrol," I reminded him. I'm going to have a Coke and go to bed."

As we shared a Coke upstairs, he told me, "Anyway, I have some good news. Leah is back. She returned tonight."

"Oh? What did you tell her?"

"I decided, what the hell, why shouldn't I tell her all about you, and

I did. We had a long talk. She's really fed up with the Society. She said all they did in Philadelphia was walk around, ring doorbells, pass out leaflets, and sign up recruits. She said the Team Leaders down there are working day and night to bring in warm bodies. They were told to promise the recruits anything. Paradise. New clothes. Courses in steno and bookkeeping. Beautiful surroundings. Wonderful dorms. As I told you, Hilly, expanding the Society is a big part of Foreman's plans."

"Have you figured out why yet?"

"No. I'm leaving that up to you. That and solving the mystery of Ginerva. . . ."

I dozed off several times, only to wake up with a start, meeting once again that beautiful face and those intent eyes studying me through the candlelight. I reviewed again and again the story of that patrol action. I was the only survivor, I had not written about it. The dead were long forgotten by everyone except their close friends and families. In the darkness I could almost hear the sergeant's laughing young voice as he carefully spelled out the name of his street. No one had been near us, we had been squatting alone in the elephant grass as the other members of the platoon poured out of the copter. Once in exasperation I pounded the bed—how the hell did she know that?

At last, near dawn, I fell into a fitful sleep, troubled by weird dreams made of the lieutenant hobbling toward me on the bloody stumps of his legs, his hand held by the young sergeant who had a gaping hole in his chest. Both were smiling and waving.

When I woke up my pajamas were soaked with sweat.

A few days later, I was going over past copies of the paper in *The Call*'s office when there were footsteps on the stairs and the door opened. I assumed it was Norman and kept reading. When there was only silence, I looked up. He was standing, grinning, in the doorway with a young and very pretty girl. She had thick, luxurious hair the color of spring wheat, alert brown eyes, a perfectly chiseled face with slightly high cheekbones. She had that sexy outdoor look and instinctively I knew she played rather good tennis and could ski.

Before he introduced us, I knew she was Leah Butler. What was it Ben had told me? "She is twenty-two and has a mind of her own."

"Hilly, I would like you to meet Leah Butler," Norman said as they stepped into the office.

Her hand was warm and slender. "Norman told me all about you and your series," she said with a smile. "May I call you Hilly?"

"Of course—Leah."

I liked her smile.

(89)

"Norman also told me you saw my father," she said. "How is he?"

"Fine. But he's worried about you, Leah. He said he would do anything to get you back home."

"Anything but the one thing I want," she said coolly.

I was puzzled. "And that is?"

"To allow me the joy and despair of making my own decisions," she said, and then quickly changed the subject. "How long do you plan to stay up here, Hilly?"

"I hope to begin writing the series by the July Fourth weekend."

"Norman told me what happened to you in San Francisco," she said softly. "But he said you still don't really believe in her. . . ."

"I guess I just find it hard to believe in miracles, Leah."

She raised her eyebrows in disbelief. "Even if you are the one who was cured?"

"That's a question. The doctors in Saigon insisted it was psycho-somatic."

She said, "But Norman said you never believed them—"

Turner called out, laughing, "Watch out, Leah, Hilly is going to prove Ginerva's a phony."

"I don't think anyone will be able to do that," she said seriously.

"Why not?" I asked.

She answered with a shrug. "That's the way I feel. Call it feminine instinct, or anything you want."

While her large brown eyes were slightly narrowed, challenging me, I told myself they could also be warm and loving.

"Is that why you came up here—to prove Ginerva's a fraud?" she asked.

"I'm neutral," I told her. "I only came here to ask questions. And to try to get answers."

"Have you succeeded?"

"Well, I haven't found out anything about her, but I'm sure the Society is a rip-off."

She sighed. "I know, it's a horrible racket."

I said bluntly, "Why stay, then?"

She said, with a hint of defiance in her voice, "Because I am sure Ginerva isn't part of this racket."

Norman hooted, "Come off it, Leah! She doesn't know those guys are ripping off millions every year?"

There was a stubborn set to her face. "I still don't believe it. I am sure Ginerva has a divine call."

"You don't really believe her stories of seeing God, Doomsday, the Almighty giving her control of the lightning, and that great white cloud that will lift everyone into Paradise, do you, Leah?" I asked.

She corrected me quickly, "She never said she actually *saw* God."

"You're right," I admitted. "In Ginerva's case it was the bright white light in the forest and that heavenly voice."

Leah smiled. "I detect a cynic."

"Skepticism rather than cynicism," I said. "But surely you must agree, Leah, her stories are far out."

"What mystical stories don't sound far out?"

"Let's assume she does have a divine command," I argued. "Why would she allow herself to be controlled by a gang of promoters and thieves? If she is a holy woman, just what is she doing here?"

She reminded me softly, "God's ways are not our ways, Hilly."

"What do we have to do to change your mind about her, Leah?" Norman called out.

She held her hands out, palms up. "Very simple. *Prove* to me she's a fraud and I'll leave immediately, go back to my father and say, 'Daddy, you were right all the time.'" She shook her head vigorously. "But I know that's not going to happen." She turned to Turner. "But I know that if you don't offer me some coffee and Danish, Norm, I'll leave *here* immediately."

We all laughed. It helped to break the ice.

"Three coffees and Danish coming up," Turner cried and rushed in with the cups.

"Norman told me about the big push for recruits going on in Philadelphia," I said, as we sat down at the table.

"Apparently not only in Philadelphia," she said. "There were two girls with me from California and Ohio. Both said their groups are planning extensive drives."

"Do you have any idea of what it means, Leah?" I asked.

She filled our cups. "The girl from California said their drive will begin when Ginerva goes on her national tour. Everyone down there was talking about the tour. Apparently Ginerva will speak in every large city from New York to L.A. Someone said it will end with the largest rally ever seen in the Giants' stadium in New Jersey."

"Foreman has big plans for that tour," Turner said. "Television, newspapers—the works."

"Norman has told me about my grandfather's plans for your series, Hilly," Leah said. "What *exactly* do you think that will accomplish?"

"We're hoping it will force the government or at least the IRS to move," I replied.

"But have you found anything to *expose?*" she asked. "I have an idea of how much money could be coming into the Society, but how can you prove they are stealing?"

Norman interjected, "I told Hilly that was impossible. If the government or the district attorney can't come up with anything, how can he?"

(9 1)

"But I didn't come up here as a detective," I told her. "I'm primarily interested in Ginerva. Did you ever hear her real name, Leah? Or where she came from? Anything on her background?"

She shook her head. "No, but is that really important?"

"You sound like her. That's what she asked me the other evening."

"Oh? You talked to her?"

After I described the evening in Ginerva's apartment, Leah frowned and said, "And she told you this about the Polish sergeant although you had never mentioned it to her or to anyone?"

I said, "There has to be a natural explanation."

"Why?" she asked soberly. "Isn't it possible that Ginerva has a special grace from God that the rest of us don't have? Why does she have to be a con artist? Or a gigantic fraud?"

Norman said scornfully, "So this holy woman with this special grace from God is surrounded by a band of thieves and doesn't know a thing that's happening. Leah, you're naive!"

I didn't intend to get into any theological discussion, so I said, "Norman was telling me about your classes, Leah—"

She gave a start and glanced at her watch. "I'm late," she said. She gave me a quick flashing smile as she jumped up.

"It was great meeting you, Hilly."

"Will you help me, Leah?" I asked.

She promised, "I'll try."

"Perhaps you can talk to Margo," I suggested.

She stopped with a puzzled look. "Margo? The girl who works in Foreman's office?"

Turner said quickly, "Hilly thinks there's something going on between her and Foreman and Sister Sloan doesn't like it."

"She's in my dorm and we're quite friendly," Leah said slowly. "Let me see what I can do."

"Suppose I go over early to the cafeteria and get us a table?" Norman said. "Will you join us, Leah?"

"I'd love to," she said and wrinkled her nose. "The company will be wonderful but the food will still be horrible."

When she hurried to the door, I noticed she had a very sensuous figure. Leah Butler, I had to admit, attracted me in many ways. . . .

"Well, what do you think of her, Hilly?" Norman asked after she had left.

"Very nice, but it's going to take a lot to convince her Ginerva is a fraud."

"She may be stubborn as hell," Turner said admiringly, "but she has a lot of guts. Foreman twice tried to get her to hold a press conference to take advantage of her name, but she not only turned him down but told him she would leave rather than do that. She's really great."

The way he said it, he really meant it.

The following morning, an Angel came by *The Call* office to bring me to Foreman.

"Any questions? Any requests?" he asked when I sat down.

"Not a thing—so far."

"Was the financial breakdown satisfactory?"

"Why, yes. I assume it was similar to the Society's IRS report?"

"Exactly. Not a penny added or deducted from the figures you received. Now I have something that might be of interest to you. A family has driven from Connecticut with their five-year-old son. About a week ago the child was struck in the head by a swing in a playground, and he has been in a coma ever since. They are asking Her Holiness for a Blessing. Would you like to come along with me to the hospital? It's only a few minutes down the road."

"I certainly would, and thank you."

"Brother Andrew is bringing the car around to the front. Why don't I meet you down there in a few minutes?"

Before I reached the door, the words of Ben were as clear to me as if he was standing there whispering in my ear. *Maybe when you're up there you can do something for this guy Foreman in the way of publicity or promotion, so he would come to depend on you. . . .*

I turned and asked, "May I make a suggestion, Brother Foreman?"

He looked up, a mixture of surprise and suspicion on his face. "Of course. What is it?"

"The wire services usually hire a local reporter they call a stringer. The one covering this area for the Associated Press is probably stationed at the White Plains courthouse. Have you called him?"

He said slowly, "I assumed Brother Troy had taken care of that. But let me check." He swung out of his chair and went into the next room. I heard the rumble of angry voices and then he came out, his eyes cold, his face set.

"Thank you for reminding me," he said grimly. "Nothing was done."

He hesitated, as if wondering what next to do.

I said, "If it will help, I'll cover it and write a hard news release on the Society's letterhead. You can have it delivered to the New York offices of the AP and UPI. I would also suggest that young Stafford come along. This could be an opportunity for some very dramatic pictures. I know the *Daily News* hasn't been very kind, but they will never turn down a good legitimate news picture, no matter who sends it in."

He gave me a grateful look. "That's an excellent idea, Mr. Hillers."

"Suppose I have Sister Sloan call Brother Stafford?" I suggested.

"Would you mind, Mr. Hillers? Have her tell him to meet us at the

Wendell Hospital in, say, fifteen minutes."

She was standing at a row of files when I came out. I noticed for the first time that she was tall and the blue sweater she was wearing did a lot for her. Without sitting down, she dialed Stafford's number, gave him Foreman's order, and turned back to me. The perfume was stronger today.

"Have you finished gathering your basic information yet?" she asked.

"Just about. I was planning to call you some night this week."

"Any night," she said with an edge to her voice. "Up here one night is the same as another."

A black limousine that seemed a block long was waiting in front of the door, with Brother Andrew behind the wheel. In the light, he had a craggy pale face and what could have been scar tissue around his eyebrows. I tagged him as a one-time club fighter who could have worked for loan sharks. I gave him a cheery "good morning" as I slid into the back seat, but he only stared at me in the overhead mirror without even a nod of recognition. In a few minutes Foreman joined us and we drove off.

"Does Her Holiness do this often?" I asked.

"No. This is a unique situation," he said. "These poor people have driven in from Connecticut and as I told Ginerva, she just can't refuse them."

"I'll find out where they came from in Connecticut."

"Is that important?"

"It will be for the Connecticut papers and television stations," I pointed out. "We'll not only give it to the wire services, but Brother Turner and I will alert the papers and the TV stations in the vicinity of where these people come from. I'll suggest to Brother Stafford that the AP use one of the shots as a wirephoto to service the Connecticut papers." I decided to belabor the obvious. "The Society and Ginerva may end up getting good press coverage on this, Brother Foreman."

"I'm sure we will." He added with a flash of anger, "I keep telling our people this is how it must be done but I can't seem to get through to them."

The hospital was a low red brick building with a large parking area in front. I was surprised to see a crowd of about a hundred, mostly young, gathered near the entrance.

"This happens all the time," Foreman said with a sigh as we got out. "They always seem to know when Ginerva will appear. Oh, here she is. . . ."

Another chauffeured limousine followed by a smaller car was turning in from the highway. The smaller car pulled past the limousine,

(94)

spun around in the parking lot, and Stafford jumped out, camera in one hand.

"Hey, what are you doing here?" he asked as I came up.

"I'm helping Foreman to get this into the papers," I said. "I want a solo shot of her when she touches that kid's head. No parents, no nurse, no doctor. Just Ginerva and the kid. Understand?"

His glance was respectful. "I gotcha."

Ginerva's face was expressionless as she followed Andrew to the hospital's front door. Foreman at her side was talking rapidly in a low voice.

The crowd milled about her. It was eerie, there was no shouting, pushing, or shoving—this was not a band of groupies; they simply reached out to touch her, most looking as though they had brushed an electrified fence. Some wept, others shook and shivered, one boy appeared to have been nailed to the concrete. She swept down the corridor, an attendant leading the way. A door opened, and we walked inside to face a young woman, her face drawn and anxious and a white-haired, distinguished looking man.

"This is my father," the woman whispered. "It was impossible for my husband to come." She clutched Ginerva's hands. "Oh, Ginerva, if you could only lay your hands on Victor's head."

Ginerva didn't answer. She looked across the room at a blond-haired little boy in a crib. There was a bandage on one side of his head and he was being fed intravenously.

"He's been in a coma ever since the swing hit him on the side of the head," the grandfather said almost apologetically. "The doctors can't seem to do anything."

As Ginerva slowly, almost reluctantly, approached the bed, I impulsively picked up a tiny bunny with floppy ears, put it by the child's face, then stepped back.

My God, you are getting to be as bad as they are. . . .

I signaled to Stafford and he moved in. The clicking of his camera was the only sound in the room. Ginerva's eyes were closed as her hand reached out to rest on the child's forehead. Then suddenly, rolling down her cheek was a solitary tear. I watched fascinated as it slowly made its way over the porcelain-smooth surface of the skin, glistening for a brief moment like a tiny polished gem as it caught the light. Before it fell I gently reached out with my handkerchief and caught it. She didn't move but her hand shook violently. After a moment, she slowly opened her eyes, smiled down at the little boy, and gently brushed the hair from his eyes. Then she turned and looked at me. It was the first indication I had that she knew I was present. Without a word she left the room, with Foreman hurrying after her.

"Please thank her," the woman sobbed. "Oh, please thank Her Holiness."

Her father put his arms around her, tears were running down his cheeks.

"You will thank her for us, won't you?" he said to me.

"God be with you," was the only banality I could think of.

"I'll bring over the prints in a few hours," Stafford said in the corridor. "What do you want to do with them?"

"I'm going back to *The Call* office to write a hard-news handout on this," I told him. "After Foreman approves it, we'll have copies made. Then I want you to bring the prints and a copy of the story to AP, UPI, the *Times*, the *News*, and the *Post*. Now I'm going in and get the old man and his daughter to pose outside for you with the car they drove from Connecticut. While you're going down to the city, Turner and I will be on the phone with the Connecticut papers and the TV stations."

"You're doing a PR job for this guy, Hilly. Why?"

I winked. "I want space on the white cloud. Let me go in and get them. . . ."

The old man and his daughter were only too eager to pose. As we walked back to the hospital, I got the details of the accident, where they came from, and the names of their local newspapers and television stations.

When I came out, the limousine with Andrew at the wheel was parked in front but Ginerva, her car, Foreman, and the crowd were gone.

"Where is Brother Foreman?" I asked Andrew when I got in.

"He went back with Her Holiness."

"How long have you been with Brother Foreman?" I asked Andrew as we moved down the highway. A slight shrug was his only answer. I decided he wasn't the talking kind so I sunk back into the luxurious seat and mentally wrote the story of Ginerva and the child. I had no doubt the Society would get some publicity, perhaps only a picture in a Connecticut paper or a few lines on the evening news program. I still didn't know what I would gain by my efforts, but I was sure I had made an impression on Foreman.

At *The Call*'s office, after I briefly told Norman what happened, I sat down to write the story while he gathered a list of newspapers and television stations which covered the area where the child's family lived.

Within a few hours I was in Foreman's office with the story and several very dramatic pictures Stafford had taken. The one of Ginerva touching the unconscious child was superb. Her eyes were closed and there was a strange look on her face; the tiny stuffed bunny didn't hurt.

"I don't know how the Society can thank you, Mr. Hillers," Foreman said after he had read the story and looked at the photographs. "This is simply marvelous."

"I wanted to do something to thank you for your kindness," I said, "I hope this helps the Society."

"Oh, it will, I'm sure it will," he said enthusiastically. This time he not only escorted me to the door but put his arm around my shoulder. "It hasn't been easy getting favorable publicity from a hostile press." He gave me a faint smile. "If you ever decide to give up teaching, Mr. Hillers . . ."

The Connecticut newspapers and television stations Turner and I called seemed interested in the local angles and promised to look at the wire copy. Later, when Leah joined us in the cafeteria, Turner told her the story.

"Well, Mr. Cynic," she asked me, "do you think it will do the child any good?"

"If the child recovers I am sure there will be a natural explanation, Leah."

"Doctors always seem to have an explanation for unexpected recoveries," she said. "It's a new technology. A new drug. A new form of therapy. But God? Never. Maybe it's because he doesn't charge a fee."

Turner uttered such a long drawn-out groan we both laughed.

"Okay, you two," she said, "some day Her Holiness will prove it."

"Prove what, Leah?" I asked.

Her smile faded. "That she has a divine command."

"When that time comes," I said, "I will genuflect."

Turner stood up and waved. "Here's Bruce," he said. We watched as Stafford weaved through the crowds to join us.

"Mission accomplished, chief," Stafford said with a grin. "The *News* liked it. When I was leaving, a rewriteman was talking to the mother at the hospital. The *Post* and *Times* said they'd look at it but both AP and UPI said they checked it and would send it out. I think we'll get some coverage." He added proudly, "The guy in charge of the *News* studio said he liked my shot of Ginerva touching the kid's forehead." He jerked his finger at me. "Have Hilly give you some tips for your crummy paper, Norm."

"Norman does the best he can," Leah said defensively.

"Only a suggestion," Bruce replied, as he inspected Leah's plate. "Oh, no, not that meat loaf again. . . ."

There had to be a romance between Leah and Turner, I told myself, and wondered why I felt a tinge of resentment.

The strange look on Ginerva's face in Stafford's photograph as she reached out to touch the child's forehead stayed with me all night. Somewhere I had seen it before. Suddenly, I remembered. The night in the St. James Theatre when the child on the stretcher had been pushed to the foot of the ramp where she was standing. I remembered how she had suddenly recoiled, a frightened look on her face, and had shaken her head until Russell whispered into her ear. Only then did she slowly, reluctantly touch the obviously very ill child.

If it was all an act, a part of this obscene scam, why would she refuse to play her role as God's courier gifted with divine powers to heal? I had no answers, I couldn't even guess. But if Ginerva remained a mystery, I was still determined to find out what had happened to the little blond-haired boy in the crib. . . .

The following morning I drove back to the hospital. To my amazement, I saw, through the half-opened door, the mother almost hysterically fondling and hugging her son as a doctor examined the child's eyes with a tiny flashlight. Apparently he was finished; he said a few words to the mother and left.

When he came out, I fell in step with him. "May I speak to you, doctor?"

He looked annoyed but stopped. "Yes, yes—what is it?"

I lied glibly. "I'm from the Associated Press. We received a tip that a woman prophetess, the one they call Ginerva, performed some kind of a miracle on that little boy yesterday by placing her—"

The doctor exploded. His face became fiery red and he sputtered before he could talk.

"You goddam reporters!" he shouted. "Playing up this nonsense! I told those people in here when they first came, and so did their physician in Connecticut, that the child was coming out of it and would be fully conscious within a few days. I happen to be this hospital's chief of staff and if I had known that phony was in there with that kid I would have personally kicked her out! Parasites like you people encourage this sort of humbug! What the hell do you think we conduct here? A school for witch doctors?"

"I'm only looking for facts, doctor," I said as humbly as possible. "So then it wasn't anything that she did—"

"Hell no!" he roared. "I have a complete report with X-rays on this case and I have spoken to their doctor in Connecticut several times. He told me he begged them not to bring the child here. But no, with you people of the press making that woman appear like the Almighty's right hand, what do you expect?"

Muttering to himself, he pounded down the hall.

"Don't believe him," a voice behind me said. "It was the hand of the Lord through Ginerva that did it."

The grandfather pushed open the door and pointed to his grandson, who held up a tiny airplane. "Grandpa! Grandpa! Mama gave me a plane."

The mother hugged the boy and wept.

The old man looked at me. "You saw him yesterday. What do *you* think?"

I avoided the question. "Would you mind if the newspapers and television news programs were notified of the child's recovery?" I asked him.

"Mind? I would love to tell the whole country about Her Holiness and the good she is doing," his daughter said fervently.

"And you, sir?" I asked her father.

"My God, man! Ginerva brought my grandson back to the living! Do you think we will be like the nine other lepers who never came back to thank the Lord? We will not only sing her praises, but I intend to make a considerable contribution to the Society."

"May I ask what you do in Connecticut, sir?"

"Ball bearings," he said proudly. "My family's been in New Hartford for over a hundred years making ball bearings." He ran his hand through his white hair. "I was very much against my daughter bringing the boy down here. I told her it was a lot of nonsense but when she insisted I called the motherhouse and spoke to Brother Foreman—"

I broke in, "Brother Foreman? You spoke to him directly?"

"Why yes." He looked concerned. "I hope all this business hasn't made him angry with me."

I said with a straight face, "Oh, no, Brother Foreman is always anxious to help someone in trouble. When you called him, did you identify yourself?"

"I told him who I was, in fact I gave him some bank references to call. I said I intended to make a sizable contribution to the Society of the Chosen no matter how it turned out, if Her Holiness would come to the hospital and bless this little fellow."

I had idly wondered what made Foreman drop his morning affairs to hustle Ginerva over here; now here was the answer. That mercenary bastard!

"The kid is named after me," the grandfather was saying, "and I love him dearly. I will do anything to keep him safe and well."

"That doctor is the chief of staff. You heard what he said. . . ."

"My grandson was returned to us by the hand of God through Ginerva," he said firmly, "and no doctor will ever convince me otherwise."

"I would like the same photographer who was here yesterday to come back and take pictures of your grandson as he is now."

"Take as many as you want," he said. "My daughter and I want the whole country to know about this miracle."

I called Turner from the lobby and told him to get Stafford back to the hospital at once.

"What's up?" he asked.

"The kid came out of his coma this morning. He's going home this afternoon. Also the grandfather is—"

Turner interrupted me, "I know. He's a big industrialist. I just hung up on the New Haven bureau of the AP. They're hot over the story. That makes another miracle for her, Hilly."

"The hell it does, I spoke to the chief of staff and he claims the kid was coming out of it naturally. But it's still a good story. Tell Stafford to get right over here."

"What should we do about the papers and the wire services?"

"I'm on my way over to see Foreman. When I get back to the office, we'll call the papers and the TV stations."

This time when I entered the motherhouse, Russell was standing at the bottom of the stairway; two Angels were seated behind the desk.

"Exactly why do you want to see Brother Foreman?" he asked roughly.

"I would like to talk to him about that child Ginerva blessed yesterday."

The mean slate-colored eyes glared at me. "Well, what about the kid?"

Drop dead, you big goon, I silently told him but aloud I said:

"Well, there are some developments I thought he might like to know, but they can wait."

I turned to the door and waited for the buzzer. I was certain the grip he used on my arm to whirl me about would leave marks.

"Hey, I asked you what about that kid?"

I'm certainly not the bravest in the world but I despise bullies. Also, it could have been a reaction to what I had seen in my three weeks at the motherhouse.

I looked down at the enormous hand on my arm and tried to keep my voice low and firm.

"Get your goddam hand off me!"

We stared at each other for a moment, with the Angels at the desk eager spectators.

He slowly relaxed his grip, then dropped his hand.

"I don't care who you are," he growled, "everyone around here obeys our security regulations."

"I agree—they should," I said. "I only asked to see Brother Foreman."

"You tried to go past us and up the stairs," he blustered. "Nobody goes up there unless *I* okay it."

Now I was an intruder and he was saving face before his Angels. I decided it was best to play along with him.

"I'm sorry if I gave you that impression, Brother Russell. I simply wanted to talk to Brother Foreman about the child Her Holiness visited."

"Wait here," he grunted, and went up the stairs. When he came down, he silently jerked his head in the direction of the second floor. The whole performance had been juvenile but I still savored the taste of my tiny victory over this hard-eyed creep.

Sister Sloan wasn't in her office, it was Margo who ushered me in to see Foreman. I studied her closely this time; she was pretty and appeared to be about twenty.

Foreman's bright dark eyes never left my face as I described what had taken place at the hospital.

"This is another miracle performed by Her Holiness," he said flatly.

I quickly pointed out, "The chief of staff at the hospital claims the child regained consciousness naturally."

"How do you know that?" he demanded sharply.

"I asked and he told me."

He waved his hands impatiently. "Doctors always say that about Ginerva's cures." His fingers began drumming. "What do you think we should do about this?"

"That's why I'm here. The return of the child to consciousness, the grandfather's position as a leading Connecticut industrialist, along with the dramatic pictures of Ginerva that Stafford took, makes this an excellent news story. I took the liberty of calling Brother Stafford back to the hospital and had him take a number of pictures of the child, mother, and grandfather. I would suggest very strongly that we contact the media at once. If it will help, I will again write the news story, including an interview I had with the grandfather and some quotes from the mother. Stafford will deliver the copy and the pictures to the same papers, wire services, and television news programs, while Brother Turner and I will contact the Connecticut papers and TV stations."

He looked thoughtful. "Do you know, Mr. Hillers, you are exactly what I have been looking for?"

"Oh? May I ask why, sir?"

"The tour," he said, looking unhappy. "The most important thing in our future, and I just can't find anyone to help me." He was silent for a moment. "And now here you are, someone with imagination and expertise in publicity and promotion." He repeated, almost lovingly, "Expertise. I'm a great believer in expertise, Mr. Hillers. Combine it with money and you can accomplish anything. Never forget that." He leaned across the desk. "I'll do whatever you suggest, Mr. Hillers."

I said, "There is one thing more. . . ."

"And that is?"

"I have quotes from the chief of the hospital medical staff. I would definitely include them in the story."

His eyes narrowed slightly. "But you said he insists the child gained consciousness naturally."

"Yes. Very frankly, he considers Ginerva a charlatan."

He looked startled. "And you want to include *that* in the story?"

"If you do, you will offer the media a complete hard-news story and not an obvious puff for Ginerva and the Society of the Chosen," I pointed out. "In that way you will gain the respect of the press. They will trust you in the future."

He thought for a moment, his fingers drumming. "You're right," he said. "I see your point."

"Expertise," I said solemnly.

He threw back his head and laughed. It was more like a bark.

I said, "I have another suggestion."

He held both hands up with a smile. "I welcome all of them."

"When the story breaks, print and television reporters will undoubtedly be banging on the front gate demanding to interview Ginerva. Her Holiness finds meeting the press disagreeable, so I would suggest that *you* have a statement prepared to read to them at the gatehouse. No questions, just read it. It should be simple, dignified, and to the point. Something about the child's recovery is still another manifestation of the power God has given to Ginerva and how happy she is for the mother and the grandfather whose belief in her was so strong they drove down here from Connecticut.

"If you wish, I will prepare the statement. By the way, I alerted the grandfather and the mother. They will undoubtedly be interviewed by the press when they leave the hospital, and I have gone over what they will say."

"Expertise," he murmured half to himself. "When will I ever get it up here?" He sighed and added, "Mr. Hillers, I can't thank you enough. Oh, by the way, how is your series shaping up?"

"Fine, sir, just fine. I believe I have enough interviews with Disciples, and I have gone over the scrapbooks Brother Turner has been keeping. This incident, of course, is excellent material. But I would like to see Her Holiness again."

"How was the last interview?"

"We reviewed her early life and how God appeared to her on the mountain trail, but, curiously, she refused to identify herself. Her name, hometown, college, or schooling. Is there any reason for that?"

"She has always refused to reveal her name or anything of her family background to any interviewer," he said quickly.

"Do you know it, sir?"

I had hoped the abrupt question would get a reaction, but he only looked grave. "Her Holiness has never divulged to me her name, the town or city where she was born and raised, or the college—"

"Was she ever an actress, Brother Foreman?"

For a flashing second I detected a slight narrowing of his eyes, but his voice remained calm and even.

"Why do you ask that?"

Rather than antagonize him I said, "It was just a thought that came to me because her delivery is so perfect, how she captivates the audience. I thought that perhaps she had studied dramatics."

"No," he said firmly. "Ginerva was never in the theatre. What you see up on the stage, Mr. Hillers, is divine power speaking through her to the people. What can we expect? This is the woman God has chosen as his courier to the world. He has given her a powerful singular grace." He gestured to me. "*You* know that." He stood up, walked around to the back of his chair, and leaned on it. "That's what we have to sell, Mr. Hillers. And don't be shocked at the word *sell* because it's the only way to describe our mission—to sell God and Ginerva. This is a busy world. People everywhere are fighting, clawing, plotting to stay alive, to raise families, to maintain a home, to find happiness in this daily struggle. They forget God, and we have to remind them they are here on earth to serve and to love their creator. Now God is angry with them and has given Ginerva a warning to the world to cast out the evil in our lives or next time he will send down the fire." He paused, and went on in a soft voice. "Look at our own country, Mr. Hillers. It's going down hill. It will take a lot to stop it, to put it back on the right course again. I intend to do that. I intend to make our leaders in Washington listen to us—"

Suddenly a buzzer sounded. Foreman looked startled for a moment, then picked up the phone, listened, and hung up.

"I'm sorry I got carried away," he said, smiling and sitting down. "That was my secretary warning me my calls are piling up."

I started to get up. "I never realized how much of your time I was taking, Brother Foreman."

He waved me back. "They can wait a few more minutes. From what I said, you must realize I have plans for the Society of the Chosen. Someday we'll talk about them." He was again the brisk executive. "Now, as for another interview with Ginerva." He thought for a moment, his fingers beginning their tapping. "This evening I will contact Her Holiness and definitely arrange for you to see her." As I

(1 0 3)

got up, he walked around the desk. "I am sure it will be productive," he said. "If there is anything else you need and I'm not immediately available, be sure to call Sister Sloan—"

When he seemed to catch himself I moved in quickly to take advantage of that opening.

"I noticed when I came in that Sister Sloan was not at her desk." I said as innocently as possible. "I hope she is not ill."

He had his arm around my shoulder as we walked to the door. "Oh, it's nothing," he said casually, "Just one of those twenty-four-hour viruses. She'll be back at her desk in a day or so. . . ."

Before pretty Margo gave me a nervous good-bye smile and the door closed behind me, I had come to the conclusion that Foreman was not only as good at lying as Ginerva was at acting, but that he had big plans for the Society of the Chosen.

And as Ben had once said, they were now beginning to sound sinister. . . .

After I had written the hard-news handout, which Stafford rushed to the various city desks and television news programs, I did the statement for Foreman. Turner delivered it to the motherhouse.

"You have done a lot for this guy," he said. "Why, Hilly?"

"Bread cast on the waters," I told him. "Maybe it will get him to open a few more doors. Who knows—perhaps I could stumble over something."

After Turner left, I drove down the highway in his van and found the Royal Coachman Motel, where I called Ben from a pay phone. To my surprise, Mrs. Caxton told me that for the last two weeks he had been "out west checking something."

"He'll be back in two or three days," she said.

"Do you know where he is or what he is doing out there?"

She laughed. "No, but you know that is not unusual, Mr. Hillers. Mr. Rice tells you only when *he* is good and ready."

I asked Mrs. Caxton to monitor the early and late TV news programs and the Manhattan newspapers for any mention of the hospital incident, and to tell Ben I would call soon to explain.

Stafford returned from the city to report enthusiastically that all the newspapers and television stations news departments had accepted his prints and my copy and immediately assigned mini-com crews and reporters to cover the departure of the mother, child, and grandfather.

"The fellow in charge of the *News* studio told me the old man is a big wheel in Connecticut," Stafford said. "They like the story. I bet they'll give it a play." He looked embarrassed. "I want to say thanks, Hilly—this will do me a lot of good."

In the late afternoon, I drove over to the hospital with Leah, Turner, and Stafford to say good-bye to the child, his mother and grandfather. The parking area was jammed with television camera crews, reporters, and still photographers.

It was the usual media circus as the very appealing child waved his floppy-eared bunny and airplane at the reporters. The grandfather and his daughter stoutly maintained it was "a miracle" performed by Ginerva that had brought the child back to the "land of the living," as the grandfather put it. It didn't hurt the scene when both broke down.

The reporters also interviewed the outraged chief of staff, who angrily described Ginerva as a charlatan and denounced the press, particularly television, for publicizing her activities. While he was ranting, I saw one cameraman slowly draw his finger across his throat.

I told Leah, "He'll be lucky if they allow him ten words. It's no contest between who will get the most of this interview—the kid, his mother and grandfather, or the chief of staff."

"The Society of the Chosen hasn't received this much publicity in years," Norman said. "You should send Foreman a bill, Hilly."

"I bet the *News* will use it on page three," Stafford said as we got into his car. "Foreman should love this."

"I can't understand it, Hilly," Leah said as she squeezed in beside me. "You help to tell the world about a miracle performed by Her Holiness that *you* don't believe."

"That was no magical cure," I told her. "I'm with the chief of staff. You heard what he said. But he won't get equal time. Who wants to listen to an angry middle-aged doctor shouting into the mike when you can show a handsome little kid who has just been raised from the dead by a glamorous prophet? Even miracles are strictly commercial these days, Leah."

She groaned, "My God, you *are* a cynic."

"Who said cynicism is only experience?" I asked, and she groaned still louder.

"Hey, here's the Royal Coachman Motel coming up," Bruce said. "I don't know about you people, but I would love to have a hamburger and a cold one. How about it?"

"The very words make me drool," Norman said.

"The treat's on me," I said.

Before we got out, Stafford turned to me and Leah. "Let's call a truce, okay? No more Ginerva. No more sick kids. No more miracles. Let's talk about the Yankees chances to—" He stopped and looked bewildered. "How about that? I've been up here so long without a radio, TV, or newspaper, I don't even know who's pitching for the Yankees!"

After we dropped Leah off at her dorm and Norman returned to *The Call*'s office, I accepted Stafford's invitation to visit his studio and look over the collection of photographs he had made for the Society during the last few years.

His studio was in a small frame building not far from a much larger one painted dark green. From the double doors under the peaked roof, I assumed it once had been a barn. The windows were shuttered and the place looked deserted.

"That's one I haven't noticed," I said. "What is it?"

He looked uneasy. "That's where the Angels work out."

"You mean it's a gym?"

"Something like that," he said shortly. He started to put his key in the lock but stopped and turned to me. "Look, Mr. Hillers, as I told you, I don't bother them and they don't bother me. Until I split from here I intend to live and let live."

Inside he switched on the lights and seemed to relax. "I don't want to appear as if I'm ducking any questions or giving you short answers," he said, "but ever since I came here I have been tiptoeing around Russell and his goon squad. At this late date I don't intend to start rubbing him the wrong way. I hope you get what I mean."

"Of course. I'm simply curious about the Angels. Do you know how they are selected?"

"I always thought that the meaner they are, the better Russell likes them. Have you seen that jerk, Matthew, who rides around with that mutt?"

"We've met."

"I found out when I first started to fool around with cameras that people love to have their pictures taken. I guess it's a kind of ego trip. Well, I took some pictures of him and his dog, enlarged one, had it framed, and gave it to him. From then on he was my buddy. A couple of times he came in here with a pint of booze and just sat here drinking. He's a boastful little thug, but I let him talk. He told me he had been busted twice by the New York cops, once for robbery with a gun, the second time for rape. He did time on Riker's Island."

"How did he ever get up here?"

"I guess cons have a grapevine. Some guy he served time with told him they were looking for what they called 'security personnel' up here and he'd certainly fit in. He said there's at least two other ex-cons among the Angels. I'm in the best of condition, but I wouldn't want to tangle with any one of them. I know I could knock Matthew's head off with one shot, but that mutt is another ball game. So I keep them all happy. That's how I exist up here."

"Have you ever been inside that place?"

"One day when I was passing and saw the door open, I took a fast look. I think it had been the barn for the estate. All I saw was a regular fully equipped gym." He hesitated. "But a few times, late at night, I thought I heard what seemed to me were hymns or chanting. It was very faint—"

"But you believe it was hymns or chanting. Like a number of people were in there?"

He shook his head. "No. It sounded more like one hell of a big stereo set, because it kept repeating the same hymns, the same chants over and over."

"Were any lights on?"

"They must have had the window covered; I didn't see a thing."

"What about that black kid, Tom?" I nodded in the direction of the barn. "Do you think they brought him in there?"

He waited for a long time to reply. "I know they did," he said at last. "It was just about twilight. I had finished in the lab and was passing that window—" he pointed to a window on my right "—when a cart pulled up outside the door. It was Russell and that creep Andrew. They had Tom between them. He looked scared, but he went in with them."

"Did you see them come out?"

He shook his head.

"Do you have any idea what they did to him in there?"

"I couldn't even guess, Mr. Hillers," he said evenly.

"Norman told me a young Disciple jumped out of a window on West Fifty-seventh Street. Did you know her, Bruce?"

"No. I only heard about it. They said she jumped from the seventeenth floor."

"And that young Chinese girl who died of an overdose of pills. Did you know her or what happened to her?"

"Look, I don't know anything about that stuff, Mr. Hillers," he said quickly. "Why don't I show you my pictures? Maybe you can pick out something you can use with your series."

He had made virtually a pictorial history of the Society of the Chosen during the time he had been at the motherhouse. There were hundreds of pictures of rallies, Blessings, meetings, Houses of Preparation across the country, and a collection of stunning photographs of Ginerva at rallies and Blessing the sick. I carefully studied one that showed her looking down at a small, horribly crippled child. Stafford's camera had captured a strange look on her face, almost one of fear.

"That was taken about a year ago at a rally in San Francisco," he explained.

"Did it ever occur to you, Bruce, that she doesn't want to do those Blessings but Foreman is forcing her to?"

He thought for a moment. "I believe I can trust you, Mr. Hillers, so I'm going to tell you something I have never told anyone else. You may be right. Once at a Midwest rally she walked away from a Blessing. It was over a kid dying of leukemia; the parents brought her to the rally to be blessed by Ginerva. I was behind a scrim with my camera waiting for the usual lineup of wheelchairs and cripples to be brought to the ramp by the Angels, when I heard Ginerva and Foreman having a hell of a fight backstage. I could see them but they couldn't see me. Ginerva was so mad she was trembling."

"Do you recall what either of them said?"

"Ginerva said she was not going out there and then Foreman told her he was damn sick and tired of her 'spells.' I think that is what he called it. Then he said, 'Just remember that morning,' and walked away."

"What did Ginerva do?"

"She stared after him, then turned around and walked back to her dressing room. I think she was crying."

"Do you have any idea of what he meant?"

"Not the slightest, Mr. Hillers." He seemed eager to change the subject, and picked up another folder and said with obvious distaste, "These are pictures I have taken of Russell, Andrew, and those creepy Angels."

There were photographs of Russell marching into a rally at the head of the Angels, on the stage with Ginerva, supervising the advance of the sick to the end of the ramp, and a series of solemn portraits. There was also a group picture of Russell, Andrew, and their corps of Angels.

"Russell loves to have his picture taken with Ginerva. He has a collection I made up for him," Bruce said. Then, with a worried look, "I don't like to keep mentioning this, Mr. Hillers, but you promised not to use any of what I'm telling you. . . ."

"It's only for my information, Bruce. I would like to know as much as possible about what is going on here behind the scenes."

"I don't really know much more. As I told you, I think this whole setup is a rip-off, and I really feel sorry for the kids who are here. But again, I've gotten a hell of a lot of practical experience. Right now I can open up a commercial studio or work as a stringer for any newspaper. So until I leave, I intend to take pictures and kiss asses. Okay, Mr. Hillers?"

It was dark when I borrowed Bruce's cart to return to *The Call*'s office. Lulled by the monotonous chugging and the soft summer's night, I let my mind drift past the events of the day: the happy grandfather, the smiling child, the weeping mother, the outraged physician. But most of all the face of Ginerva glowed in my mind, that stabbing flash of fear caught by Stafford's camera, the single tear rolling down her cheek. If only I could understand all that lay behind that tear, I told myself. . . .

Even though I had told Leah and the others I agreed with the hospital's chief of staff that the child would have emerged naturally from the coma, there were questions I asked myself.

Doctors are not infallible, the old church editor had warned me that day in San Francisco. But what would have happened to the child if Ginerva had not come to the hospital? And the tear . . . could she have been weeping for herself as well as the child? I was pondering this strange thought as I approached the opened garage under the office. Suddenly a powerful flashlight blinded me.

"Mr. Hillers?" a voice called out from the darkness.

"Yes," I replied. "Who is it? What do you want?"

"Her Holiness wishes to see you immediately."

5

Unanswered
Questions

The room was bathed in soft candlelight and shadows. Ginerva, standing by the desk, was dressed in a long flowing green dress that matched her eyes. Off to one side was a table set for two, with gleaming cutlery, lighted candles, wineglasses, and a vase filled with flowers. For the first time I noticed a kneeling bench before a beautiful silver crucifix.

"I hope you haven't had your dinner, Mr. Hillers," she said quietly.

"No, I haven't. I was just about to leave for the cafeteria."

"Fine. You can join me here," she said imperiously. The tablecloth, napkins, china, and cutlery certainly didn't come from that miserable cafeteria. I looked up, to find her studying me across the unwavering flames of the candles.

"I understand from Brother Foreman that you saw the little boy leave the hospital."

"Yes. He's completely recovered and left this afternoon with his mother and grandfather."

Suddenly I heard the door behind me open, and a young girl appeared, wheeling a serving cart. We watched silently as she swiftly and skillfully prepared our plates and salad bowls. After pouring the wine, the girl left as quietly as she had arrived.

Ginerva lifted her glass. "To you, Mr. Hillers."

I toasted her silently. I am not a wine connoisseur, but this had to be the best, like the succulent roast beef. I wondered if I should be a brash reporter and bring up the miserable nonalcoholic menu offered by her Society, or play the role of a gracious guest. I accepted the latter; the food could always be brought up, there were more important questions to ask.

She brought me back with a sharp: "Tell me, Mr. Hillers, do you believe that the child's recovery was a miracle?"

I wanted her reaction, so I replied very bluntly. "No."

The answer didn't appear to disturb her. "Why not?"

"I spoke to the hospital's chief of staff. He insisted both he and the family physician predicted the child would emerge from the coma naturally."

She sipped at her wine. "If you believed this, why then did you volunteer to help Brother Foreman publicize the whole thing? As I have been told, the story is on television tonight and in the newspapers."

I was startled at her angry tone. "I only wanted to show my appreciation to all of you for allowing me to be here. What *I* think, Your Holiness, is only one man's opinion. Undoubtedly there are tens of thousand who tonight believe you have worked a miracle."

"I don't believe these things should be publicized," she said, with a toss of her head.

"May I ask why?"

"God did not make me a divine healer, Mr. Hillers," she said abruptly and fiercely. "I am only his courier, the messenger of his warning to the world."

"Why then did you go to the hospital?"

"Brother Foreman insisted. He told me how those poor people had driven from Connecticut with this unconscious child." She added, almost helplessly, "What else could I do? I had to go!"

"Has this happened many times before, Ginerva? That you felt you did not want to perform the Blessing but were—" I looked at her across the candle flames, stiff as orange arrowheads "—urged to do so by Brother Foreman?"

"There have been times when Brother Foreman felt it was necessary." Then, impatiently, "But I didn't ask you here to discuss Brother Foreman. I asked you here to implore you not to mention any cures or miracles in your article."

I was confused by her obvious anger, which was in contrast to Foreman's eagerness for publicity. "I don't understand, Ginerva. Brother Foreman was very anxious to have me notify the media—"

She suddenly jumped up and cried, "I am not a faith healer! I have another mission—far greater than anything Man has known! I have

(111)

come with God's warning he is about to be destroyed! Don't you understand? Destroyed by the wrath of heaven! And I am the only one who can save the world!"

Her green eyes were blazing with fury, her body rigid as iron. I was startled at her outburst. All I could do was to mumble, "I had better notify Brother Foreman not to make those calls," as I started to get up.

"You will do nothing, Mr. Hillers. I have told Brother Foreman what must be done."

The anger was gone, now her voice was cool, her pose queenly. "Tell me, Mr. Hillers, do you believe in miracles?"

"I find it hard to, Your Holiness," I replied.

"But what about your limp?" she asked, so casually, so matter-of-factly, that it was a moment before I realized she had not only changed the subject but had switched it to me. I didn't answer her immediately, because I didn't know how to begin.

"You said I blessed you," she prompted.

"Yes. At a rally in San Francisco."

She touched a napkin to her lips and walked to the couch. She seemed tense and uneasy. "Do you recall what happened?"

I joined her on the couch. "Is it important?"

She leaned toward me and said, "Very important, Mr. Hillers."

The top of her gown parted, and I found myself looking down at her perfectly shaped breasts in a flimsy bra. It was hard concentrating on my answer.

"Well, I felt a great sense of peace, and then I could walk without limping. Now this only took—" I stopped at the look on her face. It was fear, swift and sudden; her eyes were fixed on me as if I was a man who had suddenly risen in his coffin.

She abruptly stood up and pushed back her hair with a hand that trembled. "Please answer me very carefully, Mr. Hillers. When you left the Saigon hospital did you believe your limp would be permanent?"

I stood up and took out the flattened piece of shrapnel from inside my shirt and handed it to her.

"This is one of the pieces they removed from my leg. It pained when I walked or stood on it for a brief period. When I left the hospital the muscles in my leg felt tight, as if the shrapnel had permanently damaged them or the tendons. Common sense told me I was limping because my leg pained and possibly had been damaged."

"Why did you come to that rally?" She pressed me intently. "Was it because you had heard I performed cures or miracles?"

"I had just returned from over five years in Vietnam. Frankly, I had never heard of you. I started to walk around the city when my leg

(112)

began to pain, so I took a cab back to the hotel. On the way we were stopped by the crowds in front of the theatre; on an impulse I went inside."

After she examined the piece of shrapnel, she looked up at me, her eyes warm and sympathetic.

"I don't think I will ever forget how you described the horrible experience of that patrol. . . ."

I blurted out, "May I ask you something, Ginerva?"

Her eyes never wavered. "Of course."

"The last time I was here, you said you had seen the lieutenant and all the members of that patrol at the throne of God, and you also told me how the Polish sergeant had joked with me about correctly spelling the name of his street. How did you know that?"

She seemed startled. "When did I tell you that?"

"When I had finished describing the ambush in the Highlands."

She stepped back, so that in the shadows her face could have been alabaster. "Did you tell me about that boy—the sergeant?"

"No. In fact I had never told anyone."

There was such a stricken look on her face I thought she was ill, and reached out to hold her arm. But she shook her head.

"No . . . no," she whispered. "It is nothing." Then she gripped my arm and pulled me toward the kneeling bench and the crucifix.

"We must pray," she said in a fierce voice. "We must both pray and ask God to save the world . . . to beg him not to destroy it with his Sea of Flame. . . . I have seen it. . . . Oh, my God, it was horrible. . . ." Her voice rose. "Horrible . . . horrible . . ."

She suddenly dropped my arm and stood there as if nailed to the floor. Now her face was transfixed, her mouth slightly open, her eyes calm, deep, serene.

She appeared to be listening. Then she nodded and said softly, "Oh, yes, Almighty Father, I will tell them. . . . I will repeat your warning and they will listen. . . ."

Slowly her face changed. Now stark fear, and her body trembled, her eyes grew wide, and she threw up her hands in front of her face as if warding off a blow.

"Please, Father, don't let me see it again."

She turned and ran across the room to slam against the wall. "No . . . No . . . Please . . ." she cried. Then, as if in resignation she looked straight ahead, tears running down her cheeks.

"I see it. . . . I see it again," she said brokenly. "The whole world is in flames. Fire like flaming water covers the earth. . . . There are no more cities . . . there is nothing . . . only the Almighty Father and his blessed son in the heavens in all their glory. . . ."

She walked slowly to the bench, knelt, and fixed her eyes on the crucifix. There wasn't a sound, only the beating of my heart.

I don't know how long I stood there. She never moved, she could have been a figure in stone.

I said at last, "Ginerva."

She didn't answer.

I repeated, "Ginerva."

Again no answer. No recognition. I reached over and touched her. Her skin was cold, her eyes were glued, unwaveringly, to the cross.

I said for the last time, now louder, "Ginerva!"

When there was no reply I left, carefully closing the door behind me, and made my way along the darkened corridor and down the stairway. My eyes were now accustomed to the darkness, and I could make out the outlines of a stage, an orchestra, and balcony. Then, to my surprise, I noticed the ceiling was like a sky, with countless stars, tiny white clouds, and a full moon. The place was so eerie I involuntarily shivered, and quickly opened the front door. An Angel was waiting in a cart, and in complete silence we drove through the warm drowsy night toward *The Call* office.

This was the second time, on leaving her, I was bewildered and confused. In that haunting candlelight, had I just witnessed a performance by a skillful actress? Was it all part of a carefully programmed drama set up by Foreman to guarantee, as Ben had said, to make me a friend in a hostile press? Or was Ginerva really some kind of a religious mystic who had been granted a divine grace to see the future? I was inclined to scoff at the last, but I always returned to that night in San Francisco when she had reached out to touch my cheek. What was most unreal was real: my limp had disappeared, my nightmares vanished.

And she knew about the sergeant.

As calmly and lucidly as possible, I reviewed what had happened from San Francisco until this evening. I wanted to see it all for what it was, to see it in the round. But in the end, I was only more confused than before; now I had more questions than answers.

Before the cart reached the office, I had come to a conclusion: I needed a few days away from this mind-bending motherhouse to regain my perspective.

In the morning, I sent a brief note to Foreman advising him I would be gone for a long weekend to start putting my notes together, and intended to return Monday or Tuesday. I couldn't get away fast enough; the whole place was becoming threatening, oppressive. As evidence of my growing paranoia about Ginerva and the Society of the Chosen, I was even fearful of telling Leah and Turner about this latest experience with Ginerva. It seemed I was meeting Angels everywhere, on the grounds, passing in carts, walking in pairs along the

(114)

paths, entering or emerging from the many buildings. And there was Russell with his silent, hostile stare. At any moment I expected to hear him climb the stairs, kick open the door of the office, enter with his Angels, and order them to take me away.

"It's going to be a long weekend," Turner said dolefully on the morning I was to leave.

"There is no doubt that you will be back?" Leah asked.

I said, laughing, "Why Leah, I didn't know you cared."

She wasn't smiling. "You haven't answered my question. Are you coming back?"

"Of course I am. First thing Monday or Tuesday morning. By the way, I'll be at the Princeton Club, if anyone wants me."

Norman said a bit stiffly, "Well, *I'll* be here, Leah."

She impulsively held his hand. "Oh, I know that, Norm. I couldn't stand it if you weren't." And then she kissed him. I thought smugly, a sweet sisterly kiss. . . .

At Grand Central I called Ben's office, only to discover from Mrs. Caxton that he was still out of town.

At lunch, Susan Kahn didn't have any more to offer about Ben. As we waited outside the restaurant for a cab, she suddenly shivered and said, "I've been getting bad vibes ever since Ben left. He just called me, said he would be gone for a week or two, then dropped out of sight. I know he's looking into Ginerva, Hilly, but I have a strange feeling about that woman. I wish you and Ben would forget her. If Butler's daughter wants to stay in that crazy place, I say let her. She's over twenty-one."

She was silent for a moment, and we both watched the doorman desperately blowing his whistle and trying to flag down a cab.

"About four this morning I suddenly sat up in bed," she said slowly. "I was sure I heard Ben calling me. It was so realistic I opened the door to see if he was in the corridor." She looked at me. "This is the second time that has happened, Hilly."

The doorman was successful, and the cab swerved to the curb. "Don't worry, Susan, Ben's fine," I assured her. "In a couple of weeks we'll be lying on the beach listening to him tell what he found out about Ginerva and how he has proof she is one big fraud."

"God, I hope so," she said. She turned as she was about to get into the cab, "Hilly, if he calls you, please tell him to come back. I'm worried."

After Susan left, I decided to walk across town to the Princeton Club. I felt frustrated and at a dead end. When I reached Fifth Avenue, I impulsively turned south until I reached the New York Public Library, no stranger to me; when I was doing my Master's thesis Room 315, American History, had been a second home. I thought that perhaps here I could find something that might give me a clue to what had happened in Ginerva's apartment. For hours I pored through books on mysticism, from Richard Rolle of Hampole, the great English mystic, to Augustine's "bright spark of the soul." It was all interesting and scholarly, but none of it answered the questions posed in my mind.

I left the library at twilight. The hours had passed quickly. A fast-food place supplied my dinner, and I walked back to the Princeton Club, my mind numb with facts about mystics and eccentrics of every age.

I had just closed the door of my room when the phone rang. The moment I heard the slightly slurred, tense voice I knew who the caller was: Tura Sloan.

"I'm in the city for the weekend," she said, with a forced laugh, "so I thought like Mohammed I would bring the interview to you."

"Wonderful. But how did you know I was at the Princeton Club?"

"I caught the note you sent to Brother Foreman."

I suggested, "Perhaps we could have breakfast."

"*Now* would be more convenient," she said quickly.

I glanced at my watch. "I wouldn't want to keep you up, Sister Sloan."

"I'm a night person," she said. Then, rather stiffly, she added, "Of course, if you don't care to make it now—"

I broke in. "Where are you?"

"At the Hilton," she said.

"I'll be there as soon as I can get a cab," I told her. On the way out I handed in my key; I was sure I would not return until much later. . . .

6

Tura

The instant I knocked, she opened the door. She was dressed in a dark blue pants suit with white trimmings, a necklace of tiny dark blue shells, and was shoeless. Her blonde glossy hair fell to her shoulders. She apparently had hastily applied her makeup; there was too much eye shadow and lipstick. I could smell whiskey.

She had a large suite. Against the wall on a rolling cart was an assortment of scotch, bourbon, rye, and club soda, with a bucket of ice. Several sections of the Sunday paper and a magazine were scattered on the bed.

"I suppose you think I'm terrible, asking you to come over at this hour," she said. "But I thought as long as we're both in the city, why not do the interview?"

"I couldn't agree with you more, Sister Sloan."

She smiled. "Can't we make it Tura and Hilly?"

"Agreed—Tura."

She turned at the bar. "What can I make you, Hilly?"

"Scotch and water will be fine."

She handed me my drink, and we clinked glasses. "To the Society of the Chosen," I said.

"To your health," she said evenly, as she sat on the edge of the bed and I took a nearby chair.

(1 1 7)

"Now where shall I start? If you're interested, my mother named me after a heroine in a soap opera."

I decided it would be a waste of time tiptoeing around her; it was obvious she had been around, and I had a strong hunch how the night was going to end. I took a deep breath. "Level with me, Tura. Do you believe in Ginerva?"

She looked startled and tried to look very dignified. "Why, of course I do. Her Holiness is God's courier! She has—"

She stopped when I got up and carefully placed my drink on the bar.

"Where—where are you going, Hilly?" she asked bewilderedly as I walked toward the door.

"Back to the Princeton Club," I told her.

She got up and hurried toward me. "But you just got here! Did I do something wrong?"

"Yes. You lied to me."

"But I haven't even started talking."

"I discovered a long time ago that when people lie in the beginning, they lie all the way. When I asked you what you really thought of Ginerva, you began by handing me the same crap they hand out to those kids up there. Let's face, it, Tura, you don't believe in Ginerva any more than you believe that babies come from the cabbage patch. Am I right or am I wrong?"

She moved back to the bed. "Sit down." When I sat down she said bitterly, "So you're just another goddam hatchet man."

"You're wrong. I intend to write as factual and as objective a series on Ginerva and the Society as possible," I told her. "But in the three weeks or more that I have been up there, all I can get is the same nonsense."

She said nervously, "You're crazy if you think I intend to help you destroy the Society of the Chosen."

"I don't want you to do that, Tura," I said, reaching out and holding her hand. "All I want are hard facts. How did you, Foreman, and Troy first meet her? How did you sell her on the Coast? Who are the Angels? Where do they come from? Facts, Tura. Facts."

"Why don't you get them from Foreman?"

"Look, I'm a stranger. It's natural that he should be careful of what he tells me."

"But how am I any different? You're a stranger to me as much as you are to Foreman!"

I squeezed her hand. "I hope not for long, Tura."

She didn't pull her hand away, and I knew she was weakening. Tonight the Society didn't mean that much to Sister Sloan.

"I give you information, it appears in a newspaper, and Foreman

(118)

puts that creep, Russell, on the trail to find out how you got it. You're gone. Then what happens to me?" She held my hand tightly. "Hilly, that guy is mean."

"No one will ever trace anything to you," I said soothingly. "I can even write it under a San Francisco dateline, claim it was from the cops—anyone."

"Maybe," she said slowly. "The cops hated our guts out there. They were always coming over to see Dave with someone who claimed we had kidnapped their kid."

"Did you get much of that, Tura? Complaints from parents?"

"Some. A lot don't give a damn."

"And some have grandmothers far away," I said gently. "Or don't have anyone."

She looked puzzled. "What do you mean by that, Hilly?"

"The kid who went out the window on West Fifty-seventh Street. The Chinese girl."

She asked quickly, "How do you know about them?"

I shrugged. "The stories were in the papers."

She finished her drink and refilled it at the bar. "They were suicides. Crazy kids."

"Is that what *you* think, Tura?"

She said, annoyed, "What is this? The prosecuting attorney?"

"It's the interview. Remember?"

"As far as I am concerned, those two kids committed suicide," she said. Then emphatically, "Just as the police said they did." She gave me a tight smile. "You sound as if you've done a lot of digging on us."

"I can tell you about the skylight in San Francisco, Tura," I said.

"You really *have* been digging," she said admiringly. "You know, I had completely forgotten about the skylight gimmick until you mentioned it." She laughed. "That was one of Dave's better ones."

"It certainly didn't do Ginerva any harm," I pointed out. "The picture won the San Francisco Photographers grand prize and has been in magazines."

"That picture made her look like she was about to ascend into heaven." She added savagely: "The bitch!"

I felt I had arrived at the crossroads. Tura Sloan was clearly a lonely, embittered woman who for some reason hated Ginerva. She was also a drinker, and you didn't have to be a clairvoyant to guess why she had come to Manhattan. While she could be the key I could use to unlock a number of the Society's secrets, she also had to be treated gently. It looked like a long night.

She refilled her glass. "I was a fool to call you."

"Do you want me to leave?"

"You know damn well I don't want you to leave," she said, her voice rising. "You know why I asked you to come over here."

"No, I don't, Tura. Why did you want me to come over here?"

There were tears in her eyes. "Because I had to talk to someone—someone other than those goddam Bible-spouting kids up there or that bastard Russell or that goof Troy!"

"What about Foreman, Tura? You told me you have been with him since the beginning."

"It's not like it was in the beginning," she said. "It's all changed now." She nervously tapped out a cigarette. "No booze. No cigarettes. No radio. No music. No TV. It's driving me nuts!"

I tried to sound casual. "What do you mean it's not the same, Tura? You mean between you and Foreman?"

"You saw her—the young kid he has working for him."

"Margo? The one with the long brown hair?"

"I warned him," she said, after almost emptying the glass with one long swallow. "I warned him that if he didn't get her out of there I'd leave."

"And what did he say?"

"You couldn't repeat on television what he told me." The rye splashed into her glass. "I had to get away for a few days."

"He said you had a virus."

"He warned me that if I left he wouldn't permit me to come back in."

"Will he?"

She said grimly. "He'd better." She stared into her drink. "I should have stayed in San Francisco, where I had it made."

I joined her at the bar and poured some scotch into my glass. "Is that where you first met Foreman, Tura?"

She went on as if she hadn't heard me. "When I walked down the streets out there, men looked at me. I had a six hundred dollar a month apartment." The words now gushed out. "Six hundred a month! I know what you're thinking, Hilly. No, I wasn't a call girl—I was in the spooky racket." She threw back her head and laughed. "Do you know what that is, honey? Mediums. Seances. I was the best. You had to make an appointment to get to see me. Nobody walked in off the street!" The smile faded. "My God, why am I telling you all this?"

Close up, there were tiny wrinkles and lines under the careless cosmetic job, but she was still a very attractive woman. When I kissed her gently, she closed her eyes and shook her head. "I'm crazy for doing this. I know I'm going to regret it. . . . Maybe we better wait. . . . I'll see you in the morning for breakfast. . . ."

She slid into my arms, and her kiss this time was anything but gentle; she had a wild lascivious tongue. She reached over and switched off the lights.

"The zipper's in the back," she whispered.

I was awakened by the scratching of the match. She was sitting on the edge of the bed lighting a cigarette, the moonlight carving a delicious silhouette of her voluptous body. I glanced at the luminous hands of my watch: nearly five o'clock.

The memory of the past several hours swept over me; it had been a wild night. I reached over and touched her back. The skin was soft and warm. She shivered, quickly turned, and bent down to kiss me. "I bet you're the most surprised guy in the world."

"Delighted—not surprised, Tura."

"Please believe me, Hilly," she said seriously, "I'm not a tramp. I could have a toss in the hay any time I want; that gorilla Russell has been stalking me for years. And that guy Andrew! I would cut my throat first. I liked you the minute I saw you in the office. I've been so damn lonely up there! I stayed up most of the nights last week moving the furniture around just for someting to do. I never lived like this. It was always a few weeks in Vegas. Or Nassau. Or Europe. No nine-to-five in a creep office surrounded by a bunch of young fanatics! That's why I blew up at Dave. He can stand it—I can't." She leaned over and kissed me again. "Now with you up there maybe it won't be so bad. Look, let's get this straight. It's not only sex. I want someone to talk to, maybe go out and have dinner somewhere on the highway. No more will I just listen to Dave talk about that goddam Ginerva and his tour! For almost a year that's all I've heard. And now he's screwing that kid Margo. That's trouble, and who needs it? How about a drink?"

Whiskey was the last thing I wanted, but I said yes only to keep her talking. Like a naked nymph she walked across the room, doing a ballet whirl as she balanced two glasses.

"Would you believe it, Hilly, if I told you I was educated by the nuns in a private school? Three years of ballet, Latin, French, and steno? I can still type a hundred words a minute and put on a seance that will shake you in your boots. You don't know how lucky you are—I'm an all-around girl!" She handed me my drink, leaned over, and whispered, "And you know I'm good at a lot of things they don't teach you in school."

"Where did you go to school, Tura?"

"Lincoln, Nebraska. As they say, 'The Home of William Jennings Bryan.' A long way from Sixth Avenue!"

She snuggled up against me and giggled. "I'm here, baby, interview me."

"Fine. Let's begin with you and Foreman. When and where did you meet?"

She suddenly sat up and leaned against a pillow. "Let's get one thing straight. I'm not going to hang David Foreman for you. Okay?"

I tried to lie as professorially as possible. "I'm really interested in a factual account of the whole background of the movement, Tura. How it actually began. How it was built up. Who is Foreman and where did he come from? What made you, Foreman, and Troy decide to join Ginerva? This is the sort of information I need. I don't see how that will hurt anyone."

"Well, no," she said hesitantly. "But let's set some ground rules. Anything I give you, you got on your own on the Coast. You never spoke to me. Okay?"

"It's a deal. Now let's start with you and Foreman. How did you two meet?"

She inhaled deeply and slowly blew out a series of perfectly shaped smoke rings. "Did you ever see anything so perfect, Hilly? It took me a long time to learn how to do this." She took a sip of her drink. "I hope I'm not letting myself in for something I'll regret."

I stroked her thigh. "From now on I'll make sure you won't be bored anymore, Tura."

"Why do women get taken in by guys like you, Hilly?" she said broodingly.

"Not like me, like Foreman. When did you first meet him?"

"Five years ago. I met him in San Francisco when he was managing a fat kid from India." She chuckled. "He was just a stupid kid who had been a waiter on a cruise ship. But his old man had been some kind of medicine man in Bombay, and he knew a few tricks. Dave got him a sitar, a turban, and a white robe, but they were struggling when I came into the picture. I taught the young jerk TM and gave him a course in Cameron's *Flowers of the East*."

"What the hell is that?"

"Cameron was an Englishman who went to India in the 1850s and became a holy man. He wrote this book before he died. It's a fantastic handbook for the making of a guru. Well, we had a good thing going until our slob began believing he was a mystic and wanted a Rolls-Royce, a yacht, and young boys. Dave had to buy off the father of a kid who was ready to file a sodomy charge. Luckily, Dave had the sense to bank our money overseas. We gave our guru fifty thousand and put him on a plane back to Bombay."

"Fifty thousand! That's a lot of money, Tura!"

"It was a drop in the bucket compared to what we'd made," she said proudly. "Dave and I split five hundred thousand. About a year later I met him in Europe and we had a fantastic time."

Another series of smoke rings floated to the ceiling.

"Was this before you and Foreman met Ginerva?"

"Two years before. Dave never really spelled out what his plans were, but something told me that with the phony Bombay mystic he was only getting his feet wet in the spooky business. The next thing he went into would be big, very big. And that is what he has now—the Society of the Chosen and his golden bitch."

"Why don't you like Ginerva, Tura?"

"I curse the day I ever let Dave talk me into backing her. She smells trouble. I warned him when this goddam thing began to get bigger and bigger, but he wouldn't listen. He's got something in his head and no one will ever shake it loose. Now don't ask me what it is, because I don't know any more than you do."

"So the only reason you don't like her is that you feel you and Foreman would have been better without her and the Society?"

"Maybe not financially, but it would have been an easier life." She ground out the cigarette. "This is only for your ears. I had a string of spooky joints going in Chicago; the law didn't look on them as a big deal. No one got hurt. Lonely widows heard from their husbands. A poor woman who lost her kid in an accident was told he was happy in Paradise. A spinster was promised her Prince Charming would soon come along. Harmless stuff. I paid the cops, and everyone was happy. One day the sister-in-law of one of the councilmen dropped dead during a seance—not at one of my places—and I was told to fold fast, which I did. I went to the West Coast and met Dave. And there are days and nights I regret that day."

"But why?"

"This thing is too big for me," she said impatiently. "You're not dumb, you must know the cash is coming in by the millions. It's legal. But it's too much. The balloon has got to burst sometime, and when it does, I don't want to be here."

"If it's all legal, why worry?"

"Let's leave that for another session," she said shortly. She leaned over and ran the tip of her tongue along the edge of my earlobe. "This is the way I want to have breakfast with you."

"You're going to make my stay at the motherhouse worth while," I told her. "What are you getting out of all the work you've done—and are doing—for Foreman and the Society, Tura?"

She groaned and rolled over. "Dammit, but you have a one-way mind!" She sighed. "I guess I better tell you before you nag me to death. I get a damn good salary. Dave gets a damn good salary. Troy is taken care of; so is Russell. We all live high on the hog. Limousines, chauffeurs. First class all the way."

"Does Foreman take anything else—in the way of money, I mean?"

Despite the dimness and the shadows, I felt her tense, her voice hardened. "Just what do you mean by that?"

I backtracked as adroitly as I could. "You know, any other fringe benefits."

"What you mean is, is Dave stealing? Isn't that it, Hilly?"

"You said it, I didn't."

"Why do I always end up with guys like you?" she said, as she angrily finished her drink and then stood up, reaching for her clothes strewn on the floor. I decided to take a long chance and let her go. If she left, I had lost a very important key to the puzzle I wanted to solve. There was also the possibility she would warn Foreman I was asking dangerous questions. On the other hand, if I won, Tura could be invaluable.

"There's a seven o'clock train for White Plains," I said, "and the coffee shop is open all night." I rolled over and gave an elaborate yawn. "I'll see you back at your concentration camp."

"You're just another no-good bastard, Hilly," she shouted, and slammed the bathroom door. She came out a few minutes later, stiff with outrage, threw her clothes in an overnight bag and left. Well, I had lost, I told myself, and perhaps when I returned to the mother-house there would be a note from Foreman asking me to leave. I wondered how I could get past the Angel on guard for one last talk with Ginerva.

About a half hour later, while I was considering what alternatives I had, I hear the key in the lock; it was Tura. She threw the bag on the floor and slumped down into the chair.

"I got to the train but couldn't get on it," she said in a choked voice. "I can't face going up there again and not having anyone to turn to."

In the first light, I could see tears in her eyes, and it made me ashamed. But then I remembered the kid she had said, "went out the window" and the young Chinese girl who had "committed suicide." It was her game, her rules, not mine.

"I told you, Tura, you don't have to be bored up there anymore."

"And what do I have to do in return, hang Dave and maybe myself for your goddam newspaper series?" she asked.

I told her, "I want the series to be as definitive and as objective as I can make it, Tura. That's why I won't take any lies. They handed me too many in Saigon."

She unbuttoned her blouse. "Don't hang me, Hilly," she whispered.

Between blowing out those crazy smoke rings, Tura told me how she and Foreman had transformed the former cabin boy into a guru with thousands of followers on the West Coast. While she set up an ashram—a Hindu retreat—in an old hall, complete with an altar, incense, and figures of Hindu deities, Foreman put on an advertising and promotion compaign, including hiring a small army of derelicts to plaster San Francisco with posters at night. As she explained with a giggle, thousands came to hear the boy's solemn lectures, all stolen from Cameron's book. When I asked how a sophisticated and cultured city like San Francisco could be hoodwinked, she explained:

"In troubled times, Hilly, no city is sophisticated. People are confused. They want assurances, promises, hope—all spiced up with some glorious mystic phrases. Like Cameron's wonderful line: 'I want to go beyond everything.'"

She laughed. "I don't know what the hell that means, but it made our customers feel good, and it soon became a standard slogan out there."

Tura also displayed hatred and contempt for Ginerva.

"She's a fraud," she said flatly. "If Dave ever heard me say that—"

"But how do you *know*? Is it possible that there could be something—"

"No! No! No!" she said with a flash of irritation. "Listen to me. I've been in the spooky business for years. I've seen a lot of fakes like her. They may sound convincing, but they are all as crooked as a guy operating a three-card monte game on Broadway."

Then I told her about the Polish sergeant. "Now you explain that."

She shrugged. "Maybe you wrote about it somewhere. Maybe you told Dave and he mentioned it to her. Maybe it was just a good guess on her part. Who knows?" She slid back under the sheet and reached out for me. "Do we have to talk about *her* all night?"

"No," I said. "Let's talk about Foreman and the money he's stealing—"

She shook her head. "No, Hilly, not now—"

"It's either that or take a walk back to Grand Central, Tura," I said softly. "Back up to the motherhouse and that lonely little house with the four walls. Remember?"

She whispered, "You are a bastard, Hilly." Then she turned her head and sighed as if in resignation. "What do you want to know?"

"Is he skimming?"

She said sullenly, "Yes."

I knew I would have to drag it out of her. "How much?"

"A hell of a lot."

"Where does he keep it?"

"Lots of places," she said, sitting up. She reached out and picked up her drink. Her hand was trembling. I could hear the ice hit the sides of the glass with tiny tinkling sounds. "Hilly, this is a bad scene."

I ignored her. "Name one place. Just one."

"The Caribbean. He bought a bank down there on an island." She shivered and came close to me. "Oh, Hilly, stop it! Please!"

(125)

I whispered in her ear, "The name of the island, Tura. Just the name of the island."

"Little Cat," she said brokenly. "The name of the island is Little Cat. The bank is on Little Cat." Then she started to cry. I kissed her.

"Now we can forget Ginerva, Tura. Foreman. The money. Little Cat. Everything. Now there's only you and me, Tura. Just you and me."

She moaned deep in her throat as she pushed up against me. "Oh, Hilly, I'm so lonely," she whispered.

Somewhere down the hall a phone rang incessantly, but after a few minutes I didn't hear it anymore.

In the morning, I dropped a satisfied but worried Tura off at Grand Central. Again and again I had to assure her that anything she told me would be attributed in my series to sources on the West Coast.

As we walked to the White Plains train gate, she warned me, "Hilly, from now on my life is in your hands. One word, one hint that I'm a snitch, and Dave would put Russell on me." She shuddered. "You just don't know Dave, Hilly. Cross him and he'll kill you."

I pulled her into an alcove, kissed her, and vowed, "You have my word, Tura—I'll protect you always."

When I came out of Grand Central, I hurried back to the New York Public Library. I had an almost overpowering desire to read the book Tura kept mentioning, Cameron's *Flowers of the East*. Apparently it had supplied the blueprint for Foreman in creating his cabin boy guru and possibly Ginerva.

I found it listed in the rare book room, but as I knew, you just don't wander in there and pick out a book. Luckily I had my old admission card, and a new one was quickly issued.

Cameron's autobiography described his adventures as a Queen's officer who had fought under Lord Canning in the Sepoy Mutiny, that famous revolt of the Bengal native army in 1857. When peace was declared, he was appointed to Canning's staff. After Canning died, Cameron retired from the army to devote the rest of his life to studying Indian religions. He became intrigued with the writings of the mystic Shankara and entered his monastery in Mysore as a monk.

After ten years as a monk, he contracted severe malaria and was forced to return to London for treatment. Several years later, when he was attached to the London Museum as an expert on Far Eastern religions, he wrote his book. Cameron had a superb eye for detail; his description of the Mutiny and its religious background, temple rites, and life in the Mysore monastery were fascinating.

In a chapter he called "A Theology of Mysticism," Cameron discussed mystics and their writings, from Thomas Aquinas's *Summa Theologica* to Shankara's works, which he had translated for the Museum. One passage caught my eye:

I have discovered that there are those who have been given the divine gift of a journey through the darkness of their soul until they can reach out to God, to hear his voice and then turn to Man to speak with a wisdom veiled in mystery.

This mystical phenomena is not only confined to the religions of the West but also in Judaism and Islam. Unfortunately, those who are blessed in this manner often lack the power to reflect articulately on their glorious experience but there are those few who can and their voices are like thunder in the night.

Such was a woman of the Ramaite sect in the south. She appeared out of nowhere to announce that the Five Gods were angry with the world and had selected her as their spokesman to Man. Crowds followed her wherever she went but when the raja and the civil administrators ignored her warnings she predicted the Gods would destroy the countryside with plagues and floods. This took place and there was a severe loss of life. I have visited the area and it is still desolate; although land is sorely needed, the natives refuse to settle there. There are myths about the woman's end; the most popular is she was borne to heaven in a chariot of fire.

That passage kept running through my mind during the train trip to White Plains. Did Foreman create Ginerva and her supernatural act after he had read Cameron's book? But the tenement super had told me Foreman, Tura, and Troy had appeared *after* Ginerva had started to attract crowds to her storefront church. Could the super have been mistaken? And if Foreman had taken the idea of a beautiful prophetess of doom from Cameron's book, what explanation was there for the child in San Francisco who had walked after her Blessing? For the young college student who recovered from leukemia? And why had my limp vanished? My nightmares?

There was also the information Tura had given me about Foreman's bank on Little Cat, that had to be checked out immediately by Ben's detectives. But I couldn't find Ben! Even Susan didn't know where he was.

By the time I reached White Plains, I was uneasy, irritated at Ben, and wondering if I should take the next train, return to the city, and dismiss the whole thing as an idea gone sour. I called Ben's office from the station but got only Mrs. Caxton, who now sounded worried. Ben still hadn't called, and she had several important legal messages waiting for him. Susan, she said, was calling at least three times a day. I assured her Ben was fine but urged her to have him call me as soon as she heard from him.

7

Beautiful Obsession

The same fat, ponderous cabdriver dropped me off at *The Call* office. As I entered the garage, I met Turner and Leah coming down the stairs. It made me feel better to see both their faces light up.

"Hilly!" Norman shouted. "We were wondering what happened to you!"

"You stayed an extra day," Leah said almost accusingly.

"I was tied up. What's happening?"

Norman looked around and lowered his voice. "Bruce Stafford came by last night asking for you. He was disappointed you weren't here." He came close to me, now almost whispering. "He said to give this to you." He handed me a key. "You were asking about that place near him. . . ."

"The green house! The Angels' gym?"

"That's the one."

"But how did he ever get this key?"

"Last Thursday one of the Angels asked Bruce to take his picture for his girl friend. Bruce took the guy's picture, and after he left he found this ring of keys on the floor where they dropped out of the guy's pocket. That night Bruce went over to the green house and tried every key until he found one that opened the door. He drives into the city every other Friday to pick up photographic supplies, and he had a copy made for you. This is it."

"That took a lot of nerve."

"He said he felt he had to do something to help you," Leah explained. "What do you intend to do with it, Hilly?"

"Get in and look around. What else?"

"Like I told Leah, I should never have given you this key," Norman said, his face troubled. "God knows what they will do if they caught you in there."

"Do either of you have any idea of what that place is?"

They both shook their heads. "And I don't want to know," Turner said.

"Suppose we drop over and see Bruce?" I suggested.

"Bruce knew you would want to do that," Leah said, "so he gave us a message to give to you. Don't visit him anymore at his studio or even act friendly toward him. And he begged us to ask you not to use that key to get into that place until after he is gone from here. He said he doesn't want to risk being connected with you in any way if you're caught."

"He sounds as though he's ready to leave."

"I asked him about that," Norman said. "Bruce likes to play it close to his vest. He just said, 'All I can tell you is that one morning you'll find I'm gone. I have planned exactly what I intend to do.'"

"Did he ever discuss his plans?"

"Never. But I believe what he says, don't you, Leah?"

"When Bruce leaves here he will either open his own studio or get a job on a newspaper," she said. "That's all he's ever talked about."

"Did that Angel ever come back for his key?" I asked.

"Bruce said he came back the next day, but when he found Bruce was in the city he went up the wall. Later on Friday he picked them up and made Bruce swear to never mention it. He said the guy was sweating as he counted every key. He told Bruce he would rather split than face Russell without those keys."

"We talked a lot last night with Bruce about you, Hilly," Leah said. "The three of us don't think you should take a chance going into that place. Bruce said it appears to be nothing but a gym."

"I have to satisfy myself. Where are you two going now?"

"Lunch. Join us?"

On the way over to the cafeteria, I told them about Ben's activities, and how he wanted to assure Norman he intended to start his civil action against the Society as soon as the investigation was finished. I didn't mention Tura; I felt it important that Leah not know. Possibly I dreaded her scorn and contempt.

We had just sat down at our table when there was the sound of a commotion at the door. We turned to see a young Disciple shouting something and waving a Bible before he ran out, followed by a stream of Disciples who left half-eaten sandwiches, bowls of soup, cups of coffee, glasses of milk.

"What's happening?" Turner called out to a passing Disciple.

"Her Holiness is walking around the grounds," he replied.

"How about it? Do we go?" Turner asked.

"Definitely," I said, and we ran for the door.

We joined the Disciples who, singly and in groups, were running across the lawn from all directions. There were looks of wild joy on their faces and many cried "Glory to Ginerva" as they passed us.

We found her under an elm, and to this day I have a vivid memory of that scene. She was dressed in a long white gown, and surrounded by hundreds of young Disciples sitting or sprawled on the grass. It was hot on the exposed lawn, but under the elm the air was cool and smelled of green things.

In a clear vibrant voice she spoke of the humble carpenter of Nazareth, the footloose Messiah, the wanderer, the strange, gentle man who never promised glory, riches, or power—only love; the man who called himself the "ransom for many." When she looked over the crowd and asked if they were ready to follow her in warning the world of the coming Doomsday, she was answered with a roar: "We are, Ginerva! We are ready!"

Then she looked up and prayed in a loud voice:

"Hear me, Almighty Father, and bless this motherhouse and these brave young people who will soon go forth to follow your command to me to tell all men to drive the evil from their hearts and fill your world with love and peace or you shall destroy it with your Sea of Flame."

She stood that way almost transfixed. Suddenly there was a shout. A bar of sunshine came through the leaves to turn her hair into shimmering copper and to bathe her face in a soft light. It was as good as any Cecil B. de Mille production. The effect was electrifying. The Disciples jumped up and began dancing about, waving their Bibles and crying out:

"Glory to Ginerva!"

"Blessed be Ginerva!"

"Save us, Ginerva!"

I looked at my wristwatch; it was just 4:00 P.M. Meanwhile Ginerva silently, slowly, walked away. By now the crowd had doubled, with Disciples pouring across the lawns and others in carts chugging frantically along the paths. Trotting across the grass came a squad of Angels. Like a precise drill team they split into two sections as they approached Ginerva, then closed ranks to completely surround her.

It was an incredible sight as we followed the crowd across the lawn toward the Grand Ballroom. Disciples danced about the emotionless Angels, while those in carts chugged alongside, calling out to her. She smiled, turning from time to time, her hand raised as if in blessing as she walked inside the square of marching Angels.

"Does she do this often?" I asked Turner.

"Every once in a while," he replied. "The same thing happens every time. Most of these kids are at the end of their session and will be leaving for other cities."

"And what will they do there?"

"Preach her doctrine—get the world's head on straight or it's the fire next time."

"So this is a sort of pep talk?"

"I would think so," he said.

"Why does it have to be a 'pep talk'?" Leah asked angrily. "Isn't it possible she simply wanted to talk to the kids about God? What's so evil about that?"

"Someone once told me," I said, "that you will never know how naive Americans are until you have managed a guru."

"Whoever told you that must have been a thief," Leah snapped. "I have to get back to my class."

Thief. I wonder how Tura would like that description?

"I told you Leah's as stubborn as a Missouri mule," Turner explained, as we watched Leah make her way through the crowd. "It's going to take a lot of proof to convince her Ginerva's a fraud."

"That may come sooner than we realize," I muttered.

We were near the *Call* office when we heard a cart approaching. It was driven by an Angel who called out: "Mr. Hillers! Her Holiness wants you to join her and Brother Foreman."

Inside the darkened Grand Ballroom I followed the path of tiny stairway lights to the top, then started down the long carpeted hallway to Ginerva's apartment. As I neared it, I heard Foreman's voice, low, intense, persuasive. The door was barely open, but I could see inside. The room was bathed in candlelight. Ginerva, who had changed into a flowery blouse with accessories to match, looked more like a stunningly beautiful model ready to pose for a travel poster than a woman who had just finished a stirring homily on the ministry of Christ. They were both sitting on the huge velvet couch. Despite the heat, Foreman wore a neat white linen suit, white shoes, dark blue tie, and white shirt with a blue trimmed handkerchief sticking out of his jacket pocket. As I watched, he leaned forward and began speaking in a low tone.

"It will be a glorious tour, Ginerva. We will go from city to city, from coast to coast, and you will deliver God's warning to hundreds of thousands. They will follow you in prayer to the Almighty Father to ask his forgiveness, to seek out his mercy and to beg him not to send down his Sea of Flame. And at the end of the tour, there will be the largest rally this country has ever known. They will wait for days to enter this huge stadium, to listen to you, to pray with you."

She was staring at him, her green eyes wide and luminous, her lips slightly parted, her face glowing.

"I will wear a white gown," she whispered, "with the blue velvet sash lined with pearls and the tiara which makes me look like a queen."

"No. No, Ginerva," Foreman protested gently. "We will have the best designers in New York create a gown that will make you more beautiful than ever. Can you see them that night, Ginerva? A sea of faces stretching to the very end of the stadium. . . . The corridors and the aisles are jammed. . . ."

He seemed to pause deliberately as if to leave the uncompleted dream hanging in the air.

"Yes. Yes," she said eagerly.

His voice rose slightly. "And when you enter, the roar of their voices rises to the heavens, to the very throne of God! And there is rejoicing in Paradise because Ginerva has won the war against Satan and she turned the world around."

She said, almost to herself, "I will speak to them that night as I have never spoken before. I will open their hearts and fill them with the glory of the Lord." She jumped to her feet and stretched out her hands. "Yes. Yes. I will make them laugh. And cry." She spun around to face him. "And be afraid. I will hold them in my hands like clay and mold them any way I wish."

He sat there, a handsome fox ready to enter the henhouse, while Ginerva still held out her hands listening to waves of thunderous applause that only she could hear. I felt goose pimples running up my arms.

"Your name will be on every man's tongue, Ginerva," he said softly. "You will be the most talked about woman in the country because of the miracles you will perform with the sick, the crippled, the blind, and the deaf. You will bless them and send them away cured and they will sing your praises."

She slowly lowered her hands and looked at him. The glow in her face winked out to be replaced by fear.

"No. No," she whispered. "Please. . . . I can't any more. . . . I won't. . . .

"God has given you this glorious gift, Ginerva," he said sternly. "It will be a sin against Heaven not to use it."

She protested, "But I'm afraid. . . . The darkness . . . the voices. . . ."

He said soothingly, "You only imagine that, Ginerva. You've been under a great strain. When the tour is over, we'll all go to Europe and stage the biggest rallies they have seen." He jumped up and clasped both of her hands in his. "You'll not only be the talk of America, but of the world!" He added earnestly, "Don't you see, Ginerva—that is why we *must* publicize your cures and your miracles. It's important to the tour. Your tour. To the success of your ministry." He suddenly became brisk and businesslike. "Now let us get ready for Mr. Hillers. He will be here any moment."

He switched on the lights, then walked over to the table and blew out the candles. He turned to her and said evenly, "Remember, Ginerva, you have changed your mind. The world must know of your cures and miracles."

She slowly nodded.

I hurried back down the hall and stairway. This time I made a great deal of noise, as if stumbling in the darkness. The lights went on and Foreman, smiling, was standing in the open doorway of the apartment.

"Please forgive me, Mr. Hillers," he called out cheerfully. "I didn't realize the hall lights were not on."

He looked polished, posed, and prepared to sell me the Brooklyn Bridge.

With his arm around my shoulder, he escorted me into the room. There was a faint odor of burnt wax. "Here is Mr. Hillers, Ginerva," he said. Then to me, "We are so glad you could join us for lunch."

This time I noticed the table was set for three.

He prompted, "Aren't we, Ginerva?"

She gave me a weak smile and said, as if on signal, "I'm so pleased you could come, Mr. Hillers."

The glow was gone from her face, she seemed subdued, there was an air of weariness, even resignation about her.

"I was told you listened to Her Holiness on the grounds today," he said.

Your intelligence network is flawless, I silently told him. "I found it inspiring," I said. "Very moving."

She didn't seem to hear me.

"Was your weekend productive?" he asked, as he waved me to a chair.

I thought of Tura and Cameron. "Very productive."

"There's nothing like cleaning out one's desk and getting one's files in order," he said stoutly. "And how does your material look at this point?"

"Excellent. I hope to start writing over the July Fourth weekend."

The door opened and two girls wheeled in a serving cart. While one prepared the plates, another poured a small portion of wine into Foreman's glass. He rolled it expertly around his tongue and announced, "Croix de Mont, 1966."

"Yes, sir." The girl seemed delighted he had guessed correctly.

We started with a marvelous soufflé. "I'm a collector of trivia, Mr. Hillers," Foreman said briskly. "Do you know who invented the soufflé?"

"No, I don't."

"Antonin Carême, in the nineteenth century," he said promptly. "Any gourmet will tell you he was the world's greatest chef. I would call this one perfect. Wouldn't you say so, Ginerva?"

She barely nodded.

He gave her a sharp look, then went on. "We asked you to join us, Mr. Hillers, to tell you I was fortunate in changing Ginerva's mind about publicizing her cures and miracles. She agrees with me now that it's important for the national tour." There was a slight edge to his voice. "Isn't that true, Ginerva?"

She toyed with her food and only slightly nodded.

He frowned and his voice rose a note. "Isn't that true, Ginerva?"

"Yes," she said in a low voice. But then she raised her head, and for the first time there was a hint of defiance in her face.

"But it is also important to let the world know that God selected me as his courier who carries his warning. . . ." There was a slight quiver in her voice. "That is my ministry. . . . That is the mission God gave me. . . ."

"Why, of course, Ginerva," Foreman said in an aggrieved voice, as if she had wrongly accused him. "Your divine command comes before everything." He leaned forward slightly. "I can promise you that before your national tour is over, even the smallest village in this country will know of God's warning! From east to west, from north to south, his words will ring out!" Now he was intoning like an archbishop. "But God also gave you this divine gift of healing, Ginerva. What of all those people who were crippled when they came to you and now can walk? What of all those who were deaf and now can hear? And the children, Ginerva—the children who are sick and crippled—yes, even dying—what of them? What do I say to their parents who come begging to be permitted to bring their precious little children to be blessed by you?" He spun around to me. "And what of Mr. Hillers? Didn't his pain and limp and those terrible nightmares from the jungles of Vietnam vanish the moment you blessed him? God sent him to us, Ginerva, sent him to help us!"

They were both staring at me. The room was very still, and I wondered if they could hear the beating of my heart.

"The gift of God is in your hands, Ginerva," Foreman said forcefully. "Not to use it, not to let the world know about it, would only be sinful." He turned to me for confirmation. "Don't you agree, Mr. Hillers?"

"Well, if there is anything that upsets Her Holiness I will gladly—"

"Not another word, Mr. Hillers," Foreman said briskly. "What would your readers think if they read a highly promoted series on Ginerva and there was no mention of her cures and miracles? Would they not think that strange? What is your opinion as a newspaperman, Mr. Hillers? Don't you think your readers would call and write in to protest?"

"That is possible."

"Of course it is," he said triumphantly. "It's all part of the glorious story of Ginerva! As much as the Angel appearing to Joseph Smith or the Angel Gabriel to the Virgin Mary!"

They were weird analogies, but I didn't want to interrupt him. Now it seemed he was lecturing Ginerva rather than talking to her.

"At every rally, Ginerva, the blind, the sick, the helpless come from all over to see you, to touch you, to be blessed by you," he said. "You can't leave them with broken hearts! They would think you had abandoned them if you didn't appear for the Blessing of the Sick."

The question just seemed to pop out of my mouth. "Is there some reason why you don't want to do that any more, Ginerva? The Blessing of the Sick?"

Her head shot up and she stared at me. For a moment I thought she was about to say something, but Foreman jumped in, this time his voice cold and hard.

"Of course not! Where did you ever get such an idea, Mr. Hillers? The Blessing of the Sick is an integral part of our rallies! The faithful demand it, look forward to it! The sick and the helpless who come are increasing! I now have instructed Brother Russell to start collecting all the wheelchairs, the hearing aids, the crutches and canes from those who have been cured, as graphic proof that the power of God rests in the hands of Ginerva! Before the Blessing of the Sick begins we will have them—"

She suddenly pushed back her chair. "I hope you will excuse me, Mr. Hillers, I feel exhausted. Perhaps it was the sun."

She hurried from the table. The door of her bedroom clicked behind her.

"Do have more wine, Mr. Hillers," Foreman said as he refilled my glass. "How was that fish? Boulangère style. Means in the style of the baker's wife. They call it that because the dish is baked with a final sprinkling of baker's bread crumbs before it's put in the oven. The fillets are folded and baked with potatoes and razor-thin onion slices. It's one of my favorites."

He held up his glass and studied the wine. "Ginerva's under a great strain these days, Mr. Hillers. The spirit of God flows through her whole being when she blesses the sick. Also, we mustn't forget, she is worried and apprehensive about her tour—"

"Has anything gone wrong, Brother Foreman?"

"Well, not exactly wrong," he said. "It's just the enormous detail and planning that must go into it. As I told you, I don't have the assistance that I should have and I've had to delay it twice already."

"Will it be from coast to coast, sir?"

"From New York to L.A.," he said proudly. "Then back to New York, where we will finish with a tremendous rally in Giants Stadium. Ginerva will appear in every large city and her name will be on the tongue of every American." He finished his wine and delicately wiped his lips. "The timing is perfect for this tour, Mr. Hillers. Just perfect. Religion is on the upswing. It's been on television, in newspapers and magazine articles. People are looking for something more than the newest appliance or keeping up with one's neighbors. This is a time of disorientation and doubt. Along with new values, Americans want answers. And Ginerva will be the force that will supply those answers." He shook his head. "But to get Her Holiness on the road is a tremendous undertaking, and I'm finding it's a staggering task to do alone."

"But there's Brother Troy and Sister Sloan?" I said. "Aren't they of any help?"

He gave a deep sigh. "Brother Troy is a fine technician who knows lighting and stage business. Sister Sloan has her own problems and is only a limited help." He sighed. "Oh well, let's get back to your series," he said. "Did you come up with any questions as you sorted out your notes?"

"Well, yes, I did, Brother Foreman. I know we talked about this before, but there is a definite gap in my material."

"What is missing?"

"Ginerva's full name and some statistics about her. Hometown. What schools she attended. Fundamental information."

"Oh, I don't think that is so important, Mr. Hillers," he said with an airy wave of his hand. "If Her Holiness wishes to keep that type of information confidential, why press her? As I told you, I don't even know those facts about her, and frankly, I couldn't care less. Do you think the thousands and thousands who believe in her really care what her name was before she was confronted by God, who gave her the name of Ginerva? And I'm certain the schools she attended would not impress them. I wouldn't let the lack of those facts bother you, Mr. Hillers."

I marveled at that smooth confident voice. He could have been one hell of a salesman.

He stood up, and I knew our session was over.

"I can't tell you how much I enjoyed you company at lunch, Mr. Hillers," he said, as he walked me to the door. "Frankly, I can't wait until I read your articles." He paused and said almost casually, "And I am sure those dramatic accounts of Ginerva's cures and miracles will provide thrilling reading."

I was unable to resist the temptation. "I do feel uneasy about using that material, Brother Foreman. After all, Ginerva did ask me not to—"

His hand once again found my shoulder. The smile was still there, indulgent, unprovoked.

"Don't worry, Mr. Hillers, I'll take full responsibility." The hand on my shoulder tightened slightly. "You *must* use it, Mr. Hillers. It's important to our tour." He added softly, "That helps to bring them in."

The following day, promptly at 4:00 P.M., I stood under the same elm, in the same spot where Ginerva had called down the blessing of the Lord. Almost to the second, the rays of the setting sun broke through the leaves and bathed me in a soft gold light. I told myself this was another coup for Foreman, and Bruce Stafford had missed what could have been a prize-winning picture.

Tura's cigarette glowed in the darkness, the smell of her perfume was heavy in the room. The air conditioner made so much noise she had insisted on shutting it off, and as a result I was dripping with sweat, my mind dull and weary from sex and booze. All afternoon I tried to get out of her what she knew of Ginerva's background, but she continued to be ambiguous and evasive.

"Are you trying to tell me you don't even know her real name? Where she came from? What she did before she arrived in San Francisco?"

I knew she was casually blowing smoke rings, and I had to grip the side of the bed not to tear that damn cigarette out of her mouth.

"I swear, honey, I don't know anything about her background."

"Tura, do you want me to walk out—now?"

"But I *really* don't know, Hilly! I would tell you if I did."

"Does Foreman know? Did he ever give you a hint?"

She hesitated for a moment. "We're not that close anymore," was her sullen answer.

"Dammit! I didn't ask you that! I asked you a simple question! Did he or did he not give you a hint of where Ginerva came from? New York? California? Florida? The North Pole?"

In the long silence, I suddenly felt such a feeling of shame and self-loathing at what I was doing that even now, years later, I can still recapture the scent of Tura's perfume, the cigarette smoke, and the nauseous feeling that swept over me. I scrambled off the bed, picked up my clothes, and went into the shower. When I came out, Tura was dressed and sitting by the window, the motel's flashing neon sign lighted up her haggard face. She had been crying, the sparkling tears still welling up along the edge of her eyelids.

"I can't tell you her real name or where she came from, Hilly," she said hoarsely, "but I can tell you she was in the theatre."

"Why do you say that?"

"I was in the chorus line when I was seventeen," she said, "and I know something about the business. One day, after we had leased the St. James in San Francisco, I saw her talking to one of the stagehands. After she left I grabbed the guy. He told me she sounded like a professional. She knew all the terms. When we first took her over, she also worked with Troy on the lights. Steve also told me she had to have been in the theatre at one time."

I told her, "Tura, it's really important that I find out as much about Ginerva as possible. Now is that all you know?"

She opened her purse and fumbled nervously with its contents. I knew she was holding something back.

"She always insisted on complete anonymity," she said finally. "She claimed it was God's wish—you know the crap she hands out. At first I didn't want any part of her. Dave can tell you that. I told him I wouldn't invest in a woman, no matter how good she was, who refused to even give us her real name. How did we know she wasn't wanted by the feds? Or some small town police department who one day would show up with a warrant for her arrest and send our investment down the drain?" She looked grim. "But stupidly I let Dave talk me into it. Once or twice, when I brought it up later, he told me to shut up or get out. I stayed. It was either that or lose my money."

"I think Foreman has something on Ginerva that keeps her in line," I said bluntly.

She stared out the window.

I said softly, insistently, "What do *you* think, Tura?"

Again she avoided a direct answer. "It was about a year after we started when I first noticed a change in her," she said. "In the beginning she was an arrogant bitch, acting as if she was the star of a Broadway hit. Suddenly it seemed Dave had cut her down to size. When I asked him what had happened between them, he just winked and laughed. One weekend Dave and I flew down to the islands to try our luck at the casinos. We were on the upswing at the time; the St. James was jammed at every rally and we had started to move out of town. Dave's not a hard drinker, in fact he seldom touches any whiskey, but this time he tied one on—and talked." She watched the flashing sign with a half smile as if remembering. "He told me he was so determined to find out something about her he had Russell intercept her mail. She was getting a flood of mail from those nuts out there but apparently Russell found one that gave them a clue to who she was and where she came from."

I handed her a drink, and she took a sip.

"What did he do about it?"

"First Russell disappeared for a while, then Dave dropped out of sight for a week or so. He told me they were searching out locations for out-of-state rallies, but at the time I suspected something was up. Then after he got drunk and told me what he had done, I put two and two together—"

I interjected, "After they intercepted the letter, they went somewhere and found out all about her?"

She sniffed. "You don't have to be Sherlock Holmes to figure that one out."

I tried to stifle my impatience. "But what did they find out, Tura?"

"You never give up, do you, Hilly?" she said.

"Dammit, Tura, what did they find out about her?" I asked, trying my best not to shout.

"You have to get the rest from Dave," she said with infuriating calmness.

"He never told you?"

"Like I said," she replied, "we're not that close anymore. That bitch spoiled everything."

I sat on the arm of the chair. "You never really told me, Tura, why you dislike her."

"When she entered the picture, things changed."

"Is it possible Foreman is sleeping with her?"

Her laugh was scornful. "No way. I can guarantee you that. She's made of ice. There's only one thing she cares about—the crowds. I swear she gets off on them. The minute she steps on that stage she becomes alive." She added grudgingly, "Oh, she's good, I'm not denying that. Probably puts Aimee Semple McPherson to shame. But . . ."

Another long pause. "But what, Tura?"

"There is something about her that gives me the creeps. Did you ever look into her eyes? Green. Like emeralds. Deep, very deep. You don't know what she's thinking." She slipped on her shoes. "I can't stay up there much longer. The place is getting to me."

"How about Foreman, Tura? Does he believe in Ginerva?"

She gave me a scornful look. "Like he believes in the Easter bunny." She shrugged. "But as I told you, Dave has an idea in the back of his head how he wants to use the Society. What it is, I don't know, and frankly, I don't care to know." She stood up, smoothed her skirt, and surveyed herself in the mirror. "Well, Hilly, now that you got everything out of me, what comes next? Do we pass on the street and you don't know me?"

"Is that what you *really* think of me?"

She gave me a faint smile. "Do you *really* want to know?"

"Now is as good a time as ever."

"I've been around a lot more than you have, Hilly, and in my opinion this series is not that important to you. There's something else."

"I would like to know what it is."

"You will do just about anything to find out what Ginerva did to you that night in San Francisco. Why did that limp disappear after she touched you? That question is bugging you, Hilly. It's hanging on your mind like a cement block. You'll never rest until you get the answer. She's become your beautiful obsession. It's the same with Dave. She's grabbed him like she's grabbed you. The both of you can't let her go. Even that moron Russell has fallen for her. In the beginning Dave promised me she would be good for only two, possibly three years, then we would go looking for something fresh. It's a hell of a lot more than two years. Now he doesn't even pay attention to me when I ask him when we are going to split from here." She gave me a malicious smile and said softly, "Hilly, maybe you're in love with her."

"Don't be ridiculous."

"Then again, there's another possibility. You may be looking for something in her."

"What would I be looking for in Ginerva?"

"Something you lost in Vietnam. Yourself. You know, Hilly, the spooky business does strange things to you. I once knew a guy in Chicago who could stage a beautiful seance. One day he put his head in an oven. He left behind a note saying he had found himself talking to his brother, who had been dead for ten years. Every time he had a customer and the lights went out, there was his brother. Finally he turned on the gas."

"What the hell does that have to do with Ginerva?"

"I always thought there was a line out there that you should never cross. In some way that guy crossed it. Maybe you found that you're on one side of that line and Ginerva is on the other. You don't want to cross it, but you have such a need to, it's gnawing at your insides."

"Tura, you're talking nonsense. You said yourself there is nothing mystical about Ginerva. You even called her a fraud."

She said, nodding, "True. I spotted her as one the moment I met her with Dave and Steve Troy in that crummy storefront church in San Francisco." She paused, then continued: "But there is also something I don't like about her, and this is the reason. She's not interested in money. And no way will either you, Dave, or any guy slip under the sheets with her. As I said, only crowds turn her on. I don't go for people like that. There are too many parts to them. I like people who let you know what they want—money, sex, booze, the horses, craps— even power. Ginerva's not like that. Do you know what I'm talking about, Hilly?"

"Do I have too many parts. Tura?" I asked teasingly, hoping to grease the way for the important question.

"There are parts of you, Hilly, that I really go for," she said, surprisingly serious. "But then again there are some parts I'll never know."

"Maybe you know the answer to this one, honey. Why does Ginerva dislike doing the Blessing of the Sick? I told you about the lunch I had with them. She wanted to drop that part of the rally, but Foreman was determined not to let her off the hook."

She looked uneasy. "It's good for contributions. One old woman gave us five thousand dollars because she claimed Ginerva had given her back the use of her arm. Why should Dave drop it? It's not against the law, and it gives hope to people. Hell, she's not the only one who does that sort of thing. You can even see them on television. After they do the wheelchair and crutches bit, some guy sweet-talks you into sending contributions to a box number." She added unbelievingly, "It's hard to believe, but people are convinced they have just seen a miracle take place on television and they send in their money!"

She had now opened the door for me to ask that really important question. "Speaking of money coming in, Tura, does Foreman do his skimming on the grounds?"

She moved restlessly. "Hilly, don't ask me those kind of questions. I told you I won't hang him!"

I quickly moved on to something else. "Well, tell me something more about the bank on Little Cat. How does he use it?"

She was silent for a moment, then said grudgingly, "That bank is the biggest laundry in the Caribbean."

For a moment I didn't get it. "Laundry!"

"Launder the money." Then she cried, "What the hell am I telling you this for?"

I gently stroked her hair. "Tura, it's only a newspaper series. But I must have facts! What's the big deal about the bank? It must be legitimate even if it's in someone's name."

"Of course it's legitimate," she replied. "Rock stars who have hit it big use offshore accounts in plaque banks. So do big New York banks. It saves paying state taxes." She said nervously, "Let's talk about something else, Hilly. Please?"

I kissed her but my thoughts were on what she had just told me. But what were plaque banks?

I pressed her, "In other words, whatever Foreman skims goes right into the Little Cat bank?"

"I'd rather not talk about it, Hilly."

I said evenly, "Tura, does the money go directly into the bank?"

She hesitated, then replied, "No. First it goes into the Fund—"

I broke in quickly, "What fund?"

"The Ginerva Evangelical Fund." She broke off and stared at me. "What am I doing?" She finished her drink in a gulp, jumped up, and said determinedly, "That's it. No more. You're getting me to say things which could get us both in trouble. I'll see you back at the motherhouse."

After she left, I slumped into the chair by the window and for a long time watched the monotonously flashing neon sign. Now I had the plaque bank on Little Cat and the Ginerva Evangelical Fund. It was obvious Tura knew a lot, and booze and sex could probably drag it out of her. But I didn't know how many more of these motel sessions I could stand. I was beginning to despise myself.

BOOK TWO

THE
SOCIETY
OF THE
CHOSEN

8

Summing Up

I didn't see Tura for a week, and then she called: the Royal Coachman Motel at four. It was the same routine, dinner in the room then we went to bed and later, after some drinks, I tried to pump her. At midnight, with most of the Jack Daniels gone, she finally began to talk. The Ginerva Evangelical Fund had a small office on Little Cat. The skimmed money was first delivered to the Fund, then deposited in the Little Cat National Bank of the Bahamas. Later the money was siphoned to other accounts in other places, but at this point Tura insisted that was all she knew. I was sure she was lying. What else she knew would have to be pulled out in bits and pieces.

Tura was also obviously frightened; despite the large amount of whiskey she had consumed, "Little Cat," "skimming," or "the Fund," as she called it, made her hands tremble. Several times she became angry and started to leave, and I had to brutally remind her that only the lonely stone house awaited her back at the motherhouse. I hated myself—but she stayed.

To avoid answering my direct, insistent questions about Foreman's manipulations, she gave me a rambling lecture on plaque banks in the Bahamas. They were simply a room with a few pieces of furniture, a plaque on the wall certifying the place was a bank—and a file.

She gave me a drunken wink. "What's in that file is important," she said in a mock dramatic whisper.

Accounts were secret and protected from outside investigative agencies; in fact a national law made it a crime to disclose details of accounts.

"And that suits Dave perfectly," she said.

As we finally prepared to leave, she said abruptly, "Maybe I'll surprise you someday, Hilly, and give you a call at your school." She studied her near-empty glass. "I've made up my mind. I'm getting out. I can't stand this place anymore, those crazies spouting the Bible all day long are driving me nuts. No way do I intend to stay here." She shook her head and finished the drink. "No way."

I asked her, "What do you intend to do, Tura, take what you can get?"

"No," she said firmly. "I'm going to lay it on the line with Dave. Hell, he's got to be fair. After all, in the beginning I did put in a lot. When he pays me off, I'm going to Vegas, Paris, Amsterdam. Anywhere to get rid of the smell of this place." She gave me a roguish wink. "Maybe I can persuade a handsome guy named Hilly to throw away his schoolbooks and join me." She gave me a wet, noisy kiss. "We could have a great time, Hilly—and all on Tura."

I gently slid out of her embrace. "But what will Foreman say, Tura, when you tell him you want out?"

She gave me another wink. "If he's wise, he'll have lots of cash on the barrelhead waiting."

"But where will he get the cash? You told me everything he skims goes down to the Caribbean."

She chuckled. "Dave will never be caught short of cash, honey. Sure, most of it goes down to Little Cat, but he keeps a lot on hand. It's grease for wheels."

"To pay off?" I suggested.

"Dave's been paying off all his life," she said, with a knowing shake of her head. "In San Francisco he had a regular payroll. You would be surprised who he was paying off. Now he's got another one. Always remember, honey, grease helps to make the wheels go round."

"Who does he pay off, Tura?"

She gave me an indignant glare. "There you go again with those damn questions!"

"Forget I asked," I said soothingly. "Let's get back to you. Suppose Foreman doesn't want you to leave and refuses to give you the money?"

She didn't answer as she slipped on her dress and began combing her long, thick blonde hair. For the first time I noticed strands of gray. Suddenly she stopped and studied herself in the mirror.

"He better have it," she said, half to herself, "because he knows I can hang him . . ."

I was standing behind her, and our eyes locked in the mirror.

"But I would never hang him for a goddam newspaper series," she said softly.

I kissed her, and she shivered. "What would you hang him for, Tura?"

"Only to save my own neck," was her prompt cold reply.

It was something to remember.

By now I had accumulated several books of notes, a shoebox filled with index cards of memoranda; several rolls of candid camera film of Disciples and of the grounds; folders of prints of Ginerva from Stafford's files and the photographs he had taken especially for me; three boxes of taped interviews and copies of *The Call*. As a precaution, I had arranged to send the material every few days to a friend who was conducting a summer school class at St. Timothy's.

What did it all sum up? I still had no proof of any illegality. What was sinister and evil lay behind the blank smiles of her Disciples, their endless chatter about God's fearsome Sea of Flame and the final victory of the Society of the Chosen when its members took their places on God's great heavenly cloud to be lifted into Paradise.

Most frustrating was that the strange and beautiful woman named Ginerva still remained an enigma.

I had no idea of what Ben would produce at our forthcoming weekend conference, although he had promised he would prove Ginerva was a fraud. Tura's story of Foreman's skimming, the bank in Little Cat, the Ginerva Evangelical Fund could only be investigated by Ben's detectives. There was also the Society's financial pattern of millions pouring into the organization through the street peddling teams and contributions.

I had gathered enough for a satisfactory newspaper series; I was sure Ben, Sir Edward, and Lord Cavendish would be impressed. Ben and Butler were confident the articles would force an official inquiry, but I did not share their confidence. The attention span of American newspaper readers is notoriously brief. Yesterday's editions are fine for historians or for cat litter, but to be effective and produce results, outrage in print must be translated into official action, and many times that "spontaneous action" has to be arranged.

At our conference I intended to share with Ben an idea which could possibly result in such national exposure of Foreman and his fellow thieves that the IRS and the Department of Justice would be forced into examining the growing menace of the Society of the Chosen.

It had to be arranged this way:

While the series was running, Tom Gray, whom Ben had boasted was well connected in Washington, would approach an ambitious senator or congressman with the suggestion he use our material and hold public hearings subpoenaing Foreman, Russell, Troy, and Ginerva to testify under oath.

What chairman of a committee would ignore a beautiful evangelist controlled by a slick promoter who had hidden millions in an obscure bank on a tiny Caribbean island?

There was also the serious question which had to face Washington and the nation in the 1980s: what can be done about these cults and sects, fascist in nature, tinged with criminality, without violating the constitutional right of their members to freedom of religion?

This combination of the sensational and a national dilemma would be an attractive package for any Washington politician seeking exposure. Obviously, such a hearing would attract wide television coverage. And as I knew from covering the alleged statesmen in Nam and the visiting Washington firemen, a television camera is to politicians what a stump speech was to Lincoln.

I dislike loose ends, and some remained untied. I had attempted several times to obtain another interview with Ginerva but curiously, Foreman had become evasive; Ginerva was either "meditating" or "out of town" or "busy on details" of the national tour. There was nothing I could do. To try to pass the Angel guarding the Grand Ballroom was impossible, and any attempt would be reported immediately to Foreman or Russell.

Neither Russell nor Andrew had been seen on the grounds for a few weeks. This bothered me, and I tried unsuccessfully to get an explanation. Norman's gossipy clerks and cafeteria help could only suggest they were out of town working on the tour.

Then there was the key Stafford had given to me. It was still hidden in a fold of my wallet. I ached to get into that mysterious green barn, but I had to respect Stafford's demands that I not make an attempt until he was gone.

"Any indication when Bruce intends to leave, Norm?" I asked Turner one night.

"The last time we talked, he said that one day he would turn up missing, and then we would know he had split," was his reply.

June's early days saw my routine become humdrum. I had finished my countless familiar interviews with just about everyone on the staff, had seen everything, except the Society's Houses of Preparation and Russell's security headquarters. The stultifying days with the endless hymn chanting and Bible quoting, the blaring of the loudspeakers delivering the maddening monotonous story of Ginerva's confrontation with God, combined with the drowsy heat, had started to numb me mentally. To break the routine, I returned to reading early file copies of *The Call*. The stuff was so badly written, the pages so badly made up and organized, it was difficult to keep from laughing.

One morning I was alone in *The Call* office when Susan called; Norman had just gone to the cafeteria to bring back some Danish and coffee.

"Hilly," she whispered. "It's me."

"I'll get back to you within fifteen minutes," I told her.

I left a note for Norman, then drove the van to the Royal Coachman and called Susan from a booth in the lobby. As soon as she heard my voice, she broke down.

"Hilly," she said sobbing, "Ben called, but now I'm worried more than ever. He's definitely in that depressed state. At times he sounded almost incoherent. What I could get out of him was that he is on the verge of getting the final piece of evidence to prove Ginerva is a fraud."

"Did he tell you where he was calling from, Susan?"

"No. He dialed direct and ignored my questions. I begged him to come back but he said he had to keep on with what he was doing. Before he hung up he gave me a very curious message for you. He said, 'Tell Hilly he and I are going to play one hell of a poker game.'"

"Do you have any idea what he meant by that, Susan?"

"Not the slightest. Most of the time he rambled. Once he called me Nancy and asked if I had taken Jody to nursery school yet." She said in a despairing voice, "Hilly, something is very wrong with Ben, and we have to do something."

Like Susan I felt helpless, but I also knew there was no sense in making any comforting meaningless promises. "Actually, there isn't much we can do, Susan, but wait it out. We both know how he goes into a deep depression at this time of year, then slowly recovers."

She asked fearfully, "Do you think we should contact the police, Hilly?"

"Where could they start looking, Susan? Then again, there's the publicity to be considered. The Missing Persons Bureau will no doubt notify the newspapers and television news programs. After all, Ben *is* a prominent Broadway theatrical attorney with many important clients both on Broadway and in Hollywood. Suppose we call in the police and a week later he appears? It would be terribly embarrassing for him, and how could he explain what he has been doing? I think we should wait it out, Susan. One of these days you'll get a call, as you always have, telling you he's back and wants to take you out to dinner!"

"Oh, Hilly, I hope so," she said fervently. "I'm so worried I don't even leave the apartment any more; I'm living on TV dinners!"

"I can't tell you to stop worrying because now *I'm* worried. But all we can do is wait. And this time when he comes back, I'm going to insist that he talk to Josh. He has to do something about that condition."

"We'll both talk to him," she promised firmly. "I can't go on like this." Then she said fiercely, "I told you I'm afraid of that woman, Hilly. There's something evil about that whole setup. Please be careful. . . . Please."

I assured her, "Don't worry, Susan, everything will turn out all right. Remember, Ben must be back for our July Fourth weekend meeting. When he calls you, have him get in touch with me at St. Timothy's. I'm leaving here a few days before the weekend."

Back at *The Call* office, I simply told Norman I had had to make a call to school to see about a faculty meeting date.

"When will you be leaving, Hilly?" Norman asked, with an apprehensive look.

"In about a week," I told him. "I plan to put my notes together, have a conference with Ben and Sir Edward, and then start writing."

Later that evening, after dinner, I joined Turner and Leah on our favorite bench.

"Hilly is leaving in about a week," Norman said quietly.

"So now it's all over," she said, looking at me.

"As far as I'm concerned it is," I said. "I've done all I could."

"But you really haven't found out anything," she pointed out.

"If you mean have I uncovered any evidence of criminality that will hold up in a court of law, the answer must be no," I replied. "But I certainly have a lot of unanswered questions."

"Questions will not put Foreman and his gang in jail," Turner observed gloomily.

"You will be surprised what happens when you ask them in big enough type."

"In other words, you hope my grandfather's newspaper will create a scandal," Leah said scornfully.

"Maybe that's what it takes to force the law to do something about this religion racket," I told her.

"But, Hilly, you don't have any proof Ginerva is a charlatan, yet you know the headlines will hint that," she protested.

"Let's face it, Leah," Norman put in, "whoever moves in on this bunch will have to hurt Ginerva. There is no other way even if she is what she claims to be."

"I should tell you both this: Ben has claimed he has discovered something in Ginerva's background which he insists will prove she's a fraud."

"Well, give, Hilly. What is it?" Norman demanded.

"I don't know any more than that. But I will over the weekend."

"I don't believe it," Leah said flatly.

Her enormous self-confidence was irritating. "Sometimes I doubt you believe the world is round," I told her.

"I hope whatever your friend claims to have is more impressive than what you dug up," she said dryly.

"What about us, Hilly?" Norman asked in an anxious voice. "Now what are we supposed to do?"

"If I were you two, I would start making plans to leave," I advised him. "Norm, why don't you split for California and lie on the beach while Ben prepares your case? Leah can—"

She coldly interrupted. "Don't tell me to return to my father."

"Why not, Leah? He's really worried about you."

She gave me a grim smile. "Someday I'll tell you about my father."

"But what will you do, Leah?" Norman asked. "Go back to drama school?"

"I just might stay here," she said.

Norman gave her a horrified look. "After Hilly's series is spread all over the country? How could you, Leah? How do we know what that moron Russell will do?"

"Why would they be suspicious of me?" she asked. "Didn't Brother Foreman instruct us to help Hilly in any way possible? I was simply following orders."

"Oh, come off it, Leah," I protested. "Norm is right. You couldn't possibly remain here after my series began. My God, it will be running in newspapers owned by your grandfather!"

"I don't believe there was ever any question of where I stood, Hilly," she said in a quiet determined way. "I believe in Ginerva, and I also believe that someday she will prove that God gave her a divine command." The sun had brought out a cluster of freckles around her nose that made her look very young and gave her face a vulnerable, almost childish innocence, offset by the cool intelligent brown eyes. "You came up here so positive you were going to produce proof she is a charlatan, but you failed. Isn't that right?"

"I only came here looking for answers, Leah."

"And you didn't find them?"

"No. But after I talk to Ben I won't have to look any longer."

She said firmly, precisely, "*Maybe*."

Finally, with the July Fourth weekend only two days away, I said good-bye to Foreman. He was still friendly and I believe sincerely sorry to see me leave, obviously only because I could offer expertise to benefit the Society. He spent most of our last session leading me back over familiar ground: the importance of the Society of the Chosen in preserving the American Way of Life; Ginerva's Glorious Mission to Mankind; Armageddon, God's Terrifying Sea of Flame; and My Own Miracle.

After some finger drumming, he adopted his favorite stance of looking out the open window at the vast expanse of lawns baking in the summer heat.

"Whatever you write about your experience with Ginerva is sure to touch the hearts of countless readers," he said, without turning around. "Remember, you are not just another feature writer, but an actual participant in one of the holiest missions in the history of mankind."

He was as solemn and glib as if he were a salesman extolling the glorious features of his latest product.

"Would there be an opportunity, even a brief one, to say good-bye to Ginerva, Brother Foreman?"

This time he did turn around. "No, I'm sorry, Brother Hillers," he said with a sigh. "There doesn't seem to be a minute. Ginerva is busy with God's work from the moment she gets up in the morning until she goes to bed late at night." He added smiling, "However, you can leave any questions with me, and I will see they are answered and sent off to you immediately."

He was now a smiling fox. I thanked him, we shook hands, and I started for the door. Before I reached it, I decided to throw out one last question and see if I could get a hint of why Russell and Andrew had been missing from the motherhouse.

"Oh, by the way, Brother Foreman, will you please say good-bye for me to Brother Russell and Brother Andrew?" I tried to look puzzled. "Come to think of it, I haven't seen them on the grounds for the last few weeks."

He was still smiling. "Oh, they are working in the fields of the Lord. I'll be sure and give them your good-bye."

Alone in the outside office, Tura clung to me. "Oh, Hilly, you don't know what your leaving will do to me."

I tried to soothe her. "You'll be fine, Tura. When you feel like talking to someone, give me a call." I said tentatively—very tentatively —"Maybe sometime we can meet in the city."

"I'm afraid," she said brokenly, "afraid of all the things I told you. I was a fool. Sure, he's treating me like a heel, but I still don't want to hang him. And, Hilly, no matter what you say or how many promises you made to me, that's what you hope to do—hang Dave and ruin the Society of the Chosen. You know that. . . .You can't lie to me." She bit her lower lip. "And I helped you. . . ."

No matter what I told her, how many promises I made, she was inconsolable, laden with guilt over what might happen to Foreman.

While she hated him, she also confessed to me, "I can't help it. He's under my skin. We're just two birds with the same feathers, singing the same songs." She added with a sad smile, "Let's face it, Hilly, Dave and I are both thieves. . . ."

Also, I knew the thought of those lonely nights in the small stone house froze her heart.

The next night, the phone rang.

It's Susan, I thought, as I picked it up. But it was Tura, her voice was so low I could barely hear it.

"Hilly," she whispered. "Hilly, Hilly. . . ."

Then there was a click.

"Who was that?" Norman asked as I hung up.

"Tura Sloan," I replied. "I could barely hear her. She just mentioned my name and hung up."

"She's probably drunk and she wants a last bit of action before you leave," he said with a grin. He yawned. "I don't know about you but I'm going to bed."

Norman was probably right, I told myself, and headed for the bathroom to take a shower. But I couldn't turn the faucet. The thought of that lonely embittered woman sitting by herself with a bottle of whiskey haunted me.

Turner, in his pajamas, came to the door of his bedroom as I was leaving.

"I can't believe it," he said disgustedly. "You're going over to see her *now?*"

"She didn't sound drunk," I said.

"Don't tell me you're going to risk getting caught by Matthew and that mutt just to hold her hand?" he said sarcastically.

"It's my paternal instinct," I told him.

There was only the orchestration of the night insects, a quarter moon, and some starlight. I now knew my way through the brush and avoided the paths and drives. Several times I stopped, listened, and took my bearings, but the estate was quiet and dark. I finally reached the stone house and found the door open. There was the sweet smell of spilled whiskey and a small pool of light from a lamp. Tura was on the floor, her back to the couch, an open bottle in one hand and a number of pills scattered across the carpet.

I ran into the living room, picked her up, and put her on the couch. She opened her eyes, they were dull, dazed. She tried to speak, but her mouth couldn't form the words.

A scene from long ago instantly came to my mind. I was in senior year at Princeton when Johnny Masters, my roommate, discovered the kid across the hall had attempted suicide by an overdose of sleeping pills after a fight with his girl friend. There were kaleidoscopic shots of Johnny and I pouring milk down the kid's throat to make him vomit, slapping him awake, forcing him to walk endless miles back and forth across the room as we supported him between us and gave him countless cups of black coffee. It was Johnny's idea, and later when I asked him how he knew his first aid, he explained he had recently read a newspaper article about poisoning.

I frantically repeated the same procedure. I was never happier than when she threw up violently on her expensive-looking rug. With her arm around my shoulder and me supporting her, we began to work in a circle around the room. At last she started to moan and her eyes began focusing.

"Let me rest, Hilly," she muttered. "Just a few winks . . ."

"Walk!" I shouted at her. "Keep walking."

We stumbled into the kitchen, where with one hand I hastily prepared the coffepot, then we continued walking around tables, in between chairs, and up and down the hall. When she seemed to slip back into unconsciousness, I slapped her awake. After what seemed a long time, she began to come out of the stupor. The coffee had perked, and while walking I forced her to drink cup after cup. At first she gagged and vomited, but I ruthlessly kept making her drink the stuff until at last she began to stumble on her own power.

It was near five o'clock when I agreed to let her sit down for a few minutes. In the pale light Tura looked drawn and haggard. Her hair was stringy and tangled, her eyes bloodshot, her hands trembled.

"Why in hell did you ever try that stupid business?" I asked.

"There didn't seem to be anything else to do," she whispered hoarsely. "I was so lonely, and afraid and sick at what I might have done to Dave."

"Tura! Talk sense!" I pleaded. "This is the guy who's cheating you! Who has pushed you aside for a kid! Who's made a fool of you! You don't owe him anything!"

"Everything you say is true, Hilly," she said, sobbing, "but I can't help it. I can't get him out of my mind. All the plans we had . . . all the good times we were going to have when the—this thing was over. Then everything went wrong. You came when I was so lonely I wished I was dead. I thought we had something going, then you said you were going away. I couldn't stand being here alone anymore . . . I just couldn't, Hilly. . . . Please don't be mad at me. . . ."

I held her and let her cry, then I told her to take a long leisurely bath while I cleaned up.

I did the best I could, and finally she came out, pale, shaking, and frightened at her close call.

"I did it on an impulse," she confessed. "At the last minute, when I knew I was passing out, I called you. Thank God you were home."

I asked, "Never again, Tura?"

She shook her head. "Never again. I was stupid. You're right, I don't owe Dave a dime. I realize how bad a guy he is. . . ." She paused. "Hilly, I'll help you all I can . . . I promise."

I was surprised to discover Tura's promise wasn't all that important; that she was alive was paramount at the moment.

I made her some toast and coffee, and after she ate, she promised she would notify Foremen she didn't feel good and spend a good part of the day in bed.

When I left, it was dawn. Halfway to the *Call* office I heard the chugging of Matthew's cart and Buck's sharp savage bark. For a moment I felt trapped. What possible explanation could I have for being out on the grounds this early?

Suddenly I had an idea. I tore off my shirt, tied it around my waist, and began running down the path. In a few minutes I met Matthew and his dog swinging out of a driveway.

He looked startled when he saw me, and the dog began barking and trying to get free of his leash.

"Hey," he yelled. "Where the hell are you going?"

"I'm jogging," I shouted. "Do it every morning to keep in shape."

I soon left him behind, a puzzled little thief with a frustrated howling animal trying to get loose to tear me apart.

I left the motherhouse the day before the July Fourth weekend. When I said good-bye to Norman and Leah, we made our final arrangements. Posing as the Jersey City printer, I would call Norman and ask to see him regarding an important correction in the copy for the *Call*. The following morning he would meet me on the parking roof of the New York Port Authority Bus Terminal so I could give him the date when the series would begin and, more importantly, reveal Ginerva's secret, dug up by Ben. Then he and Leah would make their own plans. Turner insisted that he intended to leave at once for California and remain there while Ben prepared his case against the Society of the Chosen, but when we both asked Leah what she intended to do, she only shrugged.

I was surprised to see tears in her eyes when she kissed me good-bye, but I quickly squelched a tiny voice warning me she was my responsibility. After all, she was over twenty-one and still Butler's exasperatingly stubborn spoiled brat.

But down deep I knew that when the time came, I would ride back to the motherhouse with Norman and get her out, even if I had to throw her, hands and feet tied, into the van. Leah was already becoming too precious to me to be left behind at the mercy of Foreman, Russell, or Andrew. . . .

Death in the Park

I didn't realize how numbing the experience at the motherhouse had been until I woke up that first morning in my apartment at St. Timothy's with the sun streaming through the open windows and the grounds echoing with the cries of excited summer school students playing soccer. After breakfast I began to correlate my notes and transcribe the taped interviews. Against the backdrop of the shrill young voices, the recitals of the Disciples sounded lifeless, almost mechanical.

I couldn't wait to talk to Ben. It was early when I started transcribing so I decided to work for a few hours before I called him. When there was no answer at his apartment, I tried his office, but Mrs. Caxton urged me to get in touch with Susan immediately. Her phone rang only once, as if she had been waiting.

"It's Hilly, Susan. Is Ben around?"

Her voice was low and dull with fatigue. "He never came back."

"And he never called again?"

"No. That was the last time I heard from him." She began to weep. "Hilly, something has happened to Ben."

"I'm leaving the school right now," I told her. "I'll be there as soon as possible."

When Susan opened the door of her East Sixty-seventh Street

apartment, I was shocked by her appearance; she was not the pretty carefree Susan I had known. She was wearing a robe, and her face without makeup was drawn and pale, her eyes bloodshot from weeping. She began to sob, and I held her until she took a long deep breath, pulled herself up straight, and led me to a couch in the living room.

"Tomorrow it will be almost three weeks since he called," she said. "All this time with only one call!" She nervously twisted the belt of her robe. "It has never been this way before, Hilly. A week, perhaps, and then he would snap out of it but never this long."

"And there's been nothing since that one call? A note? Postcard?"

She shook her head and reached for my hand with a sense of desperation, as if it were a link to hope. "Poker game. What did he mean by that?"

I said helplessly, "Susan, I just don't have any idea."

"Hilly, we must call the police," she said. "I'm almost out of my mind with worry."

I could see the carnival: the reporters and cameramen trooping into this apartment; Susan, nerves stretched tight, growing more frantic by the hour; phones jangling from anxious friends, nuts, and the ghoulishly curious; detectives, the possible entanglement of Sir Edward . . . and then again, what if Ben suddenly appeared?

"But where can we tell them to start?"

"I don't know," she said. "I don't know. . . . But I can't continue to sit here and do nothing." She said savagely, "If something has happened to him, Hilly, it's got to be linked to that woman." She jumped to her feet and began prowling around the room, reaching out to straighten a curtain, move a vase. "He said he was about to get what he wanted on her. He sounded tired, depressed, but still determined. Once he said, 'We should have a camera and get the look on Hilly's face when I give him this stuff I'm getting.' "

"But he didn't tell you what it was? Not even a hint?"

She stood by the window, looking out. Her voice was low and muffled. "Nothing." She paused. "I picked up the phone a dozen times to call you—to ask you to come with me up to his apartment." She turned. "But I was afraid of what I might find." She walked back to the couch, reached in her bag, and held out his key.

"Let's go," I told her.

There was a bundle of mail in the vestibule, which we went through very quickly. It was either junk or letters on legal matters. Inside the brownstone was stifling hot. Our voices had a curious echo. Even the floors creaked.

I cautiously opened the door of the living room, my stomach muscles taut for the first stench of decomposing flesh. I stood in the doorway, blocking Susan's view, but there wasn't any need; the room was only a solid block of stagnant air, with Ellen Terry looking down at us with her provocative sensual half-smile. There was nothing in the kitchen, first floor bathroom, or the cellar.

"I'll take a look upstairs," I said, hoping I sounded casual. To my relief, the master bathroom and bedroom were only dusty and hot. After I opened the windows, I returned downstairs to find Susan, a frown on her face, standing by the fireplace.

"Is there anything wrong, Susan?"

"Someone has been here, Hilly," she replied.

"How do you know that?"

She pointed to the spotlessly clean desk, the magazines, manuscripts, law journals, and *Variety*s stacked neatly in a corner, and the clean ashtrays. "Ben has never left this house this neat since I've known him," she said. "I was here the night before he left and the apartment was a shambles. In fact, I insisted that when he returned he let me clean it." She repeated, "Hilly, someone has been here!"

"Perhaps Ben brought in a cleaning service," I suggested. "Maybe you shamed him into it."

She shook her head. "Neatness was never one of Ben's virtues. He could live in a barn and be happy." Her hand was cold and trembling when I took it. "Someone was here," she said again.

I patted the large color television set and expensive tape deck. "Would thieves leave these, Susan?"

"Perhaps it wasn't thieves," she said.

"Who else would it be? What would they want with—" I stopped and we looked at each other.

"It has to do with that woman, Hilly," she whispered. "I can feel it in my bones."

"We're both getting paranoid about Ginerva," I said. "Let's close the windows and get out of here."

We walked in silence to Park Avenue South. "How about some coffee?" I suggested.

She shook her head. "I have to get back. I have a guilty conscience, leaving the phone for even this little time." She sighed as she held back the tears. "I guess we should wait a few more days, Hilly, but not much more. I won't be able to stand it."

Two days later, Ben's cousin, Dr. Josh Stackman, a psychiatrist, called me at the school. I should have sensed something was wrong when the operator identified herself as from Bellevue. First there were the bored responses of clerks and nurses as the operator traced Josh from department to department. Finally I heard his voice rising over the crackling lines, telling me the news that froze me to the chair.

"... and a motorcycle cop found him this morning. He was kneeling by a bench near Seventy-second Street. They told me ..."

Then it reached me. Ben was *dead*. "Are you crazy!" I shouted into the phone. "Have you gone out of your mind, Josh? Ben would never kill himself! He would never walk into that park after dark! It can't be him! Tell them—"

Then I dropped the phone. I couldn't talk anymore. Josh's voice kept coming out of the receiver at my feet. "Hilly, are you there? Hilly, are you okay? Listen, let me tell you what—"

Finally there was a click. I sat there by the window for most of the morning, trying to accept what I had just heard. Ben was dead, a suicide kneeling by a park bench. I found it impossible to believe that the fiercely energetic man I had known for so many years, with whom I shared so many hours and days, was dead—and dead by his own hand! Why? Did that mysterious depression, caused by the deaths of his wife and son, destroy him? But he had come out of every previous depression. Why was this any different?

Suddenly I was remembering a lot of things: Ben, from somewhere calling Susan and telling her he was on the verge of getting the evidence which would expose Ginerva, and then giving me his final message: "Tell Hilly we're going to play one hell of a poker game." What did it mean? And the curiously neat apartment. Had Susan been correct when she insisted someone had been there? But why? What could they have been looking for?

I had no heart for questions and answers and playing detective. I had to go to Susan, who was waiting by her telephone. ...

I also knew that when Ben mentioned "poker game," he wasn't talking about playing cards.

But what did he mean?

Our close friends had come and gone, and now we were alone. There were no more tears left, and we sat in silence, as the purple light closed in. Outside, Manhattan was going out for the evening; horns were honking impatiently, doormen were whistling for cabs, gears meshed, tires squealed.

"It's my fault," I said at last. "I should not have waited. I should have called in the police."

She protested softly, "Oh, Hilly, don't blame yourself. There wasn't anything we could have done. You heard what Josh said. Ben finally got to a point where he couldn't return. You know it was getting worse every year. ..."

"I know Ben even better than I know myself," I said. "No matter

(159)

how depressed he became, he would never kill himself. And as for going into that park after dark! He would never do that, he was too streetwise."

Now it was almost dark in the room. Susan's face was a pale blur, she was crying softly. I went across the room and held her.

"Why?" she sobbed. "Why, Hilly?"

I had already vowed to try to answer that question.

The services for Ben at Campbell's were impressive. The chapel overflowed with friends and clients, many of them Broadway and Hollywood stars who attracted hordes of photographers, television crews, and reporters. Sir Edward, who had flown in from London, was brief but eloquent. On the way out to the cars, he whispered: "I'm leaving. I'll call you as soon as I return."

We buried Ben on a small knoll in a Westchester cemetery. I turned away after throwing a handful of earth on the casket, realizing now that he was really gone, that never again would I hear his voice or his laughter.

Before we left the cemetery, Josh gave me a key to Ben's brownstone. "The family wants me to take care of the estate. I have an old patient who is a reputable antique dealer. When things settle down I'll have him look over the place, but before that I want you and Susan to select something—anything. You were both closer to Ben than what's left of his family."

"I can't even think of going back there, Josh."

He urged me. "Please do. It would be too much for Susan, but you get over there in the next few days. Don't think I'm a vulture, Hilly, but I know Ben made out a will some time ago and probably left her a share of his estate. But I don't mean money, stocks, or property; I'm talking about something Ben loved that should belong to her. Can you suggest anything I can offer to Susan, Hilly?" He added, almost apologetically, "Even to doctors the details of death can be very trying. We're only realistic when it's someone else."

"Give Susan the Terry portrait, Josh," I told him. "They both loved it. She kept telling him that when they were married she intended to hang it in the john."

"I know Ben really wanted to marry her," he said musingly, "but something always seemed to hold him back."

"The fire?"

He shrugged. "Possibly. Susan told me last year she intended to nag him the next time to go into analysis to see if he could lick that periodic depression, but I warned her he would never consider it."

"I could understand a feeling of sadness when the date came

around, but to Ben it was much more than sadness."

"Possibly a deep guilt complex," he said. He seemed intent on studying the occupants of the funeral cars as they passed through the gates.

"But why should he have felt a guilt? It was a complete accident. The fire marshal told me the fire had probably been started by a short in the wires in the walls. He said that's not unusual in an old house. Ben always said that he was going to take a place at the shore one summer and have the old wiring and plumbing replaced."

He said, still not looking at me, "He was in Washington overnight."

"But he had been stuck on business. Something about the contracts for that musical about the Twenties."

I was surprised at the bitterness in his voice. "And the play was a bomb, remember? It ran for three weeks and then folded. Ben always insisted the blonde lead was another Marilyn Monroe, only with brains and a great voice."

"Do you really think it was suicide, Josh?" I asked him bluntly.

He looked startled. "Of course, Hilly. Why do you say that?"

"It doesn't add up," I said. "Oh, I know what depression can do, but I also knew Ben, and no one can convince me he went into that park at night and pulled the trigger—alone."

"For God's sake, Hilly," Josh said, "Are you suggesting someone helped him?"

"At this point I don't know, but I'm going to try like hell to find out."

"Sometimes it's a good idea to let the dead rest in peace, Hilly," he said softly.

"If there was anything wrong with his death, Ben would never rest, Josh," I told him.

We watched in silence as the last cars left the cemetery, then we shook hands. "I have to get back to the office," he said. "You have my number. Give me a call if you need anything."

During the next few days, I alternately tried to mourn Ben and put together the fragmented pieces of his last days. Susan, our close friends, Mrs. Caxton, his legal associates—all were bewildered and sad but could supply no new information. Mrs. Caxton was typical: "Mr. Hillers, I wish I could help you, but I don't know a thing. Mr. Rice just dropped out of sight. He never called in, never sent me a note, and for the first time since I've been with him for all these years, he missed a court appointment. It was so unusual that when I called the judge to request a postponement, he couldn't believe it and asked if Mr. Rice was ill. . . ."

In those few days back at St. Timothy's, I soon realized that life goes on, steadily, unrelentingly, indifferently. It was probably all to the good; the puzzle of Ben's death had to be put aside temporarily and I could clear my mind.

Susan had been shattered. A few weeks after the funeral, she told me she could no longer stay in New York. She had accepted an art director's job in a Chicago advertising agency and would move there. When Josh insisted she take the Terry portrait, I agreed to deliver it.

As before, the air in the brownstone was hot, stagnant, and smelled of dust. I tossed the bundle of mail I had found in the vestibule on the couch, and opened the windows before I gently took down the portrait. Then I sat down at the desk to discard the junk and put aside the personal mail I intended to send to Josh. An envelope from an oil company caught my eye, and I opened it. The stack of flimsy receipts was for gas, oil, and minor repairs at his neighborhood garage, and I wrote a note to Josh reminding him to cancel Ben's numerous credit cards. I idly flipped through the stack when one fell out; this time it wasn't the local garage or a filling station but the Great Western Auto Rental Agency, Boise Airport, Idaho. The receipt, with Ben's scrawled signature, was for the rental of a car and mileage of two hundred and sixteen miles. The date was three weeks before his death. I felt my mouth going dry but also a heavy weight, like a cement block, slowly being lifted off my chest.

Idaho was where Ben had uncovered Ginerva's secret!

I quickly found some paper to wrap the painting, called Susan, and took a cab to her apartment. She looked drained, her face revealing only blank, empty exhaustion and sadness. When I carefully unwrapped the paper, she fought unsuccessfully to hold back the tears. I quickly went out into the kitchen, not to look for a cloth to wipe the dusty molding as I told her, but to get control of myself. The moment I saw that bright painted smile, with Susan silently appealing to me to help her, all the bulwarks I had built to hold back my own emotions began to crumble. I made sure it took a long time to find the cloth.

"I'm sorry, Hilly," Susan said when I returned. "I promise not to do it again. Josh warned me not to try to hold back the tears, but it seems that is all I have been doing. Crying, crying, and more crying." She held her fist against her lips. "Oh, Hilly, I miss him so much!"

All I could say was, "So do I, Susan, so do I."

We talked of meaningless things over a cup of coffee, and then I hung the portrait over her fireplace.

"Now, Terry, we both lost our man," she said quickly.

"There's something I found at the house, Susan," I said, and showed her the auto rental agency bill. She looked from the bill to me. "So that is where he was!"

"You never guessed it? He never mentioned Idaho?"

(162)

"Never." She quickly reread the receipt. "Is this where Ginerva comes from?"

"I haven't the faintest idea. This is the first time I've heard of Idaho in connection with either her or the Society."

"Then Idaho must be where Ben uncovered her secret!"

She read the rental car bill.

"Should we call the agency, Hilly? Perhaps they would know where he went?"

"I have found out that when you want important information, you don't use the telephone. It's too easy to be brushed off. Go yourself. Many times I have discovered the tough guy on the other end of the line is really only a mousy clerk who doesn't want to be bothered. I'm going to fly up there."

She urged, "Please, Hilly, let the police handle it. I'm afraid of that woman and her Society. Don't have anything more to do with them."

"Susan, I've been wanting to talk to you about this. I'm not convinced Ben just walked into that park alone and killed himself."

She looked startled. "What do you mean?"

"Something or someone made him pull the trigger, and I don't believe his periodical depression was the complete motive. Sure, it could have been a contributing factor, but there had to be something else. I don't know what, but I intend to find out. I'll start with the Boise Airport agency."

The owner of the Great Western Auto Rental Agency in the Boise airport was a transplanted Brooklynite—Borough Park—who had accompanied a Boise buddy home from the Korean war, fell in love with his sister, and settled here. He told me all this, then found his ledger book. Ben had hired their heaviest car. "He said he intended to do a lot of driving and wanted to go first class," the man explained. Three weeks later, he returned the car and paid his bill with his credit card. That was it.

When I asked what was in the two-hundred-mile radius of the airport, the owner pulled out a road map, made a circle with the airport in the middle, and said, "Your friend could have gone anywhere. It's all rural. Some places so small, there's only a gas pump and maybe a store."

"He didn't give any hint of where he had been?"

The man shook his head. "I remember him very well. He knew I had to be from New York, and told me Brooklyn was going to secede from Manhattan and they were going to build forts at the exit of the Brooklyn Bridge to keep out the foreigners. We had some laughs. But when he came back he was quiet, like he had something on his mind." He shrugged. "After he paid his bill, he walked over to where that stairway is,"—he pointed in the direction—"joined the two guys there, and then they all headed toward the New York gate."

I broke in quickly, "Two guys?"

"Yeah," he said. "They were twins, that's how I remember them. My grandmother usta say every time you see twins you make a wish. When I—"

"What did they look like?" I said.

Another shrug. "Like twins. I didn't get a good look at them but they were twins. You know, dressed alike. I think they wore blue suits, maybe brown. Same haircuts . . . things like that . . ."

I spent the trip back to New York working up a detailed report for myself, including facts, along with suppositions, possibilities, and things to check such as: "Talk to detectives on the case. Find the Medical Examiner's report. See Josh. Sir Edward." I hesitated, then added: "Give detectives the National Bank on Little Cat. Ginerva's Evangelical Fund."

Who were the mysterious twins? It was only another unanswered question among a legion of answered questions—including Ben's remark to Susan about a "poker game."

Josh listened to my story and my theory. in the doctors' lounge of a Queens hospital. When I had finished, he said in an unbelieving voice:

"Are you trying to tell me, Hilly, that you hope to prove those two guys, the twins at the airport, had something to do with the Society of the Chosen and actually *murdered* Ben?"

"Maybe they didn't pull the trigger, but couldn't they have done something to him psychologically?"

"You mean like the Manchurian Candidate? Well, first of all, as a psychiatrist—"

"Don't be professional with me, Josh, I'm asking as Ben's best friend. Can it be done?"

"Brainwashing is still a loaded subject, Hilly. Some psychiatrists claim it's a myth. They maintain that while people can be propagandized, they can't be forced to behave in a certain way."

I suddenly recalled the Marine corporal, an escaped POW I had interviewed in the Saigon hospital. After an orderly dropped a pan, his hands trembled so badly I had to light his cigarette. From what he told me, the VC conducted a sophisticated brain-control program in the camps to break the prisoners. Before I left, the boy slowly opened his hands. The tips of his fingers were still healing. He had pressed bamboo splinters under his nails so the pain would keep his mind alert. When I told this to Josh, he only shrugged.

"That was wartime, Hilly," he said. "But look at the Hearst trial. F.

Lee Bailey tried to prove the SLA brainwashed Patty to turn her into a robot bank robber, but the jury refused to buy that. Frankly, I consider your theory farfetched. Why would they go to all that trouble because Ben had found out something about Ginerva's past? All they had to do was outshout him like all those cults do when they're made a target."

I leaned close to him and said softly, "Josh, this is a racket drawing in millions every year. They're not going to let anyone get in their way. Also, the guy who runs the Society of the Chosen has big plans for the future. God knows what they are."

He looked startled. "I didn't realize it was that big. So you believe Ben was a threat to them?"

"Possibly the only threat since they started," I said.

"But, Hilly, you don't know a thing about those guys he was with at the airport," Josh protested. "How do we know they were skilled in mind control. They could have been two New York businessmen Ben met and the three were coming back to the city."

"That doesn't add up," I told him. "We know from Susan that Ben was in that depressed state, and I can assure you that when that time came around he didn't want anyone's company—including mine or Susan's. No, my instinct tells me these twins had something to do with the Society of the Chosen. I've come to know these people, Josh. They're ruthless. And smart. Why should they commit murder when they can simply twist Ben's mind, put a gun in his hand, and whisper in his ear to pull the trigger?"

"But Hilly, it's not that easy," he protested. "Even with a moron, you first have to prepare the ground, and as we both know, Ben was a very brilliant guy. The smartest psychologist in the world couldn't do that to him!"

"You forgot one thing—Ben wasn't normal," I reminded him. "It didn't take a psychiatrist to notice something was wrong with him around the anniversary of Nancy and Jody's deaths. For years I could spot the signs. He would become vague, restless, didn't talk much, or he repeated the same stories of how he first met Nancy at Lincoln Center or how we got drunk in the Third Avenue saloon the night Jody was born. He adored them, and to have them die like that when he wasn't even in town did something to him from which he never recovered."

He gave a deep sigh. "I know it, and I wish now with all my heart that I could have done something to help him."

"What I'm getting at is this: suppose Ben in that depressed state fell into the hands of people skilled in the techniques of brainwashing. Couldn't they in some way have found out what was troubling him, and used that information to push him into suicide?"

He thought for a long moment, then said very carefully: "They could have started with a stress interview—"

I broke in, "And what is that?"

"Probing a patient's anxieties. If they knew how to work it, they could have gotten him to talk as a release. Alcohol as a depressant would help, also being with him constantly. A stress interview could have been broken up between the two of them, one supplying the other with facts."

"Like cops interrogating a prisoner, one is the good guy, the other the villain."

"Something like that," he said. "But, Hilly, the very thought of that happening to Ben is harrowing!"

"Josh, what I want to know from you is this: *could* it have happened?"

He looked at me, then suddenly blurted out: "Hilly, I have to tell you something!" He found his cigarettes, lit one, and inhaled deeply: "I'm breaking every goddam rule of patient-physician relationship telling you this," he said, nervously twisting the match between his fingers, "but I guess under these circumstances I can be forgiven. You know Ben didn't come home the eve of the fire, but stayed in Washington."

"Yes. He was delayed because of last-minute changes in the contracts for the lead in that musical." I reminded him, "Wasn't the lead that blonde you said Ben considered another Monroe with brains and voice?"

"The same one, but it wasn't contract negotiations that delayed him. They had dinner, too many drinks, and he ended going to bed with her. He awoke about eight o'clock in the morning, raced to the airport, and came home in a cab just as the firemen were rolling up their hoses. A squad car took him down to Bellevue, where I met him. He never realized he was in the morgue, and I had just identified the bodies of Nancy and Jody." His hand trembled as he raised the cigarette. "I prayed that he would fall apart, but he didn't; he kept everything inside. And when he decided to keep the brownstone and continue to live there . . ." He shook his head sadly. "Remember when I asked you to try to presuade him to get rid of it? I warned Ben he was setting up a time bomb that one day could explode in his head, but he wouldn't listen. He was punishing himself. That's what he did every year, relive the same ghastly morning over and over and over. It was like a man putting his hand in a fire the same time every year. So now when you ask me if Ben was vulnerable to any suicidal suggestion put to him by someone skilled in brainwashing techniques, I must say yes. However, they would have had to uncover everything connected with the fire that was hidden deep in Ben's psyche to create an inner turmoil. I shudder even to think of it."

"My God, if only he had told me!"

"I only found out last year, when he came to after that last siege and told me the whole story," he said. "I begged him to go into analysis, and he said he would think about it. You know how Ben was, you could never find out what he was thinking or doing. I did suggest that he tell you the whole story and make you a release or a sounding board, which would have helped, but he said he would never do that to anyone, especially you."

"But why, Josh? We were close as brothers."

"That was the depth of his guilt complex. He couldn't let anyone share the burden of what he considered his unspeakable sin."

"But why would he tell all this to two strangers?"

"Were you ever with him during the period of his depression?"

"No. As I said, he wouldn't see me or Susan or anyone."

"There's the difference. This time he found himself in unfamiliar, even hostile surroundings, and those twins could have been friendly, comforting, understanding. It would be natural for Ben to turn to them. Perhaps in some way they were acting the roles of Ginerva's enemies."

"And is that the way it could have happened?"

"It is still only hypothesis, Hilly," he cautioned. "We are assuming that all the factors as I outlined were present."

"I believe they were," I said.

"Then I would say they could have implanted a deep-rooted desire for self-destruction," he said heavily.

After my session with Josh, I found a small restaurant near the hospital, where I brooded over a cup of coffee. I felt a mixture of a deep sadness, realizing what Ben had suffered alone all those years, along with a growing hate for Foreman, Russell, and the Society of the Chosen. I was reluctant to believe Ginerva could be linked to Ben's death, but common sense kept pointing out that, as a front for this monstrous confidence game, wouldn't she also try to protect it? Still there was some doubt—why did I keep trying to protect her?—so I decided to let her be judged by the evidence. I was convinced I was putting together at least the framework of a circumstantial case to show how Ben could have been persuaded by outside forces to pull the trigger, a case I told myself would certainly force some agency of the law to start an investigation of the Society of the Chosen, despite their First Amendment protection.

Looking back, I am surprised at my naiveté. I was soon to learn how helpless even a cynical former war correspondent could be when he attempted to tilt at municipal windmills protected by bureaucrats and politicians.

(167)

The detective who had handled Ben's case was a weary veteran of the city's violence. He listened emotionlessly to my theory and my evidence that anonymous twins skilled in thought control and in the service of the Society of the Chosen had helped Ben to kill himself.

Although he never changed expression, before I finished he had made me feel like one of those garrulous old ladies who visit newspaper offices during the full moon with stories of how the FBI is shooting rays at them from under closed doors.

He made a few half-hearted notes, then pointed to files of paperwork off to one side of his desk.

"I don't know when I can get around to looking into that," he said. "Investigating Avenging Angels expert in brainwashing who murdered a guy psychologically doesn't come across this desk every day. It's more like what I got a couple of hours ago. A faggot wanted a weenie so bad he went into the park and got his throat cut. Or the three little kids who beat in a guy's head with a brick to get his bike that cost thirty-three dollars. Homicides get priority; there are over a thousand suicides every year in this city."

I knew it would be a waste of time to continue.

"I'm sorry I bothered you," I said.

"We are always ready to serve the public," he said, deadpan.

At the morgue it took a lot of talking, flashing my correspondent's card, and shuttling from one department to another before an assistant medical examiner came out into the hallway to talk to me. He was an intense elderly man, with angry eyes and bristling white tufts for eyebrows. He grumbled to himself as he skipped through a file.

"Nothing here," he said looking up. "The man killed himself! Ballistics. Police investigation. Medical history of depression." He glared at me. "Are you a relative of the deceased? Just what is it you want, sir? What kind of information? This stuff is not public, you know. Not at all! Want to see the chief?"

I left him shouting at a maintenance man who had ground out a cigarette on the floor.

I found the patrolman who had discovered Ben's body, standing by his scooter on the Seventy-second Street traverse drive in Central Park. He was young and looked bored and tired as he wrote out a parking ticket. He told me he had found Ben kneeling by a bench about a hundred feet east of Central Park West. They had identified him from papers in his wallet. The gun was still clutched in his hand. The cop studied the passing traffic when he said it was a magnum revolver. He didn't have to spell out what a .357 caliber magnum bullet could do to a man's head.

On a hunch I returned to the precinct and the world weary detective, to ask him if they had traced the gun's serial number. He sighed at the enormity of the task, and quickly read some papers in a folder, only to tell me it was "police business" but perhaps I could learn more from the police Property Clerk's Office.

I received the same information at downtown Police Headquarters; who owned the gun or where it came from was "police business."

Mrs. Caxton gave me the name of the head of the private detective agency Ben had hired to look into the Society of the Chosen. I found the best of their reports were those of a three-man team who had followed teams of the Society's street peddlers for three weeks. The detectives discovered the jewelry sold as "handmade from the Far East" was actually manufactured in an East Side loft and sold at a 400-percent markup. All receipts were turned into a storefront office in the East Village. Detectives had not only bought the jewelry, wilted flowers, and other junk, but had also questioned a number of buyers and contributors to try to arrive at the Society's weekly take. I was gratified their figures were near mine.

The investigator I was most eager to talk to was Tom Gray, the young law student who, according to Ben, had excellent "Washington connections." But before I called Gray when I arrived in Washington, I decided to look into Ginerva's story of her missionary parents.

I now posed as a reporter for the Ranks newspaper chain researching a religious feature story. The State Department's public relations quickly shuttled me off to a patient elderly man who listened to my story, disappeared, and eventually returned to tell me there was no record of an elderly missionary couple ever killed in La Paz by a drunken American salesman. To double-check he had queried the La Paz consulate and would have an answer in the morning. Also their list of missionary groups serving in all parts of the world failed to turn up a "Society of World Christians."

An international missionary group told me the same thing, and a Spanish researcher I hired to go through a file of La Paz newspapers at the Hispanic section of the Library of Congress reported there were no stories of any missionaries killed by a car. The following afternoon, the State Department employee shook his head; the consulate had replied in the negative. No such accident involving two Americans had ever occured in La Paz and no missionary group of that name had entered Bolivia since 1900.

I had now proven that Ginerva's story was a lie. How much more of her act was just as phony?

I met Gray in the Union Station's coffee shop. He was young, blond, and bespectacled, with an almost clerical look which successfully hid a streetwise expertise and a startling inside knowledge of what was going on in the nation's capital. His father, a former Connecticut senator, had joined the sugar lobby after he had been swept out of office in the Nixon sweep. He later established a law office, now one of the most influential in Washington. Tom had worked on special assignments for the detective agency while attending George Washington Law School, and was now waiting for the results of his law boards.

"I was shocked when I read of Ben's death," he said, his pale blue eyes asking the question.

"They'll never convince me it was a suicide," I said, and told him what I had found out in Idaho.

"But can you prove it?" he asked.

"That's what I'm trying to do," I said. "I hope you will help me."

"I'll do anything I can," he said. "I really liked Ben. Where do we start?"

I told him what I had found out about Ginerva's background and described my idea for senatorial or congressional public hearings.

"Of course you don't run around knocking on the doors of congressmen or senators asking them if they want to look into the affairs of a beautiful but phony evangelist," he said. "Religion is still a very delicate question. Politicians don't want to get involved with it, and neither does the IRS or Department of Justice. What you need is someone desperate for exposure who is willing to take a chance that such a hearing might backfire."

"Do you know someone like that?"

He smiled. "The Washington woods are full of politicians desperate for exposure, but it's no use getting a tin horn or some chowderhead —and the woods are full of them. You need someone with savvy. Let me talk to my father, and I'll get back to you."

When I asked if he could help me find out the "police business" of the magnum, he laughed.

"No problem," he said. "My former roommate works in the Department of Justice. I'll give him a call. But don't expect any great surprise. This is routine police procedure. They check the serial number of the gun and forward it to the FBI. They probably found it was stolen."

"But why the big secret? Why didn't they just tell me the gun was stolen?"

"Everyone in police work has a folder, Hilly," he said with a grin. "Cops hate to give out any information from that precious folder."

We said good-bye at the train gate. "Remember Washington is only a small town built on government business," he said. "Everyone connected with that business is a gossip. Even newspapermen. Go over to the Press Club bar now and you'll find them trading items about who is doing it to whom, and why. As my father told me a long time ago, he found it was only a question of having patience in Washington; if you wait long enough and keep your eyes open and your mouth shut, you'll eventually get the answer—or at least a clue—to what you are looking for. Sure as there is an Oval Office in the White House, I'll hear something about Foreman, Russell, Ginerva, or the Society of the Chosen. But just as important, I'll learn who is a prime candidate for that hearing you suggested. When I do, I'll let you know, Hilly. And you can tell Sir Edward he won't get a bill, but I would like two orchestra seats on the aisle for his next show. I'll call you tonight about that gun."

That evening Tom Gray gave me a quick report on the gun. "No big deal, Hilly," he said. "The New York cops simply sent the number of the gun down to ballistics, who very quickly found it was part of a shipment of magnums stolen a year ago from a dock in San Francisco. It's routine. Police departments from all over the country do this every day. They pick up a gun in a holdup or any crime, and the Bureau helps them to trace it back to the original source through the serial number, manufacturer's code, license—that sort of thing."

"How the hell did Ben ever get a gun like that?"

"I would say that either he bought it under the counter or it was given to him."

"It was given to him, Tom," I said.

A gun stolen in San Francisco. The Society of the Chosen started in San Francisco. Foreman and Russell came from San Francisco. I could almost hear the click of the pieces falling into place.

10

Brother Hillers

I had been gradually feeling a change, a shift in decisions. Perhaps it had been brought about by the official cynicism I had encountered —the detective's imperturbable indifference, the stupidity of the police property clerk, the assistant medical examiner's cruel hostility— perhaps a combination of all. But whatever the reason, my quest had now become an intense mission. There were questions that demanded answers. Who had persuaded Ben to pull the trigger? What was the secret in Ginerva's life he had uncovered that was so important it had led Foreman, Russell, and the others to go to such extraordinary lengths to silence him? I had laughed at Ben's warning that Foreman's plan for the Society of the Chosen had a sinister ring; now there was a possibility Ben would prove from the grave that he was right. He had left me a sense of responsibility I could not shake off. Also, it was undeniable that my experience with Ginerva had scarred me forever. Why? I could hardly explain it to myself. However, I knew this: my mind was too rational to abandon itself to a beautiful woman with strange powers who was surrounded by confidence men, criminals, and now murderers of the man I had loved as a brother. Perhaps in finding the answers to who killed Ben, I could fit together enough pieces to solve the puzzle of who and what she was. Ben had promised to give me proof she was a fraud; now I wanted that proof more than anything else in the world, and I didn't know how I was to get it.

Then, a few mornings later, I was both stunned and exuberant to receive a call from Foreman offering me a job directing the publicity and promotion campaign for Ginerva's national tour.

"I believe I told you I am without any help in those two areas," he said. "I *must* have an experienced assistant. Frankly, I was impressed by the way you handled that child in the hospital situation. The media coverage was unbelievable. I have three full folders from our clipping service."

I pointed out, "This would mean postponing writing my series."

"Couldn't that wait?" he asked anxiously. "The national tour is terribly important to me. Details are mounting every day and there is not much time left to make preparations. Only yesterday I was forced to let two opinions on auditoriums pass because our dates were not firm. And it's too late to bring in outside help."

"When would you want a decision, Brother Foreman?" I asked.

He laughed softly. "Yesterday. But seriously, I would like a decision fairly soon."

"How about tomorrow?"

Obviously pleased, he said, "That would be wonderful. And Mr. Hillers . . ."

His voice trailed off and there was a moment of silence.

"Yes, sir."

"There can be bigger things for you in the future."

This superb stroke of luck not only answered my problem of how to infiltrate the Society of the Chosen, but it would also put me close to Foreman and allow me to observe Ginerva as an insider.

If there were answers to my questions at the motherhouse, I would find them.

I gave my resignation from St. Timothy's to a shocked Johnny Masters, who after hearing a partial explanation of what I intended to do, insisted I take a sabbatical. Sir Edward was next. In his Dakota apartment, I told him everything I had learned about Ben's death and what I intended to do.

He gave me a dubious look. "What you propose to do, Hilly, strikes me as very risky. From what you tell me, they're a bloody ruthless bunch."

"I'm no hero, Sir Edward, but if I don't do *something* I won't be able to live with myself."

He said quietly, "This has been a horrible affair, and I feel deeply responsible for Ben's death. Hilly, if there is anything I can do to help—anything . . ."

"Yes, there is, Sir Edward," I told him. "Keep those detectives available, especially Tom Gray in Washington."

"Done," he said quickly. "I will notify the agency immediately that they are to accept any assignment from you and that Mr. Gray is to be at your disposal. Good God, that's the least I can do."

"I would also suggest you have the agency send someone to Little Cat to look into their plaque bank and the Ginerva Evangelical Fund."

"Of course," he replied. "Do you think there is a possibility they would find anything down there?"

I advised him, "Nothing ventured, nothing gained. Ben outlined the difficulty of prosecuting these people. Any bit of evidence will be important."

He suggested, "Perhaps I should go back to the Attorney General?"

"I wouldn't waste your time, Sir Edward," I told him. "The AG saw you, he satisfied his wife and gave you advice. To ask for another interview would only irritate him. Do it my way."

"But what about Leah?" he asked, with a worried look. "I do want her out of there."

"It's no longer a question of what *you* want, Sir Edward," I told him. "I don't have to tell you that Leah has a mind of her own. She is convinced Ginerva is a holy woman and she told me she intends to stay."

"And there is nothing we can do to change her mind?"

"Nothing—except for me to prove to her Ginerva is a fraud."

He fiercely pounded his fist into the palm of his hand. "Hilly, you've got to do that!"

I tried to keep the sarcasm out of my voice. "I assure you, Sir Edward, I intend to try."

I next called Norman, posing as the Jersey City printer with a request he come to New Jersey to review some important editorial changes in *The Call*'s copy.

The following morning, we met on the parking roof of the Port Authority Bus Terminal, and in his van I reviewed everything that had happened since I last saw him. Norman looked stunned when I told him about Ben's death; for a moment I had forgotten how completely isolated he was in the motherhouse.

"Ben dead!" he whispered. "I can't believe it!" He gripped my arm and shook me. "Hilly, don't ask me to stay up there another day. I knew something like this would happen, I warned Ben and I warned you. They're not going to let anyone, but anyone, be a threat to their racket! You're crazy if you think you can do it alone! Sure, I'm sorry for Ben. He was a great guy. But I don't intend to wind up like him in a grave while no one on the side of the law gives a good goddam. To hell with all of it! Let them have their thirty million dollars a year! I'm getting out while I can!"

"Anything you say, Norm," I told him quietly. "Does Leah still intend to stay?"

He slammed his fist against the dashboard. "She's crazier than you are! Only yesterday she told me she plans to stay at the motherhouse —no matter what happens!"

"That will help. Maybe between the two of us we can come up with something."

"I know what you're trying to do, Hilly," he shouted. "You're trying to shame me into staying! But no way will I do that! You want to be killed like poor Ben, you go ahead. But count me out!"

I patted him on the shoulder. "Have it your way, Norman. And thanks for everything."

He didn't answer, only slammed the door behind me, swung out of the parking space, and roared down the ramp. I felt like a heel, because I knew Norman would never leave the motherhouse while Leah remained.

I called Foreman from a phone booth in the lobby of the terminal to advise him I accepted his offer. I almost choked when I told him that after my experience with Ginerva in San Francisco, I could not refuse to serve her and the Almighty Father. . . .

"This is the best news I've had in months," he said. "When can you join us?"

I told him, "Tomorrow morning."

Crossing the lobby to the escalator to take me back to the parking roof, I was accosted by one of a group of the Society's Disciples harassing the crowds. When he thrust his container at me, I put in a dollar.

"Glory to Ginerva," I told him. "I'll see you on the Great White Cloud of Salvation."

I left him with his mouth open. It might be a long time before I scored another point against them.

I spent the rest of the day preparing gifts for Foreman; a dummy of a revised *Call*, marked-up copies of the paper showing the miserable job the printer had done, the names of three nonunion print shops who told me they were willing to bid for the job, and a list of possible promotion and publicity campaigns for the Society of the Chosen.

This time when I arrived at the motherhouse, the guard at the gate greeted me cordially, a cart immediately appeared, and I was whisked past the two Angels at the foot of the stairs to Foreman's office. To my relief, Russell was not in sight. But neither was Tura. Margo, who was at her desk, gave me an apprehensive smile and quickly brought me in to Foreman.

When I sat down, he leaned across the desk and held out his hand. "Welcome to the Society of the Chosen—Hilly. Suppose you call me Dave here in the office? It can be Brother Foreman outside."

"Fine, Dave." I pushed the dummy of the revamped *Call* across the desk. "This is my idea of the new paper. I went over the copies for several months. The printer has been giving you an atrocious job. I'm prepared to tell him that one more typo and he is out."

He frowned slightly. "But his bid was the lowest."

"There are three other nonunion printers in Jersey City, one within four blocks of his place. They all told me they wanted to bid for the job."

His face cleared. "Do anything you feel is necessary"—he held up the dummy—"to bring this off. It's exactly what I want."

I pushed the list of promotion and publicity ideas across the desk. "Here are some ideas I jotted down, Dave. When you have a few minutes, look them over, and we'll discuss them."

He glanced down at them and nodded. "Wonderful. I'll get to them as soon as possible. Where do you want to begin?"

I told him, "If I intend to write about the Society, I should be acquainted with everything about it. I've covered the motherhouse, now I would like to observe your training program. Suppose I spend some time at the Staten Island House of Preparation?"

I was sure I had caught a slight narrowing of his intent dark eyes. "Why Staten Island, Hilly?" he asked softly.

I shrugged. "As I understand, it's the most efficient and the most effective."

His polished fingernails began the drumming. Finally he said thoughtfully, "Perhaps that might be a good idea. I'll have Russell make the arrangement with Brother Watson."

That was a new name, "Brother Watson? Is he in charge of the training program?"

"Brother *and* Sister Watson," he said. "A wonderful God-loving pair. True-blue Christians. You will also have an opportunity to hear Brother Singleton, one of our finest preachers. Would you like to leave tomorrow morning?"

"The sooner the better, Dave."

"Let me talk to Russell," he said. "I'll be back in a few minutes."

He went into another room and I saw one of the buttons on his phone light up; he was talking to Russell. The green files were very near his desk. I quickly reached over and tested each drawer; they were all locked. I spun the pile of papers on his desk to face me. The letter on top was from an account agency confirming a luncheon appointment, others were bills and memos discussing routine internal matters at the motherhouse. I stifled a feeling of degradation at prying into another man's private files and correspondence; from now on I had to ignore codes and rules.

"Russell will make the arrangements this afternoon," he said when he returned. "You'll be out in the woods. They don't even have a phone. Water is from a well, and the farmhouse is over a hundred years old." He laughed. "But you asked for it. By the way, do you want to continue living at the *Call* office? If not, I can arrange something better."

"The *Call* office will be fine, Dave," I assured him.

"I told Brother Turner you're the boss and he's to do anything to help you," he said. He stood up and held out his hand. "Welcome aboard, Hilly. I know we're going to do great things together for the glory of God and Ginerva."

I tried to sound casual as we walked to the door. "I didn't see Sister Sloan outside. I hope she's not ill."

"Sister Sloan has some personal problems," he said shortly. "But she'll be back in a few days."

Norman and Leah were horrified when I told them I was going to Staten Island. After a welcome-home party of coffee and the cafeteria's stale buns in the *Call* office, Norman warned me I was foolishly walking into a bear trap.

"I don't care what Foreman promised you, Hilly," he said nervously. "If Russell is setting up the arrangements, watch out. It's only common sense. You're moving in on his territory; it would be naive to believe he will sit back and take that. And I wouldn't trust Foreman as far as I can throw a baby grand. What's to prevent both of them cooking up something horrible for you out there?"

Leah broke in. "We saw some of the kids who came back from Staten Island, Hilly. They didn't look or act the same. Something had happened to them out there."

"I told you, Hilly," Turner said, "that's the place where they break in their peddling teams. The kids have to be brainwashed to do the things these teams do. And you're walking into all that? I think you're crazy."

"But both of you went through the training program," I reminded them.

"But *not* Staten Island. That's a hellhole!"

"I came up here to get answers," I told them, "and if it means taking chances, so be it. No one is going to bend my mind. Remember I was in Vietnam."

Leah said softly, "Yes, but this is a different kind of war, Hilly." She reached inside her bag and took out a small leather-bound book of crossword puzzles with a pencil stub in a holder. "When I'm in my room and those horrible loudspeakers go on, I use this to keep my sanity. Maybe it will come in handy."

"I counted presidents backwards," Norman said. He added with a grin, "I can't believe it's *Brother Hillers!*"

"We're glad you're back, Hilly," Leah said. Her lips felt warm and sweet when she kissed me. "I—we missed you. Didn't we, Norm?"

"Yeah. But I was sleeping better," he said.

She rumpled his hair. "You missed him as much as I did. How many times did you tell me?"

"Norman said you intended to stay, Leah," I said, "no matter what happened."

She said with a shrug. "I just made up my mind to stay and see how this all ends. It's got to—someday." She nudged me. "I also want to see you genuflect."

"That will be the day," I said. "Did Norman tell you about Ben Rice?"

"Yes, and I was shocked," she said soberly. "But, Hilly, how can you prove Foreman and the others forced him to commit suicide?"

"All I can do is try."

Her hand searched for mine. "I'll do anything I can to help."

"But look at what we came up with before," Norman said disgustedly. "A big, fat zero. Hilly, even you admitted it was impossible to get anything on them."

"But now it's going to be different," I told them. "Then I was an outsider, now I'm an insider—Foreman's right-hand man on the tour. As Ben said, I could stumble over something."

"Your being on that tour is not going to make Russell very happy," Norman warned.

"Hilly, be careful of that man," Leah warned me. "God knows what he will do if he ever finds out what you're up to."

Norman groaned. "And what will Russell do to *us*? I must be out of my head staying here with you two idiots."

"What about Ginerva?" Leah asked. "Do you think she knows anything about Mr. Rice's death?"

I suggested, "Doesn't common sense indicate she must know *something*?"

"You'll never get Leah to admit that," Norman said scornfully.

"Let's see what comes out of all this," Leah said quietly. "Norman said you saw my father, Hilly. How is he?"

"His new play is in production, and he is very lonely without you."

"With a play in production? Never. He's not worried about me. He's not worried about anything. There's only one thing on his mind. His play."

She didn't sound angry and there was an expression of pain and acceptance in her eyes. She smiled tightly and said with absolute certainty, "He'll never change." She looked at me. "Is he drinking?"

"No," I said. "He's in fine shape. He looks as if he has been on the wagon for months."

"That's his routine," she said grimly. "Getting into shape for the big game. Did he have a girl friend around?"

"If he did, I didn't see any." I slipped my arm around her waist. "Leah, you sound like the perfect worried daughter."

"Don't get me wrong," she said firmly. "I love my father very much. But as I told you, he just refuses to believe I'm over twenty-one, I have my own life to lead, and money can't buy everything."

"What about Ginerva?" I asked them. "Have you seen her?"

Leah told me no one had seen Ginerva on the grounds again, and Norman's gossipy clerks had her preparing for the tour. There were indications Foreman had started his big push: Norman and Leah had headed a team searching out Disciples with an art background; all had been ordered to report to tour headquarters in Manhattan.

"How did you find them?" I asked.

"From the Society's master list," Norman explained. "It's in a rear room in the library. When you enter the Society, you must fill out a long form answering all types of questions—you'll probably get one very soon. Besides basic information, they also want to know what hobbies you have, the majors you took in school, what, if any, musical instruments you play, have you ever taken part in a political campaign or do you know anyone in politics? There are all kinds of questions, even to the type of car you own."

"What's that for?"

He laughed bitterly. "They take your car and sell it—for the benefit of the Society, of course. The first day I was in the training program, the guy who was assigned to me kept asking, 'What do you want a car for, Brother Turner? You're in God's house now and Ginerva will take care of everything you need.' I had a TR-7—a beautiful car— and all paid for. I didn't want to give it up, but one night this guy brought over three more Disciples and they backed me into a corner. By the time they were finished, I had signed it over to them. Along with my mother's inheritance and our brownstone." He slammed his fist down on the table. "How could I have been so stupid?"

"So all that information is put into a master file?"

"Everything. It's all cross-indexed. There's an old woman in charge of it who drives you nuts with her Bible quotations."

"Tell Hilly what she said about the computers," Leah suggested.

"Oh, yeah. She told me Foreman is going to send her and several other Disciples to a computer school, and they're going to break down some walls and use the rear of the library for a bank of computers."

"Did she say why?"

"She said it had something to do with the street teams. I guess they want to find out how to make more money."

"Foreman made Margo an art director," Leah said. "Part of the second floor of the dorm has been turned over to the kids from out of town. She told me a bus takes them down to tour headquarters in Manhattan in the morning and brings them back at night."

"Why Margo?" I asked. "What does she know about art?"

"Oh, she's a fine artist," Leah replied. "I think she has talent. When she first came up here she did a watercolor of the motherhouse, and they have that hung in the dorm's reception room. That's how Foreman first noticed her."

"Margo was sitting in for Sloan in Foreman's office. What's with Tura?"

"A few days ago," Norman said, "Margo had dinner with us. Then we sat on our bench and talked. She told us Foreman and Sloan had had a big fight in the office downtown. She said she was bringing him some artwork to be approved and heard them even though the door was closed. She said Foreman was so mad he said he was going to throw her out the window if she didn't leave."

"Did Margo know what the fight was about?"

"No. She got there at the tail end. She said she slipped into one of the offices when Sloan came out. She said Tura was crying." Norman gave me a conspiratorial look. "That's one person around here you should duck. Something is going on between them, and I believe Foreman when he says he will throw her out a window."

"But we don't have anything to do with her, Norman," Leah protested.

"You never can tell, Leah," Turner said, still looking at me, "one of us may just run across her."

I waited until after midnight to slip out of *The Call*'s office, leaving behind an almost frantic Turner who pictured all types of things happening to me if I was caught by that pockmarked hoodlum and his monstrous guard dog. He was right; I was taking a considerable risk, one misstep and it would be all over. Yet Tura in a screaming fight with Foreman could mean anything. When I left the shadows of the *Call* building, I was almost sorry I had started; it was a bad night to be out on the grounds with the full moon, like a polished silver plate, outlining shrubs, trees, walks, and lawns. I used the back paths and lanes and finally reached the far edge of the estate and the small stone house with the white wooden fence and a birdbath. There were no lights, but I had a hunch Tura was there—where else could she go? I tried tapping on the window, and when there was no answer I rattled the heavy brass doorknob. For a long moment there was only the monotonous orchestration of the night insects, then a dull low voice asked: "Who is it?"

"It's me, Tura—Hilly."

A bolt slid back, a key turned, and the door opened. She was in a robe and the smell of whiskey was strong. When I stepped inside, she shut and bolted the door.

"I heard you were back," she said. "You damn fool!"I followed her into the living room, where the moonlight painted everything with silver; chairs, a couch, the planked varnished floor, a desk, a small portable bar, and a carved wooden elephant lamp.

I joined her on the couch, but when I leaned over to kiss her she turned her face away.

"What's all this about you coming back as Foreman's assistant on the tour?" she asked.

It would have been useless to lie to her so I decided to play it straight. "He offered me the job; I would have been stupid to refuse it. What better way can I get a close-up of the Society and Ginerva to write about them? Anything I publish must be documented."

"And I suppose I'm to help you get that information?" she asked in a harsh voice. "Is that it? Is that why you're here?"

"I can only ask, Tura," I said, and reached out for her hand. At least she didn't pull it away.

"I wondered when you would be getting to me," she said with a sharp laugh. "I knew you would be wanting something."

I had to hate myself when I leaned over, kissed her on the cheek, and stood up.

"Good night, Tura. I'm sorry I bothered you."

She didn't let me reach the door. "You can't leave me now," she said sobbing. "I need someone to talk to. I've been sitting here *alone* for two days!"

"When did you eat last?"

"Last night. Yesterday some time. I don't know. I've been sitting here making love to Jack Daniels."

"Is there anything in the refrigerator?"

"The guy who delivers the garbage the kids eat stocks my refrig with the best every week," she said, with a short hollow laugh. "That's one of my fringe benefits."

Fortunately the kitchen was as bright as day from the moonlight and there was no reason to put on a light. The refrigerator held an amazing variety of fine foods; from sliced turkey, ham, and cheese to frozen filet mignon steaks, pies, and cakes. There was enough liquor in the cupboard to open a store. I made some sandwiches and iced tea and brought them in to her.

"Have some of this and forget the booze for a while, Tura."

(1 8 1)

"What is this? The softening up process?" she asked, but pushed her drink aside and selected a sandwich.

"I like you too much to let you sit here alone drinking yourself to death. What brought this on?"

I didn't press her when she didn't answer; I was going to be up at the motherhouse for a long time.

When she finished her sandwich and tea, she asked me for a cigarette. I found a carton in the kitchen and gave her a pack. Her face was haggard and aging in the tiny flame of the match. She inhaled deeply, and we watched the smoke ring hang for a moment in the silver light, then slowly dissolve.

"Thanks, Hilly," she said, leaning back against the pillows, "but you shouldn't be here. This is not a good place. Go back to your classroom."

"It's something I must do, Tura. If you will help me, fine; if not, no hard feelings." I held her hand in both of mine. "I hope I can still come by and say hello."

"Oh. Hilly," she cried, "you will never know how lonely I am. Kiss me, please kiss me . . tell me you need me, even if you're lying . . ."

The intensity of her mouth on mine surprised me; it was as if she wanted to devour me. Her hands were shaking. I tried to calm her, but there was something urgent and insistent about her. It was more than sex; she seemed to have a desperate need, like a seeking, frantic child. Finally she lay back, breathing in deep wrenching gasps as she held on to my hand. It was eerie; her face a dripping haggard shadow in the fringes of the soft moonlight, her voice a fierce whisper.

"He said he's going to kill me, Hilly, if I don't stop asking for my money. He said he's going to turn me over to Russell, and I know what to expect!"

"Easy, Tura, easy," I told her softly. "Who said he's going to kill you?"

"Dave," she asid. "We really went at it a couple of times when I asked for my share. The last time he offered to give me a flat payment of fifty thousand, but when I laughed at him he became like a crazy man and warned me that if I didn't take that and shut up, he would have me thrown out of a window and make it look like suicide." She shuddered and clung to me. "And he can do it—I know that!"

"How do you know that, Tura? Has he done it before?"

She whispered, "Yes. Yes. But don't ask me anything about it now, Hilly. Please don't!"

She was too distraught to push her, so I quickly changed the subject. "Perhaps you should take the fifty thousand, Tura. Then you can leave here, go to Vegas or Europe and enjoy yourself."

Her voice hardened with stubbornness. "But why should I, when what I ask is peanuts compared to what they now have? I put money into this thing!" Her voice rose in righteous indignation. "I have an investment in this setup!"

"What amount did you ask for, Tura?"

"I only asked Dave for five million, but I said I would settle for two," she said, as casually as if she was talking in hundreds.

For a moment my mind could not grasp what she had said; I was staggered. When I recovered, I said, "Five million! Tura, you're insane! No wonder Foreman wanted to throw you out the window!"

Another smoke ring, gray against the silver light, slowly twisting, dissolving. "Five million is only a drop in the bucket," she said. "Now there's a hundred million dollars in the pot. . . ."

It was difficult to keep my voice under control. "How did they get so much money?"

"I told you, the money is coming in by the millions every year, and now they are skimming like there's no tomorrow."

I asked, "And it's all going to that bank on Little Cat and that fund?" She hesitated. "As far as I know."

"Is the bank in Dave's name, Tura?"

She gave me a twisted smile. "You never give up, do you, Hilly?" She shook her head. "He would be stupid to have it in his name. He has a front." She added harshly, "And for Christ's sake don't ask me the name because I don't know it." She pointed to the bottle. "I'll have a little Jack Daniels."

I mixed the drink, and she kissed my hand as I handed it to her. "Don't be mad at me, honey," she said. "I'm upset. I promised I'd help you, but don't crowd me about Dave. Not today."

"Okay," I said. "Let's forget Foreman. What about Ginerva?"

She groaned. "Do we have to talk about that bitch?"

This time I was adamant. If I was going to play nursemaid to a drunk, I wanted something in return. "No more generalities, Tura. I want information about her. Specifics. You told me you thought she could have been in the theatre, but I want to know where she came from. What is her name? Her background?"

She snuggled up against me. "I don't have that kind of information, Hilly. I swear it. But I'll get it." She looked up and kissed me. "You know something, honey, I made up my mind I'm not going to leave. He can take that fifty thousand and shove it. I'm going to hold out and get on his back until he talks real money."

"But didn't you tell me it was dangerous to cross Foreman?"

She took a deep swallow. "He knows he has to watch his step with me." But her voice faltered and she gave me a frightened look. "But what if he puts that creep, Russell, on me?" She leaned her head on

(183)

my shoulder and clung to me. "Hilly, you can't let them hurt me! You're all I got up here! Protect me, Hilly, please protect me!"

I groaned inwardly; now she had made herself my responsibility.

She had another Jack Daniels and began to get sleepy. I tried to get her to talk about Ginerva, but she only mumbled something and fell asleep. I covered her with a blanket and left. The number one hundred million echoed in my head as I cautiously made my way back to the *Call* office. This huge fortune had undoubtedly cost Ben his life. By the time I reached the office, I was dripping with sweat, and the night was not that hot.

In the morning we had returned from breakfast in the cafeteria when an Angel drove up in a cart to bring me to Russell. Norman gave me a despairing look, but I winked to show him how brave I was. In reality I had butterflies in my stomach.

Russell's office was on the ground floor of a low one-story stone building not far from the dorm.

I found myself facing a cold-eyed thug. He was wearing a short-sleeved shirt, perhaps for effect, that showed his muscular arms covered with fine blond hair. I was surprised to notice for the first time that he had a tiny American flag tattooed on the base of his thumb. Above his head was an open chest attached to the wall, with countless keys hanging from hooks.

Although he eyed me like a snake contemplating a mouse as his next meal, he was obviously under orders not to harass me.

"The place you're going is in Charleston, Staten Island," he said. "Report to Brother Watson at two P.M." He tossed a slip of paper at me. "Here's the directions." Then he leaned back in his chair. "So you're gonna handle the publicity and promotion for the tour."

"That's right," I said. "I welcome any suggestions."

"Don't expect any help from me, Hillers," he said roughly.

"What's bugging you, Russell?" I asked bluntly.

He slowly leaned forward. "I don't know who you are or what you're up to," was his soft reply, "but one of these days I'm gonna find out."

As I started to get up, he said with a smirk, "I told Watson to make sure you saw *everything*."

And then he laughed out loud and slammed his enormous open hand down on the desk. "And by Christ he will!"

11

In the
Fields of the Lord

Charleston, Staten Island, was in a remote section of dirt roads, trees, remnants of pansy farms, and clusters of split-levels with American flag decals on fenders, bicycles in driveways, and a few washlines put up by independent-minded housewives. The United Parcel truck-driver who gave me a lift was friendly until I told him I was on my way to the Society's House of Preparation.

"They're all nuts," he exclaimed indignantly. "Why the hell are you joinin' 'em?"

"I got troubles," I said. "I'm looking for peace and love of the Lord."

"It's your own business, buddy," he said, "but I think you need a few drinks and a warm body."

He was still shaking his head when he let me off on a dirt road behind a bus that was discharging passengers.

"Some of your pals," he said with a snicker, then drove off.

There were about fifty, the majority in their teens or early twenties. All white, except for one black and an Oriental. They were dressed in jeans and T-shirts. One older man wore an expensive gray suit, shirt, tie, and brogans. He had a bony face and intense eyes. A giggly fat girl clutched a violin case; when she bent over to pick up a dandelion, which she handed to the black kid, I could almost hear her protesting seams. They all carried paper bags or valises. The black kid had a bowling ball bag with a broken zipper.

I followed them up a long weed-choked walk to what appeared to be an old farmhouse surrounded by several acres of fields and woods. The farmhouse had two stories and an attic. The screens were rusty; some had holes. Spindles on the porch were missing. In the rear was a large barn. The lawn consisted of bare spots and crabgrass.

The screen door was swung open so violently a piece of the molding fell off, and a tall thin woman rushed out onto the porch. She was wearing a bizarre print dress that looked as if it had been thrown on by someone escaping a fire.

"Welcome!" she cried. "Welcome! Welcome!"

"Jesus!" the black kid said, and stared at her with an open mouth.

She leaned down and kissed the fat girl, who giggled.

"Welcome, daughter! Welcome!" she went on. "Welcome!"

Behind her appeared a huge man in pin-striped gray pants and matching vest with a gold watch chain strung across his belly. The sleeves of his white shirt were rolled up above his elbows. When he raised his arms, his full beard and feverish eyes made me think of John Curry's painting of the fanatical John Brown.

"Welcome, brothers and sisters!" His voice boomed over us like crashing surf. "Welcome to Ginerva's Society of the Chosen! Come in!"

We trooped into a dim hallway, and at his request left our suitcases or packages by the front door.

"I am Brother Watson," he said, standing above us on the stairway leading to the second floor. "And this"—indicating with a wave of a hand that looked like a club with fingers—"is my wife, Sister Watson. We welcome you as candidates who wish to be soldiers of Ginerva!"

Several grinning young men, all with whitewall haircuts and wearing dark pants and T-shirts with the printed slogan: YES WE HAVE FOUND THE WAY TO BE SAVED across the front, began circulating among us, shaking hands and saying over and over, as if they had records implanted in their heads, "Welcome. The Society of the Chosen is now your family and we are your brothers."

Although they appeared to me to be Avenging Angels, Watson introduced them as our "instructors" who would accompany us "every foot of the way along the glorious path" of our training program, as he put it. They were smiling, but their eyes were flat and emotionless; they could have come from the same mold that produced Andrew or the other Angels at the motherhouse.

They ushered us into what had once been the dining room. The walls of two smaller rooms had been torn down to make one large one. The plastering job obviously had been done by an amateur;

seams along the plasterboards were rough and uneven. Everything in the large room was painted black; floors, ceiling, and walls; even the metal chairs stacked in a corner were black. In the dusty fireplace was a mound of ashes and charred logs from the previous winter. Old-fashioned French windows were closed. There were no pictures on the walls, but above the doorway was a crudely painted figure in gold of a woman with upraised hands: Ginerva in primitive style. In front of the fireplace was a slightly raised wooden platform, probably built by the amateur plasterer; nails, bent under the glancing blows of a hammer, had been carelessly driven into the wood.

Lights attached to a metal strip along the ceiling flanked the platform. In contrast to the other amateur workmanship, they appeared professional. Some had "barn door" attachments to help focus the light beam and curb the glare, along with parabolic reflectors to shed an indirect light. A few were equipped with color filters. Troy's work, I told myself. Incongruously, off to one side was an expensive-looking stereo set and a stack of records on a chair. I caught a glimpse of the faces of Beethoven and Sousa on the jackets. On top of the piled chairs was a large blackboard and a wooden pointer.

There was an air of carefully controlled fanaticism about the place.

"Our meeting room," Watson explained.

We followed him through a kitchen with a deep eighteenth century iron sink and a hand pump.

"God's clear water," Watson thundered, "right from the heart of God's good earth! No pollution here, brothers and sisters!" As if to prove his words, he vigorously pumped the handle and water gushed out. He beamed at us; we tried to beam back.

"Man, even Harlem has faucets," the black boy said to me in a low, disappointed voice. The well-dressed guy glowered at him, but the kid gave him an impassive look and shrugged.

The dank barren cellar was our quarters. Sleeping bags were arranged in rows on slabs of foam. A toilet in the front consisted of a sink and urinal.

"You boys will have to double up in the morning," Watson said with a roaring laugh. "Just like the army! Only it's the army of the Lord!"

"Amen," the well-dressed guy called out.

The second floor, sleeping quarters for the female recruits, consisted of a series of small rooms, barren except for sleeping bags, an occasional worn chair, and exhortations in gold which read: "Join the Society of the Chosen and Be Saved!" and "Beware—Doomsday Is Near!"

Early in the evening, when we returned to the kitchen, several women, without lipstick, their hair arranged in old-fashioned buns, were preparing jugs of Kool-Aid and plates of cheese and crackers.

When we followed Watson into what I was already calling the "Black Room" and sat in a circle on the rug, the women passed paper cups of the sweet drink along with two crackers and a slice of cheese. But first Watson gave us a blessing.

"Lord God Jehovah! We are gathered here this day to teach our newly arrived Brothers and Sisters how to follow in your footsteps by serving in the Society of the Chosen to preserve our beloved country and sacred way of life. Number us among your soldiers. O Lord, fill us with your spirit and strength to obey your commands, so that we in turn will be among the Chosen when you sound the mighty Trumpets of Doom to wipe out this evil, insignificant universe! Then Lord, let us board your Golden Cloud of Heavenly Victory that will ascend into your kingdom of eternal salvation!"

Mr. Well-Dressed jumped up and shouted: "Hallelujah! Bless the Lord!"

Watson eyed him sternly. "I haven't finished, Brother."

The guy, still trembling with ecstasy, sat down, and Watson rumbled and thundered for another half hour. When he ended, I was so hungry I bolted down the cheese sandwich and drink. I was given another cup, but when I asked for a second sandwich the serving woman gave me a look that made me feel like Oliver Twist confronting Mr. Bumble.

When we finished, one of the women came in with a carpet sweeper to quickly clean up the crumbs, while others removed the cups and paper plates. At Watson's order we sat in a circle on the floor and were joined by a slender man with a large paper-thin nose. He was dressed in a shiny blue suit and looked like a Hollywood Rasputin. Watson introduced him as "Brother Singleton."

Singleton never smiled, never said hello or good-bye. Off the rostrum he seemed oblivious of the world, but on the rostrum he was a shouting, raging preacher. Before he began, Watson asked us to identify ourselves and give a brief reason why we came and what we were seeking.

Mr. Well-Dressed said he was a broker seeking God through Ginerva; the black kid admitted he was a former junkie trying to keep the monkey off his back; the others had a variety of occupations and tales of why they had come to the Society. I simply identified myself as someone assisting the Society.

Then Singleton began. He had a snarling, bitter voice that lashed us like a whip. We were sinners, the dregs of the earth, who daily crucified Christ as surely as the Roman soldiers on that Good Friday. That harsh voice pictured the lowering sullen skies, the brave dying Christ, the laughing soldiers, sorrowful, frightened John, the weeping Mother. He went on for hours, slamming his worn Bible on the rostrum, until finally, when I glanced at my watch, I discovered it was after midnight. The spotlights came on suddenly to wrap Singleton's busy frame in a weird light that slowly changed to fit his words: soft yellow, angry red, sorrowing purple. The air in the room became close, stifling; Well-Dressed might have been wearing Brooks Brothers, but he hadn't had a shower or bath in some time and he was rank. I noticed the black boy's frightened face had a sheen of sweat. A few of the young girls were weeping, and from time to time someone cried out: "Oh, God, forgive me. . . . Forgive me, Lord!"

Then it ended. Without a word the light faded and Singleton vanished.

"Now for a good old-fashioned sing-out, Brothers and Sisters," Watson roared. The women distributed smudged Xerox copies of a song sheet, a record was started on the stereo, and we all swung into "Rock of Ages."

I don't know how many hymns we sang. Like Singleton, they seemed to go on forever. The stereo was turned on to a high pitch, and in that black box of a room the mighty Mormon Tabernacle Chorus, along with Sousa's Marine Band and Beethoven's Fifth Symphony, lined up like artillery wheel to wheel to bombard us with noise until we staggered with fatigue. I found it difficult to keep awake. Most of the kids barely moved their lips, and even the evangelical broker appeared dazed. Finally it ended, and we were told to line up and place all our jewelry into a bag with our names.

By this time I was sure there was some mistake. I would observe their sessions and even listen to that fanatic, Singleton, but I didn't intend to part with the expensive watch I had bought in Saigon and my Princeton ring.

When my turn came, I started to say to Watson, "I believe there has—"

He never gave me a chance go finish. "Did Jesus wear jewels, Brother?" he bellowed at me. "Did Paul have a gold watch? A handsome ring? No, Brother, there is no need for the Devil's trinkets in the House of the Lord."

I started again. "But I came over here—"

An instructor silently held up the paper beg with my name written in crayon. It seemed useless to continue to explain; I was too weary. I dropped my ring and watch into the bag and stumbled downstairs to the cellar and my moldy blanket.

It seemed I had only been asleep for a few minutes when Watson's booming voice awakened me. As I crawled out from under the blanket to share the foul-smelling toilet with Mr. Well-Dressed, I could see by the cellar's window it was dark outside.

"What time do you think it is?" I asked the broker. As he urinated, he answered me in a weird singsong voice: "I found the Lord through Ginerva; Praise God for Ginerva!"

I wondered why fanatics were tireless.

The windows were still closed in the Black Room when we entered like a file of prisoners. Even at this early hour the room was stifling. I was determined to force either Watson or one of the instructors to listen to me. I had no intention or desire to be treated like the black kid, the little fat girl, or the crazed broker.

But I soon discovered I was like a Kafka prisoner. When I managed to slip past the instructors and get to Watson in the kitchen, he stopped me before I had a chance to begin.

"Get back to your place, Brother," he thundered. "You can't break the rules in this House of the Lord!"

I began again. "You must listen to me, Brother Watson. I'm not a Disciple. I am in charge of—"

Watson looked over my shoulder. "Take Brother Hillers back to his place," he ordered.

Two instructors whirled me around, practically dragged me back to the Black Room, and pushed me down into the circle. This time I stayed there. It was obvious I had been set up either by Russell without Foreman's knowledge, or by both of them. The latter, I suspected, was true; Russell had convinced Foreman it was better to have a brainwashed Director of Promotion and Publicity than one untested.

Singleton soon appeared, to batter us with a long sermon comparing our civilization with Sodom and Gomorrah. When he finally ended, I heard the hum of commuting traffic on some nearby highway.

Breakfast was Wheaties and a glass of milk I was sure had been watered. We marched into the kitchen to pile our plates to the tune of "Amazing Grace," then out to the backyard for vigorous setting-up exercises under the command of one of the young instructors.

I decided to take one more chance, and left the line to talk to him. He instantly jabbed me in the chest with a stiff finger.

"Back into line, Brother," he roared.

"I simply want to point out to you I am not—"

He put his face close to mine. "Back! Back into that line! Everyone does exercises! A fit body is the only temple for the Lord!"

There was nothing to do but follow his orders like the rest. For more than an hour we jumped, twisted from side to side, did kangaroo hops, and ended with pushups.

"You'll do twice that before you leave here," he promised me.

I was the only one he spoke to.

We returned to the Black Room for more prayers and another violent, seemingly endless sermon by Singleton about the evil world. Lunch was a cup of Kool-Aid—lemon this time—and a bologna sandwich.

Prayers, songs, the thunderous bombardment of the loudspeakers, and discussion; it went on all day and into the night, when Singleton returned to the rostrum. Before we went to bed we sang patriotic songs, ending with the National Anthem.

Hours in the Black Room, the songs, prayers, lectures, repressive lectures, the vigorous exercises continued for days. A regimented pattern soon became apparent. First, there was no communication with the outside world; our boundaries were the Black Room, the cellar, and a brief exercise period in the yard. I gradually felt a sense of being controlled. At first it made me uneasy, but as time passed, I felt myself accepting each program which skillfully fitted into the next. Then came a second phase, during which we were deliberately humiliated by Singleton. He selected a few to make public confessions of their sins and evil life. Sense of self, pride, and accomplishments were attacked by both Watson and Singleton. The black kid was their favorite target; weeping, tears running down his shiny cheeks, he told how he had snatched pocketbooks, mugged, and even "used the blade" to get money for drugs. Both Watson and Singleton took a licentious delight in cross-examining him about his experiences as a Times Square prostitute.

The fat little girl was quickly brought to tears as she haltingly told a classic story of rejection by a mother who was devoted to beauty parlors and cosmetics, and a father who ignored her. She had taken up the violin to please them, got acceptance from her peers in the high school orchestra, but her mother mocked her and the music teacher who was in charge of the orchestra let her stay only because she consented to take lessons from his brother. I cringed when Watson ordered her to play. It was a disaster.

I was sickened by the emotional assault on these impressionable, passive, and obviously disturbed young people.

One morning we were broken up into small groups and told to fill out an application several pages long. In addition to the basic information, there were numerous intimate questions such as salary, position; type of car owned and price; bank accounts; what people did you know who (a) had a large amount of money, stocks, or bonds, (b) had large holdings of property, (c) were in positions in which they handled large sums in banks, corporate offices, or government positions; experience in politics; acquaintance with persons active in politics or holding county, state, or government positions, length of time of friendship; details of personal property, apartment furnishings, and so on.

We answered the questions to a background of soft organ music and a woman's persuasive voice repeating the story of Ginerva meeting the Almighty. It was impossible to leave. One frightened recruit, a teenager in jeans, sneakers, and rugby jersey, returned his application to one of the instructors.

"Maybe I better think it over and talk to my parents," he said, his eyes darting nervously about the room. "You see, I got this Porsche from my uncle for my birthday. It's old, but me and my buddy worked on it all summer and now it's top grade. Man, I wouldn't want to give away that car."

"You are now a soldier of Ginerva, Brother," the instructor said, getting up. "You won't need a car anymore. There are buses and vans to take you anywhere."

"Yeah, maybe so, but I think I made a mistake coming here. I sorta had a fight with my parents and now I better talk to them. Okay?"

I could see the instructor make a gesture behind the kid's back. In seconds the boy was surrounded by five instructors who began escorting him to a door while they talked persuasively. In minutes he was gone.

There was always an instructor with a small group. The instructor who had led the exercises in the yard was with us day and night, reading us scriptures, verses from the Bible, exhorting us to believe in Ginerva and face God's threat that the end of the world was near. At first I was amused, then irritated; finally I found myself utterly bored, listening to him.

I had scoffed at Norman's warnings of what the House of Preparation could do to the human mind, and now I was discovering at first-hand how right he had been. It was one thing to be on the outside, another to be part of this deadly operation. I soon discovered why kids I had talked to at the motherhouse were robots with glazed eyes, hugging their Bibles and repeating the endless repetitive slogans and Biblical quotations.

First, the noise in that farmhouse was deafening. The windows of the Black Room were never opened, even when the smell became overpowering. Loudspeakers continually blasted out messages from God, the triumph of Ginerva, and the glory of the Society of the Chosen. Then came hymns with the decible level so high the stagnant air vibrated; when I reached out my hand I could feel sound waves flowing across my fingers like invisible water.

There was also the lack of food. Eating had never been my thing.

There had been days in the jungles of Nam when I barely tasted a mess from the cans although I was ravenously hungry. Now I found myself remembering them. The small bowls of cereal, the cup of sugar-sweetened juice, the meager slab of pressed meat on stale bread were quickly consumed by the acids in my growling stomach, to leave me dreaming of Chateaubriand for two, with crisp warm rolls, baked potatoes, and fresh string beans, topped off by homemade cherry pie—a meal Ben and I and our dates had taken for granted so often at the little restaurant on York Avenue.

After a week, I felt so weak that in the afternoon a sheen of sweat would break out on my forehead and I found my hands trembling. All this time we were being bombarded by screeching hymns, the thunder of Singleton's voice, or the blaring of Sousa's band playing partriotic numbers. This went on day and night, even when we slept.

Some mornings the Watsons refused to give us that horrible breakfast until each one stood up and recited several verses from the Bible. This was after only three hours of sleep.

Food, sleep, and silence. How I longed for them. To my horror, I discovered my mind was growing numb. I was actually listening to the garbage that poured out of the loudspeakers. When someone spoke to me, his voice sounded unreal and far away. There were no clocks in the farmhouse, we had no watches, so hours folded into one another like the bellows of an accordion. I kept a secret record of the days by making an X for every morning in the tiny book of crossword puzzles Leah had given me. Many of those days remain hazy, distorted, shapeless. But I will always remember the heat wave.

It began on one of those beautiful mornings when summer attacks the city with a maniacal glee, focusing the sun until tar melts, streets buckle, and every New Yorker feels he is on a spit being slowly turned over a bed of coals. I would have gladly exchanged the IRT rush-hour for the farmhouse. Long before dawn we took our places in the Black Room to be buffeted by the blaring loudspeakers, the Watsons, and Singleton. I was sure I was sitting in a pool of water; every pore in my body leaked moisture. The stench in the room was now part of me. I wondered if I would ever be able to wash it away with soap. The room was so crowded recruits stood against the walls in tiers. Singleton went on for hours. His face in the changing lights reminded me of an old English woodcut of Satan. Finally, one kid fell over in an epileptic fit, and in the confusion the door was opened and we fled to the yard like concentration camp prisoners running to greet their liberators. I sprawled out under a tree and vowed never again to take fresh air for granted.

That relief lasted less than an hour before we were returned to the

Black Room for another "discussion of the Scriptures" by Watson. This time the windows were opened a fraction, but homemade fans were forbidden.

"Remember what the Lord suffered in Gethsemane," Watson thundered, "as you sit in this comfortable room."

My mind was now like an engine clogged with dirt and old oil. I found it hard to put together answers. Everything seemed to be pouring in on me on the back of noise. I had so confidently boasted to Leah and Norman that no man could bend my mind, but I was shocked to realize I was listening to this noise as truth.

Ginerva is God's Courier. Praise Ginerva.

The world will be destroyed by God's Sea of Flame but the members of the Society of the Chosen will be lifted into Paradise on God's Holy Cloud.

O God, thank you for sending us Ginerva. Without her we are doomed.

I fought desperately to close my mind to the noise and torrent of voices. I remembered what Norman had suggested and began counting presidents backwards. When I exhausted that, I began reciting bits of poetry and recalled the years of the Revolution and what events took place. Trollope had always been a favorite, and I repeated to myself remembered scraps from his *Autobiography* where he described his post office years in southwest England, when dressed in a red coat and shining black boots he rode forty miles a day, an experience which provided the background for *The Warden*. Then Elizabeth Bowen's tales in *Encounters* with their marvelous *dramatis personae*.

I was an educated adult with certainly a variety of experiences and backgrounds to help me fight off the Society's deadly training program. I wondered what of the helpless kids, many high school dropouts, who entered this place? I could only feel a deep compassion for them and a sense of horror at what Ben had undoubtedly gone through at the skilled hands of the deadly twins.

The heat wave lasted a week. I was sure I had lost at least ten pounds. My pants hung on me like a sack, and although I washed the sport shirts I had brought with me, they smelled moldy and had actually started to rot along the seams. The sleeping dormitory in the cellar was a torture pit out of Poe; now there were so many recruits we virtually slept on top of one another. Once I tried to open the small solitary window, but discovered it had been nailed shut. Then Watson's "God-given water" ran out as the water table went below the old pump's prime line. Water had to be brought in pails from a nearby stream to flush the toilets, which only added to the stench in the house. Everyone was put on a daily ration. As a result, we became dehydrated from sweating for hours in the Black Room.

It was also obvious our training was becoming successful. The recruits now automatically fell into line at a simple gesture from the instructors. They gasped for air in the suffocating Black Room without complaining as Watson rambled on for hours, recited the doggerel about Ginerva and the Society as if a switch had been clicked on in their heads, and were oblivious of the noise—it was now subliminal.

Finally, so many recruits appeared at the farmhouse the Watsons were forced to erect tents in the fields. They were old with holes and so heavily coated with paraffin that one went up like a rag dipped into gasoline when a sterno stove overturned. Fortunately no one was inside.

Our indoctrination never ceased for a moment. A large part of the day was spent in the stifling Black Room. When that became impossible for even the Watsons or Singleton, we were marched out into a field where the "lectures" and "discussions" continued. There was no shade. If a recruit began nodding in the baking heat, an instructor would poke him with a pointed stick and shout:

"That's Satan closing your eyes, Brother! Banish him back to Hell!"

After sessions in the Black Room and the field, we played a daily game the instructors called "Wake Up, World! Ginerva Is Talking to You with God's Words!"

We formed a large hand-holding circle, whirling about as fast as we could, and at the same time singing out responses to the questions asked by the instructor, who stood in the middle.

It was a frenzied kind of weird playacting. A disinterested observer would have been horrified at the sight of a madly whirling circle of adults, sweat pouring off their bodies as they ran about in the stultifying heat, shouting this nonsense.

By my record, it was the eighth day when they started to give me "special attention." I was taken to the attic by two smiling instructors who informed me that because of my "superior intelligence" I was to be given an "advanced" course. It was suffocatingly hot in the dim attic. The only light was supplied by a naked bulb hanging from a wire. There were only a few straight-backed chairs, piles of old newspapers, and a sagging couch. Everything was covered with dust. When I protested and explained who I was, they smiled and ignored me. The sessions started shortly before midnight, after I had gone through a full day of lectures, Bible discussions, a barrage of noise, Singleton's blistering lecture, and had little food or water. I was bone weary and dehydrated. Despite everything I had done, my mind was staggering. There were times I found myself accepting their propaganda. *Yes, it was possible Ginerva had met God. How do we know she didn't. What can be wrong with a religion that only demands peace and love of your brother and whose goal is to drive evil from the world. Why not? The signs for Judgment Day are all in the Bible—the violence, wars, blood . . .*

Pairs of instructors worked in shifts so they remained fresh. When I started to fall asleep, they would wake me up, thrust a Bible into my hands, and demand I read with them. Just before dawn they would lead me back to the cellar; I would barely get to sleep before Watson's booming voice would wake us. The sessions continued day and night. There was no brutality, no acts of violence. Rather the instructors were always gentle, never raising their voices, always smiling, patient, considerate. But never wavering in their goal to claim me as their own.

I believe the kid in jeans, sneakers, and rugby jersey who had been taken away by the instructors some days before actually saved me from going over the brink. One morning I took my place in the circle in the Black Room. By now I felt as if I had been without sleep for weeks. I was weak from lack of food, and my body was begging for water. Twice that morning I had asked Watson for a cup, and each time he had smiled brightly and promised there would be some as soon as the pails were brought from the creek. But they never came. The young black boy usually sat next to me or that hopeless fanatic, Mr. Well-Dressed. Both had been easily won over and had become zealots, walking around clutching their Bibles and echoing phrases from Watson's lectures. They were duplicates of Thomas, that pathetic example of the Society's mind-bending program.

I started to yawn, but stopped midway. Out of the corner of my eye I had noticed it wasn't the broker or the black boy who was seated next to me, but the kid in jeans.

"How are you?" I asked.

I was shocked when he turned to me. In the dim light his eyes looked glazed, as if he was slowly recovering from a severe blow on the head. His long hair straggled about his face, and he held a Bible tightly against his chest.

"Praise the Lord for Ginerva," he said. Then he repeated, "Praise the Lord for Ginerva. She saved me. The devil was inside of me. I had demons in my brain who tried to make me run away but Ginerva reached out and saved me. Praise the Lord for giving us Ginerva."

"Are you all right?" I asked him softly.

"Praise the Lord for Ginerva," he repeated, mechanically. "She saved me from Satan . . ."

I felt so sick I could taste gall in the back of my throat. I wanted to pound my fist on the floor and hurl the kid's Bible into Watson's sweaty face. I was horrified when I realized for the first time how near I had come to slipping over the edge. I was shaken out of my lethargy, and for the first time in days looked around. The kids who had arrived with me at the farmhouse were almost unrecognizable. The fat little girl was like a sleepwalker, her mouth half opened, a dribble of saliva coming from one corner. Her eyes were rimmed with purplish shadows, her hair stringy and tangled. Everyone looked dazed, dirty, and unkempt.

At that moment, I began to fight back. When Watson went into his morning harangue, I forced my mind to concentrate on the names of the presidents. Trollope's long rides along the back roads of the six Welsh counties, and Elizabeth Bowen's Dublin childhood in her *Seven Winters.*It was a torturous task, but slowly, ever so slowly, I found I could ignite tiny sparks of resistance in my mind, so by the time I took my place in the circle for our daily game, I was alert, angry, and full of fight.

That night in the attic, for the first time I began an offensive, cross-examining the surprised instructors on their ridiculous interpretations of the Bible. I soon discovered they were not only manufactured fanatics, but fundamentally uneducated and ignorant. I knew I was getting to them when they hung loudspeakers in every corner; now noise bombarded me from the beginning to the end of every session.

From smelling like a locker room, the attic gradually took on the stench of a pigsty. They excused me from the lectures in the Black Room and stretched the attic sessions to almost around the clock. I didn't have time to shave, I had lost quite a bit of weight, but I kept up my counterattack. One day the sessions ended: I had won.

The following morning, when I resumed my place in the circle in the Black Room, Mr. Well-Dressed looked at me with distaste. "You should shave, you know," he said. "Cleanliness is next to godliness."

When I filed into the kitchen to finally receive a ration of water, I caught a glimpse of myself in the flawed mirror over the sink. My face was all hollows and planes, I had a straggly beard, and my eyes were sunk deep into my head.

That afternoon, instead of taking part in our daily game, I joined Mr. Well-Dressed, the black kid, and about thirty other recruits. We marched to the rear of the barn where folding tables had been set up. A nearby field of high grass led to the clump of woods and the stream where the Watsons got their water to prime the old pump and flush the toilets. As the crowd began milling about, I slipped into the grass and made my way to the woods, where I found the stream. I stripped off my clothes, now smelling like a vagrant's, and stretched out in the small pool. Feeling the cool fresh water pour over my body was one of the unforgettable moments of my life. I drank like a man in the Sahara who had suddenly come upon an oasis, splashed about, dunked my head again and again, and finally reluctantly dried myself with my polo shirt and dressed. I felt totally refreshed and ready to take on an army of instructors.

I expected to be harassed by the instructors about my absence, but when I returned there were only the tables. The crowd was gone, but I heard shouts and jeering coming from the front. There I found a handsome middle-aged couple standing with their backs to a station wagon and facing a crowd of recruits led by Watson and several instructors. On the porch Mrs. Watson and Singleton were shouting encouragement.

"I want to talk to my daughter alone," the man demanded loudly.

Watson glared at him with contempt. "She is no longer your daughter," he boomed. "She now belongs to the Society of the Chosen and is working in the Fields of the Lord with Her Holiness, Ginerva."

"She's our daughter," the woman protested in a quivering voice. "We want her to come with us. She is only a child. . . ."

"Pawns of Satan!" Watson cried. "Betrayers of Christ! Go back to Satan, your master, and tell him you have been defeated by Ginerva's Chosen! Back to the deepest pits of hell!"

"Infidels! Pawns of Satan!" the crowd began shouting. "Go back to hell! You have been defeated by the soldiers of Ginerva!"

The stylishly dressed woman, obviously frightened, did her best to avoid the shoving and pushing while her husband, red-faced with rage, tried to protect her.

"You crazy bastards!" he shouted as he yanked open the door of the passenger side and got his wife inside the car. "I'll get the cops after you for this."

At a signal from an instructor, the crowd moved in closer. Someone rumpled the man's hair as he fought to open the door on the driver's side. Once inside, he leaned out the window, pointed a finger into the crowd, and yelled:

"Unless you get into this car right now, Francine, you will be dead as far as I am concerned! Understand? Dead! Now are you coming with us or are you staying with these nuts?"

I was surprised to see him pointing at the fat little girl who had wanted so much to please her father by playing the violin. For a moment she seemed to hesitate, chewing intently at a fingernail. Then Watson put his arm around her and cried: "She no longer belongs to you! She is now our sister! Go back to Satan, your master!"

When one of the instructors began to slam the hood, the others followed his example, pounding the sides of the station wagon with their fists while they chanted: "She is our sister, Satan's pigs! Go back to hell!"

"Francine, you are no longer our daughter!" the man cried, his voice breaking. "You are dead to us! Dead! Do you understand?"

He gunned his engine, roared into reverse to the road, spun around with tires squealing, and was gone within minutes. For the first time in days there was a deep, complete silence. The recruits looked dazed, like grunts I had seen in Nam after their first battle when the VC had vanished like smoke in the wind, leaving dead friends at their feet.

Watson's voice broke the spell. "Praise the Lord! Our Sister Francine has helped us defeat Satan and his helpers!" He glared at the recruits. "Now do you see how Satan uses your parents to steal you from God? He's working every minute of every hour to take you away from our glorious Society of the Chosen! Close your eyes, shut your eyes, and fight back with this!" He held up his Bible. "Now let us praise Francine, who helped us win a battle for Her Holiness, Ginerva!"

It was a signal for the instructors. They began hugging the girl and ordered us to form a circle about her.

"Praise the Lord for Francine, Brothers," they shouted as we pranced about her. "She helped us to defeat Satan and all his temptations! See how the Devil uses your parents! Close your ears to their words and follow the example of Francine! All hail to Francine!"

We shouted this idiocy as we jumped around the poor kid, who was fighting back the tears and trying to force a smile. I could only guess at the shock her parents had experienced when they had first seen their daughter, pale, unwashed, bewildered, and lost.

Later that day, we were ordered into a long line and passed before a a table to "voluntarily" turn all our material possessions over to the Society of the Chosen. To impress us, the instructors opened the double doors of the barn to reveal it jammed with furniture, color television sets, bicycles, motorcycles—even a beautiful and obviously expensive canoe. All this, they told us, was property turned over to the Society by other Disciples. All cars, we were told, had to be turned over to the Society.

As each recruit approached, the contents of his paper bag were emptied out on the table and he was handed a release to sign. The instructors, notary publics, notarized each release. It was quick and efficient; I had the weird sensation I was at Auschwitz.

I fast-talked the instructor out of my Princeton ring, but I lost the expensive watch I had bought in Saigon.

The following morning, I was ordered to join a group of teenagers loading a truck with furniture and television sets, which I learned were sold by the Society in secondhand stores they operated in the larger cities across the country.

I judged the growth of the Society by the contents of the barn; it was never empty. Trucks loaded with merchandise "donated" by recruits throughout the five boroughs arrived every few days, while empty trucks backed up to take their place. From early morning until dusk I helped gangs of teenagers to load and unload the trucks. It was evident what they were trying to do to me; they had failed to break me mentally, so apparently they hoped to humiliate me, to destroy my ego. But the heavy physical labor had the opposite effect. I'd never known I had such a strong back. Stripped to the waist, I was turned the color of old leather by the broiling sun. I also avoided most of the sessions in the Black Room.

One morning while working in the barn, I overheard two Disciples discussing how the recruits would be broken up into experimental street peddling teams. This was one facet of the Society I was determined to view up close. At first I was afraid I would be left out, but it soon became evident that sending me out to peddle wilted flowers and phony jewelry was part of their program to break me.

I intended to go them one better; I was determined to be the street preacher.

The very idea of addressing a crowd of cynical New Yorkers on the glory of Ginerva and the Society of the Chosen made me feel apprehensive. But I knew when word got back to Foreman he would be impressed, while Russell would look foolish. . . .

A short time later, our dehumanizing period abruptly ended, and we began to receive unexpected favors. I was taken off the heavy labor detail, we were permitted to sleep late, the loudspeakers now only played soft, inspiring hymns, and we were given a turkey dinner presided over by a now jovial Brother and Sister Watson. The grotesque pair soon had everyone cheerful and calling out their love for Ginerva and the Society. They told us we were now ready to go out and convert a hostile society into following Ginerva, drive Satan back to the deepest pit of hell, and be prepared to be lifted into Paradise.

It was clear to me that this was part of a carefully devised program of procedures that could only lead to predictable outcomes. First there had been the emotional lashings, deprivation of sleep, the constant mind-torturing noise, Singleton's daily battering of minds and souls. Next came the confessions, the humiliations, the hard work. Now there were the favors, laughter, a sense of family, camaraderie, and, most of all, dependence.

Stuffed with fine food, still smiling and giggling over the jokes that each one had to tell, we followed Watson into the Black Room. Singleton reappeared, but this time his voice was soft, almost gentle as he repeated the story of Ginerva's confrontation with God and how He had selected her as His courier to bring His warning to the people of the earth to mend their evil ways or be consumed by the Sea of Flame that would turn the earth into a fiery ball in the solar system, an everlasting symbol of God's anger. He ended with a plea to us to help the Society build a better world—a shrewd offer to the youthful idealism of his audience.

"If any man be in Christ," he whispered, fixing us with his feverish dark eyes while the loudspeakers poured out a moving hymn, "He is a new creature. . . ." The wave of his hand took in the weeping, pathetic little fat girl, the desperate black kid clawing his way back to life, the mad broker. "Old things are passed away." His voice rose, "Behold all things become new. . . ."

Now, while the room bubbled with religious zeal, Watson came on to describe how the Society depended on its workers to get funds to carry on the Lord's and Ginerva's work. The next day, he told us we would be assigned to teams selling jewelry, fresh flowers, or soliciting contributions and recruits during the street preaching: "Just as the first Disciples did after the risen Lord had let His Spirit touch them . . . ."

That one night's decent sleep had softened us; only the crazy broker was on his feet before Watson's foghorn voice got us out of the sleeping bags.

"I'm going into the fields of the Lord!" he kept crying joyously. "Hallelujah!"

The black kid and the little fat girl hugged their Bibles and promised the Watsons they would return with bags of money and countless recruits.

A battered black bus with FOLLOW GINERVA AND BE SAVED painted on both sides, dropped us off at a warehouse in the West Village. Inside, the place was jammed with recruits lined up, waiting to be given their assignments for the day by Avenging Angels seated behind crates that served as desks. On the far side of the warehouse, an assembly line of Disciples worked on producing the goods to be sold; one group wove the crushed and broken flowers they had begged for during the night in the flower market into bouquets with ferns hiding the fading blooms; others inserted the cheap jewelry into the velvet niches of boxes while a team spray-painted cardboard containers and covered them with red, white, and blue crepe paper.

I collected the names of our group and gave them to the Angel when our turn came.

"Very good, Brother," he said. "This saves time. Now you will—"

"Brother Watson said to tell you I am to be the street preacher for today," I said. I knew they couldn't check by phone; the farmhouse didn't have any. He frowned, studied my name, and disappeared behind a partition. He was still frowning when he returned. "Are you sure Brother Watson said you were to be preaching today, Brother?" he asked.

"Positive," I told him.

He shrugged and called over his shoulder, "Brother Enders! Bring your group. We have your preacher."

Enders was about twenty, with a nervous habit of gently rubbing the tip of his nose with his thumb. We shook hands after an introduction.

"Brother Hillers will be your preacher for today, Brother Enders. This is his first time. Give him all the help you can."

I wondered why Enders, who carried a canvas money bag, wasn't doing the preaching, until he talked; he stuttered badly. Of the two boys and three girls who joined our group from Staten Island, one wore combat boots. When I asked why the Society didn't give her shoes, she said an Angel had told her, "We can't stop working for the Lord to take care of your feet." The other two were an energetic teenage blonde—a younger Sister Sloan—who had bitten her nails to the quick, and a sallow-skinned older girl who couldn't say a sentence without quoting the Bible. The boys were teenagers; one told me privately he spoke to Moses every morning and Jesus in the afternoon, "except when the Lord is busy." The other was an albino who examined every coin he took in by holding it next to his astonishingly thick lenses.

"How long do we stay out?" I asked the girl who clomped beside me in her combat boots.

"Until dark," she said, yawning. "Brother Enders said our quota today is three hundred because we have a choice location."

"Where's that?"

"Fifth and Forty-second Street—outside the New York Public Library."

Well, I had asked for it. . . .

"Flowers are good for four hundred," she went on. "If you don't get too much hassling from the cops, jewelry can bring in five or six."

"What do we do with the money?"

"Turn it in for the Lord's work," she said, looking at me as if I had asked an utterly foolish question. "It's Satan's world, so we take it from Satan and give it to the Society for good works."

"And what are the good works?"

"Last Christmas our Team Leader told us all about them," she said, with a dreamy look in her eyes. "Hospitals for the old people, drug centers, Houses of Preparation—oh, just about everything to change this evil world!"

"I never saw Ginerva," I said wistfully. "What does she look like?"

"Her Holiness is beautiful," she said in a voice filled with awe. "I'll never forget the night I saw her and how the lights turned her hair to gold. And her voice!" She closed her eyes and held my arm. "It was beautiful, Brother Hillers—like angels singing! Oh, I can't wait for that glorious day when we step onto God's great cloud to be lifted into Paradise. I only want to be at her side. . . ."

(202)

She was no more than eighteen and very attractive. I wondered what hidden demons had brought her to this place. When I asked, she only looked straight ahead. "I had a lotta personal grief," was her short answer.

When we reached the library's Fifth Avenue entrance, Miss Combat Boots told me it wasn't any use to start preaching until eleven, when office workers were returning from their coffee breaks and midday shoppers were appearing on the avenue.

A man can sneeze and gather a crowd in Manhattan, so when I finally mounted our portable pulpit, I looked down into a fairly large sea of faces. I also had a bleacher audience—the Library steps were crowded and attentive. Enders patted me on the back and gave me a *V* for victory sign, and Miss Boots shrewdly suggested I tell them anything to hold their interest, then follow up with a dish of fire and brimstone as they passed through the crowd with their containers.

My lips were dry and my mouth felt as if it had been stuffed with cotton as I searched for a familiar face and found none. I gave a stumbling start, my voice cracked and hoarse. In the rear a burly young guy carrying a box yelled: "Speak up, pal, we can't hear you!"

I took a deep breath, singled out the guy with the box, and began the story of the terrible hours of Company H. Suddenly, to my surprise I found I had captured their interest. They were intent on what I was saying. The guy with the box was nodding as if he too had been in Nam with another Company H. Then I gave them the business of how I had come back stateside only to fall into the hands of Satan and end up attending the rally in San Francisco where I had experienced Ginerva's miracle.

As Miss Boots and the others circulated among the crowd rattling the containers—Miss Boots told the members of our group to put five pennies in each one, "It makes a pitiful sound"—I begged my audience to give what they could and pictured how their contributions would help build the old age homes, the drug centers, and all the other good works the Society had promised Miss Combat Boots.

There was some scattered applause when I stepped down. Miss Boots was glowing, Enders pounded my back, and the black kid from the farmhouse looked at me with awe. I felt a singular sense of triumph when I saw the guy with the box put in a coin.

I went back up on the podium three more times that day. The last was in the late afternoon at the peak of the rush hour. The size of the crowd amazed me. By this time I was confident, my story glib and theatrical. For my last sermon, I borrowed some of Ginerva's material and knew I had captured their attention as I pictured the scene on Calvary: the howling winds, crashing thunder, the weeping Mother, and her dying son on the cross.

"Go back to your wives, your children, your parents, sweethearts, and families," I thundered down at them. "Tell them the story of Ginerva and how she was given God's warning to the world to drive the evil from their hearts or face his terrifying Sea of Flame. Read the leaflets our Disciples are passing out among you and ask yourself: shall I wait until the heavens echo with God's anger, or shall I lead my loved ones into the glorious Society of the Chosen and follow Ginerva onto the heavenly cloud of salvation and be lifted into Paradise?"

Miss Boots said my last pitch was good enough not only to fill the containers, wipe out their last flowers and pieces of junk jewelry, but also to fill their pockets with coins and bills.

"And God reached down and gave him the gift of tongues," the older girl said, patting me on the shoulder. "St. Paul to the Corinthians, chapter two, verse six."

"Someone slipped me a Canadian quarter," the albino kid complained, as he held up the coin inches from his thick glasses and the other kid wondered if the Lord would miss their daily talk.

The battered bus picked us up, and as we honked our way through the evening traffic, Miss Boots led us into "Bringing in the Sheaves." Inside the warehouse the Angels expertly separated the bills and coins, while teams of Disciples prepared to invade the flower market to beg for the next day's bouquets.

Brother Enders turned in our canvas bag of money, to return to us, smiling and holding up eight fingers.

"Glory to God! We made eight hundred!" Miss Boots shouted as she hugged me. "Brother, your magic tongue helped us get that!"

Enders shook hands with me as the rest of the group gave out with a few hallelujahs.

The Angel who had sent us offered his congratulations, but appeared puzzled. "Are you sure you never did any preaching, Brother?" he asked.

"Not a word," I told him. "In fact, I didn't have any religion until recently when Ginerva blessed me and opened the world of the Lord to me."

He looked as impressed as I had hoped he would.

We stayed at the warehouse for two weeks, sleeping in crude dormitories on the second floor and soliciting from noon until twilight. I had hit my stride as a street preacher, repeating again and again the story of Company H, Gethsemane, and Calvary. We traveled up and down Fifth Avenue, starting out at noon at the Plaza and working our way down to Grand Central. In five days we brought in $3,821.76, a bent token, eight foreign coins, an "Elect Jimmy Carter" button, three flyers shaped like dollar bills advertising "The Venetian Fingers

Massage Parlor," a New Jersey parking ticket, and several green supermarket coupons. New Yorkers, even when broke, evidently dislike passing up a collection box.

But what was of major interest to me was the cryptic remark made by the Angel who sent us out every day: "I sent word to Brother Watson about your good work," he told me.

I was sure that "word" would eventually get back to the mother-house.

Finally the day arrived when the black bus returned us to the Staten Island ferry. A short time later we were back at the farmhouse.

"Congratulations, Brother Hillers," Watson said, slapping me on the back. From what I hear, you're a natural-born street preacher."

"I was filled with the power of the Lord," I told him.

He was still smiling, but his eyes intently searched my face. "But the Angels said you told them I wanted you to do the street preachin'. I never said that!"

"Brother Watson," I told him solemnly, "after I left here I was so filled with the glory of Ginerva that if I hadn't spread it to the world, I would have exploded like a balloon brushing up against a pin. After all those wonderful lectures by you and Sister Watson and Brother Singleton, I was glowing with the love of the Lord! Praise God, Brother Watson, for your deep love of the Almighty!"

I left him nodding to himself.

I remained at the farmhouse another week. When the day arrived when our group left the farmhouse, the change in those kids was evident. Most of them chattered like robots, quoting the out-of-context Biblical phrases and distorted theological arguments from the Watsons' and Singleton's lectures, and repeating over and over the story of Ginerva's confrontation with God and how the Society must change the world before it was plunged into eternal damnation.

As we walked down the shabby walk for the last time, several vans pulled up to the front gate to unload a large crowd of curious recruits. The screen door suddenly flew open, and Sister Watson, still in her weird dress, rushed out, threw up her hands and cried out: "Welcome! Welcome!" Then she leaned down and kissed a bewildered teenager on the cheek. "Welcome, daughter! Welcome!" I was climbing into our bus when Watson appeared in his pin-striped pants and vest. The door slammed shut on his roar of "Welcome, Brothers and Sisters! Welcome to Ginerva's Society of the Chosen!"

After we drove aboard the Staten Island Ferry at St. George, I got out with the others and found an isolated spot on the top deck of the bow behind a lifeboat that cut off the wind. The water was choppy, and as the boat lumbered across the bay, I reviewed the days I had spent at the farmhouse. I shuddered at the memory of how close I had come to surrendering my mind to the Society's skillful thought-control program. I felt outraged at the laws and communities which allowed their children to be sent out into the streets from before dawn to late at night, seven days a week, existing on stale sandwiches, watered milk, and sweetened juice, to solicit money for confidence men and nonexistent public service programs. I felt sick at heart when I recalled the kid in the rugby jersey.

As I huddled in my narrow hideaway trying to avoid the sharp wind and spray, I felt the first stab of despair. After Ben's death, I had been ruled by emotionalism. I had been so confident when I predicted to Sir Edward I would bore from within, a one-man fifth column, and destroy the Society. How contemptuously I had dismissed the warnings of Leah and Norman that what went on in the shabby farmhouse on Staten Island could warp any man's mind. Certainly I had underestimated Foreman and Russell; they had taught me that while evil can be banal, it can also be damned efficient.

How could I ever produce enough evidence to prove to the cold unalterable law that they and their monstrous Society of the Chosen were devoted not to God and goodness but only to evil? That they were destroying young hearts, minds, and souls for greed and dark ambition?

And Ginerva—how could she explain all this?

I had outlasted them in the blazing hot attic, taken their humiliation and hard labor, even become one of their street preachers. But was it enough of a masquerade to fool them, to persuade them to invite me into their conspiracy? When this ferry docked, should I simply walk away and accept Josh's warning to leave the dead to rest in peace? I could easily return to St. Timothy's and write a harrowing newspaper series for Lord Cavendish's newspapers. But I knew, down deep, little or nothing would come out of the words and the headlines. I felt depressed, uneasy, and uncertain as the shabby, but magnificent skyline of downtown Manhattan suddenly loomed up and cars growled to life.

As I walked down the deck, I passed a group of elderly women, probably going into the city for shopping, a giddy one-Manhattan lunch, and a matinee.

"That's one of those fanatics from Charleston," one loudly informed the others. "I saw him getting out of that crazy bus with the others. Doesn't he look weird? I can't see why the police don't do anything about that terrible place. Do you know what our neighbor told my husband the other night? He said they—"

I suddenly felt a surge of triumph. Maybe I could pull it off after all. . . .

The bus delivered the Society's newest Disciples to brownstones, tenements, and storefront churches in Brooklyn, Queens, and Long Island. In the early afternoon the rest were dropped at the dormitories of the motherhouse, but I was driven to Foreman's office.

Russell wasn't at his usual post near the bottom of the stairs. One Angel whispered into a phone, and I was immediately waved upstairs. I was startled to be met by Tura in the outer office.

"My God, Hilly!" she whispered, "Have you been working as a lifeguard? You're dark as an Indian! And so thin! What did they do to you out there?"

"It's a long story," I told her. "When can I see you?"

She shook her head violently. "Don't come to my place. I think I'm being watched. I'll let you know." She leaned up and kissed me. "They couldn't believe you survived."

In minutes I was standing before Foreman's desk. He jumped up with a look of concern.

"I only found out this morning about that horrible mistake, Hilly," he said as he shook my hand and waved me to a chair. "I don't know what they were thinking about out there! I told Watson I want a complete report on this!" He gave me a searching look. "They certainly trimmed you down. Are you all right?"

I told him evenly, "I never felt better in my life, but I wouldn't recommend that program to anyone not in good condition."

He threw up his hands in a helpless gesture. "Hilly, it was all a mistake. I'll never send an oral message out there again—from now on everything will be in writing."

I knew he was lying. With a straight face, I said, "It's remarkable what simple food, fresh air, and exercise can do."

"But something good came out of it," he exclaimed. "Brother Watson sent me word you were the best street preacher they ever had. Are you sure you never had any experience?"

Still with a straight face, I said, "I guess I was inspired, Dave."

"I've been thinking about it," he said. "Perhaps in an emergency on the tour you can fill in for me as master of ceremonies. However, that's all in the future. Now what do you want to start on, Hilly?"

"Why don't I begin revamping *The Call*?" I suggested.

He hesitated. "Yes, I guess we should get that out of the way before we go on the tour. By the way, I thought the dummy was excellent."

"In the next issue we'll announce the tour with a statement by you, Dave," I said. "I'll write it and show it to you before it goes into proof."

"Excellent," he said, rubbing his hands together with invisible water. "Well, I guess we're on our way."

At the door, he said, with studied nonchalance, "Oh, on your way out, say hello to Brother Russell. . . ."

His handsome fox's face was impassive, but I was sure he was laughing inside.

When he closed the door, Tura said loudly, "Brother Russell is waiting for you downstairs," but typed on the piece of paper she was holding up was the warning: WATCH OUT FOR RUSSELL. HE'S AFTER YOU."

Russell and two of his Angels studied me intently as I descended the stairs. When I reached the bottom, he silently opened a door and waved me into a room that could have been a library. Floor-to-ceiling bookcases were empty and dusty. An ancient grand piano was covered with a sheet, and there were no chairs.

"Watson gave me a report on you," he said maliciously. "How did you like our program?"

"Well, it was strenuous," I replied.

"I should have been over there to give you my special attention," he said fiercely.

"Too bad you weren't," I said. "It could have been interesting."

"Perhaps we can arrange that someday," he said. "Just you and me."

"I'll be waiting," I told him.

As I started to open the door, he called out, "Hillers—just who the hell are you?"

"An Angel from the Fields of the Lord," I told him.

When I walked into *The Call* office, Leah and Turner stared at me for a moment.

"Hilly, I can't believe it's you!" Leah said, as she hugged me. "My God, you're so thin and tanned! What were you doing out there?"

"Loading and unloading trucks for a good part of the time," I said. "What's happening?"

"Nothing is new," Turner said. "We tried to get some word about you, but no one knew anything. How did it go?"

"Well, to begin, you were right and I was wrong—it's a mind-bending place." Over cups of coffee I described for them the highlights of my experience at the farmhouse.

"So I was right!" Norman said triumphantly. "Russell *was* out to get you."

"And he came damn near it," I admitted.

"So you're not Superfly," he said, grinning.

"No way," I said.

Leah looked puzzled. "You actually went out and preached on the street, Hilly?"

"There's not a corner of Fifth Avenue we didn't hit. And every dime was turned over to the Angels in the warehouse."

"Is that where they skim it, Hilly?" Norman asked.

"I don't know. I guess that's one of the things we have to find out."

We looked at one another. "How will we ever do that?" Norman said despairingly. "Did you get any ideas on Staten Island?"

"That street preaching wasn't wasted," I said. "Foreman suggested I could fill in as master of ceremonies on the tour. By the way, have you passed the Grand Ballroom lately?"

"Yesterday," Turner said. He added quickly, "And to answer the question you haven't asked—yes, there is an Angel still on guard. He never leaves the front door."

"And there is no word of what she is doing?"

"Nothing," Leah said flatly. "But she's there. One of the kids who cleans the Ballroom said she saw her going into her apartment."

"Can you suggest any way of getting in there, Norm? I've got to see her."

"There isn't any way, and don't try it," Turner warned me.

"Why do you want to see her, Hilly?" Leah asked.

"This is out of left field," I suggested, "but do you think it's possible Foreman and Russell are holding her prisoner?"

They looked at each other.

"But why would they do that?" Leah demanded.

"I don't have anything to hang my hat on," I told them. "It's only a hunch I got talking to Foreman. . . ."

"Even if you're right, forget it," Turner said. "There is just no way to get in and talk to her."

Leah said slowly, "Hilly may be right, Norm. But why would they want to keep Her Holiness against her will? Doesn't Foreman intend to use her as his big attraction on the tour?"

"Without her there is no tour," Turner pointed out.

"You are both probably right, but let's think about it," I said. "Maybe we can come up with a way to get in there."

"But suppose you do get in and find she is anything but a prisoner and is completely devoted to Foreman?" Turner advanced. "Then what happens to you?"

Leah reached out and held my hand. "Norman's right, Hilly. You would be taking a tremendous chance. Let me talk to some of the kids and see what I can find out."

"Okay. And in the meantime, Norm, you and I have to start working on that dummy for Foreman."

He held up a wrinkled sheet of brown wrapping paper. "I got some great material. This is a report from a guy in a lumber camp in Washington where they held a meeting."

"I told him not to laugh at it, Hilly," Leah said. "They got recruits to go to a House of Preparation in Seattle. Doesn't that prove the Society is growing?"

"Oh, it's growing all right," Turner said, holding up a bunch of letters and snapshots. "They're getting recruits all over the place. They even have a church in San Francisco's Chinatown."

12

Little Boy Lost

I first paid a visit to the Jersey City printer and silently spread out the copies of *The Call* I had marked with red ink.

"I'm the new editor," I told him. "One more typo or bad cut and you're finished."

He studied the papers then looked at me. "You in the business?"

"I know enough to realize you've been giving them the worst printing job I have ever seen."

He started to bluster. "I don't get any help from that kid Turner. I have to do—"

I interrupted him. "From now on you will get layouts, captions, edited copy, and all pictures will be cropped. All you will have to do is supply the type and a printing press. And no more extras they paid you for making up."

"I can't do if for that price," he said, shaking his head.

I gathered up the papers. "Very well. Thank you."

"Maybe we can talk about it?" he suggested.

"Why waste time, my friend?" I held up a card. "Here are the names of three of your competitors. One is only four blocks from here. They all want the job."

He gave in quickly. "Okay, you win. No typos, no bad cuts. No extras. But you supply layouts, captions, pictures, and clean copy."

It was a victory I could offer Foreman.

During the next few weeks, Norman and I worked hard to revamp *The Call*. Fortunately, the first editor had kept a list of correspondents who sent in material, and Norman had added to it. I ran up enormous telephone bills talking to each one, praising their past efforts, urging them to send in any news they had of the Society in their district including names, names, names. Our network of correspondents soon stretched from the eastern seaboard to as far north as Portland and as far south as New Mexico. I sent each one a mimeographed sample style sheet along with suggestions for photographs and captions. I wanted to make sure there would be no more reports written on wrinkled brown paper.

I was not an experienced editor. What we did was by trial and error, aided by suggestions from an old printing catalogue I found in *The Call*'s files. Gradually the shabby little tabloid began to emerge with an identity of its own. From Stafford's file photographs I selected a dramatic one of Ginerva taken a few years before at a Midwest rally that showed her in white robes, arms pleading to heaven, and with that eerie look on her face. I made it all of page one, superimposed the masthead with an italic head GLORY TO GINERVA!

I led page three with my byline story explaining how I had been the recipient of one of Ginerva's miraculous cures and had recently joined the Society of the Chosen. The Society's national activities had box heads for each state with one-column cuts of the correspondent. Personal vanity at times can be as strong as religious fervor.

Now there was an editorial page for the first issue of the revamped paper, with a personal message from Foreman, which I had written. The back page was devoted to a pictorial layout of Disciples in various parts of the country studying, praying, singing.

In between working on the layouts, I explored the grounds. As my face became familiar to the guards, even to Matthew and his dog, I had more freedom than on my first visit. I soon became familiar with the physical layout of the estate, even locating a hole in Russell's security. In the far northwest corner I discovered a clump of pines hiding a mound of earth piled up against the cyclone fence, its peak rising over the barbwire top. Apparently someone in the past had used this little hill to dump leaves on the other side. I tried to jump; countless layers of matted leaves made me feel as if I had fallen on a mattress. I showed the spot to Leah and Turner and told them to remember it as a possible exit.

I also sought out Steve Troy and tried to cultivate him.

"I couldn't believe it when Brother Foreman told me you had joined us, Hilly," he said when we met. "That was some surprise."

"I want you to know I'm not moving in on your department."

"No problem!" he exclaimed. "Why, I told Brother Foreman that hiring you was one of the best breaks we ever had!" He was silent for a moment, then added: "I heard you went through the training on Staten Island."

I carefully put out a feeler. "It was rough."

He looked beyond me. "Those Watsons and that guy Singleton are really somethin'."

When I asked him to give me some suggestions on *The Call*'s makeup, he accepted eagerly. I recalled Foreman's cold comment that Troy was born not to be noticed, and decided that while he was part of the conspiracy, he certainly wasn't Foreman's nightly dinner companion. A few friendly overtures might pay off.

Actually, Troy was very good on photographs, and he gave me a number of excellent suggestions. His favorite topic was Vietnam and the documentary he had made for the religious group in Missouri; undoubtedly it had been the high-water crest of his life. But while he was friendly and garrulous, he was not dumb. He carefully fielded my questions about Ginerva, innocent as they might have appeared, and looked blank when I mentioned Tura. Although he supplied little information, I decided to keep in touch with him; like Tura, he could be another possible weak link in the chain.

From time to time I drove past the Grand Ballroom, where an Avenging Angel was always on guard. Norman was right, the only way to see her was to get her out.

I waited for a note or a call from Tura, but none came. Turner's gossipy girl friends told him she was still working in Foreman's office; all I could do was wait. In the meantime, *The Call*'s pilot dummy was finished, with layouts, edited copy, and cropped cuts delivered to the printer. In a week we had galleys, and I persuaded him to page-proof the issue on slick paper after we turned in the corrected galleys. I was sure Foreman would be impressed.

Then one day, a little boy was lost. . . .

As I recall that day, I started to correct the galleys shortly after seven. I was impatient for the page proofs and wanted to get the corrections in early. Rather than eat the cafeteria's wallpaper-paste cereal, Norman brought back doughnuts and coffee, and the latest gossip of the outside world. As he tore open the bag, he said, "One of the kids told me the guy who delivers the bread said there is a lot of excitement on the highway not far from us. He said a four-year-old boy wandered off and half the county is looking for him."

"Do you think it could be a kidnapping?"

"No, just a lost kid," he said, putting the doughnuts on a plate. "How is it coming?"

"Fine. No typos. I'll be finished soon and we can ride over to Jersey and deliver them."

"Foreman should really be impressed. Those pages on slick paper should look great." He waved his doughnut at me. "What then?"

"Then to the tour."

"Do you really believe you'll get so close to Foreman he'll spill something, Hilly?"

"As I told you, Norm, I'm going to try like hell. . . ."

Within an hour we were on our way to Jersey City. A short distance from the motherhouse we had to slow down. State troopers were directing the traffic past a number of police cars and a crowd of curious milling about the edge of the highway.

"This must be where they're looking for that kid," Norman said.

As we came to a stop, a handler tugging at a brace of bloodhounds came out of the woods.

"The dogs pick up anything, Joe?" the trooper shouted.

The handler shook his head. "They lost the scent and have been out all night," he called back. "I'm bringin' em back to the barracks."

A trooper leading a party of civilians also emerged from the woods. They looked weary; some leaned against the cars, others slumped on the ground. A television mini-cam crew ran up and a reporter with a microphone began questioning the trooper; still photographers and reporters also joined the crowd.

The trooper brushed past the reporters and called out to a group of men studying a map stretched out on the hood of a car. "We did Ramsey's farm. After we take a break, we'll do the woods along the creek. But somebody should hit the woods around Miller's Pond."

"We don't have anyone," one of the men replied. "We have a squad car with a loudspeaker in the village now trying to round up more volunteers."

"What about the volunteer firemen?"

The man pointed down the highway to where two fire engines, an emergency truck, and a chief's car had been pulled off the road. Several firemen were sleeping on the ground and on the trucks.

"How long has the little boy been lost?" I asked the trooper.

"Since early yesterday," he said grimly. "If we don't reach him soon . . ." He shook his head and waved us on.

I could feel the kernel of an idea growing. We had gone less that a mile when I ordered Norman to turn around and return to the motherhouse.

"What's the matter?" he asked. "Did you forget something?"

"No," I told him. "But we're going to find something—a little boy."

Russell, who was standing by the desk at the bottom of the stairway, only glared at me when I told him I wanted to see Foreman.

"I have an idea that could possibly benefit the Society," I told him.

"Well, suppose you tell *me*," he barked.

It would have been futile to refuse, so I told him.

"You mean you want the Disciples to walk through the woods looking for a lost kid?"

"And I think Her Holiness should bless them before they start out," I said.

He stared at me incredulously. "Are you nuts, Hillers?" he said at last. "Are you trying to make fools out of us? And Ginerva?" He looked down at the two Angels seated behind the desk. "Did you hear what he said?"

"Just what did he say, Brother Russell?"

Foreman, carrying an attaché case was descending the stairs.

"There's a lost kid in the neighborhood," Russell said angrily, "and Brother Hillers thinks we should use the Disciples to look for him. And he wants Her Holiness to bless everybody."

When Foreman looked at me for an explanation, I said, "Brother Russell didn't give me a chance to explain. The police need more volunteers. All of them are exhausted; they have been out since yesterday. This would be marvelous goodwill publicity for the Society. There is at least one TV crew over there, along with newspaper photographers and reporters."

"Come in here, both of you," he said quietly.

Russell and I followed him into the room with the empty bookcases. Foreman put his attaché case on the sheet-draped piano and turned to me.

"What exactly is your idea, Brother Hillers?"

"I believe we should enlist every available Disciple on the grounds, march them up to where the police have established their base headquarters, and offer in God's name to help look for the lost child. And if it is possible, Ginerva should appear, even for a moment, and bless them before they set out." I added fervently, "Every paper in the city will be up there. Can you imagine the shot? Disciples, singing praises to God as they march hand in hand across a meadow! And Ginerva blessing them! It could be the highlight of the six and eleven o'clock news! And there is something more important: the little boy has been lost since yesterday morning. They just don't have enough people. There are hundreds of us right here. I think that God would agree that searching for a lost child is more important than sitting in a classroom, even discussing the Bible."

I held my breath for a moment. I didn't know how Foreman would react, but he didn't have a chance. Russell was all over me.

"That's the dumbest idea I've heard in years," he said furiously. Looking for lost kids is a cop's job! They can get as many volunteers as they want. We have more important things to do here!"

Foreman looked at me. "How do you know they haven't enough volunteers, Brother Hillers?"

"A state trooper told me. He also told me some of the volunteers have been searching since yesterday morning."

"What were you doing talking to state troopers at eight o'clock in the morning?" Russell demanded.

"Brother Turner and I were on our way to Jersey City to deliver the final proofs of *The Call* to the printer." I held up the package. "When the traffic slowed down, I asked a trooper about the search and he told me."

Russell was now talking directly to Foreman. "If the Disciples spend all day out there and don't come up with a thing, we'll all look like fools. And having Ginerva bless them! This is garbage! I tell you, Dave, garbage!"

"This is not a kidnapping," I said quickly. "The child will probably be found either alive or dead of natural causes. If we find the kid, the goodwill and publicity will be tremendous! And even if the child is never found or found dead, we will have demonstrated a sense of civic responsibility and good will toward our neighbors that is certainly expected of any religious community. Recent publicity about the Society has not been good. This is a chance to counterattack," I added. "Put Ginerva on the six o'clock news, the ten o'clock, and the eleven o'clock news, and before midnight she will have become a fact—a part of people's lives."

"But why does Her Holiness have to be involved?" he asked, frowning.

"As you have said, Brother Foreman," I pointed out as delicately as I could, "Ginerva *is* the Society of the Chosen. Without her there is nothing. God chose her as his courier to the world. It would make a powerful impact on television viewers to see her leading a search to help find a child." As I quoted, I hoped my face had a beatific glow. " 'Suffer the little children to come unto me. For they are the Kingdom of God.' " Then I became practical. "If we've going to do anything, we should move fast. The reporters who are there can still get something in the Wall Street editions of the P.M.s and the first editions of the A.M.s, but above all the mini-cam crews can get her on the six o'clock news." I ended with: "You might recall, Brother Foreman, what we did with the little boy in the hospital."

That did it. At least when he moved, he moved fast.

"I want a message put on the loudspeakers immediately," he told Russell, "ordering every Disciple to gather immediately on the grounds. I will address them. Instructors and employees are not included." He turned to me. "How far is it from here."

"About a half mile."

"Get every bus and van with drivers lined up in the driveway. After I give the Disciples their instructions, we'll all drive to the scene and offer our assistance. In the meantime, I'll talk to Ginerva. I am sure she will agree that this is God's work." Then, to me, "Congratulations, Brother Hillers, this is an excellent idea."

As he turned to open the door, Russell said in a cold flat voice: "I don't think we should do it, Dave."

Foreman slowly turned, and they stared at each other. I could feel the tension mounting in the silence. Then Foreman said quietly, "I think we should." He paused. "And we will."

"I don't want any part of a stupid scheme like this that will only make a fool of Ginerva," Russell said.

Foreman's lips tightened into a thin, almost invisible line. His eyes seemed to grow darker as he studied Russell. When he finally spoke, his voice was almost a whisper.

"Put the message on the loudspeakers, Brother Russell."

Russell's voice level changed; now it was harsh. "I say we wait a couple of hours. Maybe they will find the kid—"

Foreman's unexpected roar startled me. "Now! I want it done now! Do you understand? Now! This very moment!"

Russell glared at him, then slowly nodded. "Okay, if that's the way you want it. Okay."

Foreman turned to me. Just as quickly as his anger had flared up, so had it died away. His face was almost placid, his voice normal. "Please come with me, Brother Hillers. I want you to tell Ginerva exactly what you told me. . . ."

When we went out, I could feel Russell's eyes boring into my back. But I was exuberant. I had just discovered that Russell could be one of the weakest links in the chain.

Foreman made no mention of his differences with Russell as we crossed the grounds in a cart to the Grand Ballroom.

As we got out, the estate was echoing with the message blaring from the loudspeakers:

"This is an emergency! Every Disciple must report immediately on the grounds! Repeat. This is an emergency! Every Disciple is to report immediately on the grounds!"

I could see Disciples pouring out of the dormitories and the cafeteria and running across the lawns.

"There will be a small army," Foreman said. "We should be able to cover every inch of those woods."

"While you're addressing the Disciples," I said, "Brother Turner, myself, and Sister Butler will call the newspapers, wire services, and television stations as we did the last time. If you wish, Dave, I'll also write a statement for you to read to the press."

He tried to look modest. "If you think that will be necessary."

If was difficult to keep from laughing. "The press will expect it. I also think we should bring along that young photographer." I paused as if trying to recall his name.

"Brother Stafford," he said. "Very good. Use him any way you wish, Hilly. Please wait downstairs a few minutes while I brief Her Holiness on our plans."

A faint odor of floor polish hung in the darkened Grand Ballroom. As I waited, I marveled again at the magnificent ceiling of stars and moon. Suddenly Foreman appeared on the balcony and called out to me to join him.

It had been over a month since I had last seen Ginerva; it was like meeting her for the first time. Her beauty still startled me. She was dressed in a light green blouse and dark skirt and was carrying a Bible. A votive light was burning before the stunning silver cross.

"Her Holiness is spending most of her time in prayer, preparing for the tour," Foreman explained. "I have explained about the search."

She came toward me, smiling, her hand outstretched. It felt warm, soft, and fragile.

"I was delighted when Brother Foreman told me you had accepted his offer, Brother Hillers."

Foreman cleared his throat. "It was God's will, Ginerva."

I thought I caught a note of disappointment, a flash of resignation in her eyes as she slowly took her hand away. "I hope you will find peace and happiness among us," she murmured.

"I told Ginerva about the plan to use the Disciples as volunteers," Foreman said quickly.

"Oh, yes," she said, and, closing her eyes, "God, help that little boy! How terrible for his parents. We must do everything we can."

"Brother Hillers just came from there," Foreman said. "And he suggested, and I agree, that you should bless the searchers."

She stiffened. "No! No! No more Blessings!" Her voice rose, "I told you, no more Blessings!"

There was a hint of impatience in Foreman's voice. "There are television crews over there now. More are coming. There are also reporters and photographers. Exposure like this will help the tour."

I put in, "Please, Your Holiness, it will only take a moment. The volunteers have been there since yesterday. It will give them new strength to see you and to hear you. I am sure God will answer your prayers and show his divine mercy."

What I didn't say was: and your beautiful face will be on every six and eleven o'clock news program. . . .

When she shook her head, I turned to Foreman, who gave me an impassive look and said, "Will you wait downstairs for a moment, Brother Hillers? I wish to talk to Ginerva privately."

I closed the door but managed to leave it open, just a slit. I stopped halfway down the stairs and started to go back up two steps at a time, when suddenly the front door opened and the Angel on guard walked in. Fortunately, his eyes weren't accustomed to the darkness and he didn't see me until I had made a great deal of noise coming downstairs.

"Brother Foreman will escort Her Holiness down in a moment," I told him. "He asked me to wait here."

The Angel nodded, didn't reply, but continued to stand at the bottom of the stairway. In a moment the lights went on and Foreman came down the stairs.

"Her Holiness will ride with me, Brother Hillers," he said glancing at the Angel. "She'll be down in a few minutes. In the meantime, you can alert the press."

"Can I tell the media there will be a Blessing, Brother Foreman?" I asked.

"Of course," he replied. "Just as you said, it will make a wonderful shot on the six o'clock news."

If I had any doubt before that he controlled her, it was now gone. But why? And how?

As Foreman had predicted, a small army of Disciples was being formed into lines by the Angels when I returned to the grounds. Parked in the driveway and along the paths was a fleet of vans and yellow buses with GLORY TO GINERVA! BE SAVED AS A CHOSEN ONE painted on both sides.

When I saw Leah, I waved her over to my cart. "Get in. I haven't got time for too much explanation. I sold Foreman on the idea of using the Disciples to search for a little kid who's been lost since yesterday. You and I and Turner are to call the papers, wire services, and television stations, just as we did the last time. Foreman's hot over this idea, and if it comes off I could be his golden boy. Ginerva's going to bless the operation."

All she said was, "The last time I typed up a list of the media phone numbers and left it in the drawer of your desk."

You couldn't do any better than Leah.

After I explained to a bewildered Turner what we had to do, I found the media phone list and divided the numbers between us;

Leah used the one phone in the office while Norman and I found two more in the cafeteria building. After we rejoined Leah, I typed a brief statement for Foreman while Norman called Stafford, gave him a brief explanation of what was going on, and told him to meet us on the highway.

When we arrived at the driveway in our van, the last of the buses was passing through the gates, followed by Foreman's limousine. He was sitting in the back with Ginerva. Russell and Andrew were in the front seat.

"What is it with her and her Blessings?" I asked Norman and Leah, and told them what I had seen. "Why doesn't she want to do them?"

"Remember when I told you the first time we met?" Turner reminded me. "Foreman's the boss up here. When he gives an order they all jump through the hoop—even Ginerva."

"But I'm with Hilly, Norm," Leah said, puzzled. "I can't understand why she doesn't want to do the Blessings. When I first came here, the Blessing of the Sick was a big part of every rally. Ginerva never appeared reluctant, and they came by the hundreds." She turned to me. "What do you think it is, Hilly?"

"That's just another question we have to find the answer to."

Turner muttered, "We have more things to find out about this woman. . . ."

"I'm sure when Hilly becomes Brother Foreman's golden boy he will be able to answer all the questions," Leah said with a sweet smile.

Deliver me from stubborn and sarcastic women, I told myself.

We arrived at the police command off the highway, and the buses began unloading the Disciples. I noticed several Angels carried the compact shortwave sets Russell's security patrols used on the grounds. Foreman was talking to a short, stout man in a sweat-stained sweatshirt, mud-smeared dungarees, and caked boots. Standing next to them was a state police captain, trim and lean as if he were ready for parade. When I joined them, Foreman turned to me and said:

"Brother Hillers, the mayor has just informed me he will be happy to accept our volunteers."

"Happy!" the little man said loudly. "That's the understatement of the year, Brother Foreman. As the captain can tell you, our men have been on their feet since yesterday. They just can't go on without rest. How can we thank you people?"

A haggard young woman, eyes red from weeping, joined us, and the mayor put his arm around her. "Gentlemen, this is the mother of the little boy. Now, Mary, why don't you go home and get some sleep? If anything happens, the captain will send a car for you."

She shook her head and in a dull voice said, "Sleep? How can I sleep?"

There was the sound of helicopters, and we all looked up to watch a pair pass overhead.

"We have two of them," the mayor said, with a note of pride in his voice. "We're doing everything humanly possible." He hugged the woman. "Mary, we'll find your little John. " Another woman came up, and at the unspoken suggestion in the mayor's face, she gently led the mother away.

"To make things worse, her husband walked out on her last month," the mayor said grimly, "and no one knows where the son of a bitch can be found." He gave a deep sigh. "Well, captain, where do you want these wonderful people to search?"

"Let's see the map," the captain said.

He unrolled the map the mayor handed him, knelt down, and spread it out. There were a number of red crayon circles, with and without numbers inside the circles.

"The circles with numbers represent the areas searched along with the time the search began and when it ended," he said. He tapped several circles without numbers. "This is the Miller's Pond area, one of the largest sectors yet untouched. It is composed of several pastures and woodland with original growth. That means heavy underbrush, which must be thoroughly searched. The pond was dragged yesterday and our divers went down at dawn. Nothing was found. We can use your volunteers to move in a big semicircle from east to west. The area is near the child's home, and from what we know the mother has frequently taken the boy to a stable in this sector where they have pony cart rides. He could have wandered over there to see the horses. The only other sector left is the old Leigh tract. It's out of the way, and I doubt the child could have walked that far. If he was on the highway, someone could have seen him. However, it has got to be searched with all the other parts of this area. Now with the number you have brought us, we should be able to cover all these sectors before dark." He looked up at the mayor. "And that will lock up this map. If the child isn't found . . ."

The little mayor said determinedly, "Then we'll go back over every foot. The kid has got to be out there."

The captain nodded. "Let's start the sweep." He stood up carefully, brushed the dust from his knees, and said to Foreman, "Those sets your people are carrying look powerful."

"They're the best money can buy," Foreman replied. "Our security people use them to patrol the grounds."

"Excellent. Your people can keep in touch with one another," the captain said. He rolled up the map and gave it to the mayor. "The field's completely yours, Brother Foreman. Every man we had has come out of the brush utterly exhausted. Our dogs are back at the

(221)

barracks and won't be ready to return until tomorrow morning. Frankly, sir, your people arrived at the perfect time."

"We only came to help," Foreman said.

"And we thank, you," the mayor said fervently. "We all thank you, especially the mother of the boy."

"We'll form teams of fifty or more of your people," the captain said briskly. "Each should have a set to keep in touch with the other."

"Our teams will be led by Angels who will be in constant communication with our headquarters," Foreman replied. "Of course, any news will be sent to you immediately. Now I have only one request before the Disciples set out. Ginerva wishes to bless them and ask God in his infinite mercy to deliver the little boy back into his mother's arms."

And to get Ginerva and the Society of the Chosen a fabulous amount of free space and prime time, I thought. Well, as I had bargained with myself, all rules and morals had to be jettisoned in his sickening game, as a means to the end.

"Here they come," the captain said disgustedly. Sensing something was about to happen, reporters, photographers, and television crews were running toward us.

I told them, "I'll handle the press."

I briefly explained to the reporters and cameramen what was about to happen and assigned Leah and Turner to help them in any way. When they left, I found Stafford waiting by his car.

"Don't worry about anyone thinking we're buddies," I assured him, "I even told Foreman I had forgotten your name."

"Leah and Norman told me you joined the Society," he said. "Hilly, I think you're crazy."

"I want you to know I never used that key," I told him, "I won't until you're gone. Any idea when that will be?"

"Soon," he said. "Very soon. Then help yourself. I heard they sent you to Staten Island. What do you think of it?"

"Horrible. I can't believe what they do to those kids."

"Russell blew his top when he found you had made it," he said.

"How do you know that?"

"I only found out yesterday. Matthew wanted another picture of himself and his dog. He came into the darkroom to watch me develop the print and told me Russell had ordered the creeps on the island to give you 'the works.' He thought it was very funny." He gave me a curious look. "How *did* you make it?"

"It's a long story. When we have some time I'll tell you all about it. Now what I want you to do here is cover this thing as if you were working for *Life*. Your competition is television and the still photographers, but I have a hunch you can come up with something different."

(222)

He looked embarrassed. "I'll do my best, Hilly."

"Stay close to me. I don't know what will happen, but if anything does I'll be the first to know about it. I don't have to tell you what kind of picture you can get if a couple of the Disciples come running out of the woods with the kid on their shoulders. . . ."

"Gotcha," he said, smiling.

It was manufactured drama, but very effective. It was my idea to use one of the fire trucks. She was helped to the top, and against a background of ladders and hoses, with the weary, mud-stained volunteers bowing their heads along with the huge crowd of Disciples and the curious, Ginerva, long copper hair glinting in the morning sun, called out her blessing. I can't recall the exact words, but it was a moving plea to God asking for his help in finding the lost child. When she ended, the only sound in the stillness was the whirring of the television cameras and the clicking of the newspaper photographers' shutters. When I looked over at Foreman, he was studying Ginerva with a faint triumphant smile.

Ginerva was helped down from the engine and returned to the car while Foreman read to the press the statement I had prepared for him. Then the Disciples were quickly divided into fifty-member teams, each headed by an Angel equipped with a powerful shortwave. Before they disappeared into the woods, the captain told them to keep only a few feet apart and to advance slowly, watching for caves, large piles of leaves, or underbrush thick enough to hide a child.

"I'm driving back to the mother house with Ginerva," Foreman said. "Russell will be monitoring the reports of the Angels. If anything turns up, we'll have someone here immediately. You'll liaison with the press, of course."

"Definitely," I assured him. "I'll keep you informed of all developments."

"This is wonderful work, Hilly," he said, squeezing my shoulder. "God truly directed you to us."

"All glory to Ginerva," I said, hoping I sounded properly humble.

"Hilly, for God's sake be careful," Leah whispered to me as we watched their car disappear down the road. You're playing a very dangerous game."

"And you earned yourself one hell of an enemy today," Norman added. "Russell."

Like all searches for missing children, this one dragged on for hours, with the only enemy the formidable miles of trees, rocks, brush, meadows, and pastures, broken at intervals by lakes, ponds, and streams that had to be probed by firemen in rowboats using the sharp, ugly drags, and divers in wet suits. The firemen's auxiliary appeared with soda, lemonade, and sandwiches; as usual, the media gave the scene a carnival air, attracting a large crowd of the morbidly curious. It was a beautiful, languorous day with a soft, warm breeze moving across the meadows, gently bending the tips of the grass and whispering to the nodding wild flowers.

It was in the afternoon when suddenly Foreman, who seemed to come out of nowhere, was standing at my elbow.

"Dave!" I gasped. I instantly thought of the shortwave sets. "Did you hear anything? Was anything found?"

He nodded to the limousine. "Ginerva has insisted she be brought here."

I was confused. "Why, that's wonderful. I'm sure her presence will mean a great deal to the Disciples and the others."

He said abruptly, "Her Holiness has had a vision from God and knows where to find the child."

For a moment all I could do was stare at him and swallow hard. "A vision she can find the child?"

"And she wants only you to accompany her," he said.

The thought suddenly came to me—why was he so unperturbed? So calm? Doesn't he realize what this could do to his national tour?

I lowered my voice. "You realize, of course, this could backfire on us very badly. We should do it without the press knowing—"

He broke in with a firm, "Oh, but I want the press to know all about the vision Her Holiness had, Hilly! When she finds the child, won't that be glorious publicity? You could do wonders with it."

I said desperately, "But if she *doesn't* we could be the laughingstock of—"

"Have faith, Hilly," he told me. "Have faith. Ginerva will find the child as God told her in his divine vision."

She was sitting in the back seat, her eyes bright, almost feverish. Russell was in the front seat and Andrew was driving. The hate in Russell's face made me shiver.

"Is there anything I can do, Ginerva?" I asked her.

She didn't answer, but only held out her hand. I helped her out.

"The child is in a hole," she said in a quivering voice. "A deep, dark hole. There is a broken board over it and a skull nearby. I want you to go there with me.

I could repeat, helplessly, "A skull?"

"A skull," she said, "with horns."

The mayor and the captain joined us. "There's really nothing new," the mayor said, looking from Foreman to Ginerva. "I hope you will allow your people to stay on until dark."

"I don't think that will be necessary," Foreman said. "God has told Ginerva where the child is. She will lead Brother Hillers to the spot." He added sternly, "But no one else."

My heart sank as reporters, photographers, and TV crews surrounded us. I heard one reporter mutter to his cameraman: "Get her on film. She claims God is going to show her where the kid is."

"You can go anywhere you want to, of course," the obviously puzzled mayor said. "May I ask where—"

He paused and looked from Ginerva to Foreman.

Foreman calmly unrolled a sheet of paper to reveal a crudely drawn map. "Ginerva drew this at God's direction."

The mayor glanced at it, then unrolled his sector map. "Why, that must be the old Leigh tract," he said slowly. "About a half mile down this road, you turn into the first lane and go as far as you can. Then you cross a meadow and go through a small patch of woods."

The state police captain glaring at Foreman, interrupted him.

"As I said this morning, no four-year-old child could walk that far. And if he did get there, someone would have seen him on the highway. Besides, there is nothing there to attract him. No horses or farm animals, only the foundation of the old farmhouse. Instead of this nonsense, what I intend to do tomorrow at sunup is to take your people—"

Foreman's voice had a rasp to it, like a saw cutting through ice. "Who said this is nonsense, captain? This is God speaking to us through his messenger on earth!"

Before the angry officer could reply, the mayor said quickly, "You and Brother Hillers can go anywhere you want, Ginerva—and with our prayers." He handed me his car keys. "Use my car; it's that old Chevy parked over there on the side of the road. There's a lot of junk in the back, ropes, flashlights, old blankets, stuff like that. She's a jalopy but she gets me where I want to go."

When I passed Stafford I nodded, and he nonchalantly got into his car. I carefully put Ginerva in the passenger's seat and took my time fumbling with the keys to let Stafford disappear down the highway. Behind us the reporters, photographers, and TV crews were arguing with the mayor, who was telling them that if anyone disobeyed his orders not to follow us, he would have them arrested. Gung ho, but now I needed him.

As we drove, I looked at Ginerva out of the corner of my eye. She was staring straight ahead.

"You think I'm crazy, don't you, Brother Hillers?" she said abruptly.

"Why, no," I said, caught off balance. "I am sure that God in his—"

She sighed. "You don't have to lie to me, Brother Hillers." She was silent for a moment. "Why did you join us?"

"I was filled with the glory of God and want only to serve you," I told her.

Her laugh was hollow. "Don't sound like the rest of them—please!"

I decided to take a gamble. "Did you know I was out on Staten Island?"

"Yes, they told me."

"Do you know what's going on out there?"

Her answer was a sudden fierce, "No! And I don't want to know! Don't tell me!"

"I think as the head of the Society *you* should know."

She was fighting back the tears. "I didn't want it this way."

A hundred questions jumbled about in my mind. I finally got out: "Ginerva, can I help you?"

She slowly shook her head. "No one can help me," she said in a resigned voice. "It's too late."

"Nothing is too late," I said eagerly. "Perhaps if we—"

She had suddenly stiffened in her seat and grasped the edge of the dashboard with both hands. "The little boy!" she whispered. "The little boy!" Then, in a loud voice, "Yes . . . yes. . . . We are coming. . . ."

We were at the entrance to a lane, and I swung in to move down a bumpy tree-lined tunnel. Ginerva was silent, still clutching the dashboard and staring intently through the windshield.

In the overhead mirror, I saw the hood of Stafford's car entering the lane. We drove about a quarter of a mile until the lane ended in a mudhole. Off to the right was a tumbledown stone wall, a broken gate, and a pasture. Beyond was a small patch of woods. Ginerva slowly opened the car door and stepped out. She seemed in a trance as she passed the gate and started to cross the meadow. I followed. Once when I turned, I saw Stafford hesitating by the gate, and I waved him back.

She walked very slowly. I kept up with her but off to one side. I could see her lips moving as if in prayer. Her eyes were fixed on the woods. As I recall, it was early in the afternoon, about two; the gentle breeze had stopped, the air was still, and the pasture seemed to me to be a thousand miles wide. Crows lectured us raucously and once a rabbit bounded away in frantic hops. But Ginerva took no notice of anything, only the woods.

Finally we arrived at the edge. She hesitated for a moment, then went on. After the sunny pasture it was suddenly cool. The ground was covered with a thick mat of dried leaves; wild huckleberry vines reached out to pluck at her skirt; sunshine speared through the trees.

The woods had been thinned out years before, and I could see the fieldstone foundation of the farmhouse. Suddenly she stopped.

"Ginerva—are you all right?" I asked.

She seemed to be listening, then she abruptly raised her hand and with a scream that made my heart miss a beat, she pointed: "The little

(2 2 6)

boy! Get the little boy! Get the little boy in the hole! In the deep dark hole by the skull. The skull with horns!"

For a moment I was stunned. When I reached out to take her arm, she screamed again: "Hurry! Get the boy before it is too late!"

Then with a moan, she began to sag. I grabbed her and eased her onto the leaves. Her face was chalk white, her green eyes stared into nothingness, like the blind.

"Go and get him! Go get the little boy!" she whispered.

I looked to where she was pointing. There was only the underbrush and the large square of vine-covered stones. A mad woman, I told myself, completely mad.

I reached down to scoop her up in my arms. "There's no one here, Ginerva. We'll go back . . . and you can rest. . . ."

She pushed me away and started to crawl through the leaves. "He's there, I tell you," she cried. "He's there!"

As I reached for her again, I heard a tiny cry. We both froze. There was only silence. I ran in the direction I thought the sound had come from. As I passed the corner of the old foundation, I made a wild leap across a hole half hidden by the leaves. The hole wasn't too large and apparently had been covered with old boards; rotting ends stuck out from under the leaves. I crawled to the edge, and as I peered down the tiny voice came out of the damp darkness: "Mommy. . . . I want my Mommy."

I carefully pulled away some of the rotting planks and shouted: "I'm coming, son. . . . I'm coming down to get you. . . ."

As I passed Ginerva on the run, she was on her feet and headed for the hole.

Stafford was leaning against his car, his camera in one hand, when I burst out of the woods. He started to say, "Hey, what was that screaming—"

"We found the kid!" I shouted. "He's in a hole!"

He ran to the back of his car, unlocked his trunk, and held up a long powerful-looking flashlight. "This has got a hell of a beam, but I don't have any rope."

The mayor had said there was rope in the back of his car. I clawed through the pile of boots, pails, and gear and found a tangled rope, a ball of twine, two old blankets, and a smaller flashlight. Then we both raced across the meadow and into the woods. Ginerva was kneeling at the edge of the hole.

"I have been calling Peter," she said, "but he doesn't answer."

Peter? But the mayor had said to the mother, *"we will find your little John."*

"Maybe we're too late and the kid is dead?" Stafford said, as he helped me untangle the rope.

(227)

"Peter is living," Ginerva said in a dull monotone. "God will bring him back to me."

"She found the kid!" Stafford whispered to me with awe. "I can't believe it!"

"Only the kid's name is John, not Peter," I said.

He looked at me. "Then who's Peter?"

I knelt down and clicked on the flashlight. The powerful beam revealed it was a deep hole, probably a long-abandoned well. The little boy was on the bottom, lying face up in about an inch of water, eyes closed and arms outspread. I called out, but he didn't move.

I quickly wound the slender but tough hawser around my waist and tied a bowline, mentally blessing the neighborhood scoutmaster, a retired tugboat fleet supervisor who had insisted every Tenderfoot had to tie five major knots before he was admitted to the troop. I wound the rest of my rope around a tree and gave the end to Stafford.

"I don't know if the rope will be long enough," I told him. "If it isn't I'll drop the rest and stay with the kid. You go back and get the others. Tell them to bring the fire trucks with the ladders."

After we had carefully pulled away more of the crumbling planks to enlarge the hole, I slipped in and began descending, mountain-climbing style, my back to one side of the wall, my feet braced against the other side. The earth felt soggy. My one fear was that the sides might collapse, burying both of us.

I went down by inches. Once I almost lost my footing when the sharp edge of a rock sliced through my shirt and skin. I carefully dug my feet into the clay as I felt the blood running down my back. When the gash started to pain and throb, I rested for a few minutes.

Stafford's anxious voice seemed miles away. "Are you okay, Hilly?"

Mine sounded as if I was singing basso. "Everything's okay, Bruce. I'm just taking a rest."

Fortunately, the rope was long enough. I was near the bottom when I paused to reach over and turn the flashlight on the child. A chill ran through me. The beam first caught the gleaming eyes like fiery buttons, then the whole length—a gray rat as big as a cat. The child's arm was bloody from its first bite.

I took careful aim and hurled the long flashlight down like a spear. It caught the rat in the back of the head and winked out.

"Send down the other light with the twine," I shouted. "There are rats."

I dropped the rest of the way and felt the rat under my feet. I ground and pounded the furry body into the mud, and picked up the child. His small body was icy cold. I found his throat and pressed my finger against the artery. There was a faint pulse.

As I slipped the noose around my waist, they came at me from all sides, squealing, hissing, clawing at my pants leg. I kicked out at them, punched them off my pants, smashed them under my feet, and shouted to Stafford to pull me up. As the second light came down on a string, the rope went taut, and I frantically began inching up the wall, the little boy in my arms. The beam of the second light pierced the darkness to reveal that just below me the bottom of the hole was covered with crawling, hissing rats tearing at each other. I suddenly realized they had been attracted by the smell of the blood dripping off my back.

There have been times, even now, when I wake up with a start to find my face wet with sweat, my heart thumping like a frightened bird beating against the bars of its cage, because in my dreams I am once again going up the sides of that well, inch by inch, the unconscious child resting on my chest.

Ironically, I was in excellent condition from the weeks of loading and unloading the trucks on Staten Island. Yet halfway up I developed severe muscle spasms in the calves of my legs that made me stop until they passed. Each time, my body quivered with exhaustion.

But the most frightful part of the dream is the terrifying noise of the bloodthirsty rats below me. If I slipped or lost my footing, the suddenly added weight could easily yank the cord from Stafford's hands, and the child and I would go down. I drove out of my mind what would follow.

The beam of the light helped me to select rocks and niches for my feet so I could brace my back against the wall and inch up. I had gained about halfway when I paused, and heard Ginerva praying.

"Lord, your mercy is my hope. My heart rejoiced that you have returned Peter to me. I thank you, Lord, for I know the rivers of living waters shall be given to those who strike thy rock and call out to you."

Stretched out in the damp darkness, fighting off the pain of the spasms while the child lay like a dead weight on my chest, I wondered: who was Peter? Why were there always more questions than answers in anything connected with Ginerva?

I continued the weary climb upward, the patches of sky showing through the treetops gradually getting closer. Then at last the jagged ends of the rotting boards were just above my head, and Stafford was looking down at me.

"Don't worry," he said. "I tied the rope around the tree. Easy does it."

When I held the boy up, he reached in and pulled him out.

"Cover your face," he ordered, "and let me widen the hole."

I covered my face with my hands, and his fist smashed the rest of the rotted wood. I felt his hands searching for mine, and I clung to them.

"One . . . two . . . heave!" he grunted, and pulled. I went over the top and sprawled out on the grass. Ginerva was kneeling in front of me, pulling off the child's soggy, muddy clothes. She used one end of the blanket to tenderly dry the small body, blue from exposure, then wrapped him tightly in both blankets until the boy looked like a tow-headed papoose.

"God has brought you back to me, Peter," she whispered, and leaned down and kissed the child on the cheek.

I heard a click. Stafford was too much of a photographer to have forgotten his camera. Of all the pictures taken that day this one was the best; it would be on page one of most of the nation's newspapers and eventually become a moving classic of photojournalism.

I got up and staggered, almost falling. My legs were like tubes of lead, and the deep throbbing pain in my back was increasing.

"Hey, Hilly, you're bleeding!" Stafford cried and pointed.

I looked down, to see one side of my pants leg was covered with blood. Stafford ran over to me and gasped, "Man, you got a gash in your back!"

I leaned over and took Ginerva's arm. "We have to go, Your Holiness," I told her, "and get Peter to a hospital."

She slowly stood up. "God has given me Peter back," she said and hugged the child.

Stafford looked at me, the question in his eyes, but I shook my head.

"Let's get out of here," I told him. "You go on ahead. Tell them we have the kid but a doctor should check him over. I'll come after you."

He ran ahead, turned to snap a few more shots, then vanished through the trees. Ginerva and I slowly crossed the meadow, looking like a wartime family fleeing for the border. I was streaked with blood and mud from my feet to my hair. Ginerva's stocking were in shreds, her legs were scratched from the thorny vines, her blouse was soggy and splattered with mud, bits of leaves clung to her skirt. She stared straight ahead, hugging the child in the paint-splattered blankets.

"Ginerva, where do you and Peter live?" I asked.

"Far away," she said emotionlessly. "Far away."

The question jumped out. "In Idaho?"

"Yes," she said. "In Idaho." Then she called out, "Aunt Clem! Peter is back! God in his mercy gave us Peter back! We're coming, Aunt Clem!"

She was hurrying now and I was having trouble keeping up with her. "Who is Aunt Clem, Ginerva?" When she didn't answer I pressed her: "Where is Aunt Clem?"

She began to change. As we approached the car, she stopped and looked around as if she were coming out of a daze.

"The child is alive," she said slowly, and looked down at the boy in her arms as if noticing him for the first time.

"Yes, and all because of you, Ginerva," I replied. "You found him."

"But he was in a hole, a deep, dark hole and the skull was nearby," she said. She took a deep breath. "Then we were driving down a highway and you were talking to me. We crossed a meadow and entered a forest. . . ."

She stopped and shivered as if a cold wind had swept out of the forest.

I said quickly, "What happened, Ginerva?"

The child opened his eyes and moaned, "Mommy. . . . Mommy. . . ."

"We must get him back to his mother as soon as possible," she said, and got into the back seat. I had only turned on the ignition when I heard the approaching sirens. Then, in a cloud of dust, the first car swung off the highway and into the lane, followed by a fleet of patrol cars, fire engines, the media, and the curious. In seconds the lane was filled with cars, and I could hear the whistles and the shouted commands of troopers starting to divert traffic on the highway. A fleet-footed camerman, his mini-cam gear bouncing on his shoulder, came up as the captain, the mayor, and the child's mother scrambled out of the car.

"Where's the kid?" the captain shouted. "Is he all right?"

Ginerva gently kissed the boy, and I helped her out. We were quickly surrounded by troopers, firemen, and reporters shouting questions at the mother, who was pushed forward by the little mayor. Ginerva, smiling, held out the blanketed boy to his mother.

"God has returned your baby," she said.

Several reporters thrust their microphones like steel popsicles into Ginerva's face, but the mayor angrily pushed them aside.

"Can't you wait?" he cried. "Can't you wait?"

The sobbing mother hugged her son, kissing him wildly.

"Mommy. . . . Mommy," he said, whispering. "I got lost and fell into a hole. . . . It was dark and I kept calling you."

"He is cold, frightened, and hungry," Ginerva said, "but I don't think he's hurt."

The crowd pushed closer. The car's side mirror ground into my back and the stab of pain made me wince.

"How did you find the child, Ginerva?"

"How did God show you where the child was?"

"Did you have a vision, Ginerva?"

"What were your thoughts when you heard the boy?"

"Have you found lost children before this?"

Someone bellowed in my ear. "Hey, fellow, they said you got the kid out! What were your thoughts when you went down the hole? Someone said there were rats in the hole. What were your thoughts when you saw them?"

Then Foreman, who had fought his way to us, said something to the state police captain. I suddenly felt very tired. My legs were wobbling so much I had to lean against the car. I felt Ginerva's arm around me; she felt soft, warm, and sensual.

"You're hurt, Brother Hillers," she said softly. "You must go to the hospital."

Now Foreman, troopers, and volunteer firemen encircled us. Down the lane, the mother holding the child was getting into a state police car. Dome lights flashing, siren wailing, it began to weave through the parked cars and out onto the highway. Its wailing soon fading in the distance.

"We'll give you the entire story at the barracks," the captain shouted. "Now these people have to be checked at the hospital."

Someone held my arm and the circle started to move, brushing aside the press. I pulled my arm free. I knew the whole force of the drama would be lost to prime time if this pedantic cop made it his show in a staid police-barracks press conference. Ginerva and the Society of the Chosen would be secondary.

I pushed my way to Foreman's side. "You take over," I said softly. "I suggest you hold a press conference right here."

He caught on immediately. "Gentlemen," he said loudly, "Her Holiness will answer your questions within a few minutes." He said something to Ginerva in a low voice, and she bit her lower lip, but nodded.

There was a barrage of shouted questions. When they died down, she spoke quietly. "God in his infinite mercy showed me in a vision where the child was," she said to a battery of mikes. "But again I was only his courier and he led me to the spot. It was Brother Hillers who with the help of Brother Stafford brought the child out of the well. Now I intend to return to the motherhouse and thank God for returning that wonderful little boy to his mother." She paused. " All of us should remember that Jesus told the Disciples, 'Whoever accepts this little child, accepts me.' "

A woman reporter begged her, "Please, Ginerva, will you return with us to the hole, if only for a moment?"

She stiffened, but again Foreman whispered to her. With a look of resignation, she allowed him to lead her to the path and the meadow. Foreman, the captain, the mayor, weary firemen, troopers, photographers, cameramen, and reporters, chanting Disciples, and the curious trailed after us like a small bizarre army as we crossed the meadow

(232)

and entered the forest. Slowly, almost by inches, she approached the hole. One reporter knelt down, picked up the flashlight we had left behind, and thrust the beam into the hole.

"My God!" he cried! "Look at those rats! They're eating each other!"

TV cameramen and photographers fought each other to get to the hole. When a reporter picked up the child's soggy clothes and waved to his cameramen, another reporter pulled at them, and they started an angry tug of war.

"Stop it!" Ginerva shouted. "Stop it! Have you no respect for a holy place? This is where our Almighty Father spared the life of a child!"

The reporters looked embarrassed and the captain snatched away the soggy muddy clothes. I knew they would be displayed later at his barracks press conference.

"Did you hear the child cry from the hole?" the woman reporter asked. "Just how did you find him?"

"Ginerva was walking in front of me and Brother Stafford," I said. "God had told her exactly where the child was, and she pointed to this spot. Fortunately, the mayor had given us his car which had rope, flashlights, and blankets."

Foreman's gesture took in the lonely remote spot. "Who would think the child could come this far? Even the police didn't believe a four-year-old was capable of walking this distance, so that is why they let this sector be among the last to be searched." He added, "Only God knew where that little boy was fighting for his life, and he made Ginerva the instrument of his mercy."

"Please—no more. I must go," she said.

"Maybe we should run her over to the hospital," the captain suggested.

Foreman replied, "No, we will take Her Holiness back to the motherhouse." He looked at me. "But Brother Hillers needs a physician."

The little mayor called out to a fireman. "Take this gentleman over to the emergency ward right away. Use the chief's car!" He added, "We'll have you fixed up in a jiffy." He said to Ginerva, "Madam, there are times when words are inadequate. This is one of them."

Foreman, the captain, and several troopers started to escort her out of the woods. When she came up to me, she said quietly, "I will never forget this day, Brother Hillers. I am sure God in his wisdom has a reason for sending you back to us."

Then she was gone, and Leah and Turner were squeezing through the crowd to join me and the firemen.

"Oh, Hilly, we were so worried about you," she said. I was so glad to see her I leaned down and kissed her. I sensed she was surprised.

"You just don't know how worried *I* was," she whispered in my ear. "When Bruce told us how you had to fight off rats in that hole, I was petrified."

"By the way, where is Bruce?"

"He just left," Norman said. "He said he had enough pictures for ten papers."

In the emergency room, an intern cleaned and dressed the gash and gave me a tetanus shot. When we walked across the lobby toward the parking lot, a color television set was on.

"Look, Ginerva's blessing the Disciples!" Turner exclaimed.

The announcer was saying: "A few hours before, Ginerva had blessed her Disciples from a fire truck, and more than five hundred of her followers joined in the search for the four-year-old boy who had been missing for twenty-four hours. To repeat this bulletin: Ginerva, the woman who claims God has chosen her as his courier to warn the world of Armageddon, has found the lost child, who had fallen into an old well. In a brief press conference, she told reporters that God had led her to the remote spot deep in the woods. One of her Disciples descended down into the well and brought out the child. And now, for a report from our mini-cam crew at the very spot where this strange discovery was made only a short time ago . . . ."

A reporter holding a mike and, standing in the woods, pointed to the foundation of the old farmhouse. In the carefully controlled voice of a guide describing an historical site, he said: "Over there through the trees are the remains of what local residents call the 'old Leigh farmhouse,' built more than a century ago. It is a lonely place, far off the highway and familiar only to hunters. Yet it was here that Ginerva found the missing four-year-old boy at the bottom of a deep old well. She was driven down the highway from the state police command post to the end of a lane, crossed a meadow, and entered this patch of woods to find him. 'God led me to him,' was her only explanation." He walked slowly, dramatically, the camera following him to the well, and pointed down, the camera showing the opening with a few of the ragged ends of the board still sticking out from under the leaves.

"Earlier, hundreds of Her Disciples had joined the search for the missing child. But it was here, in one of the most extraordinary incidents of human phenomena, that Ginerva, the woman who claims to be the courier of God, found the frightened, cold, and hungry child who had fallen into this fortunately dried-up well covered—" he kicked at the remnants of the planks "—with these planks many years ago."

He knelt down, and now his voice held a suitable amount of awe. "Two Disciples who were with Ginerva pulled the child out of this hole. Police said the one who went down suffered severe lacerations on the back from an outcropping of rock and had to fight a raging pack of rats attracted by the smell of his blood before he could pick up the child and begin his ascent. He is now in a local hospital. The other, a photographer for the Society of the Chosen, was there—" he rose and pointed to a nearby tree—"hauling in the rope. When they finally reached the surface, Ginerva wrapped the unconscious boy in blankets. The photographer went on ahead to alert the police, and in a moving and very dramatic moment, Ginerva handed the distraught mother her lost son."

"You're a hero, Hilly," Norman observed.

"They didn't even mention your name," Leah said indignantly.

"I hope they don't," I told them. "My friends at St. Timothy's would think I had gone bananas."

"This should really put you in good," Norman pointed out.

"What is important, Norm," I said. "Is that by eleven o'clock tonight Ginerva and the Society will have received national attention on prime time. And Foreman knows the guy responsible."

"And you'll be his golden boy," Leah said.

"I intend to make sure."

"But you're forgetting Ginerva," Leah said. "Now what do you think of her?"

"I admit I'm impressed."

She stopped and looked at me, outraged. "Is that all you are, impressed? Hilly, she led you to a remote spot in the woods and found the child at the bottom of a well which has been abandoned for a century! No one helped her! Hundreds had been looking for the boy for two days! There were no clues—nothing! And you say all this only leaves you 'impressed'?"

"Okay. Maybe she has ESP, maybe she's a mystic," I said. "But this is not unusual, Leah. There have been cases where mystics have found bodies of people murdered after the police had been looking for months. Last summer there was that case in Ohio—"

"Hilly, let me ask you something?" Leah broke in impatiently. "You told us how Ginerva began screaming and pointing but there was nothing there. When you bent down to pick her up and go back to the car you heard the little boy's cry. Were you only 'impressed' at that moment?"

They both looked at me. For a moment I was back in the darkness of the well, the little boy's chilled body next to mine, my legs quivering with fatigue, braced against the side of the wall. . . .

"The truth, Hilly," Leah insisted. "What did you think?"

"Because she found the kid does not prove, at least to me, that she had a confrontation with God and that he selected her as his messenger to warn the world the Last Day is coming."

(235)

Leah groaned. "What more does this woman have to do to convince you, Hilly?"

I hugged her. "Wipe away those freckles around your nose."

We were walking across the hospital's parking lot to the chief's car. As we came up, I saw the young volunteer fireman who was our driver casually inspecting a bone-white steer's skull.

"They fix you up okay?" he asked cheerfully.

Leah made a face. "What's that?"

"Cattle skull," he explained. "One of the boys dropped it off on his way home. I'm gonna clean it up and hang it over my new garage for good luck. It certainly comes from a lucky place."

"Where's that?" Turner asked.

He nodded to me. "Where your friend brought the kid out of the well. It was only a few feet away, stuck in some huckleberry vines. Probably been there for years."

I suddenly remembered what she had cried: *"Get the little boy in the hole! In the deep dark hole by the skull with horns!"*

"Hilly, are you all right," Leah asked anxiously. "Don't you feel well?"

"I guess the whole day is finally catching up with me," I said.

The following morning, Foreman ordered me to join him immediately at the tour headquarters in New York City. The child-in-the-well story was producing an avalanche of publicity, and he wanted to get the tour started as soon as possible.

BOOK THREE

THE
TOUR

13

Planning the Tour

The offices of the national tour were on the two upper floors of a remodeled building on West Fortieth Street, opposite the New York Public Library and Bryant Park. The gold letters on the front door said Foreman Associates, but nothing about Ginerva. On each floor Foreman gave me a tour of the departments and a glowing introduction as his chief assistant. I had the sense of many insects working industriously in burrows that had deep carpeting, muted lights, and gracious eighteenth century prints on the wall. There were teams bent over drafting boards, desks, easels, and layout tables, studying films or making mock-up posters and broadsides. Some were Orientals, all were neatly dressed, no one was in shirtsleeves or jeans. I thought I recognized a few from the motherhouse.

"Are they all from the motherhouse, Dave?" I asked.

"I only started recruiting these teams during the past several months," he replied, "but everyone is dedicated to a simple purpose: making this tour a tremendous success."

"It appears you have a lot of faith in this tour," I observed.

"More than you will ever know, Hilly," he said, with a slight smile.

At the end of the corridor a small circular iron stairway led to offices on the next floor. One had a glass wall that provided a glorious view of the library, Fifth Avenue, and Bryant Park.

"This is my office," he explained. " It was once an artist's studio.

When I had the building redone, I told the architect, under penalty of death, not to touch one pane of glass." He said almost lovingly, "Isn't it a wonderful view? It makes you feel as if you own the whole island."

On the wall was a blowup of a huge crowd in an auditorium; a large banner hung from an upper tier: SOCIETY OF THE CHOSEN.

"Minneapolis, three years ago," he said proudly. "Over a thousand young people waited all night to get in." He pointed across the room to several other framed photographs of various rallies. "That's when we were first starting. Look at those young faces! Completely captivated by Ginerva. Well, here's your office."

The adjacent office that he said was mine was smaller, but tastefully furnished. Two large windows overlooked the park, there was a large and expensive-looking desk with a pile of catalogues and estimates, a couch, layout table, typewriter, and a machine with a console that I assumed was for viewing films.

"That's our Steenbeck," he explained. "We'll use it to view footage on our commercials."

"There's one more," he said, opening a door.

This room was long and narrow, with several plush chairs, a screen at one end, a projector at the other.

"This is where the agency people will show us our TV spots and slides."

Back in my office, he sat on the couch and waved me to the chair behind the cluttered desk.

"All that stuff on your desk has to do with slides, posters, clips, charts, blowups, 3Ms, hot press pasteups, and countless other things necessary for a top-flight promotion campaign. On the top of the file you will find a detailed memorandum I prepared for you, outlining my thoughts." He leaned slightly forward. "I am confident, Hilly, that between us we can put on a campaign and tour which will make Ginerva the most talked about woman in America!" He paused, then added: "And the Society of the Chosen one of the most powerful religious groups in the country."

In his restless way, he suddenly jumped up and moved to the window. He was silent for a moment, then without turning around, said softly, "Come here for a moment."

When I joined him, he pointed down at bustling Fifth Avenue. "Down there and in other cities, towns, and villages across the country are millions of young people, disillusioned, growing more distrustful, more passive, more cynical every hour of every day because of what they hear and what they see. I guess it's all because of what Vietnam and Watergate did to us. But whatever the cause, they are deserting formal religion by the thousands every year. Look at the seminaries. Convents. They are empty, or have only a few students left. Churches and temples are being sold because their people no longer attend services. Why? The answer is they are bored with the same old hymns, the same old sermons. They want a religion with some fire, a challenge, something to do with life and filled with action—even something to die for." He held up a protesting hand. "Please don't think I'm being melodramatic, but these are facts—facts confirmed by respectable polls. And who took these polls? The various religions! They had to find out why their pews were empty every Sunday, why the collection baskets gave the sound of metal, not bills."

We walked back across the room, his arm now around my shoulder. "There's a tremendous void out there, Hilly," he said as we sat down, "and I intend to fill it with followers of Ginerva in the Society of the Chosen. I intend to put on rallies across this country which will make Billy Graham's look like storefront church meetings." He pointed to the mound on my desk. "In my memo you will see I plan to use television, radio, and the media. I have a tentative budget of over three million."

I gasped involuntarily. "Three million!"

"I have decided that God can be merchandised like soap, cereal, or dog food," he said easily. "Another analogy would be Detroit. Through advertising and image making Detroit has made its cars almost living members of the American family. Why can't Jesus Christ be sold the same way as the latest Chevy, Ford, or Chrysler? Please don't think I'm sacrilegious! The insignificant knowledge I have of selling an American product has convinced me that our campaign is the only way we're going to put Ginerva and the Society of the Chosen into the homes and hearts of every American family during this tour. I want the package-goods principles applied to Her Holiness and particularly to the Society of the Chosen. We will sell an ethical product; we will encourage people to enter into a personal relationship with Christ through the message his Almighty Father gave to Ginerva. To do this, I want to put our blessed bucks into a national campaign for this tour, complete with television commercials, newspaper blurbs, billboards, radio spots—something never attempted before by an evangelical organization. I have many other ideas I want us to work on together, but they can wait until we get this tour off the ground."

"I don't know much about television, Dave, but I understand it can be terribly expensive."

"Only when you get into it, Hilly, will you realize how expensive it really is," he said wryly.

"Prime time on a national network is from sixty thousand to two hundred thousand dollars a minute, plus the cost of producing the commercial."

I could only repeat, "For *one* minute!"

"Oh, yes," he said. "*One* minute. My meetings with agency people over the last several weeks have given me a tentative idea of what this campaign will cost. Among the things I want you to plan is a good fiery commercial for the top shows, which will run about a hundred and twenty-five thousand."

He seemed pleased at the dazed look on my face.

"However, for that money we will reach between forty and fifty million viewers. If we can get through to only one percent, we will have reached five hundred thousand!" Now there was a slight flush in his cheeks and his dark eyes glowed with an inner fire. "Just imagine if you will, Hilly, a recruiting drive for the Society, using those top spots. There is no doubt we will have a tremendous impact on the American home! We will get recruits pouring into the Society of the Chosen by the hundreds of thousands! But it will be up to you to write and produce a commercial—with an agency, of course—that, as I said, will kick the American family collectively in the guts as they sit in their living rooms watching the tube."

He sat there for a moment, then slapped his hands together and said crisply: "Well, that's the general idea. Now as to your schedule. I suggest you run back to the motherhouse whenever you wish and see how Brother Turner and Sister Butler are doing with their new staff. When you feel *The Call* is in good hands, bring Sister Butler and Brother Turner down here to work with you." He smiled. "I certainly don't intend to break up a winning team."

He handed me a card. "This is for the garage down the street, where there is a car in your name. I have also arranged a number of credit cards for you. We are staying at the Hotel Lafayette on Sixty-first Street just off Fifth. You have a suite, and if you need anything, there are any number of fine men's shops on Madison Avenue. Open an account with any one. Now my office is next door, any questions, just drop in."

"There is one question, Dave," I said. "Exactly what is our theme for the expansion of the Society?"

"To put America back on an even keel," he said dramatically. "To show our people—both young and old—how to right the wrongs going on in this country. We can only do that, Hilly, by making certain people aware of our voice and our power. As of now, America is going down the drain, physically, spiritually, and mentally. Take a look at what is happening to us—to our cities! We're captives of crime! Of narcotics! Of official corruption and the incompetence of our leaders! We're drifting toward inevitable destruction! We need a national backbone again! We need people in power who can make decisions, who can organize the citizens of this country and show them how to stand once again on their own two feet! If possible, build new jails, but get the thugs off the streets! Bring back the death sentence! Put the fear of God in dope pushers!" His voice rose. "We must get across to this country the message God gave to Ginerva! Time is running out for all of us! Doomsday is near! The world will vanish in God's terrifying Sea of Flame if it doesn't listen to the message Ginerva brings from the Lord! And we must force the world to listen, Hilly—that is our theme!"

Perhaps it was the way the light came through the drapes or the shadows in the room, but for a brief moment Foreman looked evil. Not crooked—evil.

Then suddenly he changed emotions like a chameleon changes colors; he was again the brisk business executive. "So much for theology. Now let's get back to business. What you should do is absorb that stuff on your desk. Read my memo and then come in and we'll talk some more."

I pointed out, "I really don't know too much about television or advertising, Dave."

He paused at the door. "You can write, and you have a keen sense of promotion and publicity, Hilly. You proved that with the boy in the hospital and that perfectly wonderful job you did for us with that little lost boy. The revised *Call* is superb. This tour needs your talents. Don't worry about advertising and television. Money talks in both those fields—and we have enough to keep talking for a long time. If three million isn't enough, we'll double our budget." He opened the door. "Remember what I said. A good promotion campaign can sell anything—dog food, deodorant—even God."

When the door clicked behind him, I swung around in the swivel chair and looked out over Bryant Park. It had been a busy few weeks. Day after day the story of the little boy in the well had been told again and again on television and in newspapers. Although Ginerva refused to be interviewed, Foreman, at my suggestion, met the press camped outside the gates of the motherhouse twice a day. European newspapers and television reporters interviewed him on the phone or assigned stringers. Stafford's dramatic picture of Ginerva and the child was on page one of the *Daily News* and distributed nationally by the wire services. When I saw how Foreman liked the publicity, I made him the spokesman whenever it was possible and played up Stafford as the hero. He would be leaving shortly and could use the help in pulling off his dream, his own photographic service.

After the first wave of national publicity, Foreman insisted the tour had to begin at once and that I was to join him immediately at tour headquarters in Manhattan. A bright young Disciple, formerly a college journalism student, who had been recommended by Norman, was appointed the new editor, along with a staff. When I showed Foreman the slick paper page-proofs of the new *Call*, I knew I had gained still another foothold on his confidence.

But I was troubled because I had not seen Ginerva since that last wild scene in the forest by the well. I had hinted, then bluntly requested I be permitted to talk to her, but Foreman gently advised me that Ginerva was in "constant meditation" preparing for the tour and could not be disturbed. He was lying, of course, but there was nothing I could do.

The incident had left me with still more unanswered questions about her. I could not deny some strange power had led her to the well and the child. But as I had told Leah, newspaper reference rooms are filled with files of similar unexplained cases. Did Ginerva possess ESP? Was she a mystic? I didn't know. But this feat, while impressive, still had not convinced me she had been confronted by the Almighty. Leah, of course, angrily denounced me as she pointed out my own experiences with Ginerva, the overnight recovery of the child in the hospital, and this latest "miracle."

"My God, Hilly," she cried, "what more evidence do you want?"

I replied that while I was impressed by Ginerva, I still didn't intend to genuflect.

Hour after hour, while alone or dozing off to sleep at night, I had reviewed that scene by the well and later crossing the meadow. Obviously "Peter" in Idaho was a child, but whose—Ginerva's? And who was Aunt Clem?

A telephone suddenly came to life, and a hearty voice with a ready sales pitch identified himself as a representative of a slide company in Queens.

"Brother Foreman suggested a few days ago that I contact you this week to see if—"

I broke in, trying to sound very professional. "Why don't you call me next week? I'm just starting to pull things together."

The hell I am, I told the dead phone. What I don't know about this job would fill a warehouse, but just give me some time and I will make the name of Ginerva a household word and the ranks of the Society of the Chosen will be filled with recruits from the east to the west coast. . . .

Anything to hang that son of a bitch Foreman and his bully boy, Russell.

And Ginerva? I didn't know. . . .

I literally devoured Foreman's memorandum, which curiously did not go into detail but reiterated what he had said about mounting a media campaign with a strong television commercial for prime time shows. There was also a tentative route for the tour, beginning in the Midwest, then on to the South, and across to San Francisco, and finally ending with a major rally to be held in the Giants' stadium in New Jersey.

After finishing Foreman's memo, I moved in on the pile of brochures, catalogues, pamphlets, and presentations for slides, posters, and commercials. They were more earthy; typical Madison Avenue hyperbole, dollars and cents. A few days later, I sat down with Foreman.

"My orders to you, Hilly," he said, "are very simple. My memo outlined the possible route for the tour. I want you to plan and put into execution the media campaign. Give me ideas for posters, publicity, write a TV commercial—anything we can do to make this tour an incredible success."

"Will we be aiming only for the young?" I asked.

"While they are our primary target," he replied, "by no means leave out the mature adult or the elderly. We can find room in the Society for *all* followers of Ginerva."

Back in my office, I began making notes, then moved to the typewriter. I first selected our audiences; the Young, and Middle America.

We could capture Middle America through its fear: fear of this uncertain world, fear of the approaching Judgment Day, fear that Ginerva is really an instrument of God and that not to listen or follow her will mean eternal damnation.

Then our major target: the Young. Wondering what to do? Where to go? Who to follow? What to believe in?

We could win them by Ginerva's challenge to join her and straighten out the reeling world. We would appeal to the ideals of youth—so quickly smothered by cynicism and experience—to join the Society of the Chosen and under its banner stamp out corruption, evil, war. In this campaign there would be only youth, an illusion of a world in which no one grew old. Their leader was young, vibrant, beautiful, and personally selected by God.

Then came the planning of the tour. The first thing I did was order a blowup of the map of the country, large enough to cover one wall. On this I listed the name, address, and telephone number of every *Call* correspondent. I did the same with the Society's state Team Leaders, which Norman and Leah had copied from the master file in the library. I then divided the route of the national tour into sections on the map, labeling them A, B, C, D, and so on.

Each section was controlled by what I called a "Tour Guide Group." These were composed of the state Team Leaders with several of the correspondents as assistants. These groups operated from a communication headquarters within their section, with each member given a specific assignment: newspapers; radio; television; clergymen; religious organizations; municipal departments for permits and permissions; halls, auditoriums, and parks; local entertainment; boards of education; PTAs and women's clubs. One of their tasks was to determine if opposition to Ginerva and the Society of the Chosen was being organized in their locality, and if so, what was its strength and who were its leaders.

The next step was to divide the large sections into smaller divisions. Each member would also be given a specific assignment to work with village, town, city, and county newspapers, radio and television stations, church leaders, religious groups, municipal departments, and local businessmen. Thus the smaller groups would call on their more knowledgeable counterparts in the city for their advice, suggestions, authorization for major decisions, and financial assistance.

All groups, big and small, were to be supplied with large quantities of posters, broadsides, boilerplate—prepared material on the tour—tapes for radio, booklets for recruiting, and, most important, tickets for the rallies.

My plan was to distribute the tickets through coupons in newspaper ads, on radio and TV spots, and by Disciples distributing them at suburban shopping malls. On the theory that everyone loves free entertainment, I outlined a separate program for all groups in which they were urged to enlist the best of the local talent such as singing groups, award-winning marching bands, squads of cheerleaders, and if possible to recruit the season's top high school athlete to lead the opening prayer.

I also made a rough design for a large button, a white background with letters in fire-engine red: DOOMSDAY IS COMING! BE SAVED AS GINERVA'S CHOSEN!

My plan was to have Disciples across the country distribute the buttons to elementary and high schools, Sunday schools, at athletic events, shopping centers, theatres, town meetings, supermarkets, even at loading stations for school buses—anyplace the public could be encountered.

It was obvious the success of the whole campaign depended on this network of teams, large and small. On the map tacked to the wall, this national organization looked like huge wheels in each state; the main Tour Guide Groups as the hubs, with spokes attaching them to the smaller outlying organizations.

On an impulse I labeled it "Ginerva's Wheel of God."

I never dreamed that this foolish label would eventually become the keystone of a religious fervor that would shake this country as never before. But that was long after the days I spent in this office, idly watching the girls walking through Bryant Park, as I listened on the phone to some fanatic in a midwestern farming area promise me fervently that every man, woman, and child in his county would wear a "Doomsday Button," that every telephone pole would have a Ginerva poster and every important advertiser would be looking over the shoulder of his local editor to make sure he gave ample coverage to our glorious rally. . . .

I typed the presentation, read it with a great deal of revulsion and disgust, then gave it to Foreman.

It was our routine to meet in the hotel lobby at eight every morning and be driven to tour headquarters in Foreman's limousine with that goon, Andrew, acting as chauffeur. On what had been a folding bar in the back seat were warm biscuits, jam, butter, and a silver service of coffepot, creamer, and two cups. As the car moved into the heavy Fifth Avenue traffic, Foreman would pour me a cup of coffee, while I buttered a biscuit.

The morning after I had given him the presentation, I asked: "Do you see any holes in it?"

"Not a one," was his prompt answer. "Will you get on to the television commercial spot now?"

"Shake them up, Hilly," he said briskly "As I said, kick them in the guts. Leave them frightened and uneasy. No angels playing harps and heavenly choirs. Anything else?"

"Is there any doubt Ginerva will appear at every rally?"

He looked at me with a frown. "Why, no. Why would you ask that?"

"She seemed so distraught when the child was found, I thought the tour might be too much for her."

"I can guarantee you that Ginerva will appear at every rally, Hilly," he said evenly. "Is that satisfactory?"

"Of course," I said, wanting to spit in his calm handsome face.

During the next few days, I wrote the tour's commercial. Before me on my desk is a worn, much folded copy of the proof of that script. An enthusiastic agency man had written across the top: "The first spectacular live-action television commercial that will kick off the massive campaign by the Society of the Chosen, which we estimate will reach more than two hundred million people."

The script was all fire and brimstone, picturing terrorized crowds milling about a city street with a background of buildings in flames. In the distance, like molten lava, the Sea of Flame relentlessly advanced toward the camera. Of course, the dialogue reminded the viewers they had turned their backs on Ginerva and her divine message. Then a cut to a stock filmshot of a rally, with the name, telephone number, and street address to be filled in by the affiliate where free tickets to the rally could be obtained, followed by a stirring fadeout into flames, moaning winds, crashing thunder, and cries of "Ginerva Save Us."

Trite? Ludicrous? Even obscene? Of course it was all of that and more—on paper. But translated into a visual with sound effects and that voice of doom, the commercial stopped most viewers from turning the dial. It was similar to passing the scene of a terrible highway accident. Cars creep by, occupants turn away, but only after they have a glimpse of the crushed bodies, the spilled blood and twisted steel.

At the peak of our national drive, a Gallup poll revealed the shocking fact that millions of impressionable Americans were stirred emotionally by my manufactured bit of tripe that leaped out at them while they were eating dinner, waiting for the news, or during the commercial break of their favorite show.

The producer and the star of one hit TV show threatened to walk off the set unless our commercial was withdrawn. They claimed a survey showed some viewers were so upset they lost the continuity of the action.

This commercial was Foreman's favorite. He reviewed it with me and the agency people over and over, supplying suggestions or additions until he was satisfied. I then redid the audio part for a radio commercial, adding more terrifying sound effects and dialogue. During the tour, there was no escape for radio listeners; it battered them day and night, state to state, coast to coast. It was particularly effective in the rural areas—it brought the fearful out in droves. . . .

As I got deeper and deeper into the planning of the tour, I was amazed to discover that an enormous fear of the unknown existed among Americans, young and old, so strong it chilled their hearts and dulled their common sense. From the inner cities to Park Avenue, they were eager to believe in just about anything that promised to save them from the angry God's destruction of the world they were beginning to believe was near at hand.

I also learned from my team workers that anti-Ginerva groups were beginning to organize, particularly in the conservative Midwest. They were composed mostly of parents who had seen their children vanish into the Society or had found them on street corners selling flowers and soliciting contributions. In the beginning they had hired deprogrammers who kidnapped their sons or daughters, but when the courts sent some parents to jail, they began to organize in frustration and anger. Team workers reported they were becoming increasingly aggressive, with several arrested in one city after they fought both police and the Angels at a rally.

When I first arrived, Foreman had held early daily conferences with the staff. Then, from time to time, he began to leave early, asking me to take over, or he would not show up, explaining he had an important outside appointment. Finally, he would not appear in the morning for our trip downtown, but our hard-faced driver, Brother Andrew, would hand me Foreman's note requesting me to conduct the conferences and report to him later. The staff soon accepted that I was in command. One morning, Foreman unexpectedly walked into a morning meeting after it began, but sat off to one side, never issuing an order or countermanding one of mine. If someone turned to him, he would gesture impatiently in my direction.

When we left, he said quietly, "I'm glad to see that you have taken over so efficiently, Hilly."

While this was going on, I never missed an opportunity to search his desk, files, closet, or even his wastepaper baskets when I was sure he would be gone for some time. One morning he gave me his hotel room key and asked me to bring down his attaché case; I got the extra key from the room clerk and kept it. Unfortunately, I didn't find anything; either he was scrupulously clean, or very very careful. . . .

There was just so much time I could spend at the tour office before reaching the point of exploding with rage and frustration as this sinister scam I was helping to plan slowly came to life. There were moments when I asked myself if it would be better to sabotage the tour rather than make contributions, but common sense pointed out that Foreman would go on despite any obstacles. Only the original strategy would work: win his confidence to such a degree I would be indispensable to whatever he had in mind for the future of the Society of the Chosen.

Usually I had a sandwich for lunch, then spent some time leisurely exploring the New York Public Library, viewing its exhibits, sampling the index cards, skimming through the always fascinating *Official Records of the Civil War*, or reading the latest book on the Revolution. I also got to know the second-floor stack of phone booths, probably the last in Manhattan not ripped off by junkies.

One day, I impulsively called Butler. All I got was an answering service. After a third unsuccessful call, I demanded the service get in touch with Butler wherever he was and have him call me back at the booth.

It took so long, a suspicious guard demanded to know what I was doing. I finally convinced him I wasn't a bookmaker when the phone rang. It was Butler calling from Washington, where his play was preparing to open at the Kennedy Center.

He sounded harassed, upset. A rush of words revealed that his female lead had argued with her lover and was ready to walk out, his writers were still reworking the second act, and the lyricist was—

I couldn't take anymore. "Sir Edward, I don't give a good goddam about your play!" I shouted into the phone. "I called to simply let you know I'm working with Foreman! In Manhattan! On Ginerva's Tour!"

"Foreman?" he repeated slowly.

"David Foreman," I bellowed. "Ginerva's overseer! The guy we're after!"

There was a pause, as if he was gathering himself together.

"Why, that's fine, Hilly," he said at last. "That's very good. How is Leah?"

"There's nothing wrong with her, Sir Edward," I told him, "but what about your investigators? Have they found out anything? Is there anything I should know? What about the suicides of those two kids? And the plaque bank on Little Cat? Ginerva's Evangelical Fund?"

Another long pause.

"Frankly, Hilly," he said at last, "I haven't been in touch with them lately. This show is really something. We open tomorrow night and—"

I hung up. Now I knew what Leah was trying to tell me. For Sir Edward Butler, nothing mattered, family, self, money—only the play.

While the guard slowly paced up and down the corridor trying not to show he was still keeping me in view from the corner of his eye, I decided to phone *The Call* office. Before he identified himself, I recognized the voice:

"Brother Russell speaking. . . ."

I hung up.

When we met in the hotel lobby the following morning, I told Foreman that instead of going downtown I intended to drive to the motherhouse and spend a few days helping Leah, Norman, and the new staff finish up the next edition of *The Call*; most of the issue was to be devoted to the lost child incident. He surprised me by announcing that we would ride together in the limousine. He had important matters to attend to and we could return within the week.

On the ride to Westchester, Foreman was unusually quiet, even grim, I thought. His replies to my few questions were perfunctory. At the motherhouse, I bounded upstairs and into *The Call* office. The young owl-eyed editor and his staff looked up in surprise. Leah and Turner were seated off to one side of the room. They appeared tan and fit, as if they had been working outdoors.

"Hilly!" Turner called out.

"Just a routine visit," I announced cheerfully. "Brother Foreman is pleased with all of you, and I am only here to give you a hand."

"We have almost all the pages prepared," the editor proudly announced, handing me several layouts.

"Excellent," I said. "I'll go over them with Brother Turner and

(250)

Sister Butler, whose first assignment is to join me in a cup of coffee at the cafeteria."

By the time we had reached our favorite bench, hidden by a screen of bushes, Leah and Norman were visibly excited.

"Where were you, Hilly?" Turner burst out. "We've been on pins and needles for days."

"I got here as soon as I heard Russell answering the phone in the office," I told them. "What is he—"

"Forget Russell for now," Norman said, waving his hand, "Leah has something big!"

"The whole thing sounds like a bad morality play," Leah said. "It concerns Margo. Norman and I have been wondering how to get to you. Since she first came to the dorm, Margo has always asked me for advice about trivial things or stopped me in the corridor to talk. She seemed lost and eager to make a friend. I told you she has a talent for art, and she would show me what she had sketched. For the past week she stayed in her room. The Dorm Leader said she had the flu and had requested to move in with me for a few days. Of course I said yes, and we've been sharing my room. She seemed weak and was constantly throwing up. I urged her to have the Dorm Leader call a doctor, but she refused. One night I woke up to find her on the verge of hysterics and crying. Finally she told me what had happened to her—"

Norman put in eagerly, "You won't believe this, Hilly."

Leah went on, "As we know, Margo had been working downtown on the tour with Foreman, doing posters. One night, when she missed the bus that takes the kids from the city to here, Foreman asked her to stay over. Foreman insisted she have a drink with him. I believe her when she insists she never had anything stronger than Coke. She said Foreman kept filling her glass. She became woozy and remembers getting in a cab and entering a room. She woke up in bed with Foreman. She said she became hysterical, but he calmed her down with all kinds of promises; including marriage and how they would work together for the glory of Ginerva and the Society of the Chosen. When she told him she wanted to leave, he threatened to turn her over to Russell, who would make her into a good girl if she didn't follow orders. She told me she was terrified and did what he told her to do." Leah looked at me. "Margo told me she is pregnant."

Norman quickly asked, "Wouldn't it be a criminal offense if Foreman sexually abused a Disciple, Hilly?"

"True. But this isn't the Victorian Age," I pointed out. "It's Foreman's word against her charges. He can even cry blackmail. Margo's over twenty-one."

"She's sixteen, Hilly," Leah said bitterly. "A kid who ran away from

(251)

a village in Montana that's so small it consists of a gasoline pump and a diner."

Sixteen!

"She only had a few dollars when she reached the Port Authority Bus Terminal," Leah continued. "She took a room in a hotel off Times Square and ran out, leaving her luggage, after the room clerk tried to lock her in a closet. She met some Disciples collecting on Fifth Avenue and they brought her up here. Fortunately, she had just started her training program on Long Island when a Team Leader noticed her sketching and had her do posters for the rest of the time. As I told you, she first came to Foreman's attention when he saw her watercolor of the motherhouse now hanging in the dorm."

"What about her parents?"

"Her mother is dead, her father is a high school art teacher. I begged her to contact him, but she's afraid—not of her father but of Foreman."

Turner prompted: "Tell Hilly why she's afraid of Foreman."

"When she told Foreman she was pregnant," Leah continued, "he laughed it off and told her to go to an abortion clinic. When she refused he slapped her—hard enough to cut the inside of her mouth —and told her that if she didn't do what he told her, he would turn her over to Russell, who would take her to the clinic. When she told me this, I was so furious I told Norm I was going to see Her Holiness, guard or no guard."

"*You* were going to see Ginerva?"

"I almost had to tie her down while I talked some sense into her," Turner said. "Can you imagine what would have happened if she tried to push her way past that guard?"

"Thank God you didn't try it, Leah," I said.

"But somebody has to tell her!" Leah protested. "I am sure Ginerva does not know what is going on here."

"Maybe she doesn't, but then again maybe she does," I told her. "Now what about Margo?"

"Leah's been up with her nearly every night," Norman said. "She keeps crying, walking the floor, and refusing to eat or sleep."

"Why didn't you call me?" I asked.

"*Call you!*" Turner exploded. "Nobody is allowed to make any more outside calls unless they are approved by Russell! He's been over us like a blanket!"

"It started the day after you left," Leah explained. "He came to the office early in the morning and ordered all of us out on the lawn to join his physical fitness program. 'The body is God's temple,' he kept saying."

"And Matthew and his dog kept riding around us like Indians

(252)

ringing a wagon train," Turner interjected.

"Hundreds of Disciples were out there," Leah went on, "and we did exercises from six to eight."

"Pushups, jumping jacks—it was horrible," Turner said. "Some of the kids were so beat they couldn't walk."

"You two don't look the worse for it," I observed.

"No one complained about the exercises," Leah said, "that was great. We all had a lot of fun. But the exercises were only the beginning. The next day, Singleton, your wild man from Staten Island, appeared to give us an interminable lecture on the scriptures. After the lecture, we had hymn singing; that went on for another hour. Finally Russell marched us to the cafeteria. After breakfast, he escorted us unit by unit to whatever job we were doing."

"It reminded me of one of the Nazi documentaries you see on television," Turner said. "All we needed were khaki shorts and songs about Deutschland."

"Did anyone do anything about it?"

"Do what?" Turner asked. "They accept regimentation as they accept breathing. Now it's routine." He looked at Leah. "How about those Angels? Weren't they something, Leah?"

"They never smile, never talk—they're Russell's private army," Turner observed. "I always had the feeling that if Russell told one of them to slice me up into little pieces, he would do it without question."

"Didn't anyone protest about this?"

"No one. We exercised, marched, and sang, and did everything Russell told us to do."

"What did Russell do at *The Call* office?"

"He was there every day, checking all the copy that went into the paper. The new kid you made editor once asked him if that was necessary, and Russell simply gave him a look. The kid never said another word."

"Did Russell do anything besides read copy?"

"Yeah. Keep his eye on Leah," Turner said bluntly. "And that *really* worried me."

Leah reached over and squeezed his hand. "I don't know what I would have done if Norm hadn't been there."

"A few times after the others had left, he told me I could go," Turner said, "but I stayed. Russell just sat there and glared at me. But it was Troy who rode up like the cavalry."

"Troy? What did he do?"

Turner said, "After Russell made the rule that no one—including me—could leave the grounds or make an outside phone call without his permission, I began to get desperate. One day I met Troy on the grounds and told him what was happening. After that, when Russell dismissed the rest of the staff in the afternoon, Troy dropped by and told Russell you had asked him to go over the picture layouts. Well, he made a big production of redoing them, selecting other pictures, rewriting the captions, you know, just stalling. Finally late one afternoon Russell blew up, and I thought he was going to throw Troy down the stairs, but the guy stood up to him. After that Russell didn't come around anymore, but Troy warned us to watch our step."

"Perhaps that is why Foreman came back," I said. "He looked as if something was on his mind."

Leah's eyes widened. "Foreman is back here—at the motherhouse?"

"We drove up together. He said he's staying a few days and then we are to drive back."

"We can't wait, Hilly," Leah said quickly. "We have to help that girl."

"If she's sixteen, that means Foreman committed statutory rape, a felony," I told them. "But we still have to produce a case no district attorney can brush off. Now I'm not a lawyer, but so far, in my opinion, Margo's story lacks corroborative evidence."

"But she's the victim, Hilly!" Leah said indignantly. "What more does she have to give us?"

"I would think, the name of the hotel where Foreman took her."

"I never asked her that," Leah said.

"Does she know what name he registered under? Can she describe the interior of the room? All that can be important."

Leah looked dubious. "I will have to ask her, Hilly."

"Leah, can you get her to talk to *me*?"

Almost simultaneously, they both said, "In the dorm?"

"Of course not. Leah, you must talk her into meeting me outside. She must hate Foreman enough to go for it."

"Suppose I do convince her, what then?"

"When we get back to *The Call* office," I told her, "I will drive to the Royal Coachman and call the detective agency your father hired. He promised they would do anything I asked. We can get out of here tonight with Margo in the van. Before the guard at the gate realizes what is happening, we will be down the highway, meet the detectives, and turn Margo over to them. They will take her statement, check out the other evidence, and then turn the case over to the district attorney. They can bring down her father from Montana. It will be impossible for any DA to brush this one off. Also, the publicity will be devastating. It's certain to be page one—an attractive country girl raped by the leader of a nationally known and controversial cult!"

"And Her Holiness?" Leah asked in a small voice. "Where does this leave her?"

"Let's take one step at a time, Leah," I advised her. "The district attorney might suddenly discover that the Society of the Chosen is an attractive target, despite its First Amendment protection. He can't be accused of prosecuting religion. He will have a defendant charged with sexually assaulting a juvenile. His investigators could use this charge to subpoena the books and records of the Society. Leah, what you have given us could be the beginning of the end of this whole setup!"

"Hilly, I shudder for that poor girl," she said. "All the horrible publicity, her father brought here and being told what happened to his daughter. It's sickening!"

"What would you rather do?" I asked her, "turn this sixteen-year-old girl over to Russell? And let Foreman get away with it?"

It was unfair boxing her in like this, but there was no other way.

"No, I guess not," she said slowly. "I'll talk to her now."

We met again after dinner. "It took some talking, Hilly," Leah said. "But I convinced her to see you tonight. I asked her if she recalls anything about the hotel where he took her, but she can't. Maybe she's too frightened."

"Doesn't she know in what part of the city the hotel was located? Midtown? Uptown? What the outside looked like?"

Leah shook her head. "I talked to her for hours, but there is one thing I am sure of—she is frightened to death of Russell. All I have to do is mention his name and she literally trembles."

"What about Foreman? What does she say about him?"

"From what I can get out of her he's a Jekyll-and-Hyde character. She says he can suddenly break into a rage, threatening her with all kinds of things if she doesn't do as he says, and in the next minute he is very calmly assuring her she will be made the tour's director of art."

"Is she willing to give a statement to the detectives?"

"Hilly, Margo is a frightened sixteen-year-old girl who can't believe this is happening to her," Leah said wearily. "I'm sure she will do anything we tell her to do. When I mentioned her father, she broke down. She even talked suicide, but I believe it's only hysteria." She frowned. "Still, there is something not right with this whole messy business. . . ."

Norman and I looked at her in surprise. "Why do you say that, Leah?" I asked.

"I don't have anything tangible. Call it a hunch or instinct, but Margo appears to me to be holding back something."

"About what?"

"Again, I don't know," she said with an edge of impatience in her voice. "But it might be something connected with Russell. As I said, when his name comes up she actually shakes as if she had a fever."

"So do I," I said.

Turner added, "All he has to do is look at me and I fall apart."

"It's more than that," she said stubbornly. "When I asked her if Russell had harmed her in any way, she ran to the bathroom and stayed there for a long time. I could hear her throwing up."

Norman said wonderingly, "Is it possible both of them—?"

"I'll find out tonight," I said.

On the way back to the office, Norman whispered to me that the day before had been Leah's birthday—twenty-three.

The grounds of the motherhouse were being continually maintained by a corps of Disciples, but despite their work an occasional dandelion defiantly poked up its yellow head. I plucked the only one I could find and gave it to Leah.

"When we get out of this," I told her, "I'll make it roses."

This was our plan: Leah would bring Margo to meet me in the woods behind the dorm. It was difficult to estimate how long it would take us to walk from *The Call* office to the dorm. Both buildings were at extreme ends of the estate. An important and dangerous obstacle was Matthew and his dog, who regularly patrolled the grounds at night. To avoid them we would have to bypass the paths and drives and make our way back through the shrubs and bushes. I dreaded thinking of the journey when we would be burdened with a weak, frightened girl. In the meantime, Norman would have the van ready. It looked like a long, tense night. I never suspected how long . . . .

I called the head of Butler's private detective agency and outlined my plan. The agency head was eager to help, and we arranged a rendezvous on the highway, a few miles from the motherhouse. There would be two detectives, one a former policewoman who would care for Margo, and a stenographer to take down her statement. I told them that if we did not arrive at the meeting place by dawn, they were to assume the plan had fallen apart and could leave.

I was full of great expectations. If all went well, this could be the beginning of the end for Foreman. I would no longer have the continually revolting chore of preparing and promoting the tour. No district attorney could ignore Margo's sworn statement and the corroborative evidence produced by Butler's detectives; he would be forced to present the case to the grand jury. I hoped other law enforcement agencies would step in. I was certain Tura and Troy would turn state's evidence rather than go to jail to protect Foreman, Russell, and the Society of the Chosen.

As a witness before a grand jury, Ginerva would be vulnerable. The DA's questions would force her to disclose her real name and background. But the questions gnawed at me. Would all this provide the answers? How did she cure my limp? Find the lost child in a well? Cure a young woman of leukemia? And why had she called out the names of Peter and Aunt Clem? Who were they? What secret was she hiding that only Foreman knew?

Ginerva's face was continually before me. Her beautiful face glowing with that strange light on the stage in San Francisco. Her face frozen with fear as she shrank back when the child on the stretcher was wheeled before her for the Blessing of the Sick. Her dazed eyes looking into something only she could see as we crossed that sunny meadow.

Ginerva had something locked deep inside. A private fear? An unspeakable secret? A deep, shattering grief? Whatever it was, she had been able to control it by drawing on an inner strength that at times was not enough. Then something else had taken over. Guessing what it could be only left me frustrated and bewildered.

I doubted that the cold, unalterable law could supply the answers, but at the time there was nothing else I could do. As Ben had said, all we needed was an opening wedge; Foreman indicted on a rape charge could be that wedge.

I threw down the pencil. There was no way I could concentrate, there was no way I could erase Ginerva's face from my mind. She seemed to be looking at me from beyond a shield of glass, unable to reach out or be touched. I felt an inner stirring, a powerful desire to break that shield and hold her. To feel her warmth, to make her come alive. To me, Ginerva was dying inside, and I wanted to save her. To protect her. But from what, I didn't know. I couldn't put a name on it. It was nebulous but ugly, an invisible presence, an unprovable reality, an unmeasureable measure. I felt shaken when the thought ran through my mind: *there is a smell of death about her....*

No matter what happened to Foreman, I knew I could not abandon her. I would have to find her. Talk to her. Beg her to let me ask the questions whose answers I was now beginning to dread.

It was a cloudy, misty night, and I had the feeling the entire estate was covered by sweeping, giant bat wings. A few times I took my bearings by an occasional light, then returned to the cover of the dripping shrubs and bushes. In a way I was thankful; a full moon sailing across a clear night sky would have made the journey more dangerous. Finally, the squat shape of the dorm loomed up before me. When I gently tapped on the glass door, it opened immediately, and Leah whispered.

"I thought you'd never get back here!"

"It's as black as a tar bucket. Is she upstairs?"

"She just packed her bag. We'll be down in a minute. Wait in the woods. We must hurry. It's about time for that crazy Dorm Leader to get up."

I pushed back in the woods and crouched under a dripping bush. It was black, wet, and miserable. I was consoled only by the knowledge that we would soon be out of this sinister place.

I jumped up when I heard Leah's low call and found her at the edge of the woods.

"Margo is gone, Hilly!" she whispered frantically.

I was stunned. "Gone? But where could she go?"

"I don't know," she said bewilderedly. "When I left to go downstairs, she had finished packing and was ready to meet you here." She paused, then reached out to grip my arm. "Hilly, do you think they—"

She broke off as a light snapped on in a second-floor room.

"It's the Dorm Leader!" she said. "Quick, get out of here, Hilly!"

"What about you? They'll grab you when you go in."

"She goes to the chapel for a few minutes before she gets everyone up," she replied. "Please—please be careful, Hilly!" She kissed me and in a moment had slipped inside the dorm. I pushed through the wet brush, and when I came out on a path to get my bearings, I could see the lights of the second floor glowing through the mist and hear the faint drone of sullen sleepy Disciples joining in the prayers of their insomniac Dorm Leader.

Hidden branches reached out to slap me viciously with wet, stinging fingers while roots and vines lassoed my feet. My mind was in a turmoil. Perhaps Foreman and Russell had decided to do something about Margo. This was a hysterical sixteen-year-old girl who at the sight of Russell would begin to talk—and involve us. It was imperative I reach *The Call* office. Perhaps they were coming for us. We could pick up the van, get Leah, and move out. . . .

Halfway to *The Call* office, I heard the chugging of Matthew's cart, then the barking and snarling of his dog. There was a sharp turn in the driveway near where I was crouching. As the cart slowed down, I could hear Matthew's voice.

"What is it, boy? A rabbit? Want me to let you go after him? You would like that, wouldn't ya?"

Sweat rolled down from the inside of my arms. I knew that in the darkness and imprisoned by the bushes I wouldn't have much of a chance against that powerful animal. Matthew would never call off his dog. I slid deeper into the cover of the trees and began to run. If I made the hill at the end of the estate and went over the fence, there was an excellent chance Matthew would turn back.

Then that damn mutt began baying like a hungry wolf.

"Halt!" Matthew shouted. "Halt or I'll shoot!"

At that moment I knew Matthew would never shoot; he was frightened and probably had never fired a gun. His voice was high, thin, and quivering with fear. He could frighten the young Disciples, but facing the unknown in the misty darkness he was only a young, pimply-faced package thief. But he still had that deadly dog, now going berserk, barking and snarling as it fought the heavy chain.

"Shut up, dammit!" Matthew cried helplessly. "What the hell do you want to do? Wake 'em all up?"

The dog howled in pain, and his snarling became a whine. The cart began chugging forward. I jumped out into the path and began running. At any moment I expected to hear the sound of Buck's padded tread behind me, a triumphant yelp, and I would be fighting off those slashing teeth. But it didn't happen. Then I remembered the unfortunate milkman; undoubtedly Matthew had been warned by Foreman and Russell to use the dog only to intimidate but not to attack. Still they were coming up behind me, the dog growling impatiently and rattling the chain.

If Matthew even caught sight of me, I was finished.

I was completely disoriented in the misty darkness. There were no buildings, only lawns, paths, trees, and shrubbery. I left the path and plunged into the woods for a few moments, hoping the wet bushes and trees would kill my scent. But the dog never lost me. I was becoming frantic when I finally tripped over a low wooden white fence. I was sprawled out in a garden. When I reached out, my hand touched a cement birdbath.

Only a few feet away was the front door of Tura's house.

I pounded on the door and shook the lock. I could hear the faint chugging of the approaching cart. There was no answer.

I pounded frantically on the door. "Tura! It's Hilly! Open up! Please!"

I was about to give up when a bolt slid back, a lock clicked, and the door opened. I jumped inside, slammed home the bolt, and waited with my ear pressed to the door. The cart stopped and the dog went frantic.

"Damn you, Buck! Shut up!" Matthew shouted. Buck's howl broke off as Matthew tightened the leash. "Damn you for a fool dog! That's Sister Sloan's house! That guy is not in there—he's ahead of us!"

His angry muttering was lost in the chugging and the wild rattling of the chain as the dog fought the strangling leash.

I leaned against the door, my legs trembling like Jello. I was shivering—and not from the wet night.

Tura, a pale blur in the darkness, walked into the living room.

"He almost got you that time, Hilly," she said.

"Thank God you opened that door," I said as I followed her.

I bumped into the portable bar and reached for the elephant lamp.

"Don't turn on the light," she mumbled, but it was too late, I had switched it on.

Tura, a glass in one hand and a cloth pressed to her face with the other, had her back toward me. She turned slowly, and when her face entered the pool of light, I gasped with horror. She was almost unrecognizable. Both cheeks were puffed as if her mouth was stuffed with cotton; the skin was turning dark blue. Her bloody lower lip was split. One eye was completely closed, and her nose could have been broken.

"My God, Tura, what happened to you?" I whispered.

She held out the damp cloth and silently pointed to the jug of ice. When I filled it with several cubes, she held the pack to her face.

"Russell and Andrew," she said almost emotionlessly. "I told Dave this afternoon I had decided to leave and wanted my share. He didn't say a word, only pressed his desk buzzer. Russell came in, followed by Andrew. Dave just nodded. Russell hit me first. I can remember Andrew kicking me." She gently felt her side. "They know how to do it—don't bust anything, just make it hurt for days. . . ."

She wept, tears rolling down her swollen cheeks.

"Those dirty bastards," I said. When I put my arm around her, she winced with pain.

"When I got up, Andrew hit me. Then Russell. They pushed me back and forth between them, hitting me, kicking me. All the while Dave just sat there, not saying a word, not smiling, just those goddam fingers drumming on the desk." She shrugged. "But I guess he saved my life. It was like the blood lust was up in them and they wanted to finish the job. But Dave just snapped his fingers. Andrew stopped, but Russell continued to hit me. Dave got up, walked over to him, and slapped his face. Only then did he stop. I can remember how he was sweating, the sweat was rolling off his face. He could have been a ditchdigger taking a break. I was on the floor. I thought every bone in my body was broken. My head felt like a balloon trying to float away. Then Dave said, 'Get her on her feet.' They stood me up, and the room was like a ship's cabin in a storm. Tossing this way and that. Dave opened the drawer of his desk and took out an envelope. . . ."

She reached over and handed me a long white envelope.

" 'I told you before this is your share,' he said. 'Fifty thousand. Not a penny more.' "

"Then Russell said, 'Hey, Round Heels, want to count it?' Then he and Andrew laughed, but Dave just stood there looking at me as if he hated to stop his fun. 'And there's another thing,' Dave finally said. 'You're not going to leave now. We got too goddam much work to do on this tour. You're going to stay until it's over. Then when I tell you to go, you go.'"

"I felt as if I wanted to throw up and I knew I had to go to the bathroom. I tried to tell him but I couldn't form the words. Then I went all over his floor. Dave looked down and said, 'I guess Sister Sloan is not housebroken yet—rub her face in it!'"

She broke off, her chest heaving with sobs. "When I was in Vegas or San Francisco, men stopped on the street to look at me. Now they were pushing my face in my own pee like I was a dog."

I gave her a cigarette and she puffed on it. "When they had their fun, they yanked me to my feet. I don't know when I felt more terrible. I kept wishing I would die right in his office. . . ."

"And all this was only because you told him you wanted out, Tura?" I asked.

She carefuly placed the ice pack on another part of her face. "Nobody tells Dave what to do. He goes crazy when you cross him. Even Russell won't buck Dave when he gets hot. Maybe I kept on his back too much about the money, but I wasn't asking for something that's not coming to me." Her voice held a plaintive note. "Like I told him: 'You have all the money in the world and I always did right by you, why not give me my share?'" She changed the subject abruptly. "What were you doing out there, Hilly?"

I quickly improvised a story. "There was a kid in the dorm who said she was getting out and would talk to me." I said. "I never got to see her. She's gone. On the way back to *The Call* office, Matthew and his mutt found me."

She shook her head. "Hilly, you're going to get in real trouble one of these days. Why don't you get out of here? Forget that stupid series!"

"I'm not going to leave until I find out what's *really* going on around here, Tura." I paused. "Maybe now you should start talking." I leaned over and touched her hand. "Tura—this is your only way to get even. . . ."

"I've been thinking about it, Hilly," she said. "I was sitting here thinking about it when you knocked. I knew it would only be a matter of time before you got curious about what happened to me."

She got up and peered into the mirror. "Are you ready?" she asked in a harsh voice.

I didn't stop her when she started from the very beginning, repeating the story of the early years when she met Foreman in San Francisco and how together they had fashioned the former cabin boy into a guru, splitting a small fortune after the phony holy man fled to

India. Their meeting with Ginerva was as I knew it. I sat there listening, not interrupting, only refilling her ice pack, lighting her cigarettes, and replenishing her glass—mostly with water to keep her on an even keel.

Finally she reached solid gold.

"One day after the money began rolling in, we held a meeting, me, Dave, Russell, and Troy, and decided to start skimming off the top."

"Just like that? Was everything straight arrow before that?"

"No way. Let's face it—there were four of us—Foreman, Russell, Troy, and myself—and we're all thieves. Dave had been draining some away, but not too much because in the beginning we had to be careful; we had to get the IRS to view us as a church. Also, there's the Bank Secrecy Act which forces banks and financial institutions to report any cash transaction over ten thousand dollars. What Dave did in the beginning was to set salaries for all of us; on the record Dave gets fifty thousand as president, I get thirty-five thousand as secretary, Russell twenty-five thousand as head of security, and Troy twenty thousand as communications director. As soon as the IRS gave us that wonderful number—the tax-free religious status number—Dave called a meeting."

"Who was at the meeting, Tura?"

"The four of us. That's the meeting when Dave said we were going to start skimming off the top. But we still had to be careful, one slip and the IRS would hang us. Dave had heard about the Bahamian offshore bank deposits, so it was decided he and I would go down to look things over. We took a leisurely three weeks, and finally came on Little Cat with its plaque bank. I guess we were the right people at the right time. After a few dinners and lunches, the old guy sold Dave his bank and went back to England."

"Who operates it for him?"

"I don't know," she said. "I really don't. In fact I don't know a lot of things which happened down there after my first and only visit."

I gently reminded her, "Now about that fund you told me about, Tura?"

"The Ginerva Evangelical Fund," she said bitterly. "That was Dave's idea. He pays some guy to maintain an office down there. No money goes into it, everything is done on paper. But for the IRS it looks good."

"You said all the money doesn't stay in the Little Cat bank, Tura. Where does some of it go?"

"For a while he was dealing in the Eurocurrency market." She turned painfully to look at me. "Do you know what that is, school-teacher?" When I shook my head, she continued. "It's the unregulated pool of funds, four-fifth dollars that are borrowed and lent outside the country of their origin. I'm not too sure of my figures, but I think the fund market has gone way over sixty billion since the Arabs started to recycle their surplus oil dollars." She chuckled. "Know how I came by this, honey?" Without waiting for my reply, she said, "A long time ago, after he began to shut me out, I thought it would be a good idea to build up an insurance fund, so to speak, on Dave. Something I could really hang my hat on." She shook her head, remembering. "If he ever knew how many times I dipped into that file in his office. . . ."

She silently held out her cloth and I filled it with ice, trying hard not to let show my eagerness and excitement.

"Dave has an investment company set up in Amsterdam, which handles his investments. The Little Cat bank also makes loans to another investment company he had an old lawyer friend establish for him in North Carolina." She turned her battered face to me. "There was so much goddam money coming in that Dave had to invest some of it. I know he owns four hundred acres of prime timberland in North Carolina, has a portfolio of blue chips, and has that lawyer fronting for him in a fast-food chain." She said savagely, as she held up a thick white envelope, "Now do you see why I told him to shove this fifty thousand? It's only a trickle from a barrel."

I was stunned at the information she was giving me. I knew the Society of the Chosen was big business, but I never suspected it could be this incredible financial empire. I was listening to the evidence Tom Gray had begged for. But it had to be proven first. A Washington committee's staff with power of subpoena could do it. It was not difficult to visualize Tura, a woman scorned demanding her pound of flesh, shocking a Washington hearing room with these revelations. It would mean the end, and undoubtedly imprisonment for Foreman, Russell, and all the others who had perpetrated this monstrous national fraud.

She held out her glass and I carefully refilled it with mostly water.

"Are there any more investments, Tura?" I asked.

"There's about twenty million in Swiss numbered bank accounts," she said harshly. "Ten for Dave, ten for Russell. Dave promised to set up one for me and Steve, but it was only talk. As usual, he conned me into believing this would be our nest egg when we dumped the Society." She added bitterly, "I guess I can take the door prize for being the most gullible woman in the world. Me! Tura Sloan!"

I made the proper soothing response, then asked, "What about Troy? Didn't he ever complain? After all, wasn't he one of the four organizers?"

She gave me a hollow laugh. "Steve? Money doesn't mean that much to him. He's an addicted gambler. All he wants is enough to play the horses, shoot crap, and take care of a washed-out blonde he has tucked away in the Village. Steve was never any trouble to Dave; he always followed orders."

"Now for the big one, Tura," I said. "Where does the skimming take place?"

"In a room we always called the Money Room," she replied. "From there they fly the money down in our jet—"

I was startled. "Jet? What jet?"

She winced when she tried to smile. "You still have a lot to learn about what's going on here, Hilly. A couple of years ago the daughter of a Texas oilman recovered from an illness after that bitch blessed her. Dave got a big donation out of him, along with a Learjet. We use it for rallies, but mostly it's our money jet."

I gently pressed her, "Where is this Money Room, Tura?"

"It's on the grounds," she said. "But I honestly don't know where. What I do know is that once every three months or so Russell and Dave and the accountants get together there and count the money after it comes up here from the Mail Room—"

"Wait a minute! That's another new one. What is the Mail Room?"

She explained patiently, "As I told you, money never stops flowing into the Society. In the beginning Dave would make a pitch before every rally for contributions—you know, money to pay the cost of hiring the auditorium, expenses for bringing God's message of the Last Day to the world, that sort of crap. But once the suckers out there get hooked, they never let up. They all want space on that great Cloud of Salvation." She said wonderingly, "How can people be so stupid?"

"Do you know where that mail drop is, Tura?"

"That I know," she said. "It's on the top floor of the old Vandemeer building, Chambers and Church streets. By the way, we own the building. Dave has it figured out that the average contribution is between eight dollars and ten dollars. Do you know, it's a regular economic indicator? When inflation goes up, the contributions come down."

"Tura, this is another big one," I told her. "Do they keep a double set of books?"

She carefully inspected the inside of the cloth and then held it out. I filled it with ice cubes and waited.

"That could hang everyone," she said, "including me."

"I'm sure I can make a deal for you, Tura."

She stared straight ahead. "With whom?"

"With a district attorney," I said, and held my breath.

After a short pause, she said, "Are you working for the law?"

"No, Tura, I'm not working for any law enforcement agency. I didn't lie to you—I do intend to write about Ginerva and the Society.

From the first time I was up here, the whole setup had smelled bad to me. All I had to do was to talk to some of those kids about collections and a pattern of finances became clear. But it won't mean a damn how much is coming in unless the law gets those books."

"I was never a snitch, Hilly," she said. "This will take some thinking. . . ."

I said, "Look in the mirror and see what they did to you. Are you going to let them get away with it?"

"Sure I want to get even," she replied, "but I also want to be *alive* while I'm doing it. I know Dave well enough to realize what he will do to me if he ever got a hint I was informing. He would put Russell and Andrew on me, and they would not give up until they killed me. They know I know where a lot of the bodies are buried. A lot of bodies . . ."

I held both her hands in mine. "Tura, tell me about Ginerva. What part does she play in all this? Does she get a cut? What does she—"

She pulled her hands free. "I don't want to talk about her! That bitch is the cause of everything bad that has happened to me! I was a fool! When Dave first tried to talk me into backing her I should have taken my money and run like a deer!" She began sobbing. "All my troubles go back to her!"

Tears ran down her bruised cheeks and the split lip oozed blood as she pressed it with the ice pack. I certainly didn't take any pleasure at her degradation; my own feeling was one of personal shame that I was using her. But then the picture of the poor kid in the rugby jersey flashed across my mind. I didn't intend to play God, but Tura was one of Foreman's charter members; if this was her retribution . . .

"Help me, Hilly," she pleaded. "Tell me what to do."

"Hang all of them," I said roughly. "You have no choice. It's either you or them."

She rocked back and forth in her misery, the dripping ice pack making a dark spot on the rug. "I'll help you," I told her, "but it must be a two-way street. I want answers."

She said in a resigned voice, "What is it you want to know?"

"You told me she was in the theatre. Now, who is Peter?"

She stiffened and gave me a frightened look. "How do you know *that*?"

"The day Ginerva reached the well she seemed in a daze and kept calling the kid Peter. Who is Peter?"

"Her son," she said flatly. Then, after a pause: "He's dead."

"How did he die?"

She looked away. "I don't know anymore. Dave and Russell know everything."

I gently turned her face to me. "Ginerva told me she came from

Idaho. What does Foreman have on her, Tura? Is it connected with her son?"

She angrily pushed away my hand. "I'm telling you the truth. I don't know. And I don't want to know."

"Who is Aunt Clem?"

She hesitated. "Maybe her relative." She insisted vehemently, "I don't know any more, Hilly. I swear I don't. I only got little bits and pieces. Once when I asked what he had on her, he said, 'If you ever ask me that question again I will ram my fist down your throat,' so naturally I never asked that question again."

"How much does Ginerva get? What is her share of the action?"

Again she shook her head. "All that was between her and Dave. I never wanted to have anything to do with her. Dave made their deal."

"You keep calling her a phony—"

Tura shook the ice pack and said eagerly, "She is, Hilly, I swear she is! She's a fourteen-carat fraud!"

"But she found that kid in the well. That was no trick. I was with her, Tura! How can you explain that?"

She brooded over the question for a moment. "I met some people in the spooky racket who have what we call 'second sight.' They can see things. Don't ask me how they do it, I don't know. Once I went to a lecture on mysticism at the university in Chicago and when that question came up even the experts didn't have the answer. But that's as far as it goes with her. Everything else—the meeting with God, the warning of the Day of Judgment, the Sea of Flame, the nonsense about controlling the lightning, the Cloud of Salvation—they're all lies. Lies, I tell you!" Her swollen face twisted with hate. "It's all undiluted horseshit!"

"But how do you know?"

"It's a long story, but remember, I was there at the beginning!"

"You promised me Ginerva's real name, Tura. What is it?

Now there was an edge of stubbornness in her voice. "I don't know. Only Dave and Russell know that."

She slowly moved her arm and moaned with pain. "Those bastards hurt me, Hilly. I must get upstairs. I'm beginning to feel sick."

"Let me take you to a doctor, Tura."

"No. No. A doctor will only ask questions. He might even call in the cops. I don't want that. I'll take care of them in my own way. Maybe you can help me."

"I told you I would. Let me make a deal with the DA, Tura. He'll give you protection—"

"For the rest of my life?" she asked. "You know those politicians. Once you give them everything, they deep-six you over the side.

Suppose I blow the whistle on Foreman, Russell, and his Bitch Queen? How long do you think I'll last?"

"There's another way," I told her.

She looked at me. "I'm listening."

"I know someone in Washington who can arrange a hearing before a congressional or senatorial committee. You can blow them to bits, Tura—Foreman, Russell, Ginerva, the Angels, everyone. All you will have to do is testify, then vanish. Leave the country. Travel around Europe. After the hearings, Foreman and the others will have so much trouble with the feds they won't have any time to bother with you."

She looked impressed. "You really know someone in Washington, Hilly?"

"Someone who has all sorts of connections on the Hill. In fact I spoke to him about this."

"What did he say?"

"Nothing can be done unless someone from inside wants to talk. And, Tura, that must be you! It's your only solution. Just by appearing before a committee for a few hours you can pay them back double for what they did to you." I measured each word. "This time *you* can rub their noses in it!"

"Don't push me," she said. "I have to think about it. But now I feel sick. I have to go upstairs."

"One last question, Tura," I said quickly. "Where does Ginerva come from in Idaho?"

She feebly pushed me away. "No! No! I don't want to talk any more about her! Please, Hilly—"

"Is it a city? Town? Maybe a farm?" I went on.

"I don't know ... don't ask me any more questions. . . . Please, Hilly ... I got to go to bed. . . . I feel so sick. . . ."

She groaned and muttered with pain as she tried to get out of the chair. I helped her up, and she leaned heavily on me as we crossed the room.

"Come back tomorrow night," she said hoarsely, "late. Then we'll talk. I feel so sick. . . . I'm confused. . . . I can't think. . . ."

"There are two things you *must* think about, Tura," I told her. "Going down to Washington and testifying, and telling me where they keep the double set of books. Remember this—they won't use you for a punching bag the next time; they'll kill you."

"Tomorrow night," she said heavily as she slowly, painfully, began to climb the stairs, holding tightly to the banister as she kept repeating to herself, "I got to think of what I must do ... must do. . . ."

I called out, "Tura, let me help you upstairs."

She ignored me as she took one step at a time.

I felt a deep wrench of pity mixed with frustration as I watched her slowly near the top.

Now she was only a shadow. The question I wanted to ask all these months blurted out.

"Tura, stop! Listen to me!"

The shadow slowly turned.

"Who killed Ben Rice?"

I heard her gasp, then her frightened whisper. "My God, you know *that*! You're not what you say! Go away, Hilly! Go away! You're going to get us both killed!"

I started to run up the stairs, but her voice rose to a scream: "No! No! Don't come near me! You know too goddam much!"

Then she was gone and I heard the bedroom door slam and a lock click.

There was nothing to do but leave. When I reached over to turn off the lamp, I saw the money-filled envelope. I quickly counted the bills—there was fifty thousand.

And Tura had demanded millions.

14

The Room
in the Green Barn

I made my way back to *The Call* office without any incident, to find a white-faced, frightened Turner sitting on the edge of the bed.

"My God, it's almost five o'clock," he said. "Where are Margo and Leah?" He pointed to my wet, muddy shoes and soggy clothes. "What happened to you?"

I gave him a concise account of my escape from Matthew and his dog and what Tura had told me.

"Did Matthew see you, Hilly?" he asked nervously.

"Not a chance. It was too dark."

"If they grabbed Margo . . ." His voice trailed off.

I knew what he was thinking. "It's almost dawn," I pointed out. "If they had grabbed Margo and she talked, they would be here now. I say let's ride it out—at least until I see Foreman."

"But maybe you'll be walking into something, Hilly," he said nervously. "You may never come out of that place."

"Then again, maybe I will."

"What I can't understand is this: if they didn't grab Margo, who did? And why?"

"What is more important is what Tura told me. Now we know they do their skimming somewhere here on the grounds and then fly the money to that Caribbean bank. Did you know they had a jet?"

"I never heard of it. Do you think you blew it with Sloan when you mentioned Ben Rice?"

"It was a mistake, but I think she'll cool down."

"Christ, if they ever have a congressional hearing, this thing will blow apart," he said, obviously relishing the idea. "Do you think they'll subpoena us as witnesses, Hilly?"

The sheets felt cool and comforting, and my eyes began to close. "I'll talk to you later, Norm. . . . By the way, don't mention Sloan to Leah. . . ."

"Why not?" he asked mockingly. "Don't you want her to know you have been screwing an over-the-hill blonde to get information?"

My soggy shoe missed his head by inches.

"You know, Hilly, you can be a mean dude sometimes," he complained, as he clicked off the light.

I was on my feet the moment I heard footsteps on the stairs. Turner sat up in bed, his eyes wide with fear. But instead of Russell and his goons, it was Leah with containers of coffee and a bag of doughnuts.

"Anything on Margo?" I called out, as we dressed.

"Not a thing," she replied. "I don't know what happened to her. When I asked the Dorm Leader, the old witch only smiled and said she was now working in the Fields of the Lord. Hilly, I'm frightened."

"That makes two of us," Turner said.

"What should we do?" she asked.

I advised her, "Sit tight and see what happens. If they were going to do anything they would have done it when it was dark."

As we sat down at the table she said, "Oh, by the way, I hear Sister Sloan was taken away in an ambulance during the night."

Turner stared into his coffee and I went to the sink to get a glass of water.

"One of the kids in the cafeteria said he heard she fell down a flight of stairs."

I carried the local phone book to the table. "We had better check the local hospitals, police, and private ambulances."

Leah looked puzzled. "Why?"

"Doesn't two in one night sound suspicious?"

"But couldn't she have broken a leg or a hip in a fall?" Leah suggested. "That doesn't sound mysterious to me."

"Sister Sloan and Brother Foreman have not been on the best of terms," I told her. "Let's make sure it was an accident."

We were finished within an hour. There was no public record of Tura Sloan being removed in an ambulance to a hospital from the grounds of the Society of the Chosen. Leah gave me a puzzled look.

"How did you know they weren't on the best of terms, Hilly?"

I said lamely, "One day when I went to see Foreman I heard them yelling at each other. She was demanding money. You know, thieves always have a falling out. . . ."

Turner studied his coffee as if it held the answer to a grave question.

"First Margo, now Sister Sloan," Leah said, wonderment in her voice. "Hilly, do you think there is any connection?"

"I don't know. . . . I'll have to play this one by ear with Foreman."

At noon we walked to the cafeteria for a sandwich. When Norman returned to the table with three cups of rubbery Jello, his tray was shaking.

"What's wrong, Norm?" Leah asked.

He looked around the crowded room and quickly scrawled on a napkin: "Bruce Stafford is gone."

From what Leah and Norman could find out, Bruce Stafford vanished about the same time as Margo and Tura. He had left the door of his studio apartment open, and a passing, curious Disciple found the place empty. He had thoughtfully taken his expensive equipment.

"I don't see what possible connection there can be between him, Margo, and Sloan," I told Norman and Leah. "We knew he was going—he told me again the day the kid was found."

"After that picture was all over page one, he won't have any trouble finding a job," Turner said."

"Good luck to him wherever he is," I said, and opened my wallet to hold up the key he had passed on to me. "Now to see what's in that barn."

Turner groaned. "I had forgotten that damn key. Hilly, can't you skip this one?"

I pointed to the rain-streaked window. "It looks as if it will rain all night. Matthew and his mutt won't be cruising around. It will be a perfect time to get in there."

"Can I go with you, Hilly?" Leah asked.

I looked at her. She was serious.

"Do you know what will happen if I'm caught?"

"I was on track in college," she said. "I'm sure I can run as fast as you or Norman."

"Leah, are you crazy?" Turner cried. "If he wants to go, let him go! How many times do we have to stick our necks out?"

I waited until the early hours of the morning, when the storm was at its peak. The rain was riding the back of a northeaster, and it struck me with a fury that almost took my breath away. Lightning zigzagged across the darkness, and the peals of thunder were deafening. I had gone over the route in my mind, and the tiny pencil flashlight would give me an idea of what was inside the barn. I had only started out when I sensed, rather than heard, someone coming up behind me. I jumped behind a tree as two shadowy figures approached. When they came abreast of me, I stepped out in front of them.

If I had not put my hand over her mouth, Leah's scream would have raised the dead. Turner, rain rolling off his face, looked as if he was about to collapse.

"What they hell are you two doing here?" I demanded.

"We decided we should share the risks," Leah said.

"*She* decided," Turner protested.

"I know the way," Leah said. "Follow me."

Now she was the leader.

But she did know the way, and we were at the green barn in a short time. In the lightning flashes it looked eerie and deserted.

"Are you sure no Angels sleep in there?" Turner asked.

"Stafford said it was only used as a gymnasium," I told him. "Let's find out how right he is."

Inside, the pencil flashlight picked out wrestling mats, punching bags, medicine ball, and weights. Thick green drapes covered the windows. At the far end was a door, sheathed with tin like a firedoor. It was open. As we started up the stairs, I had the curious feeling of being in a vacuum. When I reached out, the walls felt rough; the flashlight showed they were paneled with cork.

There was another insulated door on the landing. I carefully inched it open, and we stood there in the darkness, listening for the sounds of sleeping men. There were none. Behind me, Turner grunted with surprise when my light ran around the walls. They were mirrored. The room was bare except for, in the middle, a single chair with straps, an enormous console of dials, levers, and knobs off to one side.

"It looks like the office of a disc jockey," Norman whispered. "What do you suppose it is, Hilly?"

"Let's look around some more," I said.

Our voices sounded as if we were speaking in a tomb.

The windows were not only sealed tight but also had heavy drapes. The ceiling was made of cork, and the rug on the floor was thick and soft as sod. We were in a soundproof room. I ran my hand along the wall and found some switches. When I clicked one on, the room was flooded with an intense white light. Our reflections stared back at us from the mirrors. When I switched on another, the walls slowly began to move.

"My God, look at that!" Norman cried.

The mirrors turned to become a wall of huge portraits of Ginerva in many poses; praying, at rallies, blessing the sick. Another switch filled the room with a deep resonant voice:

"And God confronted this holy woman on a mountain trail and said to her, 'From this moment, woman, your name shall be Ginerva, and you shall be my courier to the world.'"

Suddenly the room shook with noise so intense I had to hold my ears. Hymns, chants, blaring bands, the hysterical voices of women crying out "Glory to Ginerva! Glory to Ginerva!"

After a few minutes, the noise broke off, and in the still quivering silence a gentle voice asked:

"Dear Brother, you must accept Her Holiness! You must follow her and be counted among her Chosen Ones. You must take our hand and walk with us onto God's Great White Cloud of Salvation and be lifted with us into Paradise. Oh Brother, how much we want you to be with us!"

Silence again. Now an intense angry voice—to me it sounded like Singleton's on Staten Island—came to life from another side of the room.

"Sinner! Spawn of Satan! Do you still dare to doubt the word of Her Holiness Ginerva?" Do you still dare to question this holy woman who is trying to save the world from eternal damnation? Sinner, beg God to forgive you!"

Another harsh voice joined in, this time from the front of the room. "Beg forgiveness, spawn of Satan, for not believing in her. Vow to yourself that from now on you will do everything in your power to help the Society of the Chosen! It is your only chance to escape the deadly Sea of Flame! Say it, sinner! I swear to God to do everything to help the Society of the Chosen! Say it again! And again!"

Now from all four corners of the room came shrill accusing voices, wild chants, and thundering waves of organ music.

Again they broke off. Again there was an intense silence. The walls began to move, and the portraits were replaced by the mirrors. The lights lowered and brilliant strobes began flashing. The effect of the colored lights bouncing off the mirrors stunned the mind. Hymns, chants, blaring bands, and the angry voices began to mount higher and higher. I held out my hands and took a few steps forward. Sound waves were directed at the chair from all sides of the room. Whoever was strapped into it was the target for an incredible barrage of lights and noise.

I could see Leah screaming at me, but her voice was lost in the din. My brain was becoming numb. Turner looked as if he had been nailed to the rug.

(273)

I forced myself to stagger to the wall and click off the switches. The noise stopped; the lights went out. We stood in the darkness recovering our senses.

"Please, Hilly, get me out of here," Leah said in a shaky voice. "Please."

We stumbled down the stairs and out into the rain. Even the violent night was a relief after that ghastly room.

I knew we had found Russell's brainwashing headquarters. Perhaps this is where I would have been taken if I had been cornered by Matthew and his dog. Is this where they gave Ben the gun?

As we ran through the rain I promised: *I'll get them, Ben. I won't stop until I do. . . ."*

15

Wee Willie

In the days that followed, I concentrated on becoming Foreman's indispensable assistant. I was soon entrapped in a morass of paperwork, conferences with advertising agency people, luncheons, and endless telephone calls. I probed the brains and experience of every agency employee I came in contact with, until one asked me wonderingly, "Do you plan to open your own agency, Brother Hillers?"

I went to bed late, my mind whirling about with an accumulation of estimates, proofs, and artwork; orders and counterorders, the text and revisions of our television commercial, and the endless details that went into making it; material for press releases, posters, billboards, and even buttons. No detail was too trivial; everyone came to me. I wouldn't have it any other way. It was all according to my plan. Gradually the responsibility, long hours, and dedication began to show; it was soon evident to me that I had become the architect of Ginerva's national tour. Eventually there would come a day when, if I threatened to leave, it would be clear the project would collapse without my careful, devoted supervision.

This was also partially due to Foreman's absence from tour headquarters. A few weeks after I joined him, he had started to appear less and less. From what I could overhear and from the few scraps I found in the wastepaper basket, he was spending most of his time in Washington. I had no way of knowing who he was seeing or what he was doing in the capital. I called Tom Gray twice, only to be told by an answering service he was out of town; once I tried to follow Foreman when he left in his limousine, but my cab lost him in the traffic. So much for playing amateur detective; all I could do was search his wastepaper basket regularly and try to listen at his door whenever the phone rang.

There had been no visible repercussions over the disappearance of Margo, Tura, and Bruce Stafford. I wasn't surprised Bruce had left. After all, he had told me the morning of the search for the child in the well he intended to leave the motherhouse "soon, very soon. . . ." I assumed he had simply left to open his own photographic business, perhaps in a small town, and certainly not near any branch of the Society of the Chosen.

I had no answers for what had happened to Tura or Margo, and that worried me. There had been many nights when I had agonized over the decision of whether or not to call in the police and district attorney, only to arrive at the same answer: I had no proof, nor did anyone else, that Foreman, Russell, or the Angels had harmed either Margo or Tura. Also, there was no evidence Foreman had been aware Margo was an underage runaway, and how could anyone prove, without her presence and cooperation, that she had been raped and was pregnant? Also, Norman and Leah had discovered from their talkative friends another version of Tura's disappearance. This one did not include her falling down stairs and being rushed to the hospital. The story, as they got it, was that two Disciples, walking past the house and finding the door open, had called in to see if anything was wrong. They searched the house and discovered it was empty. If there had been an envelope with fifty thousand dollars, that item certainly would have been included in the gossip. Did Tura finally decide to take the money and go, or had the envelope been returned intact to Foreman by the Angels who finally came for her?

To alert the police about the disappearances of Tura, Margo, and Bruce would, of course, end my usefulness. And as Leah and Norman pointed out, suppose I did call in the police and they discovered Margo had simply run away again, Tura was found spending her fifty thousand gambling in Atlantic City, Vegas, or on the Riviera, and Bruce was photographing weddings in some small town?

Leah said the other Disciples had accepted the Dorm Leader's explanation that Margo was working somewhere in "The Fields of the Lord." I had no logical reason to question Foreman about her but I could bring up Tura without raising his suspicion.

Soon after the morning she had vanished, I casually mentioned I had heard that Sister Sloan was in a hospital for injuries she had received in a fall down stairs.

There was no hint of suspicion in his eyes when he looked up and sighed. "Yes, I'm afraid what you heard was correct, Hilly," he said dolefully. "Sister Sloan will be incapacitated for some time. I've been meaning to speak to you about that. I'm afraid that leaves a hole in your team. You may have to take on additional duties. . . ."

We never mentioned Tura again.

Finally Foreman agreed with me that *The Call* now appeared to be in competent hands and that Leah and Norman could join me in the midtown office. Each had a suite in the Lafayette and offices on the floor below me. They were officially listed as my assistants, doing everything on the planning of the tour from searching out municipal rally permits to deciding what local talent we should use. We frequently went out of town, ostensibly to untangle a local problem that had to do with the tour. It gave us an excellent cover to move freely—even to travel to Idaho if it became necessary. . . .

During these weeks, Ginerva remained in seclusion. Requests for her to appear on any number of prominent television shows continued to come in to us, but they were always refused. One was for "*Sixty Minutes.*" I tried to sell Foreman on doing it, which would give me an excuse to see Ginerva, but this was one of the few times he refused to accept my advice.

"I don't think so, Hilly," he said firmly. "No one can see Ginerva. She is in deep meditation, preparing for the tour."

Leah and Norman learned she had never again appeared on the grounds and left her apartment above the Grand Ballroom only infrequently, in the limousine driven by Andrew with Russell sitting in the front seat.

Again and again the possibility occurred to me: she was being held prisoner? But why? What could they gain?

Wasn't she the star of the whole national tour?

Then one day Foreman ordered me to give our agency a particular assignment: poll the residents of the Midwest to determine their problems and particular worries. The results showed a lack of trust in their government and the officials they had elected; they were worried about crime and inflation, and a number yearned for a personal peace to offset their daily struggles in a frantic lifestyle.

To sum up, the people of the Midwest were no different from other Americans.

With one exception.

In an area around Briggs, Kansas, a farming district, it appeared the most important incident in the lives of its residents was a shocking murder which had taken place the year before. A mild-mannered elderly choirmaster had been arrested for the rape murder of a popular ten-year-old member of his choir. Plodding state police work finally trapped him, and on national television he guided investigators to the child's grave in the field adjacent to his farm. The leaked details of his confession were ghastly. It developed that for years this rural Dr. Jekyll–Mr. Hyde had sexually abused many children in his choir, but they had been too frightened to speak out against this man who was so admired by their parents. However, before he could come to trial, the murderer had died in his cell of natural causes.

Controversy spread through this very conservative section of the midwestern Bible belt and the question was debated, often from the pulpit: why had God allowed this monster to escape the punishment of his peers? There were feature stories, television debates, and articles in religious journals.

Hard luck and tragedy followed his death. A drought killed a wheat crop and bankrupted many farmers as wheat prices continued to slide. A tornado which cut a wide swath across the county devastated Briggs but not its neighboring communities. Then five teenagers coming home from a prom were killed when an express train turned their car into a jumble of twisted steel. The accident took place only a short distance from the killer's farmhouse.

Pollsters reported a feeling of uneasiness hanging over the area. Some residents laughed when they said the choirmaster was still haunting them, but pollsters reported that many did not laugh as they discussed the killer's evil, which they insisted should be exorcised. All agreed that an old-fashioned religious rally would be a welcome way of presenting a Christlike solution to their problems.

At first I was puzzled as to why Foreman had ordered the poll, but when I read the report on Briggs, I thought I knew why. The morning after the agency had submitted its report, Foreman dismissed Andrew and suggested we talk over a leisurely breakfast.

When coffee was served, he tapped a copy of the poll. "What do you think?"

"Very interesting," I said. "It gives an excellent picture of what is troubling the residents of an important midwestern state. I would certainly use it if I were running for office."

"But suppose you were Brother Hillers organizing one of America's most important religious crusades?" he asked. "Then how would you use it?"

I said carefully, "I'd bring my crusade into Briggs. Obviously, the people are troubled—"

"By the ghost of a murderer," he broke in, with a thin smile. "It might sound weird in this day and age, but the people want his evil exorcised. And Ginerva can do it." He eyed me sharply. "What do you think, publicity-wise?"

"There's no doubt we can get some mileage out of it," I predicted.

"But the theme of the rally has got to be on Ginerva bringing peace to the troubled hearts of those who live under the shadow of Satan's evil—that sort of thing."

He slapped the table. "That's exactly what I wanted you to say, Hilly. This will not only be a sensational rally, but can serve as our pilot. Something to test our plans, to confirm we're on the right track. An opportunity to shake out the bugs. A preview of the national tour. What's your opinion of that?"

This was one way to see Ginerva. "I'm all for it, Dave."

"Excellent." He unfolded a sectional map attached to the poll and pointed to where he had already marked Briggs with a tiny red ring. "Briggs, Kansas. Twenty miles south of Topeka. Population thirty-two thousand four hundred, mostly wheat and dairy farmers. The area is predominantly Baptist but there are some strong segments of other religions." He handed me a color print of a beautiful white domed building. "This is the new ten-million-dollar auditorium dedicated to a man named Briggs, one of the state's early pioneers and founder of the town. The Briggs family owns the local grain station and the bank, and politically controls the county. The auditorium has proven to be a white elephant and a political liability to Mayor Briggs. He is desperate to have it used by anyone who can generate publicity. With my guarantee of national publicity for the rally, he agreed to give us the auditorium, use of his police department, and anything else we need, for a minimum fee."

"But, Dave, there's no way to guarantee how much publicity any event will get," I protested.

He gave me a sly, elliptical look, half conspiratorial, half arrogant. "Ginerva gave us the guarantee. . . ."

I was puzzled. "I'm afraid I don't understand."

He said solemnly, "As you know, Ginerva has been in deep meditation for weeks. In fact, she is the one who suggested Briggs. The reason is God has granted her a vision about the murder—"

I gasped. "A vision! But what was the vision about?"

He slowly shook his head. "Even I don't know. Ginerva will reveal it on the night she appears in the Briggs auditorium." He sipped at his coffee. "But one thing I know she will do is send that demon back to hell. That's what I mean about a guarantee for publicity. I think you can do a lot with that bit of news."

"Of course, it's something I can use," I admitted, "but I should see Ginerva immediately. Talk to her. Every newspaperman in the Midwest will have any number of questions, Dave!"

"Tell them their questions will be answered the night of the rally," he said casually. "Now I want you to begin immediately to lay the groundwork for the rally. I want to see your people in action, Hilly!"

Ginerva on national television would exorcise a demon and reveal a God-granted vision. . . .

He refilled our coffee cups. "Hilly, this pilot rally must explode over the country like an atom bomb!" he said vehemently. "I am a strong believer in beginnings—if you start with a powerful thrust, the momentum picks up along the way and you end as a winner. But if you start in a routine manner, it rubs off and your project remains drab. No flair. Mediocre." He slapped the table with the palm of his hand. "There can be nothing routine or mediocre about this tour! I want every rally to be bigger than the previous one! I want their dimes and their dollars! And the only way we are going to accomplish this is by spectacular publicity! Lots of television time! A kick-in-the-guts commercial like the one you prepared! Stories on page one to get us talked about! I don't have to tell you about word-of-mouth publicity! I discussed this in detail with Ginerva, and she has agreed. That's why she's been in seclusion, praying to the Lord." He added fervently, "Oh, prayer is very powerful, Hilly, very powerful. Never forget that!"

"And the Lord answered her," I said, trying to sound awed.

He said briskly, "The Lord in his wisdom and mercy answered her." He drained his cup and dabbed at his lips with a napkin. "We have to squeeze out every headline, every TV news spot that we can. The Briggs rally has got to launch our tour with a mighty effort!" His fingers began their measured drumming on the tablecloth as he studied me narrowly. "Briggs will also be *your* testing ground, Hilly. Let's see what you can do with a demon and a heavenly vision."

"I would like to make one suggestion," I offered. When he nodded, I went on. "Bring Troy to Briggs to film the rally."

His eyebrows went up. "But why do we need Troy? I hope you'll bring in every local station and the networks!"

"My idea is to have Troy film, edit, and produce a tight, dramatic fifteen-minute film, with free copies for every television station along the route of the national tour. After this rally, Ginerva's name will be a household word. Local stations will gladly use it as part of their hard-news program when we arrive in their city. It will be promotion and publicity you can't buy."

He thought for a moment. "But what about a crew?"

"I will have Sister Butler and Brother Turner canvass the Society's master list. Among our members we may find a few who have had experience in film. If not, we can hire a sound man and an assistant cameraman. Troy does his own lighting anyway, and he can edit the film in New York."

Our eyes met, and I felt something had passed between us. Before he spoke again, I knew that Foreman had been sold and was coming to the conclusion that I was the best gift to come down the pike in a long time.

"Excellent idea, Hilly," he said, with a slow smile. "Excellent. I'll order Troy out here immediately."

Leah and Norman, their faces slack with amazement, stared at me. "Ginerva is going to exorcise a demon on national television?" Leah gasped.

"And reveal a vision?" Norman added. "In Briggs, Kansas?"

"That's what Foreman claims," I said.

Norman said, "What is Foreman trying to sell us? That Ginerva has a hot line to God?"

Leah said slowly, "But why should he lie? Why would he take the chance of making her a national fool?"

"He's either the devil or a complete nut."

"He's neither," I assured him. "Foreman is a tough, realistic con man. He's not going to risk a thirty-million-dollar-a-year racket to promise some midwestern farmers Ginerva will take care of their personal demon unless he's sure he can pull it off."

"But how can he pull off a divine vision on some ghastly thing like a child murderer affecting people's lives," Leah said. "It doesn't make sense."

I promised them. "Someday it will, but as of now I'm as baffled as you are. I don't have the slightest idea of what he has in mind." I held up the memorandum Foreman had sent me after breakfast. "All I know is that the whole thing must have been carefully planned. He had the poll taken, the site selected, and the auditorium signed before we sat down for breakfast."

"And you're going through with this crazy project?" Norman asked unbelievingly.

"Of course I am. What did you expect me to say to Foreman? 'No, I won't go out to Briggs, Kansas, because this whole thing sounds too weird?' No way. I told you both I intend to do anything to become Foreman's Mr. Indispensable. This could be the first step. What Foreman wants, Foreman gets from me. . . ."

"Hilly, you scare me when you talk like that," Leah said, with a worried look.

"This is a time when we shelve our morals, Leah," I warned her. "We're into this thing too deep to worry about codes or rules. We owe too much to too many people—Ben, Margo, those kids on Staten Island—even Tura Sloan. How could we possibly back out now?"

"To use the immortal words of Sam Goldwyn," Norman said, 'include me out.'" Those people out there are too uptight about what has happened to their community and their lives to put up with any

(2 8 1)

nonsense. What will they do to us if it all turns out to be just another phony gimmick? They'll ride us out of town on a rail or let us rot in the local jail!"

Leah said quietly, "But suppose it's all *true*?"

Norman gave her an incredulous look. "Leah, you can't believe Ginerva had *another* meeting with God!"

Leah looked at me. "How do we know she didn't?"

I could only groan inwardly at her stubborn naivete. "Leah, this is just another scam Foreman has worked up to get publicity for his tour. He's desperate to make page one and get on television. And Ginerva is going along with it. What they intend to pull off is anyone's guess, but I can guarantee God doesn't have any part in it. Now let's get back to work. Remember that master list of the Disciples in the library at the motherhouse? Well, I'm having a Xerox copy made. It will be sent down this afternoon."

Turner looked startled. "What is that for?"

"I sold Foreman the idea of having Troy film the Briggs rally and using it as a giveaway to network affiliates for their news programs. He loved it. Troy is coming down here to work with us and do the filming. Maybe the list will help him put together a crew."

Norman asked fearfully, "Will Russell be out in Briggs?"

"Russell will be in charge of security as usual. You know you can't shake that guy. Wherever Ginerva is, he's there."

Leah pointed out, "I don't get it, Hilly. From what we saw at the motherhouse, Troy and Russell hate each other."

"That's precisely why I want Troy with us," I explained. "I hope it will make Russell jealous and help to keep him off balance. I intend to whisper in Troy's ear all about how Russell is trying to knife him in the back with Foreman. Divide and rule, Machiavelli said."

"I don't know about Machiavelli," Norman said mournfully, "but I remember what the gladiators said when they marched into the arena: '*Ave, Caesar! Morituri te salutamus.*' And that is how I feel." He looked at Leah. "How about you, Leah?"

Leah said quietly, "What's the next move, Hilly?"

"We're going to Kansas to start promoting the hell out of this rally," I told them. "Newspapers, television, commercials, posters, buttons— the whole program. In Topeka we will meet a guy named Dwight Davis, who's the Topeka Team Leader. I've talked to him a number of times on the phone. He owns a string of supermarkets in the Midwest, knows his way around politically, and is a friend of Jack Briggs, the mayor. I want to liaison with his teams and saturate the area."

"Will you make an announcement about Ginerva's vision?" Norman asked.

"Of course. That will be our gimmick. God reveals to Ginerva the inner secrets of the murdering choirmaster and guarantees to take care of their demon. It will be as good as Barnum's Jumbo."

"Instant religion," Norman said disgustedly. "Manufactured by news releases, buttons, and billboards. And a con man."

"Now I know what you meant about dumping our morals," Leah said, with an edge of bitterness in her voice.

"Trust me, Leah," I said. "That's all I ask."

"If I didn't I wouldn't be here," was her quiet reply.

I met Troy at Grand Central, drove him to the hotel, and escorted him to his room, a suite bigger and roomier than mine. There were ice, setups, and a bottle of vodka on a small bar.

He looked surprised. "I know Dave didn't set this up, he doesn't go for drinking."

"It's my welcome-home present," I said. "On the rocks?"

When he nodded, I poured each of us a stiff shot.

"That's why I ordered vodka," I said. "No smell." I toasted him. "Here's to our working together, Steve."

He said with a smile. "No more of that 'Brother' crap?"

"No way," I said. "At least while we're alone."

His gesture took in the room and bar. "Why all this, Hilly?"

"First, I want to thank you for protecting Leah and Norman from that goon Russell. They were both scared to death, and told me that if you hadn't interfered it might have turned nasty."

His eyes hardened. "My pleasure." He hesitated. "Watch yourself, Hilly, Russell is out to get you. He thinks you're moving in too fast with Dave."

"I never turn my back on him." I added nonchalantly, "He was really dead set against you coming out with us to Kansas."

"Yeah? Why?"

"I don't know how to say this, Steve—" I hoped I was enough of an actor to make it appear as though I was struggling with an important and personal decision. "Maybe I'm talking out of school. . . . After all, while I know you and Russell have been together a long time. . . ."

"I couldn't care less about that big creep," he said quickly. "What happened?"

"Well, we had a meeting on the Briggs rally, and I told Foreman we would be passing up the chance of the century if we didn't film the rally and give copies to the stations along our route to use on their news programs. Of course I said there was only one guy to do it, and that was you."

"And Russell didn't go for that," he said in a taut voice.

(283)

"He really ripped you up the back, Steve. Among other things he told Foreman—besides your not being reliable—you were a second-rate camerman."

I let that sink in.

Troy angrily pulled at his cheek. "That son of a bitch said that about me?"

"I let him finish, and then I started on you," I said. "I told Foreman I had seen you work in Nam and in my opinion you were the best documentary cameraman in Vietnam, and reminded him your film on that orphanage in Saigon won all kinds of awards."

I let that set. His face was now flushed with pleasure.

"I also told Foreman that I couldn't work with an agency camera-man. I knew you and how you worked, and along with Leah and Norman we would make an unbeatable team."

His eyes glowed with pride. "That was damn nice of you, Hilly. I won't forget it."

"I'm sincere, Steve," I told him. "I know you have your own equip-ment, so tomorrow, at your convenience, drop by one of the film supply houses and buy whatever you need. Have them send the bill to me. It all goes on the promotion budget."

His eyes were glistening. "What do you have in mind, Hilly?"

"Now I'm only suggesting, you're the expert," I told him. "But I was thinking of something in 35mm color and sound. Covering the high-lights of the rally, I want it tight, colorful, and as dramatic as your great talent can make it."

"What do you want to do with it?"

"I want to make twenty, thirty copies and spread them among the affiliated stations as free hard-news segments to be used any way they wish. They will help pave the way for the tour. The station will get a free professionally done film, and of course we will get the exposure."

"What about a crew?" he asked.

"The library at the motherhouse has sent down a copy of the Society's master list. Leah and Norman are checking to see if we have any Disciples who have had professional experience with film. If not, you will simply hire a crew, but frankly I would rather have our own people. They will have our interests at heart."

"And no union problems," he observed.

"I insisted to Foreman that you are to be in total charge of the unit," I said. "All you have to do is produce the finished product." I reached over and slapped him on the back. "Give me something terrific, Steve, so I can shove it down Russell's throat."

He said grimly, "You have my guarantee."

"Do you have any idea what Ginerva will do out in Kansas?" I asked him.

He shrugged. "I guess the usual."

This confirmed what Tura had told me. Foreman and Russell were splitting the millions and Troy was getting handouts to keep him gambling and happy. He was no longer a voting member of the original conspiracy.

After a pause, looking out the window, I said dramatically, "Steve, I'm going to tell you something to show how much I trust you. . . ."

He made no attempt to disguise his eagerness. "You can tell me anything, Hilly. I swear it won't go beyond this room."

"Do you remember about a year ago a choirmaster in the Midwest raped and murdered a little girl?"

He thoughtfully tugged at the loose flesh of his neck. "Yeah. I remember seeing something on television."

"Hold your hat," I warned him. "That murder took place in Briggs. Ginerva has had a vision about that crime, and will disclose what it is on the stage the night of the rally."

His eyes widened. "Jeez! What kind of vision?"

"I don't know anymore than that. Foreman claims he doesn't know, but he swore me to secrecy."

He said with a mixture of frustration and bitterness, "In the old days, Dave would have included me in on it from the very beginning."

I pointed out, "But *I* told you, Steve."

"Yeah. Yeah," he said hastily. "I appreciate that."

I refilled his glass, and out of the corner of my eye I saw him glancing at his wristwatch. I remembered what Tura had said about Troy's "washed-out blonde he has tucked away in the Village. . . ."

"Can I give you a lift anywhere, Steve?" I asked him. "I've been working day and night on that goddam tour, and today I just feel like taking a break."

"That will be great," he said eagerly.

I winked and in a mock whisper asked, "Does she have a friend?"

He stared at me, then burst out laughing. "Hey, you're all right, kid. Maybe next time. No, I want to put down a few bets."

"OTB?"

"Hell no," he said. "I phoned my selections in this morning. I'm looking for some real action. If I get over to the West Side in time, I can get into Wee Willie's place."

"Wee Willie?"

"Would you like to come along?" he asked. "There's not too many of these places left in Manhattan since Atlantic City opened."

"Definitely," I told him. "Wee Willie sounds interesting."

I didn't have to ask him about Russell; that was all he talked about going crosstown.

"As soon as Dave left, that son of a bitch couldn't wait to take over the motherhouse. First he put out an order stopping all outside phone calls, with every phone message brought to his office. He had his goon squad stopping everyone on the grounds to make sure they were wearing their ID card. Then he started those crazy exercises. He walks around like Wyatt Earp. That's what the kids call him behind his back—Wyatt Earp. They're scared to death of him and his Angels. I don't like a lot of things going on up there now."

I moved in cautiously. "Like what, Steve?"

"It's hard for me to pin it down, but there's something big going on and only Dave and Russell are in it. It's not like the old days, when Dave used to include me and Tura in everything."

"You don't have any idea what it could be?"

He shook his head. "I've been trying to find out, but I haven't had any luck. They're playing it close to the vest."

"Have you heard how Tura is, Steve?"

"For your own information, Hilly," he said, "Tura is a matinee drinker who began to rub Dave the wrong way. I warned her, but she didn't pay any attention to me. There's one thing you should know about Dave—when things are going his way, fine. But cross him, argue with him, and refuse to do what he wants, and bang—you're out of the box!"

I tried to sound unconcerned. "Tura must have bounced when she hit those stairs," I said with a laugh. "It's lucky she got away with a broken leg."

He looked puzzled. "Hell, Tura didn't break her leg." Then he nodded, understandingly. "Oh, yeah. That's what they told the kids. But she didn't go to any hospital. She simply split. Tura and Dave had a real blowup, so she decided the game was over and it was better to pick up her marbles and leave." He chuckled. "It was only a matter of time before she pulled out. Tura's not a girl you can keep on the reservation too long. She's like me. There's only so much of those Bible-spouting kids you can take, then you need a little action for relaxation." He studied me for a moment. "How about you, Hilly?"

"Just between us, Steve, I'm not making a career out of it."

"But you came back."

"I had a few personal problems outside," I said, "and the mother-house is a great place if you don't want people to know where you are." I added, "Let's say it involved a woman and could have ended up in a messy court action. . . ."

He nodded approvingly. "Good thinking. I know what you mean. How long do you think you'll stay?"

I said vaguely, "It's an experience. Maybe until after the tour. . . ."
When we reached Broadway, I told him, "You name it, Steve."

"We're going to a store on Thirty-eighth Street between Eighth and Ninth, called Trench's Fabrics and Remnants. You can park in a lot a few doors down."

Trench's was a typical Garment Center hole-in-the-wall remnant store, long and narrow, with an aisle running between tables piled high with bolts and pieces of goods. Prices were marked in crayon on white construction paper. There were a few girls measuring and cutting for women customers. I followed Troy, who moved expertly along the aisle and around some tables to avoid a Puerto Rican housewife arguing in Spanish with a clerk. In the rear he paused before a heavy, metal fire door, EMPLOYEES ONLY written on it in chalk.

To one side was a man seated on a barstool behind a cash register. He had beady eyes, wrinkled parchment skin, and a pulse like a fluttering bird beating in his neck. He was dressed meticulously in a blue pin-striped suit, white shirt, and blue tie. When he swung around on his stool, I was amazed to see he was a dwarf. He reminded me of Mr. Toad of Toad Hall. His voice was so deep it startled me.

"Haven't seen you lately, Steve. Been out of town?"

"Yeah. I've been out of town." He put his arm around my shoulder. "Willie, this is my friend, Hilly. Hilly, meet Willie Chambers."

The hand I accepted was tiny and warm as a child's. The dark eyes studied me.

"Please to meet you, Hilly. Come around any time."

"Hilly just blew in town," Troy explained. "I'm showing him around."

"Good boy," Willie said, and bent down to press a buzzer. I noticed he was wearing a thick black strap around his right thumb and across his hand.

"When I'm in town this is my second home," Troy said. "It's like a club. Willie's been operating for years. All the high rollers from the Garment Center come here. They all like Willie. There's no mob interest, no muscle, no strong-arm loan shark stuff. He pays off the precinct and they let him ride because he never gives them any trouble. I'll show you the reason why when we get inside."

From a small paneled foyer we entered a room that could have been a scene from *The Sting*. There were rows of telephones, cashiers, and crap, blackjack, and baccarat tables. Off to one side a chef in a tall white hat was carving slices from a big roast; there were also salads, cold cuts, and a small bar. The room was crowded, the air heavy with cigarette and cigar smoke. Most of Willie's patrons were middle-aged. The place did have the air of an old, comfortable men's club.

"Willie can beat OTB with the results," Troy explained. "You know phone calls can't go out from a track for ten minutes after each race.

Some guys tried to beat it by using the old method of having a spotter on the roof with glasses with another joker in the track giving him the results by using a finger code, but they last only a couple of days before the detectives at the track grab 'em. Willie's much smarter; he has guys in the various departments of the track who are calling out all the time. It only takes a second's phone call, then we have it here!" This is the start of the afternoon crowd. We should have ten percent of Willie's take." He pointed across the room. "That's why there is never any rough stuff in here."

He was a giant, the biggest man I had ever seen in my life. With his shaven head, thick, bristling mustache, swarthy face, and black eyes, he could have been Blackbeard's lieutenant or an eighteenth century Turkish cavalry officer. He was neatly dressed in brown slacks, sports jacket, and a shirt that showed an enormous amount of black hair. When Troy waved, the giant impassively nodded his welcome.

"You won't believe this, Hilly," he said. "They call him Omar. That's how he was billed in the circus—Omar the Strong Man. He and Willie have been pals since their circus days."

"I guess Willie was a clown?"

"Wrong," he said. "Willie was one of the best marksmen in the world. His real name is Sergi something—I can't pronounce it. But in their act Willie sat on the shoulders of Omar and shot at targets with rifles, handguns, just about anything that would shoot."

"A little man like that?"

He reminded me, "Remember, Hilly, Mr. Colt is a great equalizer. Did you notice that black strap on his right hand?" When I nodded, he explained. "That's a derringer. Willie was held up only once. That was before Omar came here. Two guys pushed their way in, scared the hell out of the players, and when Willie yelled, they threw him across the room like a football. After that Willie started carrying his little rod. He's got a license. He told me that first he's going to plug the next stickup man, and then let Omar take over." He said expansively, "Willie also owns a great restaurant on Forty-fifth Street off Eighth. Some day we'll go there and have dinner and I'll get him to show you his scrapbooks and the big poster he has in his apartment above the restaurant. It takes up most of a wall. WEE WILLIE THE WORLD'S GREATEST MARKSMAN AND OMAR HIS GIANT FRIEND. That's what it says. Willie also has a letter he got from John Ringling when he retired, calling him and Omar one of the greatest circus acts he ever hired. Where the hell would you ever find a pair like that running a gambling joint behind a fabric store except in New York?"

We spent most of the afternoon in the place with Troy finally gaining a seat at the baccarat table. It was easy to see he was a veteran gambler. When he finally stood up, he had won over two thousand dollars and was in a jovial mood.

At the entrance of the parking lot he said, "Look, Hilly, I know I can be square with you. Forget about me going back to the hotel. I can make other arrangements." He winked. "If it wasn't so late I'd ask her to get a friend."

"Sure, Steve, no problem. Like you, I need a warm body now and then."

He put his arm around my shoulder and hugged me. "I'll give you the best damn documentary you ever saw," he promised. "And we'll make the son-of-a-bitch Russell eat it."

We were comrades in arms, buddies. Fellow conspirators. Shoulder to shoulder against Russell. I decided it was a good time to gradually move in on him.

"Have you known Tura a long time, Steve?"

"From the very beginning," he said. "When Ginerva was starting up in San Francisco, Tura brought me over to her church—it was only a storefront at the time—and had me shoot some film on her."

"So you knew Tura before that?"

"I knew her before I went to Nam," he said.

"Any romance, Steve?"

He laughed. "Tura didn't go for me; it was strictly business between us."

This gave me my opening; now there would be no jealousy. "Tura and I got real friendly, Steve."

His eyes widened. "You scored with her?"

"We had a few parties," I paused. "Tura was real low down, Steve."

He rubbed his nose. "Yeah. I know. Things were not good between her and Dave."

I said softly, "Tura confided in me quite a bit, Steve. She told me a lot of things. Things about Ginerva. Her kid, Peter. Idaho. . . ."

He looked stunned. "Oh, no."

"Oh, yes, Steve. But it's all to the good. Now I know my way around. Now I know how to deal with Russell. But I need to know a lot more."

He looked as if he had just had the wind punched out of him. "Like what?" he asked weakly.

"Where's the Money Room?"

He slowly shook his head. "Jeez! Did she tell you that?"

"Where is it, Steve?"

He swallowed hard. "On the grounds." He looked frightened. "Hilly, you're asking questions that can get us both killed."

"The more I know, the more I can protect you, Steve," I said. "Where on the grounds?"

"I don't know exactly. They never brought me there."

"What's Ginerva's real name, Steve?"

He held up his hands, almost as if to ward off a blow. "I don't know that. Tura and I, we didn't know a lot. What we did know we put together when we talked."

"How about Aunt Clem? Who is she?"

He looked at me, slack-jawed, not replying.

I said in a low conspiratorial voice, "Look, Steve, we're buddies now. Tura's gone. You're going to need a friend— and that's me. Who brought you down here so Russell and his goon squad wouldn't be on your back day and night? Who told you what Ginerva was going to do in Briggs? It's got to be share and share alike, Steve. We need one another."

That hit home; he knew what I said was true. He *did* need a friend in court. . . .

He looked away, as if not facing me would take away the stain of an informer. "She's an old woman who brought her up. I don't know anything more about her."

"In other words, Aunt Clem brought up Ginerva in Idaho. Is that right?"

He licked his lips and nodded.

"Steve, one more thing. What does Foreman intend to do with the Society of the Chosen? What is he planning?"

There was a frightened look in his eyes, and he backed away slightly. "I don't know the answer to that one. . . . I really don't. . . ."

I knew he was lying, but I decided that for a beginning I had gone far enough. To make sure he realized he now belonged to me, I hugged him protectively.

"Steve, we have to stick together. If I find out anything, you will be the first to know. I hope you'll treat me the same way."

"Sure! Sure!" he muttered.

I tightened my grip. "I want you to know that any time you feel like a little action in Wee Willie's, you just take off. I'll always protect you. And that goes for the other action. . . ."

He swallowed hard. "Yeah. Thanks. I'll see you in the morning."

He started to turn away, but stopped. "Just who the hell are you, Hilly?"

"A friend, Steve," I assured him. "A very good friend."

From that day, Leah, Turner, and I treated Troy as a confidant. I showed him a map of the tour route, gave him progress reports, and continually praised his abilities as a television cameraman. I slowly gained his confidence, and after a few more trips to Wee Willie's and several drinking sessions in his room, I had some more bits and pieces to fit into the strange mosaic of Ginerva's background.

I knew she had grown up somewhere in Idaho. Her parents were either dead or divorced, and she had been raised by a woman she called Aunt Clem. She had undoubtedly been in the theatre. Troy insisted he did not know her real name or any more details of her early life. He either ignored or tried to avoid questions about the Money Room, Foreman's plan for the Society of the Chosen, or what Foreman had on Ginerva.

He pulled at his face as if it was a rubber mask. "Hilly, you're asking me about stuff that only Dave and Russell know. As I told you, it's not like it was in the beginning. Dave hasn't taken me and Tura into his confidence for a long time."

"Well, then, how do you know this much?"

He shrugged. "A little piece here, a little piece there. Whenever we could, Tura and I would put them together. Sometimes we were guessing, but because we know how Dave operates and had been in from the start in San Francisco, we were mostly right."

"What made Foreman stop trusting both of you?"

He said thoughtfully, "It wasn't a question of trust. He just didn't need us anymore. After all, he had Ginerva, his strong-arm man Russell, and his Angels."

I reminded him, "and Russell doesn't particularly like you. . . ."

He sat there for a long time without talking. I didn't interrupt his thoughts, only kept his glass filled. He was frightened, and I intended to keep him that way.

Despite a feeling of disgust at examining another man's belongings, I also continued to search Foreman's room whenever I was sure he had a luncheon or dinner appointment. With Leah in the lobby and Turner standing guard at the end of the corridor, I would search the room thoroughly. It was always scrupulously neat; closets and drawers never yielded anything, but once the wastepaper basket gave up a number of torn pieces of paper. Back in my room, we carefully put them together. It was a copy of an Amtrak reservation to Washington for the day before the Briggs rally.

I called Tom Gray in Washington, gave him a detailed report of what had happened since the last time we met, and suggested he pick up Foreman at Union Station and tail him during his stay in Washington.

"It will be a pleasure, Hilly," he said. "By the way, I have some bad news. As I told you, my former roommate works for the FBI. He put the names of Foreman and the others through the mill and didn't come up with any felony criminal records. Now that doesn't mean they're clean; who knows if they are using their real names? By the way, I saw you on television when Ginerva found that kid in the well.

Was that on the level?"

"As far as I know it was."

"How did she pull it off? I was sitting on the edge of my chair when she gave the kid back to the mother."

I told him, "I just don't have any answers, Tom. Maybe she has ESP. Maybe she's a mystic. I really don't know."

He hesitated a moment, then said, "There have been a few developments down here, Hilly, but I don't want to go into them on the phone. I'll be in touch when—and if—they shape up. But there is one thing I need to know. Were you serious about getting a committee to look into Foreman's Society of the Chosen and Ginerva?"

"Definitely. Why do you ask, Tom?"

He became vague. "It's too early for any details, Hilly, but I'll get back to you on what I found out about Foreman's trip down here."

The next day, Leah and Turner came into my office triumphantly holding up a list of Disciples they had found in the master list who had worked in films or on the periphery of filmmaking.

We had an elderly mixer so good she was occasionally called out of retirement to work on a major film; a one-time acidhead electrician; a young director who had been hailed as a genius before he ended up in Bellevue's drunk tank; two dropouts from film courses who had worked on independent productions. All were Disciples living in various parts of the country: the former acidhead was a Team Leader in Vermont, the elderly mixer lived in Florida, the dropouts sold *The Call* in midwestern cities, and the reformed drunken director worked under an assumed name in the Society's Ohio headquarters.

"What a bunch of flakes," Turner said disgustedly. "This is a crew for a documentary?"

"I did with a lot worse in Nam," Troy said proudly.

I had our ragtag crew flown into New York and settled in our hotel. The film course dropouts who carried copies of *Film Comment* along with their Bibles were intense and knowledgeable; one had experience with a camera and could assist Troy, the other was a sound-gear operator. The former acidhead electrician was a thin, nervous kid who told me that making a film of Ginerva was the greatest gift God had ever given him, while the mixer, a placid, white-haired grandmother, expressed the hope that this job would get her a special seat on God's Great White Cloud of Salvation.

The one-time youthful genius director turned out to be a religious eccentric who carried a small canvas bag of nuts, raisins, and sunflower seeds, a bottle of spring water, and a Bible with Ginerva's picture pasted on the inside cover. He claimed that when he was dying from the D.T.'s a friend had brought him into one of Ginerva's rallies in San Francisco and he was cured. He said solemnly, "It was then that I turned my back on the Whore of Babylon"—(Hollywood)—"and vowed to devote the rest of my life to serving this wonderful woman of God."

Troy told us he had neglected to add that his career as a director started to slide after he had hit a rival with a pizza during the Lincoln Center Film Festival and was arrested for kidnapping a cabbie and his fare. All had been injured in a crash following a wild chase by a fleet of police cars down Eighth Avenue.

We held a casual meeting at which everyone was introduced and the project outlined, with Troy handling the assignments. They were treated as professionals, and appeared eager to make a film as a tribute to the spiritual leader they adored.

We left for Kansas a few days later.

16

The Dead Man's Rally

In Topeka we met Dwight Davis, the area's Team Leader. He was tall, angular, and gray, but despite the genial hick role he played, I was sure he could have been at ease in any Brooklyn political club. His organization was excellent; to me it gave off more the odor of political sweat than the incense of religion.

Mayor Jack Briggs was a slender composed man, deeply tanned, with strands of gray in his dark hair and a combined air of studied affability and political shrewdness. I put him down as the man Lincoln had in mind when he was talking about a shifty politician stealing a red-hot stove. During our brief interview, in which he offered the town's complete cooperation, I noticed that his secretary and municipal workers conspicuously wore our Be-Saved-With-Ginerva buttons.

We immediately set up headquarters in the Briggs motel's "Pioneer Room," where we were surrounded by murals of cattle drives, wagon trains, and whooping cowboys entering Dodge City.

For the next two weeks, using the Topeka teams, I conducted an intensive publicity and promotion drive for the rally. "Ginerva's Wheel of God" split the state into sections. Teams assigned to Leah and Norman saturated towns, cities, and villages with posters, publicity handouts, and billboards. Every newspaper, magazine, religious publication, and farm quarterly was visited. Buttons were distributed at shopping malls, school stops, and in stores. Placards were hung in windows. Banks advised their depositors Ginerva was coming to Kansas with her glorious vision to banish the evil from their lives. Signs stretched over main streets warned those passing by not to close their ears to God's threat of Armageddon.

I used every political contact I could get out of Davis and Briggs to spread word of the rally. Merchants—who were also politicians—placed full-page ads in newspapers. The midwestern owner of a string of television stations, who owed a political favor to Davis, sent crews to Briggs for advance features, and interviews, and above all, used my handouts as hard news.

It was during these weeks of working with Leah that I found myself looking at her for the first time as a woman.One evening, she and I dined alone in the motel. Norman had volunteered to help newly arrived Disciples from Topeka set up a telephone room. The following morning, teams would be calling names on voting lists, urging them to attend the rally and hear Ginerva reveal her vision from the Almighty.

I had always been conscious that Leah was a pretty girl with a sensuous figure, but above everything she was Sir Edward's head-strong, spoiled brat, who had given him a great deal of heartache. I suddenly recalled I had never bothered to ask for her version. I had come to know her as an infuriatingly determined female with a mind of her own and an enormous confidence in her ability to control her own future. Her insistence on believing Ginerva was a holy woman and not possibly a charlatan had made me groan many times with frustration. But I had also come to admire her loyalty, honesty, stubbornness, good humor, and a façade of innocence I now knew hid a steel-trap mind.

As I studied her closely, I realized once again that Leah Butler was a pretty girl, very pretty.

"Anything wrong?" she asked, smiling, when she looked up to catch me staring at her. "Earring missing? Head on straight?"

"Would you really like to know what I was thinking?"

Her smile faded. "How you can stop me from becoming such a nuisance?"

"I was only thinking how pretty you are, Leah."

If I thought this would make her blush or become self-conscious, I was mistaken. The look she gave me was cool and measured.

"I don't think you looked at much of anything since you arrived at the motherhouse, Hilly. Sometimes I wondered, what is driving him?"

"Ben Rice was my closest friend, Leah, closer probably than a brother. To have him die like that and let these people get away with it? Never."

"I suppose you're right," she said slowly, "but I feel uneasy at what we're doing. 'Dump your morals,' you say. Is that really necessary, Hilly? Isn't there another way?"

"What other way is there Leah?" I asked. "You know the problems; we went over them. The law demands solid evidence to convict Foreman. How else can I get it? It's ironical that the very law we're trying to serve, protects him. But that's the way it is. One does what one must do."

She sighed. "I hope it will be over soon, Hilly. I'm really frightened—" she looked at me—"of what could happen to you if they found out. I never realized the power of the Society until we came out here. Wherever we go, there are Disciples willing to work twenty-four hours a day if necessary. There are Disciples in municipal governments. Housewives. Teenagers. Old men and women." She shivered. "I don't know why, but I'm suddenly afraid." She looked at me. "For you, Hilly."

"Nothing is going to happen to me, Leah," I said, with a laugh I hope sounded genuine. "All I need to find out is where they are skimming the money, and the law can take it from there."

She said suddenly, "There's another reason why I hope it all ends soon, Hilly."

"Oh? And what is that?"

"You're obsessed with Ginerva." She took a deep breath. "Are you in love with her?"

I was startled. "Whatever gave you that idea?"

She repeated, "Well, are you?"

I had never asked myself this question. Could Leah have put her finger on something I had been deliberately ignoring? Passion can grow on a man like an insidious fever. Ginerva was beautiful, mysterious, at times seemingly trapped by forces beyond her control. Was I really seeking justice for Ben, or was I unconsciously playing Lancelot trying to rescue his Guinevere? But as I thought about it, I knew Leah had to be wrong and Tura was right. Ginerva was my beautiful obsession; for some reason it was important to me to learn everything about her, even the smallest detail. It was all connected to that evening in San Francisco. It was one of those things you tell yourself must be done even if it costs your life. But love—no. . . .

She said bluntly, "You haven't answered me, Hilly."

I countered, "How could I be in love with a woman I may be sending to jail?"

"You would never do that," she said firmly. "Never."

"Leah, you are always so sure of yourself," I said, trying not to show my irritation. "Oh, I know—Ginerva is a holy woman, God's spectacular visionary who is offering his blueprint for the Last Day. Why do you refuse to admit that is all nonsense? Not believable?"

"In the absence of anything believable, Hilly, I think you should believe in yourself. I told you before, I'm not a religious fanatic. I can only tell you that something deep inside me insists Ginerva is not a fraud, and I am not going to shut my ears to that! Possibly I'm only the stubborn fool my father says I am."

I reached for her hands to press them together in mine. "That's the last thing I consider you to be, Leah—a fool. It's only knowing all we do about those crooks . . . ."

Our eyes met. I suddenly felt my mouth go dry, as I wondered how it would be to kiss those lovely lips.

She said abruptly, "For a long time I have been wanting to say something to you, Hilly. . . ." She hesitated. "Perhaps I shouldn't."

"Please say it."

"I think I know why you came to the motherhouse."

"Justice for Ben Rice—"

"That's what you tell yourself, but maybe there's another reason. Maybe you didn't even know it yourself. . . . Do you want me to go on?"

"Please do."

"Maybe you came here in the hope you could satisfy a feeling of guilt."

I felt as if she had leaned across the table and slapped me. "You're touching something that hurts, Leah."

"Norman told me," she said. "He heard it from Mr. Rice. About that patrol."

I didn't know what to say. A sudden montage of geysers of earth and stinking vegetation. Explosions, blood, shattered bodies, the calm voice of the dying lieutenant and I was burying my face in the muck. . . .

I looked up from studying our clasped hands. It was inconceivable that this lovely young girl should have guessed at what I found hard to admit even to myself.

"You can sound as skeptical as you want, Hilly," she said, "and you can call her all kinds of fraud, but I think down deep inside you have a tiny bit of doubt. You're hoping she really isn't a fraud and maybe in some way she can give you peace. . . ." She looked uneasy. "But I have said more than I should. I have no right, and I'm sorry."

"It happened a long time ago," I said. "I try to keep it buried."

"You never spoke about it," she said, "but somehow I know it is always on your mind."

"Perhaps it would have been better to talk about it," I admitted. "I always thought Ben was the only one who understood. To my dying day I will blame myself. It was supposed to be a routine patrol set up just for me. A day in the jungle with young heroes—all from our circulation area. Their deaths were so senseless. It will always remain just beneath the surface." She started to say something, but I squeezed her hand and shut her off. "Perhaps you're right, Leah, perhaps that's why I'm here, perhaps that's why I unconsciously went into that theatre in San Francisco that night, because I was desperate to find something, someone to turn to. That's how it started. She touched my cheek, and my limp disappeared along with those terrible nightmares. After that she was on my mind constantly. It suddenly became important to me to find out everything I could about her. Who is she? What is she? Where did she come from? I'm not in love with Ginerva, Leah. Someone once called her my beautiful obsession. Perhaps that best explains it. . . ."

She looked troubled as she repeated, "I had no right to say that, Hilly, and I'm sorry."

I kissed her fingertips. "Please don't be sorry. I'm glad we can talk about it."

Then Norman was suddenly staring down at us, his face tight. "I'm sorry to interrupt," he said stiffly. "The telephone room is set up. I'm going to take a shower."

He turned and left.

I let go of her hand. "I think I offended Norman."

"Why?" she asked evenly.

"Well, I assumed. . . ."

She pressed me. "What did you assume, Hilly? That I was in love with Norman?"

"You seemed very close," I observed.

"We have been good friends since the first time we met at the motherhouse," she said firmly, "and that is all."

I didn't know why, but I felt relieved when she said that. *My God,* I thought, *am I falling for Butler's very pretty and very stubborn daughter?* I almost laughed, but I quickly changed the subject.

"Leah, you never told me exactly why you joined the Society of the Chosen."

"I guess I was caught up in a whirlwind of love, peace, and save-the-world," she said ruefully. "Looking back, it's hard to believe it all happened."

"Was it really because of Ginerva that you stayed, Leah? Or because of Norman?"

She looked up and said quickly, "Norm is super, Hilly, but I could always take care of myself. When he first talked about leaving I urged him to go, but he refused. I guess I became his responsibility."

"Leah, you had everything," I pointed out. "There wasn't a thing you asked for that you didn't get. Why did you leave all that for this?"

(298)

"Everything, Hilly?" she said. "Not quite. After my mother died, my father was either in Hollywood making film, doing a play on Broadway or in London, or else on tour. He had no time for me. I realized this on my sixteenth birthday. My father had promised to be at my party, but instead of showing up he sent a check. I learned later he had been at the Cannes Film Festival with his latest mistress. She was only a few years older than I was. . . ."

She silently built a tiny wall of sugar cubes around her coffee cup. "I got so I couldn't make decisions, and that wasn't like me. That's one of the attractions of the Society; all decisions are made for you. It soon became a way of life. When I first came to the motherhouse I was swinging on an emotional tightrope. I really didn't know what I wanted. In the beginning I was surrounded by such a fantastic sense of involvement that I was desperate to become a part of it. I can remember how in the beginning we all wanted to give to one another because we believed in the same thing. Hour after hour, day after day, week after week they kept telling us we were like the first Apostles. We felt victorious, deliriously happy. But for me that soon ended." She sighed. "You can't trust completely and question at the same time."

"When did you really start to question Foreman and the others, Leah?"

"One day Foreman called me into his office," she said. "I was awed. Very few Disciples are ever called into Brother Foreman's office. He said he wanted to hold a press conference at the motherhouse during which I would denounce my father and plead with others my age to cast aside their parents and join the Society. I was shocked, and of course I refused. My father and I had differences, but to denounce him publicly as a monster was unthinkable."

"How did Foreman take that?"

"Not too well. He called me in a second time and tried to talk me into it, but again I refused. This time I was very angry, and I began asking myself questions. The third and last time, when he described the theatre as the 'Devil's Playground,' I almost laughed in his face. After this visit I thought I would be asked to leave, but I can see now that I still had publicity potential—they always included my name in any publicity sent to the newspapers— and Foreman also realized that if I was asked to leave there was the possibility I would denounce him and the Society."

I wasn't even listening. I had discovered Leah had dimples. . . .

She went on, "I met Norman, and we talked about what we should do. By this time we both knew something was wrong, but neither of us had the faintest idea of how to alert the authorities. Do you simply walk into a police precinct and tell the desk sergeant that you are both Disciples in the Society of the Chosen and you believe its president is a crook? Can you imagine the look on the desk sergeant's face or the receptionist in the New York City FBI office? They must get hundreds of fanatics and demented persons walking in with the same sort of tale."

"Did Norman tell you when Ben first contacted him?"

"We were both excited about the possibility that now something would finally be done. Then one day he returned from New York and told me the plan was to have you come up to the motherhouse and do a newspaper series exposing the Society."

"And what was your reaction?"

She said, laughing, "I didn't think much of it. All I could visualize was a wise-guy reporter who would write a tabloid kind of exposé which could do more harm than good."

She looked at me. "Then you came up. . . ."

"Smart-guy reporter," I finished.

"No," she said. "Anything but that. After we met, I told Norman I would do anything to help you."

"You have been an enormous help, Leah."

She said anxiously, "But *will* it all amount to anything, Hilly? You talk about the law and how it protects these people—"

I gently interrupted her. "Leah, this is exactly why we must make sure Foreman gets the publicity he wants. If we make this rally a huge success, I can force him to give me a piece of the action. I can put it on the line with him: cut me in or I'll leave and your tour will be wrecked! It's *my* tour now, Leah. The Team Leaders from coast to coast have been coached by *me*. The three of us have the details—the rally permits, local entertainment talent, the knowhow to saturate an area with publicity and promotional gimmicks. He's up to something in Washington, but in doing that he let me take over. It was his mistake. If we make a success of Briggs, Leah, I will be in the perfect position to make a demand."

"I worry about you, Hilly," she said anxiously, searching my face. "I can't believe Foreman will share anything with you."

"He will have no choice, Leah," I promised. "He will hate my guts, but he will have to live with me."

The waiter suddenly appeared with our dessert and Norman, scrubbed and grim looking, at his heels. Davis, he said, wanted us to attend a conference in the Pioneer Room. When we left the dining room, Leah went to the lounge and Norman and I walked to the elevators.

Suddenly Norman blurted out, "Don't hurt her, Hilly. Please don't."

He took me by surprise. "What do you mean, don't hurt her?"

"She's no round heels like Sloan, so why don't you lay off?"

I was startled. From the first day I had seen them together I suspected Norman thought a great deal of Leah, but I had never suspected how much. I felt like a villain.

"I'm sorry, Norman," I told him. "I certainly don't intend to break up anything between you and Leah. I respect her as much as you do."

He cleared his throat with embarrassment. "Leah means a lot to me, Hilly. She's the finest person I have ever met. I don't want to see her life messed up."

After a pause, Norman went on in a quiet way, not argumentative but very earnest, as though he were trying to explain a difficult problem.

"You see, Hilly, it's like this. When I first met Leah at the mother-house, she was lonely, bewildered, even homesick for that bastard of a father. She told me a lot about how she had been brought up, how her old man never had any time for her; I guess you could say she actually brought herself up. Well, we were together a lot, shoulder to shoulder, determined not to let them turn us into their walking machines but hoping in some way that we could get to Ginerva and tell her what was really going on. Then one day you arrived. Lochin var, promising to put all the bad guys in jail and straighten out the world. You should have seen how worried she was when you were out on Staten Island!" He paused, then added in a low taut voice, "I know Leah thinks a lot of you. And I'm afraid for her."

"Just what are you afraid of?" I demanded.

"Exactly this," he said defiantly. "You've been around a hell of a lot more than we have. You've known a lot of women, and I guess a lot were pushovers like Sloan. Well, I'm just telling you, Leah is not like that. So for God's sake, don't hurt her!"

He turned to the elevators and jabbed the button. I was touched. Norman Turner, for all his hundred and thirty-five pounds soaking wet, had not only courage, but class.

"Don't worry, Norman," I promised. "I'll never hurt her."

"Thank you," he said in a curiously formal way.

I only knew Ginerva had arrived late Saturday afternoon because Norman had seen Russell and Andrew in the coffee shop. I checked with the desk clerk and discovered they had the top floor of the motel, now shut off to the public. I took the elevator and found an Angel guarding the door of the suite.

"I'm sorry, sir," he said politely. "No one is allowed on this floor."

"Do you know who I am?" I asked.

"Yes, Brother Hillers, I do," he replied.

"Get Brother Russell out here," I told him. "Now!"

He hesitated, then went inside. In a moment he swung open the door. Russell was seated at a desk in a large foyer; Andrew leaned on a mantel nearby.

"You wanted something?" Russell asked..

"Where is Brother Foreman?"

"He's not here."

"Well, when is he coming?"

Russell slowly looked me up and down. "Get lost," he said softly.

I said nonchalantly, "Fine with me," and turned to the door.

I knew he could not stand this unexpected lack of protest. Before I could turn the knob, he demanded, "Where are you going?"

"To find a telephone," I said, "and call Dave."

My casualness, confidence, and easy use of Foreman's first name had an effect. He looked uncertain and stood up. "Don't make trouble for me, Hillers."

"I don't want to make trouble for you or for anyone else," I told him. "But Dave sent me out here to do a job—a very important job. There are some things Ginerva should know—"

"Dave will be in tomorrow," he said. "You can tell him."

I shrugged and opened the door. He hurried across the room and slammed it shut. "Don't you bother Dave," he blustered.

I said roughly, "Then get your ass in there and tell her I have to talk to her."

He hesitated, and I knew he was uncertain.

"She's busy."

I sat in a chair. "Then I'll wait."

He wavered under my determination and grumbled, "I'll see how busy she is," and disappeared in another room. He returned within minutes. "We'll have to wait inside while she's getting ready."

I followed him into a very large, gaudy sitting room furnished with pseudo–French Provincial furniture, a fireplace with red bulbs instead of flames, glittering chandeliers, and a full-length mirror. Russell pointed to two chairs in the shadows, and we sat down. The room was crowded with young female Disciples, some carrying hatboxes, others makeup kits; one stood guard over a hair dryer. Others came in from another room pushing an aluminum frame from which hung several gowns. There was a great deal of traffic in and out of what I assumed was Ginerva's bedroom. Suddenly she appeared in dazzling white, surrounded by a group of chattering, excited young girls, and walked to the large mirror. She was beautiful as always, but now appeared weary and almost indifferent. I started to get up, but Russell pushed me back into the chair and shook a fist the size of a large rock in front of my face.

Ginerva made several appearances to study herself in the mirror, each time in a different gown and always with her entourage. Disciples hovered over her, reaching out to pat a ruffle, fix a fold, or quickly mark a hem with pins. Once several tiaras embedded with tiny gems and displayed in a large velvet-lined box were offered for her inspection. When she tried one on, the effect was stunning; she seemed like a fairy princess.

Then came Disciples with boxes of slippers of many colors and fashions. They were slipped on her feet, viewed with a great many comments, discarded or held aside. The same thing happened with an assortment of jeweled sashes. Finally, when it was apparent Ginerva had approved of her dress and accessories—including the tiara—the Disciples packed their things and vanished as if a magician had waved his wand. Then the door of the bedroom was closed.

All during this strange show Russell had not said a word, only watched with an intense look of admiration. When the room was empty, I nudged him. He seemed startled, as if noticing me for the first time.

"What about it?" I said.

He slowly rose to what always seemed to be at least seven feet. "Wait here," he growled.

In the twilight, the room now seemed shabby and artificial. I could see a section where the wallpaper was coming loose, and the chair in which I was sitting had a loose arm. Suddenly Russell appeared, carefully closing the door behind him.

"She's gone into meditation," he said solemnly. "Nobody can reach her now—you, me, even Foreman. Nobody."

There was something in the way he said it that made me believe him.

What was Ginerva's vision? What did it have to do with the horrible murder of the child, now so much a part of the lives of the people in this farmland community? When Foreman and Ginerva met, would they discuss the vision? What else would they talk about?

These thoughts kept running through my mind as I watched the lights of Briggs wink on as the twilight slowly faded. Leah and Norman were at the auditorium, smoothing out the final details of the rally, and I had just returned from a final conference with Dwight Davis. Twenty Disciples in the telephone room were making their last calls, and as Davis reported, there wasn't a placard, poster, or button left. Reporters, photographers, and television crews from as far as Chicago had picked up their credentials at our press room and were crowding the motel bar and dining room. There was no doubt the rally would receive extensive media coverage.

I began to be conscious of how tired I was. It had been a hectic few weeks, and the confrontation with Russell and my failure to talk to Ginerva had been a disturbing preliminary to the main event. It would be most frustrating to be shut out of the meeting between Ginerva and Foreman. I had to know what went on between them and there was only one way: eavesdrop.

I first arranged for a police radio car to be outside the main entrance of the motel to escort Ginerva and Foreman to the auditorium and another to be waiting in the rear for me. The police chief was delighted by my profuse thanks for his cooperation—and by the $500 check I made out to their benevolent fund in the name of the Society of the Chosen. Then I looked up the motel's head bellman.

When I checked in, I had almost immediately classified him not as a native but as one of the restless breed that moves from state to state, hotel to motel, job to job, becoming more cynical, more greedy as the years passed.

I carefully took out a ten and gave it to him. He didn't blink; he knew what was coming.

"Ginerva has the entire top floor," I said. "Is there a suite next to her room?"

He kept staring at me with a slight smile. I gave him another ten.

"There's a small cocktail lounge," he said. "The rear wall of her suite is only corrugated cardboard covered by drapes that can be rolled back for a big party. But you can hear through the cracks." He asked quietly, confidentially, "Are you a fed?"

I didn't answer; the next bills I gave him were two fifties.

"If anyone is tipped off, you'll be in a lot of trouble," I warned.

"I intend to be working here for another year," he said. "What do you want done?"

"I want the door to that cocktail room opened tomorrow morning, along with the fire door leading to the floor."

Then I walked away. I was sure he had done this thing many times before and would continue to do it many times in the future.

I picked up a small, cheap flashlight at the lobby newsstand and then took a cab to the auditorium. It had a stunning interior, one of the finest I had ever seen. The choir on the enormous stage had just finished rehearsing a hymn, and a stocky choirmaster with piano legs was conferring with the organist. When Leah and Norman saw me, they waved and walked up the aisle.

They both looked tired and harassed "Hilly, you won't believe the details there are to this thing," Leah said, slumping down into a seat. "We haven't even had lunch! I've been going on a doughnut and a Coke since this morning."

"If it wasn't for Troy, this thing would never get off the ground,"

Norman said. "The guy's fantastic. Look what he's doing now."

Troy was in the center of the stage, holding up a clocklike instrument and several strips of cloth. Suddenly he was speared by a shaft of light. As he slowly turned the clock with a strip of cloth, he called out instructions to someone in the balcony. Each time he called, the light changed color.

"As he explained to us, nobody knows what will be the color of Ginerva's gown until she appears at the rally," Norman said, "so what he does is match the colors of all her gowns to the proper light screen he is using on the spot. He has it down to a science. He showed me his color chart—Ginerva must have gone through a thousand gowns!"

"How about the schedule?" I asked Leah.

She held up a clipboard. "I have it down minute to minute. I'll type it up and give you the original, with copies to the choirmaster, the organist, and anyone else who needs one."

"What about the high school cheerleaders? The local athletes? The ushers?"

"Norm and I went over the schedule with everyone," Leah said. "What about Ginerva?"

"I just saw her, after a hassle with Russell. She's been trying on gowns all afternoon and had her hair done."

Leah asked quickly, "Did you talk to her?"

"I couldn't. She was surrounded by Disciples, like a queen and her retinue. Then she went inside her room to meditate. Russell claimed he couldn't get to her, and I believed him. She seemed to me to be in another world."

"When does Foreman arrive?" Norman asked.

"Tomorrow afternoon. It will be an experience, watching him MC the rally."

"I wonder what her vision will be?" Leah said wonderingly.

Norman said with a yawn, "We'll know tomorrow night. . . ."

But I'll know before that, I promised myself.

17

Ginerva's Vision

Foreman arrived so late the next day that everyone, including myself, was on edge. But he appeared brisk and unruffled.

"Everything ready?" he asked me.

"The line outside the auditorium started to form about noon," I told him. "It was so hot I ordered the doors opened a few hours early. The parking fields are filled, and I've arranged for loudspeakers to be set up for the overflow crowds."

He looked pleased. "How is the press turnout?"

I gave him a list of the newspapers and television stations covering the rally. "We have someone from each of the networks, along with AP and UPI. There's a German television crew, the *L.A. Times* and Washington *Post* sent their own men, and we have a number of big midwestern dailies. We'll have national coverage."

"Excellent," he said. "I had a devil of a time getting in from the airport. The roads into Briggs are jammed. We should have a glorious rally tonight." He looked at me. "And Ginerva?"

"She's been in meditation since yesterday," I said.

He intoned, "Meditation and prayer—Ginerva's great weapons against Satan." Then, "I'm going up to her now, Hilly. You can expect us at the auditorium promptly at eight."

"I have arranged for a police escort," I said.

"Be sure the Society makes a sizable donation to their fund," he said with a smile. "I have always found it good public relations."

"I've already done that," I said.

His eyebrows raised. "Very, very good."

I recalled what Tura had said: *Dave always greases the wheels wherever he goes.*

I gave him enough time to get upstairs before I took the elevator to the floor beneath Ginerva's suite and raced up the back stairs. The bellman had done his job; the fire door was unlocked. I carefully inched it open. It was at the end of a long corridor and, fortunately, in the shadows; an Angel was guarding the elevator door.

I slipped across the hall into the cocktail room. The flashlight beam picked out stacks of dusty folding chairs, tables, and a small bar and piano pushed into a corner. One wall was rippled cardboard on a metal track. A splinter of light came through where both sides of the partition were loosely joined and covered with drapes in the suite. I could plainly hear Foreman talking to Ginerva in a low emotional voice.

"A great task faces you this evening, Ginerva," he was saying. "Probably greater than you have faced in a long time. A cloud of evil hangs over the hearts and minds of this little community. The restless soul of a murderer has brought tragedy and sadness. Satan is using that soul, Ginerva. You must ask God in his mercy and wisdom to send that soul back to where it came from and bring peace once again to this place."

His voice dropped to a whisper. "We talked about the vision God gave you, Ginerva, the vision of this dead man. This horrible murderer, returning in three days from the grave to tell the world he has not escaped punishment, that God has banished him to the fires of Hell for all eternity for his dreadful crime. . . ."

A pause, then:

"You remember that vision, Ginerva. It came when you were filled with the glory of the Lord and he granted you powers that no man has ever been given. Do you remember?"

Her voice was soft, almost melodious. "Yes, I remember. We talked about his glory and wisdom and how he came to me in the night and told me these things. He is pleased that I am doing his work, warning his people that they must drive the evil from their hearts or he will end this world with his Sea of Flame. Oh, yes. . . . His voice was like a mighty wind, and I could hear a chorus of heavenly voices praising the glory of God and his most precious son. . . ."

Foreman's voice was intent. "Yes, Ginerva, but the vision. Remember the vision? The poor damned soul returning from his grave in three days to appear before his loved ones. Remember, Ginerva, you saw him. . . ."

Her voice was now taut with fear. "Yes. . . . Yes. . . . He is a slender man in dark clothes."

Foreman prompted softly, "And his clothes are smeared with mud, Ginerva. He is walking out of the cemetery. He will appear in three days. . . ."

"And then when he leaves there will be peace in the hearts of the people." She ended. "I will ask God to send that evil soul back to eternity . . . back to Satan and the fires of Hell."

He said, "The Lord has listened to you as always, Ginerva."

"The Lord is my shepherd," she intoned, "and I shall not want . . ."

I had heard enough. Had she actually had a vision and told Foreman, or was he simply feeding the fantasies he had built in her mind? In my confusion, I stepped back and bumped into a stack of folded chairs. Metal legs grated together as I frantically held on to them.

Foreman called out sharply, "What was that?" then hurried across the room. The door of the suite slammed, and I could hear footsteps running down the hall. I had just squeezed behind the tiny bar when the door opened and a flashlight beam examined the darkness.

"There's no one in here, Dave," Russell protested. "It's only a storeroom."

"Goddammit, it was unlocked!" Foreman stormed at him. "You know my orders about rooms next to her suite! They're to be locked at all times."

He walked inside, and the beam bounced from chairs to the bar. I wondered if he would hear my breathing, and buried my face in my sleeve. At any moment I expected him to lean over and shine the flashlight into my face.

"There's nothing in here," Russell said impatiently. "We haven't got that much time to get her over there. Let's go!"

Foreman said grudgingly, "All right, but from now on make sure all doors are locked."

I was drenched with sweat and covered with dust when I crawled out of my hiding place. The door was locked, but it could be opened from the inside. Russell was talking to the guard at the elevator when I took a deep breath and crossed the hall, ran down to the next floor, and took the elevator to my room.

My dirty, sweaty face stared out from the bathroom mirror. I was covered with dust, and my white shirt had a dark smudge along the collar. I threw off my clothes, took a quick shower, put on another suit, and flew downstairs to where the police car was waiting in the rear.

The cop, stout and genial, observed, "You're cutting yourself pretty thin, young fellow." He struggled around in his seat to give me an encouraging smile. "But never you mind, I'll get you to the church on time."

Roof dome light flashing and siren wailing, he threaded his squad car in and out of the heavy traffic, sped down side streets and dirty roads, and finally came to a skidding stop at the entrance to the auditorium.

"This town needs all the prayers it can get, brother," he said, as I waved thanks and good-bye.

The choir was thundering, "Across the Jordan with the Lord" when Leah saw me pushing my way through the backstage crowd of high school cheerleaders, a local band, a group of athletes who would publicly dedicate themselves to Ginerva, stagehands, Disciples, and the statewide Team Leaders.

She put her mouth to my ear. "My God, Hilly, where have you been? Davis has been looking all over for you! The parking lots are filled and there's more than a thousand just standing around in the field. The police say all the roads into town are blocked and they have shut off the Briggs highway exits."

"Are the outside loudspeakers working?" I asked.

She nodded. "There was something wrong but Davis and Norm are out there with an electrician, and it's fixed." She pointed to a Disciple speaking into a walkie-talkie. "Davis has a team of Disciples with those things scattered all over the parking lots and with the crowds." Her eyes widened. "Do you know there was a line five blocks long outside the front entrance?"

"Tell Davis I'm here," I told her, "and to keep me informed if anything happens. I want—"

Above the voices of the choir we could hear the thin, high wail of the police sirens.

The Disciple with the walkie-talkie shouted, "Her Holiness has arrived. Ginerva is here."

In a few minutes, accompanied by Foreman, she entered backstage. She was stunning in a long green gown and a velvet sash studded with tiny ruby chips. Over her gown she wore a long black cape with a deep red lining. A glittering tiara sat on her thick copper hair. A circle of Angels surrounded her, slowly pushing through the crowd. Disciples, faces glowing, reached out to touch her; a few knelt down and bowed their heads as she passed. The young athletes stared at her with open mouths and the cheerleaders unconsciously touched their faces and hair as they drank in her beauty.

When he saw me, Foreman broke through the circle and joined me. He was dressed in a gray suit with shirt and tie to match, and he carried a worn Bible. He was calm, almost nonchalant.

I tried to look relieved. "We've been anxiously waiting, Brother Foreman," I said formally because of the crowd around us. "The choir is about finished. We have a record crowd. There's not a seat empty, and over a thousand will be listening in the adjacent field."

He glanced at his watch. "I said we would be here at eight o'clock; it's precisely eight." He smiled and patted me on the shoulder. "Congratulations, Brother Hillers, you have done a fine job. Now relax, I'll take over."

And take over is what he did.

From the moment he stepped out on the stage, he guided the rally with a skilled hand. He carefully followed our minute-to-minute schedule, never mispronounced a name or stumbled over an introduction.

His harmless jokes were greeted with waves of laughter. Bibles flipped open and fingers raced down pages seeking out the passages he quoted. Once when he cried, "Alleluia—praise be the Lord!" the packed auditorium rose to its feet and thundered back an answering, "Alleluia—praise be the Lord!"

An exhausted Turner briefly returned backstage to report the loudspeakers where working perfectly and the huge crowds outside the auditorium and in the fields were closely following the rally. Voices of the audience singing a hymn echoed over the open farmlands and could be heard for miles.

"And they're making a mint," he whispered. "Since the rally started Disciples have been moving among the crowds with baskets and containers. I saw Angels hauling away canvas bags filled with money. . . ."

For counting in the Money Room, I thought.

Ginerva had disappeared into a dressing room guarded by several Angels. Foreman gradually brought the rally to a high note of religious frenzy, and then, at a signal, the door of the dressing room opened and Ginerva stepped out. She stared straight ahead and slowly walked to the edge of the wings as Foreman finished introducing her.

The auditorium was instantly plunged into darkness. The only sounds were the uneasy shuffling of feet, a nervous cough. Then Troy's beam of soft blue light caught her in its circle. She slowly raised her hands and cried out:

"Almighty Father, we have come to praise you! To adore you! To give you thanks, to beg you for mercy and to give us courage in these dark days!"

Perhaps it was Foreman's skillful handling, plus my superhype combined with their long pent-up anxiety, superstition, and fear of what they believed were unknown forces threatening their lives. But whatever the reason, the tightly packed auditorium exploded with a sound I had never heard. It was a kind of high, wailing, anguished cry from many throats, and it made the hair on the back of my head stand up. Leah, who was standing next to me in the darkness, searched, found, and gripped my hand. It lasted for a few minutes, then slowly died away as Ginerva fixed her eyes on heaven. Camera flashguns winked continuously, and I could make out mini-cam crews jostling one another for position beyond a line of Angels who guarded the stage with an impenetrable wall of loyal flesh and fanatical devotion.

She began slowly, speaking of death, Paul's "last enemy." She was subdued, but her face quickly filled with passion and rapture as she reminded them of how Jesus had defeated death on Calvary.

"Some day we must all face death," she warned. "Someday he will come for us and then we will stand before God and give him an accounting of the stewardship of our lives. But we will not meet the compassionate Jesus who died for us, my dear Disciples, this will be the Jesus, the Judge of the World listing in the ledger of our lives, the good and the evil. Will you be rewarded with Paradise on the Last Day, or will you be condemned to eternal darkness, to the care of the Beast who rules the Hell where sinners thirst forever, a deep, racking, terrifying thirst for the God they spurned on earth?"

She closed her eyes for a long moment. There wasn't a sound, a cough, a shuffling of feet.

"What have you done with your lives, my dear brothers and sisters?" she asked in almost a whisper. "Examine your conscience. Have you cheated your neighbor? Lusted after his wife or her husband? Stolen money? Defamed someone's reputation? Turned your back on God? What sins are in your heart this very night? Have you been stung by Death, as Paul called sin? Are you prepared for the Last Day? The day God told me will soon take place unless you—the people of the world—do something about the evil that is tearing apart our Society, bringing on wars, the destruction of entire countries, the enslavement of nations? And if the world does not listen to me and God sends down his dreadful Sea of Flame to consume this planet, are you prepared to welcome that most democratic of things in this life, Death? Kings. Queens. Emperors. Dictators. Presidents. The beautiful and the damned. There will be no difference on that day, my dear brothers and sisters. Death will make us all equal."

She lifted the mike from its cradle and slowly walked along the stage, the spot following her, as she quoted Luke:

" 'Let your belts be fastened around your waists and your lamps be burning ready. Be like men awaiting their master's return from a wedding, so that when he arrives and knocks, you will open for him without delay.' "

She seemed to float in that billowing gown to the edge of the stage, where she looked out into the darkness.

"'It will go well with those servants whom the master finds wide awake on his return. I tell you, he will put on his apron, seat them at a table, and proceed to wait on them. Should he happen to come at midnight or before sunrise and find them prepared, it will go well with them. You will know as well as I that if the head of house knew when the thief was coming, he would not let him break into his house.'"

She broke off to add:

"Be on guard therefore. The Son of Man will come when you least expect Him."

Then with a loud cry she asked them:

"Will you listen to God's warning to me?"

Once again the audience was on its feet, to roar back:

"We will, Ginerva, we will!"

"Will you obey his holy commands?"

"We will, Ginerva, we will!"

She paused staring directly into the spotlight, which turned her tiara into a crown of stars. Slowly she held up a finger, and it went from side to side, covering the whole auditorium.

"For a long time an evil shadow has hung over all your hearts. One among you had sold his soul to Satan and debauched and murdered a child. You blamed God for taking him away before he could be punished for his sins and you accused your Lord of allowing this unfortunate soul to bring tragedy into your lives."

That high, moaning wail again rose from the audience, then subsided as Ginerva held out her arms as if to draw them to her.

"God has given me a vision, my dear brothers and sisters," she cried. "A vision in which he showed me his mercy and his justice. He took me to the very brink of Hell, and there among the wailing and crying of the damned he showed me the soul of that unfortunate man condemned to Hell for all eternity! And this I will say to you! Within three days that man will return from the grave to testify to what I have said!"

The spotlight winked out, the audience was plunged into darkness, and the voices of the choir filled the huge auditorium with the glory of the Lord. After a moment the lights came back on, and Foreman was standing at the microphone. The stunned audience stared up at him. When the choir finished, he said a brief closing prayer, and the rally was over. But even then they seemed reluctant to leave until the Angels began opening the doors. Only then did they get up and file out, whispering among themselves.

"God, what could she possibly mean, Hilly?" Leah asked. "A dead man returning to life to tell how he's been condemned to Hell!"

Norman said, "I told you she's crazy! She'll be the joke of the century!"

Russell met Foreman as he came off stage, and after a brief conversation Russell rushed off backstage, followed by several Angels. Foreman looked angry and disturbed when he waved me over.

"Where is Ginerva?" he snapped. "She's not in her dressing room."

"I don't know," I said. "I assumed she was with Russell."

"She's not," he said shortly, "and we've got to find her." He explained quickly, "She's been under a severe strain lately. . . ." He lowered his voice and urged me, "See what you can do about finding her, Hilly. We must search the grounds. The auditorium. Everywhere —but we must find her!"

He walked backstage, whispered to Andrew, then they both left hurriedly.

"They can't find Ginerva," I told Leah and Norman, "Check the dressing rooms upstairs. I'm going to look in the back."

The rear fire exit led me into the far end of the huge parking lot. It was a warm starshot night with a thin, curved sliver of moon. In the adjacent fields, beyond a screen of trees, cars were snarling into life as gears meshed. Whistles shrilled with authority, and the night air smelled faintly of dust mixed with oil and gasoline fumes. The cars in the lot where I was standing quickly pulled away, and in a few minutes I was standing alone in the darkness.

There was much to think about, and I began reviewing what had taken place this night, first in Ginerva's suite and later on the stage. It was incredible that Foreman, so shrewd and crafty, had allowed Ginerva to make this preposterous prediction. A dead man returning from the grave within three days?

There was also Foreman's performance in her suite. Now it was twice I had overheard him feeding her lines. Were they rehearsing an act? I had heard him say, "*the vision you told me about.*" Was it *her* vision or *his* scam?

But then in the midst of all this speculation came the real, which was always the unreal.

She had found the child in the well and called him Peter, who Tura told me was her dead son . . . .

She had cured my limp and banished my nightmares by touching my cheek. . . .

There was the young college student on the West Coast who—

I was jolted out of my thoughts by the low, bitter voice from the shadows. "Well, are you satisfied, Brother Hillers?"

She was luminous in the faint moonlight, almost wraithlike.

"It's not me you must satisfy, Ginerva, but Foreman," I said.

"They were very quiet," she said almost musingly. "Didn't they believe me?"

"How did you expect them to react, Ginerva?" I said, walking to her. "After all, a murderer returning from the grave—"

She broke in. "Do *you* believe me, Brother Hillers?"

When I hesitated, she said softly, "God granted me that vision to bring peace to the hearts of the people here."

"Or was it all Brother Foreman's idea?" I asked bluntly.

She sounded sincerely puzzled. "Brother Foreman? No. God opened his heart only to *me*. I am his courier. What do you mean, Brother Hillers?"

I moved so close our faces were almost touching. In the faint starlight, her eyes were deep and mysterious. I wondered—if I reached out, would she come into my arms?

She said abruptly, "There isn't much time, and I must tell you something."

I was startled. "What, Ginerva?"

"You will soon find peace. . . . God has told me. . . ."

For a long time I just stared at her. I didn't know what to say.

She said softly, "After I'm gone, you will find peace and great happiness."

I managed to get out, "Ben Rice. He didn't find peace."

She repeated the name bewilderedly. "Ben Rice? Who is he?"

I said, "They killed him because of you."

She stepped back. "I don't know what you are talking about, Brother Hillers."

Now she was deeper in the shadows. Behind us in the auditorium someone was playing a melancholy hymn on the organ. Beyond the trees a driver was anxiously coaxing his car to start.

"Idaho," I said. "Peter. Aunt Clem. Tell me about them, Ginerva. Tell me your secret . . . I can help you. . . ."

She never had a chance to answer. The beam of a powerful spotlight almost blinded us.

Someone shouted, "There she is!" and Foreman, Russell, and Andrew, leading several Angels, rushed out of the darkness to surround us.

"Ginerva, where have you been?" Foreman said, trying to keep his voice under control. "We've been looking all over for you."

"What have you been doing with her?" Russell said roughly to me. In the yellow light there was a mixture of rage, frustration, and relief on his sweaty face.

"Shut up," Foreman said quietly, "I'll handle this."

I was stiff with apprehension. I was sure Ginerva would tell Foreman I had mentioned Ben's name, Idaho and its secrets. Instead she said calmly, "It was so hot inside I needed some fresh air. I lost my way among the trees. Brother Hillers found me and was escorting me back to the auditorium." She looked at me and smiled. "Thank you, Brother Hillers."

"And I thank you, Brother Hillers," Foreman said. "We were all worried about Her Holiness." He offered his arm to her. "The limousine is right over there, Ginerva."

As she passed me, she said, "Always remember His words, Brother Hillers, 'For my thoughts are not your thoughts, nor are your ways my ways.'"

Then, her arm linked to Foreman's, they entered the triangle of towering Angels and were swallowed by the darkness.

"There will be a time, Ginerva," I said, "when there will be no Foreman. No Russell. No Angels. Only you and me. . . ."

On the afternoon of the third day I packed my bags, wondering how I could possibly explain Ginerva's idiot prophecy to the mob of outraged farmers and townspeople, and the reporters, photographers, and television crews whose stories had mocked us. My phone had rung continuously; the majority of the callers were anything but pious in their comments about me, the Society of the Chosen, and Ginerva. Even the mayor had publicly denounced us as charlatans who had capitalized on a tragedy. The morning following the rally Foreman, Ginerva, Russell, Andrew, and their entourage had taken the jet back to the motherhouse; I was to stay with Leah, Turner, Troy, and his crew for the full three days.

"Hilly, I want you to be on hand to take care of the press when the vision comes true," he said. He looked with gratification at the mounds of newspapers on the bed. "It appears we have received splendid coverage, and now it needs one last touch."

When he looked at me, I tried not to laugh in his face. "And that is when the murderer returns from the grave?"

"Exactly," he said evenly. Then he admonished me gravely, "Don't be Ginerva's Thomas, Hilly. 'Blessed are those who have not seen and yet have believed.'"

The third day began with a sullen hot dawn and developed into a broiling afternoon.

A few minutes before three o'clock, Norman and Leah appeared with their bags.

"Well, what do we do now?" Turner asked as they sat on the edge of the bed.

"Wait for Ginerva's dead man to stroll into the motel and hold a press conference," I replied.

"It's not funny, Hilly," Norman protested. "We went downstairs for lunch, and from the looks of the people in the lobby, if something doesn't happen soon they're not going to let us leave until they donate a coat of tar and feathers." He sniffed. "Well, we have one thing going for us. Troy is entertaining the television crews with stories of how he made his great award-winning documentary on Vietnam."

"What do you think, Leah?" I asked.

She shook her head. "I just can't believe Ginerva made that prophecy unless she really believed in it . . ."

I ended her sentence. "And Foreman let her do it."

We sat there staring morosely at each other.

Finally Norman broke the tense silence. "I brought the car around to the back," he said. "Maybe I better take the bags down. At least I won't have to go through that damn lobby." As he got up, the phone rang and he reached for it. The moment I heard Davis's hysterical voice I knew something had happened.

Norman looked stunned as he scrawled something on the pad. When he hung up his face was pale, and his hand trembled as he held out a piece of paper.

"Davis said to meet him in ten minutes at the end of Main Street. We're going over to the home of the sister of the choirmaster." He swallowed hard. "He said the state police have been called there by a doctor. The woman said her brother appeared to her in his funeral clothes and begged her to pray for him. He said he was burning in Hell for his sins."

Leah gasped, "Oh my God."

I quickly recovered my wits. Miracle or some old woman's hysteria, this was what Foreman wanted, national publicity.

"It will be all over the town within minutes," I told Turner. "Go downstairs and tell Troy to get his crew and meet us in the rear in a hurry. Don't say anything to the others. I want him to get an edge on any film."

Leah and I ran down the back stairs. Within minutes Troy and his crew in a station wagon pulled up alongside of us. Norman in the front seat leaned out and yelled, "Some of those newspaper guys wanted to know where Steve was going!"

We moved out fast and met Davis in his car near the edge of town. He waved and pointed and we followed him down the highway for several miles to finally career into a lane leading to a small, squat farmhouse with police cars parked in the driveway.

A state trooper was guarding the front door, but after Davis said something to him he waved us in. Foreman knew what he was doing when he selected this tall, angular politician-convert as his Team Leader, I told myself.

We entered an old-fashioned living room filled with heavy, almost ponderous dark furniture, an organ coverd with a tasseled cover, and framed pictures of men wearing high collars, thick mustaches, and somber clothes.

Sitting in an overstuffed armchair surrounded by several men and women, obviously her neighbors, was a distraught white-haired woman twisting a sodden handkerchief. A man with an open physician's bag on the floor was patting her hand and whispering to her. A state police captain recognized Davis and briefly spoke to him in a low voice. Then Davis introduced me, Leah, and Turner. With a minimum of noise, Troy and his crew completed their setup and began shooting the woman.

"That's his sister, Hilda," Davis said softly.

The woman looked up at us, bewildered. "I saw him," she cried. "I saw him at my bedroom window. A tapping at the screen woke me up. It was a full moon and my bedroom was as light as day. When I looked up he was staring at me through the screen." Her fist went to her mouth and the blood drained from her face. "He was in the clothes I buried him in! He just stood there, his hair long and hanging down." Her voice rose to a scream. "Like he had come up out of the grave. And he kept saying over and over, 'Hilda . . . Hilda. . . . God has condemned me to Hell for my sins. Pray for me . . . Pray for me . . . ' I could see his face as plain as if he had just come back from a choir practice."

The physician said soothingly, "Hilda, you've been under a great strain. Nerves make people think they see things which aren't there." He gave us an angry look. "With all this nonsense in the newspapers and on television . . ."

"No. No," she wailed. "Ginerva was right. God did show her my brother in Hell. It was him. . . . It was him. . . ." She suddenly held out her hand. In the palm was a tiny gold cross pin. "This was the cross he always wore in his jacket lapel," she cried. "I found it on the windowsill."

The doctor hastily searched his bag. "I'll have to give her a shot to calm her down," he said.

"It's true about that cross," the captain murmured to us. "I was with him all night in the barracks when he confessed. I noticed the cross in the lapel of his jacket. It was in the pictures in the papers and on television when he was arraigned."

"Anything outside the window?" I asked.

"Her bedroom is on the first floor," he said soberly. "There were some prints, but the neighbors she called practically wiped them out by the time we got there."

A phone rang somewhere in the house, then a trooper rushed into the room.

"Captain," he gasped. "Reverend Gibson's wife was just taken to the hospital. She hit her head when she fainted."

The captain said impatiently, "Why bother me? Call the Briggs police and tell them to send the First Aid Squad."

The trooper licked his lips. "But, captain—she fainted after they saw him. He was outside the Reverend's window!"

On the way to the hospital, while the captain drove, Davis filled us in. Reverend Wilfred Gibson had been minister of Briggs First Reformed Church for more than twenty years. Despite his eighty-odd years, he was still a forceful speaker, prominent in the life of the community, and a deeply religious man who had never completely recovered from the shock of discovering his choirmaster, an old friend, was a sadistic child murderer. In a memorable sermon he had begged the families of Briggs not to seek vengeance but to pray for the soul of the dead accused man.

"A lot of folks didn't buy that," the captain broke in. "I know I didn't. I was there when we dug up the remains of that poor kid. All I wanted was for the bleeding hearts against capital punishment to be there and see what I was seeing." He sighed. "Then he conked out in his cell. . . ."

Davis said, "Do you think it was the old lady's imagination, captain?"

The captain stared broodingly at the passing farmlands. "I've been a cop too long to believe in ghosts who leave footprints behind."

"Or gold crosses?" Davis asked.

"I feel as if I was looking at a Boris Karloff movie," the captain said. Frankly, so did I. . . .

A nurse brought Reverend Gibson into the small conference room where we were waiting. He was a distinguished-looking old man with a shock of white hair which made me think of pictures of Lloyd George. His face was sickly pale, and his hands trembled when he put on his glasses. He looked startled when Troy began shooting, but Davis introduced us and he nodded his permission.

"My wife can't talk," he explained almost apologetically, "the doctor has put her under sedation. I've been sitting in there reading the Bible and praying." He added helplessly, "That's all I can do."

When the captain asked him to tell exactly what had happened, the minister closed his eyes and shuddered. "I am eighty-three years old and have been serving the Lord since I was twenty-two. I was in France in World War I, worked with our missions in Africa and in the

Far East. I have seen many strange things in my lifetime, but what I saw a few hours ago . . ." He paused, then said half to himself, "The only explanation is divine."

The captain gently reminded him, "I believe you were in your study, Reverend?"

The minister nodded. "It was late, and I was working on next Sunday's sermon. Ironically, it was on the mystery of how God works in our lives. It had been terribly hot all day. But there was a slight breeze after the sun went down. Once I thought I heard a noise outside, but I was so engrossed in what I was doing I didn't pay any attention. I guess subconsciously I heard someone calling me. I called out to my wife, who was in the next room reading, but she said she didn't call me. I went back to my writing and suddenly, as clear as a bell, a voice called out: 'Reverend . . . Reverend. . . .'"

"When I looked, I saw a shadow at the window. The moon was full and the night was brilliant. I got up and walked to the window. Suddenly, I found myself staring into his face. His eyes were sunk deep into his skull and were glowing like coals. If you recall, he had rather thick black hair and it was long—" it seemed difficult for him to continue—"like a dead man's hair. I could still see him clearly in the moonlight. I was unable to move. All I could do was pray. I could barely hear his voice but I am sure he was saying again and again, 'Reverend . . . Reverend . . . God has condemned me to hell for my sins . . . Pray for me. . . . Pray for me. . . . '"

"At that moment my wife entered the room and walked toward me asking what was wrong. I couldn't speak. His face was perfectly clear. She screamed and fainted, striking her head on the floor. The cut is superficial, but she is in a state of shock."

The captain suggested, "Everyone has been uptight around here for some time, Reverend. The kids killed in that crash, the crop lost, and now this rally and all that publicity . . ."

"If you are suggesting my wife and I imagined something, captain," he said firmly, "you are wrong. What I saw on the veranda of my presbytery was my former choirmaster, a man I knew for more than twenty years. A man I had dinner with at least several times a year. A man whose funeral I conducted, and begged God in his infinite mercy to give us strength and faith to forgive."

Davis said, "We just came from the farmhouse, Reverend. Hilda saw him at her bedroom window."

"Oh compassionate Father, have mercy on us," the old man whispered, then left.

The captain looked at us. "There's one more place," he said.

I was gripped by the chilling presentiment of what we would discover in a very few minutes. But it could be no more incredible than what we had seen and heard during the past hour. I felt like pounding my knee with my fist in frustration. What was the answer to all this? Like the captain, I refused to believe in ghosts who left footprints and a gold cross. But if the restless soul of that horrible killer hadn't left them, who had? Was it possible that Ginerva *really* had the divine vision she revealed to Foreman?

The captain interrupted my thoughts when he spoke for the first time. "We don't have to stop at the office, I know where it is. I was here with some of my men the day they buried him. We thought there might be trouble, but nobody showed up, only his sister and Reverend Gibson, along with a thousand newspapermen. One of them almost fell into the grave."

We passed mausoleums, countless stone angels, crosses, and tombstones, to finally stop just below the crest of a small hill. It appeared this was a new part of the cemetery. The graves looked raw, with their withered wreaths and flowers. Nearby, a workman's tent covered mounds of sod and tools.

With Troy and his crew coming up in the rear, we followed the captain from the path. Suddenly he stopped and pointed. We looked down, horrified. The sunken mound had been disturbed. There was loose dirt on both sides of the grave.

The captain looked at us, then his finger went from the grave to the path.

There were footprints.

18

Bible Man

Ten minutes after I returned to my office at the national tour headquarters, Foreman summoned me. For a few minutes he studied me with those cold shrewd black eyes, then he abruptly held out his hand.

"Congratulations, Hilly," he said. "It was a magnificent job."

I slumped down wearily in the chair. It had been a hectic week since that afternoon in the cemetery. The press conferences had been wild affairs; even reporters got into arguments over supernatural appearances, vampires, ghouls, banshees, loup-garou, lemures, the Evil Eye, and the possibility of anyone returning from the grave. There were televised interviews with the state police captain, the sister, Reverend Gibson, and Dwight Davis. The case was rewritten for the Sunday supplements; one network did an hour show with an appropriate panel of experts to explain for the viewers what they had just seen. In brief, Foreman had received his national coverage. I sat there feeling a dull sense of triumph. All the long months of planning, ignoring morals, always playing the end against the means had finally paid off. Now within a few minutes I intended to make my pitch: either cut me in or I leave. . . .

He held up a thick folder of clippings. "I was just going through these when you came in." He skipped through the file, shaking his head with obvious pleasure. "A marvelous job, Hilly, simply marvelous. And your idea of bringing Troy out there really paid off."

"His documentary of the rally, the interviews with the sister and the minister, along with shots in the cemetery were the best I have ever seen," I said sincerely. Troy had indeed done a fine job. Not only the affiliates but also the network shows had used some of the film he had shot.

Then, without looking up, Foreman said abruptly, "Russell claimed you tried to get in to see Ginerva before I arrived. Why?"

The unexpected question flustered me for a moment, and I had to search for an answer. "The newspapermen were hounding me to hold a press conference with her. I didn't want to antagonize them; I thought a brief statement might help."

"I see." He closed the file and looked up. He was smiling, but his voice was cold as frosted metal. "I would like to make it clear, now and forever—" he paused and went on—"no one speaks to Ginerva unless I give my permission." Then his whole personality seemed to slide into another gear; once again he was the appreciative director, friendly and warm. "Now, I suppose we should get to the tour immediately, don't you think so, Hilly."

My mouth was dry; it felt as if I was chewing on cotton. "I agree. We should get on the road while the weather is holding."

"Have you decided on your jump-off city?"

"Yes. Cleveland."

He raised his eyebrows. "Oh? Not Philadelphia? Any reason?"

"I had our agency do a survey of both cities. They agree with me that Cleveland is more responsive to rallies—religious, rock, political campaigns. The people like to become involved. Also, the auditorium has a fine adjacent park for any overflow audiences."

He nodded approvingly. "As always, you do your homework, Hilly. I'm a great believer in careful preparation; it goes with money and expertise." He added, with a broad smile, "That wonderful combination is going to make this tour a huge success: homework, money, expertise."

I took a deep breath. He may have suspected something was coming, because the smile faded and he gave me a sharp look.

"There is only one thing about the tour, Dave."

"Oh? And that is?"

"I won't be taking it over."

He fought to control himself, but the shock was evident. His voice had a rasp to it. "May I ask why not?"

"I have decided my expertise should pay off," I told him. "I want in."

When Foreman was angry, his face never showed any emotion. No thinning of lips. No gathering of muscles along the jawline. Nothing could change his stony immobility.

"What do you have in mind?" he asked softly.

"Sixty-forty," I replied. "Sixty for you and anyone you have to split it with, and forty for me."

His piercing black eyes never left my face. "And in return, you'll do what?"

"I'll make your dreams come true. I will give you a tour that will not only make Ginerva a household word but will also give you more recruits for the Society of the Chosen then you will be able to handle." I promised him, "I'm also thinking of a European tour. Let the Society become international. Ginerva will take them by storm over there. I recently read a survey that showed Europeans are hungry for religion—not the traditional kind, but anything that has a flair, drama, pageantry, and excitement. By the time I am finished, she will be the most talked-about woman in the world." I emphasized, "Not only the United States but the *world*."

He blinked, and I suddenly knew the idea was not new; it had been on his agenda of the future, and I had struck home.

"I really don't need you," he said.

I gave a snort of disgust. "That's not worthy of you, Dave. You know I'm your kingpin. If I walk away the whole tour will collapse. The national Team Leaders are used to talking to me, they depend on me. I have arranged all the contracts, permits, and the television promotion. I have done most of the writing, the editing of the text for the commercials, brochures, even the billboards. Ask yourself, how much has the agency really done? Of course you remember how I was here in the office until eleven o'clock at night while you were away. What these trips were about I couldn't care less, that's your business. But the tour is *my* business. Whether you like it or not, I own it. Without me, it's nothing. If I left now, who would take my place? Russell? He's a thug with no brains. Troy? He's a great cameraman but mentally a lightweight. The only one who could have helped you was Tura Sloan and she's gone. It's either me or dump the tour. What will it be?"

I tried to appear as though I was brimming over with confidence when actually I was tense with expectation and apprehension.

He suddenly spun about in his chair, got up, and walked to the window to look down at Fifth Avenue. After a moment of silence, he suddenly said, almost musingly, "You really had me fooled. Here I was congratulating myself on finding one in a million—a religious, talented boob! A skilled journalist with a real flair for promotion, publicity, and pageantry, who would willingly work his heart out because he had been won over by Ginerva! Who was sure that whatever he did would be repaid when she led him aboard God's Great White Cloud of Salvation." He slowly left the window to return to lean on the back of his chair. He was grinning, more relaxed now, as though the first shock wave had passed and he had his strategy formed. At this point I knew he was double dangerous, and I carefully watched every move and followed every word.

"Congratulations, Hilly."

I made a slight gesture with my hand to acknowledge his felicitations.

Still grinning, he rocked back and forth on the back of the chair. "What a chump I was! I should have smelled something. But you were good. No, not 'good'; perfect!" In a low conspiratorial voice he added, "Tell me, Hilly, when did you plan all this? Before you came up here the first time? Are you alone in this thing? No partners? Have you worked a scam before?"

I felt like a mouse in a corner facing a hungry snake, and decided my previous edge of surprise was slipping away dangerously fast.

"Let's cut out the camaraderie," I told him. "I only want a decision from you. Do I get a cut or do I walk out?"

The grin vanished. "You said forty. Forty of what?" he snapped.

"Of everything. And that includes street sales and contributions."

"You're insane if you think I would agree to that," he said contemptuously.

"It was only an offer, Dave," I said. "Offers are negotiable. But if it doesn't fit in with your plans, I'll just move on. Good luck with your tour."

He waited until my hand was on the doorknob before he spoke. "Come back here and sit down."

When I turned around, he was sitting very stiff in his chair and his fingers had started their goddam drumming.

"Twenty-five percent," he growled as I sat down.

I countered, "Thirty."

"Without street sales," he said.

I shook my head. "No way. I was out peddling, remember?"

"Twenty-five percent with street sales," he offered.

I held out my hand. "You have yourself a deal."

He ignored my hand. "Not so fast, my friend. I have a conditon."

"I don't like conditions," I said.

"Like it or not, that's my final offer. Twenty-five percent including street sales, but on my condition."

"And that condition is?"

He sat down and leaned across the desk. "First, let's agree you did a fine job in Briggs. The promotion was excellent, the press coverage superb. But you had something even a cub reporter could have exploited: Ginerva's heavenly vision and a dead man returning from the grave. You will have to agree it was a natural, Hilly."

"Even a natural needs expertise." I tried to sound casual. "By the way, how did you pull that off?"

His smile was thin. "Ginerva is the messenger of God, remember?" The clicking of his fingernails on the glass desk top was loud in the quiet room. "Without you the tour could be hurt badly. I don't question that. But don't ever believe it would collapse or be cancelled. Maybe you sold me a bill of goods and now I'm caught short, but we could get by—money can buy a hell of a lot of expertise. That would take time and time is what we don't have a lot of, so I must cut you in. But before I do, my friend, you have to prove to me Briggs wasn't a freak."

I asked, "What do you want? Cleveland has its problems, but certainly no demons."

His smile was triumphant. "Exactly. But that's *your* problem. You're the promotion and publicity genius; *you* find a gimmick for Cleveland. A gimmick that will produce a tremendous amount of publicity both in print and on television." He leaned forward. "Now do you see what I mean, Hilly? Why should I cut you into something we both know is very very big because of one lousy rally and a great gimmick you had nothing to do with. I'm looking forward to a *national* tour. You claim you can make Ginerva's name a household word and give the Society of the Chosen more recruits than we can handle. Fine. Start with Cleveland. Show me that within five days you can come up with something which will put this rally on page one. Make it the subject of national conversation and comment. Pack that stadium out there. Have lines waiting to get in."

"And if I do that?" I asked.

He repeated, "Twenty-five percent with street sales included."

"Well, since we're talking about conditions, I also have one."

He waved me to continue.

"When we make our deal, I want to know and to see everything. Where the money is taken, how it is counted and by whom, and where if finally goes. I also want to see your double set of books and I want to know everything about Ginerva."

He arched his eyebrows. "That's quite a list!"

"Once I'm in I'll work like hell for you, Dave," I promised. "But I don't intend to be part of anything that has secrets from me. It's too easy to be left holding the bag. Well, those are my conditions. Take them or leave them."

He slowly nodded. "You bring me back the Cleveland rally on page one and on television, and you will be made a full partner, with no secrets."

(325)

Then he held out *his* hand; his grip was dry and firm.

I said, "Is it understood I am to be in complete charge in Cleveland?"

"You can do anything you want—if it means publicity for the rally, Ginerva, and the Society of the Chosen."

"And you will MC the rally as usual?"

"That's something I want to talk to you about," he said. "I'll be in Washington, so you will have to be master of ceremonies."

I was startled. "That's impossible, Dave. I've never done that before!"

"Don't be ridiculous," he said. "You were a street preacher, remember? And as I recall you did damn good. Maybe it was all part of your sales pitch. But whatever, you'll have to do it. That night you'll be publicity and promotion director and MC all in one. If you want to be a partner, you'll have to work for it!"

"What about money?"

"No problem," he said smoothly. "I'll give you bank authorization for a hundred thousand. If that's not enough, our New York bank can arrange funds."

"Will I be able to talk to Ginerva before I leave?"

"That is not possible," was his quiet answer.

I gave him a quizzical look. "I'm in command of a rally and I can't talk to the star?"

"There are reasons which someday you will understand," he said. "Anything else?"

"How will she get to Cleveland?"

"Russell and a bodyguard of Angels will escort her to Cleveland on the jet and will bring her back to the motherhouse."

"But will I be able to talk to her in Cleveland?"

Again a flat "No." Then, impatiently, "Why do you want to talk to her? This time she will only be doing her usual thing—the Last Day is coming and everyone had better get with it if they want to be saved. There is no need for you or anyone but me to talk to her. She must go into deep meditation. She can't be bothered with conversation."

"What about a Blessing of the Sick? We didn't have one in Briggs."

"In Briggs we didn't need one. From now on we will maintain our regular program, including Troy's storm as a finale."

I said cautiously, "I know she doesn't like to do—"

He snapped, "She'll do the Blessings."

"I don't want any problems once we get on the road, Dave."

"There won't be any problems," he said. "Ginerva will do the Blessing of the Sick."

"Is it so vital?"

"It brings in the coin," he said bluntly.

"Tell me, Dave, what's all this stuff about the Blessing? What's wrong with her?"

"You're not in yet," he said in a brittle voice. "Just do your job in Cleveland and let me worry about Ginerva."

"Fine," I said. "One more thing. Be sure you tell Russell I'm in charge and to keep away from me."

His smile was menacing. "I'm sure Brother Russell will dearly love you when I tell him there may be a new partner."

I said boldly, "So far the DA hasn't paid you any attention, Dave, but a couple of musclemen like Russell and Andrew can bring you into a grand jury room."

There was a hint of amusement in his voice. "You don't have to warn me about district attorneys or grand juries, my young friend. I'm well aware they exist."

"Yes, but are Russell and Andrew?" I asked as I started to get up, but he waved me back into the chair.

"You know, Hilly," he said, "I really had big plans for you. But in a way our little meeting this morning might be for the best. It will be easier working with you now that I know what you are." He smiled. "A thief."

I reminded him, "Birds of a feather. What about those plans. What do you have in mind?"

"They can hold," he said. "Let's first see what you can do in Cleveland."

I paused at the door. "Oh, by the way, you should have this information. I prepared a fifty-page report on everything I have found out about you and the Society of the Chosen and placed it in a safety deposit box. If anything should happen to me, someone I trust implicitly will turn copies over to the New York County District Attorney, the FBI, Department of Justice, and the Internal Revenue." I gave him a benign smile. "In our business it is always best to have a fire escape. Don't you agree, Dave?"

I expected him to say something, show some emotion, but he didn't. His face remained stone. Only his eyes revealed the rage churning within him.

The three of us almost closed the small restaurant on York Avenue, discussing what had taken place between me and Foreman and planning our next move. But every suggestion to make the Cleveland rally explosive and unusual was quickly discarded as unworkable and unimaginative.

"Now you're a threat to them, Hilly," Leah said in the cab going back to the Lafayette. "Who knows what they'll do?"

"Foreman is too smart to try anything after Hilly warned him about having that report in a safety deposit box," Norman said.

"Yes, but is Russell that smart?" she asked. "Or Andrew? They're both thugs. They haven't got Foreman's brains or shrewdness. What do you think Russell's reaction will be when Foreman tells him Hilly will get a cut? That he will be getting less and someone else will be in their setup?"

I tried to sound unconcerned. "Leah, please don't worry about Russell. Before we know it this whole mess will be over and they'll all be in jail. All of them."

She turned to look at me. "I have the feeling that you are now trapped by those terrible people and just waiting for their next move."

"Hilly can take care of himself, Leah," Norman said in a voice that I thought had a harsh edge to it. "I just hope they don't come after *us*."

"Don't act like a lamb being led to slaughter," I told him. "All you have to do is tell the driver to stop and get out."

He stared out the window. "You can do what you want, Hilly, but I won't leave without Leah."

Before she could answer, I posed the quetion. "Perhaps it would be better if you *both* got out now."

"No," was her flat answer. "And for God's sake, both of you stop being so macho."

We rode the rest of the way in silence.

With four days to go, Leah, Norman, and I flew to Cleveland with Steve Troy and his crew; Russell, Ginerva and her praetorian guard of Avenging Angels would follow in the Learjet. I hadn't had much sleep since my meeting with Foreman. Night and day I had been turning over ideas to sensationalize the rally, but nothing clicked. When closely examined they all seemed stale and shopworn. The Cleveland newspaper reporters and editors and the television news programs were too experienced and too sophisticated to buy any cardboard and paste stunts as hard news. We had to supply a genuine story or a happening that made news. All I could expect for a routine rally was a respectable half column on an inside page with—if we were lucky—a three column cut of the crowds or Ginerva on the stage. I pushed aside the Cleveland papers I had bought the night before at Times Square. They held only more bad news for us; we were in competition with a threatened garbage men's strike and an intriguing triangle murder involving a beautiful secretary who, unfortunately for us, had kept a diary. Both would make page one every night.

Troy slid into the seat next to me and picked up one of the Cleveland papers. "There's certainly a lot of things goin' on in that town," he observed. I groaned inwardly. Since what he called "my dead-man shots in Briggs" had been used on the networks' news programs, there was no holding him; he told the story again and again. But he had done an excellent job and I wanted to keep him on my side, so I closed my eyes, leaned back, and prepared to become a patient listener. But instead of Briggs, I heard him grunt and mutter, "Hey, Casey Ramona! Good Ol' Case is back in action. And in Cleveland!" He nudged me. "You heard of Casey Ramona, Hilly?"

Casey Ramona, reigning Queen of Rock. I had an immediate picture of *Time*'s cover; a pretty young girl who wore a fringed suede jacket, a battered cowboy hat perched on the back of a mop of tangled blonde curls, and who gripped the microphone with both hands as though she wanted to strangle it. The article had marveled at her ear-splitting voice.

"Uh-huh."

I only half listened to his story of how he knew "Ol' Case" from Wee Willie's gambling joint in the Garment Center where one afternoon he had watched her drop thirty thousand at blackjack only to return the next day to recoup her losses and win an additional ten thousand.

Troy said in an awed voice, "She sat there for hours, not saying a word, only giving the dealer a nod when as much as five gees were on a card. When they cleaned her, all she did was throw her last fifty to the dealer as a tip, lean over to kiss the top of Willie's head, and promise to be back the next day. I was there when she came back. By the time the joint closed she had her winnings piled around her. Willie had Omar drive her home, stay all night outside the door of the hotel room, then drive her to the bank in the morning. What a gambler that dame is, Hilly!"

"Is that where her money goes?" I asked more out of boredom than any desire for information about the lifestyle of Casey Ramona.

"Every dime," he said. "Know what she told me one day, Hilly?"

When I shook my head, he went on.

"We were in Willie's and she had drooped maybe five, six thousand. I remember when I loaned her ten to take a cab to her hotel, she said, 'Stevie, remember money is for spendin',' and then she laughed in that boomin' voice and walked out. The next day she gave me fifty because she said the interest rates had gone up all over town." His smile faded. "But Case better have some front money in Cleveland."

"Why is Cleveland any different than New York, Steve?"

"She's into a Cleveland bookie for thirty thousand, and from what I hear the bottom has temporarily dropped out of her money barrel. Oh, Casey is good for it, but the guys in the gamblin' business don't like to wait. I know the guy who is in charge of her TV appearances. Like he said, every time she gets paid there is a line outside her dressin' room, everyone with their hand out."

"How did she run up thirty thousand in Cleveland?"

"On her last tour stop. Horses, shootin' crap, blackjack; you name it. Like I said, Case is good for the money, but the guys she owes are impatient." His voice dropped a note. "If Case doesn't get up the green and pick up her markers she'll be marked lousy, and that means no more credit at the tables. She won't be able to put down a bet in Cleveland, New York, Chicago—anywhere—and that will kill her. Some people have it for booze; Case has it for gamblin'. . . ." He brooded for a moment. "Did you ever hear her sing, Hilly?"

"I heard some of her records in Nam."

"What a voice, and what a followin'!" he said. "She can fill a place better'n Linda Ronstadt—and to be better than Linda is to be *real* big!"

The idea was only the size of a pinpoint, but it was slowly growing.

"When you say she can fill a place, Steve, how much does she draw?"

He rubbed his face vigorously. "She's good for sixty thousand on a slow night. Maybe more when she has a hot record out."

"Does she have anything out now?"

He gave me an unbelieving look. "Hey, Hilly! You must be the only guy who doesn't know her. 'The Bible Man' is the hottest record ever made. *Variety* had a whole piece on it last month. Sales are out of sight."

"How well do you know her, Steve?"

"Real good," he replied proudly. "Any time I see her at Willie's she comes over and gives me a big hug." He shrugged. "We're gamblers, Hilly, two of a kind, what more can I tell ya?"

Now it was there, all developed, new and shining, an idea waiting to be put into motion. . . .

"Steve, I want a straight answer from you," I said. "How well do you *really* know Casey Ramona?"

He gave me a puzzled look. "Very, very good, Hilly. Like I said, we've been with Wee Willie for years. I guess we're his best customers. When I'm broke Case tosses me a C-note. When she goes under I give her cab fare, or maybe we take a cab to her hotel and have a drink. Hell, we've been doing that for about five years." He added indignantly, "Why should I lie about her? I'm not livin' with her."

"This is why I asked," I said, then explained my plan.

He looked stunned. "You mean, you want me to see the guy who runs the gamblin' joint in Cleveland, pay him off and pick up Case's markers—if she agrees to appear at our rally?"

"That's it, Steve. Thirty thousand for one appearance. But she's got to be converted, right on the stage, and sing 'Bible Man' and a few others."

(330)

"I don't get it."

"It's very simple, Steve. Dave insists we have to do something big to gain publicity for this rally.

"You mean like Briggs?"

"Exactly. We did so good in Briggs he wants a repeat. And I think your friend Casey Ramona is our answer. If she agrees, I want TV rights to the rally, and you and your crew do the camera work." I gently added: "Could be good for an Emmy nomination, Steve."

He nervously tugged at his cheek. "I don't know if Casey will go for a whole night at a religious rally. . . ."

I patiently explained, "All I want her to do is appear, announce she has been converted to the Society of the Chosen, and sing 'Bible Man' and maybe another song or two. How long will it take her? An hour? In return we pay off her gambling debts and she's free as a bird."

He hesitated. "From what I know about her, Case isn't exactly a religious person, Hilly."

"Look, Steve, you and I both know this is show biz, not religion."

"What about Ginerva? She might not go for it."

"Dave gave me complete control. She'll have to go for it."

"What about the Blessin' of the Sick? Are you gonna have one?"

"Dave insists on it. Why do you ask?"

He looked uneasy and rubbed his face. "She's not gonna do the Blessin's any more."

"How do you know that?"

He said vaguely, "I hear things. I think maybe she wants out." He looked about nervously. "I never told you this, remember?"

"It's safe with me. Steve."

"She wouldn't go for a Blessing in Briggs."

"But we didn't need one. We had more than enough."

"Okay. But Dave doesn't want to drop the Blessin' from the program. Ginerva does. She told Dave no more or she takes a walk," he whispered. "I guess I can tell you. I got it from one of the Angels who guards the Grand Ballroom. He heard them go at it."

"But why, Steve? Why doesn't she want to do the Blessings?"

"I don't know," he said slowly. "I really don't know, Hilly."

I was only half listening. I was planning the conversion of Casey Ramona, Queen of Rock, into a Disciple of the Society of the Chosen before thousands of her hooting, whistling, stomping, cheering followers . . . sixty thousand or more in Cleveland's Rally for the Lord. . . .

It would be another media event. And when it was over I would silently hand Foreman a batch of clippings and demand full partnership in this most sordid of conspiracies.

In Cleveland, Troy contacted a syndicate bookmaker who confirmed Casey Ramona owed $30,000 that had to be paid before the singer could lay down a bet.

At a meeting in a bar in Cleveland's colorful "Flats" I paid the $30,000 in cash on her promise to appear at the Cleveland rally and not only publicly announce her conversion to Ginerva and the Society of the Chosen, but also sing her hit record, "Bible Man," and several other songs.

The rally was tremendously successful. The place was jammed with young people, with mobs outside listening to the loudspeakers I had ordered Troy to place about the area. The idea of Casey Ramona, Queen of Rock, the pot-smoking, cocaine-snorting, wild young spirit joining an evangelical movement attracted the media, particularly television.

I blundered my way through as MC, attracting a great deal of good-natured hoots and jeers, until Ginerva finally appeared backstage, accompanied by a belligerent Russell and a guard of Angels. Russell ignored my pleas that I be allowed to talk to Ginerva. Finally there was nothing I could do but introduce her.

When I passed Russell in the wings, he was holding her carefully folded cloak and intently watching her, like a vassal viewing his queen.

There was something about her this night that haunted me; she looked weary, resigned, almost dazed. The kids listened to her in a respectful if bored silence, but they were enthralled and excited by Troy's fake storm. When it was over they whistled, stomped, and cheered, and then gave her an accolade from the Rock Generation: a sea of lighted matches.

Leah gasped. "My God, they're treating her like a rock star."

Before Ginerva left the stage, Norman alerted me backstage that a column of vans and ambulances was approaching. Despite Foreman's orders, I vowed there would be no Blessing of the Sick this night and ordered the police inspector in charge of crowd control to turn them away.

I had no idea what would happen when Russell came looking for me. I was determined to face him. A confrontation was inevitable; this night would be as good as any. I saw him appear backstage, then start to charge toward me. Sudenly the rear exit door swung open, and Casey Ramona, followed by her weird-looking band and a crowd of admirers, flooded backstage.

Casey saw me, waved, and roared, "Here we are, Bible Man! Let's go!"

Casey looked like her pictures: a young, pert, pretty face just beginning to show the first signs of dissipation; long brown hair under a battered cowboy hat, and an open buckskin shirt that was a waste of time for voyeurs. Her band was unbelievable; the drummer, who claimed to be a Cambodian boat refugee, had his body covered with sanskrit tattoos; her guitar player had his hair cut Mohegan warrior-style with a parrot perched on the topknot; the third member was a black painted white who fed a pen of protesting chickens during the breaks in numbers. Russell knew he was helpless; we were separated by a solid mass of yelling, singing, shouting, stoned kids. If he tried to plow through them they would undoubtedly turn on him.

He shook his fist at me, waved the Angels surrounding Ginerva to the rear exit, and they left.

I was only too happy to introduce Casey to a gratifying roar that could be heard for blocks.

When Casey took over, her booming voice filling every corner of the vast stadium, I returned backstage with plans to wrap up this rally immediately after Casey made her brief announcement she had been converted to the Society of the Chosen and finished her last song.

But it wasn't to be. Minutes later my troubles began when Leah shouted in my ear that Norman demanded I come outside at once. There was a riot in the making.

Outside the auditorium, I had my first glimpse of the organized anti-Ginerva groups in action. Waves of angry middle-aged men and women were rushing across the square, attacking the mob of young people with picket signs and empty beer cans. I saw one white-haired man break his sign over the back of a fleeing teenager, then slam the boy's rear with the stick. The big inspector, skillfully directing his men like a general in the field, soon had the groups separated, with the kids back to listening to Casey Ramona on the loudspeakers and the pickets marching up and down with a leader asking, "What do we want?" and the pickets shouting an answer: "Ginerva in Hell!"

As Norman explained to me, the police had been arguing with the drivers of the vans and ambulances, advising them to leave because there would be no Blessing of the Sick at this rally, when suddenly the young people began heckling the pickets, some tossing beer cans. Suddenly the pickets kicked over the police barricades and rushed the young crowd.

"I couldn't believe it, Hilly!" Norman exclaimed. "Those old toads went after the kids like it was Mark Rudd and Columbia in reverse!"

I observed, "They seemed to be organized."

"Organized!" he said. "Hell, yes! I walked over to where they were gathering. They have team captains, song sheets, picket signs, a fleet of buses, and they know what they're doing. After seeing them in action, Hilly, I think they're going to give Ginerva and the Society lots of trouble."

I agreed.

I returned to the auditorium to find Casey fulfilling her deal; she told a suddenly quiet auditorium how she had been converted to Ginerva and the Society of the Chosen. Then she closed the rally with her record hit "Bible Man," with the crowds roaring out the words.

When I last saw her, she and Troy were whispering together.

"What was that all about?" I asked Steve.

"She's got a friend whose brother owns a horse runnin' tomorrow," he explained. "She's bettin' a bundle."

"How about you?" I asked.

He gave me a surprised look. "Hell, you never bet on any tip you get from a gambler, Hilly!"

Later that night, when Leah, Norman, and I walked into the lobby of the hotel to have dinner and check out, the desk clerk waved me over.

"This gentleman has been calling you every half hour," he said, as he handed me the phone.

It was Tom Gray, who begged me to meet him in Washington as soon as possible.

19

The Money Room

When Tom met me at the airport, we selected a booth in the far corner of the coffee shop where for the next hour or so I gave him a detailed description of everything I had done, experienced, or found out since I had last seen him. Once I stopped and pointed to the notes he was taking.

"Why notes?"

"I'll explain later. Keep going."

When I had finished, he leaned back. "Well, Hilly, it looks like the pieces are beginning to fall into place."

"What pieces? What are you talking about?"

"Let me fill you in. It's a long story, so relax. First, do you remember what I told you outside the train gate last time you were down here? That Washington is really only a small town, that everybody knows who is doing it to whom, and if you wait long enough you'll find out what you want to know?" When I nodded, he said, "Well, that's what happened. I found out what I wanted to know. Through certain friends of my father's I heard how the daughter of a very wealthy Milwaukee banking family had joined the Society of the Chosen. I also heard how her parents were so furious when she refused to come home that they had her kidnapped and deprogrammed. Now follow my cast of characters very carefully. The banker happens to be the biggest contributor to the campaigns of

Senator Graham W. Newberry, the senior senator from Wisconsin, a very hard working and a very ambitious member of that exclusive club, the United States Senate. The banker and his wife stormed into Newberry's office and demanded that something be done about your Ginerva and her Society of the Chosen. Newberry isn't stupid, and he double-talked the banker and his wife simply because he didn't want to start juggling the very touchy issue of religion. But then the banker and his wife began pouring loads of money into an anti-Ginerva group in Wisconsin. I don't know if you realize how these anti-Ginerva groups are spreading across the country like a short-grass prairie fire. When a delegation of Newberry's wealthy supporters, led by the banker and his wife, chartered a plane and came down to see him, and when Wisconsin voters began calling his office and writing letters about your beautiful leader and her nut cult, Newberry decided it was time for him to get on the bandwagon."

"I've noticed the number of pickets at some of the rallies is increasing," I said, "but I didn't think they were that well organized."

"You're wrong, my friend," he said firmly. "They're growing every week, especially in the Midwest, and this is the reason: recruiters for the Society of the Chosen and the other cults have been working very hard among the midwestern colleges and have collected a large number of kids and hurt a lot of families. As a result, the families are starting to fight back. But let me get back to Newberry. When he realized what was happening he quietly got a subcommittee formed— the Senate Subcommittee of American Cults and Sects—and of course had himself appointed chairman."

I looked at him in amazement. "Are you telling me this guy Newberry's committee is going to investigate Ginerva and the Society of the Chosen?"

"Of course," he said brightly. He looked about, leaned over, and whispered, "Again, those certain friends of my father convinced Senator Newberry I was the country's leading expert on Ginerva and her phony cult and all the other nut groups, so he hired me as counsel to the committee." He winked. "It also helped that Newberry owed a big favor to those friends of my father." He reached over and gripped my shoulder. "Now we can really take off after those bastards, Hilly, and put them in jail where they belong!" He finished his coffee and leaned back. "Well, what do you think?"

"You're going too fast for me, Tom. What about Foreman? Did you pick him up after I called you? And Ginerva? What do you have on her? On all of them?"

He held up his hand to protest. "Let's take them one at a time." He waved over the waitress to refill our cups. "I picked up Foreman right after he left the station. Believe it or not, I stayed with him for a week, getting up with him in the morning and putting him to bed like a very conscientious private eye. I couldn't believe what I found out."

"Why didn't you call me?"

"I *did* call you. I told whoever answered the phone I was from an ad agency. They always said you were in Kansas. By the way, I want to talk to you about that Briggs business. But first let me tell you what I found out. I think Foreman is making a deal with Delbart Frey."

"Okay. I'm dumb. Just who the hell is Delbart Frey?"

Tom closed his eyes and groaned. "Hilly, for Christ's sake, you're a former newspaperman! Delbart Frey is —"

I suddenly remembered and interrupted him. "I'm sorry. Sure, I know. Delbart Frey is the last of the four brothers, the newspaper owners. Now as I think about it, Frey owns the *Washington Express*."

"For a moment I thought they had stolen some of your brains," he grumbled. He clicked off on his fingers. "The newspaper biggies in Washington are the *Post*, *Star*, and *Express*. The *Post* is number one, but the *Star* and the *Express* are fighting each other for the number two spot. After his brother Maxwell died, that left the old man alone, and it's been an open secret he's lost all interest in his properties. During the last year he had sold most of them; the small chain in the South, the weeklies in the West, the big one in Pittsburgh, his interest in the Boston daily, the one in L.A., and the two in Canada. But he's been holding onto the *Express*, which was their flagship. He's had loads of offers, not only because the paper happens to be a good one and a moneymaker but also because there's a very important TV station connected with it. Frey's about eighty-two and a bit of an eccentric. He's convinced the country is going to hell in a handbasket and blasts the Supreme Court every week for not allowing prayers to be said in public schools. His editorials claim it's all part of a commie plot to destroy the United States. Curiously, despite these faults, he's a born newspaperman, puts out a fine paper, and has built that TV station into a very powerful instrument. The combination carries lots and lots of political clout."

"You still haven't told me what all this had to do with Foreman and the Society of the Chosen."

"Be patient, my friend, all the pieces are slipping into place. Look at it this way: Foreman comes to Washington and spends a week with the publisher of one of the most powerful newspapers and TV stations in the country, who just happens to believe the evil side of man is taking over the world and his country. He also has a newspaper for sale." He lifted his coffee cup. "Now do I have to hit you over the head with this cup?"

"Are you telling me Foreman is trying to *buy* the Washington *Express*?

He shrugged. "What else? I tailed them to a bank that the Arabs have taken over, and it's loaded with petrodollars. I don't know at this point, Hilly, what that means, but I'm convinced Foreman is ready to buy Frey's newspaper."

"Perhaps he's only trying to get Frey's editorial backing for Ginerva's tour."

Tom shook his head. "The editorial backing of one paper in Washington wouldn't be worth the effort. From what you told me, Foreman is shrewd enough to know *national* publicity is needed to launch the tour—what you have been giving him. Now, Foreman wants that paper." He held the cup between his hands. "But the big question is, why?"

"So far that part of the puzzle doesn't fit, Tom."

"From where we stand now? No. But it all will before the hearings end."

"I recall your telling me that no one down here wanted any part of an investigation into religion, even nut cults. Why suddenly Newberry?"

"Very simple. He's coming up for reelection and feels he needs national exposure."

"There is one very important item," I reminded him. "I'm only inches away from having Foreman open the door of the Money Room and show me their skimming operation. If he gets word of the hearing and I am—"

He broke in. "I was coming to that part. The Department of Justice knows that we will issue a final report blasting them for allowing these thieves to operate, so they have decided to also jump on the bandwagon. I've been meeting with my former classmate, who is in the criminal end of the department. He wants to make a mark for himself, so I have been feeding him—not too much, but enough. I have indicated we have a pipeline into the Society and that pipeline will remain until they get their investigation under way."

I said wryly, "And I'm that pipeline."

"Look at it this way, Hilly," he said. "It's the difference between having this gang indicted by the federal government or by a district attorney. At our hearings you will continue to play the role of Foreman's right-hand man. It will only bring you closer to him. And when the hearings are over, you just continue on for a while until Justice gets started."

"Of course then I'll be their surprise witness?"

"Don't be sarcastic. Of course you will. Can you imagine the look on their faces when you walk into that courtroom?" He bent over and added softly, "That will be justice for Ben, Hilly."

"You're going to be the best lawyer in Washington," I told him, "or the best politician."

"Perhaps a little of both," he said casually. "Now about Ginerva. We have a man out in Idaho who hasn't been able to dig up too much. But maybe something will come out when she's testifying. Even a cold fish like Jimmy Hoffa got jittery when he was before McClellan's committee. They all know a perjury rap hangs over them from the moment they take the oath and the Senate can cite them for contempt." He finished his coffee with a gulp. "You don't have to worry about a thing from now on, Hilly. There's a senatorial committee looking into the whole setup, and with the Justice Department on the spot we'll finally get Foreman grand jury action and indictments."

I told him, "Your man Newberry still sounds like a bit of a headline hunter, Tom."

He gave me a cynical smile. "Aren't they all?"

At tour headquarters, Foreman tilted back in his chair and listened to my report of what had happened in Cleveland. After I finished, he continued to study me, then asked abruptly, "But what happened to the Blessing of the Sick? Russell said you cancelled it."

"I tried to get to talk to Ginerva but Russell wouldn't let me near her," I explained.

"Why did you want to talk to her?"

"Frankly, Dave, she didn't look up to it. She looked sick and there was no way to know what would happen if we had to let all those people into the auditorium. Hell, there was a fleet of vans and ambulances!"

Foreman said grimly, "I know. For days our people in Cleveland had been recruiting them in hospitals and old age homes."

I added hastily, "Also a mob of kids tangled with those anti-Ginerva pickets!"

"Let the cops handle that stuff," he said shortly. He leaned forward, his head jutting slightly forward, the sharp profile outlined by the morning sun. An alert fox.

"From now on I want you to remember one rule," he said grimly. "Ginerva does what I tell her to do. When I say bless the sick, she blesses the sick."

"What is it with these Blessings that she doesn't want to do them?"

He dismissed the question with a wave of his hand.

"It's in her head," he said shortly. "But I don't like it when my people don't follow orders. I wanted that Blessing of the Sick."

"There was a mob of wild kids in that audience," I told him. "We had gotten a late start and the cops were worried. I had no time to argue with that goon Russell—or even with *you*, Dave, if you had been there. All that place needed was one wrong move and it could have turned into a riot. And that, my friend, would have been *bad* publicity for the tour. *Very* bad."

There was the barest hint of a warning in his voice. "Suppose from now on you take care of the rallies and let me take care of Ginerva."

"Fine with me. But I didn't come here to discuss the Blessing of the Sick. You know what I want, Dave, so let's get to it."

He gave me a faint smile. "Twenty-five percent—partner."

I pointed to the folder of clippings. "Did I do the job you wanted?"

"You did. You kept your part of the bargain and now I'll keep mine. Let's ride."

The big black limousine with Andrew at the wheel was waiting outside. As always in the morning, there was a silver pot of coffee, cups, and Danish on the back seat.

Foreman neatly placed a napkin over his knee, handed me one, sliced the Danish, and poured our coffee. "You know, Hilly, I really missed having breakfast with you in the morning. I find an exchange of ideas helps to start the day. Don't you?"

I was determined to avoid the small talk. "What about the arrangements between us, Dave?"

He looked surprised. "Twenty-five percent, including street sales. Isn't that what you wanted?"

I was uneasy. He was surrendering too fast.

"I'm talking about money. When do I see some cash?"

"You're going to see a lot this morning," he said. "But first I want to give you a tour of our operation. If you're going to be a partner you should know everything."

I found Andrew studying me in the overhead mirror, but I stared back until he dropped his eyes.

We had crossed the West Side and were moving downtown under the old West Side Highway. I felt my pulse rate increasing; what did they have in mind for me this morning?

We turned into Chambers Street and stopped at Church Street. After Andrew drove off to park, Foreman pointed to a stately old brownstone building with deep-set nineteenth century windows and iron grillwork.

"One of our points of interest on the tour," he said, with that small smile.

Then I remembered what Tura had told me the night before she disappeared: *"The Mail Room is in the old Vandemeer Building on Chambers Street."*

When I looked up, I saw directly under the roof VANDEMEER BLOCK —1881. The bottom floor was occupied by a large hardware store, the kind that induces Jersey commuters to stagger aboard the Hudson Tube with an assortment of garden tools, all types of bolts, screws, and various fittings, and cans of weird English paste guaranteed to make all leather glow like a brigadier's boot. There was no elevator, only a wide creaking staircase. The doors were closed on the second floor, and the third was devoted to the Society's Mail Room.

Partitions had been removed, leaving one huge room dominated by a stunning color portrait of Ginerva dressed in a long flowing gown, wearing a tiara, and looking pleadingly to heaven, as though she were asking God's blessing on all those who worked in this room. Teams of elderly female Disciples sat on stools sorting mail into bins labeled with names of states and cities. The bins were emptied by others at long wooden tables who opened envelopes and pushed bills and sometimes coins into mounds. Facing teams at the tables placed the coins into coin wrappers and sorted the bills by denomination into stacks with a note of their geographical origin. Then the stacks of coin and bills were put into canvas bags, locked, and stacked against the walls. At intervals they were removed by Angels.

The envelopes, emptied of their contributions, were transferred to a conveyor which dispatched them to the floor below.

Foreman picked up several of the letters and gave them to me to read. They were simply addressed to "Ginerva, New York City, N.Y." or "Her Holiness, Ginerva, Courier of God to the World, New York, N.Y."

"The average donation is about ten dollars," he explained.

I read a few of the letters. One was from a wife who was having problems with a swinging husband and wanted Ginerva to pray that her husband would reform; another was from a family whose father had gone into the hospital for cancer surgery and wanted Ginerva to remember him in her prayers. Both had included ten dollars.

"The mail comes from all over the country," Foreman said. "Bags are brought up here every hour. I checked before we came here; since the Briggs and Cleveland rallies, the mail from those areas has doubled, so we know how effective our rallies will be in stimulating contributions."

I was repulsed by his cold, matter-of-fact voice. He could have been discussing the response of a mail-order campaign for shoes instead of the private tragedies and pleadings of heartsick people.

"While you're out with the tour," he said, "I intend to sit down with an architect and redo the whole building. That hardware store has been given an eviction notice. When they're gone I'm having the building gutted and elevators installed, along with a computerized mailing list of all the millions of names we have of past contributors, and a record of their donations. Then I want another setup that will take care of the changes of address. I'm thinking of sending out spiritual messages from Ginerva four or five times a year to maintain an active mailing list." He added, with a shrug, "It's going to take money, but it's the old story: you have to spend money to make money. Let's go downstairs."

The second floor was similar to the floor above; a large room with Ginerva's picture, and teams of elderly Disciples, this time typing envelopes.

"Each contributor is sent a personal note of thanks from Ginerva, along with her promise of prayers for the sender's intention." He picked one up. It was a brief mimeographed letter with a letterhead of Ginerva in the gown, still looking heavenward. Under it was: "Be Saved as One of Ginerva's Chosen When God Ends the World with His Sea of Flame."

"I want to expand this operation to double its size," Foreman said. Now his voice was animated, his dark eyes glowing. "I want to establish a system to sell pictures of Ginerva, big and small; plaster statues, some in pewter, gold, and silver. Postcards with her picture, lampshades, rugs, anything that will sell. The movies have proven that Americans love to buy that crap."

He pointed to the women who were typing. "I made a survey of a typical week's mail. You can break down the requests into categories. Wife wants help with a husband who's screwing around. A serious operation in the family. A kid is sick. Help with a new job. Get a raise in salary. Find peace and forgiveness for past sins. Help with a junkie son. After this tour is over, Hilly, I want you to write say, twenty or thirty form letters that will cover these categories. As the letters come in, they will be separated by computer into a particular category. Woman with a swinging husband gets a reply to fit her problem. Mother with a kid on drugs gets her reply. Each reply will include a color shot of Ginerva and a special prayer. You'll have to write that also. Within two years we'll have the biggest and most efficient organization selling religion in this country."

He was silent for a moment. "I said it before and I'll say it again: you can sell anything in this goddam country from God to deodorant —if you have the money and the expertise." The fox's face turned to me. "And now between us, that's what we have. Let's go."

"Where?" I asked.

"The Money Room," he replied almost mockingly. "Don't you want to see the highlight of the tour?"

During the ride to Westchester I was on edge, with countless ideas and questions whirling about in my mind against the background of a tiny incessant voice that warned me to be on the lookout for tricks. So far my victory had been ridiculously easy, even with the success of the Cleveland rally. I had expected some preliminary skirmishing, but there had been none. I briefly considered violence on their part but put it aside.

I had no doubt that Foreman cynically planned to use me until Ginerva's tour was ended and then have Russell dispose of me as a threat, too dangerous to live. I was safe until then, not only because I was important to the success of his operation; there was also that fictitious memorandum in that fictitious safety deposit box which my equally fictitious friend would deliver to the various authorities and newspapers if I failed to appear. When the time came, Foreman, I was sure, would consider the chair with the straps in the green barn. The endless waves of sound would easily turn my brain into mush and I would be forced to tell him the truth. Who would miss me? Leah? Turner? I had detailed for them all that had taken place between me and Tom Gray and predicted with an enormous confidence that the Washington hearing could be the beginning of the end of Foreman, his thugs, the Society of the Chosen and would hopefully dispel some of the mystery surrounding Ginerva. But now, riding with Foreman and having Andrew's broken face studying me in the overhead mirror, I felt neither confident nor brave.

Just before we turned into the main gate of the motherhouse, Foreman said after a long silence, "Last night Russell called me all kinds of fool for doing this." He turned to me. "What do you think, Hilly? Am I being a fool?"

My mouth suddenly went dry, but I managed to get out, "That would be the last thing I would call you, Dave."

He sighed. "That's what I told him. We'll soon find out if you're not what you claim to be and then—"Again the small smile. "We'll just have to take measures to protect our interests. Don't you agree?"

I said, "I'm beginning to think Russell is all mouth and no brains."

"You may have something," he said thoughtfully. "There have been times lately when Russell seems to be a bit too aggressive." He said, with an air of sadness, "You should have been with us in the beginning out on the Coast. It was more fun. Now we're big business and suddenly everyone is greedy. Well, here we are."

We had stopped at the small stone house where I had spoken to Russell the morning I left for Staten Island. Today there was a difference; cold-eyed Angels lined the corridor. I was surprised to find at its end a small elevator with a brass door.

"In case you're wondering what this is," he explained, "this elevator leads down to what was once a magnificent wine cellar. Unfortunately, there is no longer any wine." The elevator stopped, the door slid open, and we entered another corridor, also guarded by Angels. Foreman tapped the sides. "Solid rock," he said admiringly. "I have always thought this would make a fantastic air raid shelter."

At the end of the corridor, an Angel built like a champion weight

(343)

lifter swung open a door and we entered a large stone room lined with desks and files. Behind the desks, teams of what appeared to be accountants were scanning ledgers and operating adding machines. One of the men looked up at us. I recalled he was the Team Leader in the East Side headquarters where the groups of street peddlers had turned in their day's receipts. Apparently he didn't recognize me; he rubbed his eyes and returned to his ledger and machine.

Hundreds of the canvas bags I had seen in the Mail Room were stacked against the walls. One had been dumped on the floor; stacks of bills, of singles, tens, twenties, and even fifties had poured out. Several men on their knees were skillfully sorting the stacks into bundles and calling out their totals and points of origin in a dull monotone.

"Detroit. Downtown. Blocks A to F. Total: six thousand, six hundred fifty-six dollars and thirty-four cents. Detroit. Downtown. Blocks G to K. Total: eleven thousand seventy-two dollars and sixteen cents."

At the far end of the room was a large monitor manned by four men with microphones and headsets who sat in chairs facing a detailed city map on a screen. Each time a man counting the bills called out a total and its origin, a tiny light flashed on the screen.

Everyone in the room was dressed alike: dark blue pants, white shirt, dark tie. They were all young and had crew cuts.

"This is a rather sophisticated computer program," Foreman explained. "I have always thought it could have come out of Kubrick's movie *2001*. Actually, it's a voice data entry computer terminal programmed to understand and respond to a fairly large vocabulary. The Disciples manning the phones use a technique called 'isolated word recognition.' I'm really not up on computers." He leaned over and tapped one of the telephone men on the shoulder. "Brother Hoffman, isn't it?"

Hoffman snapped off his headset and jumped to his feet. "Yes, Brother Foreman."

"I'll only trouble you for a moment," Foreman said. "Will you please give Brother Hillers a brief idea of how all this works?"

Brother Hoffman regarded me very gravely. "Well, sir, first the operator must train the terminal by reading the desired vocabulary into this microphone. He repeats each word several times. The system is then ready to classify a word by the system's basic components: the intensity with which that sound is uttered, the time it takes to make that sound, and the frequency of the sound. The computer computes from the sound's intensity and duration. That frequency is then translated into a spectrogram which is digitized into patterns—"

Foreman said quickly, "And what does all that do for *us*, Brother

Hoffman?"

"It presents us with a complete evaluation of our street collections and contributions, Brother Foreman," he said proudly.

"Suppose you give us a demonstration," Foreman said, with a smile.

Hoffman spoke into his microphone, pressed some buttons, and from one side a printout appeared. This was slipped into another slot, and within moments a clear, concise evaluation of Detroit's street collections emerged.

"Detroit's area A to B. Present collections have dropped off fifteen percent as compared to last year but they are still above that of the previous year by five percent. Report Five submitted by Team Leader Seven reveals that the area is changing with seven blocks now occupied with minority tenants. Crime rate has risen by four percent with twenty-six mortgages defaulted within the present collection time slot. He recommended: cut street teams in half in that area and abandon them next year as nonproductive."

I was stunned. What this machine did was supply Foreman with a financial breakdown of every area where his street teams collected and its potential in dollars and cents!

"You got it, Hilly," Foreman said proudly as if reading my mind. "We know where every American dollar is coming from, if it is going to keep coming, and if not, why."

"How many cities do you have programmed like this?" I asked.

Foreman looked down at the boy. "How many would you say, Brother Hoffman?"

"We have every major city in the United States programmed, sir," he said.

"New York is a biggie," Foreman said with a sigh. "It takes us days to do a breakdown, doesn't it, Brother Hoffman?"

"Yes, sir, but we do it," he said boastfully.

"Now what do you think of us?" Foreman said, as we walked back through the corridor formed by the stacked bags.

"Very impressive," I said. "When do you do this breakdown?"

"Every three months. We have what we call a counting day. It's really not a day; three days to be exact."

"Where is the money kept in the meantime?"

"We have holding centers about the country," he said. "There the money is counted, packed into these canvas bags, and brought here in armored trucks. By the way, we own our own armored trucking service. It's a national organization and services not only us but many banks and companies."

"But why count it all here when it is delivered, stacked, and counted?"

"Angels can make mistakes," he said with a cold smile. "You would be shocked to know how many. And here is your friend, Brother Russell."

Russell was standing with Andrew by a desk near the door. There was a mixture of rage and frustration on his face.

"Dave," he said in a low voice, "you made the mistake of your lifetime bringing this guy here."

"Let's go into the conference room," Foreman said calmly.

The room could have been in a Wall Street investment firm. It was paneled in dark oak, the lights were recessed and muted, the long table polished, and the heavy chairs looked like no one had ever sat on them. At each place was a yellow legal pad, several sharpened pencils, a pitcher of water and a glass.

"Have a seat, gentlemen," Foreman said, as he sat down at the head of the table. Russell sat next to him, and I slid into a chair near the end of the table.

"I told you last night, Dave, and I'm telling you again," Russell said in a tight, grim voice, "you should never have brought this guy in here!"

Foreman inquired, "Why not?"

Russell turned and pointed at me. "He means trouble. I didn't buy him in the first place and I don't buy him now."

"Would you care to say anything, Hilly?" Foreman asked me quietly.

I suddenly realized Russell was forcing a kind of kangaroo court on Foreman. My heart started to pound, and my lips were so dry they seemed glued together. I fought to keep the quiver out of my voice.

"I thought we had a deal, Dave!"

"Brother Russell insists on hearing what you told me yesterday," he said. "About your report . . ."

"I told you how it was," I said. I glanced at my watch. "I should warn you I made provisions for this morning before we left. If I'm not back at tour headquarters by two P.M., someone will take that report out of the safety deposit box. If I don't appear by tomorrow morning, copies of that report will be delivered by hand to the New York offices of the Attorney General, the FBI, the IRS, and the New York County District Attorney. . . . Now are you prepared to take a chance?"

There was a moment of tense silence, then Russell said with a sneer: "I think he's full of shit."

I warned him, "Try me, musclehead."

Foreman asked, "I never thought to ask you before, Hilly, exactly what is in those reports of yours?"

"A description of how you and this big stoop have banked a hundred million dollars in that Caribbean bank you own and what you have done with it overseas. Also some side business ventures, such as that timberland in the Carolinas. I also have a few other things in that report—"

"Like what?" Russell grunted, but now he was not so aggressive.

"A few things about your girl friend, Ginerva," I said, trying to sound nonchalant.

Russell slammed his fist down on the table. "Like what?" he roared. He was now out of his chair, leaning across the table. I didn't answer because I was too frightened, but then Foreman said quietly, "Sit down and shut up!"

When Russell kept standing there, glowering down at me, Foreman again said, his voice rising, "Sit down!" This time Russell grudgingly returned to his seat.

"Someday—" he began, but Foreman, ignoring him, said to me, "Have you seen everything here you wanted to see?"

"I have a fairly good idea of the operation now," I replied.

"Very good. Let's go back downtown."

We had just left the gatehouse behind us when he said, "Can you tell me what you know about Ginerva, Hilly?"

"It's all in that report," I said.

"I don't care about Cleveland, I don't care about anything you have done," he said in a low grim voice, "there's no deal unless you tell me how much you know about her."

"I can tell you this, Dave, that if I ever leaned over and whispered the name 'Peter' or 'Aunt Clem' in Ginerva's ear, I would get one hell of a reaction from her," I said, with an air of confidence I didn't possess. "Is that enough, or do you want some more?"

His face was grim and set. "You don't have the documents."

I was now moving about in the dark, cautiously testing each step, hoping I wouldn't stumble and fall.

"I don't need the documents."

"There's no proof without them."

"How do you know someone didn't make copies?"

He considered this for a moment. "Whoever did is dead."

"They didn't bury the copies with them, Dave."

It began to rain, and the measured, swishing sound of the windshield wipers was loud in the taut silence. Then our bizarre thrust, parry, and protect fencing game continued.

"Did you go out there?"

"Yes, and everything I found out is in that report."

"Whom did you see?"

I didn't intend to move any deeper into the darkness. "Look," I said with an air of impatience, "I've told you enough. I think I've proven to you I'm not bluffing. If you don't think so, do what Russell wants and take a chance. You said this morning I'm in as a partner. Fine.

But now I want to see the books. I want to know *exactly* how much is coming in. After all, I'll be the guy out in the field working like hell to fill more of those canvas bags."

He glanced at his wristwatch. "I don't exactly keep the books in the bottom drawer of my desk. It will take a little doing to get them. Let's have lunch first."

For the rest of the trip back to Manhattan I huddled in a corner of the luxurious seat and stared out at the rain.

The tension was slowly draining away, leaving me exhausted, and I could feel my eyes closing. I dozed off, to wake up to the honking rainy-day traffic on Fifth Avenue. Foreman sat like a stone man, his grave motionless face turned to the rain. After we returned to the tour office, he said he had to make some phone calls. It was two tense hours before he opened his door and said apologetically, "I got tied up. Let's have lunch. There's a little place not far from here where they keep the kitchen open."

There were only two determined drinkers at the bar, and the dining room was deserted. We took a table near the window.

"I like the rain," Foreman said, staring out the window. "When I first came to San Francisco I roamed all over the city, rain or shine."

I couldn't resist making the thrust. "Was that before your cabin boy guru, Dave?"

He slowly turned his black eyes on me. "You dig deep, my friend. Watch out it's not your own grave."

"Once when I was in Vietnam," I told him, "I wrote a feature story about a typical jungle village. The old people had the usual bunch of aphorisms, but one stuck with me. 'It takes two men to dig a deep grave but only one to make a hangman's noose.' "

It was a long languid lunch, with Foreman insisting we have a few drinks before we ordered. I began to get suspicious when he started to tell me some rambling stories of his early days with Ginerva on the West Coast and then insisted we order dessert and more coffee. When finally we started back to the office, the dinner crowd was starting to arrive.

When he started with his story telling in the office I interrupted. "What's the reason for the stalling, Dave?"

He glanced at his wristwatch. "Do you remember when you remarked the other day that in our business we should always have a fire escape? Well, that's what I did this afternoon—gave myself a fire escape. By now there isn't a trace of money up there. It's well on its way out of the country. We don't have another counting day for three months. By that time we should know how far we can trust each other."

"So you decided there is no deal?"

(348)

"I didn't say that," he reminded me. "Of course we have a deal. From now on we're partners. I need you and you need me. To show my good faith, I intend to open an account in your name for a hundred thousand dollars in a San Francisco bank, immediately. You will be present at our next counting day, and twenty-five percent of everything that comes into the Money Room will be turned over to you to do with as you wish. Now, are you satisfied?"

"Not quite. When do I see the books?"

"No books, computer printouts. When do you want to see them?"

"Immediately."

He shook his head. "That's not possible. I told you I don't keep them handy. We'll have to fly down to the Caribbean."

"Fine with me. When do we fly down and pay a visit to the First National Bank of Little Cat?"

He raised his eyebrows. "*Very, very* good, Hilly. You've done your homework."

I pressed him. "When do we leave?"

He pointed out, "You're really in a hurry."

"I like to know the assets of any organizations I join. You're dodging the question, Dave. When do we go?"

"How about this weekend?"

"Fine. Just you and me. No Russell. No Andrew."

He hesitated. "Russell will insist on coming along. After all, *he's* also a partner."

"Let him insist all he wants. He makes me nervous. I'd rather he stay home. We don't need him."

He said, with a shade of affability, "You're making an enemy for me. . . ."

I said boldly, "I think between us we can handle that big goon. Why do you need him?"

He gave me a sharp look. "He comes in handy sometimes. What do you have in mind?"

"Troy's a bumbler and Russell's a dangerous menace. Why do you need both of them—when you have me?"

When he studied me for a long moment, I sensed I had found a crack, and dug deep to widen it. "Someday he's going to do something violent that you won't be able to cover up, Dave. Then the cops will come sniffing around. All it needs to make the walls tumble in is some curious, glory-hunting detective." I added very carefully, "Like that kid who went out the window on Fifty-seventh Street."

There was an involuntary flicker of surprise in his face. His voice was taut. "What do you mean?"

"The cops listed it as a suicide," I said. "You were lucky the kid only had an old grandmother who didn't push. There could have been

(349)

angry parents banging on the DA's office."

He said defensively, "The kid was a nut. The cops said she jumped."

I corrected him. " 'Fell or jumped' is the way the report reads. But an ambitious DA can make a lot of headlines out of even a clear case of suicide. He can order a grand jury investigation 'to determine the facts,' as they call it. But it wouldn't look good for you or Ginerva or any of the officials of the Society of the Chosen running that gauntlet of microphones and cameramen going into Criminal Court Building to testify in connection with the death of a young girl. That's what I mean, Dave; as long as Russell is here he spells trouble."

He regained his composure, and the look he gave me was almost bemused. "What would you suggest we do, Hilly, push *him* out of a window?"

I cautioned him, "Think about it, Dave. You told me you had lots of plans for this setup in the future. Someday you'll have to weigh them both: the plans or Russell." Then strategically I quickly switched the subject. "Now how about Ginerva? What kind of a cut does she get?"

He hesitated. "Let's say she is taken care of."

"You're not answering the question, Dave. How much does she get? What's her percentage?"

He said quietly, "Let's leave that on the shelf for now."

"We're supposed to be partners. I should know all the details."

"What she gets, who she is—that's not important," he said impatiently. "What she does for us is important."

"But it's important to me that she doesn't want to do the Blessing of the Sick. I can't handle that type of a problem on the road, Dave. These rallies have to be done by clockwork. You have to milk every ounce of emotion out of them, then shut it off. I can't be bothered with a prima donna."

He picked up a paper clip from a tray and angrily bent it in half. "I told you, it's something in her head."

"What do you mean? Are these sick kids and cripples getting to her?"

He shrugged. "Possibly. It started over a year ago on the Coast. One night they brought up a little kid on a stretcher. The kid was dying of an incurable disease. Probably cancer. She started to reach out to bless the kid, then froze, screamed, and ran off the stage. I didn't know what the hell happened to her. I found her backstage, trembling and crying. All she would say was that something had happened to her."

"Like what?"

"At first she refused to talk about it, but later, when I got her calmed down, she told me something had warned her she had gone too far. That's all I could get our of her."

(350)

"It sounds weird."

"Of course it's all in her head. But from then on it was uphill with her."

I said carefully, "But you have something to keep her in line."

Just as carefully he replied, "Doesn't it appear that way?"

"But what's the big deal about the Blessing of the Sick, Dave? We both know it's a gimmick. If she doesn't want to do it, why make her unhappy?"

"There are two reasons," he said briskly. "One, I don't like people to disobey my orders. Two, it means money. Before they get up to that stage they are told by the Angels that the Society must have a contribution. We have a scale. So much for cripples, wheelchair patients, stretcher cases, and so on."

I was so revolted I had to avoid those dark probing eyes by looking down at my clasped hands.

In a quiet rational voice he explained, "It may sound cold-blooded, but it isn't. Most of them are either religious fanatics, hypochondriacs, or terminal. They couldn't buy what she gives them—hope. Do you know what hope means when cancer is eating out your guts and the pills or the needles they give you can't dull the pain anymore? Or if you have a kid dying by inches and you watch Ginerva bless your kid after she had turned ten, twenty, thirty thousand or more people into whirling dervishes with her talk of God and eternal damnation? You heard her. No, they get their money's worth. It would be stupid to do away with the Blessing of the Sick simply because she believes she heard voices. It means a hell of a lot of money to us, and nobody gets hurt." He studied me silently for a moment. "I have never mentioned this before to anyone. Since that night she ran off the stage, she has actually cured people."

I couldn't trust myself to make any comment. I looked over his head and concentrated on a print on the wall. He didn't appear to notice and continued in a monotone.

"Sure, you and I know the Blessing is a gimmick, used by every money-making evangelist. The people who come up are mostly suffering from self-induced hysteria, sexual repression, hypochondria, or are religious fanatics. But believe it or not, Hilly, there have been some cases where there is no explanation for the people she cured. I know it sounds weird, but I not only talked to the people, but also to their doctors. You know how most of those doctors use mumbo jumbo medical language? But I got a couple to admit there had been no hope for their patients until the Blessing by Ginerva." Then he said abruptly, "There is something I always wondered about, Hilly. Was that business of your limp on the up-and-up?"

"Yes," I said. "I was limping when I went into that theatre, and after she touched me the limp was gone."

He looked at me. "What do you think it was?"

"I don't know. Maybe it was like the dead man in Briggs. What about it, partner? Are you going to tell me how you pulled that off?"

He grinned. "Let's skip that one for a while. After all, a magician should be allowed some secrets."

"There shouldn't be secrets between partners, Dave."

His grin faded, and there was a blunt edge to his voice. "You want to trade secrets, Hilly? I say fine with me. First you tell me: who tipped you about the Carolinas, the bank in Little Cat, and the account in Europe? Who told you about Peter and Aunt Clem?"

"Ginerva told me about Peter and Aunt Clem," I said.

The drumming broke off. He looked stunned. "Ginerva? When?"

"That day at the well after I pulled the kid out. She seemed in a daze. That was no trick, was it?"

When he ignored the question, I said, without thinking, "Perhaps she has a 'second sight.' "

He slowly got up, walked to the window, and looked out. Without turning, he said in a muffled voice. "So you got it all from Tura. I should have guessed. She was the only one who ever used that phrase —'second sight.' It came from her days in the 'spooky racket.' " He turned to look down at me. "How did you get to her, Hilly?"

I could have bitten my tongue. I tried to look puzzled. "Tura? How could that be? I was down here and she was up at the motherhouse, Dave."

"What's the difference?" he said with a shrug. "Now it's all in the family."

"Well, if it's all in the family, why not tell me what *really* happened to her?"

He returned to rock gently on the back of his chair. "If you're thinking I had Tura wasted, you're wrong. I'm not that crude. But that's not saying I won't let Russell drop her in the river if I think she's getting a loose tongue. The Society of the Chosen is too important to me to have it ruined by a forty-year-old lush who gets a yen to be laid every time she sees a nice-looking guy—like yourself. Tura just took off, that's all. I haven't the slightest idea of where she is."

He seemed restless and returned to the window. "Isn't this a fabulous view, Hilly? It was the best move I ever made, to buy this building."

For the first time in my life I wanted to kill a man. I was so filled with rage at this slick cold-blooded thief who spoke so emotionlessly of swindling dying children, cripples, and heartsick parents that I wanted to strangle him, to open that window and push him out. To commit such an act was unthinkable, but the urge was so strong I had to clasp my hands together until I could feel the thumping of my

(352)

heart in the tips of my fingers.

Now he was talking about the Society of the Chosen.

"I told you I had great plans for you, and I still have. In fact, more than ever. You know there's a hundred million in the pot, and more is coming in every minute. We have hit a nerve out there. People are afraid. Why? The answer is very simple. They have more problems every day. If it isn't Russia, it's drugs. If it isn't the chucklehead we have in the White House, it's the supermarket bill which has gone out of sight. If it isn't the temptations that surround kids as they grow up today, it's the thieves in Congress. Even the weather has turned against them. There's no war, but also there's no peace. They feel something is in the air. God can't take it any longer. So we come along and offer them Ginerva, who is delivering the message they most fear. Death. Of course they grab at the chance to win a seat on the Great White Cloud of Salvation when the earth turns into a Sea of Flame. We give them a dramatic show with wind, rain, and lightning, and they love it. They go home feeling cleansed of their sins and sure they will be saved on that Last Day. In return they send us money. Lots of money. For me and for you—"

The phone in his office began ringing. He went in to answer it, closing the door behind him. When he opened it and stood in the doorway, his face, as always, didn't show any emotion, but I had the impression the telephone call had delivered disastrous news.

"We're being investigated by a Senate subcommittee," he said tersely. "Some guy by the name of Newberry from Wisconsin. Ginerva and I, Russell, and the others—even Singleton and the Watsons on the Island are going to be subpoenaed."

It would have been useless to mention our weekend trip to Little Cat. Thanks to a leak in Tom Gray's tight little community of Washington "where everyone knows who is doing it to whom," Foreman's double set of books would continue to remain far, far away. . . .

Only a groan came through the receiver of the pay phone when I told Tom Gray late that night.

"I thought we were as tight as a drum," he said, "but I guess in this town complete security is impossible." He added quickly, "Did Foreman say anything about skipping?"

"He's with Ginerva now at the motherhouse."

"Couldn't you go along with him?"

"He said he wanted to talk to her alone. Everything was fine until that goddam phone call."

"Don't cry over spilt milk," he said soothingly. "It happens all the time. I'm going to call Newberry now. We'll jack up the hearing date and I'll have the New York marshals subpoena the whole gang in the morning. Sit tight, Hilly, and keep me informed. . . ."

20

The Gift
from Ellen Terry

My phone rang before dawn the following morning. It was Foreman.

"We've been talking all night with our lawyers, Hilly," he said. "Only Ginerva is going to take the stand. The rest of us will not be available to testify." He added, with a short laugh, "We'll be planning our international tour."

"Will you be out of the country?"

"It's best you don't know anything," he said. "If they pull you before that committee, you can truthfully swear you don't know where I am. But don't worry. I have excellent contacts in Washington who tell me that this is going to be a one-week wonder and then blow over. When it does I'll come back, and we'll dream up something for a press release."

I almost whooped with joy at the thought that at last I would be closeted with Ginerva —alone.

"But, Dave, you can't let Ginerva face that committee alone! She'll fall apart!"

"Oh, but she's not going to be there alone. You'll be with her," he replied.

"Then I will have to talk to her. Is she at the motherhouse?"

"No. She will be in seclusion until the morning of the hearing. Our attorneys have notified Newberry she will be there at ten A.M. All I want you to do is sit with her. By the way, this is at her request."

"But, Dave, if I'm going to be with her I should talk to her! We should go over her testimony!"

"That's what I will be doing every minute until the hearing," he said. "All I want you to do is to be there with her. The Angels will bring her to the hearing room and will take care of her when it's over. After this Wisconsin hotshot gets his headlines, we'll be back in business."

He continued calmly, "I always had a contingency plan. It's now in operation. There are people at the motherhouse who will make sure it will run smoothly. Nothing will change. But I want you to take over tour headquarters. Prepare the next few rallies. As soon as I get back, I want the tour to begin immediately. It's getting late in the season, so eliminate the smaller cities, concentrate on the big ones. Get all the permits ready—you know what has to be done. From time to time someone will call you. If you have anything important—really important—tell him. It will get to me at once. You'll be notified if I want to see you. So now you're on your own, Hilly. Don't worry about a thing. It's all political gas."

He hung up.

That night Leah, Norman, and I met Tom Gray in an uptown office. When I told him what Foreman had said, he shrugged.

"Ginerva will be coached up to the time she testifies," he explained. "Of course they'll duck the marshals with the subpoenas. It happens all the time. There's a committee leak and the principal witnesses disappear until the committee's hearings end—or its appropriation gives out." He brooded for a moment, doodling on a yellow legal pad.

"Foreman's a smart guy," he admitted grudgingly. "What he obviously intends to do is let Ginerva carry the ball for all of them. He knows what an impression this beautiful woman will have on a national television audience. She found a lost kid in a well. Brought a dead man back from Hell. Touched cripples who threw away their crutches. Foreman also knows Newberry is not stupid; if the senator goes after her too hard, he'll be an instant villain." He sighed. "And if he doesn't, his constituents will charge him with not doing his job and letting a bunch of crooks get away."

Norman asked, "Can't you do anything?"

"Foreman, Russell, and the others are our principal targets," Tom said. "The IRS gave Newberry a terrific team of agents who have been working day and night. Even if Foreman doesn't appear, I am sure we have enough to incorporate into a good report that will be turned over to the Department of Justice. The IRS could begin by taking away the Society's religious organization tax status. Foreman will probably be indicted for fraud. We can prove that none of the projects they promised, old age homes, halfway houses for addicts, you know, the whole phony program, was never started. We don't have the time, but the Department of Justice will go through the State Department to subpoena the records of that bank on Little Cat. The records there will lead the agents to the Carolina bank and Foreman's attorney down there. There could be a whole mess of indictments."

I said, "Level with me, Tom. How long will all that take?"

He carefully sketched a profile—it looked like Foreman's—on his pad. "I know what you're thinking, and you are right. The machinery of the State Department, the Bahama government, and the Department of Justice move exceedingly slow. It will take months."

Norman looked at him with disgust. "I can't believe they are getting away with it again! Even a Senate committee can't hurt them!" He looked at me. "Hilly, why are we wasting our time?"

"No, you're wrong, Norm," Tom said, shaking his head. "They won't get away with it. If they keep ducking the subpoenas, I'll push Newberry to have them cited for contempt of the Senate. He'll get a quick vote, and that means warrants wil be turned over to the FBI. We know Justice is going to move in on them." He added impatiently, "Hell, you people should know how difficult it is to investigate and then prosecute anyone in this country protected by the First Amendment! Sure, we all know they're crooks, but you've got to dig up the proof!"

I asked, "Will you touch on Ben's death?"

"Of course we're going to try to get into that, but actually we don't have much more than you already know, Hilly. We intended to throw a lot of questions at Foreman, Russell, and Troy—and Sloan, if we can find her—in the hopes that one of them will get nervous and start admitting something or let slip a few facts. But let's face it, the only way we or any law enforcement agency will get the inside story of why and how Ben killed himself will be from the *inside,* by one of *them* telling us. I was looking forward to getting Troy on the stand. We know he's weak. He's been around. He will realize that when he raises his hand and takes the oath, a rap of perjury hangs over his head. On the other hand, if they take the Fifth, that certainly won't look good for a religious organization and will be a green light for the IRS to step in."

"What about the business of Foreman and Frey and the *Washington Express?*"

He answered carefully, "Now that is one angle we have to deal with very carefully, Hilly. We checked, and there is no record of a sale of the newspaper. They are probably still negotiating. And don't forget, while it could make headlines, it is perfectly legal for old man Frey to sell his newspaper and TV station to anyone he pleases."

"Then all you have to do is subpoena Frey?" Leah asked. "Or is he too hot to handle?"

Tom gave her an annoyed look. "Nobody's too 'hot' for us to handle, Leah. But there's no percentage in deliberately embarrassing a man like Frey with a fishing expedition. Sure, if we get Foreman on the stand I'll question him about that—"

"And if he denies it, all you have to do is put Frey on the stand and ask him the same question under oath," Leah said innocently. "Doesn't that make sense?"

Tom sighed and looked to me for help. I decided it was time to change subjects.

"What about Ginerva, Tom? Will you go into her Idaho background?"

Tom looked relieved and said promptly, "Newberry and I will do most of the questioning, but everything will be very respectable and low key. The trick is to let her hang herself."

"I'll be with her," I said. I explained to Leah and Turner, "The committee wants me to continue as Foreman's assistant."

"As I told Hilly in Washington," Tom said, "Justice is going into the whole setup immediately after the end of our hearings. They have no choice. In our final report we will show how Ginerva, Foreman, and all the others committed fraud and did not use the contributions coming into the Society of the Chosen as they had promised. No projects were ever started. The bills for expenses can be proven to be phony, or at least questionable. But once Justice takes over Hilly has got to remain, at least for a short time, as Foreman's good right hand. He has got to feed Justice with everything he can get."

"Won't that be dangerous?" Leah asked.

"No more dangerous than it's been," Tom answered.

"Of course it will," she said stubbornly. "When these people have their backs to the wall they'll be double suspicious. If Foreman has these connections in Washington—"

"Justice will have top security measures, Leah," Tom said.

"So did your committee—until someone called Foreman," she said dryly.

He moved uneasily. "It won't happen with Justice." He turned to me. "If you get a smell of what they are up to, jump up and request a recess. Either I or Newberry will put on a bit of a show giving you a hard time, to impress Foreman, who undoubtedly will be watching the hearings on TV. Somehow we'll be in touch with you." He emphasized, "What we have to worry about are the anti-Ginerva groups who are coming to Washington in chartered buses. They intend to pack the hearing room."

"Do you expect many, Tom?" I asked.

"Hundreds, from what our man in Wisconsin reported," he replied. "Opposition to these cults, especially the Society of the Chosen, is building across the country. Parents who have seen their kids turned into fanatics or robots are organizing. Only last week they burned the headquarters of some sect in the Midwest and beat up the leaders. When the people responsible were arrested, they were immediately released on bail, a large crowd put them into an automobile and paraded them around the city, with the mayor thanking them on the steps of city hall. That will give you an indication of how irrational these people are getting. Newberry has ordered a double guard for the hearing room."

"You haven't mentioned the Money Room Hilly saw in operation, Tom," Norman said. "Wouldn't that show them up as crooks?"

"Look at it this way, Norman," Tom said. "If Hilly took the stand, he could tell an incredible story. Unfortunately, we can't use him as a witness because Justice would lose an important pipeline of information. There are still all sorts of questions to be answered. Foreman has told Hilly he has big plans in the future for the Society of the Chosen. We have to know what they are. You brought up the Washington newspaper. Just what does the head of an increasingly powerful religious organization want with an established Washington newspaper and the TV station connected with it? As for the Money Room, you must consider this: suppose we got a search warrant and broke into the place? What would we find?"

"Hilly saw a computer setup in operation that is hard to believe," Norman protested. "Couldn't you produce photographs for the hearings?"

Tom said with a deep sigh, "When Hilly first told me about the Money Room, I was all excited. That is, until I sat down and talked to our investigator who has made a survey of the major evangelical organizations in this country. Frankly, Foreman's setup is no better or no worse than others our man saw. They all have tremendous organizations. They are all hard to believe! Banks of computers. Staffs working as efficiently as any big bank. They all bring in millions. Only now do I realize that selling religion in the United States is Big Business!"

Leah, who had been listening intently, broke in. "You mentioned that you and Senator Newberry intend to do most of the questioning. Aren't there other senators on the committee?"

"Newberry is chairman," he reminded her, "and I am the committee's counsel. The other committee members aren't that interested. Or perhaps they're being cautious. You know, religion, no matter in what form, is still a delicate subject for Washington."

"You said you and Senator Newberry intend to let Ginerva 'hang herself,'" Leah said. "Just what do you mean?"

"We know Ginerva came from somewhere in Idaho," Tom said with elaborate patience. "Where we don't know. Nor do we know anything about her background or her real name. She's still a complete mystery. However, we've had a team of investigators who have dug up some stuff on her early years out on the Coast. We've interviewed some of the same people Hilly spoke to months ago, but we have more than that. Foreman admitted to Hilly they cold-bloodedly charge the sick to be blessed. Well, with the aid of bunko squad detectives and photographs of the rallies, we have been able to identify more than twenty regulars who were supposedly cured by Ginerva. They all came out of the personal injury insurance racket. You know, the elderly woman who rips off her hearing aid after she is blessed by Ginerva. The guy who throws his crutches into the air. Or the girl who very dramatically gets out of her wheelchair and cries out she had been made to walk by Ginerva. We interviewed ten and have their statements. All admitted they had been paid twenty-five dollars a night to put on a show. The only weakness is, they didn't know who paid them. Just a guy with a crew cut. It could have been any one of the Angels. But when they take the stand as witnesses, it will kick her credibility all to hell."

Leah said defensively, "I don't believe Ginerva knew anything about that."

"That's your opinion, Leah," Tom said cheerfully, "but we have more. We also have her early television interviews and newspaper feature articles in which she told the same story she told Hilly of how her missionary parents had been killed by a hit-and-run driver in LaPaz, how she was a missionary herself and eventually came to the South, where God appeared to her. We will simply read these stories to her, show the televised interviews, and ask her if they are true. Of course she will be forced to say yes. That is when we will hit her with the documentary evidence from the State Department that no such accident ever took place, reports of the various missionary societies proving there is no Society of the World Christians, and a letter from the Bolivian Ambassador in which he will say that his government has researched her story and have come to the conclusions that it is a lie. All Newberry has to do is read these letter and reports and ask a few easy questions. I can guarantee Ginerva will lie herself into a corner."

Leah suddenly broke in. "I assume it won't come as a surprise to you to know that Senator Newberry will soon start his campaign to be reelected."

"I would have to be living in Siberia not to know that, Leah," Tom said with a grin. "But what does that have to do with Ginerva?"

(359)

Leah asked coldly, "And hasn't a young heir to a Milwaukee brewing fortune announced he will run against Newberry in the primary?"

Gray's grin faded. "That's right, but I still don't see what that—"

"It's very simple," Leah broke in. "If you shame and humiliate Ginerva, won't it mean headlines for Newberry? Publicity for his coming campaign?"

"Oh, come off it, Leah," Gray said with a forced smile. "Newberry isn't so hard up for publicity that he would deliberately smear someone."

"But it's all publicity, isn't it?" she pressed him.

Tom said stiffly, "Any politician, from the president down, likes publicity. It's part of the American game of politics."

"And according to the rules of what you call the 'American game of politics,' a woman, no matter who she is or what she has done, is fair game. There's no defense—only prosecution. When you and Senator Newberry get through with Ginerva, she will appear a complete fraud, a conscienceless charlatan!"

Norman interjected, "Well, it looks like she could be that, Leah."

"Prove it," Leah said evenly.

"Watch us on TV," was Tom's savage reply.

Later that evening, after I had mollified an irritated Tom Gray, I joined Norman and Leah in the hotel's small bar. This was the first time we had done this. As Norman pointed out, with Foreman gone he intended to order the best of scotch and champagne delivered to his room every evening to sip while he watched "The Late Show."

"At least in that way I'll get some of my ninety thousand back," he said wryly.

"Tom must be furious with me, Hilly," Leah said. "I'm sorry, I didn't mean to irritate him. I should have kept my mouth shut."

I promised her, "Tom will get over it."

She reached over and squeezed my hand. "Hilly, I don't want to canonize Ginerva. If she's part of this conspiracy, she should be punished. But I just hate to think of her being used by a politician to get headlines."

I reminded her, "It's the old story, Leah. Newberry is a means to an end."

"Leah, I can't believe that after all we found out you still want to defend her!" Norman burst out. "She's a fraud, and who knows what else!"

"You have your opinions and I have mine," Leah said stubbornly. "And no one is going to change it—you, Hilly, Tom Gray, Senator Newberry, or the whole Senate. As I told you, prove it. I believe there is something about Ginerva we will never be able to answer—or prove."

"At this point I couldn't care less," Norman said with a yawn. "All I want is for this hearing to take place and have the government finally do something about these people." He looked at me. "Do you really believe the Department of Justice will move against these people, Hilly?"

"They will be forced to take action," I said. "Ginerva and the Society of the Chosen are now page-one news. Newberry will milk the hearing for what he can get out of it. Then his committee will hold a press conference and with a great deal of fanfare announce that all the evidence they have uncovered will be turned over to the Attorney General for investigating and possible indictments by the Department of Justice. Of course that puts Justice on the spot. If the AG and his department drag their heels because they don't want to get involved with the delicate question of when religion violates the criminal law, the anti-Ginerva groups who are now rapidly organizing on a national basis will pressure their congressmen and senators. They in turn will get to the White House, and what will follow will be a chain reaction. If Newberry keeps up the pressure, say with press conferences and an explosive report, Justice will be pushed into a corner. Then again, there's the local district attorneys. Somewhere, in some city, a DA will start a grand jury investigation and indict Foreman, Ginerva, the whole bunch. Why? The answer is simple: the government has legitimized the investigation of cults and sects. Now it's not investigating God, but a bunch of crooks! And of course district attorneys also have their Community Relations Directors—that's a euphemism for a press agent—who will know the news value of such investigations, indictments, and trials."

Norman said, with a frown, "How do you know all this, Hilly?"

I told him, "I spent five years in Saigon, which was a yellow-skinned Washington. It was the same play with the same characters, only different scenery; a Pentagon in miniature, fat-cat reporters, corruption, power politics, and image-making television."

"I find that disgusting," Leah said. "Politicians doing anything for a TV camera or a headline. I dread to think what Newberry and his hatchet men will do to Ginerva. She won't have a chance."

"I wouldn't worry about Ginerva," I advised her. "She can take care of herself. All she will have to do is play up to the cameras and recite a litany of cures and miracles. The best thing that will come out of all this is that the Department of Justice is finally making a move. If they get those bank records from the banks in Little Cat and Carolina, Foreman and the others will be in big trouble. And if they find Sloan, that will be it. Tura won't go to jail for Foreman and Russell."

"How do we know she's even alive, Hilly?" Leah asked with a shudder. "Who knows what those terrible people will do?"

"Thinking about it, Hilly," Norman admitted, "Leah is right. With their backs to the wall Foreman and the others will be doubly suspicious of everybody and everything. You had better watch your step."

"Please be careful, Hilly," Leah warned.

"What is this, a wake?" I said. "Tonight we should celebrate! We finally won! Somebody at last is going after this rotten racket! Maybe we'll even get justice for Ben. And that calls for champagne."

Over the champagne, we tried to picture Foreman and Russell in a courtroom with a judge sending them to prison for long terms, but somehow it all seemed flat and forced. Finally Norman said he was tired and intended to drink his champagne watching television and falling asleep. When he was gone, there was a long silence.

"Ginerva is on your mind," I said accusingly.

"I can't help it, Hilly," she confessed. "I know you think I'm foolish, but I just can't believe she knew they were charging those poor sick people." She looked at me. "Am I being gullible?"

"Let's face it, Leah, there is indisputable proof she lied about her background. She never had missionary parents in Bolivia nor were they killed there. She never did any missionary work in the South. We know she comes from Idaho. All these lies can't help but ruin her credibility. She's got to have one hell of an explanation or they'll destroy her."

"Maybe she had to tell those lies, Hilly," Leah said doggedly. "Couldn't there be a reason?"

I impulsively slid my arm around her waist. It was small, and under the thin blouse her skin felt smooth and warm. "Let's forget Ginerva for a while. Let's get some air. . . ."

"Hilly, it's after midnight," she protested. "Is it safe out there?"

"You can always protect me," I assured her.

As we walked down Madison Avenue, her arm automatically slid into mine. We peered in at gowns, shoes, antiques, and a window filled with delightful paintings of clowns.

"How did you find out Newberry was running for reelection?" I asked her.

"A girl who went to drama school with me dropped out to get married," she explained. "She works in the *Times* advertising department. One day we had lunch, and she got Xerox copies of everything their reference room had on Newberry. It was quite simple."

"You're proving to be a better reporter than I am, Leah."

"I wish everything would end with this hearing," she said suddenly.

"I have this feeling something dreadful is going to happen."

"Ginerva is the prophet, not you," I told her.

I felt a shudder go through her. "I can't joke about it, Hilly. I hate to see you go back with Foreman."

"It has to be done. It would be foolish for me to walk away now. It's what we have been hoping for, Leah. Answers. Justice for Ben. An end to this racket."

She hugged my arm. "I'm worried about Foreman's connections. It's all right for Tom to talk about security, but what security did his committee have? Why can't Foreman find out about you?"

"He won't. Trust me, Leah."

We stopped at a corner to let a car turn. Except for the light filling her eyes, her composure didn't change. "I told you before, Hilly, if I didn't trust you I wouldn't be here."

I suddenly wanted to share my innermost thoughts with her. "You once told me you were sure I had this tiny bit of doubt that Ginerva was a fraud," I said. "I've been thinking about that, Leah. Maybe you're right. Maybe I'm sort of pulling for her. There are just too many damn unanswered questions about her."

"Now you're the one who's talking about Ginerva," she chided me.

Looking back, I guess that evening I began to realize that Leah meant more to me than just a fellow conspirator. I had no clear idea of exactly what I wanted to say to her. I had always assumed that while I was a bit of a romantic, I also had a good sense of logic. I could look at things objectively, examine them again and again, and come to a reasonable conclusion. But when it came to examining my emotions about Leah, all I ended with was a jumble of confused thoughts and emotions. It was no longer possible for me to simply view her as Butler's impossible daughter, gullible, defiant, and very, very stubborn, to whom I would one day bid a relieved good-bye. Curiously, while I'm far from being a prude, I couldn't consider her a convenient bedmate. Tura, but not Leah. Perhaps unconsciously I was ashamed of how I had used Tura and that Norman knew it. Also, I couldn't forget the concern in his eyes when he had said, "Don't hurt her, Hilly."

Dammit, I thought, *why do people make me feel responsible for them?*

For some reason I didn't take to Senator Graham W. Newberry. Running every morning for five miles from his apartment to his office on the Hill. That prematurely gray hair, pale blue eyes, gaunt, almost ascetic look, and his brisk efficient manner. He was just *too* perfect. It was apparent his staff was in awe of him, and Tom Gray was all admiration.

Over breakfast in his office—if you can call Sanka and one slice of melba toast breakfast—we reviewed the facts I had given them and what their investigators had turned up. Newberry's questions were sharp and penetrating, but I had the uneasy feeling they were mostly aimed at headlines. It was quite obvious why Newberry didn't have a "legislative assistant," the Washington euphemism for press agent. He was his own. When we finished, he called several newspaper and wire service bureaus, spoke to friends, and gave them a brief but precise account of what he intended to develop during his hearings. To each one he promised, "It will be a hell of a hearing and will make good readable copy. . . ."

He congratulated me for what I had done, promised the hearings would be a "blockbuster," predicted his committee's report would be a "sizzler," and said with a smile he was sure the Department of Justice would soon prepare a grand jury investigation of Ginerva and the Society of the Chosen.

"Today will mark the beginning of the end of Ginerva, her whole gang, and the Society of the Chosen," he said dramatically.

"What about Foreman, Frey, and that *Express* deal?" I asked bluntly. "What the hell does a guy heading a national evangelist organization want with a powerful capital newspaper?"

His blue eyes studied me. "Justice is on that, Hilly. Don't worry, they'll come up with the answer."

Tom cut in quickly. "That's what I told Hilly, Senator."

Newberry smoothly slid onto another subject. "The Milwaukee papers are sending their staff people along with those Wisconsin witnesses. Our investigators tell us they really have horrendous stories to tell of what happened to their children in those damn Houses of Preparation." He shook his head in dismay. "It's hard to believe these things are going on. More like the Middle Ages."

The question of Frey, Forman, and the *Express*, I realized, had been neatly sidestepped. Leah had been right again. A Washington publisher *is* too hot for any Washington committee to handle.

It was a four-man committee, but obviously it was Newberry's show. The other three senators sat back, left the room, made a few remarks for the benefit of their constituents, or suddenly appeared when the tiny red light on the main camera swung about in their direction. I told myself that every member of a senatorial or congressional committee should be forced to get Actor's Equity cards.

The morning and afternoon sessions of the first two days of the hearings were devoted to the testimony of parents of children who had joined the Society of the Chosen. Their stories, as Newberry had told me, were "horrendous"; a mother and father finding their once handsome son turned into a frail long-haired ghost who mumbled

Biblical quotations and denounced them as messengers from Satan; a widowed mother whose brilliant daughter had left college to disappear into the Society, found her selling junk jewelry and wilted flowers and sleeping in a rat-infested San Francisco cellar; a young woman who resigned a promising career as a fashion designer to become a cook in a House of Preparation, walked out of the twentieth-story window after telling her fellow Disciples she had seen God's Heavenly Cloud of Salvation and was going to meet it . . . .

Hour after hour, a procession of weeping, angry, frustrated men and women told their stories from the witness table. Newberry was gentle and properly indignant, promising each one that "something will be done about these people."

As Tom had predicted, the hearing room was packed with anti-Ginerva groups. Outside, police separated two marching groups of pickets, those against Ginerva, and various other nut cults and sects. One picket in a loincloth and carrying a wooden staff, had a sign whose denunciation of civilization ranged from killing animals to building cars. The anti-Ginerva bands were angry and loud. Their pickets held up signs proclaiming: "GINERVA: GIVE US BACK OUR CHILDREN!" "THE SOCIETY OF THE CHOSEN—THE DEVIL'S OWN!" "WHERE IS ALL THE MONEY GOING, GINERVA?" "THE THOUGHT CONTROL SOCIETY STEALS OUR CHILDREN'S MINDS AND SOULS!" As the hours passed, their numbers increased. On the afternoon of the second day, they were louder and more aggressive. Twice they rushed the main doors, once fighting their way past the guards to reach the doors of the hearing room, where they were stopped by reinforcements.

After that scuffle, Tom said thoughtfully, "Hilly, if there is any need for it, take Ginerva into Newberry's office. Behind his coatrack is a door that leads down a stairway into the reserved parking lot."

The afternoon of the third day featured Ginerva. Shortly before the hearing began, I took my place next to her chair at the witness table; Leah and Norman were outside waiting to alert me when she arrived. The room was jammed with opponents of the Society. From the window of the second floor corridor, I could see the pickets were now in the hundreds. Most of the marchers were middle-aged men and women, but their angry chants and jeers could have matched any group of young protesters of the Sixties.

Shortly before ten o'clock, Leah hurried down the aisle to where I was sitting. "Ginerva is coming in now, Hilly," she said. "My God, those people went crazy out there! The ten Angels she had as escorts were hit with everything from handbags to picket signs!"

To a bombardment of flashbulbs, Ginerva entered the hearing room enclosed in a flying wedge of Avenging Angels. Almost as if by signal, the audience erupted into a roar. Men and woman jumped out

(365)

of their seats to rush at her, cursing, screaming, and shouting threats. The guards, joined by the Angels, fought to get her down the aisle. Newberry leaped to his feet, pounding his gavel, bellowing orders to the guards as he threatened to clear the room unless order was restored. Ginerva was almost lost in the melee. I scaled the small railing and pushed my way to her side. Finally, pushing and shoving, we got her inside the railing. Ginerva was pale, but she had not lost her composure as she took my arm and let me lead her to the witness table.

"Are you all right?" I whispered. She smiled and nodded, but eagerly accepted the glass of water I poured for her.

I leaned toward her and said in a low voice, "Ginerva, we only have a minute. Can I help you in any way?"

Her green eyes were dull. She only shook her head.

"Ginerva," I whispered, "you said you needed help. I'm prepared to do anything—"

"No one can help me," she said, staring ahead.

"I can delay the hearing," I said. "I can ask for a recess. We should talk before you testify, Ginerva!"

For the first time, she turned and studied me. "It is too late, Brother Hillers," she said in a low voice.

Then Newberry banged his gavel.

"This session will now come to order," he said, and grimly looked out at the packed audience. "If there are any more disturbances during the testimony of this witness I will order the guards to clear the hearing room." He pointed his gavel at me. "Your name, sir?"

I stood up. "Brother Hillers, sir."

"Are you a member of the Society of the Chosen?"

He was putting on a good act.

"Yes, sir."

"Are you an attorney?"

"No, sir."

"In what capacity are you here?"

"I guess you can say I am an advisor to Her Holiness, Senator."

If they were viewing this thing on TV, I wondered what Johnny Masters, the dean of St. Timothy's, or my faculty friends were thinking. Or Susan. Or Tura—if she was still alive. . . .

Tom Gray broke in. "Madam, don't you have an attorney?"

Ginerva replied in an even voice, "No. I have only God and my conscience."

"You sacrilegious bitch!" a man shouted from the audience.

Newberry leaped to his feet and pointed his gavel like a spear. "Guards! Throw that man out of this hearing room!"

Two guards reached into the row of benches and pulled out a

shouting, red-faced man in a gray suit. The guards half-dragged, half-carried him up the aisle while a small woman furiously pummeled them with a red umbrella until they opened the door and pushed both of them into the corridor. There was an angry muttering from the spectators, but under Newberry's stern gaze it slowly died away.

"This is a hearing room of the United States Senate," he said tersely, "and I refuse to allow it to be disrupted by anyone. Continue, counsel."

Gray said, "Madam, I will now read into the record a number of newspaper clippings, all interviews given by you to various members of the Los Angeles and San Francisco press. . . ."

Gray's investigators had done their homework. They had uncovered much more than I had in the *Chronicle*'s reference room and by my amateur legwork. There were stories that had appeared in small weeklies, county papers, and even obscure drug-culture sheets when Ginerva was starting with Foreman. In every one Ginerva had repeated the story of her missionary parents in Bolivia, their deaths, and her confrontation with God on the mountain trail.

Tom read them all in a monotone. Then a screen was set up, and a long time was devoted to viewing flickering clips of her early television interviews during which she told the same stories. As Tom had said, they were laying the groundwork to gradually destroy her credibility. After an hour of this, Gray then called various witnesses from missionary groups, the State Department, committee researchers who had examined files of Bolivian newspapers, and finally a representative of the Bolivian ambassador who read a letter from the ambassador to the State Department revealing his government had officially investigated Ginerva's story and had come to the conclusion that it was a lie. I looked at her. She seemed lost in thought, oblivious to everything.

In the silence following the last witness, Newberry stared down at Ginerva, then said, almost gently, "Madam, do you wish to make a statement regarding the testimony of those witnesses?"

Her voice was clear and firm. "Senator, are you trying to destroy me?"

Her aggressive answer seemed to take him by surprise, but Tom jumped in. "We are only seeking facts, madam, the truth."

"But isn't the truth out there, sir?" she replied, pointing to the television cameras. "Where drugs, disillusionment, unemployment, distrust of their government, are a way of life for America's youth?"

Foreman's strategy was now clear. Ginerva was talking to the American public by way of television, and not to the committee or her hostile audience.

(367)

"A long time ago," she continued, "they called another generation of Americans 'the lost generation.' But our young people today are *really* lost, Senator. They are begging for help and they are not getting it. More and more they are turning to God to—"

"Madam, a great deal of what you say is true," Newberry broke in, a look of annoyance on his face, "but we are not here to discuss the sociological problems of our young. You are here under subpoena to—"

She appeared not to have heard him. "They are turning to God because they have finally realized the answers to their problems—to all our problems— lies in his infinite wisdom and mercy."

Newberry's voice now had an edge. "Madam, you heard the testimony of the witnesses. Are they telling the truth? Did you lie to the media when you told them that your parents were missionaries in Bolivia and that you yourself were a missionary?"

She spoke directly to the cameras. "I have served God in every way possible with my whole heart and my whole being since he appeared before me and appointed me his messenger to warn the people of the world that the Day of Judgment is fast approaching."

Newberry moved in quickly. "You are under oath, madam." He reminded her, "Are you telling this committee that God the Almighty appeared before you to give you a message to the world?"

She looked perplexed. "But, Senator, I just told you that!"

Tom moved uneasily in his chair. He realized Ginerva had adroitly forced Newberry to move from fact to fantasy. She certainly couldn't be indicted for perjury because she claimed to have seen God. Who could prove she was a liar? Now Newberry was losing his self-control. His face was grim, his voice sharp and precise. They duelled like this for a time, with Ginerva countering his questions with questions of her own, quotations from the Bible, or a gentle rebuke for his lack of religious convictions. This last left him red-faced and sputtering; his constituency was known to be religious and politically conservative.

"I believe that *you* believe in God, Senator," she said steadily, "but when last were you on your knees before him? This morning when you woke up? Last night when you went to bed? On Sunday morning?"

"Madam, my religious beliefs are not a matter of concern to this hearing," Newberry snapped. "We are still trying to get out of you whether or not you lied to the television and print press about your background? The question requires a simple answer. Yes or no."

Tom, who had listened impatiently to the exchange, interrupted with a loud, "Madam, you *must* answer these questions. Were you born in Idaho, and if you were, under what circumstances did you leave?"

(368)

I knew he had touched a vital spot. For the first time, she faltered, hesitated, but then she regained her icy calm air.

"Why is my background so important to this committee?" she inquired gently. She turned slightly to face the cameras. "What should be more important to you—to the whole world—is the knowledge that time has run out. There is none left."

Even Tom looked startled. "What do you mean, Madam?"

"What I mean is this," she said. "The end of our world is very near. But it will not come as a surprise to those of us who have read the Bible. Ask your people in Wisconsin, Senator Newberry, ask them how many times the Bible mentions the world's end. Many, many times. And now that time is near. I repeated God's warning to the world, but the world turned its back and refused to listen."

Newberry said in an unbelieving voice, "Are you telling us the end of the world is about to take place, madam?"

She said, "That time is drawing near."

A woman in the audience jumped up and screamed, "Blasphemer! Devil's whore! You will burn in Hell for this!"

Several others joined her and began chanting, "Ginerva! Spawn of Satan! The Devil's Daughter!" Placards were held high and a man and two women ran down the aisle, a sheet stretched out between them with the words written in red paint GO BACK TO HELL, GINERVA, WHERE YOU BELONG!

Newberry was on his feet and pounding his gavel and shouting: "Guards! Throw these people out! Make them sit down!"

After a brief tussle, the woman was pushed out the door along with the pair and their bedsheet sign. When order was finally restored, Newberry, obviously frustrated, slammed down his gavel, and announced: "It is almost four o'clock. We will resume these hearings at ten o'clock tomorrow morning."

Then, followed by his aides and Gray, he entered his private office. As if by magic, the wedge of Angels entered and walked single file down the aisle.

"Thank you, Brother Hillers," Ginerva said softly. "Will you join me tomorrow morning?"

"I'll be here," I told her, "but tomorrow, no more excuses. We must talk—alone."

She didn't reply, only smiled as she entered the circle of waiting Angels. They walked back up the aisle and left the room.

Leah and Turner, who had been in one of the rear seats, joined me.

"She's not going to let them pin her down on anything," Turner said. "She'll be like mercury until Newberry is forced to end the hearing."

"She said the Last Day is near," Leah said thoughtfully. "She never said that before."

"That's only more of the same," I said. "Don't you see what she's doing? They have her coached so Newberry can't get around that double-talk."

Turner said disgustedly, "She's going to keep on quoting the Bible and talking about what God told her. She'll wear out everybody."

Then a clerk appeared and whispered that the senator wanted to see me.

"Look, suppose we meet for dinner at the hotel," I told them. "Maybe we can think of something to help out this guy."

When I entered Newberry's office, the last of the other senators were leaving. I had noticed that as the afternoon ground down to that boring exchange between him and Ginerva, the other committee members were gone for long stretches.

Newberry looked glum. "How do you like that bitch?" he asked.

"It looks like Tom had them pegged right. They coached her so she won't make an admission."

"It's going to be different tomorrow," he said savagely. "I'm going to make her admit she and Foreman and the whole gang are only a bunch of thieves and bloodsuckers." He held up a sheaf of documents. "The report of our accountants. We haven't reached this stuff. It gives a damn good view of what you saw taking place in that Money Room. Halfway houses for addicts. Homes for old people. Missionary centers across the world. It's all bull! They haven't even built an outhouse! The IRS doesn't want to get into any hassle with those religious groups so they let them slide by! When we get finished with her, I'm going to demand that the Senate expand the scope of this committee and give it power of subpoena for all records, not only of the Society, but of all these nut groups!" He glared at Tom Gray. "Tom, Hilly saw the Money Room in operation. Why can't we put him on the stand? Can you imagine the sensation his testimony would cause? It would knock her right on her ass!" He mimicked Ginerva's soft voice, " 'Senator, when have you last been on your knees in prayer?' " His voice rose. "I want to get that woman! She's a fraud and a menace to the youth of this country!" He pointed a rigid finger at the door. "You heard the story those poor unfortunate people told out there! They were sickening! We could be in the Middle Ages!"

I had to hold back an amused smile. It was not the souls of America's youth which bothered the senior senator from Wisconsin, but the television cameras. They had clearly helped Ginerva rack up many points against him.

Gray shook his head. "No way, Senator, can we put Hilly on that stand. You have forced Justice to move into an area they dislike, religion, and they would love to find an out. Having Hilly testify could be that out. They can simply say you blew the whole thing by revealing Hilly's role. That could make *you* look bad. *Real* bad. And that would *not* make the people back home very happy. Forget it, Senator."

Newberry brooded over this threat for a few minutes, then said, resignedly, "Yeah. I guess you're right." He slammed his fist on the desk. "But dammit, let's think of something for tomorrow morning that will put the fear of God in all of them!"

"Cite them for contempt," Tom suggested. "You can get a quick Senate vote. That will not only put the Bureau after them but also the marshals."

"Damn right," Newberry said happily. He visualized aloud a headline: "FBI HUNTS CULT LEADERS. That will get 'em."

"I'll see you in the morning," I said. Behind Newberry's back, Tom sighed and looked heavenward.

When I closed the door, Newberry was yelling for an aide to get him a drink.

I was staying at the Hilton. I had barely turned the key in the lock when the phone rang. I immediately recognized Susan Kahn's voice with a twinge of conscience. I hadn't called her in Chicago since she had left after I delivered the Ellen Terry portrait.

"Susan! How great to hear from you! Will you forgive me for not calling?"

There was a slight tremor in her voice. "I know how busy you've been, Hilly. I've been following the newspaper articles and watching the hearings on TV. I must see you at once. It's very important."

"Of course, Susan. Right after tomorrow's hearing ends I'll fly out to Chicago."

"I'm not in Chicago, Hilly, I'm at the Washington airport. I just flew in. I'm in a coffee shop right off the main entrance. Can you come now?"

"Stay put," I told her. "I'll be there in a few minutes."

The coffee shop was jammed, but I saw Susan in a booth, staring down at a cup of coffee she was stirring automatically.

When I slid down in the seat across from her, she leaned over and kissed me. Under the careful makeup, sorrow and sleepless nights had etched lines about her eyes.

"Susan, it's great to see you."

She studied me. "I would say you lost about ten, maybe more pounds, Hilly," she said. "You looked thin on television." She added, "And tired."

"It's all coming to an end, Susan," I told her. "After this hearing is over, the Department of Justice will start an investigation of Ginerva, Foreman, the whole gang. One day they'll all be indicted." I squeezed her hand. "They will be made to pay for what they did to Ben."

(371)

"Did they find out anything about . . . Ben's death?" she asked steadily.

"Not much. But I think one or two of the conspirators will talk rather than go to jail for Foreman. It's all bound to come out, Susan."

"And Ginerva? What have they found out about her?"

"Well, we know she came from Idaho, but they still haven't dug up her real name or where she—"

"It's Ann St. John," she said evenly, "and she came from a former mining camp called Poker Game. Her father was a carpenter who died when she was about five. Her mother and her mother's sister, Clementine—'Aunt Clem'—bought a boarding house in Poker Game and a highway diner. Did you ever hear the legend of China Polly and Johnny Bemis, Hilly?"

I could only shake my head. Poker Game! I was numb.

She continued. "Oh, it's all very romantic but true. Johnny was a miner who won this beautiful Chinese girl in a poker game in the 1870s. When he was wounded in a gunfight, she put him across the saddle of his horse, got him to his cabin, and nursed him back to health. Johnny fell in love with her, they were married and lived happily ever after."

"Susan, what does all this have to do with Ginerva?" I asked, bewildered.

"It has a lot to do with Ginerva," she replied. She pushed a large brown envelope toward me. I was shocked to see my name in Ben's handwriting. "That's right, Hilly. It's all in there," she said, her voice trembling. "It's a report of everything Ben found out about Ginerva in Idaho."

"My God, Susan, where did you get this?" I asked.

She tried to smile. "Ellen Terry gave it to me. You know, when the nights or the weekends get too long for a sad woman, housework can be therapy. I must have changed that damn Chicago apartment around times. The last time, Terry's portrait looked dusty. I was about to take it to a professional to be cleaned when I decided to try it myself.

"It took me most of the afternoon, but I did a respectable job, and then started on the frame. Do you remember how heavy that oak frame was with all those weird curlicues?" When I nodded, she continued. "I did one side, and then I thought the screws holding the wire needed tightening. They were large, brass, and shaped into a horse's head. When I turned one with the screwdriver, there was a loud click, and part of the lower frame snapped open. I almost had a heart attack. Staring right up at me was this envelope with your name written in Ben's handwriting."

She bit her lower lip, her eyes glistening with unshed tears. "Hilly, it was as if Ben had reached out and touched me. It was so like Ben. He loved to surprise us. And this was his big surprise for you, Hilly—the secret of Ginerva." Her hand covered mine as I started to open the envelope. "Don't read it while I'm here, Hilly," she begged me. "I've read it over and over. Ben found the answers to a lot of your questions."

A waitress hovered uncertainly at our booth. "Please order something, Susan, you must be starved."

"I had dinner on the plane," she said. "I'm not going to stay. I just have enough time to make the flight back to Chicago. I've been reading everything in the papers about her—and about you. She's a strange woman, Hilly, and while Ben found out a lot of answers, I believe there are some questions about her that will never be answered."

She leaned over and kissed me. "Goodbye, Hilly, and please be careful. Those people can be dangerous."

"Susan, one question. What does Foreman have on her?"

She said in a low voice, "She murdered her illegitimate son. He was Mongoloid."

She squeezed my hand, slid out of the booth, and in a moment was gone.

Ben's Report

I fought the temptation to read the contents of the envelope in the booth. Instead, I raced back to my hotel room, poured myself a stiff slug of bourbon, and dumped the contents of the envelope out on the bed. A chill ran up my back as I recognized Ben's handwriting. I could almost hear his mocking laugh: *"I told you I would get the stuff on her, Hilly."*

I first skimmed through the sheaf of copies of official documents. These included the search and sale of the boarding house, diner, and gasoline franchise by Ginerva's Aunt Clem; various birth and death certificates; and with bits and pieces from public records around which Ben carefully reconstructed the life of Ann St. John, former queen of Poker Game's Frontier Week, murderess, and finally Ginerva, self-proclaimed courier of God, delivering His warning to the world that the Last Day was coming.

During the weeks he had spent in Idaho investigating Ginerva, Ben had written a series of reports describing the various steps he had taken, the people he had met, and what he had found out.

The reports had been typed on Holiday Inn stationery. It was clear that he had gone over his reports several times, editing out words, filling in names with comments in brackets, preparing the material for his secretary, Mrs. Caxton, to type with the original for me. The reports had not been written in one day or night but over a period of time. I determined that he had finished the last one shortly after he had called Susan for the last time. The final date was the anniversary of the deaths of his wife and son in the fire. The last few showed how his troubled mind was slowly slipping into a deep depression.

(Mrs. Caxton: Please type as is. The original for Mr. Hillers, one dupe for our files, and one is to be sent to Sir Edward Butler. Please check with his secretary where it should be sent, to his Manhattan apartment or to where he is staying in Washington. B.R.)

My investigation of Ginerva's background began shortly after I had lunch with a client (see Sumner file, contractual violations, box office revenues, musical, *Sing a Song of Sixpence*). During lunch he casually mentioned that the prophet Ginerva he was reading about actually came from a small mining town in Idaho named Poker Game. At first I couldn't believe what I was hearing. When I asked him how he knew this, he explained that his father had been a partner for many years in a small stock company that played every state in the west from California to Washington, from right after World War II up to his father's death some years ago. His father's partner, an older man who had started touring in the 1920s, was now in the Actors' Home in Englewood, N.J. The old man had no living relatives so my client said he made it a habit to drop by and see the old man every few weeks. This one day, he said, the old fellow had a newspaper picture of Ginerva and told him he was sure her name was Ann St. John and her mother and aunt had owned the boardinghouse in Poker Game, Idaho, where he, my client's father, and their small stock company had stayed many times. I told my client I had someone whose daughter had become involved with Ginerva's Society of the Chosen and asked him if he would bring me over to Englewood to see the old man. He readily consented, so the next morning we drove over to Jersey.

(I bought a Polaroid and took shots of the old guy holding a copy of the *New York Times* to establish the date.)

I found the old fellow possessed a remarkable memory, and he gave me a detailed account of Ann St. John, whom he described as a beautiful, talented, and sometimes strange child. When I asked him what he meant by "strange," he explained that she appeared to have been brought up in a fantasy world by her Aunt Clementine—"Aunt Clem." He described her as having long hair the color of raw copper in the sun, deep green eyes, a wonderful disposition, and a tremendous love of the theatre, which she no doubt got from her aunt who had played small roles on Broadway and had a lead in a WPA touring stock company.

(375)

According to his description the aunt—Clementine Langford —had "papered" the walls of the boardinghouse with mementoes of her theatrical career: theatrical photographs, posters, newspaper clippings, and copies of *Playbill* with her name in the cast underlined in red. A sewing room, the old man said, had been turned into a backstage dressing room complete with homemade costumes, a makeup table, and a full-length mirror where the aunt taught her niece the tricks of posturing, facial expressions, and makeup.

(From what I have been able to find out over the telephone from one of the curators at the New York Public Library's theatrical collection in Lincoln Center, a Clementine Langford played several minor roles in Broadway productions and had the lead in two WPA stock companies that toured Idaho, Wyoming, Colorado, and Montana from 1936 to 1938. There are no pictures of her on file.)

Salesmen and stock companies usually stayed at the boardinghouse run by the two women, the old man said, because of its reputation for good food and clean beds. It wasn't unusual, he said, for Aunt Clem and the child to put on a skit in the living room after dinner, with an actor or actress to give them a hand.

"If you refused her," he said, "you were made to feel as if you had just turned down an opportunity to do a scene with the Lunts. Everyone said yes, of course, not only because they were actors but it also meant that Aunt Clem—everyone called her that—would let you pick up your tab the next time around if you were short. We also noticed that anyone who played a scene with them got the bigger helpings."

He had an old cigar box filled with photographs and mementos, one showing him on the porch of the boardinghouse. A copy is among the exhibits and snapshots. It was a large Victorian type, big lawn, veranda, many rooms, gables and an old barn. He said the house was kept scrupulously clean by the two women. When I asked about Ginerva's father, he said he had been a carpenter and had died when Ginerva was about five. He assumed they came to this isolated place because, as Aunt Clem once told him, she had passed through it in her WPA days and liked the country. What Ginerva's mother did or where she came from originally he did not know.

With my client's permission, I visited the old gentleman three times and talked to him for hours. His stories of his early days in the stock company were fascinating, especially when he described how he and my client's father and their tiny company played Shakespeare in car barns, American Legion posts, on riverboats, and in barns lighted by kerosene lamps. Many times, he said, they took produce and livestock for payment. Once they had a crate of chickens in the trucks they used and lived off the eggs until they reached the next town.

After I had exhausted his memories about Ann St. John, our elusive Ginerva, I went to Idaho to see what I could find out about her. I first rented a car at the Boise airport and set out for Poker Game, roughly a hundred miles east of Boise. To my dismay, I discovered the village and a large part of the district had for years been under water, ever since a dam had been built. However, from newspaper files and what public records I could locate, I was able to put together a picture of Poker Game—and Ginerva.

Originally it had been a mining camp, but by World War I the mines had been exhausted and the village became an obscure backwoods home for a few families. It took on new life in the Thirties when the state built a highway that passed along its edge. A diner was opened for truckers.

From what the old fellow told me, I estimated Ginerva was about five when her mother and aunt bought the diner. At first they lived in the boardinghouse, which the two women later bought. This was before the story of China Polly and Johnny Bemis became known; a story from Idaho's frontier history that was to change all their lives.

(According to the man I spoke to in the State Development Bureau, the story of Johnny and Polly was first uncovered by a reporter for a Boise newspaper. It is incredibly romantic but factually true. I checked it out with the Idaho Historical Society. The story was a hit and the reporter wrote an outline and sold it to "Playhouse 90" in the 1950s. It got excellent reviews and was sold to an independent producer, who made a movie out of it using Poker Game as the original setting.)

In brief, this is the story: Johnny Bemis was a twenty-two-year-old miner who came to Idaho during one of the gold strikes. He loved to play poker. One night he got into a game with a Chinese mandarin (this is true) who had charge of a number of Chinese who were working as laborers in the local mine. After Johnny cleaned him out, he put up this young pretty teenage girl as a wager. It was for one hand. Again Johnny won, and the mandarin ordered the girl to join him. Later, in a saloon there was a gunfight and Johnny was seriously wounded. Somehow the young girl got him across the saddle of his horse and let the horse take them home to Johnny's log cabin, where she nursed him back to health. They fell in love, were married, and lived happily ever after. (I know it sounds like a Wild West whopper but so help me, it's true. One of the things I want to do when I get back is to get a copy of the movie.)

Even though it was the "western period," the movie bombed at the box office. (I have a friend at Variety who is digging up the original review.) Instead of treating it as a moving love story, the producer shot it as a bang-bang western with two has-beens in the leads. However, a California promoter latched on to the story, bought the rights, and came to Idaho to put on an annual Frontier Week highlighted by an outdoor pageant retelling the story of Johnny Bemis and China Polly.

Obviously, he was trying to duplicate that very beautiful outdoor show in the Carolinas based on the Cherokees' Trail of Tears, which has become such a big tourist hit. For publicity purposes the promoter used some of the families in Poker Game as extras, and Aunt Clem badgered the promoter to give Ann-Ginerva—from now on I'll call her that—a reading. The promoter was impressed enough to give her a part. The kid undoubtedly had talent, and during the summer they kept shifting her to better parts. The second year they did the same thing, until she was given one very good scene, the role of Johnny's young sweetheart, who is replaced by China Polly. I read some of the reviews of that year and they all called her performance outstanding.

The third year she was given the lead, complete with a black wig and slanted eyes, and was a hit. But after a successful summer, her mother caught a cold in the fall. She ignored it and had walking pneumonia by the time Aunt Clem insisted she enter a hospital. She lasted a week and died.

Ann-Ginerva was devastated; she had no alternative but to stay in Poker Game—she was still in high school—and the boardinghouse and diner had to go on. Her aunt insisted she continue her plans to take up drama at the state university. She was fanatical in her determination that her niece one day would be a Broadway star. She hired a few local women to help with the diner and boardinghouse, and life went on.

Ann-Ginerva continued to play China Polly in the pageant. The promoters weren't making a fortune but the thing was growing and they raised her salary to $150 a week. When they finally invested in a national promotional and advertising campaign, the state became interested.

So far all the stuff I dug up is strong enough to discredit her tales of missionary parents and missionary work in Bolivia and down south, but I really hit pay dirt one day when I was going through the files of one of the newspapers and came upon the enclosed Xerox copy of the clipping that stated that nine-month-old Peter St. John, son of Ann St. John who played the role of China Polly in the pageant, had accidentally drowned while being bathed by his aunt.

Ann-Ginerva married! I knew that if she had been married the newspaper's reference room would have some clippings; Idaho's newspapers had nothing on that. Also there was no marriage record in the county files.

I recalled what you said about Foreman having something on Ginerva to keep her in line, and I began to sense that perhaps the death of this child might have some connection.

But there was one major obstacle to this conclusion. Even if the child were illegitimate, how could Foreman use a tragic accident to intimidate her?

Poker Game certainly never had a police department, so any death, even one that was accidental, would have to come under the jurisdication of the sheriff's office or the state police. Most of the county was under water, but the state police gave me a roster of the sheriff and the three deputies who had been in office during that period. The sheriff and one deputy were dead, another had left the state and was reportedly working somewhere in the Northwest, but the wife of the third deputy yelled over the phone that I could find "that no-good husband of mine getting drunk as usual at Bailey's bar" and hung up.

The bar turned out to be a typical backwoods gin mill with the former deputy the only morning customer. I was in luck. He had just returned from being fired from a security guard's job in Vegas, and was broke and hungry for money. Two hundred gave him what one New York detective once described to me as "the snitch's diarrhea of the jawbone."

Curiously, this guy had not connected the beautiful girl of Poker Game who had played the role of China Polly with the evangelist Ginerva. However, that is not surprising to me; no one out here has done that, as far as I can find out. The reason is simple. The old families are gone, this entire area is beautiful but isolated, its residents, hardworking farmers and ranchers proud of their frontier heritage, are certainly not concerned with the affairs and events of the big cities, particularly in the East. They don't have too many television channels, and to them the price of hogs is more important than some nut cult flourishing beyond the mountains.

The former deputy accepted my explanation without question; I was an attorney from Chicago investigating a marital case. My client had married the girl known as Ann St. John from Poker Game and I was gathering background material for a divorce action. In fact he was glad to help me; he insisted his "bad luck" started with "that bitch."

He said the original call of the child's death had come into the sheriff's office from a member of the local volunteer rescue squad. He and a deputy, who had since died, were given the case, but on their way to Poker Game the other deputy was assigned to a fatal highway accident so he dropped my man off at Poker Game and continued on his way. This is the story my deputy told me. Hold your hat.

That year Ann-Ginerva was seventeen and had graduated from high school. She was preparing to enter the drama school of the state university. As usual she had spent the summer playing the role of China Polly and helping her aunt at the boardinghouse, which now had a waiting list of tourists. The diner was crowded every day, they had installed a gas pump and hired two men to make repairs and pump gas. Aunt Clem had bought a nearby barn and planned to turn it into a garage. From all accounts they were a very happy pair.

As I have pointed out, this was the *big* year for the pageant. The state had announced plans to build an outdoor theatre and the governor, who was in Washington, had sent his representative, a young and ambitious politician, to make the main address at the annual dinner that opened Frontier Week. (I never got to talk to the politician; last year he was killed in a California highway accident. Blood tests taken by the Highway Patrol showed he was drunk. The young girl with him was also killed.)

From what the deputy told me, the politician, handsome and a fast talker, had a reputation in the capital as a womanizer. He stayed at the boardinghouse and yes, you guessed it, the inevitable happened. Ann-Ginerva, the beautiful little country kid who had only been to Boise twice, was seduced. The politico had another score, but left behind a frightened teenager who was to discover she was pregnant. She told her aunt, who was stunned.

Aunt Clem went to the capital and attempted to see the politician, but was brushed off. It must have been a horrible time for both of them in that very conservative, backwoods, God-fearing community. Abortion was out of the question. The girl was getting nauseous and once had to leave the pageant's stage. Finally she dropped out with the excuse of being ill, and Aunt Clem sent her to live with an old stock-company friend in Salt Lake City.

Now the story takes an ugly turn. The child was born Mongoloid, blind and helplessly retarded. I spoke to the Salt Lake City woman, who now lives with her daughter there, and she confirmed that part of this guy's story.

She said it was like the end of the world for both Aunt Clem and her niece. The doctors at the hospital told them the child could live to be about four or five years old. Aunt Clem, who I can only admire, sold the boardinghouse and diner and gas franchise and what property she had accumulated, and vowed to her friend to devote the rest of her life to her niece and the helpless child. This woman told me Ann-Ginerva was deeply depressed, refusing to go out. Apparently the aunt and niece shared a deep guilt complex.

Aunt Clem moved them to a small farm miles from nowhere. To their friends in Poker Game they had dropped out of sight as though the earth had swallowed them. No one knew about the child.

I would imagine life in that lonely farmhouse had been hell on earth for both of them. The child screamed continuously. From a stunning young beauty, Ann-Ginerva turned into a frail, weary, uncommunicative, bitter woman.

As the months passed, the infant's health began to deteriorate. The screaming went on day and night. Both women were worn to the bone.

Finally, one morning Aunt Clem bathed the child as usual. Ann-Ginerva was in the next room. The aunt followed her routine of emptying the baby's bath, dried and powdered the infant, and put him back in his crib. For days the little boy had been very irritable and refused to eat. His day and night crying, she later told her friend, was "heart-rending."

She went upstairs to get some of the baby's clothes, and thought she heard the water running. She called to her niece, but there was no answer. Apprehensive, she hurried down stairs. When she entered the kitchen, she saw Ann-Ginerva holding the baby's body under water while she mumbled, "Stop screaming. . . . Stop screaming. . . ."

The aunt frantically tried to revive the baby, but it was too late. He was dead. Ann-Ginerva appeared to be in shock. Before she called the local rescue squad, Aunt Clem devised a plan. She would take responsibility for the infant's death. Her story was that she had left the child unattended for a few minutes and he had slipped under the water. She told that to the volunteers who pronounced the baby dead and notified the sheriff's office.

From the beginning, the deputy said, he had never bought Aunt Clem's story. He said she kept changing details, and once Ann-Ginerva told him, "I murdered my baby. I held him under the water. I wanted God to take him."

The county prosecutor had been in office for many years and knew Aunt Clem and Ann-Ginerva's mother. It was a sad, distasteful case, and he knew what a media circus it would turn out to be if she was formally charged with her son's mercy killing. He warned the deputy it would cost him his job if he tried to press the murder angle.

While the deputy is, as his wife called him, "a drunken son of a bitch" he is no fool. To protect himself, he insisted that the prosecutor and sheriff allow him to write a full report including all the evidence he had accumulated along with the statements he had gathered that he insisted proved Ann-Ginerva had murdered her son. To keep the guy quiet, the sheriff and the prosecutor allowed him to do just that, but they made sure the stuff never saw the light of day. The case was formally written off as an accidental death and the newspapers gave it noncommital coverage.

The sheriff is dead. I finally located the prosecutor in a nursing home; he is senile and drooling. He thought I was his grandson.

The deputy said he kept his mouth shut simply because he

had to survive. He knew one word from the prosecutor or the sheriff and he would be fired, lose his pension, and never get another county job. He eventually lost out several years later when a new administration came in, but by that time, as he said, "Who cared?"

After the formal inquiry was over and the baby's death was listed as accidental, Ann-Ginerva disappeared and Aunt Clem entered a nursing home. A few years later the whole area was put under water. The state never built the outdoor theatre, the pageant moved to another old mining camp, and life went on. It seemed as though the backwoods tragedy was buried forever.

Then one day two men appeared at the nursing home. One was slender, dark-haired, dark-eyed. The other was tall with a blond crew cut. (From your description, Hilly, they *have* to be Foreman and Russell.) The dark-haired man introduced himself as "Ann's producer from Hollywood"; the other simply said he was his "assistant." The dark-eyed guy explained to the head nurse they were planning a tour of a play starring Ann-Ginerva and at her request had stopped off at the home to give her regards to her aunt and to set up an account for her at the local bank to be used as she wished.

(The local bank said the account was under three thousand dollars. At her death the remaining funds of about $2,760 were willed to the supervising nurse.)

The nurse told me the old lady was overjoyed. The two told her stories of how her niece had made it "big" on the Coast and they even showed her a picture of Ann-Ginerva in a long white gown which they said was from a rehearsal of Shaw's *Joan*, which had always been one of their favorite roles.

The pair spent a great deal of time with the old lady, who later told the nurse: "They are the most wonderful men in the world. We just talked and talked about Ann. They seemed to know a lot about her but I told them some things they didn't know."

The nurse thought it was a bit peculiar that two sophisticated theatrical guys were spending so much time with the old lady, but they seemed to make her so happy so she never gave them a second thought. Finally they left. What I think is this: Foreman and Russell somehow found out about the murder of the child and persuaded the aunt to spell out the details. Perhaps they got the old woman on tape or had her sign an affidavit—that con man Foreman could easily talk an old woman like that into doing anything he wanted—then they checked the prosecutor's file and unsuccessfully tried to find the hard-nosed deputy.

The deputy confirms this. He said that some years after the incident he and his wife had a fight and he took a job as a security guard with a small traveling carnival and was gone for a year. When he returned home, his wife told him two guys had offered her all kinds of money to put them in touch with her husband. They told her they were private detectives working on a case. She gave her husband their phone number, but he lost it when he got drunk.

Now get this: when I went through the county prosecutor's office—I told him I was an attorney checking out the survivors of an estate—I found the case file for the death of Ann-Ginerva's son, but it was empty! The chief clerk made a big show of trying to find it among other files but he never came up with it.

The deputy swore to me that he had written and signed that affidavit and a year later, still protecting his flank, had examined the file and saw it among all the other papers. He is a lush and petty grafter, but I believe him.

Now, Hilly, this development has just taken place, and I believe it will help me wind up the story of Ann-Ginerva and her Idaho background.

I was spending my last week in Ketchum, talking to this night nurse and going through newspaper files and county records. (By the way, this is where Hemingway shot and killed himself. Every time I go into a bar at night I get hit with Hemingway stories.) One afternoon when I came back from checking records in the county seat, I found these two guys waiting for me. Believe it or not, they are twin private detectives from Chicago, also looking into Ginerva! They had been hired by a wealthy California banker whose daughter is in the Society of the Chosen, and claim to have unlimited funds. The father wants them to develop something "sensational" on Ginerva so he can use it in a Supreme Court action to get their daughter out of the Society.

They want to trade information. Of course I double-talked them during dinner and the next day checked out their firm myself. Later I got their supervisor on the phone from my room and he agreed to let them show me what they had in exchange for what I had dug up.

They floored me when they said they had bribed someone to slip them the original file on Ginerva. When I tested them as to its contents, they unhesitatingly told me it contained the deputy's original report accusing Ginerva of murdering her son. They also said the file included statements and affidavits the deputy had collected at the time, all strong circumstantial evidence confirming his murder accusation. They said they had been in Idaho for a month and had come across my path in the county records office. The only thing they did not have was a present-day interview with the deputy, who they told me was working as a security guard in Vegas. It was plain they were not aware he had returned. When I told them I had located the guard and paid him for an affidavit reviewing the entire case and pointing out how the prosecutor had refused to indict Ann-Ginerva, they became very eager to read it, but I told them to wait until trading time.

(383)

Now, Hilly, this is a report of what I have been doing and what I have uncovered up to this date. In a few days I hope to find out what these two guys have and make a trade.

In the meantime, let's examine what we have and how important it is.

1. There is little doubt we have uncovered Ginerva's secret, which Foreman has been using to keep her in line. The one chapter in your series recounting all this business in Poker Game should have a shattering effect on Ginerva and the future of the Society of the Chosen. Hilly, I realize this is an ugly business, but I hope you agree with me the whole business is ugly and deserves only the most ruthless methods to uproot it from American society. From the very first time I went into Foreman and his Society I had a feeling it was evil, for all its army of chaste, blank-eyed kids who walk the streets of the nation's biggest cities shrilling their Bible quotations and promises of good will.

2. The documentary evidence enclosed completely shatters Ginerva's story to you and others of her missionary parents, their deaths by a hit-and-run driver, her own missionary work in Bolivia and other South American countries, and finally her assignment to that nonexistent missionary group in the South where she finally had her confrontation with God. What we have labels her a liar and a fraud.

3. However, there is still a big gap that must be filled in. We have a story of a young girl who murdered her helpless imbecile son and who was not indicted because of the prosecutor's friendship with the family and his personal distaste for the case. Yet the law is the law and murder is still the taking of a human life by another. If the prosecutor had gone through with it, the grand jury would have indicted her for manslaughter, there would have been a quick guilty plea and a suspended sentence. But the case would have been sensational, and with this wild-eyed deputy anything could have happened. I can see the prosecutor's point.

What we need is proof the prosecutor *deliberately* let her off the hook although he knew she was guilty and the case should have gone to a grand jury which would have had to indict Ann-Ginerva. It would add just that much more to the authenticity of your series. I have a hunch it's all in that file those two guys stole. I don't want to appear too eager to trade, but I'm not going to let them out of my sight. From now on we're buddies.

4. There is one very important element lacking in all of this: what was Ann-Ginerva's motive in becoming this charlatan? Why did this country kid allow herself to become part of a conspiracy with such sinister overtones? What deep personal reasons prompted her to dream up that preposterous story of meeting God?

5. What happened to Ginerva from the day she dropped out

(384)

of sight after the case was officially classified as accidental death? Aunt Clem sold her property and eventually went into the nursing home after the waters of the dam covered the area. But what happened to her niece? What had taken place in her life from the time she left Idaho to the time she appeared for the first time in her San Francisco storefront church?

6. The old lady in Salt Lake City, Aunt Clem's friend from their stock company days, told me Aunt Clem had a "big bank account" and "lots of government bonds" from the sale of her real estate. The bank won't surrender any of its accounts unless directed by a court subpoena, but they did give me the date the account was closed out. Comparing this with the nursing home dates reveals she drew out her money shortly before she entered the home. What happened to the money in her "big" account? Did Aunt Clem give it to her niece? If so what did her niece do with it? It was far from a fortune but it could have been substantial.

I am sure, Hilly, that you will want to reconstruct this woman's life very carefully for your series, backed by documentary evidence, so these questions must be answered to give your work the unmistakable note of authenticity. (Would they consider this series for the Pulitzer Prize? I'm serious.)

At this point I really don't know how we will proceed to fill in these gaps. I don't know what success you eventually will have with Ann-Ginerva, but let's make filling in these gaps our number-one goal.

We will talk about this over the July Fourth weekend.

This was the end of the first report. There were three more. The second described a dinner he had with the twins.

Now there is no doubt in my mind that these two guys have done a tremendous amount of work investigating Ann-Ginerva's background. As they repeated, their client is willing to spend an unlimited amount of money to get something on Ann-Ginerva to spring in court.

Over dinner they would not show me the prosecutor's stolen folder. In dealing with these people you must give something to get something. So in return for letting me read a letter from the prosecutor in which he refused to convene a grand jury to allow the deputy to testify Ann-Ginerva was a murderess, I told them where they could find the deputy.

The folder, they said, contained "dynamite," and I believe them.

This morning over breakfast they were very cheerful. They had found the deputy and for another two hundred he had given them the same affidavit he had given me. They did not tell him who Ann-Ginerva was, but simply said they represented another party in my investigation. They said the deputy was so drunk he couldn't stand up, so they drove him home.

Frankly, today I don't intend to do much of anything. After breakfast I went back to my room and stayed there until the twins came knocking, wondering why I hadn't come down.

I'm not in a mood for Ann-Ginerva. But to keep them friendly, I joined them for dinner, then went back to their room where we boozed it all night. They knew I was low and tried their best to cheer me up.

I'm weary of Ann-Ginerva. I really am.

The next report was dated several days later. It was evident Ben was gradually slipping into his deep depression.

I should be getting out of here, but these two private eyes have started to feed me bits and pieces. They have promised to let me read the letters the deputy wrote to the prosecutor accusing him of covering up a mercy killing and his letters to the state's attorney general demanding that a special prosecutor be called in. Now this is strong stuff. That goddam deputy never told me that. I went looking for him, but he wasn't in the saloon and the bartender said he hadn't seen him since "two guys who looked like twins picked him up." His wife simply yelled over the phone, "that son of a bitch is on another binge."

I guess he went on a toot with our combined money.

That night over dinner they not only showed me the deputy's letters but the originals of the exchange between the prosecutor and the AG in which the AG first advised the prosecutor he had his letter from the deputy sheriff and asking what the hell was the case all about? (It is evident from the tone of the letters they were old friends and political buddies.)

The prosecutor replied that he had "conclusive evidence" the case was a "tragic accident" and he had nothing to indicate it was a homicide. He denied he was covering up and called the deputy an "irresponsible drunk." This of course now makes it an official cover-up of Ann-Ginerva's murder of her son.

The following morning I again called the bar, but the deputy still had not made an appearance. His wife just repeated her story he was on a "binge," which I assumed happens from time to time.

I didn't care a hell of a lot. It's that time of year again. All I think about is the fire. Memories of Nancy and Jody keep crowding in on me.

When the twins came around to my room, they saw I was depressed and sat with me for hours. Maybe it was the booze or the loneliness or the feeling those damn mountains have cut me off from everyone—you, Susan, the world—or a combination of all three, but I began to talk to them about the fire and how I felt.

(386)

I know the sensible thing for me to do is not to be talking to these two strangers but to simply call that little feeder airline, make a reservation to Salt Lake City, and get back home. I could be with you and Susan by the evening. But somehow I can't get up the energy. Believe me, Hilly, it's an effort to even type these notes. But I am determined not to leave here until I find out every scrap of information about your Ann-Ginerva. I know how obsessed you are with her, so I promise I will prove to you she is a fraud. These two strange guys have it all wrapped up in the folder and I intend to get what it contains.

Isn't it strange how that bitch has become an albatross around our necks?

The next was one badly typed page.

Can't understand what happened to that deputy. I stayed at the gin mill all morning but he never showed up. The bartender said the deputy's wife is getting uneasy; he has taken off before but he always called her after a few days to let her know where he was.

This was typed later.

Later in the afternoon the bartender called me. A passing motorist who had stopped to fix a flat had spotted the deputy's badly burned car in the bottom of a gully. The state police told his wife they had found a quart bottle of whiskey on the driver's seat. The bartender said there was one thing he couldn't understand; in all the years he had served this guy he had only drunk rye. He claimed scotch gave him heartburn.

The bottle in the car contained scotch.

I can't describe how depressed I am tonight. I keep telling myself that if I had not given that poor guy the two hundred— and led the twins to him with an additional two hundred he might be alive today. Why does violent death follow me, Hilly?

The twins wouldn't let me remain alone in my room. They insisted on ordering me something, and then we sat around again talking and drinking. (One reason why I want to get out of here. I'm drinking as much as that poor deputy.) I know what's wrong with me. In a few days, it will be the anniversary of the fire. They kept telling me it would be better if I talked about it, it would help ease my mind, and I did. That's all I talked about— the fire and Nancy and Jody. I knew what the trouble is—I'm afraid to go to sleep, afraid of the nightmares, which have started again. I think I broke down once. For two total strangers they were very sympathetic. I must get out of here.

The next was typed on the back of the page.

(387)

That was last night. Between the booze, the death of the deputy, and the anniversary of the fire, I feel miserable. Maybe it was the whiskey, but the nightmares were so real I break out in a cold sweat when I recall them. There's the fire, Nancy and Jody are screaming but no sound is coming out of their mouths. The flames are solid, like a wall, and I can't get to them. That was the phone. The twins are coming down, they think I need help. God, I certainly do.

Hilly, when I get back there is something I must tell you about the fire. When I stayed

That final report broke off abruptly. All that was left was a handwritten note that chilled me. It was brief, the words large and scrawled like a child's.

Hilly. I'm going back to New York with them. I must. They promised to show me how to gain peace. No more nightmares. No more fire. I just see Susan.

Then:

They're coming back with the gun. It's hard to think. They put me in that room. Mirrors. Help me, Hilly. I can hear them at the front door. They have a key. Ellen Terry. Ellen Terry. I want peace. Fire

I put the reports and documents back into the envelope and finished the bourbon. Here was the explanation of Ben's enigmatic "poker game" and the mission of the murdering twins. It was clear what had happened. After Foreman and Russell obtained the secret of Ginerva from her aunt, they had bought the file and paid someone to alert them if anyone appeared inquiring about the case.

Someone, undoubtedly Foreman, had sent the twins to Idaho after Ben appeared. I could only guess what had followed. Ben, his tortured mind controlled by the twins, was finally strapped in the chair in the mirrored room to be bombarded by those recorded screams, chants, cries, warnings of doom, and thundering music until he begged them for the gun.

Ben said we would have to fill in the gaps in the story of Ann-Ginerva. Before tomorrow's hearing was over, I vowed to myself, she would do just that. In some way, despite the Angels, I would get her alone. Me and Ann St. John, China Polly in a black wig and slanted eyes who became God's courier to the world. And my beautiful obsession. Tomorrow there would be answers. Answers. Answers.

Great Signs
in the Heavens

In the corridor a short distance from the hearing room, Leah and Turner listened in stunned silence as I quickly described my meeting with Susan and what was in the envelope.

"What do you intend to do with it, Hilly?" Leah asked.

"Frankly, I don't know," I told her. "I want to think about it."

"You can't give it to that politician, Hilly, until you at least talk to her," Leah explained. "That's a terrifying story!"

"She's a fraud," Norman said grimly. "This proves it."

"There is nothing in what Hilly told us that *proves* she's a fraud," Leah snapped.

"It certainly proves she's a murderer," Norman replied "She killed her own son!"

Leah turned to me. "You told us what Susan said, 'She's a strange woman and there are some questions about her no one will ever answer.' I agree with Susan—there *are* some strange things about this woman. I have always thought that. Hilly, face her with what you have. Get answers, but don't let these politicians use her tragedy to make headlines. Please, Hilly."

I protested, "That's easier said than done. It's impossible to talk to her alone. The Angels come out of the woodwork."

"Maybe you can insist Newberry wants to talk to her in private," she suggested. "Do anything, but give her a chance. I can't believe she had anything to do with those terrible things."

The elevator door opened and Newberry and other members of the committee came swinging down the corridor. When he saw us, he waved.

"We'll get her this time," he called out with a grin.

"Oh God," Leah said, half aloud. She looked at me.

"Okay," I said, "I'll try to get to her."

When I arrived in the hearing room, Ginerva was already seated at the table. She gave me a small, apprehensive smile as Newberry, followed by the other senators, Tom Gray, their aides, and the steno typist, filed into the hearing room. The TV crews, undoubtedly tipped there would be action and hard news at this morning's session, immediately swung into action.

Newberry banged his gavel and announced: "Tomorrow this committee will hear witnesses from Briggs, Kansas, including a state police captain, who will testify as to certain events which took place there following a rally staged there by the Society of the Chosen."

Tom gave me a slight triumphant smile.

"I now wish to make a statement for the record," Newberry was saying. "United States Marshals with subpoenas issued by this committee have been diligently trying to serve David Foreman, president of the Society of the Chosen, Brother Russell, head of their security, Sister Sloan, the Society's secretary-treasurer, and Brother Troy, in charge of their communications, in an effort to get them before this committee to answer our questions. It is evident from reports of the marshals that these witnesses have deliberately avoided service by this committee. At a meeting of this committee held last night, contempt citations have been voted against those I have named, and their cases have been referred to the full Senate for a vote that will take place this afternoon. I will then turn the matter over to the Department of Justice for appropriate action."

The audience began cheering and stamping their feet, and some held up picket signs. Now Newberry wasn't the fastest man in Washington with a gavel. He nodded grimly, waited until the cameras got some good shots of the cheering audience, then gently tapped for order. When the room finally became quiet, he said briskly, "Counsel, start your questioning of the witness."

As Tom leaned toward his microphone, Ginerva said abruptly, "I wish to make a statement."

Tom looked up, startled. He was no more surprised than I was. I quickly put my hand over the mike and asked her in a whisper, "What do you intend to say?"

She replied calmly, "I wish to make a prophecy."

"A prophecy! What kind of prophecy!"

There was a dreamlike expression on her face. "There will be great

(390)

signs in the heavens," she said softly. "God will show his anger in many ways."

"Why, Ginerva? Why all this?"

"God is angry at His people," she replied. "They have ignored the warning God gave to me."

Newberry asked impatiently, "Are you finished, Brother Hillers?"

I asked her, "Is this what Foreman told you, Ginerva?"

"No," she said, "this is what God told me. Now let me speak to the committee."

I took my hand off the mike. "Senator, Her Holiness wishes to make a statement to the committee."

"Very well, madam," Newberry replied with a slight frown. "You may begin."

In a clear unwavering voice, she began:

"God has told me that he is angry with his people for ignoring the message he gave to me for the world and he will show his anger by great signs in the heavens and other manifestations. Many will die by fire and the sword and there will—"

She never finished. The audience exploded with shouts, jeers, and stamping. The big man in the gray suit who had been ejected the day before leaped to his feet, bellowing and shaking his fist.

"Are we going to let this charlatan get away with this?"

The woman who had beaten the guards over the head with her red umbrella was at his side, shrilling: "No. . . . No. She's a messenger from Satan. . . . Send her back to hell where she belongs. . . ."

It was a catalyst that touched off the hate, frustration, and outrage simmering for days in that hearing room.

Men and women booed, jeered, and waved signs denouncing Ginerva and the Society of the Chosen. They ignored the threatening guards and Newberry's gavel and shrill demands that order be restored. Finally he shrugged, waved a hand at the other members of the committee, and shouted an announcement that hearings were adjourned temporarily but that Ginerva was subject to recall. As I turned to leave, Tom caught my eye and nodded in the direction of Newberry's office. When the jeering angry crowd made no attempt to leave the hearing room, I led Ginerva into the office.

This was one way to get her alone.

"It's too dangerous to go out the front way," I told her. "We'll use the senator's private exit."

She started to protest. "But the Angels—"

I ignored her and led her down a winding spiral iron staircase. We came out at one end of a huge parking lot filled with cars of government employees; the reserved section had names of senators painted in the spaces. The exit for the lot into Pennsylvania Avenue had a striped wooden arm that a guard raised and lowered. As we ran across the lot to where my car was parked, I saw a single file of Angels coming from around one end of the building. Behind them was a large crowd of screaming pickets waving banners and signs.

I pressed the gas pedal to the floor and roared down the long aisle of cars to the exit. Out of the corner of my eye I could see the Angels hurtling the hoods of cars in an attempt to head me off. A driver slowly pulling out tried desperately to back in. I could feel Ginerva's nails digging into my arm as we missed the car by inches.

When the guard at the gate saw what was happening, he lifted the wooden arm so we roared into Pennsylvania Avenue cutting off a bus and a cab to a wild chorus of protesting horns.

I left the avenue as soon as possible, weaving in and out of side streets. There was no sign of the Angels. Finally, a short distance from the Capital Beltway, I parked in a quiet tree-lined street.

"Well, where will it be?" I asked her. "A motel? Hotel? Or shall we ride into Virginia and find a quiet place?"

She stared straight ahead. "Why do you want to take me there, Brother Hillers?"

I said, "You promised answers. Remember?"

"I must go back to the motherhouse," she began, but I shook my head.

"It's all over, Ginerva. I know who you are. Where you came from. And what Foreman has on you. Poker Game. Aunt Clem. The baby in the bathtub. Do you want me to go on?"

She was silent for a long time, then she said, "Drive to Barondale. It's a village in the Catskills."

I couldn't believe what I was hearing. "The Catskills? What's up there?"

"The Hill of God's Word," she said quietly, "and your answers."

I drove steadily at top speed, with only brief stops to gas up and buy coffee and hamburgers, which she barely touched. For the entire trip she stared out the window, occupied with her own thoughts. Only once she said abruptly: "Those people back there hated me, didn't they?"

"They certainly didn't want to love you," I told her. "But can you blame them after what you have done to them and their families?"

She looked puzzled. "But what have I done?"

I looked at her. "Don't you know?"

"But I only did as God told me to do," she protested. "I only wanted them to help me warn the world."

I gripped the wheel with rage and frustration. "Is this all I'm going to get out of you?"

She leaned her head on the back of the seat and closed her eyes. "Please take me to the Hill of God's Word, Brother Hillers. Please."

BOOK FOUR

THE
HILL
OF
GOD'S WORD

Ginerva's Secret

Barondale was a typical Catskill village: a main street, bank, real estate office, a few churches, synagogue, pizza parlor, service station, and a stagnant pond with a few tired-looking ducks. A few miles outside the village we left the blacktop highway to swing into a lane that led to the entrance of one of the most beautiful valleys I had ever seen. Its bright, flowered, billowy meadows were bordered by pine forests. At the far end was a low, squat hill with what appeared to be an old wagon road leading to the top. From the lane the hill resembled a green apple with its top sliced off.

There was something on the top. The lowering sun made it difficult to make out, but when I shaded my eyes I could see outlined against the sky, the ruins of a smokestack, the frame of an abandoned windmill, and a utility pole with a crossbar.

"Don't tell me we're going to have a picnic," I said, as we got out.

She ignored the feeble joke and pointed to the hill. "That is the Hill of God's Word," she said solemnly.

"Well, what do we do now?"

She didn't reply, but moved through the grass toward the base of the hill. There wasn't anything to do but follow her.

The dying day was heavy with the smell of pine. The sides of the wagon road leading to the top were thick with wild rose and strawberry vines. Once a family of blue jays broke from cover to wheel over us, their raucous complaints echoing across the valley. Off to one side, a creek twisted around the hill to disappear into the woods.

When we reached the top, I could see the creek behind the hill had been dammed to create a small waterfall and a cattle pond. At the base of the chimney, the fire-scorched foundation of a farmhouse was almost hidden by wild ground cover. Between the rusty frame of the windmill and the sagging telegraph pole was a rough stone grotto with a silver crucifix.

"Quite a setting," I said sarcastically. "Is this meant to impress me?"

"Last summer I started to come up here to pray," she explained.

The sight of the cross disturbed and angered me. "Is this the spot where your heavenly cloud will scoop up the Chosen?"

"After what you found out about me, I don't blame you," she said. She walked to the rim of the hill and looked out across the valley. After a few moments, she said, "It will end here."

"Before we begin, spare me any of that," I told her. "I got you off the hook with the committee—at least for a while—I saved you from that mob. I drove you to this godforsaken place. Now can we forget the fairy tales and *really* start talking?"

"That's why I brought you here," she said. "I want to tell you everything."

She sat in the grass on the rim of the hill, and I joined her. It was a stunning view of the great bowl of the valley, circled by the stately pine trees.

"My dream was to someday build a church up here," she said. "It would never be closed to anyone who was seeking peace through prayer."

"I'm sure that would be very impressive," I said. "Now suppose we start with you, Aunt Clem, and Poker Game."

"From the very beginning," she said softly.

I repeated, "From the very beginning. In the boardinghouse. When you and Aunt Clem entertained the boarders."

"It seems so long ago," she said wistfully. "Aunt Clem was fanatical on the subject of my career as an actress. I could not possibly hope for a great career unless I had the basics: Shakespeare, the Bible, great plays, the gentility of fine breeding. Mother agreed with her, so from the time I started to walk that was my program. Aunt Clem's number-one commandment of the theatre was that every actress had to penetrate the heart of her character until she actually became that character on the stage and in that way could draw the audience into her fantasy world. Her favorite topic on the long winter nights was to describe for mother and me her vision of me as the star of a Broadway hit. Opening night the audience would give me a standing ovation.

Baskets of flowers would be brought to the stage. Outside the stage door a crowd would applaud me wildly. Reporters and photographers would besiege me while a small army of autograph seekers would trail me to my chauffeured limousine, begging for my autograph. Oh, yes, there would be a handsome millionaire waiting with his hand outstretched. Aunt Clem was a superb actress." She paused. "I came to believe it. . . ."

"It's getting late," I said. "Maybe we can skip that."

"Yes, I murdered my son, Brother Hillers," she said evenly. "I put both my hands on his tiny body and held him under the water until he was dead." Her eyes glistened with tears. "Isn't that what you want me to say?"

The abruptness of her confession startled me. Before I could reply, she continued in a rigidly controlled voice.

"It wasn't deliberate. I didn't plan a cold-blooded mercy killing, as that deputy insisted I had done. I loved my son; no one will ever know how much I loved him. It was something that happened so fast I didn't know it had happened until I looked down and realized it was *my* hands that were holding *my* son under water."

Suddenly her control gave way, and her voice was filled with a quiet passion. "It was *my* son and *I* had killed him! And I loved Peter so much! So *very* much!"

She was speaking as if it was important that I believed it was not only an accident but that she had *loved* her son.

The words tumbled out in a rush. "After the funeral I was in such a state of depression I wanted only to die. Aunt Clem saved me. She literally forced me back into the world of fantasy she had created when I was a little girl. She first started with the Bible and made me read chapters. Then Shakespeare. She made costumes and made me put them on and say the lines. I screamed at her, but she kept pushing me, threatening to leave me, anything until, half crying, half laughing hysterically, I read the lines. But she finally won. I didn't realize it, but she saved my life. Before long I was looking forward to those few hours of make-believe every afternoon."

It was not difficult to visualize the eerie scene: two lonely women, the older desperately trying to save the younger from slipping over the brink, playing their roles in grotesque costumes against the wallpaper backdrop of the isolated farmhouse.

What I wanted to do now was reach out and touch her. To hold her. To feel her slide into my arms. I wanted to protect her from those crazies in the courtroom and the ruthless politicians like Newberry, who was ready to use her for his headlines.

I wanted to save her from that locked-in sense of doom that hung about her.

From far, far away I heard the echo of Tura's mocking: *You're hooked by her, Hilly. . . .*

She was saying, "Do you want me to go on?"

"Yes, please do."

"It's Hilly, isn't it?" she asked quietly.

"That's what they call me."

"May I?"

"Of course."

"One day the phone rang," she said. "When Aunt Clem came back into the living room, she was smiling. 'That was the prosecutor,' she said. 'There will be no grand jury investigation. Peter's death is now officially an accident.' I just sat there looking at her. I didn't know what to say or what to do. Aunt Clem decided that. That same afternoon, she drove into town and came back with two envelopes. 'Go away, honey,' she said. 'There's nothing here for you anymore. Go to New York, enroll in a good drama school, make friends, and get into the theatre. You have talent, you'll be a success. Wipe out the past. All I ask is that you keep in touch, let me know where you are and how you are. Remember, I love you very much and I'll always be here ready to do anything I can for you.'

"Then she handed me the envelopes. One contained a New York bank savings book with thirty-two thousand dollars on deposit in my name. The other had the names, addresses, and phone numbers of three of her old friends whose families had some connection with the theatre, along with the names and addresses of two very reputable New York drama schools that had advised Aunt Clem they were prepared to interview me as an applicant. She told me that she and my mother had started the account soon after the boardinghouse had become successful, and had agreed that if I was ever dissatisfied with the state university they would give me the account and advise me to go to New York with their blessing. If I finished the university, the account was to be turned over to me on graduation day to do with as I wished." She sighed. "It was a rosy dream that never came true. Three days later, Aunt Clem drove me to Boise airport. By nightfall I was in a cab going from LaGuardia airport to Manhattan, positive my name would soon be in lights on Broadway. What a dreamer!"

I tried to peer behind the beautiful face looking out across the valley. When I came to this place, I didn't know what I would find: evasions, lies, hysteria? At least the answers to my questions of how and why. But never did I expect this elaborate description of her tormented life and dreams.

She said bitterly, "It was the usual cliché scenario. You must know it. Novelists, playwrights, feature writers, even fan magazines have used the plot until it's threadbare. Country girl goes to the Big City, enrolls in a drama school, wins the coveted award, attends countless auditions and tryouts, and ends up in a dog food commercial. That's right, a dog food commercial. I led the dog out to face the camera while the pitchman went into his act. Following that were three off-off-Broadway roles, you know, the plays that never get beyond the one week in a church cellar, warehouse, or a meeting hall. I was an understudy for a summer in a Jersey shore theatre and spent six months in a nasty smelling frog costume in a TV morning kiddie show. I was part of the usual group of young hopefuls who sat around, passing a joint, drinking wine, and assuring each other it was only a matter of time before some producer would discover our brilliant talents."

She turned to look at me. There was a quiet appeal in her voice.

"Please believe me, Hilly, everything I'm telling you is the truth."

"Did you stay in New York?"

"For another year—another year of disappointments. Then a couple starting a stock company hired me to play the lead in Shaw's *Joan*. It was one of my favorite roles, and I was deliriously happy. I should have realized there was a catch to it. We opened at the Little Strand Theatre in Pasadena. It was a shabby rundown place, but the audience was wonderful and we received a number of curtain calls. I was sure I was now on my way. That night the owner of the company described what I had to do in return for playing the lead. I didn't care anymore. I would have done anything to play this role. So I became his mistress on the road. I hated every minute. He was a failed actor, a vain, weak man who had a shrew for a wife. Small companies are usually filled with petty hates and enormous egos; this one wasn't any different. Someone wanted my role, so a note was sent to his wife. One night, when she was supposed to be visiting friends, she caught us. Of course he blamed me. I had seduced him. After a horrible scene, I was on my way back to New York with a week's salary. I was months without a job until I got a minor role in summer stock playing the hotels in the Catskills."

She took a deep breath and for a few minutes silently gazed out over the valley. "I found this hill and valley, and promised myself that someday I would buy them." She turned to me with a bitter smile. "Well, I finally did, but only after I became Ginerva, God's courier to the world. Isn't that a stupid name? It was Foreman's idea; he said it would help to give me an air of mystery."

"So you made it all up."

"Everything," she admitted, "after sitting on this hill and making an inventory of my life. What a failure it was. An actress whose one big success was a walk-on in a dog food commercial, a bit player in a smelly frog costume who jumped around for the benefit of hundreds of thousands of kids whose mothers had made me their baby-sitter. Minor roles in plays that never surfaced. A brief leading lady in a third-rate stock company who kept her role not by her acting ability but because she shared the owner's bed. I was so heartbroken I cried. Suddenly the thought came to me: suppose God appeared on this hill and appointed me his messenger to bring news of Judgment Day to the world? Could I make anyone believe such a wild story? It was a challenge, and the more I thought of it the more convinced I became that I could do it. I *could* act. I *could* make an audience cry. I *could* make them laugh. I *could* make them pray. I *could* even frighten them. I sat here all afternoon and thought about it. After all, who could prove or disprove my story? When I walked down the road to where I had parked my car, I was ready to resign from the stock company to become God's courier with a message to the world that Doomsday was coming."

"And Foreman peddled it like a deodorant?"

"I never believed him when he told me he could sell anything in this country—from dog food to God—if he had the money and the expertise." She looked at me. "You helped him prove that, Hilly."

"Let's go back to San Francisco," I said. "Why did you start there?"

"Can you name a better place for what I had in mind?" she asked, with a slight smile. "I had some money left from the bank account, which was enough to live on for a year and pay a small amount of rent on a storefront church. I guess the local neighborhood looked on me as a kind of a nut, but gradually the store began to fill up. It was very strange. No one questioned me. I had rehearsed this completely fantastic story over and over, and I suppose it just sounded true." Her voice was tense and husky. "I certainly never meant to hurt anyone. All I did was tell them this silly story and beg them to pray, obey God's laws, and love their neighbor. I found that I could make them laugh, cry, and pray. I proved to myself I was an actress. They believed in me. They listened to me."

"Did you bless any children in that storefront church?"

She hesitated and bit her lower lip. "A little boy," she said. "Later they told me he was recovering. I told myself it was only a coincidence. Then other people began asking me to bless them. Most of the time I refused. I told them instead to pray to God and ask for his mercy."

"But why didn't you want to bless them?"

She shook her head. "I don't know," she said slowly. "It made me uneasy, as if I wasn't play-acting anymore. . . ."

"Let's get to that later, Ann. What about Foreman?"

"First Troy came, and later he brought Foreman and Tura Sloan.

They said they were impressed with me and felt sure they could make me one of the country's most important evangelists."

"Wait a minute. Did you tell them you had made it all up, that this was a scam?"

"They never asked me and I never told them," she said bluntly. "Foreman said he would prove what he said, and the next week I was interviewed by a religion editor and had my picture taken by a photographer. Before they came, Foreman walked around the store and noticed there was a skylight. When he pulled the chain, a shaft of sunshine came down into the store. He had me sit on a chair in that sunlight and decided the interview and picture-taking would take place at the time the sun appeared over that skylight. That's exactly what happened, and the photographer did get a striking picture, which Foreman used on all our posters."

"But didn't that give you a hint he was a real con man?"

She sighed. "Frankly, I was so caught up in myself I didn't care. They took care of everything. I insisted on anonymity. I never told them my name or where I came from, and Foreman never pressed me. I couldn't believe how the audiences began to grow. First there were a few hundred, then a thousand. One night tens of thousands greeted me with a roar that shook the building. I was never better." Her eyes glistened as she relived that long-ago night. "I made them weep. I made them pray. I made them laugh. And when it was all over, they kept singing, and refused to leave until I came out on the stage again and again. There were flowers. . . . It was like the opening night of a sensational Broadway hit. . . ." She paused. "It was Aunt Clem's dream come true."

"And you were manipulating those poor fools."

"I won't deny it, Hilly," she said softly. "Of course I was. What evangelist doesn't? As the months went on, the audiences grew larger and larger. The storefront church was left far behind; we leased auditoriums, old theatres, stadiums. Now there were always reporters and photographers. I know what you intend to ask—the money. How much did I get? Where do I have it hidden? The truth is, I don't have any money. Money never interested me. I didn't care what Foreman and the others did with the money. I had what I wanted: audiences in the thousands, men and women I could hold spellbound. Who believed in what I had told them. Who cheered me, who loved me. Oh, I had a twinge of conscience, but I justified what I was doing by telling myself that I was only telling people to pray, to read the Bible, to prepare for the end of the world that the Bible predicts again and again. What I told them is preached every Sunday from a thousand pulpits."

(401)

"With one major exception," I told her. "A con man is not behind those pulpits. Now what about the Society of the Chosen? Whose idea was that?"

She said wryly, "Foreman's, of course. He had all the ideas. It sounded simple and harmless as he outlined it; a national organization of young people dedicated to prayer, to drive evil from the world and prepare humanity for the Last Day." She closed her eyes and shuddered. "I never dreamed it would come to this."

"I can't believe you didn't know about the money coming in," I told her. "Aren't you aware they have over a hundred million dollars hidden in bank accounts, in investments, and overseas? They even own a bank in the Caribbean!"

She said calmly, "I never took a penny. You must believe that. You *must* believe that."

"What's the difference if I believe you? The people you will have to convince will be the IRS and the Department of Justice."

There was a stark silence, so total I could hear the moaning of the rising late-afternoon breeze in the treetops.

"So they are finally after us," she said in a small voice.

"You didn't expect this to go on forever, did you?"

Her hands rested in her lap. The way she was sitting, the sun outlined her perfect profile with a golden knife. She turned to me with a look of bewildered innocence.

"Everything happened so fast. The days, the months, and the years passed by so quickly. I was caught up in it. . . ."

"But not so fast you didn't include a good thing like the Blessing of the Sick," I reminded her. She was shaking her head violently, but I went on, "But why not include that one? There was a price for everything, from little kids dying of cancer to the very old who had no one else to turn to."

I will never forget that stricken beautiful face.

"No. . . . No. . . . You must not say that. . . . Please. . . ." she said almost frantically. "I don't know about the money part. I never had anything to do with money. At the rallies there were all kinds of sick people. Foreman insisted I bless them. I told him I didn't want to do that. He kept insisting, telling me there would be no claim of cures, that I would give them hope if I simply reached out and touched them. Finally I stupidly agreed. The first night, I was shocked to see a long line of sick people on stretchers, in wheelchairs, and on crutches moving toward the stage. All I did was reach out and touch them. I was amazed to see some of them throw away their crutches, hold up their hearing aids, even leap out of their wheelchairs. . . ."

I said disgustedly, "Don't tell me you didn't know they were injury insurance swindlers hired by Foreman."

Her green eyes were cold with anger. "I suspected something when I began to see the same faces, but they assured me fanatical repeaters appeared at every religious rally. I told myself that maybe I was giving the really sick people hope."

"How very touching. But why did you suddenly not want to keep doing that? Wasn't your cut big enough?"

She gave a deep, shuddering moan. "This is why I didn't want to do the Blessing of the Sick anymore. One night they brought this little child." She broke off and sat very still, her eyes fixed in the distance, her fingers locked together. Then slowly she went on. "She was a beautiful little one about four, dying of some dread disease. On the stretcher she looked no bigger than a doll. She had enormous blue eyes, and when they wheeled her up she said, 'Mommy said you and God will help me, Ginerva.'"

I listened with mingled emotions. I wanted to interrupt her and ask in a cruel sarcastic voice if she would like violin strings as a backdrop, but something in her face stopped me. She seemed far away, remote. Her voice was hollow, emotionless.

"As I reached out to bless the child, something happened to me. I was in a deep black pit, with voices warning me I had now gone too far. I must be punished. I could barely lift my hand from the child's forehead. The blood seemed like ice in my veins, the voices were loud in my ears. I wondered if anyone could hear them. Then I found myself standing there looking down at the child. I was so frightened I ran from the stage. The same thing happened to me at other rallies. I began to have nightmares. They were the same, over and over. I was in the midst of this terrifying storm when suddenly God reached down from heaven to hand me a bolt of lightning. It didn't burn in my hand, only felt warm. The dream was so vivid that when I woke up I could almost feel the warmth in my palm."

As if remembering, she tightened the grip on her fingers, but couldn't control her trembling.

"It was then that I told Foreman I was finished. I couldn't go on. He told me the Society of the Chosen was too big, he had too many plans for the future. I had to stay. When I told him I simply intended to drop out of sight, he opened a drawer and handed me a folder. It was the prosecutor's folder he had stolen. In it was the whole story of Peter's death. He said that if I didn't continue as Ginerva, he would announce I had left because he had exposed me as a murderess who had killed her son. There wasn't anything left for me to do but go on."

"But how did Foreman ever find out about Poker Game and what happened there?"

She shrugged. "Very simple. He intercepted Aunt Clem's letters. In one she spoke of Peter, and that got Foreman to thinking. Then he and Russell went up there, filled my aunt with lies, and got her talking. She didn't know it, but Foreman taped her story of what happened. They also had someone steal the original file on the case."

"You never heard of Ben Rice?" I asked.

She slowly shook her head. "The only time I heard that name was when you mentioned it, Hilly."

"And your child's death was what Foreman held over you?"

"I felt trapped," she said. "There didn't seem any way out. I thought of killing myself, but then one night God *finally* spoke to me."

Everything shattered like fine glass under a hammer blow. I asked in a dumb way, "What did you say?"

"God spoke to me," she said calmly. "I was having this same dream, and woke up to find a real storm taking place. Perhaps the thunder had awakened me. I was petrified. I forced myself to get out of bed and close the blinds. Before I reached them, there were tremendous bolts of lightning mixed with peals of thunder that shook the building."

Her hands involuntarily went to her ears as if to shut out the sound. She remained like that for a few moments, then slowly lowered her hands.

She whispered, "God stood before me in a sheet of flame. I didn't see his face, but his voice was like thunder. He told me I had committed a grievous sin, but he had forgiven me. He said I was to continue to warn the world to prepare for the Last Day, because he was angry with the evil man had permitted to exist and he was ready to send his Blessed Son to judge us all. . . ."

Her face was filled with anguish, her eyes wide with fear, as she got to her feet and walked to the edge of the hill.

She raised her hands to heaven, pleading. "They turned their backs on me, Lord! They have laughed at me! They have called me a false prophet! . . ." She seemed to be listening. Then: "Yes. . . . Yes. . . . I will."

Sobbing and crying incoherently, she turned and ran down the wagon road. I jumped up and followed her. She was as fleet as a deer, but I caught her in the meadow and wrestled her down into the grass. She lay on her back, one hand flung across her face.

"Let me go," she sobbed, "I must return. God wants me to go back."

"There is no more Society of the Chosen, Ginerva," I told her. "It's over. Finished."

"No," she replied fiercely. "The Society will never die. It belongs to me, I dedicated it to God."

She tried to get up, but I gently pushed her back and pinned down her outstretched arms. She began tossing from side to side with short, gasping sobs. I slipped my arm under her head and held her until finally she lay still and the sobbing ceased. At last she sighed, her body relaxed, her face pressed against my arm. From her deep, even breathing, I knew she had fallen asleep. I remained in that position until my arm became numb and I carefully moved it. Only then did I realize that twilight had faded into darkness and the meadow and hill were painted silver by the rising moon.

I stood up, studied the pine forest with its silvered top, and wept. I had found Ginerva's real secret: she was mad.

I sat there until the moon was high. Once she cried out, and when I went to her she was sitting up, staring straight ahead. She was whispering, holding her clasped hands to her breast.

"No. . . . No. . . ." she kept repeating. "Dear God, no. . . ."

When I reached out for her, she didn't appear to recognize me. Her hands went to her mouth to stifle an eerie cry that made me shudder.

"I'm here, Ginerva," I told her. "I'm here. Nothing can hurt you any more. I'm here. Cry. . . . cry . . ."

Racking sobs tore through her body. She clung to me, nails digging into my arms, and wept until the breath came rasping from her throat. Finally she lay exhausted, her head on my chest.

"Please take me back to the motherhouse," she begged in a dull weary voice.

"Why go back there, Ginerva?" I asked. "They'll soon get Foreman, Russell, and the others and it will be all over."

"I have much more of God's work to do," she replied.

"Tell me, Ginerva," I asked softly, "was it God who told you where to find the child in the well?"

"God in his infinite mercy granted me a vision and showed me where the child was," she replied.

I prompted, "Perhaps it was Brother Foreman. . . ."

She went on as if she had not heard me. "It was Peter in the well. . . . I heard him calling me. . . . This was not the first time God gave me a vision. . . . There was that evil man in the deepest pit of Hell. . . . God revealed to me how this unclean spirit would return to show how no man can escape the wrath of God. . . . He also showed me the great signs in the heavens . . .testimony of his warning that the Day of Judgment is near. . . ." She paused, then in a low voice quoted Paul's letter to the Corinthians: " 'The time is now short. . . . Those who weep should live as if they were not weeping and those who rejoice should live as if they were not rejoicing. . . . Buyers should conduct themselves as if they owned nothing, for the world as we know it is passing away. . . .' "

When I helped her up, she clung to me. "There is much I must do and there is so little time. . . . Please take me back, Hilly."

"I'll take you back, Ginerva," I promised, "and I will never allow anyone to hurt you again."

When we reached the car, I looked back. The night breeze was rippling the valley's grass, turning it into a mysterious, restless, silver sea. The ruins of the chimney, the iron framework of the windmill, and the crossbars of the utility pole were stark against the night sky. I turned to the car, but something forced me to look back. I suddenly felt cold all over, as if someone had pressed the blade of a knife against my throat.

I knew I would see this valley and hill again, and I dreaded what that day held for me. . . .

24

Buck

Once we left the valley, Ginerva withdrew into an impenetrable vacuum. When we finally reached the Grand Ballroom, the Angel on guard hurried out of the shadows. Before he opened the door, I pleaded with her not to stay, but she only shook her head and replied, "I must. God has ordered me to remain. There is not much time left. . . ."

When she got out, the Angel gasped with surprise. "Your Holiness! I didn't know—"

She ignored him, to lean down and press something in my hand.

"Someday you will need this," she said softly.

In a moment she was gone. The Angel peered in at me. "Oh, Brother Hillers," he said.

I was sure word would soon get to Foreman.

As I drove off, I glanced down at what she had given me. It was a plain cross, set in a strange five-pointed gold star. A mad woman's trinket, I told myself. . . .

Shortly before six, the phone rang in my hotel room. It was a far-off echo in a violent nightmare in which Ginerva stood on the Hill of God's Word, wrapped in flames that hissed in the rain. I woke up, my heart pounding. Outside the dawn was lemon-colored, and a sanitation department truck crew was testing the durability of the city's trash cans.

When I picked up the phone, a soft voice said; "Brother Foreman wishes to see you this morning at this address. Do you have a pencil?"

There was a pen and pad by the phone. The voice gave me an address in the Hamptons and hung up.

I lay back on the bed and thought of the trip back from the valley; the warm world of the car and Ginerva's pale face barely visible in the glow of the dashboard lights. Road signs darting in and out of the darkness. The swish of an occasional passing car, the hypnotic white line of the highway, and the silence of the woman next to me that spoke of unshared mysteries. Now I knew. Ginerva was schizophrenic. The terrifying days with the screaming deformed child. The tragic murder. The bizarre play-acting of the two lonely women in that isolated farmhouse, followed by years of disappointment and humiliation, had been too much for her. Somewhere, possibly the day she had first sat by herself on the peak of that hill overlooking the peaceful valley, reality had ceased to exist, and China Polly became Ginerva, God's courier and the beautiful prophet who stunned a nation by finding a lost child in a well and revealing that a dead man would return from the grave.

I was convinced that while Ginerva believed she was controlled by Foreman because he knew her secret of what had taken place in that farmhouse kitchen, the truth was that Foreman had become her alter ego, her second self who shared her fantasy world, who skillfully supplied the howling winds and lightning, the cheering crowds and applause—and the cures and miracles.

But how much of what had happened was really Foreman's fiction? If she had divine powers, where did they end and his scam begin?

Perhaps I would find the answer in the Hamptons . . . .

I shaved, showered quickly, dressed—at the last moment I put Ginerva's cross in my pocket—and had breakfast in the coffee shop before I called Leah.

"My God, Hilly, where have you been?" she exclaimed when she heard my voice. "Norman and I have been up most of the night waiting to hear from you. Where did you go with Ginerva?"

"It's a long story, Leah. I'll tell you when I get back."

"Get back? Get back from where?"

"To see Foreman where he's hiding out in the Hamptons. He had someone call me."

"I'm coming with you."

"No," I almost shouted in the phone. "You stay here and watch out for any calls from Tom. He's probably up a tree by now, wondering what happened. Tell him I'll call him the moment I get back here."

Her voice was apprehensive. "Hilly, please be careful? Please?"

It was a chilly, gray morning, with a hint of rain in the air. There was little traffic on the expressway, and I made the Hamptons in fairly good time. A gas station attendant gave me directions, and I found the house at the end of a long, winding lane overlooking the ocean. It was typical of the area, large and sprawling, old-fashioned floor-to-ceiling windows, cedar shingles bleached bone white by the winds and intense sun. The scene was gloomy; gray brooding sky, damp chilling wind, and the sullen booming of the surf.

I was surprised to find Russell answering the door. His slate-colored eyes were cold and hostile under the strange, long, blond lashes. Without saying a word he led me into a room that smelled of wood smoke as if a city boy had struggled for a long time to keep alive the tiny blaze that seemed lost in the massive fieldstone fireplace.

Foreman was seated in a large brocaded chair before the fireplace. He was wearing a sweater, and his face had a gray look. He reached for a poker, stabbed the smoldering log, and said without looking up: "Where did you take her?"

"You must have seen the mob on TV," I replied. "They were ready to tear her apart."

He repeated in a low taut voice, "Where did you take her?"

"I drove her back to the motherhouse."

Russell was studying me intently. I squeezed the cross in my pocket and felt the tiny points of the star press into the flesh. I wondered what I would do if Russell jumped me.

Foreman said, "That was after midnight. Where were you and what were you doing with her in between?"

"The Angels said he took off like a bat from that lot," Russell blurted out.

"Shut up," Foreman snapped. For the first time he looked up at me. His eyes were bloodshot, and I noticed his hands were grimy, his manicured nails dirty, as if he had been struggling with the fire. "Well, what about it?" he demanded.

I decided to play it straight and innocent. "She ordered me to drive her to a place called Barondale in the Catskills."

Russell grunted as if he recognized the name, and I felt instinctively I was moving in the right direction. "When we arrived there she wanted to go to a place she called The Hill of God's Word. It was just a small hill and big, open valley. I followed her to the top of the hill, where she knelt down and prayed before a silver crucifix for a long time. When she was ready to leave, I drove her back to the mother-house. That's all that happened."

I put on a show of being angry and said accusingly, "You never told me she was a nut."

Foreman pushed a chair toward me. "Who says she's a nut?"

"I do," I replied as I sat down. "She's a schizo, Dave, and you know it."

"What difference does it make?" he said with a shrug. "She brings them in—and that's what counts."

I pressed him. "But you know there's something wrong—"

He hesitated, then said suddenly, unexpectedly, "I've known it for a long time. That's why I'm pushing this tour. I don't know how long she can last. Those spells are getting more frequent."

"What spells?"

He carefully poked the log and a shower of sparks flew up. "Goddam fire," he murmured.

I repeated, "What spells?"

He leaned back. "I told you she got hysterical one night while doing the Blessing of the Sick. At the time I thought it was just the strain of looking at those horrible people." He shuddered. "Some of them are really awful. But a week later it happened again. She kept insisting God was talking to her, threatening to punish her if she didn't stop. I told her it was all in her head, but after that I had a hell of a time with her."

"What about that dead guy in Briggs, Dave?" I asked. "How did you pull that one off?"

Russell broke in, "Don't tell this guy anything, Dave. I'm warning you."

Foreman looked up at him. "What are *you* supposed to be doing?"

"Don't worry, I'll get to it," he said belligerently.

"You're not going to *get* to it," Foreman roared. "You're going to *do* it now!"

"Wait a minute, Dave," Russell said, pointing to me. "You can't talk to me like that in front of him!"

Foreman leaped to his feet. "Will you get the hell out of here and do what you're supposed to be doing? It's your fault they got away! Do you want them to hang us?"

"I told you I'll find them," Russell said sullenly.

"Then get the hell out of here and find them!"

Russell hesitated as if for a split second he was debating whether to continue arguing with Foreman. It was all there on his coarse-looking face, which tightened into a look of anger and frustration before he whirled around and left the room. The front door slammed, a car sputtered into life, gears meshed, and it screeched out of the lane and into the highway.

"Find who?" I asked, but I knew and dreaded to hear his answer.

"Steve and Tura," he replied. "I told him that if he didn't find them and take care of them not to come back."

A tiny pit of intense cold began to form in my stomach. "What do you mean 'take care of them,' Dave?"

"Just what do you *think* I mean?"

"Take care of them," I said.

"No witnesses, no case," he said coldly. "Do you think I'm going to let a couple of frightened snitches destroy what I have built?" He shook his head vigorously. "Never."

"Let's get back to Briggs, Dave. How did—"

"Forget it," he shouted. "I don't want to hear any more about it. I have enough on my mind. That son-of-a-bitch Newberry is going to jail us for contempt. The Bureau has agents on my tail."

I was startled. "How do you know that?"

He gave me a cold smile. "Money. Expertise. And homework. I did a lot of it while I was down in Washington. Now it's paying off." He frowned. "I want you to keep Ginerva under control until this thing blows over. Go back to the motherhouse and make sure she returns to Washington if the committee wants her. She's perfect. Did you see the show she put on down there? Talking about how God is going to produce great signs in the heavens! And will punish us all with fire and sword! It was great, I tell you!"

"Is that another one of your scams, Dave?" I asked.

He picked up the poker and cautiously nudged the logs.

"Is it, Dave?" I insisted.

"Why don't you wait and see?" he suggested mildly.

"Dave, what will I do with her?" I asked him.

He looked surprised. "Take care of her, Hilly. What else? We'll use her as long as she lasts. When she cracks up, we'll gradually phase her out. The Society is growing every day. That's important."

I asked him bluntly, "What plans do you have for it?"

"They're big," he replied promptly. "Very big. And you're part of them. But that's all in the future. Now it's Ginerva. She's not all gone yet, and is still very important to us."

I felt a barbarous anger and was shaken by the unbearable thought of how I could kill him. The desire was so strong that to hide it I clasped my hands together and avoided looking at the heavy poker.

"What about my split?" I managed to get out.

"No problem," he said casually. "As soon as this committee business is finished we'll sit down in the Money Room and talk business."

"And if your muscleman catches up with Steve and Tura?"

"He will," he said savagely. He glowered down at the struggling fire, then glanced at his wristwatch. "I have to be moving out of here shortly. You better get back to the motherhouse and see what she's doing."

He walked me to the door. And said in a cold, contemptuous voice, "If she wants to know where I am and what I'm doing, tell her I'm in deep meditation and talking to the Lord."

I did a lot of thinking on the way back to Manhattan. I felt a profound pity for Ginerva used by a cruel rogue such as Foreman. Few would fully realize the magnitude of his evil as I did. His ruthlessness revolted me. There was now a double score to settle with him: Ben and Ginerva. Once again I wondered if I could kill him, but the very suggestion was so alien, so shocking I dismissed it. I could never pull the trigger in cold blood. I had to see him led off in handcuffs and face me in a courtroom. It was now easy to understand how he operated. Foreman was a skillful confidence man with grandiose if sinister plans. Ginerva, the beautiful, the mysterious, the helpless, was his perfect foil. He thought up the gimmicks, she pulled them off. But a tiny nagging voice continued to warn me there had to be something more. Foreman could not have invented that touch of her hand on my cheek on that long-ago night in San Francisco that banished my limp and nightmares. Nor could he have found the child in the well, cured the student and the little boy in San Francisco. He had hinted the dead returning from the grave in Briggs was a trick, but suppose it wasn't? And what of her prophecy before the committee of great signs in the skies and God's threat to punish his people. . . .

Even now I couldn't let go of her. Mad woman. Scam artist. Charlatan. Liar. Fraud. Still there had never been anyone like her in my life.

The minutes inside that well. In the moonlight on that hill. They would never go away. There were still loose ends to be tied, still more questions to be answered.

If they could be answered

I was on the Long Island Expressway nearing the Cross Island Parkway when the first bulletin came over the radio. In Illinois an anti-Ginerva mob of pickets had turned ugly and burned a House of Preparation. Seven were arrested; there were only minor injuries.

The second bulletin described a riotous scene in a Wisconsin courtroom where several Disciples had been arraigned for distributing literature without a permit. Angry pickets, led by the father of a young girl who was among the Disciples, jumped them when they were leaving the courtroom after paying a small fine.

I was approaching the Whitestone Bridge when the third bulletin came over.

"Westchester police report more than three hundred pickets, who earlier had been peacefully parading up and down outside the motherhouse of the Society of the Chosen, have clashed with a group of Avenging Angels, the cult's security force. Police said the Angels rushed out of the main gate and attempted to wrestle signs from the pickets."

Then at the Bronx end of the Whitestone came the fourth bulletin.

"A serious clash is now taking place between anti-Ginerva pickets and security forces for the Society of the Chosen on the grounds of the cult's motherhouse in Westchester County. Two bus loads of pickets, apparently waiting to become part of a large demonstration against Ginerva, the cult's beautiful and mysterious leader, rushed to the scene when they heard their members had been attacked by the Avenging Angels who protect Ginerva and patrol the grounds of the huge estate. There have been reports of other disturbances across the country by anti-Ginerva groups and opponents of other cults and sects. The disturbances were apparently touched off by the recent appearance of Ginerva before a Senate subcommittee during which she made a prophecy of great signs in the heavens and that many will die by fire and sword. At the conclusion of that hearing, angry pickets who had packed the hearing room . . ."

The highways were familiar, the rush hour was over, and I made good time to the motherhouse. From far down the highway I could see the orange glow of burning buildings reflected in the twilight sky and hear the faint wail of sirens. I knew police cars, fire engines, hoses, and emergency squads would have that part of the highway blocked, so I made a wide circle and backtracked to the northern boundary of the estate. I parked my car, climbed the fence, and entered the grounds by way of the small dirt hill.

The south end was in flames. I could hear far-off shouts and jeering as I made my way to the Grand Ballroom. The heavy door was open. There was no guard. It was eerie inside with the ceiling of fake clouds, stars, and moon seemingly frozen in space. The tiny lights embedded into the stairway were still on, and I made my way to her apartment. The door was open, and I caught the faint scent of her perfume. I called her name, and my voice echoed off in the darkness, leaving the only sound the beating of my heart.

The lights I switched on showed the room was not disturbed. The silver figure on the cross looked down at me. I made my way downstairs and out into the fading twilight that smelled of wood smoke. The jeering and shouting had become louder. Once I thought I heard the sound of a shot. Now it was dark, with a misty moon and some starlight. I moved through the bushes to the motherhouse. It was engulfed in flames, with the silhouettes of jeering and shouting men and women marching up and down. Suddenly a wave of chugging carts emerged from the darkness and headed toward the marchers. This time there was the unmistakable sound of shots. I saw one marcher stagger and fall. Others picked him up and ran to a line of parked yellow buses, followed by the charging carts.

It was an eerie updating of an old western movie.

There were more shots, this time from the buses. One cart spun around and stopped. I decided to return to the fence and leave this frightening world. Then I heard Buck's drawn-out howl, like the leader of a wolf pack running down a deer. It was far off to the left, so I left the woods for the paths to put as much distance between me and that monstrous dog as possible. I started running, but was caught in the beam of a powerful spotlight.

"Halt! State police!" A voice commanded, "Who are you?"

I said the first thing to come to my mind. "AP from the White Plains Courthouse."

The beam switched off. "Get back to the gatehouse where the press is with our spokesman," the voice ordered. "We can't be responsible for you people out here. There are too many crazies on the grounds."

The group started to move off through the darkness, but a figure detached itself and approached me. "Wait up, AP. I'll come along."

I was stumped by that voice. When he came up to me, I struck a match and held it up to Bruce Stafford's face.

"Hilly!" he gasped. "What the hell are you doing here?"

"I might ask you the same thing." Now I could make out the bag he was carrying over one shoulder and the camera in his hand. When the match burned itself out, he stopped me as I was about to strike another one.

"Don't do it," he warned. "Those cops are right. You wouldn't believe what I've taken pictures of tonight. But what are you doing here?"

"I came looking for Ginerva."

"She got away with Leah and Turner and a guy from the Newberry committee."

"Where are they now?"

I could sense a shrug. "I guess Ginerva's in his custody. Christ, that was a hell of a hearing. Margo and I couldn't get over seeing you on the tube."

I shouted, "Margo?"

He broke off. I could visualize his face; he was cursing himself for being all kinds of fool.

"Yeah," he said shortly, "We're married."

"How in the hell did—"

He said with a rush, "Look, Hilly, I haven't time to go into details. I have my own studio in New Rochelle and I'm doing great free-lancing for the papers and the wire services." He thrust a card into my hand. "I got to get this stuff downtown while it's hot. Drop by later and we'll

(4 1 4)

tell you what happened—everything, the whole story. Okay? Hilly, it was great seeing you."

He ran off into the darkness.

I stood there for a moment, completely bewildered. Margo and Stafford married! What else would this weird night produce?

I started back toward the fence and my car. On one of the paths I stumbled over something. It was the canopy of an overturned cart. Scattered about were clubs, pipes, and bats. I selected a pipe, neatly taped on one end. Russell, it appeared, had equipped his thugs with only the best.

I was near the base of the mound when I heard Buck's howl off to one side. For a moment I was petrified and ran up the path. Someone below me shouted, "There's one of 'em! Let the dog go."

I had reached the top and the first pine trees when I heard someone running up the path. In the moonlight I could see it was one of the Angels, a big man waving a rifle.

"Don't let the bastard get away," he shouted.

He was probably one of a group of Angels patrolling the grounds with Matthew and the dog, looking for victims. I was about to yell out and identify myself, but common sense told me they didn't care who was in front of them in the darkness. They only wanted to kill someone, anyone, to let Buck tear someone apart.

As I stood there feeling terribly helpless, the words of the little sergeant come back to me as we crouched in the elephant grass waiting for the others to leave the helicopter:

"Remember, Mr. Hillers, when you're fighting the VC it's either you or him. Get to him first."

That is what I did.

As the Angel came abreast of the tree I was standing behind, I put out my foot and he went sprawling, rolling over and over. He started to bounce up, but the floor of pine needles was slippery and he fell to one knee. As he got up, I hit him across the temple with the pipe. He went down, rolled over, and lay still.

As I reached the fence, I heard the padded pounding and Buck's eager savage growls. Instinctively I jumped to one side, and the huge body brushed me, slashing fangs missing my neck by inches. Buck crashed into the underbrush rolling over, paws kicking and clawing for a hold on the slippery pine needles, his outraged howls echoing through the forest. Running up the path Matthew was shouting: "Get him, Buck! Kill him, Buck!"

In a second I had leaped from the fence into a deep pile of leaves. Above me, outlined against the starlight, Buck looked as big as King Kong. The animal hesitated for a moment, then jumped down, missing me and thrashing about in the leaves. As I got to my knees, the dog lunged at me. I cried out in pain as teeth ripped through my jacket and into the flesh. Then, with all my strength I swung at the furry head. Buck yelped once in surprise, slid back and rolled over, hindquarters jerking. The animal sighed once, then lay still.

There was a thud as Matthew landed next to me. "You killed Buck!" he shouted, tugging at his belt. "You killed my dog!"

When I grabbed his hand, he was holding a gun. I yanked it away and threw it as far as I could. When he came at me, I slapped him across the face. He staggered back, whimpering. I was beginning to feel light-headed, and I knew from the stickiness along my arm that Buck's teeth had reached the bone.

Matthew dropped to his knees to cradle the dog's head. "It's okay, boy," he cried almost hysterically. "It's okay. I'll get you to the vet, and he'll fix you up. It's nothing, boy, it's all right."

"It's not all right, you son-of-a-bitch," I told him. "Buck is dead and I wish it was you instead."

Then I walked off through the trees, feeling my way along the fence until I reached the car.

I was just another casualty in the very busy emergency room of the local hospital. I left with twelve stitches and headed for New Rochelle and Margo, whom I needed to fill in some gaps of this ghastly puzzle.

Margo

The business card read STAFFORD'S STUDIO. WEDDINGS. PASSPORT PHOTOS. PORTRAITS.

It was an old one-family frame house on a side street. A sign in the window repeated the wording on the business card. Margo answered the doorbell. She had put on a little weight, was pale with lines about her large violet-colored eyes that gave her a vague, haunted look. She was a very pretty girl and decidedly *not* pregnant. Her hand involuntarily went to her mouth when she saw me.

"Who is it, honey?" Stafford called out as he stood in the hall, holding a dripping print. When she didn't answer, he joined her. "Oh," he said. "You didn't waste any time. Come in." As I passed them, he pointed to my arm. "Did you tangle with those nuts up there?"

A wall mirror showed I was unshaven, hollow-eyed, with a long scratch down one side of my face, probably from Buck's claws. My jacket was dirty and torn, the bandage showing.

"I met Matthew and Buck," I explained.

He whistled. "Man, that dog is big."

"*Was*," I said.

They both looked at me. "Honey, how about getting some coffee and a couple of English," Stafford said. "Hilly looks like he could use

(417)

something." She smiled and hurried into the kitchen to fill a coffeepot and split some English muffins as Bruce spread the wet print out on a drying board. "I got ninety percent of the best stuff down there already," he explained. "The picture editor on the *News* called a few minutes ago to tell me it's the best I've ever turned in." He gave me a sharp look, quickly poured a glass of whiskey, and handed it to me. I discovered my hand was trembling so badly I could barely lift the glass. The whiskey exploded in the pit of my stomach, sending waves of relaxing heat throughout my body.

Margo abruptly turned from the toaster and said, "I want to thank you, Brother—Mr. Hillers, for how you tried to help me that night. We felt terrible about leaving and not letting you know."

I looked at Bruce. "*We?*"

"Okay, let's start from the beginning," he said. "First of all, as you can see, Margo was never pregnant. She used that as an excuse to get away from Foreman." His face hardened. "I'm not going to hold anything back. He did get Margo, but thank God nothing happened. The true story is this: you know about that girl who went out of the window on West Fifty-seventh Street?"

"The kid who committed suicide?"

"Only it wasn't suicide, Hilly," he said softly. "Russell pushed her out that window."

I looked from one to the other. Margo, holding onto the edge of the sink, looked on the verge of fainting. Stafford jumped up and held her tightly.

"My God, how do you know that?"

"Margo saw it," Bruce said. "This is what happened. In the beginning the girl was a dedicated Disciple. Like Margo, she was an artist working on posters in the tour office. Every once in a while Foreman would select a young girl, always a dedicated Disciple, and really give her a snow job. Most of the kids were from out of town and very unsophisticated. His method was really cornball; he either talked them into it or kept them late and fed them booze. Well, he had a hell of a time with this one girl. He didn't get any static from her parents. She only had an old grandmother somewhere in the Northwest, but she was caught by a guard trying to get into the Grand Ballroom to tell Ginerva what had happened. Then she began to make all kinds of threats. Foreman brushed them off, but one he didn't. She told him she had an appointment with a lawyer in the West Fifty-seventh Street building to take her to the district attorney's office to sign a rape complaint against him."

He looked at Margo. "Right, honey?"

Margo nodded. "She told me she called him a devil right to his face, and said now she knew why Chen Ling had killed herself."

"That's the Chinese girl who was found dead from an overdose of pills in the hotel room," I said.

"Maybe it wasn't suicide," Stafford interjected. "But let Margo tell it."

"She said that Foreman jumped out of the chair and began slapping her and warning her that if she ever went to that lawyer or tried to see Ginerva again he would kill her and have it made to appear like an accident," Margo continued. "I hadn't believed half of what she had told me before, but when I saw her face all puffed up, then I knew she was telling me the truth. She was frantic, and told me she knew Foreman wasn't fooling, that he would kill her. She didn't know what to do. That's when he started on me." She bit her lower lip. "I was frightened to death of him. When he insisted I had to stay and work that night on the posters, I wanted to run away. But I was as much afraid of being alone in the city as I was of him." She shook her head. "It only happened once. I told myself I would rather kill myself than have this continue. So I talked to the other girl, and we decided to both go to that lawyer on West Fifty-seventh Street and ask him to take us to the district attorney."

She began weeping and Bruce held her close, whispering to her and kissing her cheek.

"I'm sorry," she said, wiping her eyes.

"Russell found out where they were going," Bruce went on. "He forced them to ride up to the seventeenth floor where there are stock rooms or something, no offices. Then he told Margo to leave, and that if she said anything he would take care of her. Margo went down one floor, then decided she couldn't leave the other girl. She walked back up the one flight and was just opening the exit door when Russell was shoving the kid out of the window."

I said, "My God, didn't she scream, or fight?"

Margo began sobbing. Stafford, grim-faced, said, "Margo said the girl looked as if she was stricken dumb. She said she will never forget the unbelieving look on her face as Russell pushed her out on the edge. It was about a foot wide. She tottered for a moment then fell backwards. Sure, the cops said fell or jumped."

"And Margo?"

"She carefully closed the door and ran down the seventeen flights of stairs. Russell was waiting in the lobby. He simply grabbed her and brought her back to the tour headquarters. Foreman told her the other girl was mentally unbalanced and had committed suicide by jumping from the building after Russell left her. He told the cops the same story; that the girl was showing signs of instability and they had pleaded with her to enter a hospital but she had refused. The next thing they had heard was that she had killed herself. The cops had no

(419)

alternative but to list it as jumped or fell."

I said, "You know what this means, Bruce?"

"I know," he said slowly. "At first I said to hell with it, we're happy now, why get involved? But it was no use. Margo kept tuning in those hearings, and when I came home she would be crying. All she did was cry. It was on my conscience, too. Only a couple of days ago, after seeing you on TV, we decided to get in touch with you." He sighed. "There's more to it, Hilly," he added, and left the room. In a few moments he returned with a large string envelope.

"You probably know the reason Margo was working at tour head-quarters was because she is an artist. I think a damn good one. I've been trying to get her to go back to painting, but this thing is so on her mind she can't even think straight." He slipped a folded paper napkin and a page torn from a sketchbook from the envelope and handed them to me.

"The first sketch she did was in the cafeteria on that paper napkin when she returned from midtown," he said. "That night she was almost hysterical. I had a hell of a time calming her down. A few days later I insisted she redo the sketch."

It was a ghastly but riveting charcoal sketch. Russell, standing in the hallway, had just pushed the girl out on the window ledge; her face was frozen with horror, she had thrown up her arms and was falling backwards.

"My God, this is horrible," I said. "Why did you make her do this?"

He said evenly, "Insurance. For both of us to get out of the mother-house—if there was no other way."

Margo came in with the buttered muffins and coffee on a tray. She was trying hard to hold back the tears. She gave a start when she saw the drawings.

"We had to show them to Hilly, honey," Bruce said. "You know we agreed to go through with it."

"Will I have to take the witness stand against them?" she whispered.

Stafford hugged her. "You don't have to worry about anything. I'll be with you every minute."

"You still haven't told me how you both got out of the grounds," I said.

"Margo and I had been planning for a long time to split out of there and get married," Stafford explained. "After that incident, I knew I had to move fast. We never expected Leah to bring you into it. The night Leah planned to have Margo meet you outside the dorm was the night we were going to get out. I knew there was one sure way, to use Tura Sloan's car. She came in and out of the grounds at all hours, and the guard at the gate knew better than to stop and question her. After Leah left to go downstairs to watch for you, we slipped out of a

(420)

side entrance and headed for Sloan's garage, which is attached to the house.

"We were in the garage when that moron Matthew tried to get you with his dog. We heard the barking and the howling coming nearer."

Margo squeezed Stafford's hand. "Bruce had a big wrench and said if the dog went for you he was going out to help."

"I figgered, what the hell, both of us could take care of that creep and the Stilson I had was heavy enough to bash in the head of that mutt," he said. "But then we heard the front door slam, and Matthew and the dog passed. All we could do was stand there in the darkened garage. I knew you were inside the house because we could hear voices. Finally we heard Sloan shout something and the upstairs door slammed and then you left."

"It was scary in that garage," Margo said with a shudder. "I kept holding on to Bruce."

He picked up the story. "We waited a while, then I started to work with a flashlight. I know cars, and there was no problem jumping the wires. My plan was to yank up the garage door, gun the motor, and get the hell out of there. I had finished with the wiring, Margo was in the car, and I was about to grab the garage door, when suddenly the garage lights went on! Tura was standing on the steps with a little bag in her hand. She looked horrible. Her face was all puffed and bruised. 'What are you doing with my car?' she asked.

"I told her, 'We're getting out of here and I want to use your car. I'll call you and tell you where I'll leave it. But don't try to stop us. Please."

"She stood there for a moment just staring at us. Then suddenly she began to laugh. A wild kind of laugh. When she stopped she said, 'This is great, kids.' She walked down the steps and threw her bag into the car. 'What are you doing?' I asked her.

"'Doing?' she said. 'Just what the hell do you think I'm doing? I'm leaving with you!'"

Bruce flung up his hands. "So that's how we left—with Sister Sloan's car and with her in it!"

They looked at each other, exchanging small conspiratorial smiles.

"So you got out. But then what happened?"

"That crazy Sloan," Bruce said, shaking his head. "She insisted we fly out to Montana and get the blessing of Margo's father. So we all did. She put up the money, from a roll that would choke a horse. When I asked her if she had held up a bank, she only laughed and said Foreman had given her a pension."

Margo interjected, "My father loved her."

"All I can say is, she treated us great," Stafford said. "When we came back, she insisted on lending me five thousand as a down payment on this house and to buy what equipment I didn't take with me from the motherhouse. I knew I had given them ten times what the stuff was worth in hard work. Tura stayed with us for a couple of weeks, then left. She said she wasn't cut out for suburban living."

I pointed out, "But isn't staying this close to the motherhouse dangerous? I thought you might have established a studio in some small midwestern town."

"I had made a lot of good contacts on the wire services and the dailies in the city," he explained. "It made Tura nervous but—" He tapped the sketches and said quietly, "I knew that these would take care of any trouble."

"And Tura?" I asked eagerly.

"She called us the day the hearings opened, then that morning the senator announced they all would be cited for contempt. She really sounded nervous and said she might try to get to Europe. I warned her they might have agents watching the airlines. Then Margo asked her to come up here until it blew over, but she said she was going to stay in the city for a few days until she decided what she wanted to do. She called late that same night and said she intended to check into the Edgeworth Hotel on East Seventy-second Street and would call us from there. She said that maybe she would come up here for a while. I knew she checked into the Edgeworth because I called, but there was no answer in her room."

I left with Margo's sketches in the envelope and her promise that she would testify to watching Russell push the girl out of the window of the seventeenth floor of the Fifty-seventh Street building. Obviously it was enough evidence to indict Russell and possibly Foreman for first-degree murder and to reopen the death of the Chinese Disciple. . . .

Now it was becoming clear that my part in all this was almost over. But curiously, instead of being elated, I felt weary, depressed, under a shroud of pervasive gloom, as I drove to Manhattan. I could only think of Ginerva and how she looked so mad and so beautiful in the moonlight on the peak of the Hill of God's Word. What would become of her?

Tura wasn't at the hotel. A bored desk clerk said she had checked out the same night she had checked in; there was no forwarding address. I began to feel the damage done by Buck's fangs as I stood on the corner near a newsstand wondering what next to do. I idly studied a tabloid headline: GAMBLING HOUSE BUST NABS 20.

Just another one-day wonder for the reporters covering police headquarters, I told myself, and was about to turn away when the words "gambling house" echoed in my head.

Troy had said, *"Wee Willie's is my second home, when I'm in town."*

The fat, elderly Puerto Rican woman was folding up batches of fabric when I entered the store.

"Closing," she said. "Come back tomorrow."

I brushed past her and walked to the back where Wee Willie was sitting on his stool checking some figures in a ledger. It took him a few minutes to recognize me.

"Hilly," I reminded him. "I'm looking for Steve. This time I have money."

"Oh, yeah," he said in that strange deep voice. "Steve's inside. Only an hour more, then we're closed. Okay?"

"I think I can clean you out in that time," I said.

His answer was a bored, "Where did I hear that before?"

Troy was standing behind a blackjack table watching a player empty a boot. When I tapped him on the shoulder, he turned and made a soft moaning sound in his throat.

"Let's go outside and talk," I suggested.

"I'm the next player, Hilly," he said, looking around the room. The giant Omar was at the far end, leaning over, listening to a player.

"Don't try to alert that big guy, Steve," I warned him. "Don't make any trouble. There are two agents outside."

He closed his eyes and moaned again.

"You're not in trouble, Steve," I assured him, "only Foreman and Russell."

He reluctantly followed me out, with the dwarf giving us a look of surprise, then suspicion.

"Leaving so soon?" Then to Steve, "Everything all right, Steve?"

"Yeah, I'm all right, Willie," Troy mumbled.

On the street I flagged down a cab. "Where are the agents?" he asked when we got in.

"I told them I didn't need any agents, that we were friends and I could talk to you, Steve."

"What about?" he asked.

"Wait until we get to the hotel," I said. Then to the driver, "The Hilton."

I told the suspicious room clerk we had been in an automobile crash and wanted to have dinner and get some rest before taking the late train to Connecticut. He was properly sympathetic, and the curious bellman was satisfied with a healthy tip. Room service brought up sandwiches and a setup with a bottle of scotch. The food helped to revive me, but every muscle and heartbeat were begging for sleep and the pain in my arm was increasing.

Troy pointed to my bandaged arm. "What happened?"

"Matthew's dog. I had to kill him."

He stared at me unbelievingly. "*You* killed that big mutt?"

(423)

"Did you see what was happening up there on television?"

"I saw it on the news," he said, nodding." I couldn't believe it when I saw the motherhouse burning. Where's Dave?"

"He has Russell looking for you." I deliberately paused, then added, as melodramatically as I could, "I don't want to frighten you, Steve, but he has Russell looking for you and Tura. He told Russell he wants you both killed. I was there when he gave the orders."

He licked his lips. "I knew he would. I intended to buy a piece tomorrow so when he came looking for me I would be ready." He added, "This blowup's been a long time comin', Hilly."

I pulled up the pillows and leaned back. The scotch was helping to dull the pain.

"Steve, who killed Ben Rice?" He jumped as if he had touched a live wire. "Who?" I knew he was stalling.

"Ben," and then I slowly spelled out the name: "R-i-c-e. He blew his head off in Central Park with a magnum after he had found out about Ginerva in Idaho," I added.

"Jeez," he exclaimed, "just who the hell are you?"

"Ben Rice was my closest friend. I'm working with the Newberry committee." I repeated, "Who killed him, Steve?"

He said doggedly, "I don't know anything about it. I swear I don't."

I slowly unwound the string envelope. His eyes were glued on me. "What do you have there?"

Without answering, I handed him the charcoal sketch. He stared, then ran into the bathroom. I could hear him vomiting. When I came in, he was running the water and splashing his pale face.

"Jeez! What a hell of a thing to do to a guy," he said.

"You lousy son-of-a-bitch!" I shouted. "That's a sketch made by an eyewitness of a young girl being thrown out of a seventeenth-floor window by Russell!"

"Hilly, I wasn't any part of it!" he cried. "I wasn't! It was Russell! Dave had him do it!"

"How do you know?" I asked.

"Tura told me," he said. "She told me the whole story a couple of nights ago when she found me in Willie's."

"How does she know?"

"Dave told her," he said. He slumped down in a chair, splashed some whiskey in a glass, and swallowed it in one gulp. "And she knows about your friend Rice. She said Dave found out he was in Idaho and sent two guys up there to take care of him."

"Who were they?"

"Two guys Tura knew from the spooky racket. They're twins and they're expert hypnotists. Tura said they work high-class parties where they get a line for jewel heists."

"How did they talk Ben into killing himself?"

He tugged at the flesh on his cheek. "Hilly, as God is my witness, I don't know anything more. I told Tura I didn't want to know about it. All I'm trying to do is get some bucks together so I can get the hell out of this city. I'm through with Dave and this Society stuff. I don't want any part of that hearin'."

"As of now you're a committee witness," I told him. "It's either that or run from Russell. And he's not far behind."

He buried his face in his hands. "I gotta get out of here. That guy's crazy, Hilly. He'll either bust you with his hands, throw you out a window, or make you swallow a bottle of sleepin' pills. He's nuts."

"Is that what he did with the Chinese girl?"

He stared dully at the floor and slowly nodded. "Tura knows that, too."

"Tell me this. How did Foreman work that Briggs gimmick—the dead man coming back?"

He shook his head. "Like I said, Dave didn't need me anymore. I don't know what scam he worked." He clasped his hands together. "I should've bought a piece before this. I had a feelin' that if the DA or anyone started lookin' into the Society Dave would put Russell on me. I warned Tura, but she refused to believe Dave would do anythin' to hurt us."

"You don't need a gun," I told him. "I'm going to make a deal with the committee to get your contempt citation lifted. All you have to do is appear as a witness and tell them everything they want to know."

He nervously stretched the skin of his neck until it looked like rubber. "Hilly, I can't go on as a snitch . . . on television. . . ."

"With the committee you're safe," I told him, and pointed to the window. "Outside there's Russell. You have no choice. What do you want it to be?" I picked up the sketch. "Maybe this will help you."

He drew back his chair. "No. . . . No. . . . Don't show it to me, Hilly. You're right. I'll go down there and make a deal. You'll stay with me, right?"

"All the way," I promised. "Now where's Tura?"

He swallowed hard. "She's stayin' in Wee Willie's apartment over his restaurant. The Center Ring on West Forty-fifth Street, near Eighth. I told Willie she was in deep to loan sharks and couldn't pay. He agreed to let her stay there until she squared herself. I think the little guy has taken a shine to her. He won't let anyone upstairs without my okay, and makes Omar sleep outside the door. How do you like that? Having a giant sleeping outside your door like a watchdog?"

"That's great," I said. "Now let's go down and see Tura."

In the cab he kept pulling at his face and neck and bemoaning his luck. I only half listened. Newberry was getting his headlines, gift-wrapped.

The Center Ring was a typical theatre district restaurant; down three steps and into a bar. Off to the right was a dining room with walls of red raw brick papered with replicas of old-time circus posters. The menu was chalked on a blackboard, the tables had checkered tablecloths, and the waiters were all actors waiting to be discovered. It was late. There were only a few diners left but the bar was crowded.

Wee Willie was perched on a stool near the door. Towering over him was Omar, dressed in a suit with a white shirt and dark tie. With his gleaming bald head and hoop earrings, he could have been Mr. Clean waiting for his date.

There was curiosity on the midget's tight parchmentlike face. "Hiya, Steve. Back so soon?" He ignored me. There must have been some prearranged signal between Willie and Omar because the giant looked down and studied me. "How did you do today?"

"Okay," Troy grunted. Lowering his voice, he said, "I got to see Tura. Me and her boy friend."

Willie frowned and said in that deep voice, "Tura never told me anything about a boy friend." As if I didn't exist, he added, "What's this boy friend's name?"

"Hilly. You met him. Look, Willie, don't play games. This is important. We got to see Tura right away."

The giant casually put his arm, thick as an oak tree, across the entrance to the dining room.

Troy gave me an agonized look.

"Wait a minute," I said. "Suppose you let Tura decide who she wants to see? Tell her Hilly is here and see what *she* says."

The little man snapped his fingers and the bartender hurried up with a box of cigars. He selected one, carefully clipped an end with a tiny gold scissors, lit it, puffed a few times, then told the giant. "Okay. Go up and tell her Hilly is here and wants to talk to her." He turned to me for the first time. "If she says no you buy me a drink and say good-bye. No hard feelings. Right?"

"Right," I said.

It was an interminable five minutes before Omar appeared and nodded to Willie.

"Okay, Steve," Willie said. "You and her friend go up. She knows that if she wants anything, all she has to do is yell. She yells and my boy here goes up to see what the trouble is."

"Believe me, there won't be any trouble, Willie." Troy said, with a relieved look.

As if the thought had suddenly come to him, Willie snapped, "Is this guy from the sharks?"

Steve shook his head violently. "No. Nothing like that."

Omar guided us to the rear of the dining room, where he opened a door and pointed to a stairway. When I passed him, the smell of garlic was very strong. Troy knocked on the first door. When a low voice said to come in, we stepped inside. The apartment consisted of a small kitchen with a breakfast bar, a bathroom, and an enormous living room with red brick walls like the restaurant. One side was almost covered by a large circus poster showing a dwarf dressed as a cowboy riding the shoulders of a giant and aiming a rifle at a tiny white ball. Large block letters read ANNIE OAKLEY'S LITTLE BROTHER WEE WILLIE THE WORLD'S GREATEST MARKSMAN AND HIS FRIEND OMAR THE GIANT.

Tura was sitting on a couch, her feet drawn up under her. A bottle of whiskey, glasses, and a bowl of ice were on a cocktail table in front of the couch. She was wearing a wrinkled robe and looked older, dumpier, her face pale and drawn. She glared at Troy as we sat down.

"You just couldn't wait to let out where I was, could you?" she said bitterly.

"Believe me, Tura, I didn't want to do it," he said pleadingly, "but Hilly insisted he had to see you. He knows a lot, Tura, he really does. And Dave has got Russell after us. Hilly heard him give the order. He wants to waste us, Tura." He turned and beseeched me, "Tell her, Hilly."

Her mouth tightened and her chin came up when she looked over at me. "So you know everything?"

"Ginerva murdered her Mongoloid son in Poker Game, Idaho," I said. "Her Aunt Clem took the blame. But that's not all Foreman has been holding over her. She's mad, and he's been feeding her fantasies. He's her Doctor Frankenstein. Do you want to hear any more?"

Tura looked shaken, and her hand trembled when she held out a glass. I made her a drink and gave it to her.

"We have a lot of talking to do, Tura," I told her.

She looked from me to Troy. "Willie has his blackjack setup going in the back room downstairs," she said. She reached in her bag and took out a handfull of bills. "Go down and try your luck. I want to talk to Hilly alone."

Troy seemed eager to leave. When he was gone, Tura sighed. "I knew I couldn't trust him, but he was the only one I could turn to." She gave me a tight smile. "*You* know I can't stand four walls and an empty room."

"It's not his fault, Tura. I twisted his arm."

"So you know everything?" she asked. "Who told you?"

I said evenly, "Ben Rice."

There was a stricken look on her face. "What do you mean?"

"He left behind a complete report of what he had found out in Idaho, Tura," I said softly. "Now give. You know those two guys—the twins. Who are they? What did they do to Ben?"

She held her hands to her face and began weeping.

"I told Dave I didn't want any part of it. But he made me."

I pulled her hands from her face. "Made you do what?"

"I didn't want to do it, Hilly, I swear," she sobbed. "But you don't know what he can do to you."

I repeated, "Who were they and what did they do to Ben?"

"I met them a long time ago when I was working the spooky racket in Chicago," she said, wiping her eyes. "They had a mind-reading act, you know, someone in the audience holds up an object and the blindfolded guy indentifies it. It's an old carny trick. They are also the best hypnotists in the business and they took courses in mind control."

"Did Foreman bring them to teach Russell and the others?"

She nodded. "These guys are slick talkers, and they convinced Dave they could teach a small group of selected Angels the technique of mind control, which could be used at the motherhouse to keep trouble-makers in line."

"Is that why they fixed up the room in the green barn?" I prompted.

She closed her eyes and, moaning, moved her head from side to side. "Dave set that up. I told him it was dangerous. I didn't want any part of it. Ask Steve, he can tell you that."

"Is that where they took Ben?"

She bit her lower lip and bowed her head. I reached over and pulled her close to me.

"Tura, no more playing games. All I have to do is call Dave and tell him where you're hiding and you're dead. I don't have to tell you about Russell. That big freak downstairs won't stop him. The last time he only slapped you around. This time . . ."

She held my hand and begged, "I'll tell you, Hilly. I'll tell you all I know. I swear it. Andrew told me. He was trying to get around me one day and talked a lot. Shortly after they came back to New York from Idaho with your friend, they brought him up to the barn. Andrew said they worked him over in that room until he was turned into a dummy. That's what he called him, 'a dummy.' They had it fixed so he wanted to kill himself. Andrew said it had something to do with his dead wife. I don't know the story. Russell gave him the gun and they drove him down to Central Park. Andrew said they waited until they heard the gun go off and they knew he was dead. It was all Dave's orders. He said Ginerva belonged to him. He made her and he owned her and nobody was going to interfere with his plans."

Tura was only confirming what I had suspected. But I felt such a surge of rage I had to drop my hand from her robe so I wouldn't strangle her.

"Don't blame me, Hilly," she whispered. "Who knew it was going to end like this? I went in on a scam. Like I told you, when I saw I was in over my head, I wanted out. Dave wouldn't let me go until he worked me over and gave me that fifty thousand."

"Let's get back to Idaho," I ordered. "Who sent the twins there to take care of Ben?"

"Dave," she said hastily. "He and Russell knew about the kid Ginerva killed, from one of the letters her aunt had sent her when we were first starting in San Francisco. Then he and Russell conned the old lady to tell them the story. They paid someone to lift the file, and then they paid someone to keep their eyes and ears open if anyone came asking for that file." She took a deep breath. "That's how Dave knew Ben Rice was up there snooping around." She stopped and said with a frown, "What is this guy Rice to you, Hilly?"

"My best friend," I said.

"So that's why you screwed me all these months," she said, with a harsh laugh. "Sex for information. Right?" She seemed to be gaining back some of her confidence. "You, the DA, even the committee haven't got a thing on me. I had nothing to do with forcing your friend to kill himself. There's no money in my name, only the cash Dave gave me. I didn't—"

I opened the envelope and slid Margo's sketches in front of her. She gave a short yelp of terror and flung herself back on the couch.

"Oh my God. . . . No. . . ."

I joined her on the couch. "That's Russell throwing the girl out of the window on West Fifty-seventh Street. It was drawn by Margo, who will be an eyewitness. What do you think the grand jury will do when they see this? You're a conspirator, Tura, a conspirator to kill that kid."

Her eyes were wide, her ashen face covered with a sheen of sweat. "No. Don't say that, Hilly. I can't even kill a fly. It was Dave who did it. And Russell. He does anything Dave tells him to. And that guy Andrew."

I leaned close to her. "Did Foreman order Russell to throw this kid out the window.

She nodded and began to sob.

"How do you know?"

"He told me. He said he had no choice. The kid was going to the DA."

"And Russell also forced the Chinese Disciple to swallow a bottle of pills, didn't he?"

Another nod.

"Did he tell you that?"

Her voice was a muffled whisper. "Dave told me everything on the trip to Little Cat . . . when he still loved me . . ."

I leaned back. There was the first degree murder case against Foreman and Russell.

"How did he work the Briggs scam? The dead-man-coming-back business?"

She looked up, tears running down her cheeks. "I swear I don't know, Hilly. Remember, I was gone when he pulled that off."

"And the kid in the well?"

She shook her head. "That I don't know." She added hopefully, "But I can tell you about the Polish sergeant and how he kidded you about spelling the name of his street."

I was startled. "Ginerva told me that the first night I met her."

"Sure she did," Tura said, with a short laugh. "Dave fed it to her in one of their sessions."

"But how did *he* know about that sergeant? I had even forgotten him."

"All the stuff I pulled in the spooky racket is simple—once you know how it works," she said. "This is how that worked. When the publisher in Boston—I don't remember his name—"

"Ranks?"

"That's him. When Dave checked with him about you, they spent over an hour on the phone." She smirked. "I know. I was listening in. That old guy really sold you to Dave. One of the things he did was to read a letter he got from the mother of that Polish kid, praising you to the sky. It seems her nephew had been in a nearby outfit and had spent the night with her son before he went on that patrol. I guessed the kid bragged you were going along. One of the things he told his cousin was how he intended to kid you about the spelling of the name of his street—Kosciusko. Dave just made a lot of notes as Ranks talked, and later he fed them to Ginerva." She pleaded, "So now you see how it was, Hilly? Everything that happened was Dave's fault." She moaned softly. "In the beginning it was a simple scam, nobody got hurt. But it got out of hand. Too much money came in. How can anyone handle all that dough and not get hurt?" She shrugged. "We got hurt."

I poured some whiskey in her glass, and she took it eagerly, her eyes searching my face for a clue to what I intended to do. I felt drained, exhausted, degraded, and my arm was paining. As Tura said, it was all very simple when you know how it worked. . . .

"One very important question, Tura. And I want a straight answer. Where are those twin bastards now?"

"They left after Dave paid them off," she replied. "I heard they're operating with some society jewel thieves. They entertain at parties, spot the stuff, and tip off the mob. Don't ask me their names because

(430)

they change them every week. They're the best in the spooky business. Once when they were working in England they conned their way into a university where they lectured on mysticism. They're good and they're dangerous."

She took a deep long breath that seemed to clog her throat when she exhaled. "Hilly, what's going to happen to me? I'm afraid." She leaned against me. I suddenly felt a surge of pity for her. We both had been caught in the same web. I held her close until she finished sobbing. Then I kissed her gently. There was lots of gray in her hair.

"Don't hate me, Hilly," she said brokenly. "I never wanted any of the bad things that went with this scam. Like I said, in the beginning it was simple. She was beautiful, she had a message that appealed to lots of people, so Dave said let's invest a few grand, make a big profit, and dump it. But I didn't like the idea from the beginning. I never liked working a religious con. I felt it was walking into the unknown, and that can be dangerous. . . . When we started it was so easy . . . now I have government agents looking for me!" Her hand gripped my jacket. "What can I do, Hilly? I'm going out of my mind in this crazy place, with that freaky little guy who carries a tiny gun in the palm of his hand all the time and his bald-headed monster . . ."

I gently pulled her away. "Tura, you have to appear before the committee."

She shuddered. "Oh my God."

"There's no way you and Steve can avoid that. The committee will give you protection, and after it's all over they'll provide you with a new identity. You can go to Europe or anyplace you want."

She daubed at her eyes and said in a resigned voice, "Will they help to get me to Europe?"

"Of course they will. I'll have the counsel for the committee give you his promise. But I don't want to fool you, Tura. The Department of Justice and probably the New York DA are moving in, and you and Steve will have to testify before grand juries and against Foreman, Russell, and the others."

She said slowly, "So I will have to hang Dave."

"That's the way it is, Tura."

Her hand searched for mine, and I held it. "I feel so alone, Hilly. Will you sort of be around?"

"Of course."

She said with a smile. "Will you kiss me again?"

I kissed her.

"That little guy's very nice, but I know that some night he's going to ask if he can sleep with me," she said. She thought for a moment, then giggled. "Well, there's a first time for everything."

(431)

By now the dining room was filling up with late theatregoers and the bar was packed. Willie was still sitting on his stool by the doorway greeting a group of laughing customers. Standing beside him was Omar, his dark eyes never still as he surveyed the customers and the busy bartenders. Troy, looking unhappy, was seated at a table in the bar, pushing an empty glass about on the checked cloth. When he saw me, his face lighted up.

"Jeez! You were up there a long time!"

"Tura has agreed to testify—just as you're going to do," I told him.

"They'll give us protection, right?"

"Stop worrying. I will have the counsel of the committee personally guarantee you'll get all the protection you need."

He followed me when I joined Willie. As before, the dwarf spoke to Troy, mentioning me in the third person as if I weren't present.

"He must be an old friend. He was up there half the night."

"Thanks for looking out for her," I said.

He ignored me. "You sure he's not sent by the sharks?"

Before Troy could answer, I said, "Tura is in big trouble, Willie. Not with me, not with the loan sharks, but with Washington. She's going to appear down there as a witness before a Senate committee."

Willie, still ignoring me, gave Troy an angry look. "You never told me she was in trouble with the feds. I don't like that. I don't want any trouble with Uncle. What does he mean, she's in big trouble? What kind of trouble?"

"A committee is lookin' for her, Willie," Steve said. "Somethin', somethin' to do with the spooky business."

"Nobody will make trouble for you, Willie," I assured him.

For the first time he looked at me. "Who the hell are you? The president?"

He turned to Steve. "You hung one on me, Steve."

There was a sheen of sweat on Troy's forehead. "Somebody's after her, Willie. I didn't want her to get hurt."

I interjected, "Please let her stay here, Willie. Give me twenty-four hours and she'll be gone. No one will ever know where she stayed."

"She's a nice woman," he said. "I don't like to see a woman like that get hurt." He said to Troy, "You bum, why did you let her get in this spot? Why didn't you take care of her?"

Troy looked at me and shrugged hopelessly.

"Twenty-four hours, Willie, that's all I ask," I said.

He carefully tapped his cigar on the edge of an ashtray. "Okay. But not for you and not for this bum—only for her." He eyed me. "You with this committee?"

"I'm working with Mr. Gray, the general counsel of the Newberry committee."

"I have your word I won't be involved? It's bad for business."

"You have my word. We'll be here tomorrow night."

He studied the glowing end of his cigar. "Who is 'we'? The Bureau? IRS?"

"Mr. Gray, the committee's counsel."

He sighed. "Okay." The parchment face was tight. "Steve. From now on stay out of my place."

Troy said hesitantly, "I thought maybe I could stay here also, Willie."

But the little man wasn't listening. He was reaching out to shake the hands of a man and his wife who said they were in from Dallas and some friends had said they could always get a marvelous late supper at Willie's Center Ring. . . .

My mind was now staggering with fatigue. In the cab, I put my head on the back of the seat and let Troy babble on.

"When I get some bucks I'll come back and make it up to Willie," he said, half to himself. "I'll prove to him he didn't get hurt takin' care of Tura. Hey! Maybe she'll take care of him . . . Tura never minded a bit of kinky sex. . . . The little guy really likes her. . ."

I finally got him in the hotel room, poured him a stiff drink from the quart of scotch, and warned him not to answer the phone or the door until I came back the following day with Tom Gray.

He stood by the door, rubbing his frightened face. "I got your word, Hilly. They'll protect me. Right?"

"Nobody is going to hurt you, Steve," I promised him. "Finish your drink, take a shower, and go to bed. I'll find Gray and bring him back here to talk to you. Don't leave this room for any reason."

I decided to return to the Lafayette. It was the only place where Foreman could get in touch with me.

I barely made it to the room. The night clerk and the lone bellboy exchanged glances. A strip of stainless steel in the elevator showed me I looked as if I had just come off the Bowery. When I got into my room, I carefully took off my jacket. My arm was stiff, and when I lifted it out of the sleeve I moaned from the stab of pain that shot through me. I felt feverish and almost emptied the jug of ice water on the bureau. When I sprawled out on the bed, I could feel the weariness draining out of me. I wanted to kick off my shoes, but I didn't have the strength. I closed my eyes and felt myself slipping down a long black tunnel made of velvet. Faster . . . faster . . . and faster. . . . Now there was someone with me. . . . It was Ginerva, holding tight to a little boy with blond hair. . . . She was screaming but I couldn't hear her voice. . . . But from her lips I knew she was crying, "Help me, Hilly, help me. . . ."

It was the telephone, ringing incessantly. It seemed to be saying, *Get up. I know you're there.* I kept hoping it would go away, but it didn't. At last I picked it up. The same soft voice answered my hello.

"Brother Foreman suggested you turn on your radio. I'll call you back shortly."

There was a click.

It was a few minutes before five. The first radio station I tried had a long-range weather report read by a weary announcer; on another an all night phone-in talk show was discussing flying saucers. Finally I found a news station with phony bells clanging to simulate a wire service bulletin.

"Reports are still coming in from several states of strange lights and explosions in the sky," the announcer said. "During the night police of fifteen states have been deluged with calls from residents who have described explosions and weird bright lights flaming across the sky. One man in Tennessee said he saw a scarlet cross in the heavens. Oregon newspapers and police were called by many residents who said they heard loud blasts in the sky and saw dull green lights which lasted for several minutes. In Chicago thousands described a glittering white star that hung in the darkness, then slowly vanished.

"All this, combined with last night's explosion of a natural gas tank in southern Illinois, which so far has taken the lives of four firemen and several workers, and the shocking tragedy of only a few hours ago when an apparently deranged man hacked to death ten men, women, and children in a Harlem tenement with a swordlike weapon used for cutting sugar cane, have many recalling the recent prophecy of the prophet, Ginerva, before the Newberry committee. The controversial cult figure predicted there would be strange signs in the heavens and an angry God would punish his people with the fire and the sword.

"In Washington, Senator Newberry told the Associated Press he would hold an important press conference this morning, while in several cities large crowds have gathered in streets and parks to hold prayer vigils."

I turned on the television, and instead of a late, late movie, the color picture slowly took shape of a reporter overlooking a sea of flickering candles in an open-air auditorium.

"Since the lights and explosions began to appear in the skies, thousands have joined this praying group of Disciples of the Society of the Chosen. Some are in their night clothes and are clearly frightened. Many I spoke to insist that the controversial prophet Ginerva is right and the Day of Judgment is at hand. Attempts to find Ginerva have been unsuccessful. She has been in seclusion since the riot at her motherhouse when anti-Ginerva pickets clashed with the Society's security forces."

When the telephone rang again, I had a pad and a pen. The soft voice ordered:

"A train will leave Grand Central for White Plains in precisely thirty-one minutes. Brother Foreman wants you on that train. Don't use the front entrance of the hotel. A cab is parked in the rear waiting for you. You will be met at the White Plains station. Brother Foreman said it is vital that you meet him in the Money Room. The computer printouts have just come in from the Little Cat bank, and he insists you be given your share immediately."

Then he hung up.

I tried to write down the message, but the damn pen was dry, all I got were scrawls. But the message was simple. Be on that White Plains train and come up to the Money Room to collect. . . .

There was no sense in calling Tom Gray; he wasn't in Washington. Bruce Stafford had told me Gray, Leah, and Turner had taken Ginerva out of the motherhouse. Leah and Turner's rooms didn't answer. I thought of calling the Manhattan FBI office, but even the slightest hassle with some officious nightside agent or clerk would delay me. Those precious minutes were ticking by.

I was wobbling with fatigue, and now that I was awake my arm began again, a deep throbbing pain that went from shoulder to elbow. I hastily shaved, struggled into a new shirt, and found the cab in the rear of the hotel. The driver was a sleepy kid with long hair and a Greek fisherman's hat. All he could tell me was that someone picked him up in midtown, drove to the hotel, and gave him ten dollars to wait for me in the rear.

I arrived at Grand Central Station in time to gulp down a cup of coffee and a stale bun.

The late *News* had a terrifying front-page picture of the tank explosion with a head BLASTS, LIGHTS IN U.S. SKIES with a key line over it, GINERVA'S PROPHECY?

The story from combined wire services told how mysterious lights and blasts in the heavens had awakened countless thousands in several states, and police in some sections reported growing panic. In Ohio a police captain compared it to the terror produced by the famous Orson Welles radio show, "The War of the Worlds."

"The precinct's telephone board is lit up like a Christmas tree," he said. "They're all talking about Ginerva's prophecy and they say they intend to start praying."

As the train passed through Harlem, looking as if it were greeting the dawn with a curse, I asked myself how this could be another

Foreman scam. How could he produce lights in the night sky, tear apart a natural gas tank, and send a maddened killer on a rampage—with a sword—to hack ten people to death? I felt a combination of rage and frustration. Only a few hours ago the puzzle was almost finished. Now, once again, it was in a shambles, with more pieces missing than before. If this was her prediction come true, then Ginerva wasn't mad. But I knew she had to be. I had seen her, a completely mad woman in the moonlight of that silvered meadow at the foot of the little hill. . . .

To keep my mind from whirling about, I concentrated on the pain in my arm. It was clean, sharp, intense; I savored every stabbing thrust.

The White Plains station was deserted except for a bus pulling out with a few passengers. Parked nearby were the fat cabdriver, who could have been dozing, and a long black limousine with Andrew behind the wheel. He looked up at me impassively, then reached over and opened the door.

We didn't exchange a word during the short trip to the grounds or when we passed through the gates of the grounds. Before us loomed the shell of the motherhouse. The roof had fallen in. Only parts of walls were left, like a row of stumpy black teeth outlined against the glowing morning sky. But he didn't drive to the small stone house where Foreman had showed me the Money Room. He was driving down a path and at its end was the green barn. I lunged for the door, but they were electrically controlled. I met Andrew's eyes in the overhead mirror. For the first time, his face was showing some emotion. He was grinning.

26

The Room of Mirrors

The gymnasium was incongruously neat. The heavy weights were stacked, rows of boxing gloves hung from hooks, and three basketballs were in a large box. The chair they had pushed me into was directly in front of Foreman, who sat behind a small desk. He was dressed almost casually, sport shirt, slacks, and white shoes; he could have been on his way to a tennis match. Russell wore a dark blue short-sleeved knit shirt that showed off his powerful arms and chest. He had greeted me with a laugh, but now he was staring down at me, his eyes filled with a murderous hate.

"There really is a lot we have to talk about, Hilly," Foreman said with a sigh, "but fortunately there just isn't any time. That's one of the reasons why I didn't turn you over to Brother Russell and Brother Andrew. They wanted so much to be alone with you."

"One hour, Dave," Russell said softly. "Just one hour."

Foreman waved him into silence. "We're saving everything for you upstairs," he said. "But before we turn you into a very obedient young man, Hilly, I suppose I do owe you some kind of an explanation." He leaned back and gave me a mocking, benevolent smile. "First of all I'm going to satisfy your curiosity about Briggs. Really, it was very simple. I know a perfectly marvelous actor who has worked any number of scams, mostly seances and that sort of thing. I had gathered newspaper stories and pictures of the killer, so we knew what he looked like. My actor is an expert at makeup and disguise. He looked so much like that dead guy he gave me the shivers. Your very wonderful publicity and promotional campaign had psyched those fools out there so the two old people were in a very receptive mood when our actor appeared. They reacted exactly as I knew they would. As I told you, Hilly, you just can't beat money and expertise."

"But what about the grave and the footprints?" I asked.

He laughed. "Oh, my actor is an ingenious fellow. He slipped in there the night before, did a little digging around the grave with a hand trowel, and made the appropriate footprints. Now I suppose you want to know what we did about the cross he left behind on the sill of the old lady's window?" He smirked. "I'm really proud of that one. I noticed in all the newspaper pictures that the choirmaster wore a cross in his lapel. All we did was buy a similar one. It took some looking but Andrew found one—of all places, in a religious store!" He frowned. "For a time I thought that state police captain might give us some trouble. He was the only one who didn't buy the whole performance; he wanted to dig up the corpse and see if the pin was really gone. But fortunately the old lady threatened to go to court to stop him. So he let it drop. From what I heard it's accepted out there Ginerva summoned a dead man from the grave." He added, "By the way, Ginerva is with your friends in Sir Edward Butler's apartment. They intend to bring her to Washington to testify before the committee about the rockets, but, poor woman, she doesn't know a damn thing about them. She thinks they came from God—"

"Rockets?" I asked. "What rockets?"

"Those lights in the skies were powerful rockets, the finest you can buy," he said, laughing. "They were set off simultaneously across the country by teams we have been training for months. You would be surprised what you can get people to do in the name of the Lord." He shrugged. "But you know what they say about the best of plans. One of our bases in the Cascades exploded and two Disciples were killed. The survivor talked. Now Newberry will have a field day."

I was confused. "But that wasn't on the radio or television."

"Didn't you hear Newberry announce he was holding an important press conference this morning?" he asked. When I nodded, he continued, "That's when he will make his disclosure. They flew parts of the rockets down to Washington and he intends to show it on TV." He said savagely, "Those idiots! Everything went off perfectly—except for them!"

"Wait a minute," I said. "They said Newberry was going to hold an important press conference but they didn't mention anything about rockets. . . ." As the horrible thought came to me, my voice died away.

Foreman was smiling, the other two were laughing.

"That's right, Hilly," Foreman explained. "We have a contact on the committee." He looked over at Russell. "Suppose we tell Hilly who our contact is? After all, what difference will it make? In a few hours he won't even know his name."

"I'm going to like that," Russell said. I had the immediate impression he was aching to cut my throat. "Sweet Brother Hillers will be my good Disciple who will do everything I tell him. . . ."

Foreman leaned forward. "Our contact is right in the committee, Hilly. His name is—" He slowly spelled out the letters. "G-R-A-Y. Tom Gray." He obviously enjoyed the stunned look on my face. "That's our boy. Newberry's counsel. It took a lot of wire pulling to get next to him, but we finally bought him the other night. Isn't it terrible what people will do for money and political favors? So far he has been perfect." He shook his head. "One thing, Hilly. You completely fooled him. He warned me you're a dangerous fanatic who could explode at any minute." His eyes narrowed. "But I can't blame Gray. You fooled a lot of people, including me. And I'm not easily fooled!"

"But he didn't fool me," Russell said roughly. "I spotted him the minute I saw him. Didn't I warn you, Dave? But you wouldn't listen."

"Well, I'm listening to you now," Foreman said grimly.

"But what about that exploding gas tank? The crazy man in Harlem with the sword?"

Foreman gave me a look of disgust. "Oh, come off it, Hilly, you're smarter than that. How could I possibly pull those off? They just happened. But of course we have already claimed them as part of Ginerva's prophecy. This country is very uptight these days, my friend, and it doesn't take much to create a panic. And that's exactly what we're doing now—creating a national panic in the name of the Lord. Team Leaders across the country are holding open prayer meetings, reciting Ginerva's prophecy and message over and over. Remember what Goebbels said about repetition? No matter what Newberry says or displays at his press conference, by tonight millions of Americans will believe our rockets were signs of God's anger with man and that gas tank explosion and that psycho in Harlem were all part of her prophecy that this is the beginning of the end for all of us."

Andrew spoke up for the first time. I expected his voice to be harsh, almost gutteral, but it was surprisingly soft, almost feminine. "The kid in the well, Dave. Let him in on that."

"Oh, that was superb," Foreman said, shaking his head in admiration. "And most of the credit must go to Brother Russell." He bowed in the direction of Russell who was grinning.

"I must admit, you had a good idea. Hilly," he said. "Disciples searching for that kid was a natural for publicity for Ginerva—and of course for the tour. But there was one hitch. That bitch was giving me a hard time about doing the Blessings, and as you pointed out, this one we needed for the news programs. Frankly, it took some doing to get her to come over there with me. Then while you and those two kids, Butler and Turner, were calling the papers and the TV stations, Russell came over to see me with a glorious idea—"

I pointed out, "But when we left you had just told him off and ordered him to do it your way. Remember?"

He nodded. "That's true. We've had many differences in the past, but they never amounted to anything." He looked over at Russell. "Right, Russ?"

Russell grinned and said proudly, "Tell him about my plan, Dave."

"His idea was superb," Foreman said with a slight smile. "As he pointed out, we had enough Disciples to cover twice that area, and if the kid hadn't been found by now there was an excellent chance he would be discovered by one of our teams. The plan was to have every Angel acting as a Team Leader equipped with one of the powerful shortwave sets the security patrols used. They were to keep in constant touch with him at our communications center. As Russell pointed out, if one of our teams found the kid, we would be first to know and in some way we could use that, perhaps to get Ginerva over there in a hurry." He smiled. "Well, one of the teams was lucky and heard the kid wailing in the well. The Angel turned in a detailed physical report of what they had found. He was ordered to leave the area with his people and await orders. Naturally the Angel and the Disciples were perfectly disciplined and did what they were told. That's when I got the idea—why not have Ginerva find the kid?"

"But how?" I asked.

Even before he answered, I knew Foreman was going to tell me their deepest secrets. His ego demanded it.

"It was easy," he said, his eyes shining with self-satisfaction. "I sold her the idea that God had told her where the kid was in the well. Hell, I even gave her the stuff about the skull the Angel had used as a landmark."

I insisted, "But how?"

"Hilly, don't be stupid," he said frowning, impatiently. "She's schizophrenic! Ask any psychiatrist, they're the easiest to manipulate. First you set the scene"—he grinned—"that candlelight gimmick was great—then you carefully build up their fantasy world, and at the right time plant in their heads whatever you want. By now with Ginerva it was easy. She's no longer playing the role—she's living it!"

"But there was a map you gave the mayor."

He smirked. "Sure, drawn by God—through me."

"And those idiots believed every word of it," Russell said contemptuously.

"You rotten bastard," I said to Foreman. "How could you have done that to her?"

He arched his brows in mock indignation. "What did I do to her? She was never more happy than when I supplied her with a divine vision! There she was on national television, led by the hand of God to that poor little lamb about to be torn apart by rats at the bottom of the well." He said to Russell, "We'll never top that one. Never. The rocket scam can't compare with it."

"Once I thought of killing you," I told him, "but the very thought revolted me. Not now."

"Now—or anytime—you could never do it, Hilly," he said gravely. "You're not the killing type. You could never pull the trigger. He shook his head. "You're not like me. Once I started this thing, I made a promise to myself not to let anything or anybody get in my way." He threw up his hands. "And I didn't. And that's how—"

I ended the sentence for him, "You got together a hundred million dollars."

"We have to get out of this guy who he's working for, Dave," Russell said harshly. "And this isn't the way to do it."

"Just who are you, Hilly?" Foreman asked quietly. "Who are you working for?"

"I'm not working for anyone," I told him. I took a deep breath and said, "My best friend was Ben Rice."

Foreman's face never changed, but I was sure I caught the flicker of surprise in his eyes. "Well, what about Ben Rice?"

"I simply wanted to find out what happened to him."

Russell laughed. "He blew off his head in Central Park."

Foreman ignored him and said quickly, "So that's why you entered the Society?"

"Yes. And I found my answer in Poker Game."

Russell and Foreman exchanged glances.

I suggested, "I still think we can make a deal, Dave."

When Foreman seemed to hesitate, Russell jumped up and smashed his fist on the desk, glaring down at Foreman.

"He's stalling," he said. "Now! No more talk!"

They looked at each other, eyes locked. But this time it was Foreman who wavered and broke. He looked at me and shrugged. When Russell moved around the desk I leaped out of the chair, but Andrew caught me from behind and pinioned my arms. The last thing I saw was the triumphant grin on Russell's rough face and his fist, big and hard as the head of a sledge, coming directly at me. Then there was an explosion of stars in my head.

I came to with someone nudging me. The room slowly swam into focus. It was paneled and bare, except for the mat I was lying on. There were no windows, a recessed light was in the ceiling. Foreman was standing over me. Apparently he had nudged me back to consciousness with his foot. Twice I tried to sit up; the third time I succeeded. My fingers told me my jaw was swollen. I tested it gingerly. It wasn't broken, and I had all my teeth.

"That was stupid, Hilly," he said. "You should have known that big goon was aching for you to start something."

"Well, what are you waiting for?" I asked.

"I'm ready to make a deal," he said. "Tell me all you know and I promise to make it easy for you."

"What do you mean 'easy'?"

"Do you know what sound waves can do to the human brain?"

I was so frightened I couldn't answer.

He went on, "Before your brain is completely damaged you will suffer pain so intense, so piercing, it is impossible to describe. After you break, laser beams, passing through a computer and then through film, will create three-dimensional figures so real they still scare the hell out of me. Those figures will take you on a trip through Hell which will etch such terrifying scenes on what's left of your brain that you will be on your knees for the rest of your life praying to Ginerva to save you a seat on her heavenly Cloud of Salvation. When you leave here you will be a constantly smiling idiot, hugging the Bible and jumping to obey every command we give you. After a month or so, some of your memory machinery will return, but it will be mostly reflexes, like what talents you have and we'll use them. Now I can make it easy for you, Hilly. I can give you a sedative so you will simply go in there like a robot and come out like a robot. It's guaranteed to save you a great deal of suffering. . . ."

"Is this what you did to Ben Rice after the twins got through with him in Idaho?"

Again there was that flicker of uncertainty in his eyes. "You see, Hilly, that's what I mean. I must know where you got your information. Would you like to tell me some more?"

I repeated, "Is this where you brought Ben Rice?"

He shrugged. "There isn't any reason why you shouldn't know. Actually your friend Rice scared the hell out of us when he found that drunken Idaho deputy. The twins, of course, took care of the drunk and then really moved in on Rice. They both admitted that, while they were very good, they would have had a difficult job with Rice if he had not been in that depressed state. They brought him back from Idaho to his apartment, where they softened him up and then took him here. In a way Rice surprised us. It took two days to break him. But when it was finally all over, he did everything we told him to do. You should have seen him—hugging his Bible and praising Ginerva and the Lord. We told him we were going to give him peace and let him rejoin his wife and child. So we gave him the magnum—part of a shipment stolen on the Coast, I should point out—and Russell and Andrew drove him to Central Park, where he blew his brains out. Now I think that explains just about everything. Oh, one more thing. Your bluff about the letter, the report in the safety deposit box, and that mysterious friend who was going to rush copies to the DA and so on—well, we came to the conclusion it was a pipe dream. Isn't that true, Hilly?"

"You'll find out very shortly," I said, still bluffing, still hoping.

He shrugged. "Well, if you want to continue to play the hero, be my guest. Now let me tell you something about the treatment Rice got and what you will get very shortly."

He thought for a moment, then continued in a monotone, as if he were a professor lecturing his students. "The velocity of sound in free air is affected by the wind, by the slightest breeze, and by temperature, especially humidity. But in an airtight compartment—such as the one you will be taken to—sound becomes a terrifying weapon. Powerful, invisible, and at stages beyond the hearing of man. You may be still conscious when the mirrors in that room start splintering. And for this reason. In addition to the sound cones in the four corners of the room, which will be directly targeted at you, there are vents along the top of the walls near the ceiling line. Behind these vents are powerful quartz oscillators. They spin at such high speed their sound cannot be heard, but they will be creating what the scientists call wave 'fronts'—like waves"—his hands shaped the rolling surf—"coming into shore. They will get steeper and steeper until finally they will crack right over you." He paused to sadly add: "By this time of course you will no longer be conscious. In fact, you will no longer be a sane man." He became brisk. "Now, Hilly, we don't have the two days for you as we had for Rice, which means the plateaus of sound will be condensed. You will therefore pass through the plateaus more rapidly and your suffering will be twice what Rice went through. Now do we have a deal? The pill for information?"

It took a great effort to get to my feet. He watched me smilingly. Finally, as I stood there swaying, I spat in his face. He didn't say a word or change expression; he simply wiped his face with a clean handkerchief, which he carefully folded and put back into his pocket. The door operated like an electrically powered overhead garage door. He had a small box in his hand, which he pressed. As the door slowly descended, he said, "I'll give you that pill—but only after you clean my shoes by licking them. . . . And by the way, we have an idea where that bitch, Tura, and that drunken slob, Troy, can be found . . . ."

Now that the first flash of fear had passed, my mind was almost unnaturally clear as I began to plan to fight for my life—and my mind. Foreman had made one mistake—telling how Tom had described me as a fanatic ready to explode. This could only mean Tom was working some plan. But where was he? In the meantime, I had to find some way to get out. I walked about the room, examining every foot. It was almost hygienically clean, without a speck of dirt or a crack in the walls. I ran my hands along the smooth surface, even trying with my nails to widen the seams of the door. I knew Foreman was not exaggerating what they could do to me in that mirrored room; Ben's death and that pathetic black boy, Thomas, were their proof. If escape was impossible, the only way I could survive was to control my mind. But how?

Suddenly I remembered the POW in the Saigon hospital. I had only to close my eyes and see him sitting on the edge of the bed, chain-smoking and nervously running his hands through his hair as he told me how he had survived their torture:

"They first used music, then sounds pitched as high as they could make them. Fortunately for me, their equipment was primitive. But it went on for hours, the noise bouncing off the walls. Gradually my head seemed to be swelling, getting larger and larger until I imagined it was as big as a basketball. I knew I was near cracking. That's when I pulled the bamboo splinters from my bed frame and began shoving them under my fingernails. I tell you, the pain never felt so good. I concentrated on it, screaming my fool head off, but it helped me from breaking. . . . Those gooks had a lot of respect for me after that. . . . They said I was the only one who didn't break. My fingers swelled like sausages but it was worth it, beating those bastards at their own game."

I began searching for splinters. But there weren't any. The oak panels were expertly joined together, the varnished floor was as smooth as aluminum. Then suddenly I remembered Ginerva's tiny gold cross within the jeweled five-pointed star.

"*Someday you will need this,*" she had said.

The points were needle sharp, and when I thrust one under my nail, the sharp, intense pain made me jerk my hand away.

Then there was the click of a lock and the door slowly slid up to admit a grinning Russell and an impassive Andrew.

"You going to come quietly or do you want any more?" Russell asked, holding up his fist. "Dave said not to work you over, but if you make any trouble—"

Andrew moved to my other side. Now I was between them.

"Andy was a good boy in the ring," Russell said. "Maybe he took too many in the head, but he can still turn your face into hamburger. When he gets tired, I start in." He held out his open hands; they were enormous. "I won't punch you. I'll just slap you. What's left of your face will just explode—that's all. Well, what do you say"—he emphasized the name—"Brother Hillers?"

"I'm not a fool," I said. "But some way, somehow, you'll be taken care of. . . ."

"Yeah. Maybe that dead guy will come back and haunt me," he said as he flung me toward the door. When my bandaged arm slammed against the doorjamb, the pain which swept through me was so intense I almost threw up. As they dragged me along the corridor I wondered—how long would I last?

Foreman watched silently as they forced me down into the chair and put the strap across my chest and feet. In the mirrored wall I looked like a man trussed into an electric chair waiting for the executioner to pull the switch.

Foreman said, glancing at his watch, "I would estimate that you will start screaming within two hours. Of course you know this room is soundproof."

I tried desperately to appear calm, and I think this bothered him. He gave me a curious look and said, "Are there any other questions you would like answered while you still have your senses?"

Keep him talking, I thought, stall him as much as possible. Soothe his ego, make him preen—The Year's Outstanding Salesman.

"There's one thing you beat me on, Dave," I said humbly. "What were you doing with Frey, the Washington publisher?"

For the first time the surprise was clear in his face. "So you *do* know a lot!"

"Suppose we talk about it?" I suggested. "You have your goons take off these straps and—"

When Foreman frowned and looked thoughtful, Russell shouted, "No way, Dave, are we going to talk anymore to this guy! You sold me on him once, and see where it got us?"

I hastily took a wild shot. "That paper is connected with your plans for the Society, isn't it, Dave?"

The temptation was too much for his ego. "Sure I'll tell you —why not?" The words rolled about the mouth as if he were savoring a fine wine. "I'm buying an Invisible Government."

I could only stare at him.

He repeated with obvious enjoyment. "An Invisible Government. That's what I call the media. It's no longer the Fourth Estate: now it's a power all by itself. The public didn't realize that until Watergate. And now I'm going to own a piece of it. I'm buying the Washington *Express* and its affiliated TV station. I'm putting the fix in to get by that foolish cross-media ownership rule—you know, the rule that you can't own a broadcasting company and print news in the same community. Next year I intend to buy a small but influential chain of newspapers in the Midwest. Then later there's a big one here in New York I know I can get. They're in trouble and it's only a question of waiting. I've been tipped off that they're bringing in an efficiency man who will use a hatchet on the budget, and that's always the beginning of the end . . ."

"To hell with that crap, Dave," Russell snarled. "Let's get going with this guy."

Foreman ignored him. There was a glow in his eyes and his voice was exuberant. "If you want power these days, control the media—it's better than money. Look at the 1972 Democratic primary in New Hampshire. It was the press that paved the way for McGovern. And look what they did in '68. They forgot to inform the public Johnson got more votes than McCarthy. Every four years a new, small, but powerful community of journalists helps to make our history by telling us what the candidates are doing but forget to tell us what they are saying. As for Watergate, it was the press who toppled a President, the most powerful man in the world . . ."

Russell shouted, "For Christ's sake, shut up! Let's go!"

Foreman glanced at him, then returned to me. "It's unfortunate I have to be surrounded by Neanderthals. That's why I had great plans for us, Hilly. The name of the Society of the Chosen will never appear in the *Express* or any newspaper or be mentioned on any television station we own. They will be used for something far more important: politics. First I intend to start selecting and backing local candidates, then move on to bigger offices, say a senator or a governor. The Society will be used as a vote bloc. How can they beat us? A controlled media and controlled fanatics! The organization you set up was just the thing I needed. This Newberry committee is only a big bag of political wind. When it collapses, I intend to move into the national scene. Through fronts, of course. Within five years I will control an Invisible Government of newspapers and TV stations that will stretch from coast to coast, from north to south. Even now we are in the process of finding young attractive candidates."

"Why?" I asked.

He shrugged. "Power. The ability to make other people do what you want. Isn't that the name of the game these days?"

"Dave!" Russell roared. "Forget it! We don't have the time!"

"That's true," Foreman repeated sadly. "We don't have the time." He looked down at me. "You can believe it or not, Hilly, but I am truly sorry it has to end this way. I believe we could have done great things together. This religious racket has incredible potential. All you need is an army of fanatics who believe in your gimmick, money, and expertise." He raised a finger. "And of course you have to do your homework."

Then he turned and walked out of the room, followed by Andew.

As the door slowly descended, Russell said softly, "This one I'm going to enjoy."

"Drop dead, creep," I told him.

When the door closed, I gently squeezed the metal star in my fist and felt its points dig into my flesh. Then I waited. It didn't take long for them to begin.

The first sounds from four corners of the room were animal cries of terror, of women wailing over and over, "Ginerva! Courier of God, save us!" The volume gradually increased until the words were no longer distinguishable. They became a high-pitched whine as the wall of mirrors slowly turned into giant posters of Ginerva dressed in white, her arms stretched upward to heaven. Then suddenly the whine was replaced by a tremendous crash of drums, followed by a brass section. The walls turned back into mirrors, then back to Ginerva. Lights went out. There were crashes of thunder, flashes of lightning. All the time the volume of the noise kept mounting.

I don't know how long this went on. Suddenly it broke off, and the silence was actually deafening. Echoes reverberated in my head while a light appeared in the ceiling that was so intense it seemed to be burning the eyes out of my skull. This was followed by darkness, complete, without the tiniest glimmer of light. I found myself becoming disoriented. After a brief period, the intense light returned, accompanied by a different type of sound. This time I heard the fans starting up; they sounded oiled, efficient, deadly. Gradually they became a whine. The velocity increased until I could no longer hear them, but I could almost feel invisible waves crowding against me, growing higher and higher—the "fronts" Foreman had predicted.

I was passing through the plateaus. Sound had now gone beyond the range of the human ear. I wasn't prepared for the stabbing pain, as if someone had thrust a wire-thin stiletto through my head from ear to ear and was wobbling the blade back and forth. I never knew I was screaming until the sound broke off and in the silence my screams bounced off the walls. Darkness followed. When the lights came on again the fans started. This time joined by the shrieking sounds aimed at me from the four corners of the room.

I lost all sense of time. I was in a vacuum filled with sound producing pain so intense it filled my whole being. It pierced my head, seeking out the remotest part of my brain. I sensed, rather than saw, the mirrors crumbling, one by one. At times I felt I was in the bottom of a deep canyon trying to flee from those invisible waves flowing in and out of my head.

I must have bitten through my lower lip because I felt blood dripping off my chin. In one brief lucid moment I remembered Ginerva's cross in the star, and I squeezed into my hand with all my strength.

The pain was almost exquisite as the metal tore through the flesh. When the sound waves mounted, I pushed the star in deeper. It became a struggle between me and my own brain. I commanded it to obey my personal pain, to ignore the outside forces. Somehow I hung on. Then the sound waves broke off, and the images appeared. Satan was standing in front of me; his face reminded me of Foreman's— thin, handsome like an evil fox. He was dressed in a long red cloak and was pointing to figures with frightening ravaged faces who reached out for me. I fought against the straps, but they seemed to be pulling me toward a pit in which men and women were imprisoned with chains to a bed of coals. Their wailing filled my ears. I fought the straps, I knew I was screaming . . . . I pounded my fist on my knee trying to drive the metal deeper into my palm . . . .

Suddenly the images vanished, the lights came on, and the door slowly rose with Tom Gray standing there; then Leah and Norman . . . . They stood looking at me, Leah's hand to her mouth. Tom and Norman called out to me but I couldn't hear them . . . .

I slowly slipped away into a soft comforting darkness.

27

Wee Willie's Place

The sedation they gave me made me sleep for twenty-four hours. I came to in St. Vincent's as a surgeon was changing the dressing on my hand. The violent tugging against the straps had torn open the stitches from Buck's bite, which had to be replaced, and now several more were needed to close the deep wound in the palm of my hand. Tom silently handed me Ginerva's metal star. One part was bent into the shape of a hook.

The condition of my hearing was more serious than the wounds. Specialists warned me to expect some impairment, and as I grew older I would eventually be forced to wear a hearing aid. Another hour or so in that room, and not only my hearing but my brain would have been destroyed.

My hearing was slowly returning, but the doctors said it would take at least a week before it would be fully restored. Now, in voices that seemed to come from far off, Leah, Tom, and Turner told me what had happened.

After leaving Ginerva in Sir Edward Butler's apartment with two U.S. marshals on guard, they came to the hotel looking for me. When there was no answer, Tom had the hotel's security man use a passkey. They found a great deal of blood on the bed where my arm had started bleeding during the night, and while Tom phoned Washington, Leah discovered the pad by the phone. Fortunately, the ink-less ballpoint had traced "White Plains Station . . . Foreman . . . Money Room . . ." into the paper. Tom alerted Newberry, who contacted the Department of Justice and the FBI. At the station, the fat cabbie told them he had seen me getting into one of the Society's limousines. Leah and Turner suggested the green barn; a shootout followed.

It was strange to barely hear my own voice as I told Tom how Foreman had boasted he had bought him. He studied me soberly, then loked at Leah who nodded, put her lips close to my ear, and said:

"Tom couldn't help it, Hilly. He had to set you up for Foreman. The Department of Justice insisted you had to be used as bait to get him. The were afraid he was about to skip out of the country."

"Thanks very much," I said. "But at least you got him and Russell."

They had a strange look on their faces. Leah slowly shook her head and again leaned down.

"Andrew and three Angels were killed," she said, "but Foreman and Russell got away."

I couldn't believe what she was saying.

Norman said something to her and she nodded.

"Ginerva's gone. My father said one moment they were talking about the theatre and the next moment, when he went into the kitchen to make sure the marshals were being fed, she was gone."

Tom looked so stricken I felt sorry for him.

"Never mind," I started to say. "We'll find—"

Then I stopped, stared at them, and shouted so loud I could hear myself: "Tura! Troy! Russell is after them!"

As I started to get out of bed, Tom and Leah tried to hold me back, but I shook them off. "Tura and Troy are waiting to see you, Tom. They have agreed to become witnesses before the committee. Steve is at the Hilton and Tura is in Wee Willie's apartment!"

I could almost read Tom's lips. "Who the hell is Wee Willie?"

It was agreed that Leah and Norman would return to Sir Edward's apartment in the hope that perhaps Ginerva would return, while Tom and I rushed to the Hilton. It was the peak of the rush hour, and getting uptown was the usual New Yorker's daily nightmare of blocked side streets, honking horns, and imbecile cabdrivers. Tom shouted some more details of what had happened, but I couldn't concentrate on what he was saying. I was remembering what Foreman had said as the door lowered:

"By the way, we have an idea where that bitch Tura and that drunken slob Troy can be found."

As the cab swung into the Hilton, I noticed a police car in the driveway reserved for cabs; three maintenance men were hosing down the sidewalk. I was about to enter the revolving door when I stopped; Tom bounced off me and hit the door. I turned and forced myself to walk to the man with the hose. There was a shoe at the curb and the water in the gutter was bright red.

We both stared down at it for a moment, then ran back to the hotel. A few minutes later, the cop who had been making out his report in the manager's office handed us a torn clipping and a color photograph in a plastic case. It showed a smiling Troy, and on the back was written: "Stephen A. Troy receiving the award of the Council of Midwestern Churches for the outstanding religious television documentary of the Vietnam War."

The clipping was from a television column: "The extraordinary film on Channel Four News last night of Ginerva's prophecy of the dead man in Kansas returning from the grave, was taken by Stephen A. Troy, a professional TV cameraman who is an official of the Society of the Chosen. Troy won an award for a religious documentary he did on the Vietnam War. . . ."

The cop told us a chambermaid had seen Troy returning to his room with a package that looked like a bottle. Before he opened the door, a man approached him, and they went inside the room. A short time later, Troy's body landed on the sidewalk.

Tom showed me the chambermaid's description of the man: "About six four, very powerful, short-sleeve blue sport shirt, blond crew cut. . . ."

The cop's call to the precinct quickly produced a number of detectives, a fingerprint man, and a homicide squad captain who had a cast in one eye that gave me the eerie feeling he was always looking at me twice. When he heard our story, he immediately rushed us to his car, and we wailed across town to Wee Willie's Center Ring. He double-parked and we ran to the front door. The restaurant was dark, the door locked.

The captain stepped back, eyed the door, then expertly kicked it in.

We stepped into the dark bar that smelled faintly of stale beer. When the captain looked at us, we pointed to the dining room and the door at its rear. He took the steps two at a time.

The door of the apartment was open. The giant had never heard the footsteps above his snoring. The knife was buried in his heart to the hilt.

We followed the captain inside. Russell had caught them in bed. A big patch of blood on the circus poster showed where he had hurled the midget across the room like a rag doll. Then he went for Tura. The horror was frozen in her blue blotted face, the thin piano-wire noose buried so deep in the folds of her throat it was no longer visible.

The captain studied the poster, then Willie. He knelt down and carefully turned over the dwarf's right hand with the black leather thong around the thumb.

In the palm was a tiny dark blue revolver as small as a toy. The officer smelled the tip of the barrel, looked up, and said something to Tom, who repeated it in my ear.

The greatest marksman in the world had never had a chance to use his little gun. . . .

Lady of the Lightning

A week later, Senator Newberry announced in Washington that Ginerva would soon appear to call down the lightning of the Lord to prove to the world she was not a charlatan. The day before Newberry called his press conference, Tom read us the letter, written in an obviously feminine hand on a single sheet of white paper. It was signed simply, "Ginerva."

> On television you have called me a fraud, a liar, and a cheat. What happened was brought about by men of evil. I knew nothing of their deeds. I served only God and tried to get the world to listen to his message. Now there is no more time left for me. I have failed in my divine mission. But God has forgiven me. He has listened to my prayers and has promised that I will control his lightning during a storm.
>
> God will not allow me to be harmed. This will prove to the world that I was indeed his messenger and not the charlatan you have pictured me.
>
> I will soon announce where I will appear and where the storm will take place.
>
> God have mercy on all of us,
> Ginerva.

"How do you know this isn't just another crank letter?" I asked Tom.

He held out his hand. "This came with it." In his palm was a tiny gold cross within a circle of five stars.

"Is the FBI looking for her?" Norman asked.

"Only unofficially," Tom said. "There's really no reason for them to pick her up. She's still under the committee's subpoena and will be in contempt only if she fails to show up when the hearings resume."

"When will that be?" Leah asked.

"Shortly," he said. "Now that it's open season on the Society of the Chosen, every federal agency is cooperating. IRS will announce they have lifted their religious tax status and have turned over to us quite a bit of evidence dug up by their investigators. There is no doubt the Society is finished."

"But where were they yesterday?" I asked. "The FBI? Treasury? IRS?"

But Tom only shrugged.

Leah said bitterly. "And they keep asking why young people want nothing to do with politics."

As always Tom changed that subject. "How are you feeling, Hilly?" he asked hastily.

I wasn't too bad physically, although Leah insisted I now had more stitches than a Raggedy Andy doll. Russell's fist had cracked a wisdom tooth, which tortured me for a night and was extracted the following morning, but my arm and hand were healing fast, and my hearing had returned, although there were brief periods when I felt an intense pain in my ears. This would gradually vanish, the doctors had told me. But mentally I wasn't all that good. Although I did my best to hide it, I felt depressed. The one shoe on the bloody sidewalk and Tura's blue, bloated face would remain with me forever. Now they joined the platoon of Company H, whom I had never left behind in the jungles of Vietnam. I blamed myself for Tura and Troy's deaths, although Tom, Leah, and Turner argued that this was the game they had played and if what happened to them was their retribution, so be it.

But I didn't like playing God.

"It could be worse," I told Tom.

A week passed with no developments. Then one night when we were at dinner, Tom was called to the phone. He returned ashen-faced.

"They just found Foreman dead in a Park Avenue apartment," he announced. "He was strangled by Russell."

A short time later Tom, Norman, and I—Leah refused to come—were admitted by an FBI agent into a luxurious Park Avenue apartment just off Seventy-fifth Street. It was crowded with agents and homicide detectives under the direction of the captain who had taken us to Wee Willie's restaurant.

He pointed across the room to Foreman's body outlined on the rug by chalk. A police photographer was taking his last pictures. There was a stunned look on Foreman's face, as if he could not believe death was about to claim him.

The captain indicated the swollen dark blue neck. "This time Russell didn't use any piano wire. That guy must have hands like an ape," he observed. "The medical examiner said he crushed every bone in Foreman's neck."

"How do you know it was Russell?" Tom asked.

"The doorman and neighbors identified him," the captain explained. "He came here several times to visit Foreman. Apparently this time they had an argument. The woman next door said she heard them shouting and then there was a lot of noise. She called downstairs, but before the doorman came up Russell rushed out." His wave took in the apartment. "The guy put up a hell of a fight. . . ."

Tables were overturned, chairs broken, and a drape hung in shreds. The captain said musingly, "I wonder why Russell did that?"

A small color portrait of Ginerva, the type sold at the rallies—similar to one in my wallet—had been placed on a splintered table carefully propped up against the wall. In front of it was a single rose.

"Maybe he's sentimental," the captain suggested.

The murder of Foreman fed the headlines. The story of the investigation of Ginerva and the Society of the Chosen, her disappearance, and Newberry's promises of explosive developments in his future hearings were on page one of the majority of the nation's newspapers and featured on the nightly TV news programs. The major speculation was why Russell had murdered his close friend, associate, and mentor. The homicide captain's theory was they had fought over the huge loot; the FBI insisted it was for the leadership of the Society of the Chosen. But I knew a reason none of them could guess—Ginerva.

Looking back, I was surprised to recall the many signs of devotion to Ginerva Russell had displayed: the look of admiration on his face as we watched her prepare for the Briggs rally that afternoon in the motel suite; how he tenderly folded and held her cape when she went on the stage in Cleveland; the look of relief when he discovered she was in the parking lot; his collection of pictures of himself in Ginerva's company, supplied by Bruce Stafford; Tura's observation that Russell was in love with Ginerva.

I should have suspected a long time ago that this Neanderthal was helplessly in love with his beautiful, mad princess. . . .

The more I thought about it, the more I was convinced my theory was correct. Russell would not have fought with Foreman over money; as Tura had told me, there was ten million in his name in a Swiss bank account. And the leadership of the Society was not Russell's dream; he was content with his little army of Avenging Angels dedicated to protecting Ginerva. Something Foreman had said about Ginerva, had touched off Russell's uncontrollable rage.

I thought about her constantly, mostly at night, staring into the darkness against the muted backdrop of the city. Then in the early hours of a morning not long after Foreman's murder, when I was asking myself the question of where could Ginerva be hiding, the answer came like the stroke of a gong:

The Hill of God's Word!

I recall I was sprawled across the bed, half-listening to some idiotic late movie, when I jumped up and looked out of the window. In my mind I could see the low squat hill in the serene valley.

This was the logical place for her to go. There was no other security against the frightening world of reality pressing in on her. Didn't she tell me that this was where she had found peace and one day would build herself a church on the peak for all who sought peace of soul and mind through prayer?

When we had been there she had said, "This is where it will end. . . ."

In her fantasy the Hill of God's Word could be the place where the Lord would send down his mystical lightning to bathe her in fire yet leave her unharmed.

I began dressing. I had to go there. On an impulse, I put the twisted five-pointed star and cross, on the chain with the piece of shrapnel.

On my way out of the hotel, I started to pick up the house phone to call Leah. But then I decided this was something I had to do alone.

The highways were empty and I made good time. When I reached Barondale there was a light in the east, a bakery truck was unloading, and early morning workers were buying newspapers at a stationery store. I swung off the highway and parked near the lane that led to the valley. The pine-scented air was clear and birds were heralding the dawn as I approached the meadow.

Then behind a screen of trees I saw the car, a long black limousine. Ginerva's limousine.

I approached it cautiously. It was empty; from the dew on the hood and the roof it obviously had been parked in this spot all night. Before I entered the meadow I studied the hill. The framework of the old windmill, the utility pole and its crossbar, and the ruined chimney were outlined against the gray sky like crosses. I could feel a cold shiver go down my back.

Calvary.

I stayed there for a long time but nothing moved on the hill. Rather than cross the open meadow, I decided to make a wide circle through the woods and follow the creek to the rear slope. It was getting light when I reached the old cattle pond and waterfall and started to climb. There was no path. Wild raspberry vines, snaking through the woods, were as strong as barbed wire; there were trees and branches blown down in past storms. I was halfway up the slope when I heard a noise behind me. The shadowy figure of a powerfully built man was moving through the woods. Before he reached a clear spot, I knew it was Russell.

He still wore the blue knit shirt, but there was a large dark brown spot on one side. Blood. He was grinning when he emerged from the trees to stand below me.

"I knew you would show up," he said.

"Where is Ginerva?" I asked.

"Up on top of the hill," he said, "but you're not going to see her, Hillers."

Out of the corner of my eye I had caught a glimpse of a nearby broken limb on the ground, with branches and a pointed end. I kept talking as I inched toward it.

"Why not, musclehead?"

"Because I'm going to kill you," he said, and flexed his huge hands. "With these. After your mother won't recognize you, I'll teach you some karate." He shook his head slowly. "I can't believe my luck. Now it's just you and me, schoolteacher."

I tried to keep my voice even, almost casual. "Why did you kill Dave?"

For a moment he hesitated; he was debating with himself. Should he answer the question, should he keep talking to this man he intended to kill? But I had guessed right. He hadn't planned Foreman's murder. It had been done in a burst of homicidal rage. He still found it impossible to believe what he had done. He wanted to talk about it, to rationalize, even without knowing it, to beg forgiveness. For Russell knew that without Foreman he was only what Foreman had called him, a Neanderthal.

"I tried to reason with Dave," he said, with a hint of bewilderment in his voice, "but you couldn't reason with him. . . . He wanted me to waste her. . . . When I said I would never do that, he said he would do it himself. . . ." His voice hardened. "He said she was a nut and would be better off . . ."

His voice trailed off and he stared at me, the cold calculating stare of a stalking wolf.

"Everything was fine until you came along, Hillers," he continued. "I kept warning Dave there was something wrong about you, but he wouldn't listen. . . . He said he would do it his way. . . . If only he had listened to me. . . ." He held up his hands like huge claws and said, "But now I'm going to fix all that."

"You can't kill me, stupid," I said as he started up the slope.

Russell could never cope with the unexpected. He stopped, frowning.

"Yeah? Why not?"

The branch was nearer. I also wanted to keep him several feet below me; it would put him at a disadvantage.

"How can you kill anyone without a window? Remember the poor kid you killed on Fifty-seventh Street? And how about Steve Troy? And Tura? But you didn't need a window for her, you used piano wire."

"Talk all you want," he said doggedly, "I'm still gonna kill you."

I needed less than a foot. "Tura told me a lot about you, Russell," I called out.

He stopped again, and seemed to be debating with himself whether to get on with it or find out what Tura had said.

"Maybe you're afraid to find out," I said. The branch was very near.

"She was a lush," he said belligerently.

Finally the branch was at my feet. I had never been a physical match for Russell, and now with a stitched arm and hand I could offer only so much resistance. But I resolved that before he killed me he would know he had been in a fight. I could feel the energy, blood sugar, and adrenaline pumping through my body, tightening my muscles, making me unusually alert. In Vietnam I had always felt this way every time the helicopter began descending to drop us off to view some action.

I said softly, "Tura told me you were queer, Russell. That you can only make it with little boys. Is that true, faggot?"

With a wild cry, he ran up the slope. The advantage of a few extra seconds gave me the chance to pick up the branch, aim, and hurl it like a lance at his face. He was so intent on reaching me he was taken by surprise and barely had time to duck. The limb's sharp end opened a bloody gash on the side of his head. It wasn't heavy enough to stun him, but the branches clung like tentacles to his knit shirt and he had to tear them away.

I was set when he came at me. With every bit of my strength, I hit him on the cheekbone. I felt the bone give way, and he staggered back to slam up against a tree. He shook his head like a clubhouse fighter

(458)

and charged at me. I had found another piece of branch and used it as a club. When it shattered into splinters on his forearm, he swung with his open hand. I ducked, but not fast enough. There was an explosion of stars and I was sent lurching through the trees. His open hand pulled back, but he slipped on the leaves, soggy from the dew.

I leaped into the brush and began running. I could hear him behind me like a bull elephant crashing through the jungle. But then suddenly I slammed into something and bounced back; I could barely see the rusty wire fence in the brush. I started to turn to my left, down the slope, when he caught me.

He whirled me about and the open hand caught me on the side of the head. When I fell, he yanked me to my feet and hit me again. I remembered what he had threatened in the barn: "*I'll only use my open hand until your face explodes. . . .*"

After another shower of lights, I knew I couldn't stand much more. The next time he pulled me to my feet, I kneed him in the groin. His hands dropped involuntarily and I drove my thumb into his eye. He bellowed with rage and stepped back; this time I drop-kicked him in the stomach. I knew I had hurt him, but stupidly I moved in, hoping to drive a fist into his face. Another open-handed blow almost tore my head from my shoulders. When I got to one knee, he was reaching for me. I felt around me, but there was nothing, only wet leaves—I threw a handful of leaves and dirt into his face.

He stopped to rub his eyes but he was far from blind, as I discovered. When I got up and tried to run past him, he reached out, grabbed my arm, whirled me about, and slammed me against a tree. The pain in my arm was so great I cried out. But a wild raspberry vine was wrapped around the tree, so in turn I rubbed his hand against the thorns and he loosened his grip.

For a few minutes we became partners in a wild ballet as I tried to avoid his searching hands.

I made the mistake of trying the same trick twice. When I bent down to scoop up another handful of leaves and dirt, he caught my collar. In the struggle he tore my shirt to shreds, but forced me down to grasp my throat in his hands. I frantically battered his face with my fists, but it was like punishing granite. He never said a word as the vise tightened about my throat. I could barely breathe, there was a loud roaring in my ears and the light was growing dim.

Then suddenly her words came back to me: *Someday you will need this.*

I yanked the bent metal star from the chain. I had no idea how I could use it. Everything was growing dark, the roaring in my ears was a sound from a giant seashell. I dimly recall slashing at his face and neck. Suddenly his grip around my throat loosened, and he staggered to his feet.

When I sat up, the brush whirled about then slowly returned to normal. Russell was standing against a tree. The pupils of his eyes had turned up in his head. His mouth was open and blood was pumping out of the jagged slash in his throat where the hooklike star had found the jugular. I will always remember the grotesque look of surprise on his face as he slowly crumpled. I knew he was dead before he hit the ground.

For a long moment I just sat there, numbed, barely able to move. My fingers told me one side of my face was swollen like a melon. A rhythmic throbbing pain had started in my arm.

I finally got to my feet and stumbled, crawled, and clawed my way to the peak. I found her kneeling before the small stone grotto with the silver cross.

"Ginerva," I whispered.

When she didn't turn around, I reached out and touched her shoulder. Her skin was dry and cold.

"Ginerva," I said again. When there was no answer, I stepped to one side. Her eyes were staring and empty. The pulse in her throat was barely discernible.

"I'll take you home, Ginerva," I said softly, and lifted her to her feet. The sun was half a gold coin perched on the rim of the distant hills and its soft light filled her face.

I knew no one could ever hurt her again.

There isn't much more to tell. Ginerva and her Society will be debated for years by theologians. We listened to them testify under Tom's questioning before the Newberry Committee. Some denounced her as a false prophet who had suffered God's wrath, others hailed her as a new Joan of Arc who had desperately tried to deliver God's warning to a cynical world and had sacrificed herself to save us all.

As for Ginerva, she had disappeared into the darkness of her own soul when I found her kneeling before the stone grotto on the Hill of God's Word. She never emerged from that catatonic state and never spoke again. She was finally committed to an upstate asylum, but she had to be shifted from institution to institution to avoid the fanatics, the curious, and the still-loyal members of the Society of the Chosen who insisted she had really been a divine messenger.

Every year "anniversary" feature stories and documentaries resurrect the whole ghastly business. I came to appreciate what anyone involved in a news story must go through: the endless repetitious questions, the phone calls from London where a chance remark or a hasty word makes a sensational headline. It was Fleet Street which first dubbed her the "The Lady of the Lightning."

One network did a two-hour documentary on Ginerva, and it was scary watching the graphic scenes, such as the child in the well, return to life. . . .

Ironically, despite the avalanche of publicity, sensational disclosures by Newberry's Committee of the looted millions, the mirrored room, the brainwashing, the Money Room, the political deals and offshore bank accounts, there was little justice for Ben Rice. Tom described in shocking detail for the committee how Ben had finally become the Society's Manchurian Candidate who was finally given a stolen gun and taken to Central Park where he killed himself, but it was impossible to build a case of murder against anyone.

No witnesses, no case.

The deadly twin hypnotists, who had been taken into custody, insisted they had met Ben briefly while passing through Ketchum after appearing at a benefit in Boise—a fact which was later confirmed. They denied knowing Foreman, Russell, or Tura, or teaching a mind control program at the motherhouse. Who could disprove their statements?

No witnesses, no case.

When they appeared before the committee, the pair turned out to be slick showmen with a kind of hideous pride in their claim that they were the best hypnotists and sleight-of-hand men in show business. At first they made the committee and the audience laugh at their tricks. But Tom slowly led them down the road of their varied criminal careers, arrest by arrest, with their celebrated lawyer, who usually got a five-figure retainer, loudly protesting. In the end Tom finally showed them to be what they really were: a pair of cold-blooded crooks who had a deadly knowledge of hypnotism and elementary psychology. When they stood up after testifying, sweaty but still arrogant, two FBI agents happily took them into custody; the Bureau had uncovered a warrant for their arrests as conspirators in a society jewel robbery. One of the other thieves had become a government witness, Tom said, so there was an excellent chance the pair would finally serve time.

We all toasted Tom that night with champagne. Leah wondered out loud, "Is there any place free from evil?" She called me a miserable cynic when I answered that there is no such place and never will be as long as there are men of free will. . . .

The Newberry Committee hearings finally ended with a bombastic —and probably insignificant—final report denouncing the cults and sects suspected of victimizing the young, the impressionable, the lonely, and the lost, for their own profit and sinister goals.

In my opinion the Newberry Committee's major contribution was to raise the still unanswered question of the 1980s before America:

What can be done about these cults and sects, tinged with fascism and criminality, without infringing on the constitutional rights of cult members to practice freedom of religion?

I finally wrote my series for Lord Cavendish's newspaper chain, with a free copy for Mr. Ranks in Boston—who didn't forget to remind his audience I was his former Vietnam "chief corre- spondent." He also used that cliché picture of me, unshaven and worn, glaring down at my typewriter as if Errol Flynn was peering over my shoulder.

At Lord Cavendish's request I expanded the series into a book, which had a wide sale and touched off a number of articles about Ginerva, some thoughtful, many lurid.

She is never far from my thoughts. In idle moments I close my eyes and see her beautiful, delicate face in the candlelight as I had seen it that night so long ago in her apartment above the Grand Ballroom. What happened all those months—from Briggs to the harrowing moments in the mirrored room—now has a dreamlike quality. At times scenes seem fuzzy, out-of-focus snapshots, and I have to convince myself that it all really happened.

I believe now that Ginerva must be placed in that most incompre- hensible of companies, the mystics, the saints, and the unexplainable. Her mystery lies somewhere in between all three, a mystery I am sure will never be explained by cool medical terms or fire and brimstone from the pulpit. It has been argued that her "miracles" were in fact only manufactured scams or natural coincidences. I suppose I should agree. But I have found coincidences are far less convincing when one is an eyewitness or a participant.

Now that the dust has settled and Ginerva is confined to the Sunday supplements, it has occurred to me that perhaps God's almost arbi- trary use of grace had transformed her from a meddling intruder, engulfed in her own careless evil, into what could be called a sort of sanctified sinner, more likely to receive a divine command than the rest of us alleged humanitarians. Finally the inscrutable ways of heaven brought her to the hill and to her tragic end. . . .

When I suggested this in my series and book, pointing out that God's ways are unknown to man and therefore must remain inex- plicable, I was inundated by an avalanche of mail, some from clergy- men who scornfully described my suggestion as theological absurdity and said that my intimation that Ginerva was anything more than a pathetic madwoman or a shrewd con artist, had to be classified as pure invention.

As for me, I know now that Tura was right. Ginerva had become my obsession, my beautiful obsession, from the moment she touched my cheek that night in San Francisco. I had to find the answers, to solve her mystery, to find her secret at any cost.

But had I?

I was at loose ends after the hearings. Ranks offered me the dream assignment of writing a column, going where I wanted and writing what I wanted. There were other offers. But I returned to my seniors at St. Timothy's. One spring afternoon, Leah and I were married in the school's chapel with Tom as my best man and Norman as our usher. Sir Edward gave us a handsome check as a wedding present, and we took a leisurely trip across the country.

The day after our return, Tom called to tell us that Ginerva had died in her sleep in a small asylum in upstate New York. To avoid a public spectacle, the institution's superintendent planned to have her buried quietly.

With Tom and Norman, we drove upstate. We saw her for the last time in the asylum's tiny chapel. Despite the institutional plain gray dress, she appeared as beautiful and ageless as ever. We sat in the shadows in the last pew during the perfunctory service, then followed the casket to the grave in the far corner of the graveyard. Later, when we asked permission to raise a headstone, the superintendent begged us not to place her name on it for fear it would become a shrine.

So instead of her name there are only the words of Isaiah that she had quoted to me:

"For my thoughts are not your thoughts nor are your ways my ways."

Leah and I went up there alone to watch when the stone was delivered and placed at the head of her grave.

"Well, Hilly," Leah asked suddenly, "was she or wasn't she?"

I didn't have an answer then, nor do I have one now.